Iain Sinclair

DOWNRIVER

(Or, The Vessels of Wrath)
A Narrative in Twelve Tales

Granta Books
London

Granta Publications, 2/3 Hanover Yard, London N1 8BE

First published in Great Britain by Paladin, 1991
First published in paperback by Vintage, 1995
This edition published by Granta Books 2002

A CIP catalogue record for this book
is available from the British Library.

1 3 5 7 9 10 8 6 4 2

Printed and bound in Great Britain
by Mackays of Chatham plc

Contents

Offered to those contrary spirits,
Mike Goldmark and Patrick Wright

'As I walked, trying to understand this, filled with this as with some pure intelligible security, I heard the first wraths of the guns at the Thames' mouth below Tilbury. The wraths so soon to be answered by shrapnel screaming in the air ...'

Mary Butts, *The Crystal Cabinet*

I

He Walked Amongst the Trial Men

He Walked Amongst the Trial Men

'He walked amongst the Trial Men
In a suit of shabby grey;
A cricket cap was on his head,
And his step seemed light and gay ...'

Oscar Wilde,
The Ballad of Reading Gaol

'And what,' Sabella insisted, 'is the *opposite* of a dog?'

Her husband, Henry Milditch, continued to ignore her. This was not easy. Sabella had been painting all afternoon, and was now flagrantly drunk. She poked a pint-sized coffee mug into his midriff. The red wine splashed on to his shirt. He wheezed cigar smoke like a leaking radiator.

'You two are as boring as those old farts on "Test Match Special". Everything's finished, burnt out. Nothing is what it used to be. Every book you mention is "a dog", "a howling dog", "an absolute dog". I want to know what *else* there is in the world.'

Milditch, up to now, had kept his life in separate compartments. But, with the move out of Hackney, everything was coming to pieces. His wife was roaming free in his book room in an old rugby shirt that she filled very adequately, even though she had put it on back to front. And her daughter was doing her best to climb into my lap and interest me in an odd volume of nautical memoirs.

'You're a pair of rheum-eyed mongrels.' Sabella spun on me. 'You whine about dragging yourselves to Groucho's. Why don't you take us along? I don't mind male bimbos. Some of them are quite tasty. And all of them have more to say than you do. Who the hell wants to spend their life stuck out in a Suffolk fish dock, ploughing through reprints of Wilkie Collins, and watching fat opera queens pull themselves out of taxis?'

Milditch compulsively reshelved his yellowbacks. He muttered something incoherently decent-minded about inner-city schools and the rising tide of litter and urban violence.

'*Bollocks* to urban violence,' Sabella screamed. 'You'll dump me out in the sticks with your rotten kids, while you slide down the motorway. You'll only crawl back when you need a few quiet days to sleep off the excitement.'

Milditch picked her up, carried her out, and locked the door. She kicked against it steadily for ten minutes or so, until she damaged her naked foot. Then she sat in the corridor, and sobbed. Quite musically.

I turned my back on the small pile of books I was about, unenthusiastically, to carry away; I looked out of the bay window at the lovely green lung of Victoria Park. A tame prairie that kept me sane through a difficult winter. This was the house of some old sea captain. It was oddly proportioned, with each room decorated in a distinct style – as if warring tribes had camped there. When the park was finally butchered and buried under tarmac by the threatened road schemes, it would all be over. There would be nothing left. The Widow and her gang had decided that Hackney was bad news and the best option was simply to get rid of it, chop it into fragments, and choke it in the most offensive heap of civil engineering since the Berlin Wall.

Then Milditch dropped the hint. Which was, I suppose, why I let it lie fallow for so many months. He gave things away only when they were fatally tainted, or drained of all their vital fluids. He wouldn't pass on an infection, unless he could swop it for a superior one. He must have been unnerved by the weeping of his children, the curses and the threats of his wife. He looked, pacing his den, obsessively delousing his ginger beard, like a veteran foot-soldier from the Katowice midfield, a slightly sandblasted Tommy Smith.

'Tilbury,' he mumbled. A confession that he instantly suppressed. 'Tell Dryfeld and I'll kill you. I don't want this surfacing in the guidebook. It's still too hot.'

Who was Milditch anyway? His birth name had dissolved, long since, into the borders of the River Lea, the industrial sumplands; out there among the thickets of intemperately abandoned motors, the odd shoes, the cat sacks, the dusty banks of albino nettles. *Milditch* fitted better at the foot of the credits. It went unnoticed. It sounded so damp and wormy and English. The obscure fogs of his Baltic destiny had been exchanged for a manic restlessness, which partly masked his lifelong quest for revenge. He made deals. He shuffled telephones. He haunted the dead zones of the city looking for connections that only he could activate.

He had another angle: he acted. And cornered the market in disposable villains, donkey jackets, and third policemen. He underacted to the point of being, clinically speaking, brain-dead. He once made base camp for a three-part Mini Series push-on-the-Pole; which was routed, for the convenience of the Money Men, through Angmagssalik, Greenland. He pocketed quite a provocative compensation cheque when a wind-machine, hurling polypropylene chips in a simulated blizzard, cut his face to ribbons. No matter. Convalescent, swathed in ice-crusted band-ages, he turned up a stash of pornographic novels – dumped by a crew of drill-bit technicians, en route to the Gulf – and shuffled them, at a modest profit, into the deep parka pockets of the Second Unit.

Milditch's survival depended upon his anonymity. If he became a 'face', he was redundant. He let his hair grow and went about unshaven, glowering; then reversed it, scalped himself, grinned like a monkey, and razored his jowls into the consistency of expectorated bubblegum.

I knew him as a book dealer. An acquaintance of mine met him selling cold fish on a beach. Others swore that he dabbled in property. Cer-tainly, he was known to all the casting directors. He was always shooting down the M4 to Bristol; taping his two sentences from some repeatable radio classic; gathering the scripts from his fellow thespians for immediate resale; scouting the Clifton bookshops: only to return to his gloomy captain's cabin, to make the inevitable phonecalls, while he watched the shadows lengthen across the troubled ocean of the park.

'Tilbury,' said Milditch, reluctantly activating a light switch, 'looks well worth a visit. The floor was covered in books. That's good. Nothing in cupboards or on shelves. So they don't do the fairs. The place probably opens once a year, for an hour, while the owner airs his alsatians. I'd cane it myself – but I'm marooned in Uppingham in a duff production of Calderon's *The Surgeon of Honour*, sponsored by some local nutter who's trying to revive rural England by importing Soviet chess champions. Just send me a nice sweetener, mate, if he drops his trousers.'

I knew then that my days as a dealer were almost over. I didn't want to touch whatever lay on the floor of the Tilbury shop. But I had the queasy sensation there ought to be a story in it.

A swollen pink finger, like the thumb from an inflated rubber glove, rose above the London plane trees, and twisted in the evening air. I could still make out the slogan, 'Celebrate JESUS!' The tent-show season was on us already. It was time to be out on the road.

II

The train out of Fenchurch Street has been salvaged from some condemned fairground. It shakes the boardwalk at Limehouse so fiercely
that the station threatens to collapse into a heap of rotten timber. The
guards, pouting with boredom, hands lost in pockets, twitchy, surfeited
on nipple-sheets, have been thoroughly schooled in circumlocution.
They have no ambition beyond stranding any person misguided enough
to commit themselves to their protection on the poisoned sands of
Canvey Island: a gulag of sinking caravans, overlooked by decommissioned storage tanks.

'And this also has been one of the dark places of the earth,' I quoted,
straining the portentous ripeness of another Pole over the drowned
fanns of Essex.

Thin winter light suppurated between towerblocks and shabby
graveyards, picking out the glinting scabs of rusty water. A network of
ditches offered to flood the low fields, to hide the disgraced enclosures of
fast-breeding motors, that were herded, unlicensed, for conversion to
paddocks of weed-choked scrap.

If there was an open *mesa* left, it was soon bunkered into a firing
range. Red flags kicked in the breeze. The occasional lop-sided barn, a
heritage token, had been preserved for the well-fancied combat of
imported pit-bulls.

And always, beyond the pain – the river: black, costive, drawing me
on; flaunting the posthumous brilliance of its history.

III

Tilbury Town is a single street, and it is shut. European rain brings
down the dirt that floats so enticingly out from the massed pipes of the
power station. The innocent sightseer abandons his guidebook to relish a
haberdasher's grease-streaked window, which features underwear so
outdated it has all the nostalgic allure of a fetishist's catalogue. There is a
'Financial Consultant' with a twenty-four-hour sideline in radio-
controlled mini cabs. And yet more mini cabs. The chief industry of the
place is providing the means to escape from it.

Cranes from the docks seal the set, and diminish it; preposterous as the
Bureau de Change that is gratefully dying into its varnish.

After a couple of hundred yards the buildings simply give up. I am
lost among the terminal hobs. Locked yards with sheeted secrets,

contracts that lack a signature, consignments that were never collected: a killing ground for lorries, misdirected, with an inadequate cargo.

On the inshore edge, between the point where the speculators ran out of ideas and the storm's horizon, is a pisshouse, half-demolished; a municipal *jeu d'esprit*, with green tile pagoda roof. The exterior walls are still favoured by local sentimentalists, staggering home with a skinful – and a singular method of celebrating the resonance of location. And here, on the very precipice of oblivion, propped by a flying buttress of ex-Launderette washing machines, is a lit shopfront: a mirage that could almost pass for Milditch's legendary Antique Haven.

There is a man inside, smoking, warming his hands over a two-bar electric fire. The CLOSED sign is nailed into place. The man looks at me, at my rain-plastered scalp, my dripping coat, my hungry red eyes. Turns back to the fire. Which has a more profitable animation: it throws out sparks. With luck it will burn the place down. He cleans his ear with a matchstick, and rolls the result between his fingers. I rap the window sharply with a coin. He lights another cigarette; rummages under the table, finds a second fire, a fan-blower, and plugs that in.

The existential pathos of this mute Conversation Piece could have endured for a generation. The rain reconstituting my shirt as tie-dyed woodpulp. The junkman's thoughts set morbidly on poll-tax forms and the price of electricity. A sheet of dirty glass dividing us into Subject and Object, observer and observed. My eyes feverishly annotating the bedlam for a book that would justify this manic quest. Jugs, biscuit tins, trays of bent forks, cracked picture frames. None of it held any interest for him. He might have been hired to sit there. He probably couldn't escape. The washing machines, like an unrecorded ice age, blocked his exit. He had not chosen any of these things. He hated them. People died; he stored whatever they did not take on their journey. The dead dominated him. I was also a threat: I might want to force even more stock on to the premises.

The tremulous balance of the situation was ravished by a gunshot from the corner of the street. I rapped, with a little more force. The key holder surfaced, gasping, from his control experiment in suspended animation. More shots, skidding tyres, crashed gears ... and a Morris Traveller, lacking its side-windows, mounted the kerb. And drew up, a yard shy of my kneecaps.

In the world of junk shops and resurrectionist scavenging, there are no surprises. The unexpected is what we are most comfortable with. My old market colleague, Iddo Okoli – for whom Field Marshal Amin was the cadet version – stepped from his smoking wreck, and removed his bowler, to execute a formal bow. Lion-hearted; he gripped me to his chest, growling dangerously, like a flesh-eating king.

The excavated proprietor shuffled to the door. I followed Iddo inside.

IV

They lay under the pear tree: smeared with themselves, torn, sore, and thirsty. They lay apart, panting. Their tongues lolled in the dirt. They dribbled, slippery with melting 'KY' jelly. Then the fatter one, Bobby, crawled off, sick to his heart, unbalanced, and looking for air that he could breathe. His creamy lace-trimmed basque pinched false breasts from his abundant flesh. His varnished skin was marbled with a perplexity of contusions. His black silk stockings were split; revealing spidery tufts of man-hair. He was dragging his insides after him across the gravel: a dead dog. They were still trapped in the thatch of a barren orchard.

What could be more depressing than the interval between orgies? Bobby wondered if he would *ever* summon up the enthusiasm to begin it all again. How could he avoid catching sight of last night's partners? How could he avoid paying them? Always problems for the creative mind.

As he crossed the path, he begged the single stones to pierce him. He relished the sluggish ripples of discomfort. It could have been an hour, or a day, before he reached the concrete steps of the redoubt, and hauled himself on to the river wall, the East Gun Line.

'Speer's Theatre', his friend the painter had called it; wistfully invoking the classical pretensions of the Third Reich. The steps were all that was left. A meaningless piece of something. The outer rim of a Temple of Atrocities. He wanted to lick bloodstains from the cold stone. He wanted to touch the water. The morning light on the river was his salvation.

Wooden stumps in the mud. The ruin of a jetty. The tide was turning: a slime-caked causeway, plastered in filth and sediment, pointed at Gravesend. He often boasted, without much justification, that Magwitch faltered here, escaping from the hulks; and was brought to shore. The last pub in the world, the World's End.

From beyond the curve of the power station, Bobby saw them coming up on the tide: from the Hope into the Reach. The familiar nightmare. The early light followed, like an attendant; grey, crumbling, flaky. It broke them apart, into a flood of false lumber. They floated in never-connecting circles; going under, dipping from sight. They were all dead. They swam to fetch him. Wavelets, drowned angels; pale-green billows. There were women in hats, holding their children above the waterline. Infants slipping from their arms, slipping from sight. The river's net was churned; and the ropes were cut.

'Not again,' Bobby whimpered, 'I swear on my life. I'll never do it again.' Hot tears bruised the kohl, blackened his eyes, inflicted damage.

More ropes than faces. He knew it would be the same. It could not change. The living location imprisons incomplete instants of time. Sex acts release demons. But the morning light would resolve it, sweep away the visible traces. Except the Indian woman. She was always there. Walking across the water towards him, daintily stepping from wave crest to wave crest: down from the church, court habit, throat hidden in a ruff of sea-bone, most severe.

'*You called him father, being in his land a stranger. And by the same reason so must I you. Fear you here I should call you father? I tell you then I will, and you shall call me child, and so I will remain for ever and ever your countryman.*'

The mantic shine of fever. Sewage breath. Her voice in his mouth.

Then the howl; the compressed madhouse shriek of the power station. Steam alarms. Whistle. Dread. The unrinsable taste of sperm in the throat.

V

The curtains were drawn. The doors of the pub closed against the vulgar world. The inner circle of the Connoisseurs of Crime paddled yet again through the shallows of forensic legend; traded atrocities. They dominated, complacently, a log fire powered by gas jets. Errlund, his desert boots on Hywood's chair, was hogging the conversation.

'"Sir" graciously took me along to the Beefsteak,' he droned. 'Too many flapping ears at the Athenaeum. The old pansy didn't want his posh pals to catch him hobnobbing with a scribbler. Yes, he'd try the fish – a palsied scrape of cod. Difficulties with his choppers. Nearly spat them on to the plate every time he opened his mouth. *Une belle horreur!*'

'Spare us the complete rollcall of domestic details this time, old boy,' Hywood yawned. He'd heard it all before. And it wasn't improving. Some fool had mentioned Errlund in the same breath as Marcel Proust, and it had gone, quite disastrously, to his head. The reviewer had, of course, been discussing types of morbid pathology, and not literary style.

'I followed him,' Errlund continued, impervious to cynicism, or any other form of moral censorship, short of an iron muzzle. 'I followed him into the dining room. Have you noticed how he walks these days? Waddles, I should say. He lurched between the tables, like a circus elephant with the squitters. Nodded seigneurial acknowledgement to complete strangers. They thought I was doing the decent thing – bringing him out for the afternoon from the nuthatch.'

'For God's sake, Errlund. Drop the Chips Channon routine, and get on to the serial killings. Are you going to publish the surgeon's papers in full, or are you going to "summarize" them, and bend whatever you find there to fit with your own theories?' Hywood tugged at his earlobe in annoyance. He'd given the advantage to Errlund. He'd betrayed *interest*. Now the bastard would pad it out until all the chaps forgot it was his turn to get in a round.

'When we finally eased him into his seat, he had the greatest difficulty remembering where he was,' Errlund sailed on, serenely. 'He stared up at me over his half-moons in a perfect rictus of terror. He must have concluded I was his valet, or bumboy, and he simply couldn't imagine why I was sitting down with him at table. He was far too *gentil* to mention it, of course. All that shit flogged into him at Eton and Balliol. His fine grey eyes were watering slightly, and there was just a hint of rouge on his cortisone-puffy cheeks.'

Errlund paused. His timing was perfect. Hywood's eyes were shut. But he was faking. 'Get on with it, man,' he growled. 'Or do you want me to finish it for you? "If you do this thing ..." Is that right?'

'Quite right,' Errlund conceded. 'He gazed at me for a few moments, in silence, to convince me of his seriousness. "If you do this thing," he croaked, "you'll be blackballed. No decent club will touch you. You'll never see your name in the Honours List. Your K will remain a pipedream." Then he excused himself; his "secret sorrow", problems with the waterworks. One of the waiters carried him back, trouser-cuffs steaming. He counted his cold sprouts and gave me a very significant look.'

A snort from Hywood, followed by a jaw-cracking yawn, indicated that he was crossing the borderland of sleep. Errlund's narrative was underwriting his nightmare. Hywood had joined them at the table.

'His concentration was fading fast,' said Errlund mercilessly, 'but he managed to signal for the custard. "Make me a promise," he trembled. "You will never again associate that noble name with those tedious crimes. They can never pay you enough blood-money. Leave it to the Penny Dreadfuls, old chap. What can it possibly matter to the civilized portion of society if a few whores are slit from nape to navel? I've never myself cared for sports, but these hulking and vigorous young blackguards must sow their wild oats. Let them keep it to the streets, and pray they do not frighten the horses."'

Hywood sat up with a start. 'Did he actually confirm that your man was the guilty party?'

'Oh no,' said Errlund, 'he was much too far gone. He'd wandered off among the yolky richness of Kentish brickwork, honey-coloured Cotswold stone, Winston, Guy, Jim Lees-Milne. "Must say," he drawled, *à propos de rien*, "quite surprised, glancing out of the jarvey on the way over – the vast numbers of coloured people passing unmolested down the Haymarket." Then, without warning, he shoved a bundle of letters towards me, under cover of the cheeseboard; coughing into his sleeve, and fluttering his eyelashes like a Venetian concubine. "You see, Errlund?" he broke out again. "You take my point? You have a contribution to make. Your name is often spoken aloud on the wireless. I can arrange for you to view all the private papers. I'll give you another man altogether, a sick soul. A much better yarn. What can the 'truth' matter now – when you set it against an advance from an honourable publisher? Your fame is assured. Take your time, go down to the country. It will be marked in the right places, I promise you. Drop in, any Thursday, at the Albany. My day, you know." I had to lift his hand from my knee. When I walked out, he was still talking to the empty chair. The waiter was taking a brandy glass to his lips, then patting him dry with the folded edge of an Irish-linen napkin.'

Bobby, the publican and sinner, the gold-maned 'television personality', posed for a moment in the doorway, then tottered to the bar and shot a very large gin into a dirty glass. 'Cunts,' he whispered, superstitiously. And pressed his glass against the tiny shoulders of the dispenser.

A Romanesque docker, head slicked with sump oil, sleeves rolled threateningly above the elbow, kept his back to the fireside cabal of Crime Connoisseurs, while he indulged in some serious drinking. He was being talked to, whined at, flattered, flirted with, and altogether patronized by Conlin, the notorious Lowlife photographer. An evil-smelling dwarf who had lost his christian name, thirty years before, in a strict discipline Naval Training Establishment for delinquent boys. His Leica was on the stool beside him. The great Conlin! The man who had shot, and later destroyed, the definitive portrait of John Minton. Beads of salt-sweat rolled down the contours of his coarse-grained skin. Smirking, then sniffing, he began to excavate the docker's ear with his tongue. Without hurrying, or spilling a drop, the docker finished his drink. He stood up, rolled his shoulders, and clamped his vast hands around the back of Conlin's neck. He looked for a long moment into the photographer's eyes: then he nutted him. And watched him drop, screaming, on to the floor.

Gamely, Bobby rushed forward to hook Conlin's elbows back on to the bar. Blood was dripping from the photographer's broken nose into his vodka. Bobby teased a cigarette between Conlin's trembling lips, and lit it with his own.

The board behind the line of inverted spirit bottles was decorated with exotic postcards from Bobby's collection: jungles, ivory poachers, whips, balconies. Bobby tried to take his mind off things by constructing a fiction that would animate these static images.

Recklessly inspired, he groped for Conlin's camera. He propped the wilting photographer between the docker and his mate; then fidgeted the group, until the sign, BUOYS, could be clearly read on the left of the composition. He carefully framed out the corresponding door, marked GULLS.

The dockers were rigid, severe; breathless. One of them mimed danger, by fingering a kiss curl; while the other excited a detumescent bicep.

Bobby, the artist, was not quite satisfied. After prolonged meditation, and a final check through the viewfinder of his fingers, he darted forward to unzip Conlin, fumble him, shake him out. The earwig! Now satisfied, he snapped the shutter on another fragment of his one-day-to-be-published tribute to a lost generation: the Tilbury Group. He might give his agent a tinkle.

VI

Iddo Okoli, savage in Middle Temple mufti – pin-striped, wing-collared, with soup-stained tie – progressed benevolently through the collapsed markets, smiling on chaos. His wife, broad, dignified, sheet-wrapped, followed in his slipstream. His children, in a file, struggled with suitcases of outdated textbooks. How his optimism survived, nobody knew. He bellowed at back-counters. He shook the plaster from damp ceilings. He beat on tables. There had been good days when he almost covered his bus fare.

His prospects changed with a small piece of theatre that became apocryphal in the trade. A literary graveyard, lurking between the Royal Academy and the Museum of Mankind, was 'rationalizing' its stock, and adjusting to market forces (prior to becoming an airline office), by reshelving directly into a builder's skip. Iddo watched, hands on hips, as the nocturnal assistants blinked into the brilliance of the street, carrying as many as three books each; which they dropped, with great precision, on to the growing heap.

Iddo removed his bowler, and mopped his brow. He examined a few items in this reserve collection. He nominated a dozen or so, on the grounds of weight and size; bounced the hernia-dodging juniors, like so many jackals, and made for the shop, three steps at a time. He attacked the counter and gavelled it ferociously with his fist, until the buyer appeared; yawning and pale with anguish. Iddo was not the most sought-after of 'runners'. The buyer, fretful, and slightly hungover, inspected the current selection.

'Um, yes. Better, Iddo.' He could hardly believe it. 'Quite presentable. The best books you've ever located.' He prised open the jaws of the till, slipped Iddo the customary paper to sign, and let him get away with a fiver and three singles. Iddo was in the big time.

By now the skip was attracting the attention of a few lesser carrion; 'outpatients' on bicycles, shuffling dead stock between Shepherd's Bush Green and the Charing Cross Road. Iddo palmed them aside and waded, waist-deep, into the unreconstructed dreck. A dredged armful and back to the counter. *Three* blue ones!

At the close of trade, Iddo staked himself to a lethally trashed set of wheels. His horizons detonated. No longer was he trapped within the confines of a fifty-pence bus ride. He could risk Penn, Brackley, Colchester, Guildford. He was one of us.

And here was I, once his patron, staggering into a docklands junkshop, under a washing machine that was leaking what I hoped was water down the front of my trousers. There were two more machines waiting outside in the Traveller. And a brace of spin dryers on the roof-rack.

While the junkman and Iddo debated this lump of cargo-cult plunder, I subsided into the books. I rapidly cast aside the usual trench-foot volumes of First War photographs. These are loved only by antique dealers, sternly refusing to sell them to bookmen, who wouldn't give them house room if the dustwrappers were woven out of dollar bills. I spurned the damaged glitz of Edwardian decorative covers: the unreadable in the process of becoming the unsaleable. I was left with five hardcore targets to consider.

The Tilbury Catalogue. Spring, 1988. Codeword: Hopeless.

(1) A defective first edition of Joseph Conrad's *Youth*, Blackwood, 1902. Pale green linen-grain cloth, with marginal tracery of cigarette burns (Craven A, *c.*1952). Endpapers somewhat

nicotine-tanned. 'The End of the Tether', pp. 313–17, torn away
and used as spills. A distressed copy that has not quite given up
the ghost.

(Verdict? Better have it. My friend Joblard, the sculptor, wants
to sample *Heart of Darkness.*)

(2) *In Tropical Lands: Recent Travels to the Sources of the Amazon, the
West Indian Islands, and Ceylon.* Published by Wyllie of Aberdeen in partnership with Ferguson of Ceylon, 1895. Despite a
trivial dusting of mushroom mulch, a *nice* copy. Author's name
suppressed under the imploded corpse of a potentially uncommon spider. The creature in question *might* have posed for the
illustration on p. 103, giving this item the additional interest of
being an association copy. We make no surcharge on this
account.

(Verdict? Forget it. Anything with a map costs too much
money. And Dryfeld is always saying that you can't sell
S. America.)

(3–5) The final three volumes constitute an incomplete collection of
the works of Patrick Hanbury, Director, Department of
Medical Entomology, London School of Hygiene and Tropical
Medicine. We can offer a yard of research on *The Natural History
of Tsetse Flies*; and a slim octavo volume, complete with the
uncommon ash-grey dustwrapper, produced in a version of the
Fortune Press house style, and emphatically titled, *The Louse.*

This last item, a cornerstone in any library, is illustrated, in
line, with an exceptionally delicate study of *Phthirus Pubis*
(female), from above. An alarmingly vivid section throws a new
light on 'Methods of Rearing' – by means of lice boxes attached
to the skin, in a garter beneath the sock. '*The louse feeds only on
man, and must do so frequently; it has to be reared on human beings and
it should be kept on the skin for long periods every day. The most
convenient method of rearing the insect was developed by Nuttall …*'

Increased costs of publication do not allow us to do justice to
the ultimate volume: *Researches in Polynesia and Melanesia, An
Account of Investigations in Samoa, Tonga, the Ellice Group and the
New Hebrides.* The author's sensitive use of the plate-camera
presents extreme forms of physical deformity in the guise of
decorative art. Disease-ripe flesh bursts and fruits, escaping from
the stunned dignity of gracious native specimens. Never before,
in our opinion, has Surrealism courted the analytical eye of
Science to such effect. Disbelief wrestles with pathos. The gross

excitements of the Freak Show are enclosed within the discretion of the ethnologist's cabinet.

(Verdict? Irresistible!)

Iddo and the junkman had not wasted their time. While I have been browsing among the beached detritus of the Imperial Dream, they have slapped hands to celebrate the resolution of their infamous deal. Iddo alternately squeezed and pommelled the junkman, until he swallowed his still-burning fag. The junkman, in revenge, pelted Iddo with bank-notes, and worried him in the general direction of the river.

Any offer for my fancied books is redundant to the thrust of the moment. Iddo's motor – with fresh detonations, smoke clouds, the singe of chicken feathers – buffets him back to his self-inflicted Apocalypse. Normality creeps awkwardly on to the set. The junkman resumes his brave attempt to cook himself between two fires. Money does not interest him. A hip-flask does. He brews up; growing weary of the exercise long before the water boils. Condensed milk, Camp coffee, sewage water, whisky. We achieve a kind of bleak, post-bellum fellow-ship. And he is happy to elucidate the nature of the scam.

He has cornered the market in the unloved. The streets are awash with non-functioning electrical hardware. He gives it shelter. He operates an unsung Battersea Dogs' Home for Zanussi, Hoover, Indesit, Electra, Hotpoint, Bosch, Bendix, Creda, Electrolux, Philips. All the tribes of brutalized and deserted dishwashers, vacuum cleaners, and tumble dryers. They were never turned from his door. He has a backer, a deal-maker; some local publican with media connections, contacts on the Ivory Coast. They wait until they can cram a dozen containers, then set keel from what's left of the docks, to Lagos. Top dollar!

'We're webbed up, squire,' the junkman smirked. 'All the way to the Generals. There's a nobbled Russian geezer with the Third World Aid delegation who loves to bilk the "sooties". We sweetened him with a nicked Harrods charge card and enough small change to play the slot-machines for a fortnight.'

Apparently, the dosh has to be laundered through a government-funded education programme: heavyweight Industrial Training Films. A category that has fallen into sad disfavour since the days of Lindsay Anderson and 'Free Cinema'. Now a few bearded Dutchmen, cut off in their prime by the Civil War, rush around with U-boat cameras and outdated stock trying to incite their students, who are interested only in wearing bow ties and driving around in air-conditioned Cadillacs, to recapture the fire of John Grierson's social visionaries. They project, in furtive cellars, romantic images of steel furnaces, backlit assembly lines, and naked sweating workers. But the students want only to be Game Show anchormen, with travel allowances to Bangkok. The Dutch instructors have to deal in black-market primitive art to survive. They are almost always caught. The police are tipped off by the traders, who buy back their own goods at a 'special' price. The film-makers pay their way out of prison, or die in chains.

None of this concerns the junkman. A few modest currency fiddles on the side, and he's in clover. A detached residence that backs on to the railway track at East Tilbury; heated swimming pool, cocktail lounge, pebble-dash portico, closed-circuit security system, Mercedes: and a panoramic view across the biggest rubbish dump in Essex to the Romano-British settlements now tactfully concealed beneath river mud. As Glyn H. Morgan remarks in his seminal work, *Forgotten Thameside* (*sic*), Letchworth, 1966: 'In spite of the recent disappearance of the hut circles the scene is still well worth a visit.'

Wade in, traveller, and stick fast. Try to imagine, as you go under, Claudius bringing his legions over from the Kent shore. This is where it happened. This was the place.

Look on these new men: Princes of Ruin, Lords of Squalor.

VII

A few weeks later I was back. It wasn't going to be easy to shake free of this place. I needed to investigate without the frenzied rush of hunting for negotiable books. I walked from Tilbury to Tilbury Riverside. I wanted to take a longer look at the station concourse, the Custom House, the Fort, the Gravesend Ferry – and I invited Joblard to accompany me. We would identify the stretch of water, where the *Princess Alice* went down with the loss of six hundred and forty lives: salvaged bodies exhibited on three piers. Our motives were, as always, opaque and spiritually unsound.

Pensioned trading hulks rusted in the docks: fantastic voyages that would never be consummated. The cranes had become another forest to be culled for their scrap value, another location for 'Dempsey and Makepeace'. The rampant dereliction of the present site was as much an open invitation to the manipulators of venture capital as the original marshlands had been to the speculators and promoters who dug out the deepwater basins, and laid thirty miles of railway track in 1886. When artists walk through a wilderness in epiphanous 'bliss-out', fiddling with polaroids, grim estate agents dog their footsteps. And when the first gay squatters arrive, bearing futons ... the agents smile, and reach for their chequebooks. The visionary reclaims the ground of his nightmares only to present it, framed in perspex, to the Docklands Development Board.

Cowboy hauliers, chancers with transport, trade the freight that is still worth bringing in as a cover story: tractors that metamorphose into rocket launchers, heroin-impregnated madonnas, all the miraculous shape-shifting cargoes.

We broke into a ghost-hut masquerading as a Seaman's Hostel; a spectacular and previously unrecorded brochure of photo opportunities. The roof had been bombed. Curtains of red dust fell through the chilled air. Voices of departed voyagers. Quarrels, drink. Tall tales, unfinished reminiscences. Shards of mirror glass sanded the stone floor: a lake of dangerous powder, from which you might reassemble a version of the past – by sweeping this snowstorm backwards into the projector.

The station itself is a mausoleum built to house the absence of Empire; Empire as a way of escape, of plundering the exotic, defrauding our impossible dream of some remote garden of paradise. A cantilevered shed, epic in scale, runs away to piers, Custom Houses, platforms that might once have connected with the city. But now you will have to conjure from your grandfather's memory the oak-panelled saloons, upholstered in tapestry, the floors covered with Turkey felt.

The place is shrill with the traffic of the dead: furs, cabin trunks, porters. There are mesmerizing patches of sunlight on the bald stone flags that it is impossible not to acknowledge. We move slowly, talk in whispers: a cathedral of evictions.

We followed the tunnel down to the Gravesend Ferry, the TSS *Edith*. Everybody wants to get away. The officers from Tilbury Fort chose to live on the other side, among the decayed Regency splendour, where there was some remnant of life and society. Their 'pressed' men were either invalid, or had to be locked at night into their barracks to prevent them from deserting.

No time, on this excursion, for the World's End; a low tumble-down weather-boarded building, once the baggage store where troops crossing the river left their equipment. Tables for stripping the drowned. We skirt the pub and its stunted orchard, reluctantly; passing on, to enter the Fort by the ashlar-faced Water Gate.

Immediately the shades press on you. The lack of any ordinary human presence makes the survival of this enclosure remarkable, and daunting. The tourist feels responsible for the silence. The cobbles of the parade are beaten fears. Bone faces crowd the upper windows of the Officers' Quarters. Sand spills from the water pump. Someone has placed a dead bird in the mouth of the ceremonial cannon. In the chapel the caretaker inscribes the names of the Jacobite prisoners who died at the Fort, hidden from sight in the tunnels of the powder magazine. Spent weapons, hostages. Highlanders brought by sea from Inverness, for eventual transportation. A museum of madness and suffering set into a vicious – but disguised – pentagon. Redoubts and ravelins spike the surrounding swamplands: the Water Gate can empty the moat and inundate these outlying paddy fields.

There is a scratching mockery in the movement of the caretaker's quill, as he columns his pastiche ledger with real names. *Cameron, Macfie, MacGillivray, MacGregor*. The east wind courses through brick-work passageways, caponiers, and ramps; outflanking the petrified weaponry.

Among the cabinets of gas masks, mortars, knives, and bandage boxes is a map that illustrates the lines of fire between Tilbury and Gravesend, as proposed by Thomas Hyde Page in 1778. The river at its narrowest point, eight hundred yards, shore to shore, is tightly laced by invisible threads: a stitched vulva. The only entrance to the heat of the city is denied. A pattern is woven over the waters; which remains unactivated to this day. And, therefore, most hazardous.

The only blood shed in anger was during a cricket match. An Essex batsman, his wicket flattened, held petulantly to his ground, demanding that the strength of the breeze be taken into account. The incensed Kentish outfielders sprinted to the guardroom: most of them moving for the first time that afternoon. The skipper snatched up a rifle, and shot the defaulter where he stood. An elderly invalid, intervening with the garrulous wisdom of his years, was bayoneted through the throat. The sergeant in temporary charge of the Fort, while his officer promenaded the terrace of the Clarendon, was butchered in his nightshirt on the balcony of the Sutler's House: prefiguring that famous icon of General Gordon, waiting on the steps of the Governor's Palace at Khartoum for the spears of the fanatics, children of the Mahdi, redeemer at the end of time. (In an earlier incarnation, as Captain Charles Gordon, the stern Bible-puncher had commanded the Royal Engineers at Gravesend – where a small plaque honours him for his devotion to 'the poor and sick' of the town.)

The men of Kent escaped from this horror across the river. The Essex ten, claiming a moral – if pyrrhic – victory, ran off over the drawbridge into the sunken levels.

A photograph, promoting the glories of the station concourse at Tilbury, before the reconstruction, features a newspaper kiosk, with the day's headlines clearly visible: BIRTHDAY HONOURS. BATTLE IN THE SUDAN. Six massively moustached porters stand at ease, barring all bogus claimants from the Third Class Waiting Room.

Joblard and I, subdued, retreated; by bulwark and counterscarp, through *fausse-braye* and *cunette*, to the Dead House. We passed out by the Landport Gate and turned towards the hope of the World's End. On the far shore of the outer moat was the dark tangle of a wild orchard: the gentle flicker of candlelight behind shaded windows. Shrill laughter on the evening air.

VIII

When does a victim realize that he is the chosen one? When does a 'fall guy' receive the first intimations of vertigo?

Arthur Singleton, his whites held in place by a knotted Kingston Park tie, stood queasy and distempered, leaning breathless against the brass line of zero longitude. A pale stripe of virtue ran away from his navel and down Maze Hill, between the twin domes of Greenwich Hospital, across the river, and far around the red-splashed globe: to pierce, on its return, his psychic body. A shocking, but unremarked, jolt in the lower spine. He had completed his preparation. He did not salute the bullet-pocked plinth of General James Wolfe, abseiler-extraordinary, and exporter of 'high degree' Freemasonry to the North American continent. He walked, head bowed, along the broad avenue towards the heath. He was bent to his fate, tapping his bat on the ground at every third stride.

Singleton felt a tingling in his palms; the sympathy pains of martyrdom that presaged an heroic contest. He could sense the stigmata sweating blood into his white gloves. Today would be exceptional. He rested and fed all his doubts into a giant oak. The tree was a metaphor for the innings he would play. The roots were laid in the vision of the city, seen from the hill. The trunk was the slow build-up of confidence: 'seeing' the ball, before it left the bowler's hand. And then the branching out, the flowering. The strokes all round the wicket, sketching the tree's shape into the ground for ever. He had only a necessary fear of the opposition, coupled with the still greater fear of losing 'face' among his fellows; the cramming masters, curates, and medical men of Blackheath who would this afternoon meet Lord Harris's eleven in a charity match, for the benefit of the dependants of the drowned, in the tragedy of the sinking of the paddle-steamer, the *Princess Alice*. The sky was bruised and purple, racing, livid with threat and prophecy.

Dr Grace, the Hon. Alfred Lyttleton, Lockwood: names set into the earth like pillars of a temple. Arthur was at the wicket and taking guard with no memory of the preliminary courtesies; the introductions, the toss, the early collapse of the local men. He was wholly detached from the scene, which could have been an engraving in the *London Illustrated News*. His foot moved towards the first delivery – short on the leg side – and the spectators were applauding a boundary.

The heath was enclosed in a bell jar of wild light, high clouds chased and harried. He was standing on the world's curve – and he stood erect, shaping each drive, timing each cut, chipping wide of the stolidly planted fielders. Dr Grace was shaking him by the hand. His voice was unexpectedly high in pitch. Arthur could not understand what he was saying. He walked off. The fever-drained grass stretched into an endless plain. The dark houses slid from his sight. 'Singleton, well done! Capital display, sir! Fine knock, Arthur!'

He forced a passage through the press of friends and strangers: the ladies, their parasols, their billowing dresses. Soaked. Dripping on to the ground. Shadows that could drown him. Uncovered bodies. Did they need to bring them here? Hair shapeless and obscuring their faces. No eyes. Tongues like slaughtered animals. White mud. *Don't touch.* Their cold hands scorch his arm. The dead ones block him. Their fingers twist around his heart. '*I felt I was going to be like Mother and the best thing for me was to die.*'

Mother was waiting. She offered me her cheek. She had come back, to watch. 'Arthur, my boy, what has disturbed you? And where is your wig? Surely, you cannot intend to enter court in this undress?'

The boundary ring has been posted with the unfortunates. They are laid out – a catch, a pale harvest – upon wrinkled black tarpaulin sheets. They shine in pitch. They have been hooked and drawn from the river. The heaped poor. They are swollen with death. They did not learn to swim. We have scraped the water from them like a caul of skin.

Now they are calling for the doctors. 'Doctor, a moment. Your signature, sir. For my godson. Would you oblige me ... your name ...' *Bury me! Blind me! Cut out my tongue!* Now the umpires, the white coats, are at my elbows. 'He must rest.' Clear him; carry him to a secure place. A place in history. Justice will be done in *Wisden's Almanac*. Arthur Singleton's stout innings on a sticky wicket against the established men of England. An obituary tribute to a fine cricketer, and a gentleman; a Wykehamist, a scholar of New College, Oxford.

Leaning on his bat, Arthur is led from the field. He passes through a narrow gate in the wall, and into a private garden. He taps his willow, with every third stride, on the gravel.

We stood outside the World's End, reluctant to enter, to break the spell of silence. Shadow blades of the pear tree thrash the sailcloth windows. Tupping marionettes. Remote voices. Wood smoke. '*The dead are dancing with the dead.*' This clapboard shanty has been sifted from the spoils of the river; nailed together out of drowned timber – spar set to mast, pegleg to oar – ramped out of chaos. World's End, *fin du globe*.

The door was not locked. We pushed through to the bar. And backed our drinks into a remote corner. Uninvited guests at the requiem for an orgy that was still waiting to happen.

I put the photocopies I had made from Patrick Hanbury's *Researches in Polynesia and Melanesia* on to the table, to show them to Joblard – who had a taste for the impossible. He liked to stretch the boundaries of disbelief until he achieved a frisson of naked panic. He used his fear to kick-start a slumbering consciousness.

'Certain spots,' wrote Hanbury, 'particularly those associated with death, are haunted. I recollect that two members of the hospital staff met a devil … and were so terrified that they dropped most of their clothes, but would not return to find them.'

Hanbury's photographs are a metaphor for the story of tribal contact with Europe, and the cruel refinements of European light. They demonstrate, in growths of outlandish tissue, our need to capture the extraordinary: to analyse, convert, *to put a price on*. The amused subjects stand willingly before the hooded stranger and his tripod. They accept the presence of the black box that will reduce them; shift them to a generality, an illustration of a definable tendency. Delicate ritual markings become 'deformities'. Pattern succumbs to elephantiasis; a vast strawberry richness. The scrotum sagging from the warrior to the ground beneath him. Clusters of enlarged follicles. The truly monstrous is calmed by its context. Ulcers, yaws, lesions.

We are ashamed. We turn away. The calm acceptance in the face of the natives forces us to close the book, and drop it into my bag. But that is not enough. We search for something, anything, to carry us into a safer narrative.

Then we recognize, with distaste, both the turtle-necked figure sprawled at the fireside, and the fleshy publican; his eyelids stroked with kingfisher blue *ultima*, his lips violet, above small rabbit-sharp teeth. They are the recorders and violators of the myth of the unsolved serial murders. They convert that slaughter into a brotherhood of remembrance. They honour the imagined (and nicknamed) psychopath who brought the four of them together as the 'Connoisseurs of Crime'.

Errlund, Bobby Younger, Nick Hywood, Sgt Roughdew: the philosopher, the publican, the journalist, and the keeper of the Black Museum.

Errlund was boring his friends with the latest anecdote dug out by his
researchers from the Bishopsgate Institute. He had the reputation of
never having actually to write a single word of any of his books. 'He was
doing cut-ups when William Burroughs was still getting his kicks from
dropping aspirin into Coca-Cola,' Hywood said of him. 'He's the first
of the Post Moderns. The ultimate technician of disinterested commer-
cialism.'

'One of the pleasure-seekers on the *Princess Alice* – or so she claimed –
was "Long Liz", the Ripper's third victim,' Errlund began. 'She was
perfectly respectable then, dolled up for the excursion; three layers of
petticoat, and no drawers. *Petite bourgeoise*. Sheerness, North Woolwich.
Can you hear the band out there, midstream, hacking away at "Nancy
Lee"? Cockney hordes packed into the saloon; bawling, shoving, belching stout, dressed to the nines. Nothing changes. A few "commer-
cials", tradesmen with their popsies, fathers feeding misinformation to
their brats on the upper foredeck. Beneath them, the great wheels were
churning, bringing her about. On the bridge a seaman screams, "My
God, Captain, that man is starboarding his helm!" And the *Bywell
Castle*, an iron-screw steamer, comes straight on them. "Thin as egg-
shell", the *Alice* breaks up directly. Singing becomes screaming. They
were in the water. The idlers on the river wall could see the light die in
their eyes. They were only yards from the shore. Their fingers clawing
without purchase at the cold tide. Layers of muslin belling into strange
shapes, getting heavier, wrapping them in cement.'

'And you suggest,' said Roughdew, hoping to edit a wearisome
exposition, 'that this experience launched "Long Liz" on the fatal phase
of her career? She felt somehow that she did not deserve to survive? She
was looking, ever after, for a second chance to die?'

'She had been escorted.' Errlund was not so easily diverted. 'Her
husband, and her two dear ones. She would not give them up. She
snatched at a rope trailed from a small craft. It was already full and low
in the water. The baby was dragged from her arms by the undertow. A
man climbed on to her back, using her like a ladder, kicking for dear life.
She lost her front teeth. But she held to the rope. Ropes were threaded
all over the river, a great net of holes. Ropes and lanterns. A grim trawl.
She was two hours in the water. They brought her off, finally; got her
ashore. Greenwich. Horse-blanket, brandy, a complimentary ticket
from the London and Blackwall Railway. Before the stars were out, she
was back in her lodgings. It might never have happened.'

'Amen!' muttered Hywood.

Errlund plunged on, intoxicated by his own rhetoric. 'But that was her story, the drowning; that was her justification. Small ghosts accompanied her into every public house in Whitechapel. They did for Michael Kidney, a dockside labourer she was living with. "I couldn't share a pillow," he said, "with two dead angels." The lies that Liz told became the truth of it. Her single encounter with the crush and weight of water, the overwhelming force of the river, carried her away. Spindrift. She drank in revenge. Diluted the Thames with gin. Until that night when, at last, she went with a "wrong-un"; up from Cable Street, factory gateway. She was split open, severed from the phantoms she could not bring to term. The victim of a monster she could exploit, neither for gain nor sympathy.'

'Very pretty,' said Hywood, 'but what was the fate of the surrogate Ripper, the *Bywell Castle*?'

Errlund made a show of checking his papers. 'She left Alexandria,' he said, 'with a cargo of linen, bound for Tilbury – and was never seen again. There were rumours that she'd rounded Cape Corvoeris. And then, nothing. Off the map, lost, gone to Atlantis. She'd served her purpose. You go downstream with impunity only once. If you get safely past Blythe Sands, you're in a different story.'

X

The hill was smoking: it seemed to have been shelled by some infernal ordnance. 'I am walking into hell,' thought Arthur Singleton. The trees were a sham. Elizabethan veterans: hollow, dry as chalk, held upright by ties and staves. There had been some unimportant tragedy. A mistake, an accident. Pieces of smouldering black cloth were caught on the bushes. The air was burnt and sour. Fragments of bone were trodden into the earth.

Arthur walked between the umpires. As they walked, they dropped pebbles into his pockets. One pebble, he surmised, for each run scored; for every stroke of his life.

They cut directly through the contours of the maze, did not meander, or pace out the mystery. They snapped the invisible strings, plunging down towards the dance of light that flickered so transiently on the water. They were reading his confession to him. They told him the things he had done. The letter was placed next to his heart.

Now Arthur saw the raised spear of a white church between the twin domes of the hospital. There were masts and ladders. Courtyards, narrow passageways. Stone steps, green with algae.

He paddled carefully out from the dark and narrow beach, until he was moving freely. And without effort. The mud did not settle on his white trousers. He slid. The steep gradient went away from him. He drifted. He opened his arms. The water flowed into his veins. He crossed over.

XI

Bobby Younger sat in the back of the curtained limousine between two officials. The keeper of the Black Museum had tapped him, sliced his reverie, asked him to step outside: some gentlemen wanted a word. Then Bobby was squeezed. He was sweated, cold. Photographs confronted him that might once have provoked a private pleasure, but were now contextualized into raw fear. Rough, shirtless boys pouted: he was accused by every mark that he could identify. Old letters, written in heat, without thought, were sealed in pouches of plastic – like rare literary holographs. There were documents, typed in blue ink, defaced with official stamps. There were reports from West Africa; facts and fictions. Duplicates, invoices, VAT returns, sworn statements. The junkman had rambled like a speed-freak. Bobby's unwritten autobiography had been violently sub-edited, ghosted by professionals: it was offered to the world in instalments of lurid sensation. The Tilbury Group was defaced into the Wild Bunch. Bobby had been nominated, and would now oblige. Always. And for ever.

He had been shadowed and eavesdropped – as we are all eavesdropped – and now he was put to use. He would serve. Or he would cease to be. His London days were a scrapbook to barter; but Bobby himself was no longer credible. His parking space at the studios had already been requisitioned. He would take the offered advance and step westwards. A bungalow on the edge of a golf course. He would speak only in quotations. He would disappear from view. Confessions would be supplied; private papers, forgeries. The Black Museum was at his disposal. He would shape an account of the murders that would point the finger where the finger should be pointed. He was 'on the firm'.

Arthur Singleton's name had been promoted to the head of the list. The seals were broken on all the files. Arthur Singleton should therefore bear the solitary brand of guilt. His was the honour. He was the 'madman', the 'invert', the 'suicide'. He was the Judas Goat, by appointment.

'We'll make it easy for you,' the thin one said, offering Bobby a

cigarette, and dropping, without embarrassment, into the parrot-speak
of his trade. 'We'll supply you with the opening paragraph.'

Bobby was trembling. He had to move a finger slowly along the line
of words to make any sense of them. *'When does a victim realize he is the
chosen one? When does a "fall guy" receive the first intimations of vertigo?'*

XII

I stayed in my corner, doing nothing; swirling the liquid yellow stain in
an almost empty glass. Joblard's thirst was painful to watch. He
drummed his fingers, waiting doggedly at the bar for Bobby Younger's
return. The shifty rump of the Connoisseurs of Crime had tumbled out
of a side-door, like an audience fleeing from the National Anthem. We
were alone.

Joblard used this suspended interval of time in arranging the twelve
postcards, on the board behind the spirit bottles, into a coherent tale: a
fiction that would carry him out on the tide, and away from the sullen
gravity of Tilbury Riverside. The postcards were our only hope of
escape.

Joblard's HEART OF DARKNESS. A Narrative in Twelve Postcards.

(1) Sepia filter: the tanned light of dead time. Heat haze. A three-
master rides at anchor. Two small islands float, unfocused, like
derelict submarines, covered in vegetation. The photographer has
been unable to describe the point at which the sea melts into the
sky.

(2) A rivermouth, obliquely approached. A slave fort, or another
island, shimmering in mid-channel. A tall bare tree lifting from
the scrub that runs down to the water's edge. The sharp black
gradient of an infected beach.

(3) Five native 'boys' rowing a longboat through the shallows.
Perhaps to oblige the photographer? He would not be able to do
justice to the cultivated moustaches of the pilot from a greater
distance. The rudder strings hang limply in the lap of a corpulent
and ugly Dutchman, or Low German trader. He sits, straight-
backed, his hands cupped protectively over his genitals: as if to
shield them from the eyes of the oarsmen – who have nowhere
else to look. Their reflections, broken and butchered, follow them
through the water.

(4) Two African 'bloods' are travestied as South Sea Cannibals. They have feathers poked in their crinkly hair; and they are wearing grass skirts. One appears to smoke a clay pipe, while the other chews a cigar. Stiff cellophane collars clamp their throats, like slave-chokers. The suggestion is that they have eaten a Missionary to obtain them. They are playing billiards. 'An easy shot' is the card's ambiguous title. Does it refer to the cannon on offer? Or to this unarmed brace of smoking-room intruders? Will their heads fit onto the wall between the decorative white nudes and the framed photograph of the 'Central Hotel'? The postcard was printed in Saxony.

(5) *Adamorisha, Lagos*. Six draped figures, probably male. Their hands and feet are hidden in loose blankets. Their faces are covered with cloths. They are holding sticks and wands and shotguns. Straw hats, either Spanish or Mexican, keep their head-coverings in place. The effect is bizarre: nuns playing at cowboys. Or, more accurately, a renegade sect overcome by the need to 'fix' the moment before a massacre. A record that will not hang them. The man who took the photograph was obviously slaughtered at the completion of his task. Possession of this postcard is a potential sentence of death.

(6) The hunt: a dead crocodile, its jaws set in a terminal yawn. Twenty-five white men in hats pose around the corpse. Most wear moustaches. A naval officer is bearded. They all bristle with rifles, hand-guns, bandoleers. The dominant member of the group is also the fattest. He rests his boot on the crocodile's neck. It is the Dutchman from the longboat. The scaly victim, too old to make a decent suitcase, has been hired for the occasion. Does it take a posse of twenty-five grotesquely over-armed and over-dressed colonials to eliminate one elderly reptile? These men are going somewhere else. They are travelling downriver. And they will, at the very least, burn a village, rape the cattle, and annex a piece of territory the size of Portugal.

(7) *Chef de Village (Congo Français)*. He glowers in creased jacket and cheap beads. He wears a bowler hat with the lining turned out, in the form of a sweaty leather skullcap. He hides beneath the shade of a golfing umbrella. His infant son stands beside him: stone-smooth, sculpted head reaching over the rim of a table, that has been set out to resemble a roadside stall. Two empty beer flagons and a corked bottle of 'Natural Bilin Water'. A jaggedly-opened

tin of tomatoes. An upended bowl that keeps the flies from some invisible delicacy. What is the chief's son staring at in such perplexity? Whose shadow falls across the corner of the table? Has a great chief been reduced to the status of a roadside huckster? Or has a surviving huckster been found to impersonate a chief?

(8)   A secret place. A clearing in the jungle. Young boys in loose white shifts stand in a pool beneath a waterfall, that drifts like ectoplasm from the overhanging foliage. A man and an older boy are perched on the rocks above them. They lean on sticks. The boy might be blind, or a leper. Balanced, on the edge of the card, is a second youth: a bugle raised to his lips. A European lies beside him; bald and bearded, in a greasy soutane. A Jesuitical dwarf, in stockinged feet, whose eye sockets are markings in the red earth. Deeper into the shadows are further figures, still as plants. The lacy spray rises like smoke from a hole in the cliff. It is a real temptation to reverse the card, and turn the composition on its head. This reading is stranger, but calmer. The boys now hang from the walls of a cave, like so many scholarly bats. The waterfall is, of course, unchanged.

(9)   Ivory poachers. A white man closing his hands around the long barrel of a rifle. He has borrowed General Gordon's tasselled smoking cap. He could be Sinclair's grandfather. He has that mixture of ferocity and sunken-eyed cunning. Eleven naked and muscular blacks pose around him, with the arrogant self-possession of Yardies. They have been chosen and arranged like a touring cricket team. The 'head boy' wears a moulting stovepipe hat. In the centre of the composition is a trophy table, supporting the solitary tusk of a bull elephant. From the arrangement, and the design of the plates, it is possible to deduce that this table once belonged to the *Chef de Village*. He is no longer to be seen. Neither the *Chef*, nor his son.

(10)   An uprising, or dispute among bandits. The slaughter is 'staged' outside a corrugated-iron shed. Riders on mules. Half a bicyclist. A raised whip. A man in the dirt, arm outstretched, flinches from the carefully aimed rifle. A loss of 'sharpness' in the foreground melts a group of bearded fanatics into a single unit: a triple-headed monster *physically demonstrating* the miracle of the Trinity. One of the victims is smiling, and giving the game away. Impossible to tell. Is this faked photograph a rehearsal for an atrocity that has yet to be enacted? Or is it a reconstruction of some repellent

episode, already well on its way towards entering the history
books? A mustard-yellow fingerprint spins through the trees like
a dying sun. It is still not too late to bring the criminals to justice.

(11) The golden hour. Three colonists, or 'interlopers', are gathered
for their sundowners in the corner of a verandah. They are
'meditative, and fit for nothing but placid staring'. The planked
balcony on which they sit is also a kind of deck, set high above a
deserted street. There is a wine bottle on the bamboo table. Their
glasses are charged, but they are waiting patiently for a signal
from the photographer. Obviously, they have something to
celebrate – if it is only their good fortune in possessing an
undrunk bottle of claret. Our angle of approach is indirect; we are
eavesdropping on this scene – with the tacit collaboration of the
participants. Beneath the cane chair of the bullet-headed man is a
riverboat captain's cap. He has the predatory smile, and the arched
eyebrows, of an avatar of Sir James Goldsmith. Cross-legged,
straight-backed as ever, squatting on the floor, is our Dutchman: a
bronze idol in a crisp white suit. The third man, with a glass
frozen halfway towards his preposterous moustache, is a father-
in-law, glancing hopefully out of shot for the assistant director's
call for 'action' in a minor Mack Sennett comedy. Above the
heads of this complacent drinking school two sharp-spoked
wooden wheels have been placed: almost Japanese in their effect.
They have returned from an expedition. They are alive. They
want to parade their triumph in the face of posterity, like a
one-finger salute.

(12) A little later, on the same verandah. Everybody is slightly
drunker. The photograph itself is inebriated. And the features of
the riverboat captain, who leans forward to 'top up' the
comedian's glass, have been burnt out like a flaring match-head.
The colonists have slipped from focus, but the balcony of the
adjacent bungalow has sharpened. The street has gone, leaving in
its place a tall bare tree. It is as if the whole set had slid back to the
shore. Yarns of the ocean will now be put to the test. The sun has
dropped behind the Japanese wheels, giving them an heraldic
status. And the photographer has slipped to the floor. He includes
most of the tin roof in his composition: a flapping dark sail. A
sinister development. But there are more troubling implications.
The Dutchman has disappeared; and another man, younger, with
the same moustache, has taken his place. He *could*, very nearly, be
the Dutchman, at another time, ten or fifteen years before:

reincarnated, by occult trickery, for this special valedictory piss-up. It is easy to imagine this trio meeting every evening, taking up their invariable positions, drinking their invariable drinks, making the invariable remarks. The second version of the balcony scene might then be an *earlier* party: aped, to greater effect, in the first postcard. But the fact that the riverboat captain and the comedian are unchanged would seem to contradict this explanation. No, it is much more obvious than that. *The Dutchman has taken over the camera.* Legless and wobbly, he is attempting to reproduce the original portrait. Perhaps, each man in turn will be the recorder: before returning to reoccupy his place as a bit-player. But all the other postcards, if they were not flawed in processing, have now been lost. And cannot be described. The new face, the man who has been responsible, until this moment, for the pictorial record, is an actor, an ironist. He precisely mimics the Dutchman's way of lifting his glass with a mannerist delicacy about the positioning of his fingers. He could be the double of Paul Klee, photographed in 1906, in the garden of his parents' house in Obstbergweg, Berne. He is the true author of this fiction that could, of course, be reassembled in any order, and read in whatever way suits the current narrator. These dim postcards are as neutral as a Tarot pack.

Joblard's thirst was unassuaged. The game was over. He wanted more. He leant across the bar and plucked the postcards from their board. He fondled them, and sniffed them. He held them against his cheek, and he shuffled them. He turned them over. THIS SPACE, AS WELL AS THE BACK, MAY NOW BE USED FOR COMMUNICATION, BUT FOR INLAND ONLY. The warning proved unnecessary. All the cards – except one – were blank, virgin. The owner could not bear to part with them. They would find their way into a scrapbook. But the billiard-playing cannibals *had* received the red king's head, and was postmarked LEYTONSTONE. 3 P.M. SP23. 04. So this tale of the exotic had not been stolen out of the dark continent, *but dispatched to greet it.* Nothing could match the mysteries shrouding the heart of Leytonstone. The sender had no word to add to the image. He identified his potential audience, spelt out, with some difficulty, an address – and left it at that. Who could, in all conscience, ask for more? Demented investigators, and bounty-hunting snoops, should search out the descendants of 'F. Wilson, Esq., Santa Isabel, Fernando Poo, S.W.C. Africa'.

2

Riverside Opportunities

Riverside Opportunities

'Let's to terrestrial flesh, or
bid good-night, I thought.
I said, I'm unversed, I said
nor a clerk of nigromantics ...'

David Jones,
The Lady of the Pool

The marmosets have gone. Why else would we meet in this place? A graveyard detached from its host: a church tower faking a period grandeur, while its body tumbles wantonly into decay behind corrugated-iron fencing. From the low steps of St John's, Scandrett Street, I mourn the loss of another secret locale. A *temenos* remaining sacred because we do not need to visit it. It is there, and that is enough. The balance in our psychic map of the city is unharmed. But now another disregarded inscape has been noticed and dragged from cyclical time to pragmatic time; has been asked to justify itself. *Shannon Landscapes* are the chosen agents of 'reality': red bearded, slow-moving giants in check shirts have the renovation contract. The nautical graves are bulldozed, and the sepulchres retained as captive features. The brute undergrowth has been uprooted, and the ghosts put to the torch. The totemic animals have fled.

Marmosets, lemurs, genets, tamarins and sugar gliders were brought ashore, covertly, and traded from public houses along the Highway. Across the tables of the Old Rose bundles were passed. From under stiff seamen's jerseys, small hot lives were drawn, living hearts. The locals adopted them without certificates or rabies clearance, without quarantine. These tamed exotics enriched their primal soot. Panicked beasts were drawn down into the dark houses, were petted – or pained – to early death.

But some marmosets broke free: forward-thrusting jaws, bark strippers. They were able to tolerate the hostile temperatures. They took cover behind the walls of this graveyard with its fox-mangy London planes, its chestnuts. They cowered among the white blossoms. From the warehouses came the scents of their homeland; from Cinnamon Street, sacked essences. The slow presence of the river chilled their benign hysteria. With their pinched skull-faces and their tufting professorial hair, they resembled a tribe of pygmy Longfords – flinching, purse-lipped from the pain of the world. Delicate human hands fluttered vaporously, or masturbated in absorbed lethargy. The minimum requirement for their survival was a lack of attention. Unseen, they were immortal. And always beneath them, granting them gravity, lay the children of sea captains and merchants: their mouths stopped with shale. Dead daughters, stacked five to the grave, outlasted by some mute father, who will never be able to forgive them their mortality. Bleak histories whose chiselled narratives are fed with lichen. Now, sitting here as the light died, I projected false images of Guiana on to the mustard-colour bricks. I heard the promise of stone cities in their shrill birdlike voices.

But I was not alone in my interest. Juveniles from the tenements, scavengers of the wastelots, netted them, clubbed them, pelted them with stones. Hereditary enemies: killing what they cannot eat. They trapped and sold them. Peeled them for gloves. The marmosets were caged in huts and experimental basements. Mild theoreticians in white coats probed with blades for the sources of memory. Simple tasks were rewarded. Bells rung brought nuts and chocolate drops. Pieces of their brain were cut away. And still the tasks were performed. Further excavations; cells burnt with hot wire. The performance was slower, but it was completed. The skull, finally, was a hollow membrane, lit by torches: 'memory' was active – and unlocated. The landscape is destroyed, but the dream of it is everywhere.

I heard the urgent click and drag of Todd Sileen's approach. A troubled leathern creaking, nautical and obscure: like wind in the riggings, or the pull of an unoiled wheel. You felt Sileen's presence, before you could find him. The temperature dropped, and plants died. 'Baron Saturday', the urchins called him – from a safe distance, crouching, heads in caps, from terror of his unpupilled eye. They saw him in their fevers. He put stones under their tongues. He slept on a mattress of skulls. He cast no shadow. Breathing heavily, he lowered himself on to the step beside me: a damaged manifest. His leg thrown out, stiff as a plank.

'We're in, boss.' Sileen spoke from the throat: abrupt, punched sentences. He coated each syllable in phlegm, like a craftsman varnishing a dubious 'Old Master'. His shifty glance checked the corners, frisked me for a hidden microphone. 'He'll see us at twelve o'clock, "railway time". One minute out, either way, and the deal's off.'

He pushed himself up. He was away, and motoring. His exaggerated roll – a man dancing on logs – swept him forward at a pace I could hardly match. He cornered on one heel, and hopped over kerbs. But living within a gentle full toss of Wapping Stairs had not helped his style. The damp had got at him, rusted his humour. Too close an association with water has always worked on the physiology of the darker strain of fictional hero. And the lower limbs are the first to suffer. The literary icon finds himself turning, from the feet up, into a carved figurehead. Todd Sileen was another Ahab, a forked man lurching on a single prong. As a skilled carpenter, he might easily have whittled himself a trusty peg – but that was another country, another life. Time was against him. He was against time.

Sileen had a guilty secret: he was gathering about him the works of Joseph Conrad. All of them; every envelope, every (certified) drop of ink. *Why* he was doing this was a thornier question. Let's skip the psychology and call him a run-of-the-mill headbanger: the kind of pest who sleeps outside the post office to get his catalogue before you do. We were together because he had a use for me. He wanted me, in my capacity as a bona fide crook, to front him; to work the discounts, list the remnants, and speed the duplicates on their way to California.

Whenever Sileen chose to leave this rancid backwater, it would be finished. He was the last human. Scandrett Street would never again be what it was, on this day, in this light, on this square of pavement.

We entered the Cuckoo, Wapping Lane, in an elegiac mood, touching the tables to make sure they were solid; keeping a weather eye on the door, in immediate expectation of a demolition squad. When we had secured our pints and a bowl of depilated prawns, we reviewed our tactics. The public bar was empty; sunlight filtered through the frosted window, picking up the heraldic colours, to spill them, recklessly, over the floor. The moment was eternal: whoever spoke first was damned.

It appeared that one mile downriver, in a studio apartment, Dr Adam Tenbrücke of Narrow Street was hoarding a shelf of Conrads he had painlessly amputated from the David Garnett Collection. Tenbrücke specialized in 'Judaica'; with sidelines in Holocaust mementoes, the more saline Expressionists, and anything occult, involving ritual sacrifice – preferably human, young, and female. He had his own vineyards on the Rhine, and he always wintered in the Cape. He favoured cigars that might have been rolled in human skin, stitched over a morbid blend of camel dung. He smiled effortlessly, but without meaning.

Tenbrücke had accepted the Conrads, with sighs and shrugs, as part-payment in a currency deal that had gone sour. 'You cut off a head only once,' he remarked, 'the gonads you can always squeeze.'

These books meant nothing to him. His price would therefore be impossible to meet. It was the best method of milking some pleasure from the affair. He would hold out until the sweat was rolling, in steel bearings, down Sileen's neck; until his tongue stuck to the roof of his mouth. How Sileen knew this, ahead of the event, I could not begin to guess. He did his homework without leaving his fireside. He consulted the messages in the flames. He was inevitably putting the phone back on its cradle as you entered the room. He lived in whispers, behind closed blinds: at midnight, he took to the streets.

Sileen never admitted to owning a car — it was my business to drive him — but now, as we passed one, parked with its nearside wheels on the pavement, he stopped and put a key in its lock. It could have been any car. He seemed to have picked this one simply because he was tired of walking. He was in second gear, and away, before I had worked out how to shut the door.

II

'This house once belonged to Francis Bacon: a painter.' Tenbrücke brushed aside any formal introductions and began lecturing us, as if we shared *exactly* his sense of the cynicism and venality of the world: a vision he tried, with scrupulous politeness, to mirror in all his dealings. 'Left nothing behind him. Not a tube of any description, nor a knife. What did he do here? He never lifted a brush. Sat quiet with his back to the window. The river-light modelled his head with an interesting syphilitic effect; the dying claret going green at the edges. He looked as if he had been flayed.'

Sileen and I, side by side, Tweedledum and Tweedledee, sat stiffly on the edge of a merciless Bauhaus shelf; polished leather thongs on an armature of brass. We were auditioning for something. Tenbrücke put a flame-thrower to his Brechtian cigar: with the relish of an interrogator.

'You don't smoke?' he stated, between slow puffs.

'Only cigars,' I replied, hopefully.

'Ah, good. Very good.' Tenbrücke nodded, without passing the box. 'You really should try these some time. A little shop in Amsterdam.'

He wanted to show us everything: inscriptions, photographs, woodcuts of dockside crucifixions, autographed menus (authenticated with chicken fat), skulls in the rubble, sabre massacres, caricatures of vast hook-nosed profiteers fellating gold from the enslaved and mesmerized masses. He reared above these boxed and gilt-edged images. He caressed velvet; he fingered, he teased. He slid open drawers with well-rehearsed gestures. He oozed and glistened: his mouth melted with soft metals. He ran his hand inside a closely-buttoned suede waistcoat — a slash of hunting pink — to massage the heart of a slaughtered animal. Sugar-dusted lumps in a silver bowl were pressed on us. Rubber cubes disguising a kernel of pinewood.

'Saturday afternoons, do you ever visit the Porchester Hall Turkish Baths?' Tenbrücke wasn't ready to give Sileen an opening. 'It helps to steam Farringdon Road out of the pores, I find. I'm not fit for anything else. I'm too old for Bell Street and Portobello. They're all there.' He laughed. 'All the faces. Property, Television, Boxing, Snooker. All the agents, the brokers, Tin Pan Alley. Terence Stamp? Of course. Rolex watches? Oysters? Half-price, and better for cash!' He bared his wrist.

Sileen made for the window. He gave up on the shelves of black fetishes. There wasn't a book in the place.

'Shoes?' Tenbrücke gestured, pleased that he was finally getting to his man. 'Brogues? You want a nice pair of Church's? Straight from the box. Any size you fancy — as long as it's a ten.' He heaved up a trouser-leg and flashed something bloody and well-bulled at us. I hoped, fervently, we were not moving on to the underwear.

'A Burberry for the wife? I'm serious.' Tenbrücke mistook Sileen's snarl of rage for a smile. 'Guess how much? Go on. As new, never worn. On my life, we're not talking "seconds". A hundred notes? A hundred and fifty? Forget it. Sixty. Sixty pounds, and I'm down to the garage to open the boot. Did you clock the Merc, on your way up? Nipped over to Germany in the spring. Business and pleasure. Only twelve thou on the dial, and she runs like quicksilver.'

I was beginning to enjoy this, wondering how long Tenbrücke could keep the Sidney Tafler routine going. He was well over the Race Relations limit, and drifting into pure pastiche. But it served its purpose. It turned Sileen into a wolf-man. He was ready to bite.

'Some advice, boys.' Tenbrücke had nailed his victim to the floor. He was ready to wind up the sideshow. 'Never buy anything but the best, the brand-leaders. I'm robbing myself, but I'm going to let you walk away with the pair of Burberrys for a oncer. Keep the girlfriend happy, and save the other for your wedding anniversary. This is vital: make sure the ladies in your life take the same size. It stands to reason. Your slag will pay her way in discounts.'

Tenbrücke yawned. And, for a moment, his eyes went dead. Then he took a small ivory box from his desk, and threw back a handful of pills, which he chewed noisily. The box was the real thing. It had cost some narwhal a tusk.

'Every Saturday, Porchester Row. We hear everything before it begins to happen.' He spoke automatically, like a dying tape. His spirits always sank with the sun, but he was incapable of making a move to bring light to the room. Sileen had won. He had to wait a few moments more: stolid, immovable, but unwilling to be the one to broach the business that was the sole purpose of our visit. Waiting was what Sileen did best. The Thames would freeze before he would be diverted from his self-imposed quest.

Now the combatants battled into the night in a monumental drinking bout. Tenbrücke fought his 'black dog' mood with cases of sweet yellow German wine. Sileen threw back whatever was put in front of him, grim-jawed, expressionless: the experience seemed, if anything, to sober the man. But, as bottle succeeded bottle, Tenbrücke's coarse humour was activated. He frisked again. He unlocked cupboards; he fiddled with wall-safes. He laid tissue-leafed folders in Sileen's lap; gently, like virgin brides. Nobody spoke. The world retreated. Remote sounds drifted from the river, as from another empire; muffled by glass and heavy drapes. Sileen could be neither shocked, nor provoked. The etchings were spread on the table in front of him: a dangerous challenge to an already replete gourmet. Men, women, children; freaks and beasts – in every possible combination. A terrible grimoire of possibilities, taken to its logical conclusion. The living savaged the dead. The unborn were mutilated.

Tenbrücke's mouth was liquid with excitement. His pink thyroidal eyes bulged in a net of broken veins. His cigar butt was black with gingivitic drool.

I realized that if I, as the disinterested party, did not act fast, we would be condemned to stay here for ever; witnessing this obscene and absolute self-exposure. Tenbrücke was a sick soul, begging us to forgive him – by sharing in his sickness. He was describing himself by showing us each and every object that he had collected. I attempted to pull him back from the brink, by the magical act of naming. 'Teodor Korzeniowski,' I said, 'otherwise, Joseph Conrad.'

It was enough. The very sound of it bored him. 'A dreary fellow, this Old Man of the Sea. A bourgeois mandarin. I never deal in Poles. I don't want herrings. I don't want promises. I want gold bars, furs, fine art. Sell these books, if you can, to the pug in the Holy See. Life's too short to haggle with silk-knickered wops.'

But we have to understand that, naturally, the items in question cannot be given away. Without respect, a deal has no meaning; it would not be binding. Tenbrücke's hand swallows Sileen's cheque, only to drop it with a pained shrug. Sileen had dated it '1888'. 'A final drink, gentlemen. And away.'

I carry the boxes out to the car. The one-legged man, kicking out his customized limb, swivels, grinning, down the spiral staircase.

III

Todd Sileen had captured, for this era, a couple of council properties, tucked away between blocks of undeveloped industrial warehouses and a spate of wild gardens. His sense of when to strike, and when to move on, was unmatched – and would have made him a rich man in some purer sphere of speculation: land, drugs, literary brokerage. Sileen didn't need wages. Without apparent income or occupation, he moved freely over the country and the continent, just as the seasons took him. And all the time, the body of Joseph Conrad – as it could be excavated from documents, letters, and sketches – was re-forming around him. He was nailing himself inside another man's shroud. He was willing Conrad's *physical* immortality; turning this Wapping hutch into an immaculate death-barque. When the very last item in the bibliography was secured, Sileen would cease to exist; and the thing he had made would be there through all the lives of the unsuspecting speculators, rushing to their doom on the river.

He was also working hard at taking over the redundant public library – the rest of the public having obediently decamped – to make it his own. To this end, he brandished his deformity as a credential; crawling into the Borough Housing Office on his hands and knee. But points on that waiting list were an unnecessary luxury. The council had taken power by offering an ear to every Valium-gobbling fanatic. They put themselves forward as the shock-absorbers of disenfranchised anguish; then dutifully dissipated the pain by identifying the most popular scapegoats. And passing out the brickbats. Renegade socialists muttered in pubs that these scoundrels were the barely acceptable face of skinhead fascism in 'liberal' drag. The party championed 'local' issues; when, in truth, there was no locality left. Employment was a sentimental memory: the whole corridor from Tower Bridge to the Isle of Dogs was in limbo. It was waiting to be called up. A cold wind ruffled the drowning pools, the labyrinthine walkways, the dumping pits. A few sponsored artists kept a window on the riverfront polished for the developers. There were lofts of hand-made paper waiting for the best offer.

Sileen was in clover. One of these days they would buy him out. If today's councillors were caught with their fingers in the till, there were plenty more to replace them. Meanwhile, he cultivated his balcony: an explosion of green life, lovingly watered by his amiable provincial girlfriend. She tolerated all his foibles, and cooked with such natural artistry that loungers hung about on the street corner soliciting a dinner invitation. Her life, shared only in certain areas, remained robustly independent in all others. Her presence in the flat humanized the unmannered bluntness of Sileen's dogma.

I watched, awed, as Sileen sank, puffing out his coarse sporran-moustache, into the swamp of an old armchair. He savoured these newest treasures: books to be slotted into place on the shelves that ran out from his shoulders like a benevolent crucifixion. I knew he did not have to read these things, or even handle them. The particular arrange-ment, by colour and texture of cloth, conferred power. Their touch was stunning to the skin.

Sileen opened a goatskin volume and, without needing to search for the place, tapped out a letter from Henry James. 'The news of Conrad's collaboration with Hueffer is to me like a bad dream which one relates before breakfast, their traditions are so dissimilar. It is inconceivable ...'

The letter was plucked from my hands. And replaced by a late photograph, executed by Boris Conrad: his father, leaning back, eyes firmly closed in a transport of exquisitely simulated agony. He offered me an autographed schooner, waiting on the tide. I admired, in turn, postcards of rivers, forts, crocodiles, ivory poachers. I slowed to the asthmatic breath of this Edwardian domesticity. Salvaged chairs emitted comfortable tobacco-replays; released from their depths carelessly incar-cerated farts.

Now Sileen, madly by lamplight, checked the oversize photocopied sheets of Conrad's bibliographer, *Smith*; cackling as he ticked off his recent purchases. He had made an authentic capture I could not under-stand or evaluate. But I knew that I was incontinently eager to escape from it.

IV

With no view from his window – no vision to accuse him – Sileen survived. Tenbrücke was made miserable by the presence of the river. He could do nothing with it. Yet he could never bring himself to pull the drapes and blank the world out. It would still be there. And he would see it. He covered his eyes with his hands. He felt his brain drowning in occult semen; pearly slime dripping slowly on to sawdust; cold honey leaking from the sharp lip of a teaspoon.

His residence was a controlled environment. Each object smirked in self-justification. It knew its value. It had the advantage. It 'appreciated' as fast as its curator, Tenbrücke, was dying, decaying, sweating himself away. Even the wooden blocks of the floor shone in aggressively shifting patterns: arrowheads pointing the path to extinction.

Tenbrücke willed himself quite deliberately to let the knuckle of dead cigar ash drop on to the white Afghan rug – but he could not do it. Terror beaded the stubble of his skull. Angry boils erupted on his neck. Tubercles insinuated in his oxters. His stomach spasmed convulsively. But the Waterford-crystal glasses on the silver tray remained unsmeared, brittle. The seals on the bottles were unbroken. The lemons were unblemished anchorites: worthy of Zurbaran. Tenbrücke, like Sileen, was a man who spent much of his time alone in his chosen space. He had married late – and too wisely – a much younger woman; an innocent who hoped, one day, to inherit most of Caithness. For now, she was safely occupied in the city. She satisfied his lack of desire. They ate out.

Tenbrücke fiddled with the knobs of the shower unit. He left the perfectly adjusted stream of water running, but he did not undress. He sat on the edge of the bed, feeding the black coverlet through his fingers. He was melting. He could smell animal-death on his body: a beast hunted to climax. He tasted ash mixed with rain. Something was wrong. One of the floor tiles was – *of its own volition* – lifting, coming away. A light was hidden beneath, and a light was lifting it. There must be a hole in the ceiling of the flat below. Tenbrücke would have to ring the agents with a formal complaint: or, better, instruct his lawyers to hit them for a completely new floor. He was tired of tiles. He wanted weathered marble, inset with birds, branches, flames; lapis-lazuli, veins of silver. The light was so strong: what were they doing? There must be an unlicensed photographic session in progress. The riverside apartments were very popular with New Wave pornographers.

He found that, without moving, he was able to look directly into the hole and – although this defied the laws of physics – he could see everything they were doing. It was just as if he was in the room with them. He *was* in the room with them. He joined them in their circle of salt: a circle of names he knew had been stolen from the Kabbalah, the Book of Spirits. Now he breathed as they breathed, faster and faster; choking, a claw at his throat. His eyes watered from the smoke of burning incense. He heard the repeated whispering of the name: *Belial. Be-li-al. Be-li-al. Be-li-al. Be-li-al.* It was his own voice. A polished dish was in his hands. And he saw in it a distorted face, a face of fire: bearded Falstaff; laughing, high-eared, red. He bared his teeth. And bit through the flesh of his cheeks, until the blood ran out from his mouth.

The pain brought him back. It was over. He slid open a drawer. Customized handcuffs, thongs, and a leather mask lay on top of two neat stacks of folded and ironed pyjamas. He tore off his shirt, losing buttons; mopped his malarial torso with a pyjama jacket, which he then put on.

He wanted to write something down, to leave a note for his wife. He needed to imagine her, still in her scarf and Barbour, searching for him, calling his name: the square of blue paper, unread, in her hand. But it was impossible. He was trembling too much to hold a pen. He pulled on a camelhair coat, stuffed the handcuffs into his pocket, and ran out of the flat for the last time.

V

A shifty unshaven polymath nebbish, with a cocky drone, and a patter so tedious it could have been marketed as a blood-coagulant, was lecturing a dangerously healthy-looking Californian couple. They were shrink-wrapped, sterile, irradiated like a pair of Death Valley grapes. They socked vitamin-enhanced aerobic vitality at you, so hard you could wish on them nothing but a catalogue of all the most repellent diseases of skin and bone and tissue; all the worst back numbers from the cursing books of Ur, Uruk, and Kish. You were obliged to super-impose on their boastful skeletons the historic treasures of old London: growths, malignancies, rickets, nose-warts, furry haemorrhoids, palsies, fevers, sweats, bubos, wens, mouth-fungus, trembles, and pox scabs. They were so heavily insured against disaster that they were almost *obliged* to justify the premiums by dropping dead before they overdrew another breath.

The woman kept dabbing her lipstick with a Kleenex, and flinching visibly from the sneering intimacies of the tour-guide; who last had his teeth investigated in celebration of the election of Clement Attlee and the coming Socialist Dawn. Harold Wilson's white-hot technology of dentures, he ignored. The husband wondered how the same soft drink he used in Soquel could taste so *strange* in London, England. What did they do to it, for chrissakes? Maybe the dyes for the logo had some kind of freaky half-life? This frigging town was awash with terrorists bran-dishing poisoned umbrellas, crazy Irish bombers, Arabs spitting in your food, and fall-out from Russia stripping the trees. If you could find a train that was moving, it was sure to explode. They couldn't even keep the beer cold. They sure as hell imported the formula, but were too dumb, or too greedy, to follow it. Ugly bunch of chicken-shit dick-heads! Skin like bath-scum. Fughh!

The guide was in spate, and lying outrageously. He appeared to be rehearsing for an occasional column in *The Times Literary Supplement*, that would get up everybody's nose with its preening erudition. They swallowed what they wanted of it, and wondered if they could survive yet another evening in the National Theatre before cutting their losses and skipping to the Hemingway Conference in Venice.

'Can you believe what those English critics wrote about *Serious Money*?' the woman whined. 'We just found it was totally without soul. It was so *shallow*. It didn't confront the real issues. And the theatre! My God! No air-conditioning: you're practically sitting in some guy's lap. No wonder the English are all sex criminals. I felt so *dirty*. Believe me, it wasn't easy to get those tickets. I'm sorry to say this, but we were conned. We won't be back in a hurry, will we, Bob?'

'You are standing,' said the guide, a little wobbly himself; his arm thrown affectionately around the gibbet, 'on the very site of the infamous "hanging dock" that saw the execution of so many pirates; including, of course, Captain Kidd. You probably recall the name from the cinematographic version – 1945 – with Mr Charles Laughton, Randolph Scott, John Carradine, Gilbert Roland ...'

'Errol Flynn,' said the Californian bookman. 'Errol Flynn did all the pirates.'

'I beg your pardon. No, sir. Flynn was a colonial, son of the Empire. Born Hobart, Tasmania, circa 1909. There is some debate about that, I grant you. Two schools of thought. Tedd Thomey suggests ... But I won't bore you with scholarship. Flynn played Captain Blood in 1935 for Michael Curtiz (or, Mihaly Kertesz, if you prefer it), an extrovert Hungarian gentleman, later acclaimed for the film *Casablanca*, made in ...'

'Randolph Scott only made Westerns,' said Bob the bookman, grimly. 'He was never in a pirate picture. I like Randolph Scott. I've got all his stuff on video.'

'Indeed, sir, the performer in question is widely admired, particularly by our European cousins, for the mythopoeic Western films made with that fine amateur of the *corrida*, Budd Boetticher. Some critics laud the cycle for its moral austerity in the use of landscape – while others, more cynically, put the bleakness down to Harry Joe Brown's tight control of the budget. For myself, I would have ...'

'Listen, jackoff,' screamed the Californian wife, edging ominously close to a full-blown attack of the vapours, 'get your act together, or forget your gratuity.' She wanted to be safely back in their own room at the Tower Hotel before she was forced to gamble on the facilities of the 'Little Girl's Room' in a dockside public house selected, for the worst possible reasons, by their now discredited guide and mentor.

'You will notice, recently restored,' the guide continued, unabashed, 'the actual gallows on which maritime offenders were stretched for the entertainment of the local populace. They were left dangling, bowels vacated...' (He had the godalmighty nerve at this point, as the wife recalled later, to leer directly into her face) '... before being suspended in chains, from that post, to be washed over by three tides.'

'Why three?' said the woman. 'Wasn't that being a little excessive?'

'Reasons of arcane ritual, Madame, difficult for visitors from an infant culture to comprehend. The three tides symbolized the three branches of the awful machinery of state. First, there was the Executive. Next, the Legislature. And, finally ... to make sure they had bloody snuffed it. Same thing up the road, wasn't it? They staked the heart of the Ratcliffe Highway vampire. Simple insurance, lady. No snivelling about miscarriages of justice after three good black Thames tides. Bring it back, I say. The corpses looked like cuttlefish. And had about as much to say for themselves.'

The Californian temptress turned her back on him, for a reviving snort of duty-free, Chanel No. 19, *Eau De Toilette* spray. She was beginning to hyperventilate; and was trying to regain control by essaying a sequence of prescribed facial exercises – leaving onlookers to assume she was about to suffer a quite interesting epileptiform seizure.

The gibbet itself, now being quizzically tapped by the man from Soquel, was no more than an effete sample of contemporary piracy on behalf of the Town of Ramsgate public house. In season, for a couple of weeks in June, it was much snapped, taped, and committed to polaroid. It was located near enough to the true site of the Hanging Dock to provide a Hammer-film frisson for twilight drinkers in the walled garden.

The Californians did not care, at this time, to venture down the steep ramp and on to the foreshore of the Thames for a view of Tower Bridge with the tide out: the curious rocks, sacks, and spokes revealed in the slurping mud. They passed back down a narrow alleyway to their valet-serviced gondola, slotted, so inconspicuously, alongside a clutch of showroom-quality Porsches, Range Rovers, and Jaguars. The guide, following closely on their heels, in case they made a run for it, decided on the instant to scrub around his usual Ratcliffe Highway number: the *patron* of the Crown and Dolphin had been less than generous with his little 'drink' on the last visit.

The guide turned his script, seamlessly, towards Rotherhithe, which was becoming a notably tasty shrine to the Fictitious Past. They could start at the Picture Research Library, where they could admire the utterly authentic accumulation of detail that went into making the utterly inauthentic *Little Dorrit*. And, if they were lucky, they might get to share a *demi-tasse* with the lady-director herself. ('Do we call her Christine or Christina?' 'Well, it's spelled ... but her husband. Honestly, it doesn't matter. She's a lovely person. She's got absolutely no side.') Then there's the Heritage Museum, the Glass Works, the Knot Garden, and the site of Edward III's Manor House, presently indistinguishable from a six-hundred-year-old midden.

'Right, that's favourite,' the enterprising nebbish thought. 'Straight down the tunnel, drinks on the deck of the Mayflower pub, swift shuffle around Prince Lee Boo's sepulchre – and it's three fish platters, guv'nor, and a bottle of Chablis at the Famous Angel.'

Dr Adam Tenbrücke, only yards from the gibbet, went unnoticed by the fact-grubbing tourists. He had decided to take his violet suicide note as a 'performance-text' and to give it the full treatment. He slithered down the scummy steps, and hobbled across the sharp stones of the over-welcoming septic beach. His red brogues were licked with green-grey mud. A heavy chain dangled from the mesozoic timbers of the wharfside; part of the décor of an otherwise uninspired set.

Tenbrücke sank down gratefully beside it. He took out the handcuffs and – well practised in these matters – secured his wrists behind his back. He fumbled, blindly, for the large ring on the wall. He was safe. No more decisions to be made. He was bait to the furies: a maggot of chance. There was just enough play in the chain for him to pitch forward. He could kneel, his head on his chest, in the damp slurry. And wait.

VI

I remember Joblard telling me once that as a child he had stayed with relatives in Rotherhithe, among the Surrey Commercial Docks. He had woken on the first morning, wiped the misted window with his pyjama sleeve, and seen through the porthole a great liner of ice – as he thought – sliding, with tragic inevitability, down the street; pressing close between the curtained blocks. Not sure if he was asleep, the boy rubbed his face against the cold glass – until he felt a vein in his cheek beating *inside* this new and frozen skin. The tenement itself had become a vessel; they were voyaging out, unpiloted, into desolate wastes. He tried, without success, to force open the window. Icebergs were locking on the tide; clanking together, smoking in collision: advancing on the city in a blue-lipped armada of destruction. The Pleistocene was revived. It was welcomed. Bison would herd together in lumber yards. Antlered shamans would carve the marks of power on the walls of the Underground; would initiate fires in long-deleted stations.

One of the stokers, up on the deck, leaning on the rails, noticed the boy watching from the circle within the opaque window. He waved. In that terrible moment, Joblard realized his own mortality. *He also could be seen*; his existence was no longer a secret, and never would be again.

Later that morning, with his two cousins, he made the discovery of a ventilation shaft leading down into the Rotherhithe Tunnel. They spent the day scouring the streets for old nails and bolts, lockjaw-inducing lumps of rust; until they had stuffed to the brim several large brown-paper bags. They climbed up on to the grille that covered the mouth of the shaft, and skilfully aimed their missiles on to the huge fan-blades beneath them. The noise, in that enclosed space, was most gratifying. It was the Sands of Iwo Jima, Hamburg, the *Graf Spee* rolled into one. The scavenged shrapnel was hurtled into the tunnel; devastating the traffic, and maiming a solitary cyclist. The satisfaction they derived was that of the disinterested artist: it was wholly imagined. There were no curtain calls. The perpetrators were already out of Brunel Road and halfway up Clack Street; their socks around their ankles, chortling and punching, distrusting the shrill vehemence of their own laughter.

VII

From that moment, Tenbrücke felt better. He tilted the burden of his head. There was so much sky. Passengers on the river, glancing back at him, thought he had made a discovery: he was excavating a shard of Roman pottery from the shallows – with his teeth. While he looked over at the far bank, he forgot why he had come to this place. He had stopped trembling, and he felt light and, for the first time, a little frivolous. The river plashed, a soup of mud, swooshing the immortal rubbish, backwards and forwards, in a lullaby motion. He heard voices above him.

'Down there, girl. Just look at it. Fucking filth! Ignorant bleedin' bastards. What happens? The tide shifts it off of 'ere. So they build a

Thames fucking Barrier to stop it getting away. All right? Next morning it's all bleedin' back again. Fucking ridiculous.'

This premature ecologist, sickened by the perfidy of the planners (and all the other 'thems' who never have to answer to the people for their actions), let his obsolete fag packet float from his hand to freshen the collage of neap-wrack. Uncertain footsteps in retreat: the wheeze of the pub door.

Tenbrücke set himself to assess the riverscape on the far side of the choppy water; to fix the limits of his vision, and to make them final. Rotherhithe was not a place to which he had previously given much consideration. It looked foreign, and somewhat estranged from itself. The significance of this apparently random assembly of buildings awed him. He became aware of patterns, meanings, distributions of unexpended energy. His sense of colour was overwhelmingly *personal*. It hurt. It hurt his blood. The horrifyingly *soft* green spire of the Norsk Kirke flooded his throat with bile: of exactly the same concentration. Cheesewhey oozed from beneath his fingernails. The Famous Angel, the tower of St James's, Bermondsey, were ancient offences that only he could redeem. Pubs and churches, derelict and decaying wharfs. A solitary odd thin building; a slab of something left behind from a previous incarnation. Tenbrücke thought he remembered a woman at a drinks party telling him Lord Snowdon had once lived there: before he was inducted into 'The Family', of course. Bachelor days. Clubs. Paragraphs in 'William Hickey'. Demobbed photographers, models, gangsters, characters from the Rag Trade. All the big hooters and the weak chins: horse mouths, taffeta, fag smoke, suicide.

He heard the muffled and distorted voices of pleasure-boat spielers, identifying the notable stones. They were talking under the water. They made no sense. *Silver Marlin, Captain James Cook*. Fins of sour lace froth followed in their wake. They tore the fabric of the river: pushing a false tide towards Tenbrücke's inlet. The water was on him.

Occasionally, a tourist waved to him from a boat, and was disappointed to be ignored – poncy Cockneys. But, as the light started to go, Tenbrücke had a moment of curious intensity. He had what amounted to an involuntary close-up of a golden dragon; its claws hooked to a polished globe. This was the weather-vane of St James's church, more than a mile away – but now so near him, he could see the paint flaking from the dragon's scales. He was drowning in physical detail: breathless, aroused. They sang out: the chips of blue-painted ceramic tile, the sharp knuckles knocked from coffee mugs, the wounded bricks. He felt their history, felt the warm hands of their owners, felt the energy of their decay. It was all pouring into him. The light was unopposed. He was swept out of himself, strung on a chain of shimmering beads that absorbed each and every particle of his private anchorage. Gulliver Agonistes: he could not turn Wapping to account. Number the crystals. Unknot the threads that kept the water from the air. *Hekinah degul!*

When the tide was at his throat, he almost changed his mind. Came to a consciousness of where he was. Tore his flesh; putting weight and strength against the cuffs and the ring. Then he softened, settled himself; his back against the wharf. A cloud of midges drifted from the slime-covered stone blocks of the Old Stairs. He could see straight through them. They had abandoned him, the familiar desires. There was no fret left in them. And he noticed now another set of steps leading upwards, leading nowhere, ending in a wooden fence. He opened his mouth and swallowed everything that was coming.

VIII

When I returned to Wapping after the agreed three months – to collect my share of the divvy – everything had changed; it was *Kristallnacht*. There were roadblocks, searchlights, dogs on chains. Chanting hysteria breathed a new life into the poisoned varnish of the walls. Riot-shields, flaming milk bottles, horses.

I dodged, and weaved, among the scarlet snakes, the video-contrails; ignoring contradictory orders howled through megaphones that converted the human voice to a form of millennial robot-speak. I had to abandon my car on Cannon Street Road and walk back, clambering over fences, and slithering down heaps of rubble; wary of rats and fanatics. The riverside acres were a battleground, a no man's land; barricaded, fought to the point of inertia, by private armies and absentee War Lords; protected by beam-operated grilles. The contractors had parcelled up the docks and were trawling for names that would mist the eyes, suspend disbelief, and sell the proud owner a share in our maritime heritage: the Anchorage, Silver Walk, Sir Thomas More Court, Pageant Steps, Tobacco Dock. Paid researchers burrowed in the files; they plated nostalgia.

There were deck-planks nailed across Sileen's window. The greenery was dead and the flower pots smashed. Repeated knocks drew a pensioner from the balcony above – sole tenant of the ant heap – who assured me, from a safe distance, while pacifying a monstrous hound, that Sileen had gone: 'him and his boxes'. A taxi, early one morning. Nobody had seen him since: you could hear the phone ringing behind the padlocked door. His girlfriend, receiving no word from him, had moved out; crossed the river.

And so it ended, an unremarkable incident. I had mislaid plenty of other customers and potential benefactors – 'not known at this address' – before and since; dozens of promised postal orders never quite materialized. But there remained a disturbing niggle of curiosity: that Sileen should quit what appeared, to outside eyes, as such a grove of benevolence. The plants, the spices, the charm of his companion, the calmed space between the walls of books. Had his quest been brought so close to completion? There is no entrance to another man's life. Why should we expect one? What is presented to us is often the most disposable of assets: the motor is elsewhere, an impenetrable secret. Sileen had upset me only by opting out of the fictional curve I had prepared for him. He had ceased to exist. He was written out of the story.

A few years later I thought I saw the girl, or someone very like her – with the sort of coat she favoured draped about her shoulders – sitting in the corner of an obscure Southwark pub. The man with her had an African drum in his lap, which he was obsessively mapping with be-ringed, prehensile fingers. I left the bar, on the instant, by a side-door; without attempting to speak to her. I had no desire to confirm or deny the reality of her presence.

IX

Joblard rang me to 'discuss the likelihood' of my driving him to Norwich to collect a vanload of scrap; and, in passing, as a sweetener, he mentioned the discovery of Adam Tenbrücke's swollen body, by a couple of metal-detecting beachcombers. This low-key event had been nudged from the local news coverage by the Wapping Riots. Then, for some reason I have still to discover, I flashed to an earlier episode that had definitively blighted my faith in this ill-defined zone. It was all to do with the Rotherhithe Tunnel: a most unnatural feature. It had a 'bad karma' – holding together the irreconcilable differences of the two shores in an evil marriage. The children were deformed and ugly, always seeking for a way to strike back.

A day's aimless exploration – walking to escape, rather than to make any discovery – had ended. I was, in truth, fleeing from an image in the Herb Garret of the old St Thomas's Hospital. Hanging in a corridor, outside the restored operating theatre, is an engraving of a late-eighteenth-century amputation. The wild-eyed victim struggles with the brawny porters. The saw is frozen, inches deep in the fat of his thigh.

And, notable in the front row of the audience, is a formally-jacketed
Pacific islander; fine-featured, beside the gross and sniggering assistants.
This distinguished alien evidently reads the event as a required sacrifice,
a test of will, an initiation – and not as some banal exhibition of
virtuosity on the part of the surgeon. The mortal intensity of his
expression drove me from that place and out along the Surrey shore;
diving, after Tower Bridge, into the obscurities of Horselydown,
Curlew Street, and Jamaica Road. If I had not broken away from the
stranger's mesmeric gaze, I knew that I would very soon be seeing the
precise shape of terror he had identified in the aqueous humour of the
victim's eye. The engraving was another sorcerer's mirror. I was reading
De Quincey then, and – obsessed with spiral stairways, opaque and
smoky domes, potential mysteries – I decided to come back across to
Shadwell and the homelands by way of the Rotherhithe Tunnel.

If you want to sample the worst London can offer, follow me down
that slow incline. The tunnel drips with warnings: DO NOT STOP. Seal
your windows. Hold your breath. This is not reassuring to the pedestrian, who wobbles along a thin strip of paving, fearing to let go of the
tiled wall: working the grime into his icy hand. Your heart fills your
mouth, like a shelled and pulsing crab. Why are there no other walkers?
Traffic scrapes so narrowly past: the drivers are mean-faced and locked
into sadistic fantasies. White abattoir walls solicit vivid splashes of blood.
You *feel* the brain-stem ineluctably dying, releasing, at its margins, dim
and flaccid hallucinations.

Half-naked labourers splashing through the darkness, struggling in
the heightened air pressure that was necessary to keep back the waters;
falling victim to 'caisson disease', as they excavated, inch by sullen inch,
the mile and a quarter of clay and gravel.

DO NOT STOP. Seal your windows. Read the scars and striations, and
wonder if some juggernaut will spread you into them. Keep moving –
but not *too* fast. Don't breathe so deeply. We're still going down. It's the
wrong tunnel. I must be halfway to France. Don't hyperventilate. Even
if I do get out of here, it's too late, my brain will be pumice stone. Stop
then; rest, sit – you're dead.

The tunnel covertly opens a vein between two distinct systems, two
descriptions of time. The outfall of the city is bled into drained marshlands. Electrical faults animate the rotting convict hulks, spin the wheels
of coaches that clatter towards the channel ports. Reports of foreign
wars, remote revolutions, run into the stacked trophy rooms of Empire.
A voice is forged, a bone whisper, that belongs to neither bank. The
tunnel is the ghost of something that never had the chance to die. Niches
in the laboratory light of this shrine lack their votive skulls. Unfocused

demands slide over the white tiles, searching for their oracle. The shaft should be a *vertical* stroke, and not linked to profit. But instead it was, as always, a boastful speculation, celebrated with bands and flags; stifling at birth its true purpose. The mists of Ultima Thule are dispersed by giant fans. To walk here is to blaspheme. The tunnel can achieve meaning only if it remains unused and silent.

I decided that 'research' could be pushed just so far. I had been under the river for ... I don't know, perhaps half an hour ... when I came upon a ventilation shaft – with a stairwell. Blades spun angrily in their cage, paying out, with the worst of humours, a sallow dole of air. A dark flourish of metal led upwards towards a hope of the light. I must, by now, be back on familiar ground. I felt certain I had trudged to the outskirts of Cambridge. I vaulted a low barrier, ignored the prohibitions, and dragged myself, step by step, into the cool night.

It was the unresolved hour, early evening; dim buildings bent over me: I walked away as fast as I could. But the townscape would not settle into any recognizable pattern. Disturbingly, everything was *almost* familiar – but from the wrong period. I was navigating with a map whose symbols had been perversely shifted to some arcane and impenetrable system.

I stopped a man in a donkey jacket, and asked him if he knew where the Highway was. He stared at me blankly, then mumbled something that sounded as if it had been inefficiently dubbed. A chemist's shop was open – but it was signed *Apoteker*. The realization came over me: I was dead. My hallucination in the Rotherhithe Tunnel was to believe that *I was still alive*! I must have stumbled, fallen; crushed my head. I was now beached in the suburbs of purgatory. I walked faster – clammy-handed, scrotum tightened with fear – trying to escape from my own shadow. I ran for the sanctuary of a squat and depressing building – because the lettering above its entrance appeared to be in English. I knew that the language of the dead would be a dreary cuneiform Esperanto. The building was revealed as the Evangelical Church of the Deaf! A hellish vision. Bleak sermons of damnation thundered at a cowed congregation, their faces hidden in their gloves. I sprinted. Paradise Row led me, through dark shells of decay, to a stygian river.

I searched the far bank for the outline of the Famous Angel. I willed the skeleton of Tower Bridge to rise from the waters. Close passageways between tenements brought me to Hope (Sufferance) Wharf, and the church of St Mary the Virgin. I passed through the gates and into the churchyard. There was a single distinguished tomb, railed off: beyond it, across cobblestones, I could see a finely proportioned late-eighteenth-century house; oil lamps burning at an upstairs window. Standing proud from the building, floating, turned away from each other, were two children; stunted – but not quite deformed – fingers clutching books. If the books slipped from their grasp, the children would fall to the ground: the trancelike spell of this levitation would be shattered. They were both dressed in woad-extracted blue. The boy wore a full-skirted coat, with yellow hose; and the girl – a long dress, clean pinafore, mob cap. Their lips were not altogether innocent of cosmetic enhancement. They stared expectantly towards the river. Their stillness was unsettling, other-worldly. They were not so much children as incomplete adults. But no force that I could summon would turn them or bring them to speech. Their language would never be negotiable in this elided diocese.

The breath goes out of me. I collapse on to the preserved tomb: all its neighbours have been reduced to an unreconstructed heap of slabs and broken angelic forms. I am confronted with the legend of Prince Lee Boo. He is here: open-eyed, separated from me by a single sheet of stone – which becomes, as I lie facing him, a two-way mirror. I excavate his life from the letters on his grave. I am forced to listen to the story from his own lips, as they move in synch with the words that I read. The words are subtitles, cut in braille, for this kingdom of the deaf. Lee Boo is condemned endlessly to repeat the authorized version of what his short life has become. He must make do with whatever audience he can secure. Until he is allowed to move, I cannot move. That is the price the stone-mirror requires.

Dean Swift, infallible with rage, anticipated the affair by half a century. The East India packet, the *Antelope*, sailing from Rotherhithe in 1783, under the command of Captain Henry Wilson, was shadowed by its already-wrecked fictional namesake and double. A coral reef was breaking the surface, before the pilot was dropped at Gravesend. Sheerness, in the evening sunlight, became Oroolong. The surgeon, Lemuel Gulliver, led the crew ashore, disappearing into the pink sand like a damp stain in the midday sun.

The islanders of Coorooraa, modest and sharp-witted, offered their friendship, while the mariners constructed a new schooner to carry them back to their homeland. In exchange, the white men demonstrated the magic of toys and bright instruments. They settled local wars. The chief (or Rupack), the Abba Thulle, decreed that his second son, Prince Lee Boo, should travel, under the protection of Captain Wilson, to learn the secrets of glass and fire. Wilson left behind him, as an article of good faith, Madan Blanchard; a feeble-minded youth who gloried in the honour of his selection for this solitary – and lifelong – glory.

By this typically one-sided act of enterprise trading, Lee Boo was imported into Rotherhithe as exotic ballast. He was paraded at balloon-launches, prize fights, and 'all ticket' amputations. He was fortunate that Groucho's had not yet opened its doors. It only required his rapid demise to convert him into a theatrical 'smash': an operetta with dances and sentimental speeches, a pantomime. The flyers can be examined to this day at the Picture Research Library.

Lee Boo dutifully made study of magnifying glasses and telescopes. He watched the stars as they hid within torn fragments of cloth, or flew up from the flame of a candle. He followed the track of the river, as it pulsed through his wrist. He saw his own death floating above the water, nailed to the prow of a warship. With a 'glass-eye' stick he could read the stories that had been, and the future he was retreating into. The white man, Blanchard, had taken his place as the son of Abba Thulle. It was *his* duty therefore to die, and to free the pale exile from his dark twin. He remembered the tale of the brothers, Longorik and Longolap. And the warning: in a strange land when you are offered the choice, for your bath, between clean and dirty water – take the dirty.

Within six months of his arrival at Captain Wilson's house in Paradise Row, Rotherhithe, Lee Boo was dead. Coconut meat was laid upon his eyelids, so that his eyes should always appear to be open. And so they remain. A link was forged with Madan Blanchard. A few spade-weights of ground in this churchyard and in Coorooraa – removed from local ministrations – became places of mediation, of respite and sanctuary. A true tunnel, unpromoted – and available only to the crazed, the sick, and the dying – had been dug.

Coorooraa was unvisited, ignored by the trading nations, until 1967, when John Boorman brought ashore an alternative Lee, the hard-drinking Mr Marvin: paid to confront, in single combat, the ex-Samurai, Toshiro Mifune, for *Hell in the Pacific*. I like to think that some insignificant member of the crew, a 'focus-puller' or 'clapper-loader', with the forlorn ambition of becoming a novelist, sat, away from the others for his evening joint, in the clearing where Madan Blanchard had been laid to rest. He would discover a sentence, whose import he could not yet comprehend, coming into his mind. He would 'see' a graveyard in London, somewhere near the river. '*The marmosets have gone.*' He jots the words, trustingly, into his red-and-black notebook.

The interval, resting on the sepulchre, had calmed me. The known world crept back. It was now so obvious! I had made the mistake of climbing out of a ventilation shaft on the same side of the river that I had embarked from. I had in fact never left Rotherhithe. But an involuntary return to the point of departure is, without doubt, the most disturbing of all journeys.

With the disappearance of Sileen and the death of Tenbrücke, it became obvious that an inhibition had been removed: one version of the past had been effectively erased. And, as I attempted to write their story, I mutilated the truth, with faults in emphasis and diction; so that the pain lost its yeast. It was unreal. The past that I had described was not Sileen's past, nor was the death of Tenbrücke justified by my account of it. If the 'correct' selection of words — a pure and imagined order of sentences — has the power of animating, and bringing to life; then a failure to obey the Voice *must* bring forth zombies, breathe the force into monsters. There is speed without focus, action without meaning.

Wharfs developed into concept dormitories. Rancid docks were reclaimed and rechristened. The insolent calligraphy of Harry's Java Brasserie affronted Sileen's abandoned hutch. The whole Wapping ditch was converted overnight to estates and protected enclaves. These bespoke 'riverside opportunities' are so many stock points; painted counters. They are sold before they are inhabited. Investors shuffle the deeds to other investors, and take their profits. The empty spaces appreciate. Now thrive the chippies.

I met one such in the rain. An eyeball-to-eyeball organist, a Northerner, who slept in a church loft that would soon, under pressure of 'market forces', have to be sold. He was on two hundred notes *a day*, hanging doors. But had no prospects of buying into the area on such starvation wages. 'They target you,' he told me, 'at forty doors a session. Hang 'em high, and hang 'em fast. Then double-check the showflat. I'm in work for years — repairing the damage.' These unoccupied shells are already crumbling around their hacienda fountains and dockside viewing platforms: *Marie-Céleste* villages of decamped Lego folk.

'There's a nice line going,' the organist said, 'in rent books. You can pick up two k, down the local, selling them to runners, fronting for Estate Agents — who are themselves fronting for the big Property Combos, who are fronting for God knows what evil blood-bargains of Moloch greed and paranormal enforcement.' I excused his youthful rhetoric: a man who squats on ecclesiastical land must be allowed to read these matters in nostalgic hellfire terms.

'Anyone with a rent book,' he continued, 'qualifies as a local resident; and is graciously allowed to purchase one of the token flats set aside at a "controlled" price, to allow the fellaheen to acquire a small corner of what used to be their own cantref. In reality, this public-relations charity is smartly turned around into profits of fifty or a hundred thousand per unit: which makes a down payment — thanks to the "capital-friendly" terms on offer in the Enterprise Zone – on a deepwater marina. The Brink's-Mat mob laundered £750,000 on a couple of wind-blown jetties, and cleared a million and a quarter. There are far bigger killings on the Isle of Dogs – with far fewer risks – than in knocking over a bonded warehouse. And meanwhile, the now bookless *rentiers*, having burnt their two thousand in an orgy of hire-purchase video madness, are bouncing on an awayday ticket to Cardboard City.'

Warm, refreshing rain. I stood by the dome of the sealed entrance to the Rotherhithe Tunnel in King Edward's Memorial Park, Shadwell. This route has been aborted; the pilgrimage to the shrine of Prince Lee Boo in the churchyard of St Mary the Virgin is now a folk memory. I turned from the ironwork – with its obsolete frets and curls, celebrating the initials of the London County Council – and walked away down an avenue of pollarded trees towards the Highway.

I had meant, for years, while tramping its verges, to take a closer look at St Paul, Shadwell: 'traditionally known as the Church of Sea Captains'. Here were baptized the mother of Thomas Jefferson; the eldest son of Captain Cook; and Walter Pater, a confirmed bachelor. The church grounds, now cruelly abbreviated, ran down to the river's edge. The present structure, rebuilt in 1820 as a 'Waterloo Church', is a workmanlike branch-line station, knocked up by the railway architect, John Walters. It is plain-spoken, untemperamental: a refuge that quietly offsets the portland-clad baroque grandeur of Hawksmoor's St George-in-the-East. Easily ignored, St Paul stands as a sanctuary from this other sanctuary – which has recently been assaulted by devil-worshipping poets and dealers in the junk bonds of fiction. The crypt, Joblard informs me, was used as a campsite for the embarking Angolan mercenaries.

These superficial intimations of grace are suddenly challenged by a manic drumming, a ringing of handbells, a torrent of deep-throat chicken-slaughter chants in honour of *Les Invisibles*. The red church doors are flung open and, down the steps on to the rain-slicked stones, comes a mad voudoun (Catholic, Pentecostal, Masonic, speaking-in-tongues, Judaic lost tribe) funerary procession. A weaving wailing convocation of all the religions, faiths, and superstitions: bay-leaf-swatting cardinals, swordsmen, aproned dignitaries, bearded patriarchs, crusaders with the cross of Malta, and foxy ladies slithering electrically on stilt heels. Comes a mute gaggle of shock-white cockney shufflers, in wraparound shades, manipulating – on bone shoulders – the flower-decked canoe. Comes the pendulum of incense, the sweat-flecked drummer, the jigging and jiving roll-eye smokers. Comes Iddo Okoli, the giant; hat in hand, overcoated, weeping. He waves a great handkerchief like a flag of surrender. He is floating the death-canoe on a tide of faith. He is launched. And all can view the handsome face of the still child: marked with tribal scars, so that his beauty should not excite envy and hatred.

The wailing of the women is unbroken. A dagger-point of heat between my shoulders: I am pressed forward, stumbling up the steps of the church. I enter the darkness. At the head of the aisle is a clay jar, a *govi*, in which is trapped the *gros-bon-ange*, the double of the child. His water-shadow. The jar is set between candles, in a pentacle of white sand. It is guarded by the *vever* for Agwé: twin craft with patterned sails, a toy flag, and the word, IMMAMOU.

I kneel and -- with an unpremeditated gesture – touch a finger to the water, break the surface. The grip of the conditioned mind falters, something unshaped moves through my stunned defences. I am 'mounted', in such a way that I cannot speak, or choose the order of my words. My ego is stopped, and in that moment of dizziness, blood rushing to my head – I can only make a report, I cannot act. I have brought with me, as an offering, the unresolved death of Tenbrücke, and I have received the *esprit* of Iddo Okoli's son. I am suspended between them. I know now that above the walls of this church is another church; above this shamed city is a bright twin. All the barren space we can imagine is named and guarded, sacred; each moment of the day has its angel, to be recognized and honoured. Detail sharpens: the texture of the wood is numinous, living. The walls shine and open.

The body of the child, the returning ancestor, is carried in his canoe out on to the Highway. The drums of the procession stutter and fade: after-images blown into the distance, lost. It never happened. The door is wide. The candle flames shiver in a gentle wind. Shafts of pale sunlight break through the low clouds.

But, looking into the neck of the *govi*, I see the true procession break away from this other, and return to the riverside, to Wapping Stairs: marmosets chattering on the shoulders of the men, oracular birds restored to the trees. I see the white vessel launched from the beach. I see trailing flowers catch and absorb the death of Tenbrücke. The tide sweeps the craft into the Lower Pool. And I know I have no choice: by whatever distance I fall short, I must begin my attempt in this place.

3

Horse Spittle
(*The Eros of Maps*)

Horse Spittle
(*The Eros of Maps*)

'Fly, I sispected – Horse, I dint'

George Herriman, *Krazy Kat*

Fredrik Hanbury, the writer, sat opposite me, across a pine table; drumming his thumbs. Roland Bowman stood at its head, moving backwards and forwards, pausing, smiling, gliding to the stove, the shutters, the foot of the stairs; peering up, finger to his lips, in case his mother should call. Roland's knitted waistcoat – a sunburst among the calculated minimalism of the basement – could not be bought at any counter: you felt Roland had always owned it, it had been passed on to him at some discreet family initiation. You also felt, noticing the ease with which he possessed his space, that while he remained in this kitchen Roland would never age. He was weathered, fit, tanned; beached, safely, on the far shore of thirty. And would be true to that condition for as long as his tenure in Fournier Street lasted. He slid gracefully over the flags of stained-glass sunlight, gesturing, talking; a red coffee pot pivoting on his outstretched arm. Here, beneath the level of the street, it was dim, caged: cool stone floor, smooth wood panels muted in gesso. Everything was slow, calm, concentrated. Whatever was spoken was burnt, momentarily, into the air; and could be read, before it was heard. Roland refilled our hand-painted mugs with his strong black brew. I tasted the grains with my tongue.

'She was a very unusual person.' Roland caught me trying to decode the framed photograph. Was it contemporary? Or was it one of those theatrical poses that certain stallholders try to pass off as 'Art Deco', 'Art Nouveau', or anything else with 'art' in the title: straining to make the mere sound of the words inject a nostalgia for the robed, the remote, the indecent ... the expensive. A girl, they suggested, had also to be a flower, the twisted stem of a glass, or a wind-tossed flounce of drapery. But the point with the portrait that had taken my fancy was that the subject, this girl, was obviously *aware* of the camera, and its technical limitations; and yet the result seemed natural, spontaneous, a challenge. She was naked. The print was deceptively grey and soft – which made it difficult to date. The photographer had been careful not to impose a queasy subtext: to make a confession of his own inadequacy. He was not 'saying' anything. He could have been blind. The starkness and brutal directness of the final image suggested that the girl had taken the shot by an act of will, controlling the light and the focus for the precise exposure she wished to celebrate. 'This,' she said, 'is how I want to remember myself.'

Then Mother did call, unshrill, an interested upstairs voice; and Roland, indulgent, went to her, taking her a cup of coffee, an onion roll warm from the oven. He held the jug out, as if it were guiding him, an oil lamp: he pirouetted the tight stairway, talking back to us over his shoulder. Now Fredrik, who was fretted by a restless and finger-jabbing energy – who talked best on his feet – came around the table, to take the photograph into his hands: he gave his tribute gladly, to the beauty, the strength, and the potential mystery of the girl. We were happy, on the instant, to jettison the original, and rather dubious, pretext for our visit: we would draw breath, wait, follow whatever announced itself to us. If we did not impose the reflex inhibitions of disbelief, we would surely come, without strain, to the heart of the tale. We no longer believed in 'Spitalfields' as a concept: in 'zones of transition', New Georgians, 'the deal', or any of that exhausted journalistic stuff. We had something much better: a story we did not understand. It is always much more enjoyable to play at detectives than at 'researchers', who gather the evidence to justify the synopsis they have already sold.

The girl, on her knees, arms thrown back, was a dancer. She was effecting some kind of Isadora Duncan, swan-raped, *Noh* swoon: demonstrating both her 'inner stillness' and the power she exercised over her body. If there *had* been an assistant, he (or she) had lit the undecorated set to the key of the disturbing mood the dancer was insisting on: the self-exposure was posthumous, and fiercely erotic. She lay upon a memorial slab, the chrome maquette of a notorious torture baron. We could do nothing at all to get closer, either to this presentation, or to the girl herself: the implied narrative. It was too late to withdraw. Our interest was aroused, feverish. We would have to wait. Take whatever Roland chose to give us. It couldn't be forced. Now there was a streak of tension to fracture the restored empathy of the underground Huguenot kitchen. No florid and sentimental inscription defaced the photograph. It could have been sold in its thousands, sepia-tinted, a gaiety postcard; but we were convinced this was the only surviving copy. We were also convinced we would have to travel back through the dancer's grainy window to enter the story she had already persuaded us to demand from her.

Roland, returning with a tray, set it down on the table, assumed Fredrik's abandoned chair and – unprompted – told us about his friend, Edith Cadiz, the dancer. She was originally, he supposed – the matter was never discussed – an unconvinced Canadian. He didn't blame her for that. He'd never met any other kind. But it did leave an ineradicable trace, the faintest whiff of bear grease; and a clear-eyed, unEnglish humour to qualify her almost masculine assertion of self. You noticed next the unnatural smoothness of her body: the smoothness of the professional performer. The fierce options she enforced on her body only stressed the essentially private nature of her quest. She recognized the same loneliness in Roland, the same pattern of wounds. They were alone because they would not compromise the defiance of their solitude. They had been touched, and often, and would continue to be touched; but they would never drop that shield of protective charm. They cultivated the closeness of orphans, or revolutionary comrades in exile; making no demands on each other; seeing each other accidentally, for – much prized – afternoons of gossip and silence.

Edith came to this country, modestly funded, with money her mother saw as a final pay-off: she settled in Palliser Road, Baron's Court – a piece of ground given back to a squabble of more or less house-trained colonials, as being otherwise unfit for human habitation. She embarked, unenthusiastically, on the usual acting, modelling, and wait-ressing courses that she was far too intelligent, and singular, to complete. She was not without ego, and a certain talent for showing off; but she preferred not to demonstrate her capabilities, while some anthropoid agent's hairy chaingang-paw crawled up her skirts. It wasn't so much that she felt her virtue was worth more than a couple of bottles of Retsina: she wearied of the invariable bullshit surrounding this banal and ugly transaction. They never said, 'Fuck me and I'll get you the Royal Court.' The fatherly monologues were so repetitive, so punctuated with sincere smiles, and confidence-inducing pats on the thigh. They could have been put on disk: (a) boastful lists of possessions, (b) holiday yarns, (c) ingratitude of former clients, (d) venality of producers, (e) excellent prospects of increased earning capacity, (f) desirability for prolonged discussion in more congenial environment.

Neither was Edith keen to transform herself into a sunsilk bimbo, gagging on rampant chocolate-coated members, and conducting furtive assignations with a jar of coffee. She didn't want to pick up brownie points hanging around holes in the ground with Peggy Ashcroft and Ian

McKellen, or picket embassies to get the parts that Julie Christie turned down. She wanted to be left alone to discover the limits of what she could become. She wanted to relish performance for its own sake, to use her power to the full – because that, more than anything else, gave her satisfaction.

Roland, as he explained, had not initially been involved with whatever it was she was working on. She called around for a cup of tea. She chatted with Mother. She ate Roland's biscuits. Sometimes she slept for two or three nights in Fournier Street. And then, out of the blue, one August morning, she knocked on the street-door, and invited Roland to come and see her show. She was leading a dog on a chain: a heavy-pelted wolf cousin, a male. Roland went with her. The show was amazing: ferocious, insulting, funny. And performed in the most unlikely – and previously resistant – setting: the Seven Stars, Brick Lane.

Our current obsession with colonizing the past – as the only place where access is free – had made available, courtesy of the Borough Library, a collection of reproduction maps of East London: gaudy fakes to authenticate any cocktail bar. They were inexpensive, printed on stiff card; with roads, the colour of dried mustard, sprouting from the empurpled lamb's heart of the City. You could walk your fingers in imaginary journeys, and sneeze from the real dust that you disturbed. The Thames was alive; a slithering green serpent, a cramp in the belly.

Edith's particular favourite was *Laurie & Whittle's New Map of London with its Environs, including the Recent Improvements 1819*. And she had constructed, with paste and a heavy needle, a costume shaped from this map: part Edward Gordon-Craig, part Maori kite-bird – a feathered storm-disperser. Wearing it, she became an angel of threat; or a demon of bliss. She respected the traditional accoutrements of her trade – the cloak, the gloves, the boots, the thong – but she elaborated their shape, the angle of the shoulders, the constriction of the waist, until she turned herself into a living artefact, a weapon. She played with her make-up: her slightest movement provoked a paradoxical reading of the history of the patch of ground on which her audience were standing. She was increasingly absorbed, excited. Colour printers in Wilson Street provided enlargements of especially libidinous zones: *The Victualling Office, Sugar Loaf Green, Callico Houses, Morning Lane*.

But before she appeared in her 'special' costume, Edith Cadiz attacked them with a dance that was savage in its invitation. She was naked, too soon; shuddering and leaping, with no accompaniment, to wild sounds of her own invention. She laughed in their faces. She flashed them with spiders and rods of iron. She showed them wounds they knew they would inherit; then forced them back against the walls, by spinning pebbles of fear. The attention of the punters was fully engaged: they were unsexed, wary. It was what they had come for, but it was not right. Dry-mouthed, they could not swallow their beer.

After the subdued interval, in which they were able to recover their identities, Edith walked among them, collecting her tithe. They had paid, so they looked at her, and over her – as they had the courage for it: they made jokes. She was naked still, her smoothness glistened with pearly beads. There was a heat and a honey-sweetness on her. Two points – where high cheekbones stretched her face into a mask – had been pinched into colour; otherwise, she was pale, stiff, without animation. She shook out her hair. They dropped their furtive coins into an alopecic and grease-stained bowler.

The tension is broken. Conversation revives. Edith tells the publican that her hat once belonged to T. S. Eliot. He thinks she is alluding to the 'Chocolate-coloured Coon', and suspects that the hat is illegal, contraband: 'worth a few bob'. He is almost tempted to make an offer.

For the second half of the show, Edith does not move at all: a wartime Windmill nude, exposed to a ring of 'breathers', their knees heaving and bumping beneath rubberized police-issue raincoats. She wears her costume of maps. There are rings sewn to districts that have previously been cut so they will tear away, at a touch. Heard from the street, the sound of the audience is elongated and alarming. They are out of control. They feel their tongues being slowly split with rusty shears.

Edith Cadiz invites her sweating jackals to sing out the street names: *Heneage, Chicksand, Woodseer, Thrawl, Mulberry*. She gives them a voice to relieve their tension. And – if they nominate a name that has been prepared – her wolf-dog leaps from the audience, rushes to her, takes the brass ring in his wet mouth, and pulls away a Spitalfields terrace with a twist of his powerful neck. The jagged gap reveals new streets, fresh relations: Edenic glimpses. The tired city is transformed: a dustpit fades to expose an orchard, a church lifts through a sandbank, a hospital (with blazing windows) slides beneath the surface of a slow-moving river. The punters are maddened. The Thames attacks Hornsey. Leadenhall Market removes to Chingford.

The affair was too rich and strange. It was talked about, but it was not popular. They felt safer with the black leather bike-girls, cracking whips in their faces; and the others, the contortionists whose trick muscles could suck coins out of the sawdust, without using their mouths or hands. Edith was left alone on stage, in a scatter of torn paper. She was bruised and scratched by the dog's claws, his slavering enthusiasm. Some of the colour had run with her sweat: it was moving over her shoulders, down across her belly. Her wounds were an urban survey, promoting fresh deltas and rivulets, revitalizing dead hamlets, soon to be linked by fantastic railways of silver and bronze: animal-headed marvels, belching fire. She had succeeded; but she was not sure what that meant. She found herself, suddenly and dangerously, prophetic.

Roland too had witnessed something forbidden: something he could not shrive by making a report of it. Without malign intent, he left the fatal black spot in my hands.

II

A couple of weeks later, hustled by his producers, Fredrik rang me. We arranged to meet for a drink in the Chesham Arms, Mehetabel Road, Hackney: just down the ramp from Sutton House, a genuine, but well-disguised Tudor Manor that had probably survived thanks to the obscurity of its location. 'They' had not yet decided which motorway would bury it. The planners assumed this weather-boarded relic was another bankrupt mock-Tudor sandwich bar, and they left it alone: 'Turn that one over to the Pest Squad, Ron!' The building was sealed, and guarded by a depressed gaggle of ghosts and clinically-reticent poltergeists. It burst into life, infrequently, as opposing factions argued about its purpose, or jemmied away the skirting boards to reveal – in triumph – stubs of rat-gnawed chalk or some defunct grammarian's detention exercises. Both parties would fervently claim these rodent droppings as the evidence that clinched the very case they were attempting to prove. Then the whole business would sink back once more into perpetual limbo.

We made it to the bar on the stroke of opening time, getting our drinks in, before the place was invaded by a scream of grim-faced 'alternative comedians' – the alternative, I suppose, would consist of being funny – who 'wrote' nose-picking duologues for a pair of infamous vodka-swilling slobs. These dyspeptic businessmen nerved themselves to face the odd TV 'special', enough to keep their images polished for the advertising slots that provided most of their real income. They gazed in naked envy at the queens of 'Voice Over', with their villas in Tuscany; and they gritted their teeth over the video empires of clapped-out stand-up comics, who could now afford the best psychotherapy that money could buy. But the nerve-jangling hell of sitting for an hour, trapped in the back of a cab, while the failed 'Mastermind' at the wheel performed his audition, made them wonder if the street-cred of an office in Hackney was worth the candle. Their bosses, compulsively over-achieving bonzos, subtly emphasized their superior status by dressing in a gross parody of City uniforms. We hold the equity, brothers. And don't, for one minute, forget it. Charcoal-grey suits, with silk linings, the colour of rancid ice-cream; no ties. An uneasy compromise between wide-nostrilled insider-dealer and scrap-metal show-off, cased up for the dogs. The pack shuffled and sparred around the two luminaries, spitting and swearing, trying to look as if they had just boogied in off a building site, in their trainers, dirty socks, and shaving-foam basketball boots. The benzedrine thrust of their social vision demanded a constant spray of obscenities, aimed exclusively at other television programmes; and a dozen imbecile schemes to resurrect the Tottenham Hotspur midfield by importing a brace of 'total foot-ballers', whose names they could neither remember, nor pronounce. But this did not inhibit them from chanting these names, loudly, as they topped each other in flights of absurdity and pretension: until the affair lost all focus, erupting into a face-slapping, foot-stamping, 'knee-him-in-the-nuts, Sidney' squabble. They were ejected. 'A good working lunch' would be the favourite description: 'creative tension'. They stood around on the kerb, filling out forms to claim their expenses, and composing complicated requests, to be delivered by mini cab from the Mare Street deli. They were ready to recharge their batteries. The best of them were snoring on the pavement, as they waited for the fleet to arrive.

We had the bar to ourselves. Fredrik was evidently experiencing some difficulty in recalling what we were doing here. He never had fewer than twelve projects on the boil at the same time; pacifying demented, near-suicidal producers, not by delivering his script, but by suggesting, over a three-hour lunch, ever more wondrous possibilities: glittering ratings-winners, replete with intellectual and moral credibility, certain to confirm reputations and make, as an incidental by-product, fortunes. But he needed time, 'seed money', equipment, secretaries. He'd go to his grave, pelted in a hailstorm of writs.

Excited, making notes for an article on whisky labels, and another on pub telephones, Fredrik broke off: to slide the neighbourhood fright sheet across the table. There were a couple of paras about a missing nurse, last seen on the platform at Homerton, now presumed to be another victim of the 'Railway Vampire'. This was unexceptional, a mild filler; the equivalent of a Flower Show critique. It was buried among the ranks of block-headline teasers: MAN LOSES EYE IN ACID ATTACK; EPILEPTIC RAPED DURING FIT; GUARD JAILED FOR SEX WITH DAUGHTERS; ARMED SWOOP ON EMPTY HOUSE. An interesting form of 'new journalism' was developing, uncredited, in these local weeklies: a calculated splicing together of the most surreal samples of proletarian life, with an ever-expanding, colour-enhanced section on property speculation. ENJOY FACILITIES OF DOCKLANDS; INVESTMENT OPPORTUNITY; FIRST TIME RELEASE, ONLY MINUTES FROM THE CITY! ONE MILE FROM CITY ... 800 YARDS FROM BISHOPSGATE. The provocation is stark: throw open your windows, you can pee into the river.

But the horror tales – BLACK THUGS WITH HOME-MADE SPIKED BALL AND CHAIN RUN AMOK ON TERROR TRAIN – serve another, more sinister, purpose: they drive out the crumblies, the garden cultivators, to the forest clearings, to Loughton, to Ongar, or the poulticed mudflats of the Thames Estuary, the ultimate boneyards of Essex. More Victorian family homes, strong on 'character', and low on plumbing, are released on to a greedy market. Hard-boiled feminist crime writers, and stringers for *City Limits*, peddle across town, from Camden and Muswell Hill, to take up the slack. 'Baroque realists', and tame voyeurs fixated on entropy, tremble in paroxysms of excitement and distaste. There hasn't been such *hot* material lying around in the streets since they nobbled public hangings and bear baiting. Suddenly, we're all Henry Mayhew and Jack London. It's – *shudder* – unbelievable, terrible. We rush to our word-processors, the hot line to Channel 4. We're going to get the lead story, with photograph, in the *London Review of Books*.

Fredrik's wife, a lady of great charm, wise enough to prepare herself for Hackney life with two or three Liberal Arts degrees, and a wicked sense of humour, was now a psychiatric consultant at the Hackney Hospital: this being the only kind they went in for. She had, Fredrik explained, recognized the snapshot of the nurse that accompanied the story of the railway vanishing act in *The Gazette*. The girl's name was Edith. Edith Cordoba? Edith Drake? She couldn't remember. But she wasn't English. She was sure of that. East Coast American? Wore expensive shoes. Had worked in the hospital for almost a year, which constituted some kind of record. And she wasn't even on Valium, with Noveril chasers.

Could it be? Edith Cadiz a nurse? It was time to visit this hospital, to trace the infected fantasy to its source. Fredrik knew where some of the bodies were buried. He had been working around here shooting standard-issue inner-city squalor, that could be assembled fast to provide a poverty-row back-up for a 'major Statement' that a 'Very Important Personage' wanted to deliver, at peak viewing time, to his future subjects. 'One' had been suffering lately from a rather disquieting sensation that 'something ought to be done'. His uncle felt much the same way about South Wales. Much good had it done him. Or them. A lecture was even now being hammered out by half the unemployed architects in the country, who could – under the protection of the blue-blooded ecologist – safely savage the half who *had* managed to climb off the drawing board.

I left Fredrik to his task; blowing foam into the pub phone, while he sold a potential essay to Germany, analysing … the reformist uses of the very instrument he was now clutching in a stranglehold. 'Discontinued alternatives,' he was screaming, while he waited for a simultaneous translation. I would adopt my usual method, and circumnavigate the hospital walls; see what the stones had to say.

The hospital site covered ancient parkland, and might yet be profitably developed. It had, in the meantime, been designated the dumping ground for all the swamp-field crazies, the ranters, the ultimate referrals. Leave here, and there is only the river. The shakers were swept in – or delivered themselves, gibbering, at the gates: they were rapidly tranquillized, liquid-coshed, and given a painted door to contemplate. The only other ticket of admittance led, by way of the left-hand path, to the Drug Dependency Unit; which attempted, by methods traditional and experimental, to wean the helpless and the hopeless from their sugary addictions. The main thrust of this enterprise – stilling the inarticulate voice of rage – merely created a host of new, and more exploitable, addictions. Only the pharmacists and the Swiss turned a dollar. The wicked old days of brain-burning and skull-excavation (with soiled agricultural instruments) were a folk-memory. That machinery was too expensive to replace. A wimpish revulsion against water treatments led, logically, to the gradual suspension of all bath-house activities. Whole wings were simply abandoned to nature; eagerly exploited by rodents, squatters – and smack dealers who traded their scripts without quitting the sanctuary of the hospital enclave.

Looking up from the east end of Victoria Park, or out of a shuddering train, the hospital was minatory and impressive: a castle of doom. The endless circuit of its walls betrayed no secret entrances. Window slits flickered with nervous strip-lighting. Grimy muslin strips muted any forbidden glimpses of the interior: recycled bandages. The steep slate roofs were made ridiculous by a flock of iron curlicues.

An increasingly anorexic budget was dissipated in child-sex questionnaires, plague warnings, and reports (in six languages) justifying the cleaning and catering contracts. The nurses, to survive, established their own private kingdoms. The doctors kept their heads down, writing papers for the *Lancet*, that might catch the eye of some multinational talent scout. Better Saudi, or Houston, than this besieged stockade. They sampled, with reckless courage, bumper cocktails from their own stock cupboards.

My circuit was complete. I was back where I had started: in Homer-

ton High Street. I had discovered nothing. My notebook was scrawled
with gnomic doodles that might, at some future date, be worked into a
jaunty polemic. Of the dancer, there was no trace. I would return. And I
would be armed with a camera. Without a blush of shame, I was starting
to enjoy myself.

III

Edith Cadiz had never felt so much at her ease. She found herself, for the
first time in her life, 'disappearing into the present'. There was a physical
lift of pleasure each morning, as she climbed the sharply tilted street
from Homerton Station. The day was not long enough. She ran the
palms of her hands against the warmth trapped in the bricks: she grazed
them, lightly. She held her breath, relishing to the full the rashers of
moist cloud in the broken windows of the East Wing. Often she stayed
on her feet for twelve hours; not taking the meal breaks that were her
due. She was absorbed in the horrors that confronted her. No human
effort could combat them. Ambulances clanged up the High Street:
security barriers lifting and falling, like a starved guillotine. This was a
world that Edith had previously known as a persistent, but remote,
vision: a microcosm city. There was nothing like it in her reclaimed
Canadian wilderness: an impenetrable heart, with its broken cogs,
shattered wheels, and stuttering drive-belts. Her dispersed mosaic of
dreams allowed these damaged machine-parts to escape from 'place' and
into time. The victims, vanished within the hospital walls, grew smooth
with loss. They dribbled, or voided themselves in distraction, staring at,
but *not* out of, narrow pillbox windows. They were all – the tired
metaphor came to her – in the same boat: drifting, orphaned by
circumstance, unable to justify the continuing futility of their existence.

And it was endless: floor after floor, deck after deck – unfenced
suffering. There was no pause in her labour; nothing to achieve. It could
never satisfy her. Faces above sheets: amputated from the social body.
They did not know what they were asking. They took all her gifts, and
put no name to them. The shape of her hands around a glass of water
held no meaning.

Each nurse laid claim to some part of the building as territory that she
could control: imposing her own rules, her own fantasies. It might be a
special chair dragged into a broom cupboard. It might be a cup and
saucer, instead of the institutional mug. It might be a favoured cushion,
or a colour photograph cut from a magazine, presenting some immacu-

late white linen table on a terrace overlooking a vineyard: *Provence*, *Samos*, *Gozo*, the *Algarve*.

Edith made her decision. She rescued all the children she found lost within the inferno of the wards. They were not always easy to recognize. Some pensioners had discovered the secret of eternal youth. They shone: without blame. They remembered events, and believed they were happening for the first time. They entered chambers of memory from which no shock could move them. They were small and un-scratched: they learnt to make themselves insignificant. But some children were fit to pass directly into the senile wards; never having experienced puberty or adult life. They were overcome, shrunken, shrivelled; hidden behind unblinking porcelain eyes. Most did not speak. They should not have been there. They were waiting to be moved on, 'relocated'. Their papers were lost. Some were uncontrolled, hurtling against the walls, on a hawser of wild electricity. They would leap and tear and shout, spit obscenities. They would punch her. Or cling, and stick against her skirts, burrs: huge heads pressed painfully against her thighs. One child would lie for hours at her feet, and be dead. Another barked like an abused dog.

The room that Edith commandeered in a remote, and now shunned, south-facing tower gamely aped one of those seaside hotels, built in the 1930s, to pastiche the glamour of a blue-ribbon ocean liner. There were wooden handrails, and a salty curved window overlooking the sparkling tributary of the railway, that ran from Hackney, through Homerton, to the cancelled village of Hackney Wick – and on, in the imagination of the idlers, across the marshes to Stratford, to Silvertown, to the graveyard of steam engines at North Woolwich. Another more stable vision was also there for the taking: security systems, tenement blocks, pubs, breakers' yards, a Catholic outstation with albino saints and blackberry-lipped virgins, and the green-rim sanctuary of Victoria Park.

For a week Edith swept and scrubbed, polished and painted. She stole food and begged for toys and books. She was determined to impose a formal regime; to re-create a High Victorian Dame School. She wanted canvas maps, sailing boats, new yellow pencils, wide bowls of exotic fruit. She wanted music. Their strange thin voices drifting out over the hidden yards and storehouses. Her stolen children, playing at something, came – by degrees – to accept its reality. They were boarders, sent from distant colonies, to learn 'the English way'. They were no longer solitary: they were a troop. They even, covertly, took exercise. They left the hospital: walking down the Hill in a mad, mutually-clinging crocodile, over the Rec to the Marshes. They were too frightened to breathe: not deviating, by one inch, from the white lines on the football pitches – climbing over obstacles, cracking corner-flags, tramping through dog shit. They huddled, a lost tribe, under massive skies. The rubble of pre-war London was beneath their feet. They walked over streets whose names had been obliterated. They could have dived down through the grass into escarpments of medieval brickwork; corner shops, tin churches, prisons, markets, tiled swimming pools. On the horizon were the bright-orange tents of the summer visitors; the Dutch and the Germans who processed in a remorseless circuit between the shower-block and their VW campers.

Over the months, Edith coaxed the children towards language. Or shocked it from them: in tears, and in fits of laughter. The railway passengers noticed this single window, blazing with light.

Other unlocated souls made themselves known to her. Orwin Fair-childe, cushion-cheeked, chemically castrated, had been turned out of the ward as 'insufficiently disturbed': he could not escape its pull. He pretended to be part of the queue of outpatients that formed early at the gates: a queue from which never more than one or two highly-strung potential travellers hauled themselves aboard any vehicle foolish enough to slow down. Cars kept their doors and windows locked. The other loiterers remained – until dusk fell – leaning against the hospital wall; picking up sheets of old newspaper, greeting unknown friends, or screaming challenges at imaginary enemies. The queue was perpetual and self-generating: an unfunded 'halfway house' between the hospital and the insanity of the world at large. The people who mattered offered a loud '*Yo!*' to Orwin's oracular question: 'Are you in the queue, man?'

Orwin polished his bottle-glass spectacles on his shirt-tails. Then he set up his elaborate, but eccentric, sound system. He Scotch-taped his sheet music to the side of a bus shelter, and dived, scowling, into 'Greensleeves'. He plucked at the strings of an Aria-Pro (II) electric guitar – as if he was extracting porcupine-spines from his bulging thigh. The noise was hellish. He sealed his eyes, and entered some dim cave of absolute concentration.

It became a ritual of Edith's to take Orwin for a drink in the Spread Eagle on her way to the station. He would roll a cigarette and offer it to her. She would refuse, and offer him a drink: which he, in his turn, declined – on religious grounds. He spoke about the Ethiopian Saints who had lost themselves in this City of Sin; but who would certainly acknowledge Orwin as a fellow spirit, by spotting the coded note-sequences in his music. The Saints left messages for him in books. But, of course, the libraries would not let him get his hands on them: claiming that he could not read. The teachers had all been bribed to keep him in ignorance.

Dr Adam Tenbrücke also spent time as a temporary guest of the hospital. He had been found, weeping and shaking, running his head at the door of a warehouse-gallery on the perimeter of London Fields; which featured, at the time, a chamber flooded with sump oil. This was instantly optioned by the Saatchis. The owner, a claque of tame critics, and a few jealous hangers-on rushed outside, squawking, 'Did Doris ring?' – bursting to break the news to any passing drifters. They tumbled, in a heap, over Tenbrücke, who was rocking back on his heels, imitating a blind monkey. Smelling the weirdness of 'real' money, the owner dragged him inside.

Tenbrücke pointedly refused to sign his name in the Visitors' Book, and would speak only in German. The Gallery Man, now suspecting the devious hand of the encamped 'travellers', rang for the snatch-squad – who were only too happy to tranquillize the gibbering doctor with their truncheons. He was delivered – a knot of terror – to the reception cages. He would talk of nothing but suicide. 'I'm drowning in filth,' he whispered. In other words, he was depressingly normal. He sounded like a politician. They frisked him, hit him with enough stuff to stop a runaway horse, and turned him loose. He tore off his clothes and – howling Aryan marching songs – stumbled down Marsh Hill. He walked back to Limehouse Basin along the River Lea: white, and fat, and stark-naked. But he went unmolested; just another long-distance health freak jogging into obscurity.

It was still quite possible to survive on a nurse's salary; but not to eat, to travel, to take decisions over your own life. Therefore, most of the nurses moonlighted as cleaners, or as barmaids. Even their uniforms were rented – warmed by their bodies – to a drinking club on the Stoke Newington borders; where they were worn, with minimal adjustments, by hostesses who catered to a certifiably specialist clientele.

But it was the opening of the Dalston/Kingsland to Whitechapel rail link that granted Edith's continued presence at the hospital an economic viability. Now, at the end of her working day, she could take the North London line to Dalston, change, and step out within half an hour on Whitechapel High Street. Time to read, once again, her faded pink copy of *The Four Quartets*. '*And so each venture / Is a new beginning, a raid on the inarticulate …*' The generous arches and lamps of the London Hospital penetrated the gloom like a Viennese opera house. Edith slipped Mr Eliot back into her raincoat pocket.

The balance was achieved. Edith Cadiz could nurse by day, and supplement her earnings by unselective prostitution at night; 'blowing'

the priapic hauliers, who were working out the last days of the Spitalfields Vegetable Market. It would be simplistic to suggest that Edith's
was a mechanical response to circumstantial poverty. The twist was
more complex: if she was unable to live as a nurse, she was also unable to
live as a prostitute. The attractions of these twinned survival-modes
were quite different. They were separate, but equal. In both theatres of
risk, Edith was involved with external demand-systems that gave her
unexpected courage, and fed her dramatic sense of self. The risks she
took brought to life a scenario, in which she could not quite believe that
she participated. She maintained, to the end, an inviolate sense of silence.
The emissions of the lorry drivers, she trusted, would somehow en-
gender language for the mute children, safely secreted in their ruined
tower.

Edith was an unusual person.

IV

The great shame, and dishonour, of the present regime is its failure to
procure a decent opposition. Never have there been so many complacent dinner parties, from Highbury to Wandsworth Common,
rehearsing their despair: a wilderness of quotations and anecdotes. 'My
dear,' a Camden Passage 'screamer' smirked, as I cleared a few boxes of
inherited books from his cellar, 'we never get asked to Mayfair any
more – it's always Hackney. Wherever that is.' Writers were glutted on
hard-edged images of blight. They gobbled and spat, in their race to be
first to preview the quips that would surface in next week's *Statesman*; or
to steal, from some Town Hall booby, statistics to lend credence to a
Guardian profile. Literary bounty-hunters – bounced publishers, and the
like – scouted out-of-print anthologies for any Eastern European poets,
in wretched health, who had not yet been 'targeted' for an obituary.
They fell over each other to finger these deservedly-forgotten scribblers
at thirty pounds a hit.

And if the Spitalfields weaver's loft, or the country house, wistfully
rendered in a mouthwash of Piper twilight, staggered on as icons of a
vanquished civilization, then the fire-blackened cityscape of the Blitz
was the setting increasingly invoked by the barbarians of the free
market. Exquisitely made-up young ladies tottered out on Saturday
mornings to hawk the *Socialist Worker*, for an hour, outside Sainsbury's.
Duty done, they nipped inside to stock up on pâté, gruyère, olives,
French bread, and Frascati for an alfresco committee meeting. The worse

things got, the more we rubbed our hands. We were safely removed from any possibility of power: blind rhetoric without responsibility. Essays, spiked with venom, were the talk of the common rooms. Meddlesome clerics fought for the pulpit. The most savage (and the wittiest) practitioners were never free from the telephone. Review copies clattered on to the mat, obsequiously eager to face the treatment. TV lunches were grim as public floggings. Government narks listened at every door. Nobody wanted it to end. Jerome Bosch art-directed the steaming imagery. It was positively Spanish: Index, Inquisition, *Auto-da-Fé*. Nobody wanted to be the one to hammer the first stake through this absence of a heart. We'd have nothing to write about, except ley lines and unexplained circles among the crops.

The 'Standing Member', Meic Triscombe – a stoop-shouldered, flat-footed, arm-flailing shambler, whose delicate porcine features were lost in the barren disk of his face – haunted his electoral boundaries like the Witchfinder-General. His nose, a detumescent erection, twitched after conspiracies, winks in the council chamber, wobbly handshakes. He favoured quarrelsome lime-striped shirts; always untucked, fanning out behind him; quite loud enough to set the dogs barking, and causing women to miscarry in the streets. Asthmatic – and allergic to almost all life-forms – he gasped and sneezed, turning his frailty to advantage, by pretending to be overcome by emotion: a Shakespearean soliloquy of pity for the human condition. Choking and spluttering, he drenched his audience in a spray of peppermint-tasting mucus; desperately running the sleeve of his blazer across his watery eyes. There was no other calling in which he could parade his disabilities in such a favourable light. On the telephone he could be genuinely alarming. And had been reported several times as a pervert.

His constituents – or unemployment statistics, as he thought of them – were bow-legged, small-skulled, foul-mouthed, impertinent; fff-ing rapid-fire dirges of complaint, out of the corners of mouths tilted into half-zipped wounds. Triscombe could not bend low enough – an old rugby injury – to make out what they said. His slight hearing difficulty, mostly a build-up of cerumen rammed into the external auditory meatus with the tip of his black Biro, was an aristocratic trait, and no hindrance in the chamber: he thought of Harold Macmillan. As did so many others, now that the old confidence-man was safely removed from the scene. Triscombe did not need to sift the words of the fellaheen; he was their voice. He could articulate their primitive and amorphic wails for attention. On their behalf, he dined on rumours, played squash at a City health club; denounced scandals he was too late to get in on. He thought of himself as the 'people's tribune' and he lived among them. Or, at least, *reasonably* adjacent to them. While he waited for his personal *Belgrano* to cruise down the Hertford Union Canal.

His wife, estranged, and with a cast-iron investment portfolio behind her, refused to set foot in the grime of East London. The property Triscombe acquired in a partly-renovated Early Victorian Square (okayed by John Betjeman), within safe hailing distance of the Islington borders, lease signed three weeks before the election, had proved a decent enough speculation when he 'let it go' six months later – well before 'Black Monday'. These large crumbling mansions, built for sober city magnates, had given refuge, in the era of Wilsonian Social Democracy, to some of the more acceptable – and only distantly related – members of that premature Free Market combo, the notorious 'Firm': before the towerblocks marched in like triffids. The square, a quadrangle of submerged aspirations and cringing modesty, now preened itself on an actively 'ruralist' identity. It was a village under siege from marauding misfits, razor-gangs, crack dealers, and fast-breeding aliens. The gentle bohemian newcomers of the 1960s uprooted the comfrey and the cannabis, persuaded someone to take on the cleaning lady, and took flight into the silicon-chip countryside; draining, in the process, the last dregs of their inherited capital. Sadly, this was the ultimate shuffle of the brewery shares. Their homes, now seen as a solid 'first step on the ladder', passed into the hands of food-photographers, marine insurance trouble-shooters, rising tele actors going into their second Stoppard, and Bengalis shifting from supermarket chains to oil percentages.

Triscombe took his profit and went east, to the summit of the Ant Hill. When in doubt, climb. The nude temptations of worldly power: he loved to look down on the beaten spread of the Borough and say, 'All this is mine!' There was a reborn credibility in stashing himself among the photogenic ruins of Homerton: it added considerable colour to his CV. A satellite development had been jobbed onto the shabby grandeur that clung to the coat-tails of Sutton House. The estate's title was worked in flourishes of wrought iron into the entrance gates, like something out of *Citizen Kane*. Security guards, a nice blend of ex-para and ex-Parkhurst, patrolled the walkways, Moorish arches, and plashing fountains of this Neo-Alhambra. The tower of St John of Hackney rose proud above the camera-scanned walls, with intimations of vanished Templar glory. The panoramic view towards Leytonstone was not so hot: a set of low-rise blocks, let in by the planners on the dubious grounds that, at least, they were not high-rise blocks. These were the ultimate *barrios* of despair, and behind them lifted a futuristic silver tube:

the burning chimney of the Hackney Hospital, belching forth mistakes, ex-humans, and assorted bandaged filth.

Meic Triscombe was a shire-horse among whippets. Red ears pricked for multinational conspiracies, tongue like a dagger, equine teeth set to savage the 'Secret State' Whitehall plotters: a stallion of wrath! He stamped and snorted; he reared up. He also tended, rather too frequently for comfort, to fall down; so that one, or more, of his limbs was perpetually cased in plaster. An ardent all-night debate on the abolition of the ILEA caused him to tumble the length of a spiral staircase in the terrace house of a female member of his steering committee: cradling in his arms a not-quite-empty bottle of Southern Comfort. A barstool shattered under the sudden imposition of his weight, leaving its shrapnel in his left buttock, while he was denouncing the iniquity of a system that permitted whispering nocturnal trainloads of uranium waste to pass unchallenged through 'Nuclear Free' Hackney. He suffered an attack of acute food-poisoning, with attendant sweats, cramps, and trumpeting flatulence, on a 'fact-finding' tour of ethnic restaurants between Lower Clapton and Green Lanes. Meic Triscombe was not unknown to the Hackney Hospital. A procession of mini cabs heaved him out at the gates; where 'security' told him, firmly, to try elsewhere. They had no facilities for dealing with accidents, emergencies, amputations, inebriations, childbirth, chewed-off ears, grievous bodily harms, or spontaneous combustions: or, indeed, anyone at all who was not actually frothing at the mouth, bug-eyed, and belted into restraint like an 'Old Kingdom' mummy.

So it was that the stallion, Triscombe, became one of Edith Cadiz's lambs: another unrecognized messenger found babbling on the pavement. He limped across Homerton High Street, leaning heavily on her shoulders, to the Adam and Eve, for a pick-me-up, a bottle or so of medicinal Cognac. His eye, guileless aesthete, admired the relief carvings above the pub entrance – a naked couple, daring divine retribution – while his fingers, unoriginal sinners, tried to sneak a touch at Edith's nipple. It wasn't just the liberating effect of firewater on his sweat glands: Triscombe was amazed to discover that Edith did not need to be seduced by gusts of Bevanite eloquence. Neither did she succumb to the vapours on his moral high ground. This time he did not have to present himself as 'the Last Socialist out-of-captivity': the hotshot cocksman who had never sold out. Tears filled his eyes as he spoke of the miners, the hunger marches, the lock-outs. Edith yawned. She wouldn't be shamed into surrender. She was willing: this clown was the agent of fate she had been waiting to snare.

But Triscombe, saturated in the hypocrisy of his calling, was congenitally incapable of taking 'yes' for an answer. Puppy-eager, he tongued her neck, as he pitched an over-familiar yarn about the slime deals that would see the hospital razed to make way for yet another 'riverside opportunity'. Even if it took a clear day and a powerful periscope to find the river in question. It was an accepted natural law that any piece of ground overlooking a puddle of water − river, canal, sewer, or open-plan cesspit − would be a golden handshake for a speculative builder: 'minutes from the City, offering all the advantages of country life'. The Government's public-relations machine had very effectively stolen all this water imagery from its traditional proletarian base. The canal bank had served, from the Social Realists of the 1930s to Alex Trocchi's *Young Adam*, as a dour backdrop for relationships poisoned by industrial dereliction. Now, in the coming blush of privatization, water is declared to be 'sexy'.

Edith required no such dialectic. She took Triscombe's drink. And she asked him how much money he had. '*How much money?*'

Triscombe's mounting excitement tangled him more completely into his usual state of impotence. The horse of panic. He was about to break something. The barmaid shifted a religious statuette out of reach. The landlord shrouded his parrot. 'How much money?' Trembling, he started to turn out his capacious pockets. She did not mean that: the petty cash for a knee-shaker under the viaduct. She meant *income*, stock-points, retainers, kick-backs, research contracts, leaks to the *Eye*. Could he afford her − *on a regular basis*? Would she fit, snugly, on to the payroll? Because that was all that mattered. To clear, for her own exclusive use, an uninfected stretch of time.

What Triscombe actually wanted, when they returned to his impersonal apartment, was difficult to speak about, to spell out in precise detail. Edith waited, legs tucked under her, in a bucket-chair, running her fingers, caressingly, through the golden muff that hung under the belly of Triscombe's alsatian: the guardian that slept at her feet. Guarding against what? Special Branch, 'The Company', Mossad, MI5, MI6? The Widow's favourite chalk-monitors, Ad Hoc Splinter Groups, spooks, wire-tappers? The fellaheen hordes, black gypsy petrol-bombers, Iranian fanatic Jews tooled with castrating shears? Trotskyites, the Red Brigade? Lesbian rapists? This dog, he felt − and he wanted Edith to feel it too − had absorbed most of his own masculine virtues: by close association. The beast manifested his warrior soul: it represented his power, but without the inhibitions of his public standing.

Edith soon understood *exactly* what Triscombe wanted, but she remained perfectly relaxed, detached: there was so much time waiting to

be paid for in this room. She would not burn it. Let him get there when
he would. She understood that this would be one of the most effective
acts of theatre she had been able to conjure. It was truly monstrous, and
also quite simple. She would involve herself in a performance that was,
by statute, criminal, and degrading; mythic in its blasphemy. She would
devour the substance and the essence of taboo – with the bulging,
pleading eyes of the instigator following her every movement: the
paradigm of an audience. It was Triscombe's vision; he was its victim.
She wanted to make an account of this. To repeat the act in language, to
perfect and refine it. She slid a notebook from her handbag and started
to write.

White-cheeked and musty, Triscombe faced her: his back arched
against the wall. A thick blue vein was pulsing on the side of his head,
like a worm digging its way out. She thought he might be sick. His
breath smelt like wet rope. She spoke to him reassuringly, softly,
outlining her demands. 'A standing order': the phrase made her smile. A
sum, calculated on the spur of the moment, to be paid, monthly, into
her account. A selection of Deer Brand black notebooks with red cloth
corners. Some Japanese drawing pens. A watercolour by John Bellany
that she had always coveted. Afternoons.

Anything. Absolutely. He agreed. His hands were palsied. He had
lived with this image since boyhood. Its safety was that it remained an
image. Therefore, he was human. Therefore, he could denounce the
corruption of the world. Man's man, people's tribune – stallion of the
virtues. But now this woman was starting to act it out. *Jesus Christ, the
curtains!* In a fever, he checked them. Edith Cadiz was sinking, very
slowly, stretching on the floor with the dog, who was turning, waking,
yawning his meat yawn. Teased, he growled, and showed his teeth.
Edith unzipped her dress. Triscombe was transfixed, a stone man. He no
longer wanted any of this. It was agony to him. Edith draped the dog's
head in red silk. It looked as if she had wounded him. She spoke; she
blew in his ear. The beast responded, with a show of anger, to these
preliminary caresses.

The spread of her arms. Triscombe enters a colour-plate, the childhood illustration he longs to bring to life: *Blodeuwedd's Invitation to
Gronw Pebyr.* It has been said that fairy stories are erotic novels for
children. But they are worse than that, as Triscombe is discovering. A
low-cut bodice, with a tightly-laced dress. She heaves with terror.
Savage streaks of blooded light escape from the forest: some massacre or
sacrifice to pagan gods. The white horse stamping through the fast-
flowing river, hoof raised, searching for a dry rock, or … the head of a
dog. A hound that will scrabble up the bank, shake himself, and soak the

dress of his mistress. She is trapped within its clinging stiffness. She lifts the embroidered hem. The dog nuzzles, thrusting his otter-head between her naked thighs. His rough, salty tongue laps and scratches. She grasps him by the ears, guiding him. Her breath comes faster. She swoons to ...

No, no, no. This is all wrong. It is Gelert the Faithful, blood-muzzled in his greeting. Slain in error: destroyer of the wolf-threat, not the sleeping infant. Triscombe is a one-handed reader, slithering among nursery icons, coded legends. He presses his cold nose to the tint of damp pages: the salmon runs, the gold shimmer, the white froth of water breaking around the horse's raised leg. Edith Cadiz is the raven-haired temptress worming out the secret of the Triple Death. She will destroy him. Her hair covers her face. She is without identity.

Choking spasms of language gushed from Triscombe's mouth. Things he thought he heard. Voices on trains. 'She's a dog, mate.' *Dogmate.* 'On heat all the time, like a fucking dog.' 'Came home for his dinner, didn't he, and gave her one.' *Dogfuck.* 'I know all the bouncers. Every time I borrow a few quid I say, "Cunt, shut your fucking mouth." That's why you never get any.' *Cuntmouth.* He's growling, rolling, hurt in his throat; biting at the fur on his wrist, pulling out the waxy skin in a red pinch of flesh. 'She's a fucking diamond, son.'

Triscombe is dribbling; grey bubbles of mucilage slather down his chin. Rasping, harsh breath: a file across his lungs. 'Took 'er down the 'ospital.' *Horse spittle. Whore's spital. Clap-shop.* The bitch. 'Fucking 'ore.' The cunt. The dog.

He drops, stunned, into a black imageless sleep. A poleaxed carthorse.

And Edith writes, steadily and fast, her account of events that connect with these events; but which are *not* these events, and are *not* an account. She does not describe what has happened. She describes something else, which exists, independently, beyond the confines of this close room.

Naked, Edith looks into the bathroom mirror, and is — for the first time — troubled. She sees: '*The eyes of a familiar compound ghost / Both intimate and unidentifiable.*' She does not know herself. Her excitement is now as compulsive and primary as Triscombe's was, when he watched her. She does not make more of this than her written structure can contain. She is satisfied. She has committed herself. She believes that, at last, she has gone too far: there is no way back.

Edith left him, stretched on the floor: she walked, unshowered, down the High Street to the hospital.

V

It is not known, and I do not know, what happened to Edith Cadiz. Some urgent sense of the mystery of the story, locked into her Fournier Street photograph, sent me once again along the railway line from Dalston/Kingsland to Hackney Wick. The Wick had now been relegated, by an unsightly forest of concrete conifers, to the status of the Liechtenstein of the Lee Valley: lacking only the advantages of a competent fiscal laundry service. Once it was a shopping centre, somewhere to travel towards, a destination: the name alone survives. A hoop of gutted enterprises caught between the East Way and the rat-infested river. A station platform boasts of easy access to the Marshlands; where, in the twilight mists, razor-blade-chewing loners wait for their victims to stroll out of domestic banality into a definitive hothouse fantasy. The elevation of the tracks offers a momentary vision – through nicotine-shadowed windows – of the hospital blocks; the Gormenghast on the hill, the Citadel of Transformation. Drawing my last optimistic breath, I suffer the familiar dank whiff of tranquillized dreams, flesh-burns, piss and mindless fear.

I toiled slowly uphill towards a site that I knew had been abandoned. I stared into wild gardens. I ran my knuckles over broken bricks. I photographed reflections in dusty daggers of glass. The trail was cold. All the narrative excitement had returned to its source: the silver-framed photograph in the basement kitchen in Spitalfields. Edith's actions, the magick she had practised, had been translated into an indefinable quality of light. I was forced to invent and extend the fragments of plot her teasing sense of theatre had scattered over these wasted streets. She no longer had any connection with this place. The hospital was a dead set from which the principal actor had vanished: without her, it was unbearable in its implications.

At the Texaco Filling Station, a seventeen-stone black, Sumo-flanked, in yellow satin Bermuda shorts, was causing a little chaos: and rather enjoying it. Orwin Fairchilde. He was dominating the confessional-slit of the cashier's window, puffing out his cheeks, like a finalist in a hot-water-bottle-inflating competition. The flesh of his face was a network of scars, some suppurating, some freshly self-inflicted with a Stanley knife. Orwin's grime-encrusted spectacles magnified his eyes into menacing white balls. The cashier was fascinated. He could actually see the eyes inching out of their sockets. He found himself sliding a 'free offer' cocktail glass across the counter, to catch them. It was late afternoon and the door to his office had, thankfully, been security-locked. But the queue of angry punters was growing all the time. Horns were punched, and held. Those at the back, frantic to turn in from the kamikaze madness of the High Street, were more strident in their complaints than those close enough to take a good look at Orwin's shoulders.

'Gimme *Rizla* papers, man, an' a box a matches.' Orwin's desires were as specific, and as irritable in their expression, as any dowager's. 'Not tha' one, stoopid. Take it back. I got tha' picture, in' I? Said wha', man? *How* much? You crazee? Arright then, 'alf a box. Gimme 'alf a box a matches. Tha's right. *Count* 'em. Count 'em all out where I see 'em. Don' fuckin' sell me short, man. Gimme Juicy Fruit. Jew-cee Fruu-t. Nooo, iz torn. Tha' one, *tha' one*. You deaf, or sumpin'?'

Now the petrol-freaks are ready to slash Orwin to ribbons with their credit cards. He doesn't budge. He holds a bucket-sized fist in the air, saluting the world. He, very slowly, counts out the few coins he can dredge from his deep pocket: a common-market capful of busker's droppings. But hold up here: something has caught Orwin's jackdaw eye. This enterprising garage is lending its support to local arts and crafts by featuring a gravity-defying display of 'exotic' underwear, sculpted, with buckles and hooks, from pink rayon ribbons and panels of spray-black plastic. Rigid duelling suits for solitary posers. But Orwin would like – if the cashier has no objection – to fondle the merchandise. It might make a very suitable gift for his mum. She's been a bit down, lately.

Orwin's no mug. He knows exactly where it's at. He's foxy. He can anticipate to the second the little Paki's decision to reach for the telephone. The catcher's van will be summoned. There'll be a brief, and pleasantly bloody, altercation. Then, it's tea and medicaments. And a reserved armchair in the front row of the dayroom: fade into 'Neighbours'.

Marsh Hill: red walls of the secure compound. Internal exile. Shovel the flotsam into these hulks of stone. It's the humane alternative to transportation. Better the lash, and the carcinoma-inducing sun. The ghosts fade from sight. Children, without speech, wake in empty flats, and creep, hungry, to school; wearing the clothes they slept in – not knowing if they are expected.

Edith Cadiz, as a nurse, no longer existed. There is no record that she was ever here. The turnover is too high. Doctors put in for a transfer before they drive, for the first time, through the gates. Nurses suffer breakdowns that would once have merited a chapter in any medical memoir. All I have learnt is that the quest for the woman and her journals – if pursued – will initiate abrupt retribution. It is safer to return to the photograph, which is itself a kind of death. I will speak of 'composition', 'grain texture', and the 'magnificent eloquence' of her flung-back arms. But is this a gesture of triumphant completion – or a dancer terminated by a sniper's bullet?

VI

In 1868 an Australian Aboriginal, 'King Cole' (as he had been named by his sponsors), stepped ashore on English soil at Tilbury. Shaven-headed convicts, social defaulters, premature Trade Unionists, and supernumerary Irishmen had been regularly exported to the antipodean wilderness, in chains, from the far shore: shells of the hulks lay there still, rotting in the black mud, between Woolwich and Crayford Ness. Now was the time to trade, to exchange these criminals for good yellow gold and nigger cricketers.

'Nothing else of interest,' commented the *Daily Telegraph*, 'has come out of that blighted desert'; adding, in jocular parenthesis, that it might prove to the advantage of all godfearing Christian gentlemen if Mr Charles Darwin booked passage with the dusky savages, when they returned to their wilderness. He should question them closely, demanding anecdotes of their grandfathers, the monkeys. Indeed, with their fine dark beards, slanting brows, and deep-set eyes, did not these sportsmen bear a striking resemblance to the Fenland Sage? They would surely take him, on a more intimate acquaintance, for a god; and cause him to revise his blasphemous works – in the light of his personal knowledge of the labours of divinity.

King Cole, standing at the rail of the *Parramatta*, watching the pilot-boat butt its way across Gravesend Reach, knew that this was the Land of Death. He had dreamt this place and, therefore, it had become familiar. He was returning, without fear, to the country of the Dog Men, the destroyers. A great tree had followed him for many days over the ocean: the eucalyptus that must grow from the stone of his heart.

Johnny Cuzens, Dick-a-Dick, Mosquito, Jim Crow, Twopenny, Red Cap, Mullagh, Peter, Sundown, Bullocky: they were dressed in ill-fitting gamekeeper's waistcoats, bow ties, flat hats. They walked in silence, close together, carrying their own bags up the creaking gangway towards the Immigration Hall. King Cole recognized these planks immediately, as they all did: the Bridge of Hazards. If they walked beyond it, there was nothing but the Leaping Place of Souls.

King Cole was prepared: his fingers ran rapidly over the painted markings on the wall, the priapic pinmen at their dance. The loving encounters of women and animal-ancestors. So they came into an arching cathedral of sunlight, of voices, and confusion, and movement. They kept together. The dead man with the others.

They were covered in black smoke. Smoke surrounded them, warning them of the city. The voices of trees were hidden in the smoke. The carriage doors were slammed by porters: the pages of iron books, a collapsing library. Shouts, waves: as of the drowning. The Immigration Hall was once more deserted. And the station photographer had nothing to record but their absence, the subtle alterations in temperature that their passage had provoked. He infected his plate: the kiosk, the clock, the soul-snaring patterns in the stone flags of the floor. Officials watched from behind their moustaches, legs spread, at ease: the returned soldiers. A faded placard: '*Birthday Honours*'.

The glass plate, coated with white of egg sensitized with potassium iodide, washed with an acid solution of silver nitrate, developed with gallic acid, was fixed; and made available for close examination, long after the anonymous photographer was dead and forgotten. The positive image, when it appeared, uncredited, years later, in a nostalgic album celebrating 'the steam era', revealed – by some fault in the processing, some fret of time, or trick of the light – that the roof of the Hall had become a version of the river, a reflection of water from the dock: ropes, hawsers, hull-shadows, ripples of tide. Tons of water hung, and floated in the air, above the heads of the porters who were sternly facing the demands of posterity: emptying themselves into the shrouded camera, so that they could remain forever 'on call'. And the river would flow above them, until they ceased – or we ceased – to believe in it; when they would be swept away entirely.

The notion of an Aboriginal cricket team proved a rewarding speculation for the hotelier (and former Surrey man) Charles Lawrence, and his partners, the 'shadowy' W. G. Graham, and George Smith of Manly. The demand for novelty they stimulated was such that, within ten years, a troop of white Australians followed them over – to the disgust of several elderly MCC members, who felt they had been cozened into wasting time on a cheap fraud. 'Demm'd fellers can't be Australian. They ain't even half-black.'

The 1868 'darkies' drew a large crowd to Lord's, six thousand of the curious, sportsmen and their ladies – despite the counter-attractions of the Ascot meeting – to watch the Aboriginals face up to a side that included the Earl of Coventry, Viscount Downe, and Lieutenant-Colonel F. H. Bathurst who, statisticians will recall, 'bagged a pair', falling twice to the wiles of Johnny Cuzens. King Cole limited himself to half a dozen overs of under-arm lobs, which he bent dangerously, or pitched into the sun – to drop directly on to the stumps.

At the close of play, the Aboriginals put on another kind of show: running the hundred-yard sprint backwards, throwing boomerangs and spears, executing tribal dances, and dodging the cricket balls that young blades were invited to hurl at them.

King Cole spat blood on to a white cloth. The linen absorbed the outline of the stain, a map of his lungs. A nurse folded and removed the soiled towel; but the place was recognized. King Cole was eager to relive his death. He found the infection he needed in cow's milk; he had to release it. Nodular lesions spread through the weakened tissue. His lungs were paper, patched with paper. They were beyond use. Night sweats, fevers: he melted. They could not look at him. He returned the name they had given him in a triumphant pun: his eyes burnt like coals.

Two weeks after the circus at Thomas Lord's cricket ground, King Cole lay dead in Southwark. They brought him from Guy's Hospital to a pauper's grave in Victoria Park Cemetery, East London; long accepted as a necropolis of the unregarded. They carried him on a board, past the domed scalloped alcove, a cross-section igloo, built from the Portland stone blocks of Old London Bridge; and they aimed him at its twin, across the river, in the far reaches of the park, beyond the cricket grounds. The particular site where they folded King Cole into the earth is now diligently disguised as 'Meath Gardens': a light-repelling reservation, amputated from its original host by the twin cuts of Old Ford and Roman Road.

And here, Meic Triscombe – a powerful advocate of Aboriginal Land Rights ('Land is Life') – was instrumental in arranging that a hardy eucalyptus tree (sacred to caterpillar dreaming), and supplied courtesy of Hillier's Nurseries, should be planted by some noted local figure, who was known to be sympathetic to the Cause; and who could be relied upon to conduct himself, and the difficult ceremonies, with dignity – but also with passion, subdued fire. Triscombe thought he knew just such a person. He would not have to travel a million miles to find him. The memory of King Cole would stay forever sharp in Tower Hamlets.

A cricket match would follow on a specially laid synthetic strip, donated by Tru-Bounce (Wanstead). There might be a little low-key television coverage. A quirky, heart-on-the-sleeve account by some local pundit to pitch for the Saturday *Guardian*. Who lived in the Borough these days? Alun Owen? Andrew Motion? Fredrik Hanbury? Triscombe could call in the favours. He would emerge, rightly, on the international stage, confronting global issues: genocide, torture, acid rain. He'd stuff the greeny yellowy whale-bait on their own patch. Sponsorship, by Qantas, was assured. This was the 'Qantas Aboriginal cricket tour'. A nice conceit: 'Qantas' Aboriginals, presumably living in burnt-out fuselages, and hunting by jet. The 'souvenir programme' already credited: Slazenger, Puma, Barclays Bank, Nescafé, Cell Link (suppliers of mobile phones), Wood of Bournemouth (supplier of BMW), TNT Magazine, Benson & Hedges, East Midland Electricity Board, Arcade Badge Embroidery Co., Australian Wool, and Contagious Films. Triscombe's in-house humour would have to be aimed with great care; some of these jokers could be touchy.

The commemorative match in Victoria Park, between the 'Qantas' Aboriginals and Clive Lloyd's eleven, was a modest affair, a sober success. The bespectacled and ageing panther gathers the ball at extra cover and returns it, straight to the wicket-keeper's gloves, with an effortless flick. His young team-mates do the running for him, giving away the odd 'overthrow' on the bumpy daisy-dusted turf. The Aboriginals conduct themselves in the accepted all-purpose style, that could mean a team of cigar-chewing Dutchmen, headhunters with filed teeth, or morally stunted mercenaries going anywhere to chase a krugerrand.

A knot of local black kids, in the tea interval, picked up the rudiments of boomerang throwing: the blade held upright, spun twisting into the wind. They returned the following evening, to drop an incautious grey squirrel from a plane tree; and to watch while it was chewed – then abandoned – by a yelping levy of over-fed pooches.

My son was restless. Cricket was not his game. It was too far away. And too cold an afternoon. I had seen as much as I needed. Conscious of the sacrilege, we set off for home before the game was concluded. I did not witness the end of Clive Lloyd's brief innings.

VII

In Meath Gardens, off Roman Road, the hands of the clock were edging to attention at midday; a group of fit, dark-skinned young men, in green blazers, stood over a hole in the ground, practising late cuts and cover drives with their rolled umbrellas. A publicity girl from Qantas, who had miscalculated – by one – the number of buttons to leave undone on her starched blouse, was fending off the attentions of the sole representative of the English Press, a papillous 'stringer' from the *East London Advertiser*.

Edith Cadiz, in a startling white raincoat, had detached herself from what she was seeing. She leant against a pollarded English elm, and looked across the insistent wave-pattern of the reclaimed graveyard to the allotments. The dull grass was like a coarse hospital blanket too hastily pulled over a corpse that refuses to shut its eyes. Edith tightened her grip on the Eliot. She 'heard another's voice cry: "What! Are *you* here?" / Although we were not.' If she had painted this scene she would have omitted herself altogether. She reached for her dark glasses: believing, like a child playing hide and seek, that if she could not see, then nobody could see her. She was no longer an actor in anything she was forced to observe. Men, she decided, could never aspire to play any role but the audience. She remembered St Paul: '*Their mouths were like open graves.*' She knew that Triscombe would come, but that is not what she was waiting for. The notebooks were all filled: her presence was no longer necessary. She wanted to read them, one by one, to Triscombe; so that he would be fatally infected. The story would stay with him, and – in time – he would die of it. Gentle, westward-drifting rain lacquered her fine red hair to her skull. She was unaware of it. Let this scene finish. Return once more to the Fournier Street refuge; to Roland's basement kitchen. The pine table, the red coffee pot. A cigarette. Make a perform-ance of it, pass the burden.

Triscombe's black Jaguar came through the arched entrance gate, with its weathered heraldic shields, its eroded script, *Victoria Park Cemetery 1845*; and drew up, shy of the ceremonial site – engine running, windows steamed over. Two council gardeners rested on their spades, waiting for the signal, and calculating the precise amount of overtime they would earn. They had a small side-bet running on whether the eucalyptus would last a month.

The dog, Gelert, once Triscombe's guardian, lay at Edith's feet, scarcely breathing; his pelt heavy with the rain. He was faithful to whoever fed him. The dark darkened. Commuter trains hissed and clattered on the elevated railway that marked the boundary of the field. Sparks were struck from the overhead wires. The Victorian headstones had been broken up, carried away, incorporated into municipal building projects. The ground was shaken by its agitated past. It was humped, pocked, pitted: lacking a glossary of the original names. The memorial site elected to remain anonymous, remembering nothing. A seismic disturbance had gashed the earth, so that the dead walked free. They clustered in the feathery trees. And the trees bore it: mutilated into eccentricity, dense with voices, wind-serving. They took on strange ancestral forms. They were cartoons of abdicated tribal power.

Morkul-kua-luan: only the Spirit of the Long Grass knew King Cole. Rogue eddies whirled from the speed of the railway; seeking animal heat, untwisting the vines and insipid clusters of green that masked the allotment. A recollection of rage surfaced among the Qantas cricketers:

the stone of their hearts broke open, and fell from them. They stood with their fathers; they were men. They made a circle around the hole where the tree would be planted.

Triscombe lumbered from the car; a leather-jacketed researcher, up on his toes, to keep a golfing umbrella over the great man's streaky pate. Ever the politician, Triscombe squinted through the rain to identify the weightier journalists, the position of the video cameras and the microphones. *Nothing!* He evidently had all the pulling power of a flatulent concrete poet. He had drawn two gardeners who were scowling at their boots (self-evident members of the electorally unwashed), and a dozen sullen – and disenfranchised – darkies. Was it for this that Triscombe had been sitting for ten minutes in his car, pumping himself to give his blessing to King Cole, for his voyage through the Dreamtime. There was no going back. Why had he bothered? There was no ethnic percentage in Abos. Now that he thought about it, he convinced himself that there weren't any in Hackney. We had everything else: Blacks, Indians, Pakis, Turks, Kurds, Greeks, Yids, Fascists, Pinkos, Greens, Gays – but hardly an. Australian of any type. A few back-packing antipodean dykes got into the schools; but they moved on fast. And good riddance. No, this was all a bad mistake. Or worse, a miscalculation. His firebrand eloquence would have to be spat at the wart-decorated flasher with his notebook – who might turn out to be nothing more than a peculiarly unselective autograph-hound.

Then Triscombe noticed Edith. That eucalyptus hole, he thought, will never be big enough. He whispered something to his researcher.

He plunged – fists flailing, loose strands of hair flicking the faces of his small audience, like a cow's tail chasing flies – straight into the heat of the matter: the slaughter of a whole people, sacred innocents, keepers of the dream, by rapacious and sadistic land thieves, backed by puppet governments and mega-corporations. He named names. He spoke of genetic mutations, ancestral sites poisoned for millennia; of enforced sterilization; drink-sadness; deaths in custody. He described back-country cells that looked like abattoirs. He poured out all the well-rehearsed routines his researcher had fed him over a leisurely breakfast of kidneys, burnt bacon, and fried bread that dripped white grease when he pressed it with his fork. And it was all true. But because *he* was saying it that truth was lost. He merely participated in the crimes; and, by naming them – without heart-directed anger – he softened their edges, generalized them to impotent rhetoric. The tree-planting had become a second burial for King Cole, a display.

Now Triscombe was sure. He was aroused by the false demons of his well-crafted performance. He was excited by the extinct emotions he had touched within his hidden self; and he had to disguise the physical manifestation of that excitement by immediately plunging his hands into his trouser pockets. He was *genuinely* moved, both by the tragic stupidity of genocide, the termination of a non-renewable human resource, and by the solitary courage of Edith Cadiz. He was inspired, but his solution was extreme. He wanted to – as he saw it – arrange a marriage: between the spirit of King Cole and the warm body of his former mistress. He wanted Edith to be buried alive.

He turned away. The gardeners were stamping down the earth, hammering in a stake to support the tender growth: they were shuffling back to their shed. But the woman was the crime. A taboo had been wilfully broken. She had witnessed a moment of ceremonial magic. Punishment was inevitable. Triscombe was not implicated. '*The rest is not our business.*'

Edith was smiling: none of this mattered. It was happening to somebody she had known once, and left behind. The researcher tried to cross the park towards her; but time was frozen, the 'long second' of science fiction – everybody else was moving so slowly through solid air that was turning into ice. He closed his fist around Gelert's collar and hauled him, choking, back to the Jaguar. A track was visible where the animal's weight had resisted, and flattened the wet grass. The engine was over-revving: the car backed up over the flower beds, spinning earth, then jolted out under the arch, and away into the traffic of Roman Road.

Playing its part, the rain began to fall with more purpose. Edith turned up her collar. She seemed to be quite alone, under the tree, on that dismal ground. Even if she had been searching for one, there was no way out: she was trapped, blocked in by the flats and the railway. Then some men, who had been casually watching, talking among themselves, walked out of the pool of shadows beneath the embankment wall, and came quickly towards her.

4

Living in Restaurants

Living in Restaurants

'The beetles dying of the plague
don't care what railways are like'

Benjamin Péret,
The Girls' Schools are Too Small

We had hardly begun: we were no more than two or three lunches into the project when I first heard the term 'kill fee'. The trainee director assigned to vet our suitability let it fall from a peak of feigned excitement and urgency: as if this film was the *one* he had been searching for to launch not only his career, but ... ours as well. Together we were a dream-ticket: Ken Loach paired with ... Tom Wolfe. We were irresistible. He smiled, and looked from Fredrik's face to mine in the vain hope of approval. I thought his team sounded, well, a little ... over the hill. Museum-bait, in fact. Kitchen-table socialism vampirizing a seizure of good-old Southern-style carpetbaggery. And there was a definite limit, now rapidly approaching, to the number of metaphorical pause-bubbles (...) I could swallow, without punching the over-articulate director in the mouth. I was prepared to suffer just so much in the cause of gluttony.

Our boy was clearly a non-combatant. And we were the end of the line. A good way of stiffing him from the payroll. We were a dangerous mess, waiting for some fool to tread in it. There was, sadly, a saturation point to how much flaky carnival footage this man could pump through the schedules on the 'ethnic guilt' quota, before somebody noticed. It was time to make his play. 'Kill fee': it hung there, slightly obscene, a dagger of ice suspended over the pink lawn tablecloth; reminding us of exactly who held the whiphand, and who we were working for. One unjustifiable paragraph, one location more than half a mile from a three-star diner, and we were back on the street, with not much more than our bus fare to show for four months of heroic eating.

The 'Corporation', as is well known, is a Christian version of the Vatican, with all the immemorial chains of command, schisms, heresies, court favourites, interrogations, excommunications, icons, martyr-doms, and public burnings: thickets of conspiracy in which the left hand denies all knowledge of the pocket the right hand is picking. The Vatican has its global responsibilities (getting the dirt out of banknotes, and promoting moon-tested golf-buggies); but the Corporation yields nothing as a fountainhead of dogma. White papers, touched by the hand of Reith, are eternal and infallible:

(1) There are two sides (and only two) to every argument.
(2) We shall offer them, without fear or favour, equal air-time.
(3) The only good book is a dead book. (And grant, O Lord, that it be set in Africa.)
(4) Yesterday's dross, if repeated often enough, is today's classic. (Memo to *Contracts*: Tighten up on those Repeat Fees.)
(5) It is always better to *employ* Irish Jokes, than to tell them. We are never vulgar. Especially about money.
(6) If the Irish are 'men of violence' they may speak only in subtitles.
(7) It is a short step from the Department of Religious Affairs to the throne of the Director-General.
(8) Only Accountancy is a Higher Calling. The 'Accountant' is the person who is accountable to no one (except, of course, She-Whose-Name-May-Not-Be-Taken-In-Vain).

The Corporation, in its perpetual and never satisfied search for 'The New', operates a nervous compromise between greed and caution: a sinister cloud of anti-matter, giving off odours of sanctity and expensive aftershave, trawls for virgin energies to subvert. Two of the sharpest headhunters, pulling their faces out of their coffee cups with an audible 'Eureka!', stumbled, *at the same moment*, on the name of Fredrik Hanbury: who was so prolific in his journalism, so much in demand, he seemed to be reviewing half-digested pastiches of his own work, flashing from magazine to newspaper in an exuberantly Socratic dialogue that only he was fast enough to follow. This banal coincidence in the recognition of a name it was harder to avoid than to notice was elevated – by a species of desperate occultism that lurks in all stagnant bureaucra-cies – into a significantly compelling *synchronicity*. And so, only a year after his seminal book of essays went out of print, the word from the Bush was – bring me the head of Fredrik Hanbury!

Fredrik had done a number in the *London Review of Books* on a novel I had recently published; which would otherwise, despite the gallantly double-glazed 'doorstepping' of my publisher, have sunk into necessary and well-deserved obscurity. Fredrik suggested that Spitalfields was, currently, a battleground of some interest; a zone of 'disappearances', mysteries, conflicts, and 'baroque realism'. Nominated champions of good and evil were locking horns in a picaresque contest to nail the ultimate definition of 'the deal'. We had to get it on. There were not going to be any winners. If we didn't move fast, any halfway-sharp surrealist could blunder in and pick up the whole pot.

'Spitalfields': the *consiglieri* liked the sound of it, the authentic whiff of heritage, drifting like cordite from the razed ghetto. But, please, do not call it 'Whitechapel', or whisper the dreaded 'Tower Hamlets'. Spital-fields meant Architecture, the Prince, Development Schemes: it meant gay vicars swishing incense, and charity-ward crusaders finding the peons to refill the poor benches, and submit to total-immersion baptism. It meant Property Sharks, and New Georgians promoting wallpaper catalogues. It meant video cams tracking remorselessly over interior *detail*, and out, over lampholders, finials, doorcases, motifs, cast-iron balconies; fruity post-synch, lashings of Purcell. And bulldozers, noise, dust; snarling angry machines. Ball-and-chain demolitions. *Sold!* There's nothing the cutting-room boys like as much as a good ball-and-chain: especially with some hair-gelled noddy in a pin-stripe suit at the controls. Skin-deep Aztec fantasies of glass and steel lifting in a self-reflecting glitter of irony from the ruins. Spitalfields was this week's buzz-word. And Spitalfields meant lunches.

But lunches also have their hierarchies. You start on your own doorstep. A sciolist, call him Sonny Jaques, with a gold stud earring, and a doctorate in Romance Languages (from, let us guess, Southampton University), sounds you out about the nearest 'little Italian place' that takes credit cards.

'Jaques? I suppose you pronounce that "J'accuse"?' said Fredrik, to get the ball rolling.

'Jake-Ez, actually,' the director replied, too self-absorbed to be so effortlessly insulted.

The trattoria we located, in a backwater off the Kingsland Road, had just opened in a lather of misplaced optimism. I gave it slightly less chance than the *Titanic*. It would be an off licence within the month. Then a fire-damaged shell. Then a sealed hazard; waiting for the insurance investigators to settle the claim.

Today it was empty: salmon-pink tablecloths, freshly laundered, and sharp enough to cut you off at the knees; wild flowers; silver service; napkins erupting out of fluted wine glasses. The gaffer – in his black, open-to-the-navel blouse – leapt on Sonny, as if he was a practice manikin for a mouth-to-mouth-resuscitation class. The man had packed his bags, and most of the silver. He was ready to chuck in the lease when – as his finger closed on the trigger – the BBC arrived. It had to happen. Glorious visions cut in on each other: telephone reservations, cigars, signing sessions, assignations, bankable painters doodling on the menu cards, group photographs on the walls (lavishly inscribed), talent scouts begging to be called by their christian names. He wants to join in, to proffer advice. He wants to sit on Sonny's lap, and 'kick around' a few casting concepts.

But Sonny is going up in smoke; he is live with morbid energy. As Fredrik soliloquizes, he angrily abuses the tiny pages of his notebook. The green pen-tip breaks the surface of the paper. He accumulates the evidence that will be held against us. 'Right!' he enthuses, at regular intervals, banging the table; so that our host has to slide from his bench, with an apologetic smile, to catch the flower holders. Sonny glances from Fredrik to me, then back again. 'Right? That one's a definite maybe. Excellent. It's all coming together.' But nothing is agreed, nothing is made clear: nobody has the bad manners to mention money. Lowlife anecdotes are really what turn Sonny on – but how do we translate them into the script? '8mm Diary footage? We can use that. Send it in for transfer. Work on textural variety. I like it.'

He is wringing our hands: the restaurateur froths with compliments and invitations, as he struggles to reinsert Sonny into a yellow pigskin jacket. Sonny assures us that we give 'good lunch'; the project is 'looking great'. We have to go home, stick at it, stay cool, and wait for the call. Unfortunately, by an oversight, Sonny's pack of credit cards fails to produce a valid one. No problem; Fredrik and I empty our pockets and manage to cover the bill. 'Just put it on the chitty, boys,' Sonny says, 'and claim a couple of taxis while you're at it.'

Now the caravan rolls on to downside Shepherd's Bush. Our table rates at least two producers. We are not substantial enough to score anyone from 'Religious Affairs'; but we get one apiece from 'Architecture' and 'Literature'. Who knows what slot this thing might fit into? Why spike it for the price of a *Grade IV (Writers and Talking Heads)* binge? There's a whole cluster of modest *Nouvelle Cuisine* joints sticking bravely together in the warren, north of Addison Gardens, entirely targeted at working lunches for the Corporation. Every time the budget is slashed on 'The Late Show', two of them go out of business. They serve minute, and beautifully arranged, portions – and charge no more than they would for a side of bloody Aberdeen Angus, with all the coronary trimmings. Everybody starves a little, and feels the glow of virtue.

The architectural producer – the one with the serious tweed jacket, who 'used to know your friend, the poet, Eric Whatsisname' – is a man who understands the value of time. He calls loudly for a second platter of new potatoes before we've finalized our power-plays over the seating arrangements. The potatoes are dwarf hybrids, the size of slightly pregnant peas. You get five each. The serious jacket is working on a calculation of their weight by volume. He has that combative attitude so prevalent among people who spend their lives bluffing genuine enthusiasts into believing they know nothing about their own subject. And will need a sturdy lifeline from a sympathetic producer. He had been co-opted into Architecture from the London School of Economics; and – having made two films in five years – was generally held to be doing an excellent job, in not wasting public money.

The other nob is distinctly 'Arts'; and proves it, by arriving just in time for the lemon sorbet – and still securing more than his fair share of the Austrian anti-freeze. He's one of the Nigels. The first thing people ask about them is: 'Is he the one who made a cunt of himself with Genet?' It *always* is. Very nice fella, Nigel. Won't hear a word against him. He should worry; on £40,000 a year, and enough 'allowed' days to bang out a novel for one of the posh houses. Some of these Nigels turn eventually into Nicks, and transfer – without fuss – to London Weekend. But this one is still, quite definitely, a Nigel. He knows how to keep the wine flowing. And we all sit in a formaldehyde line, trading blank-verse anecdotes – like late T. S. Eliot at the Edinburgh Festival. Nobody has actually said anything about the film. *What film?* We must be auditioning for the Masons. It's a quick handshake, a peppermint, and back to the office.

On the pavement, the moment before we are cast adrift, Sonny tips us the big wink. The project, he assures us, is 'on'. We can start mapping the camera angles. Secret signals were, apparently, exchanged across the lunch table. You can read a lot into the way your neighbour turns his fork, or flashes his wine label. We'll have a production number by the end of the month.

The feeding, from this point, falls on us. The second (working) stage belongs to kitchens. You begin to understand why notes were kept. Motorcycle messengers lacerate the city bearing triplicate summaries: within the hour, the scenes we have written are returned to us, translated into an ersatz and shifty language. A simple instruction, such as: *Camera moves from street into synagogue*, is inflated into a page of tortuous explanation. A party of schoolkids is invented, so that the camera will not have to be switched on without a justification that would stand up in a court of law.

In the old days, the 1960s, it was taxis: an endless circuit of cabs with solitary cans of film, script revisions, hampers. Now there's more *gravitas*: we talk to agents who talk to agents (and charge us for the privilege); we talk 'repeats', and we talk 'kill fees'. We'll have to put a nine-month gestation into this script for an initial payment of – what – £200? See how that floats at the next lunch. We could be scheduled, or we could be looking at some very 'creative' expenses.

We have come in from the cold. We have not yet taken the blood-oath, and signed the Official Secrets form, but we do have an interesting collection of phone numbers. And the promise of an actual contract.

II

'Research' was the excuse for a day or two walking the labyrinth: markets and breakfasts. Fredrik wanted to call on Roland Bowman, an actor he had met at a party, who was restoring a house in Fournier Street. Roland had staged, in the tragic basement that once held the Hebrew Dramatic Club (scene of the 1887 false-fire panic, and death-on-the-stairs of seventeen members of the audience), a millennial version of Wilde's first play, *Vera; or The Nihilists*. He brought out the *Rose-Croix* ritual that Wilde had coded into the piece. And his own perform-ance, as Vera, in this all-male production, gained the unexpressed approval of his neighbours, Gilbert and George.

Roland was no card-carrying Huguenot. He had been drawn here down a track of dreams. He remembered what the house would become. It was all inevitable, and his talent lay in not opposing the current that was already carrying him along. The ruin was now a valuable property in which he camped with his mother, while he breathed life into a shell of bricks and plaster. He was living far beyond his apparently modest means in keeping faith with this vision. Market forces would conspire, in time, to expel him. But that was the nature of the place. The human element was optional.

At the back of the house was a narrow, walled garden. Roland pointed out the hops he had cultivated, as a gesture of solidarity with the earlier benefactors of this soil, and with the prevailing winds that gifted us with all the odours of Truman's Brewery: odours you can taste, Whitechapel's *madeleine*. Fredrik, of course, had a dissertation handy, culled from the journals of a Quaker brewmaster, asserting that the heady scent of the hops made men drowsy and women lascivious. He knew the Latin names of all the flowers.

We settled on a bench, all of us sharing a notion that this was slightly unreal, a posed photograph. We wanted to arrive at the story that lay ahead, but there was no way of rushing it. Roland was fascinated by his own wrists. He stroked his fingers obsessively down the length of his arm, gesturing, encircling the wrist; as if he could not believe in its delicacy. He is ageless, benign; a chaste Dorian Gray. He moves in clean lines against a plain background. Nothing is hurried. His arms are thin, but a braid of muscle bunches under the short sleeve of his matelot jersey.

He showed us the house: we eavesdropped on his private space. What we relished, we also exploited. Our brief from the Corporation insisted that each minute particular be generalized: it must stand for something, an articulated tendency. If we could not explain it, then it did not exist.

From the first-floor window I looked back over the garden, and north towards Princelet Street; and I was amazed to discover how much of this area was still covert: hidden space, old courts, outhouses, industrial yards tethered in hawsers of convolvulus, protected by hedges of thorn and nettles. The heart of Whitechapel remained in purdah, sheathed in a prophylactic neglect: from the streets there was no hint that this unexploited kingdom even existed. Had I stumbled, after all these years, on a method of painlessly visiting the past?

On the other side of the house, facing the magnificent threat of Christ Church, Roland was in the process of creating a room that would set the key for his entire scheme: the minimal decorations he had so far effected were both ritualistic and meaningful. One wall was covered with a painted backdrop; a Strindbergian victim, whose hair, and silent scream, shakes a liquid jungle of intestinal ropes and vines. She is drowning in fire. This hot flush of expressionist bravado is countered by a pale and handsome fireplace, freshly installed: on its mantelpiece is the Spy cartoon of Oscar Wilde.

Roland was ahead of us. 'Yes, the fireplace did, in fact, once belong to Wilde,' he said. 'And, I suppose, I like to believe that it still does. Sympathizers rescued what they could from Tite Street after the crash. The fireplace passed, for generations, among friends: who could appreciate its value, and its charms, without wishing to obliterate those qualities in a sordid monetary transaction.' Roland was making a speech, and he knew it. He floated upstage from the mantelpiece, so that he could spin, dramatically, on his heel, and allow the sunlight in the window to fluster the red in his hair. 'I cling to the conceit,' he continued, 'that when I've finished the job, Oscar will walk in, smoking his blonde cigarettes; ready to accept the sensational role of a character, literally unresolved between life and art. It's what he always wanted.'

Slightly embarrassed by this infusion of greasepaint, I began to shuffle a stack of books that stood alongside the framed Wilde caricature: six mint copies of a celebrated 'bestseller' that attributed the most peculiar properties to the local churches. The critics promised your money back if you did not die of terror as you read it. Many of the New Georgian squatters kept a copy in the close chamber, though privately decrying the thing, as a calumny on the disinterested aesthetics of Baroque Architecture. But even as a talismanic icon, I felt that six units was stronging it.

'When Mother and I moved here,' said Roland, with the frankness that characterized his conversation, 'and because our interests are well known, all our chums kept making us presents of that book. I haven't got around to reading it yet. Something holds me back. I couldn't *bear* to be disappointed. I liked the Wilde novel so much I wrote to the author, through his publishers, inviting him to trot along for a cup of tea, and a look at the fireplace. He never replied. And I realized afterwards, with utter shame, that my letter must have read like some terrible gauche come-on.'

'Don't worry,' I told him, 'the publishers probably shredded it. He's far too much of a goldmine to be interrupted with tea ceremonies.'

This prompted Fredrik – who had been silent for about two minutes, and was turning a dangerous rectal-purple colour – to vault into an improvisational theory that I soon lost track of: it concerned 'prophetic curvatures of time', vampire-clones, and hermetic sexuality. He posited an 'eternal return'; whereby certain figures are unable to escape the Wheel of Fate. Those cultists who look longingly on such as Wilde, Chatterton, Rimbaud, Blake, Stevenson, or Keats are themselves trapped, *as in a liquid mirror*. Obsession matures into spiritual paralysis. The cultist relives borrowed lives, is bound to gross matter; to ghosts of the undead, and the always-dying. But the created grids of energy can be consulted like a tarot pack: so that, for example, Peter Ackroyd's *The Great Fire of London* can anticipate the coming 'heritage' triumph of *Little Dorrit*, and the shift in focus that would make the Thames itself an assertive template from which the new London would be built. This is the confection we are now required to worship: a 'view' by the Venetian mercenary, Canaletto.

Roland was actively infected by this madness. He responded to a theme that must have been buried far beneath what Fredrik was actually saying. He shunted us on to the familiar *fin de siècle* notion of the 'time-halting' magic of the photograph, or portrait, where the photographer does not deflect the intensity of the subject: the Dorian Gray syndrome. The person who submits to this, who allows themself to be caught, is caught for ever. They are no longer free to draw breath. The evidence is used, *and will continue to be used*, against them. 'Neither is the photographer immune,' Roland insisted. 'It happened with Robert Mapplethorpe. The love-objects he was driven – so calculatingly – to capture, returned the compliment. And fixed the relationship in a now definitive form.'

It was, Roland thought, Wilde's photograph, the reckless arrogance of it, taken in New York, January 1882, Napoleon Sarony, that finished him. Wilde posed, with all the insane courage of the damned, in the Masonic costume of the Apollo Lodge, Oxford: knee-breeches, silk stockings, pumps. He had been inducted into the *Rose-Croix* Chapter, which offered the promise of a ritual of death and resurrection. The regalia included a lambskin apron, of which he was almost indecently fond. From the second Sarony hooded his lens, Wilde's card was marked; he had only to wait for it. The brothers were going to nail him.

Turning my back on the fetid heat of the room, I walked over to the unshuttered window. I could see across the street into the rectory of Christ Church, Spitalfields: the shadowy, dark-wood staircase designed by Nicholas Hawksmoor. An inaccessible ladder in time.

III

There is a grove in Victoria Park much favoured by a snaked-haired former 'rent boy', and his inherited dog. Tucked contentedly into his fifties, he remains clear-eyed, unlined; though tolerably weather-beaten. His shaggy dust-powdered mane – unremarked in the Living Theatre years – now drew the odd disapproving sniff from brutally-cropped joggers. Expensive orthodontia (the gift of a fastidious oralist) is being gently eroded by a compulsive fondness for lethally dyed gobstoppers. He dribbles constantly from the corners of a wide and slack-lipped grin. He is known, to those who cannot avoid him, as 'The Mad Mason'; or, more recently, as 'Neb' or 'Nebby'. This sobriquet deriving from his tendency to crawl along the ground, searching for lost coins, and spirit-messages from the wind. Neb was another who had been '*driven from men, and did eat grass as oxen, and his body was wet with the dew of heaven, till his hairs were grown like eagles' feathers, and his nails like birds' claws*'. William Blake might have been using a polaroid when he caught Neb's likeness in 1795. But 'The Mason' retained, above everything, a mad and reckless joy. Nose among dog turds, he laughed. He lived in an irreparable feud with himself: loud, ungoverned, shouting and punching at shadows. Like a streetwise tom cat he chewed the coarse-spined grass only to make himself sick, to retch up the poisons of the city.

If you spoke to him he would not look at you, because he did not believe you were really there. He plucked obsessively at the lobes of his ears; he gouged his cheeks. Flesh fell from him: turbid fruit. But he had survived the gloomy medical predictions – the venereal probes, the brain wires – by many years; and now his pre-twilight days were spent roaming the broad estates of the people's park. Within the circumference of what he had already discovered, Neb was a free man.

But he was certainly not one of your usual dog fanciers: an evil category that have conspired to turn London into a steaming slough of inefficiently recycled horse-pieces. Those yelping pragmatists, the dog-owning tendency, huddled together beside a bench, in a circle of dead white earth, talking of 'points', diets, canine bowel movements: so many mothers at the school gates. They watched, with barely-concealed pride, as their brain-damaged inbreeds did unspeakable things to the legs of collapsed cyclists, or knocked over a howling toddler. They only came to life if any mere pedestrian retaliated and spoke sharply to their darlings; and then they would scream the foulest obscenities, and call on their protector, PC Plod. Park-keepers and policemen, possibly through some kind of genetic deficiency, have a sentimental fondness for these hideous beasts. And, by law, the first bite is on the house. It goes unpunished. Count yourself lucky if you don't get rabies.

Neb's grove, fringed with Edwardian trees, was shunned by the dog people. But they paused, in their flight, to monitor their pets while they strained at the stool, legs rigid, eyes on stalks, tails erect, panting knots of concentration. 'You better watch it, Missus,' Neb would invariably shout, resenting the trespass. 'They're going to let the Koreans build a camp here. That dog of yourn'll be dizzy, turning on a hot spit. They'll think this place is a takeaway.'

It was a game. Neb did not care. He was sifting the rubbish the wind had blown against the fence of the keeper's house. No bagman, Neb stuffed his pockets with scraps of old newspaper; which, later, in his Well Street garret, he would assemble into a promethean scrapbook of unconnected narratives. The *Daily Telegraph* and the *Hackney Gazette* were particular friends.

'SEX CHANGE WIFE' MURDERED AFTER WITCH'S WEDDING. *Husband wanted affair with another man, court told.* DERANGED KILLER IS LOCKED AWAY FOR EVER – *54-year-old man's fingernails were ripped off with pliers* – *Mr Berman was a loner.* CLASS WAR DENY ATTACK. DRUGS DOCTOR BACK ON REGISTER. WOMAN RAPED BY GANG WHO LACED DRINK – *as the evening progressed a group of 'nice Chinese lads' introduced themselves* – *when she awoke she was surrounded by a group of men, giggling hysterically, who pinned her down and took it in turns to rape her, she said. The East London Licensed*

Victuallers' Association emphasized that they have never discriminated against gypsies. There is a difference between gypsies and Travellers. As a shopkeeper born and bred in Stoke Newington ... I am writing a documentary TV programme about people with original jobs and driving ambition ... Stamford Hill, where she was beaten, slashed with a knife, forced to sleep in a broom cupboard and warned that if she breathed a word she would be visited by black magic spirits.

The book-running days ended for Neb four years ago, shortly before the legendary Nicholas Lane went into exile. Neb had an obscure commission to purchase any items appearing on the stalls that touched on the Masonic Craft. But this was not enough for him: he lectured loudly on the corruptions of the Brotherhood to all who would, or would not, listen. He flapped, he spat: beak-nosed pamphleteer, bog-leveller. A William Prynne, born again. He broke the oath of silence, he waggled his tongue: on flyleafs, he sketched the secret seals. Browsers, picking effetely at Ardizzone squiggles, were initiated into the outlandish mysteries of the Bora Ceremony.

Inevitably, Neb was noticed. There was a rival: black-suited, loose-wigged, a silver dealer, with leather gloves, and the pallor of a stagnant urine sample. A man who bought, and removed from view, anything that even *hinted* at knowledge of the Ancient and Accepted Rites, the Higher Degrees. He would explode with gaseous ripples of fury, in a chain-reaction bilious attack, if these forbidden books were not, on the instant, polished, triple-bagged, and slid from the sight of the vulgar.

Then came the fateful day when the Mad One – who was beginning to mix the polemic rant with shrill anecdotes of some of his stickier 'rent-boy' triumphs – spotted a punter, debating with his wife the purchase of a pair of sugar tongs, and yelled, 'I had your old man, Missus, *twice*: in the pergola by Manor House Hospital. You know it? Just off the Heath. He wasn't much. Do you have to start him talking dirty?' The death-kit, silver-hoarding Masonic hitman cornered, unexpectedly, at that moment, bearing some swag from the Georgian Village. He appeared – with a look of lemur-like paralysis – to recognize Neb: in both his capacities. But it was too late. Neb was flying.

'Wouldn't melt in his mouth. Look at him.' Neb's voice leapt into the equine register of a Frankie Howerd impersonator. He was enjoying himself. The punter's wife was calcified; while the accused man, in reflex shame, was stuffing his pockets with all the silver snuffboxes on the stall. The stallholder, swathed in money belts like a Zapataist guerrilla, was puffing herself up, cobra-fashion, ready to emit a scream that would take out most of the windows between the canal and Barnsbury. 'Tight-arsed bugger. You should see what he did to me. I can't walk down to the Job Centre without leaning over. Don't let him near you, love, when he's got a broom-handle.'

One of Neb's flailing manic arms caught Nicholas Lane's wine glass, and spun it into the air – a chalice of blood – causing it to invert, and the blush of cheap red claret to soak gratefully into the pages of J. S. M. Ward's *Freemasonry and the Ancient Gods*. As Neb reached forward to repair the damage, he succeeded only in tearing, into two unequal portions, the fold-out plate illustrating *The Templar Charter of Trans- mission*. He stood there, open-mouthed; flapping ineffectively at the wine stain with the ravished drawing.

If it had been possible, the hitman would have paled: his complexion was already on the unconvinced side of goat's whey. He was a back-door johnny staggering home from an all-night blood-transfusion party.

He stared directly into the lens of Neb's left eye; he gained entrance. The Mad One was head-clamped, zapped with a stun-gun. The heat drained from him. It was as if a mirror had been implanted between Neb and the world. There was no longer anything he could touch without passing this incorruptible guardian; the self that had died, one micro- second before. Therefore, he did not age. He was without purchase on life, a harmless thing. He stumbled from the market. And he never returned. He had, in that swift division of time, been emasculated; banished to the reservation of those who live without light. The inherited dog joined him; a protector to keep off the curious, a buddy to see him through to the end. Neb had found the beast, wandering half-starved, in Meath Gardens.

The Mad One was effortlessly replaced – a new boy was on the streets before he had reached Haggerston – but his charge stood. Masonry is a certain recipe for a bestseller. Anything on that topic will be bought by the brothers to keep it out of the hands of the uninitiated. And bought. And bought again. It is the 'investigative' author who does not always enjoy his royalties. He suffers: the mad late-night phonecalls; the hand- printed letters, leavened with non-sequiturs; the blinding headaches. Is the paranoid, as William Burroughs says, in possession of all the facts – the only sane man in a tilted world – or has he merely initiated an irreversible conspiracy against *his own sanity*?

Neb was arrested two or three times, out beyond the cricket square, for exposing himself; but this was more carelessness than any desire to boast, or to engage yet again in human commerce. He was finished with all that. The tape was running backwards: as he circumnavigated the grass ocean, he re-enacted incidents from his past; he triumphed in ancient conflicts. The limits of the park became the limits of his world-picture. His childhood was visited among the swings and sheds:

chapped legs, and the smell of warm pee. His adolescence was associated with water: the boating lake and its islands. Hiding from eyes and stones; scratchy with secrets, unregistered library books under his jacket. He missed the ugly plaster dogs on their plinths. They had been hacked off for renovation. And would be replaced by freshly painted fakes. Death lurked, Neb felt, in the misted windows of the Burdett-Coutts Tower. The evil moment of his conception kept him clear of the twin stone igloos culled from the block masonry of old London Bridge.

These igloos were the subject of one of Neb's perpetual monologues. He muttered as he stalked: he clapped his hands. The mason's marks, hidden behind the capstone, obsessed him. The triangle, the circle, and the cross. Shiva the Destroyer; flame on the funeral pyre. 'Lifted from the river; the medieval bridge, the chapel,' he nodded, as if making the discovery for the first time. 'They stole the stones – two for Vicky Park, one for Guy's! You won't get me out on the water. Under the arch? Never!' He prophesied disaster; drowning, lung-burst. What other kind of prophet was there?

He spoke of the alcoves as 'dream-helmets'. And it is true that they were generally avoided. Cyclists kept cycling. Adulterers stayed in their vehicles, as if frightened of the lions. 'Sleep in those things,' said Neb,

Mason's Mark, found in the stone alcoves at
Victoria Park and Guy's Hospital, Southwark

'and you'll incubate your own death. You'll be forced to dream all the nightmares that have ever flowed down the river, all the plagues and executions. Why do you think they look like the Thames Barrier? Because the real job of the Barrier is to retain the sleep of the city; not to let our dreams – the most precious of all resources – escape.'

Neb was very tired now, but he kept on walking.

IV

The grass was flat and white where Colonel 'Colt' Swinefoot's tents had stood. The evangelist, his caravan, and his shock troops, had moved east, to offer a much-needed blessing for West Ham FC. But the colonel's apocalyptic warnings hung in the air, like the heavy scorch of frying onions, compressed beef, and temporary repentance: 'It is the hour of the Antichrist. The mark of the beast is branded into our cheeks. Our tongues shall blacken and swell, until our very mouths are filled. *Amen!* We will be dragged, cursing, into hellfire.' And more of the same. Much more. Three hours on his feet was as nothing to Colt. Sweat rolled from his brow. The chorus stamped and sang. Fire buckets rattled with coin. Colt's sermon, fiendishly amplified, blasted the walls of the old Victoria Park Lido; which had been recently ordained as East London's first privately-funded lazaret. Neb took it on himself, unpaid, and uninvited, to become one of the angels.

AIDS was a fifth-floor disease, in a four-floor culture. There had to be somewhere – preferably outside the inhabitable zone – where a buck could be turned coping with one of the few genuine growth areas that was still, always excepting the West Coast, scandalously under-exploited. Fortunes would be made when a tested antidote was brought in – but that was the big one, Nobel stuff, the Holy Grail. Meanwhile the name of the game is counselling, care, discretion, and check the credit cards before the first transfusion. Things were happening fast. There was now a state far worse than being an 'outpatient'. The agents of Venture Capital had identified a brand of 'quarantine' that had much in common with other hermetic encampments, kept for aliens in time of war.

The lazaret stood just inside the park gates, at the Grove Road end, beyond a notice announcing that 'these premises are protected by Barbican Security Services'. The red-brick Stalinist folly with the sea-green pantiled entrance had functioned for many years as a swimming pool. Now it looked as if the set for *Fifty-five Days at Peking* had been requisitioned for a *Living Dead* video-quickie. Neb blundered among the enfeebled inmates in their fugitive exile; the HIV-positives, the 'black spot' carriers. He ran messages, he went shopping; and, if he was incapable of listening to any instruction, he was ready to talk without hypocrisy or fear. He rushed through the pallets, arms waving like a bird scarer, beating off the gathering darkness. Dame Nightingale: he buddied the sick. He gave them their first strange taste of life-after-death.

Spies reported a fierce debate in the council chambers concerning the fate of this abandoned municipal swimming pool, one of Lansbury's finest lidos. It was a symbol of a vanished *Health and Efficiency* era; a huge, chlorine-weeping, corn-plaster-infested trench – where Neb had achieved some of his most spectacular conquests – which should, without doubt, be restored and streamlined as an 'investment opportunity'. The public purse no longer ran to filling it with water (perish the thought, better to fill it with oil!) for the unbathed peons to splash about, urinating, exposing their unsightly flab, and floating their beer-cans and fag packets. No instruction had, as yet, been received from above to make a charge for entrance to the park: a 'reserved vehicle area' was being enlarged and fenced, marked out for the ticket machines. It was perhaps premature, before all the tenders were sifted, to pass any binding resolution. The decision-makers contented themselves, for the present, with covertly enclosing more and more of the open ground; creating a no man's land, a causeway of conveniently storm-felled trees.

The Controller moved his office into the upper chamber of the Burdett-Coutts Tower; a structure that seemed to have evolved from an unlikely collaboration between Albert Speer and Rowland Emett. Hierarchic steps, and pillars of pink Peterhead granite, gave way to eccentric decoration; clocks, twirls, twists, stone fruits, and weather-damaged puns. The titular spirits were four seriously overweight cherubs: only one of whom had held on to his wings. Their eyes were debauched with red paint. Their pudgy feet rested on squirming fish. Unwillingly – and after an obvious struggle – they had been surgically initiated, made kosher: with full subincision rites. Their off-white pigeon bellies hosted the usual braggart scrawls: I ALWAYS FUCK MY MUM! BONGO + COLL + SPAM. Above their hydrocephalic heads, in Gothic Script, ran the sad legend, 'For Love of God and Country'. Amen, Colonel, to that.

From his crow-high porthole the Controller weighed the options, comparing, unfavourably, the visible reality of the broken-down lido with the optimistic and rhetorical plans that were spread out on a table at his elbow. The Four Horsemen romped across the paddy – and with them a hook on which he could surely hang his future. *Plague!* They should get it corralled fast, put their brand on it; make it pay.

Within hours a crude conversion was under way that retained the original concentration-camp fencing and watchtowers, while shifting the pool itself into a 'basically Neo-Templar ambience': from hydro to hospice in fourteen days. The ironies implicit in this transaction were thrown away on its perpetrators: a primary source of infection should find itself recast as the ashram of its final flowering.

The pool was submerged in drapes of lemon-and-white canvas, divided into individual cubicles. The surround was tiled, and saturated with fountains. The feel the architect wanted to go for was 'non-denominational Moorish'. No disturbing images to invoke the past. Just the wind in the trees; reflections of clouds; plashing water falling on stone. The once-sordid changing sheds became 'day rooms', with low couches and the (piped) music of strings.

On fine afternoons the living skeletons lay outside on recliners, gazing listlessly at the agitated sails of the trees; as they shifted and quivered, and breathed. There was something heroic and improvised about the whole affair. In the fullness of time, naturally, the baths could be 'themed' from diving boards to buffet, and a reasonable charge levied: payable in advance. The destitute could take out insurance, or make their own arrangements, under the sponsorship of caring libraries – if they could find any. This was a transitional phase. The developers were ready, on the nod, to 'get into bed' with the council. They were quite willing to sponsor the publication of leaflets, available on request, from all registered gyms, saunas, launderettes, and secondary schools: 'Holy Communion – Is There a *Safe Method* of Using the Chalice?' 'AIDS and the Trade Unions'.

The local authority that had once tolerated Roland Bowman's T3 Classes (Therapy-through-Theatre) now transferred him to the lazaret. It was easier to turn the 'outpatients' loose than to have them poncing about on a stage, 'expressing themselves' and getting ideas. They'd had more than enough of Roland's subversive readings of the minor classics: all-male, all-female; all paid for by the taxpayer. There was no percentage in it. Roland was a nuisance. One of these days a bored critic might leave Shaftesbury Avenue and review a play staged in a synagogue. They saw their chance and 'invited' Roland to develop a scenario that had proved highly popular in San Francisco: 'How to enjoy a fully satisfying relationship with a mortally-disadvantaged partner.'

Does love end with death? The sunshine theory was that it did not; many spiritual climaxes lay ahead – if the groundwork was tactfully handled. The bones of the thing had been shamelessly lifted from the Natural Childbirth propagandists – 'breathing', stages, levels of pain: unashamed Tupperware Buddhism. The dying were to be taken, step by step, *through* death; which was, apparently, a kind of wind. They learned to sing their way out, to cut free from their old lives and their worn flesh. They joined with the wind. They moved among the leaves of the trees. They faced what lay ahead. They were instructed to fantasize a picture of the beloved one; then to strip the picture of all its physical attributes, reduce it to a flame; to step into that flame, burning away all memories, all regrets. Love curves around them, like a fault.

As Roland instructed them, with disinterested affection, and with strength, they did indeed begin to taste smells, to hear colour. Their sensuous faculties had never been so acute, because they no longer had the will to oppose them. They were able, *by their own volition*, to enter a place of safety; a place of which Roland had no knowledge whatever.

Neb and his inherited dog leapt joyously around the fringes of this mantra-chanting seminar, performing his own spinning-dervish celebration. He took in marginal details that were of no value to any other human creature: blue plastic streamers caught on the wire, or the last red rays of sunlight picking out the jagged glass fragments in the windows, making them into maps, outlines of islands to be visited by the saints. The tranced neophytes swayed and moaned, while Neb muttered his dark imprecations to the older gods. His lips bubbled with white pellets. The shape of Roland's dance had conjured a truce with time. His naked white-bone feet were scarcely touching the cool green tiles. The low drone ran out across the park, shadow-spokes through the dark grass: the angry courage of the dying men.

V

Sonny Jaques, the director, had learned by rote the rules that he now preached with all the fervour of a convert. The camera could *never* remain still for more than nine seconds. The camera may not move unless it is following some person on a legitimate quest. When in doubt: cross-cut. Somehow, half a dozen stock situations, visited briefly, in and out like a milkman, were assumed to be more interesting than any solitary sequence doomed to stand on its own feet. The validity of this argument was always endorsed by quoting the success of 'EastEnders'. At which point, Fredrik swallowed hard, and thought of the kill fee.

Sonny had to admit, after a night of agony, that he was 'unhappy' with Roland. (He had, at the last head count, been sufficiently unhappy with Dryfeld and Joblard to pogrom them from the script altogether. Poor Milditch never made it, even as a kitchen concept.) He liked Roland. Of course he did. He *loved* him. There was enormous 'potential' there, but ... we didn't *quite* have it in focus yet. I knew we were heading for trouble when I saw those pause bubbles (...) streaming from Sonny's nostrils.

When Sonny was in a state of doubt, his face gelled into a grin set in plaster of Paris. I wanted to tap him with a hammer, and watch it shatter. He kept an admonitory finger wagging, chopping steadily like a Sabatier blade against a herb-board. 'Um, um, um. Ah, ah. Um. Ah.' The tension ran out in rings. The coffee turned to mesozoic mud in our cups. I was all for resolving the matter, unilaterally, with a swift kick in the nuts; but Fredrik had a wonderful way of simply ignoring these local difficulties, cranking the scene on as if they had never occurred. He would suck in a long breath, swallow all the philosophical loose ends still lying on the table, and let rip with a twelve-minute speech, which totally anaesthetized all resistance, and caused the flies to drop dead from the ceiling.

What Sonny wanted to know was: how could we write *anything* down before we knew what was going to happen? And, if we didn't write it down, so that it could be approved by three producers and a finance watchdog, then nothing would happen ... ever. These ephemeral and unreasonable ideas had to be stiffened up: our ghosts had to be *solid*, so that we could cut away from them. We had to appreciate the awkwardness of his dilemma.

As he talked Sonny liked to pace, and also to eat; so that we were dutifully swivelling, backwards and forwards across the table, like the crowd in the Hitchcock tennis match, following him as he made his way to the refrigerator for another handful of black olives. (The family supper had dwindled by this time to a carton of leather-skinned yogurt and an anchovy that was waiting to be carbon-dated.) When Sonny had accumulated a dozen or so stones in his paw, he would arrive at the head of the table and roll them emphatically towards us, like poker dice. 'Ah, um. Ah.'

The pitch that Sonny went for – the only concept with *filmic* possibilities – was the notion that Roland should act out some play, it didn't matter what, in the deconsecrated synagogue at Princelet Street. We can light it with millions of candles, swing incense, wave flags: let's go for it. *Ivan the Terrible, part 3!*

'But hold up, boys, don't get carried away too soon. If living actors are involved, we're hung up on paying union rates, the budget is blown: we'll have to lunch in some bug-infested Brick Lane rat hole. That's serious stuff. The catering is not your department. Just give me seven and a half sheets of negotiable paper that I can take upstairs, without getting egg on my face.'

VI

I drank coffee with Roland Bowman in his basement kitchen. As we chatted, I searched for the photograph of the dancer, Edith Cadiz; but it was no longer on show. Secretly, this pleased me. I didn't want to know if the photograph had changed: if it showed some fresh aspect of Edith's disappearance that I would have to act upon. Any minor alteration in the image would mean an alteration in the account I had already written of it.

Roland was perfectly willing to discuss the director's latest temporary enthusiasm. Previous experiences with the Corporation had resigned him to any twists of fate, however bizarre. He was excited to be involved, but knew in his heart nothing would come of it. He had been in the synagogue once before, with a Firbank adaptation, that had drawn the town, but passed unnoticed in Fleet Street. Now curiously, Fleet Street had marched – like Birnam Wood – to the Isle of Dogs, while Roland held, blindly, to his ground.

It was happening again: the preternatural sensitivity of this ambiguous setting. Nothing was fixed in age, or in gender; only 'place' was constant. Roland anticipated the request I had not yet brought myself to make. He shot upstairs and returned with a large brown envelope containing Edith's notes for the play she wanted him to stage. The play had been delivered, in a woeful state, by a wild-haired messenger, whose condition paralleled the package he was carrying. A dog kept him company. A dog that Roland recognized. The animal had been to Fournier Street before.

The synagogue was now part of the Spitalfields Heritage Centre (by rumour, a front for storing Georgian plunder), so there should be no problem about using it for the performance. We'd take our spot in the queue, behind the primitive artists and the stockbroker wedding receptions. Roland made only one condition. He would not give us sight of his script until there had been a private 'run through', which Fredrik and I would attend: no lights, cameras, or crew were, at this stage, to be involved.

VII

The house in Well Street, Hackney, where Neb lodged was a curious one, but no more curious than its landlord. Elgin MacDiarmuid was a premature New Georgian: he might well have survived, under a preservation order, and several layers of black animal fat, from the era of the slobbering Hanoverians. He lived, and had for years, before cults or articles, in absolute squalor. He broke his fast, when he was 'off the gargle', on bottles of sweet South African sherry; dropping, painlessly, into an insulin-coma that necessitated long sandal-flapping treks out along the canal, and into the leafy suburbs: brooding on ancient glories, or the wives that were flown, along with his inheritance and his favourite four-poster bed. In these sere and yellowed years – he had now turned forty – the 'black dog' was much with him. He sulked in kitchens, he moaned; and sucked for comfort on loose strands of hair, thereby fulfilling most of his dietary requirements. He was amused, as a compensatory fantasy, to announce himself as the hereditary 'Lord of the Isles' – 'dear boy' – or, at the very least, his younger brother. He woke daily in the expectation of a piper at the door. He took to attending clan gatherings, sodden wakes, packed with embalming-fluid-perfumed Canadians, and canny lowland advocates who charged these foreign puddocks a fierce price for two or three nights of rough-hewn crofter living.

Elgin was running down the last of the family properties; hanging grimly on until the concept of 'Docklands' could be stretched to include Hackney. Or until they buried him under a motorway sliproad. The family had been traditionally 'turncoat'; betrayers of Parnell, dinner guests of Black Tim Healy, friends of the Castle. They had thrived on it, to the extent of a brace of hotels in the Joyce Country, and a scatter of London hideaways for the drunks and the gamblers, too far gone to pick a decent American pocket.

Elgin's father's frock coat, a skimpy thing, torn at the seams, and green as moss, barely covered a snuff-stained string vest, and a heaving gut, that would have bulged, if it had not long since collapsed utterly, to hang dead over his leather-belted moleskins: the only surviving legacy of too many nights of 'great crack' and inferior bottled Guinness.

CRACK. The word proved something of a liability when Elgin bellowed it to the world at large: drawing DHSS snoops, vagrants, and outpatients on walkabout, down on his parlour. 'Great crack, lads. You should have been there last night,' he would cry, even to the fur-tongued companions who had stuck with him to the unforgiving steel of dawn. Now *barrio*-rats, and spike-skulled squatters from distressed chip vans, broke surface; to nail these rumours that worried them, like the smell of baking bread in a starving city. They turned the place over, ripped up the floors, slashed the mattresses, and sprayed the walls with libellous assertions. In their justifiable vexation, they set fire to crates of Elgin's scrolled genealogies, his family portraits. He hardly noticed. Worse things, by far, waited every time he closed his eyelids.

The wiring in Elgin's den burst from the walls in a shower of sparks; vines or snake trophies, inadequately disguised by layers of paper that rivalled a definitive V & A catalogue. The plumbing was authentically Georgian (i.e. there wasn't any); and what substitutes Elgin contrived, he also spilled as he struggled in terror from his bed, to place his foot straight in it, or to retrieve a floating sandal from an overloaded receptacle. His sheets ... but there are limits beyond which even the hardened 'Baroque Realist' falters.

To maintain the stable character of the household Elgin picked his lodgers from among a Johnsonian gathering of riffraff, not yet barred from an Islington hostelry much patronized by antique dealers (or, more accurately, 'runners' to antique dealers): most of whom vanished like quicksilver at close of trade, to Golders Green, Muswell Hill, or Seven Kings; or dived into back rooms to whisper with furtive connections. Some of Elgin's boys threatened to become actors. Some 'restored' prints. Some fronted expense-account restaurants. All were prepared to drink. And most were, with no wild enthusiasm, homosexual in persuasion.

Neb, oddly, had not drifted in by this route. He didn't drink: which made him immediately suspect. 'The creature's a soot-smeared, melon-headed Ulsterman; a horse-fucker,' growled Elgin. 'You'd better lock up the candles.' But, despite the landlord's primitive caveat, Neb had been successfully smuggled in, and established, by a props man from Sadler's Wells; who later survived an attempted self-crucifixion on Hampstead Heath, and dined out on it through half the green rooms in Europe. Neb contrived not to be noticed. He stuck to his attic like a tame crow. He paid his rent, and he went out early. If, by some evil chance, Elgin met him on the stairs, the landlord crossed himself, spat twice on his hands, and prayed he'd be gone in the morning.

Most nights there was a party. Elgin would not allow his tenants to escape so lightly to bed: dues must be paid. 'Did I ever tell you, dear boy, about the time my grandfather, Lord Cloghal, killed a pig with a polo mallet?' Bed was, in truth, all that was left to him. The wives, English and high-born, had cleaned out the rest; abandoning him to the 'crack' and the incendiary levees. These became so common that the fire brigade refused to turn up to bear witness. A blackened residue of 'slipper stew' was what held the pans together. Heavy curtains danced seductively in the candle-light. Orange-crowned fags dropped from tired hands on to pillows of straw.

One of Elgin's fly-by-night guests, a not very resourceful book thief – who simply removed plate-books from the London Library, gutted, and sold them; watermarks, stamps, and library labels – was in a flat

panic to obtain a tube of sufficiently unctuous ointment. Elgin Mac-
Diarmuid, being asked for 'jelly', pictured calves' feet, nursery tea,
nanny's starched apron; and he fell, with an almost audible crash, into a
brown study. 'Gone for ever, dear boy. All gone.'

The pederast, who went under the name of David DeLeon, was bent
double, scarcely able to walk, quite ruptured with urgency: suppressing
a pitiful sob, he begged from door to door. His catamite lay waiting,
with few visible signs of impatience; picking his pimples and squirting
the result over a yellowback Sapper novel, that a previous tenant had
tried forlornly to collect.

The heat was on. The thief knew the net was closing around him.
Even the dim and gentlemanly bookmen like to see the odd knuckle
cracked, to witness the uppity bender take a public caning. DeLeon's
shirt melted; he smelt of cages. The hideous sounds of Elgin's subterranean melancholy – clinking bottles, bog songs, tears – only reinforced
his sense of inevitable confinement. Tonight might be his last chance to
feast with panthers.

The thief pounded at Neb's door: without success. He had reduced
the grandeur of his demands from vaseline to baby lotion; or butter,
polyunsaturated margarine, linseed oil, mayonnaise, louse shampoo.
Anything. This wasn't the moment to count calories. His mouth was far
too dry simply to spit on the snake, and hope for the best. He knew Neb
was in there. He could hear the inherited dog scratching at the far side of
the bolted door. He snapped: converting the imps of lust to demons of
wrath. He snatched up a hammer, and a mouthful of nails from the
frame-maker's cupboard, and proceeded, with yelps of rage, to seal Neb
into his mansard garret.

Neb, at the first blow, transformed himself into an item of furniture;
mute, uncomplaining, clasping his scrapbook to his heart. DeLeon
completed his task with the aid of a few loose floorboards. And went
below to find a bottle.

Not for nothing had Neb studied the ways of the East. He could feed,
for months, on his own karma. He withdrew: he retreated into a
floating world of headlines; narrative collages that opened so many
possible avenues. He would begin at once on an obituary notice.

GAY ARISTO AND RENT BOY IN THIEVES' KITCHEN SHOCK. IRISH ANGLE
SUSPECTED. *A delegation of notables, including the Standing Member, Meic
Triscombe, and several faces from the cast of 'EastEnders', today broke into the
attic room of a house in Well Street, claimed by its owner, Elgrun MacDonald
(68), to be of 'immense historical importance'. The delegation had intended
making an award to a long-serving social worker, Nebuchadnezzar Spurgeon,
whose selfless activities on behalf of the Grove Road Lazaret (plc) have won*

him universal acclaim. However, when the doors were broken down by sanitary operatives, it was revealed that the 'artist's garret' was uninhabited. Obscure books on the occult by Colin Wilson, W. H. Hodgson and others were removed for forensic examination. A pile of brown dust was said by one of the actors to be 'in the shape of a dog'. 'This mystery will rival the Marie Celeste,' claimed a Townhall Spokesperson. 'It is straight out of Edger Allen Poe [sic].'

Elgin MacDiarmuid, soul-crushed, sunk into a shameless candle-cupping pose: his skull was a parchment membrane. Nightmare shadows stretched and yawned against the walls. A capuchin monkey plucked at his sleeve. Beast faces winked in the panels of the windows. The slop bucket of his fears had been spilled, and the swamp dwellers were loose. There was now no barrier between past and future, between naked panic and its uglier manifestations. He saw DeLeon as he really was. And he called for a shotgun. DeLeon belonged in the trophy room.

A fabulous smell, the spittling sweetness of roasting pork, filled the basement; drool seeped from Elgin's snoring mouth: it stung the absurd, pre-pubertal pliancy of his skin. His skin was his memory: the retarded child held within this abused and rotting carcase. Elgin screamed aloud, woken by pain; and dropped the candle which was gently cooking his venus mounds. Hungry flames licked across his bare mattress, leaping deliriously from pools of congealed chicken fat to liquid rivulets of chip grease. Sportingly, the fire outlined Elgin's shape in the bed: the man's animal traces burnt like a sacrifice. The bog landlord looked down at where he should have been lying. It was a small conflagration: nothing in that. The walls were already black as a holocaust; and several windows were missing, where agitated lovers had done a header into the streets.

Roars of torment from the bull-baited MacDiarmuid roused the pack of lodgers and associates, who tumbled into the night in various stages of undress, inebriation, and sexual attainment. Sheets of flame escaped gratefully into the clean air. The draggletails, their lice and their parasites, sprawled in the gutter on the far side of the street, to watch the show. There had been nothing like it since the Smithfield barbecues.

From the dark safety of the coppice, Elgin saw the Big House. The brute laughter of the peasantry. He had been burnt out, driven from his inheritance: four hundred years of culture trampled in the mud. 'Save the Rowlandsons,' he howled. 'Who will carry out Hogarth's "Roast Beef of Old England!"? A gold sovereign for any brave lad who dares the flames.' The fond tricks of the mind, that can promote one of the lesser insurrectionists to a chief among Wicker Men. Elgin the Torch heard the skirl of the pipes on the crown of the hill: the heavy smoke of the hospital incinerator. The road to the isles opened before him.

All that remained of the sorry affair was to witness the figure of Neb, translated from grass gobbler to Blake's *Cain*; his hair on fire, white hands tearing at his scalp. He was trapped in the mansard window, like a negative within a square of film. The heat would print his image into the glass. He lifted the blazing dog above his head, as if the animal were a flaming brand, or the true source of the fire; then he hurled it out in a frosted shatter of moth-sharp fragments. And the beast fell, an incandescent log, through the cold air, down and down, towards the distant street.

VIII

We sat on either side of the Ladies' Gallery in the Princelet Street Synagogue: I took the East, and Fredrik took the West. The keys were in my pocket. We had locked ourselves into the building. The candle holders, hanging in front of us, were eggs of brass, from which writhed serpentine tendrils. They swayed perilously, revolving in a breeze that had no obvious source. They were muted in a thick dust of bone, masonry, cloth, and prayer; and were crowned by strange doubleheaded birds, Hapsburg eagles, whose necks twisted against threat from any quarter of the compass. Lamps had been lit on the floor beneath us: necessary oils sputtered. The chamber was dim and anxious. This first stage involved an attempt to stop-down the rush of time, to chill this event, to allow the setting to absorb, and swallow, our invading presences.

Roland concentrated solely on the management of his own performance; following closely the guidelines he recovered from Edith's frantic and inelegant script. The hints Roland dropped suggested that Edith had not written anything in the form of a play. There were, for example, no speeches or stage instructions. No, what she had done was to ensure that anyone who read her notes with attention would be led to 're-enact' the sequential prophetic curve that any play has to be. The script was a series of physical proposals for a séance that would deliver the event Edith was imagining. Wisely, Roland allowed the ritual site to look after itself. His only 'theatrical' contribution was to drape the expressionist backcloth from his Oscar Wilde drawing room over the raised *bimah*; making a tent from which we assumed he would, in his own time, emerge.

I don't know how long we waited. Light died in the sloped glass roof over our heads: it grew strong again, illuminating the cracks, the broken webs of long neglect. I'm sure that neither of us slept, or lost consciousness for more than a few seconds. Very slowly, the shaking and the rolling of past worshippers faded: the silver bells, the pomegranates; the stiffened yolks of eggs, unpeeled from dead faces; the steam from the bath house melted away. And we heard the low whining of a solitary dog. It seemed to come, not from the floor of the synagogue, but from beneath it: a melancholy and inhuman *kaddish* of loss. The hair rose on our necks. We heard the claws of the dog scratching on tile: turning, circling; faster, faster, from end to end of the cellar that enclosed him. Our sense of the animal developed: a lion-headed, tail-thrashing, back-arched revenger, bumping against the floor that could no longer contain it. The beast was growing. It would burst through the feeble bricks.

Our veins closed, stopping the surge of blood to spasms of pain. The room was filled with suspended heat. We flinched from the rails on which we were leaning. We dug our nails into the palms of our hands.

Now there was a cooler sound, metallic; a length of chain dropping into a dry well. A small gridiron in the floor of the main chamber was lifting itself, falling back into place; lifting again. A stutter of untraceable images flooded in behind the sound. A cloaked sleeper, living or dead. A peasant-priest stalking the circumference, barefoot; drawing his own breath from a glass-flute, in which locusts are imprisoned. Horizontal confessions. Crimes of passion. The supplicant lies, face down, upon the synagogue floor, and whispers his (her) guilt through the grille to an unseen confessor; or into a pool of accumulated evil. The priest is standing on a chair in the inundated cellar, neck twisted, lifting his mouth to catch her (his) spit. The penance involves cleaning with the tongue these loops of cold iron. And it is shared between priest and victim.

With a wild rush of yellow, of thorn and sand, the lion-thing was at the door: it thundered, its breath was rage. We did not want to see it, but we could not move.

Roland Bowman was naked, red, on all fours; crawling like some obsolete chess piece, across the worn boards towards a restored pool of decorated tiles. His movements were precise, but they did not appear to be premeditated. He *was* the inherited dog, burnt of its fur; birth-shivering, as it aligned itself to enter once more the geography of its ordained narrative. Scalded, raw, vulnerable; Roland pushed himself pitifully along the floor, until we felt the waves of displaced pain enter our own knees and wrists. His muscular control was astonishing.

I gave no credence to what I was seeing. I was the right eye, Fredrik was the left eye: we had both to concentrate to bring this vision into focus. I could not judge its distance from my own amorphous fears and desires. I could not guess what part of this scene Fredrik was censoring with his intelligence. But what I saw shocked me. The dog's swollen pizzle, emerging like a piston of peeled, pink flesh from its holster of fur. Nothing of Roland was left. He was overwhelmed by this assertion of the animal's unthinking maleness. I did not believe Roland would ever break free from the creature whose spirit he had so convincingly summoned.

The dog salt-licked the blue pigment from the dutch tiles. He put his shoulder, in turn, to each of the six pillars. He acknowledged the *amud*, and bent his head before the Ark. Now the vigour drained from him. He was beaten. He dragged on broken legs. His spine was twisted, his head lolled. The crushed beast slunk from our sight under the painted cloth of the tent – and re-emerged, on the instant, by some conjuring effect; erect, strutting, arms thrown wide, parading the cloak of maps. The dog was Edith Cadiz. Or a switch had been made. Roland had volunteered to vanish in her place from this story. He was robed once more in the cardboard streets that surrounded his house. He was dressed in the tale he had told us at his kitchen table, the woman's life.

Roland's body – hairless, pale, disciplined – had the miraculous capability of allowing any other life to be 'projected' over his own. He was neutral; the dream actor. A man, a woman, an animal: he could be a cardinal or a horse, a prostitute or a surgeon. The watchers would witness whatever transformations they dared to conceive.

For this role Roland's make-up was predatory and exulting. He laughed, and he licked his white teeth. He ran a finger teasingly over his lips. He shook out the red-gold hair that flowed down his back. Edith was producing a wicked pastiche of the Roland who laid claim to her identity, by making himself the sole curator of her legend. There is no salvation in dumb reverence. Loving admiration metamorphoses to soul-theft. The glamour of the risks that Edith provoked had been peeled like a mask from the bone of Roland's skull. Neither party could break from this terrible contract: the telling and the showing, the being and the dying. The mirror had frozen hard about them.

There was only the sound of bare feet sliding on the boards. Roland spun to face the Four Quarters of the World: he stretched out his arms. He was passing down a track already flattened in the wet grass, under the arch, and out of Meath Gardens: rain in his face, he brushed against the drooping purple heads of buddleia. Eyes shut, following the wind; he crossed Roman Road towards the corroded green effigy of a blind man tethered to a stone dog. He could go no further. He was enclosed by a crescent of water; which he drew, at once, into the unsuspecting air. Faith kept the shining column in balance on his hand, a liquid wand.

Fredrik, coughing fiercely, stood up, a handkerchief clutched to his lips: he loomed alarmingly over the balcony rail. Shadows from the swinging lamp aged him; grew a dark judicial beard. He challenged the woman who stood beneath us on the floor of the synagogue. He spoke, but the voice was not his own: it was chalky and base. He rose to defuse the gathering tension of the moment: only to discover that he was now the dominant part of the act. He was implicated: the necessary articulator of a written voice.

'Who is he who gives you this authority?' Fredrik choked out the words he was hearing for the first time. His fingers closed on his throat, so that he could feel them, and assess their truth.

Edith countered his assault with movement, the steps of a dance: she glissaded, turned, showed her back. She ripped the sleeve from her cloak, and let it float into the unlit margin of the stage.

'What business do you have with Hebrew ceremonies, the taint of idolatry, and the like?' Fredrik continued his cabalistic interrogation.

With a sound like dry flame rushing over a tinder-trail, Edith split open her costume of maps: it hung loose from her shoulders, drowned wings. A sudden leap obscured her: she was hidden behind one of the red pillars.

'By the power of the four princes I require your submission.' Fredrik slumped back into his seat. He was stripped of his borrowed dignity. He did not speak again.

But Edith Cadiz was instructed by her angel and would suffer no governance. Roland, naked once more, had the body of a woman.

IX

We returned to the house in Fournier Street: it was a clean, fresh morning. Vagrants were already standing around their perpetual oil-drum fires. Nobody ever saw one of these fires being started. Forklifts were shuttling the vegetable market; odd, single trays of exotic fruits were carried to taxis. It was still quiet enough to enjoy the agitated cicada-hum of the sewing machines. We waited for Roland in his mother's sitting room. But there was no clear space into which our turbulent imaginings could skulk, searching for respite. The room was crowded with so many gathered mosaic-fragments of the old woman's previous lives. It was one floor higher, but the same shape as Roland's Wildean chamber: it seemed smaller, packed as it was with occasional tables, mementoes, knick-knacks, votive offerings.

While Fredrik gossiped happily with Mrs Bowman about Canada – where he had spent a few fugitive years finding out that he was not an academic, and that Black Mountain poets, individually or *en masse*, would never produce anything but aggravation – I picked up the photograph of Edith Cadiz which I had excitedly rediscovered among the ranked portraits of husbands, ballet masters, loved enemies, and lost friends. I suppose I was expecting, or projecting, the ultimate Dorian Gray transformation: that the silver print would now represent Roland Bowman in Edith's skin. Our night in the synagogue *had* to clarify the insane ambiguities that infected this house (and all its visitors). I was, by temperament, much happier analysing glass slides with finite examples of captured time, than scrambling across the living face of Whitechapel. The story, in all decency, should end here. I revolved the frame in my hands. I tried every angle. There was no change. That elegiac aggression was as strong as it had ever been: the pearly smoothness of light on her body. The gesture of the arms that refused a definitive interpretation. It was undoubtedly the same woman.

Mrs Bowman, bird-eyed, caught me at my investigations. 'Quite pretty, isn't it?' she said. 'I'm very fond of that frame: cost me thirty-five pounds in Bermondsey. I couldn't get Alfie to shift on the price. Girl's quite attractive too. Absolutely the right period. That's why I've never bothered to change her. I felt she went so well with the frame. And, when you've only a son left, well, you do tend to collect another little family to keep you company.' She laughed. 'I think of them as quite real. I make up all sorts of stories about them. But only for friends, of course. Yes, I do find myself wondering, from time to time, who she was; and if her life was anything like the one I have saddled her with.'

I could only stare at her, with ill-mannered bluntness, and will some saving breath of 'Bates Motel' transvestite shape-shifting slaughter. Roland would surely emerge from behind the wig, a carving knife in his upraised arm. But, no, sadly; this was a small, voluble, and wholly convincing woman. Then I heard a key turn in the lock of the street door, and light fast footsteps, that could only be Roland's, raced towards us, up the long flights of stairs.

5

The Solemn Mystery
of the Disappearing Room

The Solemn Mystery
of the Disappearing Room

'Then to the tower to watch'

William Hope Hodgson,
The House on the Borderland

Arthur, who was also, obscurely, known as 'Monty' or 'The Boy',
opened his sticky seropic eyes in a room that had bent around him in the
night; that had contracted to a necklace of tyres. He could not draw
breath in it. There were no corners to the walls. He was alone, abandoned, far from ground, amputated from memory: a trustee with a
black ribbon sewn to his sleeve. He no longer had to suffer the linoleum
wards, or the dormitories with their milky puddles of disinfectant, their
anguish, sprayed threats and sudden, random blows. He did not need to
twist on his mattress at the mercy of some communal nightmare; or to
wake, on this fine morning, to the bite of another man's parasites,
inherited from a foam pillow, still saturated with unshriven dreams.

But at this altitude there was no purchase; Arthur's mind slipped,
forcing him to bury his face in a pink and threadbare cricket cap. All
night he had been remembering his teeth, seeing himself wrap them in
soft purloined lavatory paper: then the discovery of his secret hiding
place by some dark and stalking double. Shame. Anger. His breakfast
extended over the entire day, as he sucked his string of rind towards a
slow and salty dissolution. No, he had been too cunning for that. They
were gone. His teeth were the past, a squandered inheritance, wilfully
forfeited.

Once the twin towers of the Monster Doss House had been decorated
with flags: the pride of the fleet, a red-brick leviathan, studded with
portholes. An Imperial fantasy: Wembley Stadium set in a grassless
desert. It had been photographed, part of the social record, for the first,
October 1903, edition of Jack London's *The People of the Abyss* – where
it can still be found, sheltering between page 240 and page 241. In its

pomp the Doss House had shaken to the snores of a thousand men, snorting and gobbing the choked filth of their lungs. But now the half-dozen tolerated vagrants were forced to hide themselves – even from each other – somewhere in its telary vastness; camped in locked corridors, they fought for the remaining blankets with patients too bizarrely infected to be accepted, even as charity-appeal posters, by the London Hospital. They were not 'star material', and would never get a call from Mel Brooks, or be played on Broadway by David Bowie. They died, slowly, in unrecorded cupboards.

Sticking to the damp walls of this pest seminary were plagues without names, that would test the recall of even the most diligent antiquarians of medical science: fibrillations, lesions, scabs, lymphs, bubonoceles, swellings, welts, knots, discharges and seizures unidentified even in the holograph manuscripts of medieval Spanish apothecaries. This sad rump of nostalgic vagrancy, these stinking heritage ghosts, clung to life only to bleed the fundraisers; scratching their way into the casting directories of documentary film-makers, or whining their mendacious auto-biographies from doorstep to doorstep through Bloomsbury. They were the 'house guests' of the developers until the Monster Doss House could make its appearance in the brochures as 'an historical site', and City-based newcomers could get their rocks off recolonizing a genuine Poor Law survival ward. They could make pets of the cockroaches. This fired-clay alp was built to last for ever by planners in the grip of dynastic certainties. Features of the original plumbing would be in-corporated with no surcharge. Speculators, on the instant, were sweat-ing to buy a piece of it. They were dumping wine bars in the Old Kent Road, like so many cat sacks, just to stay liquid. But – until the first ruched sorbet curtains dressed the portholes – the dead men had a role to play as walk-on 'local colour'.

The porthole, looking out to the west, was no longer a temptation for Arthur. His turret room, a literal crow's nest, had once been a privilege the inmates had fought to achieve: wrestling through gutters, ambu-scading the key holder with sand-filled stockings, biting and clawing to be first man at the evening window. They had to hobble Scotch Dave with a paraquat and British Sherry cocktail, when he took to protecting his claim by sleeping all afternoon on the Doss House steps. Joey the Jumper actually dug himself into the refuse bin of the London Hospital's surgical ward, so that he could maintain a death-watch on the padlocked door. He was submerged, head on knees, in a canister of mustard slime, pus, and gungy dressings – but he couldn't control the compulsive drumming of his heels, or gag his endlessly rotated mantra of early Christian martyrs. 'Stephen, James the Apostle, James the Righteous,

Paul and Peter, Symeon, Ignatius, Rufus and Zosimus, Telesphorus, Germanicus, Polycarp.' One of the warty roundhead orange-boys put a lucifer to a trailing tongue of bandage that spilled from the bin's lid, and Joey was deep-fried in his own fat.

The mysterious attraction of the west window was no difficult matter to explain: the unashamed voyeurism of the incarcerated onanist. Monkeys in zoos, or lifers in strip-cell confinement, obey the same imperatives – without any visual stimulation. Before the ochre-brick 'Espresso Mosque' had been grafted on to Whitechapel Road it had been possible for these one-handed visionaries to stand unbuttoned at the grimy porthole, and to sweat cobs with the effort of focusing red eyes on the overnight lorry park beneath them. They stood through all the tedious hours of darkness, hammering against the sill, bruising strained flesh in an orgy of untargeted self-mutilation. They hung as if 'on the rope', suspended over the pulsing violet ghetto. They learnt to 'see' with their ears, to follow the subtlest shifts and arrangements of human commerce: tree-breath, water whispering under the paving stones. Their fathers rebuked them from the throats of birds.

Then, as dawn broke, blooding the slate and the wet tarmac, they caught the first tremble in the curtained cabs of the long-distance hauliers. They saw the gay girls stretch out their legs, skirts riding high, risking the drop back on to firm ground. The girls were inevitably overweight, with make-up spattered like an autistic action painting; or scrawny, nerve-ticked, scratched, pimpled, and frantic to score – wriggling in satin, torn fish-net, split and smeared saddle-leather. But the vagrants were not disillusioned. These were their saints. The distant mechanisms of exchange became a portfolio of detached details: knees metamorphosed to skulls, tangled in rat fingers; black gearshifts; elbow joints; neck hair; segments of wheel fur. Laughter died in blows; threats, whispers. Lights flared along the windscreens in promiscuous delight. Cigarettes burnt cruelly through the hooded darkness. Thumbs agitated belt buckles. Hands swallowed stiff banknotes. The watchers were implicated, mumbling, taking sides; making their selection from a repertoire of pain and pleasure; wanking themselves into vacancy, letting their brains run from their sudorific noses in streams of unwiped silver.

But that view was gone for ever. *The Garden of Earthly Delights* was strictly off limits. The *muezzin* who wailed his exotic arias over the pantiled roofs, the sprouting chimneys, and the glistening gutters, had captured the townscape. It was his: to curse, to anathematize, to hurl fire and brimstone on to the sublimely indifferent heads of sinners, as they gurgled like hogs, shoving their lips into the triangular wounds on cans of export lager. The gun turret of this Disneyland mosque, behind its bullet-proof glass, was empty. The summons, bringing the devout traders to their knees, was pre-recorded. Mercifully, the holy man was spared even a glimpse of these unamputated follies.

No need for Arthur to waste precious minutes on his toilet. He rolled from his mattress, fully dressed, in waistcoat, collar and cuffs, fingerless gloves: he reached for the once-white dustercoat that served as a blanket. He was lost without it; a disbarred hairdresser. The coat was his comforter, and his calendar. One pocket, when he inherited the garment, contained six limestone pebbles. Therefore, Arthur lived by a six-day week: the day of rest was an option he rarely needed to invoke. His existence was perfectly adjustable to the symmetrical paradigm of cricket. His philosophy discovered, in the end-to-end, turn-and-turn-about duality of the game, a Manichaean implication. The strictly regimented numerology satisfied him in a way that was too deep to articulate.

Each morning, buttoned into his overall, Arthur shifted one stone. 'Another night gone,' he would mutter, grimly. But when all the stones were disposed of, safely lodged in the originally barren pocket, it was necessary to begin the cycle again; using the untainted hand to trundle the heated pebbles back, one by one, to their starting place. Any small calculation (in the way of purchasing bread or a newspaper) that might require the aid of the stones had to be entered into only as a last resort: or the crucial mensuration of passing time was thrown into chaos. Midweek saw Arthur at his most balanced. By the end, he sagged; weighed down by the bias of a full pouch. A severe strain was placed on an area already disputed between ilium, ischium, and pubis. He walked like a man conscious of the fact that his trousers are held up by faith alone. He rattled: enemies were warned, friends scattered.

Nauseous, and light-headed with fasting, Arthur manoeuvred around the sharp spiral of stairs towards the street door. His coat-tails spun out; the pebbles striking the wall a muffled blow at each revolution. Once outside there was no return until dusk fell: the heavy door, operated by a cunningly weighted device, locked behind him.

He did not have far to travel: jobbed on to the Palace of Dossers was a parasitical structure (which may, in fact, have preceded it), the Spear of Destiny; an inn distinguished by several entrances, close passages, and the dubious suggestion that a way might be found into the saloon bar from the cellars of the adjoining pesthouse. Unfortunately this dream, though much discussed, had never been realized. The bones of the searchers lay buried beneath a mass of ugly bricks, licked white by indigenous rodents.

Hands sunk in deep pockets, tolling on his rosary of pebbles, Arthur waited: exiled indefinitely at 'square leg'. Two hours passed before the window above the pub sign opened – and a wicker basket was lowered on a rope. A swift inspection revealed four lonely coins, but no written instruction. No instruction was necessary. No word or glance was ever exchanged between Arthur and the invisible donor.

The Bangladeshi grocer who had inherited, along with the business, the title of 'Mickser' (the *aka* of a shady and excessively mobile Dubliner from the North Side), parked his Rover *Vitesse* on the kerb, set its alarms, and scuttled across Fieldgate Street to unchain his plate-glass door, before it was terminally violated by Arthur's palsied fist. Mickser was genial, even at this ungodly hour, smooth-skinned, balding more gracefully than Frank Sinatra: an incipient pot belly damaged the clean lines of his stylish shirt. The customer who took the till's hymen demanded a certain deference. 'What's wrong with your bed, Arthur? Too much rub-a-dub, mate. No good at your age, you old bastard.' Mickser was enjoying himself so much he didn't bother to 'adjust' the change. Slowly, Arthur filled his basket: eggs you could see through, red-top milk, pilchards, sour cream, *Mail on Sunday*, sliced white loaf. It was calculated to the penny. Arthur pocketed the coins that were returned to him; his most regular income. The hooked rope was waiting, dangling from the pub window; the basket was rapidly pulled from his sight. His brief glory as a discerning consumer was over.

His tribute paid, and his crust earned, Arthur moved south, down Romford Street – a tight chasm between refurbished tenements – shuffling towards the Commercial Road, testing the cracks in the paving stones with an imaginary willow. He kept to his own warren, did not stray from the force-field of the gentle aliens, the brown faces and the unrequired artists: a plantation of sorrows. He had his routes, his benches; but they were fast cutting them down around him, nibbling at the violated brain-stem. The map by which Arthur navigated had been refined to a network of razor strokes on the palm of his hand: scarlet traces scabbing the ingrained dirt. His apparently unmotivated perambulations gave him the leisure to preach a recital of Jesuit sins, to muddy the skirts of the Whore of Rome. He pleaded his innocence to the skies, and caressed the rope burns on his neck: water, he shunned. In the window of a knife shop, he caught his own mocking reflection: how could he remain suspended in time, unaging, and soft as cheese? What was the nature of his crime? He spat a dry pellet of venom at the lying portrait. And cancelled it with a smeared circuit of his arm.

The river, guilty as ever, glimpsed between warehouses, stalled him: his heart went out, he spun on his heel, tramped back, head down, plodding in his extinguished footsteps; demanding sanctuary of *The Spear of Destiny*. He arrived just as the exanimous sun fell behind the Mosque, innocently emphasizing the glory of its bilious brickwork – against which lurched the lengthening shadows of the unquenched vagrants.

The immense hands – flashy with *senile lentigo*, trellised with hard blue veins – that Arthur had last seen gathering up the wicker basket, now lay, without threat, on the polished mahogany surface of the bar. This horizontal mirror of ancient wood played back the transaction as a sepia-tinted reverse-angle shot. A signet ring, the size of a Klondike nugget, stood out from the publican's paw like a supplementary knuckle. Its owner seemed simply to have allowed it to grow, *in situ*: it was worth more than the pub's freehold. The man himself was composed equally of bone and metal. His shoulders were Detroit fenders, and his bullneck would have blunted any chainsaw. He was formidable, long-skulled, spike-haired, with calcitic eyes and brows like cutlass slashes. He commanded the deck of the pub by the slightest twitch of his nostrils. He offered Arthur no greeting. A bottle of barley wine was opened and slid towards him. No payment was exacted, and no glass was produced.

Arthur retreated to his corner in the snug, to watch over the tables and to empty the ashtrays (usually, into his own pockets). If anyone else had been occupying Arthur's favoured chair he would have thought nothing to plonking himself down directly in their lap: the social gaff was never repeated. But 'The Boy' – this decrepit and weather-stained adolescent – was not regarded by his peers as a serious drinking man. Half a dozen barley wines, and any dregs left in the pots, saw him through a single session. The Irish considered him, for all practical purposes, a teetotaller; a snivelling chapel-haunting bogtrotter who wouldn't stand his round; a sheep-tickling gombeen eejit suckled on rainwater dripping from the arse-hairs of a spavined donkey. And that was when they were in a conciliatory mood, badgering Arthur to slip them a bottle of lavatory cleaner to give 'a bit of body' to the Hanger Lane stout.

The Paddies shared the front bar, in an uneasy truce, with a school of choleric and pop-eyed Jocks, who were ready, after a dozen Youngers, cut with blue, to let fly at anything that moved. These amiable exiles were easily recognized by their pinched and blistered lower lips; eaten away by spitting a perpetual stream of *f*-sounds, 'Jimmie', from behind what was left of their upper teeth. Rabid and posthumous men, without social identity, they had followed William Hare, the resurrectionist, on the long road south. '*Hang Burke, banish Hare, / Burn Knox in Surgeon's*

Square.' Hare, having narrowly escaped the gallows – where Burke dangled for almost an hour – was released from gaol on 5 February 1829, and 'put on a train south'. He travelled under the name of 'Mr Black'; to vanish for ever into the streets of Whitechapel. Another blind beggar, another silent volume.

By day, the Micks worked Euston; not having the imagination to travel further afield than the spot where they fell off the Liverpool train. The younger lads walked about with their hands out, waiting for some philanthropist to stick a shovel in them. They mingled awkwardly with the wall-whores; drinking anything that was put in front of them, and stripping to the bone the first man to drop, or take a fit. Only the strongest warriors begged a path back to the safety of the Doss House. The unfortunate, and the sick, received abrupt cosmetic surgery on the end of a broken bottle, or were brutally culled by the refuse departments of the state – tumbling to their deaths from visionary staircases that appeared before them in solitary cells; gibbering-out in controlled pharmaceutical experiments.

But the landlord, Jerzy the Count, could call the whole pack to order by the simple act of heaving himself down the length of the bar, snapping open his personal cigar box, withdrawing a Cuban dynamite-stick, which he rammed between his lips, primed like a blowpipe, to spatter defaulters with high-velocity dumdums. He thumped the lid shut, causing the unboiled teeth, in the confectioner's glass jar on the shelf behind him, to rattle. Jerzy acted as unofficial dentist to the Doss House; knotting a red handkerchief around the fangs of any swollen-cheeked supplicant mad enough to moan over his drink; he swiftly extracted the decayed stump. Then cleaned out the bone fragments with a pair of pliers. Many halfway-healthy canines, incisors, premolars, and molars had also been recklessly sacrificed for the free tot of neat Polish spirits that concluded the operation. The raw shock of the first gulp numbed the tongue, froze the eyeballs in tent-peg horror, and even, momentarily, silenced the Glaswegians. Some of Jerzy's trophies, enamelled veterans, were capped in gold, souvenirs of plumier days; most were yellow pebbles, cabbage-coloured drachma.

All this Hogarthian stuff was beneath the notice of the Count's wife, the Lady Eleanor, who kept to the burgundy-flock cave of the snug, standing guard over her inscribed portraits of Bobby Moore, Archie Moore, Kenny Lynch, Charlie Magri, 'Babs' Windsor, and assorted bracelet-waving gangsters. She perched, a silver-dipped cockatoo, on her high stool; scarlet of claw, dragging deep on menthol-flavoured fags, and tossing back thimbles of obscure but highly-scented liqueurs.

Joblard and his *camarade* were among the familiars of Eleanor's bosky covert. They were, once again, in temporary retreat from the slings and arrows of bailiffs and bankers, estranged families, over-eager disciples and equally impoverished friends. They were potless, and squatting in a borrowed cell among shelves of authenticated nouveaux proles: dope dealers, outworkers, arts administrators and the like. But, while they lived within the shadow of the Doss House, it had not yet become a final reality, a fixed abode. The old vision Joblard suffered – of destitution, memory loss, vagrancy, wine – merely simmered on the back burner: his face returned to him from the scabs and rags of some passing mendicant. They were welcomed to the pub as friends, and courtiers, with no interrogation as to their past or their future. The Spear was gradually revealed, over the months of leisurely intoxication, as an independent principality – with its own laws, health service, banishments and forfeits.

One evening, two of the 'potato-heads' began to fight; ineffectively, a solid table between them – but with sufficient spunk to attract the sporting instincts of the assembled Jocks, who were so bored that they were watching a foam-flecked nutter spit out segments of his own tongue. Luckily for the amateur combatants, Jerzy was not in the bar. Occasionally he would withdraw – fingering a swiss roll of crisp new banknotes – to conduct a 'bit of business' upstairs with dark-suited associates, who arrived in the alleyway, bearing heavy suitcases and well-wrapped packages. And who left, unsteadily, without them. Bursts of strident martial music may have been timed to baffle obscure blood rituals, or overheated currency debates – but they led to rumours, never more, of planned coups: *Knights of the Rosy Cross*, *Timber Wolves*, worshippers at the flame of racial purity.

The Lady Eleanor had been left alone to cope with any dramas, short of a visitation from the angel with the key to the bottomless pit. Unable to lever herself from the adhesive surface of the stool, or to show her face in the retort of the street bar, she essayed a rising sequence of hysterical fit-inducing hisses and whistles. Joblard, ever the gent, was constrained to stagger forward; partly from a nice sense of social obligation, but mostly in quest of serviceable lowlife anecdotes, should it prove necessary – as it so often did – to sing for his supper around the dinner tables of such recently humanized investment opportunities as Finsbury Park or South-west Hackney.

The first Paddy, late of County Offaly – a sullen, custard-pallor student of Aquinas – made skilful use of a well-seasoned crutch; jabbing with dogmatic insistence at his opponent's sauce-stained waistcoat, while mumbling a succession of discredited Latin tags. The cumulative effect of these guerrilla raids was to enrage his elderly adversary to the point of a massive sunrise apoplexy. The man's spectacles – more decorative than functional – sported only to sustain the *gravitas* of a former 'boy curate' at Mooney's House, Pearse Street, shattered when the sharpened crutch-tip caught him a spiteful blow behind the ear; bringing his misshapen blackberry-crusted nose into sudden and violent contact with the formica.

The engrossed but watchful North Britons saw their chance and, punting the crutch under a bench, left the Offaly sciolist grounded and cursing, while they dragged the honourably-discharged potman – whom they correctly assessed as the weaker vessel – out into the yard; where they proceeded to kick what remained of the living daylights out of him.

The potman's fury was unabated; he was unusually blessed in still having a few functional grinders left in his mouth – which he clamped, with commendable pluck, in the green calf of the nearest Scotsman, whose howls brought the children in from the streets, and gathered quite a crowd of disengaged ladies of the night. Murder, cannibalism – or the first dentally-performed amputation – was narrowly avoided by the swift action of Joblard, who summoned the Count. Annoyed at being diverted by this puny affray from the imminent sacrifice of a non-Aryan fowl, Jerzy produced a baroque service revolver from behind the bar, and began to pistol-whip the Caledonian raiding party. They were put to ignominious flight, leapfrogging each other, through the liquid mush of an upturned bin, to reach the safety of the Doss House. It was Culloden Moor revisited.

So this was the curious social sketch with which Joblard lured me into a meet: at the modest cost of a couple of rounds of beer, and a probable tandoori luncheon. There was already a dotted 'tear here' track running down my spine. I was ready to split wide open. I trembled in that state of mingled inspiration and paranoid-dementia, in which the strangest characters I could capture on paper, after many sleepless nights, would interrupt my agonized efforts at composition with a brisk knock on the door. They only wanted to introduce themselves, to put a few simple questions about 'the geometry of time and transformation'. They begged to confess, dragging sacks of documents into the hallway. They recited, with perfect recall, the legends I had not yet nerved myself to complete. Once, as I passed a cinema, on my way home from the bank (in the usual catatonic depression), a man I had only that morning 'killed' in the most hideous way, stepped out and touched me on the shoulder. Would I care to inspect the building's haunted attic?

Unfortunately, there was no way I could resist the pre-fictional content of Joblard's expertly pitched outline. A pub that seemed to have been christened by Rudolf Steiner? A Polish Count, with a potentially renegade past, who never left the safety of his protected enclave? What was the true history of this Billy Bones of Fieldgate Street: the door watcher, hugging his revolver to his chest, and having his food delivered in a basket on the end of a rope? Was it significant that he bore a remarkable resemblance to his fellow countryman, Karol Wojtyla, the Supreme Pontiff? Who was this bruiser in silks, this man of secrets? I could not wait to be initiated into these latest mysteries – even though I knew that my own fears had whistled them from the woodwork, like a bacterial culture from sweating gorgonzola.

II

There are mornings when the iron clouds do not press, when it all lifts, and your stride across the cobblestones is light and turf-sprung. You are accompanied by a sense of wellbeing; the world moves through an ease of recognition, and Fieldgate Street opens into a discreet metaphor of itself. The present stain – bricks, dirty windows, furnaces, generators – is accepted, but does nothing to damage the older sense, still vital; the unassumed joy of entering into the original field. *White Chappell* spreads out before us, muscular and calm, without fences or limits, expanding as far as we let the sight of it run. The great minatory blocks of the Monster Doss House and the London Hospital sink beneath their own folly; are absorbed in dunes of marram grass. That boundary, or edge of what is known, visited only in sleep, and towards the end of the night, is now gently insistent. Beyond the dry river of New Road, ruffled and buffeted by a false wind from vehicles attending only to the irrational need to be elsewhere, is the unachieved and unachievable meadow: the imagined shrine, solace to pilgrim and vagrant. The healing shadow of this resurrected earth mound, a clay Silbury, is set outside the severe concentration of the city.

Looking – a wild hunch – for something worth reading on the subject of runes, I turned to J. H. Prynne's *Pedantic Note in Two Parts*, and found myself, at once, linked, or inspired by this text, to demand that the black sentences be made manifest in these streets: I would see the words take a physical form, painted on floating sheets of glass. '*The runic concentration,*' Prynne writes, '*is in each case the power of longing to include its desired end, to traverse the field without moral debate or transcendent abstraction; joy as the complete ground underfoot.*'

And so it was: the inn sign of The Spear of Destiny was revealed as a barrier, or challenge, dropped across my track; visible to all deranged souls fleeing from their destiny with enough resolution to discover gehenna in this dusty warren: to go no further.

A familiar figure, puffing out his cheeks with the effort, clung precariously to the tilting signboard, while completing the last dramatic flourishes of a bogus calligraphy. What he had conjured, in a hailstorm of *tachist* enamel, was some solvent-abusing Siegfried's vision of a bolt of lightning shattering an anvil of blue ice: more of a lager video than a primal race-memory. The lettering was a chaos of pastiched runes, based on a vague pictorial resemblance between the letters of the alphabet and the rune-marks on a Novelty Shop chart that the artist was consulting with great deliberation, by rubbing his nose against the plastic card. The steroid-pumped 'S' of Spear was represented by the rune of 'wholeness', *sowelu*; and the 'p' by the axelike *purisaz*. The system was a sham, mere decoration, artfully faked so that the letters seemed to have been cut into the wood. The covert occultism of this attempt was dispersed, made futile – and yet the cunning of the artisan, his painful snail-knuckled precision, created a shield of defence that, as it faded and took dirt, would achieve a significance unintended by its perpetrator. This benevolent dwarf honoured Prynne's demand that '*formulae of power*' should be '*compact and anonymous*'.

I held the ladder while Woolf Haince descended. They didn't come more compact, or more anonymous than Woolf. He was a man of infinite, but astigmatic, courtesy. He recognized only those things that he could touch. As we shook hands he stared and sniffed until the connection was made. In another existence, Woolf had painted signboards for the smaller antique shops around Camden Passage; most of them changed hands every quarter, when the rents were 'reviewed' and the Italians and Americans were still staying at home. It was, for a time, a good business to be occupied with: he survived, earning enough change to pose, cash in hand, as a bona fide customer for the bookstalls. That's how I met him, hopping from foot to foot, wiping his nose with his sleeve in an agony of indecision. I supplied him with the reassurance that the mantle of mysteries was intact: he fondled promiscuous paperback fables of Atlantis, Borley Rectory, UFOs, pyramid power, Spring-heeled Jack, talking stones, spontaneous combustions. He nodded over them, a woodpecker with the shakes – twitching, stroking, muttering incantations – before he ended my suspense, dropped a couple of icy coins into my hand, and slid the chosen volume swiftly from sight, into the deep pockets of a Petersburgh Hay Market overcoat. He never needed to extract or consult these books: he absorbed their essence directly into his bloodstream. They kept him warm in winter, padding him – from neck to ankle – in a protective armour of reference. Woolf Haince was a walking library.

Sadly, the sign-painting dwarf, martyred by the exactions of his calling, was now half-blind, capped in a horn of comforting darkness. I led him by the elbow into the depths of the pub. Joblard was waiting, chatting to Eleanor: the introductions were made. Woolf was so diminutive that as we talked, his chin resting on the edge of the table, he turned with anguished deference, a rotating gargoyle, from face to face, in quest of the meaning of these sounds he could not quite bring himself to capture. He weighed each syllable so carefully that he was left far behind in the mad rush of our fragmented and competing narratives.

The matter Joblard wanted to nail was far ahead of him; he could only circumnavigate it, making raids by means of a notebook and a fine black pen. He identified a sequence of abrupt pictographs, cancelled suggestions, hints, flickbook mappings that ran over several nervously turned pages.

'*Seated winged figure with gold hands waits in boredom?*' He searches for the image that might confirm this risky quotation. '*Plaster of Paris map and four white African moths?*' Too late, they have fluttered out from between the imprisoning pages: he has obliterated them with a gesturing paw.

Eleanor, with enormous tact, had turned herself into a stuffed and lacquered bird. Her smile is fixed and the drinks are jerked into her tight mouth, like coins swallowed by a chocolate-coloured toy. Woolf is also adrift. His life was solitary. He had barely acquired the habit of speech. The sound of his own voice terrified him. He sunk into his coat, tugging down a curtain of uncombed hair. He calmed himself by picking a louse from his celluloid collar and snapping it between horny fingernails.

We had been drinking for two or three hours (during which time Woolf toyed with a half-pint of orange cordial; dipping a lurid tongue into his glass and spreading the stain, as he licked compulsively at his blistered lips, into a rictal deformity) when the little man suddenly darted a hand into a bottomless pocket and pulled out something white and tightly folded. He ironed the scrap with the heel of his hand, indicating by the rapid movements of his head that we were free to examine it.

The design meant nothing to me: a narrow rectangle, small circles at the four corners, dotted lines to cut the diagonals. Our benign but uncomprehending stares seemed to excite Woolf, like burning tapers applied to the soles of his feet. He ran a paint-stained finger along the base of the rectangle. 'See?' he choked, 'Fieldgate Doss House, the twin towers.' We nodded, returned empty smiles; waited. He jerked his thumb to the head of the map. 'Princelet.' Then, with greater emphasis, 'Princelet again!' This still provided us with only the loosest sense of a scheme that was evidently of critical importance to the dwarf. Snorting, he leapt to his feet, and – snatching at my sleeve – dragged me out of the twilight bar and on to the street. Joblard, pausing only to throw back his chaser, and to make a snatch at mine, followed us.

Drawing a length of rough twine from around his neck, Woolf fished out an enormous key. He stood before us, posed against the bars of afternoon sunlight, like some blasphemous parody of a boy-bishop by Mantegna: hands outstretched, he inched his way up the steps, leading us into the belly of the Monster Doss House. Woolf, it seems, had claimed – by default – the temporary status of caretaker, and lived in the topmost room of the east tower.

The view to the south, obviously of no interest to Woolf, judging by the state of his windows, was breathtaking: and would be featured in all the developer's brochures. Beyond the litter of roads and railways, the cranes and the scaffolds, we caught a glimpse of the white extravagance of St-George-in-the-East. Closer at hand was a furtive peek into Joblard's flat, where his young friend was evidently enjoying a post-prandial nap: a vision the other denizens of the Doss House would have killed for.

The world at large did not concern Woolf. What interested him stood on the table: an ancient Grundig tape-recorder, a spectral deed box. We waited expectantly, but it was not yet the right moment. Joblard took the only seat in the room and interested himself in rolling a cigarette. Idly, I picked up one of the books I had sold Woolf, long ago, never having got beyond the first page, on which my staggeringly modest price was still inscribed: *Men of Wisdom, Lavishly Illustrated: Master Eckhart and the Rhineland Mystics.* The pictorial wrapper was now grey with a sticky film of dust, but – beneath it – I could just recover the image of a monk and his Bible. I played an old game that never lost its charm, and flipped the book open, to read a couple of lines at random. '*I answer: One work remains to a man truly and properly, that is the annihilation of himself.*'

Woolf's monastic self-neglect spread chokingly through the confines of this cabin. It was as if he excreted dust with every movement; it sweated from him, dandruff and mercury, crumbling over everything. Even the sour corner of an abandoned loaf was grey as pumice stone. The bed was unmade. His books were heaped over the floor, collapsed columns, a millennial ruin; pages were folded back and covers torn. Woolf made his own dim light; he scratched it, in miserly quantities, from an irritated skin – enough to locate the tape spools in their box, or to hack open another tin of mortuary beef. He had accepted a consignment, in lieu of payment, from a Tooley Street dealer who had gone into receivership.

We sat in silence. Woolf's cold-blood calm was beginning to spook me. He seemed to exist on the far shore of some unspeakable trauma, doomed to pick through the rags of a past he had never legitimately inhabited. One of his arms disappeared into the folds of his library coat and emerged with a roll of masking tape that he used in his work. He placed his sketch of the occult rectangle on top of one of the spools of the Grundig, and stuck it down. I knew from our earlier market conversations that Woolf experimented: he was intent upon locating the voices of the dead, using blank tape as a medium: he concentrated on nothing, emptied himself, gave access to the unobliterated residues of past and future events.

Now he moved for the first time towards the window; and I noticed that a light came on in the uncurtained west tower – as if triggered by the removal of Woolf's spectacles. The energy of this remote orange cell was being stolen directly from Woolf. He knew what was revealed; he did not need to see it. A man in a pink cricket cap was staring at us, back across the chilled void. Woolf was satisfied: he felt a primary connection had been established, the second man *could not break away*. He would be eviscerated into our machine, wound out like linen. Gasping for breath, sweating heavily, Woolf pressed down the square grey button. There was a click. And the creaking spools began to revolve.

III

Fredrik Hanbury was on the phone early. A being of marvellous enthusiasm, he drove directly at whatever was out there to be grasped, with all the centrifugal desperation of a man who has somewhere lost time and is determined to recover it – whatever the cost. He had turned up a tale that might prove to be the kernel of our Spitalfields film: the myth of the disappearance of David Rodinsky.

Rodinsky, a Polish Jew from Plotsk or Lublin or wherever, was the caretaker and resident poltergeist of the Princelet Street synagogue: an undistinguished *chevra* without the funds to support a scholar in residence. He perched under the eaves, a night-crow, unremarked and unremarkable – until that day in the early 1960s when he achieved the Great Work, and became invisible.

It is uncertain how many weeks, or years, passed before anyone noticed Rodinsky's absence. He had evaporated, and would survive as municipal pulverulence, his name unspoken, to be resurrected only as 'a feature', an italicized selling point, in the occult fabulation of the zone that the estate agents demanded to justify a vertiginous increase in property values. The legend had escaped and the double doors were padlocked behind it; the windows were sealed in plasterboard versions of themselves. Rodinsky's room was left as he had abandoned it: books on the table, grease-caked pyjamas, cheap calendar with the reproduction of Millet's 'Angelus', fixed for ever at January 1963.

The Newcomers, salivating over an excavated frigacy of chicken, followed by smoked collops and green flummery, had discovered a quaint fairy tale of their own – without blood and entrails, a Vanishing Jew! They fell upon it like a fluted entablature, or a weaver's bobbin. The synagogue, complete with dark secret, passed rapidly into the hands of the Spitalfields Heritage Centre; under whose sponsorship, with the aid of a good torch, it is possible to climb the damaged stairs and – by confronting the room – recover the man. 'He's all about us,' whisper the shrine-hoppers, with a delicious shiver.

Fredrik's forefinger jabbed against my chest in uncontained excitement; an aboriginal pointing stick, a magnetized bone. It was his cudgel and his compass. We charged south along Queensbridge Road, over the humpback bridge and into bounty-hunting territory. Over his shoulder, Fredrik tossed a scarf of wild cultural references. His method was to heap idea on idea, layer after layer, until the edifice either commanded attention or collapsed into rubble. Leaving him, if he was lucky, holding one serviceable catchphrase: 'a post-hoc fable of the immigrant quarter'. The things Fredrik noticed were the things that mattered. He had about a yard's advantage over me in height. He could stare, without stretching, into bedroom windows. Today he was magnificently Cromwellian, fanning his moral fervour under a bouncing helmet of Saxon hair.

'This is Poland,' he shouted, 'old Kraków. The attics, the cobbles; rag-pickers scavenging a living out of nothing. Unbelievable! The landscape of the Blitz. Brandt's photographs. Any day now we'll have acorn coffee and shoes made from tyres.'

We bounded down the Lane – I was jogging steadily to keep up with him – shunned the hot bagels, passed under the railway bridge. I noticed the old woman who always stands smiling against the wall, not begging, nor soliciting charity, but 'available' to collect her tithe from the uneasy consciences of social explorers.

'Chequebook modernism,' Fredrik spat at the Brewery's glasshouse façade. 'By reflecting nothing but its own image, this structure hopes to repel the shadows of past crimes. Listen, I've been reading the journals of the Quaker Brewmasters – fascinating – did you know families actually starved to death on this spot, had their fingers chewed off by their own dogs?'

The turn into Princelet Street, from Brick Lane's fetishist gulch of competing credit-card caves, is stunning. One of those welcome moments of cardiac arrest, when you know that you have been absorbed into the scene you are looking at: for a single heartbeat, time freezes.

We are sucked, by a vortex of expectation, into the synagogue, and up the unlit stairs: we are returning, approaching something that has always been there. The movement is inevitable. But we also sensed immediately that we were trespassing on a space that could soon be neutralized as a 'Museum of Immigration': as if immigration could be anything other than an active response to untenable circumstances – a brave, mad, greedy charge at some vision of the future; a thrusting forward of the unborn into a region they could neither claim nor desire. Immigration is a blowtorch held against an anthill. It can always be sentimentalized, but never re-created. It is as persistent and irreversible as the passage of glaciers and cannot – without diminishing its courage – be codified, and trapped in cases of nostalgia. But we ourselves were ethical Luddites, forcibly entering the reality of David Rodinsky's territorial self: the apparent squalor and the imposed mystery.

There *was* no mystery, except the one we manufactured in our quest for the unknowable: shocking ourselves into a sense of our own human vulnerability. We were a future race of barbarians, too tall for the room in which we were standing. We fell gratefully upon the accumulation of detail: debased agents, resurrectionists with cheap Japanese cameras.

We dug, we competed, we whispered our discoveries. There was the hard evidence of a weighing-machine ticket, wedged into a Hebrew grammar, that presented Rodinsky at twelve stone twelve pounds (what numerological perfection!) on 2 August 1957. We estimated his height by holding up an ugly charity jacket from his wardrobe. We felt a footstep-on-your-grave tremor as we read his handwritten name in an empty spectacle case. We sniffed at the boxed bed in its corner, and the rugs that had coagulated into planks. We fondled pokers, gasmasks, kettles. We scraped at the mould in the saucepans. We would have interrogated the rats in the skirting boards, or depth-profiled the vagrants who had skippered in this deserted set. We knew the names of the films that Rodinsky had attended, and the records he had played. We snorted dust from the heaps of morbid newspapers; sifted foreign wars, forgotten crimes, spasms of violence, royalty, incest, boot polish, dentures and haemorrhoids.

Books were everywhere, covering the tables, spilling out of drawers and boxes: dictionaries, primers, code-breakers, histories, explanations of anti-Semitism. Inversion, agglutination, fusion, analogical extension were Rodinsky's familiars. He took a Letts Schoolgirls' Diary – 'begun Tuesday 20 December 1961' – and converted it into a system of universal time. Julian, Gregorian and cabalistic versions tumbling into the Highway Code, and out again into Aramaic, Hebrew, Latin or Greek. There was a desperation to crack the crust, to get beyond language. '*KÍ-BI-MA ... SPEAK!*'

'It's a lock,' as the TV boys say. The Carnival Season would soon be over, and Sonny Jaques would be shuttling back from the Caribbean, refreshed and ready for another round of discussions, rewrites, revisions, lunching drafts. But we'd deny him even a cheese dip until he agreed to see this room for himself. It is the prize exhibit, a sealed environment; even the light breaks hesitantly through cracks in the boards that cover the windows.

Rodinsky's diary-script reveals one last frenzied charge at the cuneiform tablets, the king-lists. We are shaking out locusts and cinders. The final entry is almost illegible. '*By he she / aren't so not take.*' '*Not take.*' The command is ignored, Fredrik slips into his pocket the scarlet document the curators have ignored. In failing to feature the Letts Diaries, they missed the chance to turn the Princelet Street synagogue into as big a commercial attraction as the Anne Frank House. They removed everything else: the books with colour plates, the ziggurat snapshots, all the significant bric-a-brac. Urchins and sneak-thieves completed the job, cargo-culting the swag to the fences of Cheshire Street and Cutler Street.

Now I began to understand the nature of the trap. I was like the fox who philosophically accepts that he has made a bad decision – only when he has to chew off his own leg to escape. There was nothing astonishing in the disappearance of this man. He could not be more available. It was all still here: the wrappings, the culture, the work he had attempted, his breath on the glass – and even, if we carried it away, his story. We could provide the missing element, fiction, using only the clues that Rodinsky had so blatantly planted. Fredrik's fateful choice in picking up the diary made it certain that the unfinished work of this chamber would be taken to its inevitable, though still unresolved, conclusion.

The man remains, *it is the room itself that vanishes*. You are looking into a facsimile, a cunning fake, as unreal as the mock-up of Thomas Hardy's study in Dorchester Museum. But the fake was crafted by none other than the apparent victim! The room's original has shifted to another place, achieved another level of reality. You would have to share Rodinsky's fate to find it. There is no use in stripping the panels from the walls for your Docklands condo, or reviving the set for a Gothic Tour (designed by Edward Gorey?) taking in New York and Chicago. The heritage is despair and the heritage is the measure by which we fail in visiting this grim module. It can be marketed only as a suicide-kit; a death by aesthetic suffocation, an empathy attack.

The room emerges as a deconsecrated shrine, sucking in the unwary, tying them by their hair to the weighted furniture. No one who crosses the threshold is unmarked. These psychic tourists escape with modest relics, souvenirs that breed and multiply in their pockets like pieces of the true cross. They propagate a dangerous heresy. They are scorched by shadows that do not belong to any three-dimensional object. Rodinsky is assembled, like a golem, in the heat of their attention. He is present in all the curious and seductive fragments left in this cell. And whatever was ferreted away behind all this stimulating rubbish has completely evaporated.

Chastened, I stand with Fredrik in the domestic ruin of the back kitchen, looking north towards the brewery. The true history of Whitechapel is here, unseen, invisible from the public streets. Lost gardens, courtyards whose entrances have been eliminated, shacks buried in vegetation like Mayan temples – so that only a previous intimacy could establish the meaning of these mysterious shapes. The ground is unused and unlisted: it does not age. You could hack a path into the thicket and converse – as a contemporary – with the dead centuries. You could discover the secret of time-travel: nobody ever 'goes back'; rather, you die into what you see, you slow down, choke, peel layers from the bone until you become aware of the stranger crossing the garden towards you, recklessly parting the damp greenery, picking thorns from his wrist – the man who has your face.

At a distance now, in the safety of my study, I write. My pen moves over the paper, as nervously stimulated as an electrocardiogram tracing. The scarlet leatherette diary is open in my left hand. In August Rodinsky interested himself in the laws governing *shechitah* (ritual slaughter); the flawless blade, the uninterrupted stroke. He made notes from the Babylonian Talmud, as codified by Joseph Karo (those fated initials again, denoting aggressive victims and reluctant predators!). I can only repeat, edit, copy – '*Damascus … Ahab the Israelite … I and you gods … so take*' – acknowledge the conflicting impulses, or drift into the diary's flattened pre-Columbian world map, with its anachronistic 'shipping lanes and railways'.

Almost unnoticed, at the side of Rodinsky's room, is a blind passage that leads nowhere, quilted in newspaper bundles, wine bottles, broken slates. A man's naked shoulders rub against the plaster walls, streaking them with blood. His hearing, sensitized by privation, is pitched to the rush of vital fluids within the bricks; to the telltale creak on the remembered stairs; to the public world of the street that is far beyond the reach of his restricting chain.

A news cutting, disturbed by my agitated shuffling of the pages, floats from the diary on to my desk: a codling moth, or flake of ash. I try to avoid it, but it sticks to my hand. A photograph: hollow cheeks, a dead-eyed man with the shadow-moustache of malignant fate. An involuntary traveller covering his face against a photo-degraded blizzard. '*And here is Yasha, seen in this Nazi-released picture after his capture.*' Why had Rodinsky preserved this image from among the mounds of unscissored newspapers? I was glad that I did not have to know.

I reseal the diary into its jiffy bag, wrap it in felt, secure the package with string. I drip hot wax over the knots. I can no longer allow that book to draw breath in my room. But – as the power of its dictation subsides – all the annotated ephemera of the Princelet Street attic also pales, and bleaches from sight. What remains, and will not be displaced, is a solitary brass key, lying on the shelf in Rodinsky's wardrobe. Everything else, I am now certain, is a sorcerer's smokescreen.

IV

The looped tape ran on with its mesmerizing impersonation of silence. We concentrated on the squeaking and grinding of its untended mechanism. Woolf Haince was alert, cradling his toy like a case of pet locusts; ear cupped, he nodded in recognition. 'From the fourth corner, six to ten princes,' he murmured, 'the fire.'

Joblard, at the turret window, could see the dim bulb in Arthur's hutch, a lemurian smear; but 'The Boy' himself had sunk from sight, sparked out, without memory. He lived in the eternal present of the vagrant, submerged, primed to mere survival. Arthur was a drowned man, returned. He had been wiped clean by his hours in the water. He was 'Monty'. His flesh was soft, rotten blue, unmarked by razor: a prebendary pout outlined in shabby down. He was dying slowly into his portrait, exchanging breath with a single captured moment: post-coital sulks daguerreotyped on to florid card. Ruined Arthur was smoking-room bait; a gamy valentine stitched in lemon satin. The lie of his life was lost, inscribed on a sentimental flyleaf, bound in canary vellum, pillaged by bumbailiffs; auctioned, sacked, snatched, scattered. He cannot escape from any of it – rectal damage, *sobranie*, flushed velvet: he remembers nothing. A lurid afternoon, the clouds spinning his sickness; he lurches towards the river. He has been filed and forgotten; wormed, silver-fished, tanned to powder. Arthur in his pomp: long-necked, a curious centre parting; lavender water, spoiled Bloomsbury. Virginia Stephen dressed for some jape in her brother's cricket togs! (And, incidentally, there is an extant snapshot of Vanessa batting, *c.*1892, while sister Virginia cradles the ball, like a harmonica, to her pursed lips. Vanessa's forward 'push' is hampered by a woefully inadequate, cack-handed grip. Her front leg is nowhere. And her eyes are either firmly shut, or grounded in despair. In other words, she looks every inch the missing England opener.) Arthur Singleton is transfixed by a guilt he has done nothing to earn. In justice, he is doubly punished.

As the weakened vagrant went under, let go, the reels speeded: the machine lurched and spat. The tape was flesh. The Grundig was skinning Arthur alive, peeling his memory. The spools travelled so fast, they did not move at all. Escaping sounds were coarsened in a spindle of autopsy bandages. Sound was light. Woolf made frantic motions, as if lathering his hands with soap. His tongue, still glowing like sodium vapour, lizard-flicked for imaginary flies. This passage of the tape was tidal, impregnated, sweeping over obstacles. There was a shower of static: panicked feet running the cobbles.

A moist darkness muffled the world, wrapped the tower in living felt, sooted the floorboards. Woolf waved us back; so that we formed our own rectangle, as we pressed against the walls of the circular chamber: Joblard, myself, Woolf and the Grundig. Suddenly there was no focus for our attention; we made no attempt to listen. The tape took over our critical functions: it drew our breath, massaged our heart-pumps. We were submerged in our own reveries. We had forgotten if Woolf was recording or playing; transmitting, or forcing us to transmit to other, as yet unidentified, attics.

I drifted into a sort of uninspired lethargy: sounds without images, bands of mute colour, violet-grey lesions, persistent green moulds, puddles of crushed chalk. Joblard's roll-up had ignited his mouth: it spread in a lycanthropic grin. I became convinced that his lips were on fire, his cheeks were salt and his eyes had rolled into scorched feather-balls. His whole head was a dog of flame. And now – at this moment – the tape began to release gasps of fear; the asthma of sex-seizures, closed throats, trauma. It grated and rattled. The pain was intense, lungs shredding as they drowned in hot sand. I had to close my eyes and cover them. But it was useless. The tape was 'passing' a worm of clotted black blood. Absurd guitars and hollow Tijuana brass had infiltrated the cupboard walls, the boards clattered and shook with stamping heels. Mad skullhouse laughter, halothane submersion: the words of the chorus stretching into phantom Yiddish. We were helpless, slithering towards extinction; 'wet-brained' like a six-day wine school, retching on our own bad air.

The rim of the porthole-window was a spinning disk of heat, in which it was possible to transcribe the cracks and dirt-veins as runic violations, bad will, attempts to seize the power of an ill-directed sacrifice.

The sound of a loose tape-end, repetitively thwacking against the spool, died: the machinery was running down. Nothing was moving. A faint spiral, or fountain of light, lifted in an uncontrolled vortex. It was more a comical irrelevance than any kind of grail or chalice: a trumpet in a sham séance. The voices of which it was composed competed for the dominant roles in a meaningless operetta. We had begun to 'see' – or perhaps to be seen – but that was not astonishing, and would not open the path to the field we desired, without daring to approach.

In the morning, over a late breakfast in the Market Café, Woolf asked if we had experienced it. 'Yes,' I said, 'the terror of being trapped underground by fire, choking on black smoke. I couldn't breathe.'

'Fire?' replied Joblard. 'You mean drowning, going under. I saw black trails of river-slurry sliding from your nostrils. You were going down for the third time in the corner of that room. Then mud packed close around my skeleton. I couldn't raise my hands from the floor. I was a living fossil; lying beneath the Thames, watching my own past float over my head, exhibitionist and unforgiving.'

Woolf Haince, post-human, nodded; mumbled; picked up and set down his canvas satchel of paints and brushes. He refused to adjudicate between our competing visions. Or to tell us what we 'should' have seen. Nothing surprised him: he lived at such a pitch of nerve that every moment was his first. He was not implicated in his own destiny. He had seen the worst, and passed through it. He was stamped and registered in a book that was marked for the furnace. He made no claim for this place, above any other.

We walked with him, and we walked alone – Woolf had withdrawn into an impenetrable cocoon of melancholy – up Wilkes Street towards the Heritage Centre. A little, pigtailed girl with polished black shoes and tailored overcoat was standing in the doorway of a refurbished Georgian residence, plucking at the handle of her new travelling bag; while her father, impatiently stretching his cuffs, rotated on his heels, staring up and down for the taxi he had ordered. The perfect proportions of his Doric doorcase with the regional rustication, so little used outside

Spitalfields, gave him no comfort. 'Do stop that, darling,' he scolded.
And 'darling', recognizing the danger signal, obeyed. The desired cab
was, in fact, stalled within thirty yards of its goal; the cabbie cursing and
mouthing, leaning on his horn, trapped behind a double-parked van,
into which a sharply cased pair of Bengali disco-dancers were waltzing a
herd of heavy-odour leather coats, for the traildrive 'Up West'. They
could have given the girl a lift to Knightsbridge, and lowered Daddy's
blood pressure which was beginning to pump the mercury, gathering
itself for the big bolt, as he *heard* the crash of markets, screen-glitch, the
runaway numbers, the futures that were all used up.

Cornering into Princelet Street, we paused to admire Woolf's handi-
work, the *trompe-l'oeil* versions he had painted over the plasterboard
windows of the synagogue. But, before we could advance on Brick
Lane, Woolf plucked at my shirt-tail and dragged me into the building.
In the hallway was a table, on which had been spread a rack of sponsored
booklets, produced for the Museum of the Jewish East End: everything
you never realized you needed to know about 'East End Synagogues' or
'Yiddish Theatre'.

'The fourth corner! Six to Ten, Princes,' Woolf insisted, stamping his
plimsolls, 'the address! Here, this street, last century, used to be called
"Princes", not "Princelet". Got changed, didn't it, 1893? Too many,
they said, princes in the East End. January 18, 1887, remember, the
Hebrew Dramatic Club? Lenin spoke there once, they're trying to get
the money.' He held the red guidebook up against his face, pretending
to read, turning the pages, backwards and forwards, until he found the
passage he wanted. Then pointed across the road to the Club's exact
location. He closed the book, recited by rote, at speed; a frantic,
unpunctuated single rush of breath.

'William Cohen, a weaver of Brick Lane, Spitalfields, described what
happened to a reporter from Reynolds Newspaper:

> "The piece played was the 'Spanish Gypsy Girl' and it being a
> favourite in this quarter the club room in Princes Street was
> literally packed ... Everything went smoothly up to the last act,
> and five minutes after that had commenced I heard the sounds of a
> disturbance in the gallery. I thought at first it was only a fight, but
> presently I heard a cry that the gas was escaping, followed by a
> shout of fire. A fearful panic was created: everyone rushed towards
> the doors. Simultaneously someone turned out the gas; the build-
> ing was then enveloped in darkness ... the screams of the women
> and children were deafening and heartrending ... presently some
> candle lights were brought on to the stage, and then I saw a fearful

sight. Round about the doors bodies were piled up to the height of several feet ... the stream coming down from the gallery had met the stream from the body of the hall and every minute some one was falling, only to be trampled upon. Presently a policeman appeared on the scene ..."

'Seventeen people lost their lives in the tragedy. In fact there had been no fire, and the inquest failed to establish whether there had indeed been a gas leak, or whether, as Abraham Smith the manager suggested, the accident might have been deliberately caused by the jealousy of a rival clubowner, Mr Rubinstein of the Russian National Club in Lambeth Street ...'

I walked with Woolf through the body of the synagogue. Potted histories, simplifications, and reproduced photographs were tacked to the walls – maps of the Diaspora – nailing us to a censored version of the past. The names of the dead, and the amounts of their family donations, were painted on panels beneath the Ladies' Gallery.

'Lovely bit of lettering, that,' Woolf offered his approval, turning away from me towards the place where the Ark would have been kept, bending his head. 'The fire was first,' he said, 'before the tape, before I could trap and hold it. Fire against water. It was close behind me, scorching my heels, burning the shadows. Fire is the essence of voices. It is what you cannot reduce to ash. It's all that's left. Last night I saw nothing. I have never seen anything.'

'But there was no fire.' I couldn't resist playing the pedant. 'It was a false alarm. Someone imagined the smell of gas, someone else freaked out and screamed. Claustrophobia, a mass hallucination. Skulduggery by rival anarchists. A premature panic reaction, anticipating the ...'

'No cellar fire,' Woolf grunted, chin on chest, making a confession. '*It was our fire, transmitted*: the fear I can never see. We lifted it last night, gave it entrance. And the skins of those poor people blistered, came away in flaps and patches. The shock singed their coats, blackened their hair. They were like limbs of timber, raked from the ashes. Our self-inflicted terror gained access to that Princes Street Club and caused the first shriek from some exhausted working woman.'

Joblard, who had wandered upstairs for another look at Rodinsky's room, now rejoined us. He wanted to know what it was that Woolf had seen in the night.

Woolf shook his head, shuffled back towards his faked windows. He had seen nothing. Neither had Joblard anything to report from the golem's attic. Bottles of rare dust, books, an unmade bed, the calendar with Millet's 'Angelus'. He was moving across the room to tear off the leaf for January 1963 (which for some reason caused him irrational annoyance), when an unexpected light from across the street caught his eye: flames breaking from the ground, a basement transformed into a clay oven. He smelt gas, a solution of bitter almonds. He had taken up the key from the wardrobe and – pressing it to his forehead – had drunk all the coldness of the metal, calmed himself. His skin was marked, flushed with the jagged, angry imprint. He replaced the key, with enormous care – his hand trembling – so that it lay once more, *precisely*, within its own outline in the dust of the shelf. Nothing in the room had been disturbed by his presence.

V

Still high, and not yet ready to come down, I thought I'd drop in at Fredrik's house on my way home, and feed him a selection of these latest picaresque retrievals; sound him out, see if we could work them into the Spitalfields film – which was, I suspected, a dead duck, well on its way towards the proverbial 'spike'. 'Look here, no problem,' Fredrik reassured. 'We've got a production number, so we're OK. Yes?' I'd read these entrails before. When a property's 'hot', you get a phonecall every day, in the late afternoon, as soon as the producer comes in from lunch. Then it cools to once a fortnight – in the morning: from the production secretary. Then silence. Alarmed for the fate of your loving months of research, you crack, lose your cool, ring in. The office has been given over to a think-tank of graduate juveniles who are working up the fillers for the new culture season. Our bossman, we learn, is taking a well-deserved sabbatical at Oxford, recharging the batteries, browsing in libraries (who knows where that could lead?), locking horns with some radical frontline thinkers, and punishing the claret. He was – so the word went – 'lunched out', and had taken to snapping, 'But where's your justification?' And: 'I'll have to take that one upstairs.' His wife couldn't get a decision out of him on next year's holiday plans, and his boyfriend did not know who was kosher for the dinner-at-home list.

The 'oral history' scam was now, apparently, considered slightly – very very slightly – *passé*, out of kilter, a little bit … earnest. There was no directive, as such, but the whisper from on high indicated that the technique led to whingeing from 'certain quarters', complaints about 'lack of spunk'. The concept was distinctly on the damp side. No; what the revamped programme had to target was the 'One Pair of Eyes', side-of-the-mouth, back-of-the-hand, word-to-the-wise humour (Alan Bennett, right?): a flavour perhaps of gay, but *loyal*, cynicism. 'Go for those nutty characters you write about; off-the-wall eccentrics, head-bangers with *chutzpah*. Leave the think-stuff to the professionals, love. Dig them out and we'll shoot them. That's a promise. You wait, we'll share a table for the BAFTAs yet. Give me that surreal, subhuman cartoon feel you're so good at.'

Fredrik's house lay in a zone of deceptive calm, within the ambiance of the old German Hospital, around which he had, doubtless, already gathered a fine clutch of anecdotes (cross-referenced and inserted on floppy disk). It was tucked away from the traffic on a patch of ground still ripe in the memory of its days as a market garden. Orchards of iron, sour apples of anguish, had buried the scrumping enclosures that made the mean dystopia of city life tolerable – by bordering it with neat fields, streams, farms. Fredrik's bower reminded me: there had once been an outside, a skin, a chimera of *beyond*.

A baby tucked under his arm, one telephone pinioned by a raised shoulder, another in his pocket, cats clawing up his corduroys; Fredrik answered my knock. 'Hey, Iain, very good! Just hang on a moment.' He was tall enough to scoop the drooling infant on to the top of a cupboard, while he juggled phones – 'look, let's have a drink sometime, yes?' – and dictated the getout of a promised review, for a book that was now going into its third paperback reprint. The tiny child sensed its danger, eyes open, smiling in trust; game to relish the experience.

'Listen listen listen,' Fredrik prepared to move into a higher gear, 'this is all very agreeable.' He varied the pitch of his voice so that his monologue became, in turn, an invitation, a whispered confidence, a lecture, a stand-off. 'Look here!' He patted the head of the telephone and shook the baby. Agents were goaded, producers wheedled, editors repulsed, speeches accepted that he would have to prepare in the train to Cambridge: and all the time, with his stockinged foot, he turned the laminated pages of a picture book that a second, larger child was following with some animation, occasionally hammering Fredrik's knee with a wooden brick to show his appreciation. All three male Hanburys emitted regular bronchial barks and coughs: the price of living in a reclaimed swamp.

Unfazed by all this commonplace fury, Fredrik contrived to produce a competent pot of coffee, and I was able to edge sideways into the narrative of my latest Whitechapel adventures. I was beginning to see the 'zone of disappearances' in a new light – as a focusing lens by which everything that was vague, loose, indistinct, was made clear; given an outline and an identity. Whitechapel created beings who were so much a part of where they were that outsiders – murky in motive, and greedy to do good – could not see what was being put in front of them. They wanted something that simply was not there, and – not finding it – insisted that it must have vanished.

From the Irongate Stairs (by the Tower) streams of the dispersed, the scattered and unhoused, processed through the Minories, or Mansell Street, into the indifferent grasp of the labyrinth: within its protection their old markings were erased. 'Disappearance' is what we *wish* on them, so that we can expose what they never were. We can dump our ruin in the space that they vacate.

The 'newcomers' fade into frenzy, and emerge in other disguises. Excesses of poverty and privation, outlandish sacrifices, draw the prying eyes of the 'concerned' world (Baroness Coutts, Mr Dickens, Dr Barnado, James Hinton): pull down a few tenements, start a soup kitchen, grant exilic status to disgraced politicians (a nice reversal, now they flee to Whitechapel to get away from whores!). Rodinsky's room is untouched, immune. It is the *absolute still centre* of the maze; walls of furious wind break around it. It is preserved by the uncaring velocity of the street business that surrounds and disguises it. It is safe because – until now – it is unmentioned.

The man himself was out of history, so calm, so unwilling to announce his presence by any sudden movement, that it was safe to cry: he is gone! We were rushing too fast, too much taken with the 'importance' of the mystery. If we enter, and publicly expose this chamber of silence, shame will surely follow us, tearing everything apart. The walls of the labyrinth will tumble out like a tract of virgin rain forest.

Fredrik was amused by the pretensions of my argument; but well able to trump me. He had received that morning a package sent on by the curator at Princelet Street, documents gathered in response to his Spitalfields essay in *The London Review of Books*.

The first item, given in evidence, was a paper-clipped pair of photographs of Rodinsky's room, taken from almost identical positions: one, just after the vanishing act – and the second, within the last year, to illustrate Fredrik's article. The contrast was astonishing. The abandoned room of the 1960s is neat and sparely furnished: no sign of the books, and romantic clutter. On the wall, where there is now an empty wooden frame, was once a large-scale reproduction of the 'Angelus'. The calendar, repeating the image, hung closer to the bed. The tide of time, with the passing decades, has washed all the gash – the diaries, bottles, pans, suits – back from the void. The uninhabited set has been deluged with artefacts that attempt to reconstruct a deleted personality. What has happened, inexplicably, is that each visitor has been compelled to leave something behind. The room, as we are now presented with it, is entirely staged: it is as unreal as the shadowland Hermann Warm painted for *Das Kabinett des Dr Caligari*.

Next, there was a letter, headed 'A Mystery Solved', photocopied from the *Jewish Chronicle* of 24 June 1988.

> As a boy in the late 1930s David Rodinsky was 'boarded out' with my mother and father, who were Jewish Board of Guardians foster parents.
>
> Many years later, around 1967, I came across him again in the course of my work as a JWB social worker, and by then he was living at the synagogue.
>
> More recently the room was 'discovered' with his books and personal effects left untouched, as though he had just walked out. Rabbi Hugo Gryn asked me if I could shed some light on his background, and I searched for the JWB file which I knew went back to about 1930, but unfortunately it had been destroyed.
>
> Incidentally, he did not disappear; he died of a stroke when he was in his mid-forties.
>
> Michael Jimack,
> Research and Information Officer,
> Federation of Jewish Family Services.

'*Unfortunately it had been destroyed*!' Fredrik snorted, and caressed his wart, 'exactly what they told me about the Princelet Street collection, "lost in transit, can't be located at this time". Do you imagine that Simon Wiesenthal ever "destroyed" a file? It's unheard of, yes? These people will hunt a rogue spoor through the centuries, through any wilderness of shredded documents: there is no place on earth to hide from them. They're still hot on the trail of the descendants of the pogrom-initiators, and the blood-crazed racist fanatics from the time of the crusades.'

Fredrik was so excited that he began to juggle a cat and a child, switching them – to the delight of the infant and the horror of the animal – from hand to hand, in a manic version of 'find-the-lady'. 'No, listen, it won't wash: something is seriously out of synch. The affair takes on the gristle-plasma texture of Kennedy Assassination paranoia: the shift where, suddenly, everything is true. And worse. These genealogical "dicks" are deliberately keeping the lid on, burying Rodinsky as an atypical incident. They've stamped the trunk: "Do Not Open Until the Millennium." They don't want any Second Coming.'

Now, with a flourish, Fredrik passed me the final item, another letter, written by hand, to Michael Jimack, responding to his note in the *Jewish*

Chronicle. These sheets of lined paper remain the only surviving human report on Rodinsky and his family. As I read them I felt the temperature change: the natural and immediate tone of voice dropped me into a tale that Dostoevsky never got around to completing.

4.7.88　　　　　　　　　　　　　　　　Stoke Newington

Dear Mr Jimack

Having read your letter about David Rodinsky, I am prompted to write to you, which is now a matter of history.

I am the last surviving son-in-law of the late Myer Reback, who was shamash of the Princelet Synagogue, & I married his daughter (now deceased) in 1937.

I was no stranger to the Rodinsky family & knew them well. They occupied a two-roomed flat above the living rooms of the late Mr and Mrs Myer Reback, & I made a few visits to them.

There was the mother a widow, & she had two children, a girl named Bessie, who unfortunately was mentally backward, spending most of her life at Clayberry Mental hospital. Her visits were very rare to Princelet Street & there was David, the son, who always looked pasty-faced & the flat was always like a 'hagdesh'. The mother was not over-bright, she was toothless, & always walked about with a blanket over her shoulders. Please forgive me, but I gave her the name of 'Ghandi', & by that name she is still mentioned by the Reback family to this day. Her life was full of worry for the future, & the Reback family helped her in various ways, under her poor circumstances; all in all, the mother & son lived like hermits on the top-floor flat above the synagogue. Now about David: he was not bright in his youth, his complexion was very sallow, something about him in his speech was rather hesitant in conversation. My daughter Lorna (who is 49) knew him quite well & remembers him, as she spent many hours at her grandfather & grandmother's flat when she was quite young.

In 1939, I was called up to serve in the RAMC through the military hospital reserve, & having seen service in the Middle East, India & Burma, I returned to England (a trained nurse) in 1946, & my connection with the synagogue was history. It was in 1948, while working at the German Hospital in Dalston as a male nurse, I attended a bar mitzvah at the Heneage Street Synagogue, & to my surprise I met David, he was there for the Kiddush!

He recognized me immediately, in the few years of my absence he had grown taller, more manly, & very coherent. He still lived at

No 19 Princelet Street, & to my surprise he was quite fluent speaking Arabic. This came about when I told him of the many places I had visited, & could converse to him in Arabic, as I had seen service at the Suez Canal & Cairo. This was my last meeting with him, & this ends my story.

Princelet Street has a history of well-known personages. Next door the synagogue, Miriam Moses' father had his sweatshop for tailors; the story is that he obtained his employees from the immigrants of 1890, by going to the London docks, & getting men who spoke no English & paying them 1 gold sovereign for 6 days' work, the hours were 6 a.m. to 12 p.m. at which time he turned off the gas light! 'Jewey Cook', the boxer, lived in a tenement next door, & he would sit on the doorstep displaying his Lonsdale Belt with pride. His real name was Cohen, his father was a retired Polish tailor, who was well known to the Polish tailors of the West End, where he could be found begging in his old age. 'Jewey Cook's' cousin is married to Vera Lynn, he is a trumpeter & bandleader, original name of Cohen, but has anglicized it. The last I knew of 'Jewey Cook' was 1936, he told me he worked as a labourer in a travelling circus. There is a large house, no doubt having belonged a Huguenot silk weaver, immediately opposite the synagogue. Here lived the Rev. Yellin, the mohel; there may be circumcision certificates still around.

> To close, with best regards, from
> (Mr) Ian Shames

PS Would like to hear from you!

VI

'Died of a stroke.' Stroked to death. A word of such fascinating ambivalence; it is brushed with shock. Apoplexy: out of the blue, a sudden attack, without anger; an interruption in the flow of blood to the brain. And suffered, we have been told, by the masonic Magus, William Gull, *before* the Whitechapel Murders – removing him from guilt? A blessing then; freeing other impulses, opening locked doors. A way out. An excuse.

Arthur Singleton shared a bed one night with a 'wet brain' who told – eyes open and blazing, without thought or hesitation, the same mad loop of rhetoric – how he had gone down into the country, the marshlands, with a troop of gypos. Romany-Jewish, he said, been in Whitechapel since the place was named.

All day the gang directed him, with kicks and blows, to load turnip sacks on to a barge; they kept him chained beneath their lorry at night. But he had never seen things more clearly; leashed like a dog to this tight circumference, free, within the limits of his chain, crawling from behind the wheels to piss himself, or hold his mouth open under the water tap. The cold stars! Pleasure had never been so acute: the sensation that bliss was measured in each slow drip, each pearl that fell – if he could only calm himself to wait – from the cruel metal spout. This hard-won knowledge that moments of release from pain are divided among us, and that we will all achieve our portion, however mean and brief. The edge of things shone and grew bright! He saw the clapboard sheds float, like lions, above the mud. He was not staked – but *freed from movement*, and from choice. The flame of panic was doused. He lay down and, gratefully, pressed his cheek to the ground.

And he wept, Arthur said that he wept; lids rolled back, staring fixedly at the ceiling's flaws – the snorts and coughs of the other men. It was all over now; he had escaped, broken away, run through the sedge and soaking fields, dogs at his heels, curses, shotguns, threats. All finished, done.

Without a pause, tears rolling from his unblinking eyes, he was forced to begin again; always the same tale, how the gypos had untied him from these streets and he had gone down with them, freely, into the marshlands.

6

Eisenbahnangst
(into the Fourth Square)

Eisenbahnangst (*into the Fourth Square*)

'The voices didn't join in, *this* time, as she hadn't spoken, but to her great surprise, they all *thought in chorus* ... Better say nothing at all'

Lewis Carroll, *Through the Looking-glass (And What Alice Found There)*

I had chased the rumours from Highgate to Stratford, from Spitalfields Market to the Minories – but they eluded me, sliding feline around the next corner, spraying the cobblestones. I caught whispers in back-bars, sudden hunched-shoulder silences. Gnomic hints, clues masked in obscenity, had been inscribed, a foot from the pavings, on the locked doors of the Fournier Street mosque: *Spring-Heeled Jack had returned*.

It began soon after they closed the market down and the methsmen infiltrated the catacombs. They had been driven from the ramps in Fieldgate Street, ferreted from their holes in the ground by the restoration of St-George-in-the-East; burnt or flooded from their skippers. The tides of benevolence outpaced them. Undeveloped bombsites were protected by razor-wire, trick paint that took the skin from your hands, chained wolves. The old trenches and bunkers were transformed by spectral floodlights into a pageant of futurist aesthetics: pecked and raked by overhead cameras. The jake-fanciers, blues boys, and cider-heads had gone under: burrowing into the earth, they renounced the light. Even their final sanctuary, the Monster Doss House, was sealed 'for renovation'.

But it wasn't until the third of the Railway Murders – VAMPIRE AND BRIDE-TO-BE IN DOCKLANDS HORROR – that some ambitious nerd on the *East London Advertiser*, scenting a future 'paperback original', invoked Jack; and triggered the inevitable climate of compulsory mass hallucination. Letters poured in from a fools' pilgrimage of state-sponsored zombies, table-tappers, and hoarders of 'Old Boys' Annuals'. Penny Dreadful buffs stumbled gibbering out of Leytonstone with a tale to tell on local radio.

A man had been noticed on the platform at Hackney Wick by an Afro-Caribbean SRN, entrained for North Woolwich, 'visiting the sister'. She was committed to a monologue concerning a recent wedding party, to which she had *not* been invited – when she distinctly saw, as she repeated to the *Advertiser*'s yawning hack, 'a dirty, long-haired fellow, gypsy-looking, nicotine-coloured: like he needed a strong evacuant, man'. He was wearing a kind of fancy-dress voodoo cape, 'Batman thing', and pretending – so she believed – to wait for the Richmond train. She had travelled the borough in the course of her duties, and handled 'all sorts'. This joker was a bad one. She remembers saying to her friend, 'Some people are still, well, I got to say it, not entirely liberated from prejudice'; a movement caught her eye, she glanced out. The gypsy had reappeared on the opposite platform, and was staring straight in at them with his great red eyes, like a big savage dog. It was as if he had *jumped right over their heads*! There was no other way. No time to have gone around the train, or even under it. He couldn't cross the line. But the way he was holding his finger up to his lips, and licking it – uggh, so suggestive! As the train began to move, she opened the window, to take his details: he had vanished. Gave her the shakes, just to talk about it.

There had been another incident – reported in confidence at the muscat-sipping close of a dinner party – where a publisher, returning from a Götterdämmerung of a book-launch, emerged a little tentatively from the underground at Highbury Corner and started to tap his way across the Fields; taking plenty of 'breathers' while he steamed the bark from an avenue of lime trees. He was not surprised, and only slightly annoyed, when a figure he described as 'a Hal Ellson punk, revamped by Clive Barker' took to 'posing' repeatedly in front of him, 'like an escaped Ballantine Books sensationalist wrapper'. The publisher admitted, to his cruelly sniggering audience, that he had probably not even noticed the freak the first two or three times: it was all he could do to prop up the trees as they threatened to fall and crush him. He assumed he was being solicited by one of the more short-sighted of the homeless predators who claimed the Fields for their habitat. And anyway, as he confessed, he was 'weary of tongue, smoked raw, stimulated to the point of spontaneous detonation'; his neck creased into folds from nodding a reluctant agreement to the demands of total strangers, bearing contracts for signature.

But, even to this cerebrum-abusing inkbug, the visionary pest on his path was unavoidable: as he managed to navigate around the subhuman entity, so the creature somehow contrived to 'manifest' itself six or eight yards further towards the east, his shelter and destination. There was a tedious sweat-handed familiarity about all this. We were back in the halcyon days of mirror-trips, bad acid; meals that re-formed from the traces of vomit on your desert boots. The threat of mugging did not disturb the publisher. He would have welcomed it as a pragmatic solution. It would excuse the present condition of his head. He had been polished by the dry cheek-busses of fluttering PR parrakeets, breathed on by garlic-chewing agents, assaulted by demented authors with saga proposals longer than their own doorstopper scripts. He snapped: lowered his naked scalp and charged, blind, at the sneering phantom. *Nothing!* A breeze of soft fire: like singeing the hairs on your hands, when you are too drunk to notice. Gone, *disparu*. A slightly chilled column of air.

The publisher, call him Alex Roe, dined out so often on this fable that he began, in the end, to think of it affectionately as another over-seductive synopsis; a blockbuster, commissioned but never delivered. The one that got away.

The only other report of spring-heeled weirdness that I managed to trace brought me back, once again, to Princelet Street. A persistent film student, going under the name of Davy Locke, had been working on a project suggested by my account – published in the *Guardian* – of the apparent mystery of Rodinsky's room. Using the contacts Davy developed, we were able to spend several days sifting the files, documents, and notebooks discovered among the promiscuous chaos of the Heritage Centre office. As always, we operated against the encroachments of cartels, and deal-makers who were sharp enough to sense that something was about to happen in this place, and to demand a piece of it: any piece. The narrow synagogue hallway filled with multicolour turbans bobbling, like weevils in a pail, as they huddled together to whisper their propositions; before being shunted aside by a buffalo-gang of Hasidic hitmen in black, ankle-length coats and bullet-catching beards. The tumbling shadows, the muffled collisions of these debates fell across the doorway to the office, where Davy Locke had shaken the dust from yet another 'last surviving' Letts Schoolgirls' Diary. It was prefaced by Rodinsky's translations of the most effective curses and warnings he could dredge from all his collected Books of the Dead.

After weeks of deliberation, lengthy discussions in the poolroom of the Seven Stars, Davy decided to risk his four hundred feet of 16mm film over one autumn weekend: go for bust. He invited me to perform a single take in which I would mumble inconclusively: feeling most fervently that the moment when the shutters were removed from the window, to allow this shot, was the moment when the last vestiges of 'mystery' would dissolve. The light held among the chosen objects and specimens would fuse with the world.

We pushed our way through the stacks of newspaper, along Rodinsky's ghost-corridor, and out on to the parapet; to sit and watch the sun move behind the portland dagger of Christ Church, and on to illuminate the Babylonian advance of the City's jagged towers. We were unnecessary. Under the slats of weather-boarded garrets, machinists pedalled furiously; oblivious of the alternative realities that would soon envelop them. The street beneath us was poised, finely balanced, between its own time and our projection of it. It remained uncaptured, immune.

The shoot was over. Boxes of film-making equipment, used by the professionals only for sitting on, were manhandled down the springy and unlit stairs. I touched palms with the cameraman and the two girls, sound and continuity, who waited with the boxes while Davy went to retrieve their van. I was eager to return to my typewriter; and the unresolved peculiarities of Woolf Haince's Grundig.

A few weeks later, when I went to St Martin's to view the rough-cut, I took the opportunity of questioning the members of the crew, separately, about what they claimed had happened after I left them outside the synagogue. This was not easy. Davy couldn't let up: he had become so involved with the nature and quality of Princelet Street that he had been returning obsessively, spending days poring over the diaries. He even read some prophetic significance into the tattered 'Angelus' calendar. He cited Dali's painting of 1933, 'Gala et l'Angélus de Millet précédant l'arrivée imminente des anamorphes coniques'. The calendar was a magician's 'window'; the figures of the man and woman, the rake and the cart were runic letters forging some motive word of power. By his lingering close-ups Davy had incubated the Angelus, and speeded the arrival of the 'anamorphes coniques'. We could expect to encounter, at any moment, a lobster-crowned revenger out of Arcimboldi: the figure lurking at Dali's open door.

Davy witnessed the moment when Rodinsky's books were brought back from the vaults of the Museum of London; fifty uniform cases, prayers, primers, fold-out plates of inscriptions and king-lists. But the event that excited him most occurred when he replaced the shutters on the windows of the attic room. A beam of light shafted from a fault in the boards on to the dusty surface of an open drawer in the bedside cupboard. A white ring, or disk, played speculatively across the enclosed tray: 'a camera obscura'. The drawer became a miniature theatre in which light itself was the prime mover, articulating this drama of reduced and abandoned objects. Davy was still worrying at this epiphany – which, he felt, proved the inadequacy of his attempt to capture the essence of the mystery on film – as he walked away to loop the projector, and to dim the lights. I was able, at last, to probe the witnesses I had come to see.

The little Scots girl said she hadn't really noticed anything. She was so pleased to get away from the awful chill of that room, and the dust – which she was starting to think of as Rodinsky's disintegrated body. He had not vanished: he had come apart, haemorrhaging motes of unspoken language, ancestral slights, persecutions. She felt the crew were trespassing: the relief of being on the pavements overwhelmed her. She screwed up her eyes to cancel that invaded space. She may have dozed off, nodded out on her feet: a strange lethargy came over her. She remembers being in the van driving away; when, suddenly, they all wanted to talk at once.

Her friend, the dark handsome one, was more specific. A man 'appeared' at the far, west end of the street. The sun was setting behind him. It was, she swears, like *Nosferatu* or *Der Golem*: long tumbledown houses tilting, windows on fire, and this guy, 'quite good-looking, in a lizardy way', standing absolutely still, and *casting no shadow*. He definitely hadn't stepped out of a doorway, or up from a basement. She'd been thinking of making a sketch of the view towards Wilkes Street – 'it was amazing, a time shift' – then *there* he was. A red-bronze colour, with shoulder-length hair. He was naked, and prodigious. 'You know, *built*.' The girls giggled. Enormous, 'hung like a stallion'.

'Bollocks!' The cameraman took off his beret. He *knew* the dude had abseiled down from the church tower. And he was wearing some kind of parachute-harness.

Three solid days of walking, circling, doubling back on my tracks, buying drinks for the endemically loquacious – those who have seen almost everything, and remembered nothing – took me no further into the tale. My cash-flow was critical. I was ready to jack it in and hump a few crates of my best stock to John Adrian's shop in Cecil Court (where he is always available for Fagin impersonations), when I noticed the dog. It had been there from the first morning, but it kept its distance. Now it was *ahead* of me; when I grew tired, it waited: shough, water-rug, demi-wolf; a skulking black mat; stump-tailed, dripping, a flat-snout cur. Head tilted grimly forward, it led me through a maze of obscure streets, and windowless warehouses; beyond the Aldgate boundary and deep into the Minories.

As I climbed wearily up the steps towards Fenchurch Street Station, the dog turned – and I recognized it. The beast had somehow earned remission from beneath the hoofs of the Knight's horse: uncelebrated, it guided the trail from Southwark in William Blake's engraving of Chaucer's *Canterbury Pilgrims*. While the other pilgrims look fondly back on the arches and spires of the city, talk among themselves, flirt or boast, the wretched animal stares straight ahead: beyond the illusion of achievement, he plods; collared, unable to deviate from a course for which he has no relish, no hope of salvation. The pilgrimage offers sixty miles of agony, and the constant possibility of being trampled into an undignified pulp.

Things had improved; my guardian, and familiar, had lost his collar – but not the weals that reminded him of its once-irritant presence. The cur waited at the head of the stairs, hieratic, dribbling in the dirt, posed for me to appreciate its startling defect: it had no eyes. I do not mean that it was blind, or that its eyes had been gouged out by handlers preparing it for some specialized dogfight. Coarse hair covered the place where the sockets should have been. The skull was smooth as wood. The animal had never possessed eyes, and did not appear to miss them.

An answer – the wrong one – came to me, in response to Sabella Milditch's oracular riddle. 'What is the opposite of a dog?' 'An Andalusian dog': the 'encounter between two dreams'.

II

The privatization of the railways carried us straight back into all the original excitements – and most of the chaos – that attended the birth of the system. Unchallenged social changes generated their own hubris: anything was possible. Demons slipped the leash. We were lords of creation. We could tear down and reshape cities; send iron ladders steepling out over the unregistered landscape. Holding Companies were cobbled together in wine bars, floated on breakfast telephones, sealed with a snort or a massage: new lines were recklessly launched and abandoned – to fail in Ongar, or out among the mudflats of Sheppey. Viaducts sauntered elegantly across watersport docklands; then waited, in shivering embarrassment, for the ring of Dynasty XXI fortresses they would service to be completed.

When the line was projected from London Bridge to Greenwich in 1834, St Thomas's Hospital was uprooted (leaving the Surgical Tower as an amputated stump), rookeries were flattened, graveyards were excavated to support the piers. 'Deregulated' energies frolic like Vikings, boast and ravish: paperwork is retrospective. A gang of Irish navvies, sixty strong, appear on your doorstep, grinning, with picks and shovels. Your house comes down that morning. The letter from the council remains 'in the post'. The viaduct blitzkriegs the market gardens of Deptford; recouping some of the capital investment by graciously allowing the punters to use the edge of the track as a rusticated esplanade, catching glimpses of the mothering river – beyond the hedgerows and the mounds of rubble.

Nothing is wasted. The nice idea was 'what-if'd' of rehousing the traumatized and homeless tenants in model dwellings constructed in the arches of the viaducts: cave-squatters in Rotherhithe, awaiting a visitation from Ansel Adams. And, meanwhile, engravings were commissioned, replete with idealized gardens – bell jars, bee hives, pedestrians in a narcoleptic trance. A church spire lifts from the domesticated woodlands.

The reality, sadly, was a lesser thing. The constant passage of steam trains overhead fouled the laundry, choked the kitchens, rattled the stone 'sleepers', and brought down plaster from the ceiling. Cracks formed, like emergent river systems; water streamed down the curved walls, stimulating moulds and previously unrecorded mosses. The inhabitants fled; black-faced, white-eyed, trembling. The caverns among the arches were translated overnight into brothels and grog shops: they shuddered to other, self-induced, rhythms. The unbroken revelry was drowned by the clattering of the rails. Street traders, and unlicensed hawkers, weaseled the now unrented spaces. Animals were bartered. A tunnel of covert merchandise burrowed its way through the orchards; giving entrance to rats, phlegm taints, cholera. Amateur sportsmen peppered with buckshot anything that moved among the saplings. Indigenous labour mobs disputed points of etiquette with the Irish navvies, invoking the aid of crowbars and shovels still heavy with graveyard clay.

The advantage of this new wave of millennial railway promoters – visionaries in pin-stripe suits and hard hats – is that they are prepared to take a flier on all the eccentric early-Victorian routes: so wantonly trimmed by pragmatists and penny-pinching mandarins. These muzzled sharks burnt to reactivate such fantasies as the mad curve from Fenchurch Street to Chalk Farm: the scenic route, by way of Bow, Victoria Park (or Hackney Wick), Hackney and Highbury. They didn't care where the trains went; the attraction lay in tying up the station concourse. The slower and more complicated the service, the better for business: a captive scatter of sullen consumers bored into stockpiling reserve sets of dollar-signed boxer shorts, croissants, paperbacks, gasmasks, ties to hang themselves ... the potential yield had them drooling. Soon there were more stations than railways. Shopping malls, from Peterborough to Portsmouth, were designed to look as if you needed an 'away day' ticket to ride the elevators. Combat-fatigued office vets found themselves reserving a seat in some burger bar, and asking to be put off at Colchester. Others set out as usual for the city and were never seen again.

Committed to the black dog's – potentially lethal – offer of Fenchurch Street, I elbowed an opening towards the ticket office, shoving through this demented set of fancy-dress vagrants, muffin men, and wenches whose wobbling chests were displayed on trays decorated by orange-segment chocolates. A pair of security men with commendations from the Scrubs were bouncing a genuine wino, who had wandered in looking for small change, down the length of the pink marble staircase. Everywhere there were posters in celebration of the first 'railway murder', authenticated by H. B. Irving, actor and author. This assassin, Franz Müller, was depicted as a moody passed-over curate, swallowed in a miasma of pew-guilt and self-abuse. '*Ja, ich habe es gethan.*'

A contemporary account revealed that the victim, Thomas Briggs, was discovered on the tracks, 'his feet towards London – his head towards Hackney'. The object of the crime, a gold albert chain, was traded in the Cheapside shop of a jeweller called Death. Müller fled to America, attempting to subsidize his voyage by devouring, as a wager, five pounds of German sausages at a sitting. He failed: his dry mouth refusing the slippery and uncooked cargo.

The effete whiggery of the neo-Palladian concourse was coming in for some foot-first roundhead aggro. A one-man militant tendency I took, at first horrified glance, for some hireling *doppelgänger* of Müller was storming between the colour-co-ordinated barriers; ploughing all before him with a chieftain among bicycles, varnished in radioactive puke. He was wearing a rough-weather set of golfing tweeds, in purple-and-lemon checks that would have brought Jeeves to the edge of apoplexy; and which now succeeded, where all else failed, in driving off the sightless dog. A modest morning's work for my old comrade in adversity, the unchristened Dryfeld.

'I have, sir, no desire to urinate on your property. I want a ticket for my bicycle.' At the sound of his voice: families, climbing out of taxis, climbed straight back in again. The security men developed a pressing interest in railway timetables. Fathers hid their children's faces in unsuitable magazines.

A *posse comitatus* of minor uniformed officials were urgently striving to explain that their award-winning reproduction short-haul carriages – though mounted on metal frames with spring buffers, upholstered, horsehair-cushioned, smooth as a diligence in their flight over the city – had no corridors, no guard's van, no toilet facilities, and no space reserved for bicycles. The journey was too short, too spectacular, to be of value to cyclists – who liked to keep their heads down, while they ground, masochistically, at the pedals. The line did not cater, and did not intend to cater, for that sort of person: the trouser-clipped, yellow-bandaged anarchist.

'Well, it caters for me!' the Magwitch-lookalike growled, immovable. 'And I *never* pee.'

This was true. He would not give the time to it. The daylight hours were for scavenging, not eating or pleasuring, or indulging the whims of a caffeine-twitchy bladder. In decent darkness he gorged himself to the boundaries of immobility on trays of innocent vegetables. He evacuated his bowels, massively, once every full moon; according to the opening hours of remote provincial bookshops, and the dictates of his personal lunar calendar.

The lovingly re-created teak compartments of the Chalk Farm Special, shimmering in maroon and canary yellow, were intended to carry only human ballast. Cyclists cycled: for health, economy, the liberation of womankind, and shapely calf muscles. Dryfeld chose to disagree: firmly. The first railway murder of the new system was imminent.

A compromise was finally arrived at – with the yelped assistance of half a hundred gun-jumping middle-management chickens who were trying to make a run from the city, before they let the advance wave of lager louts out of their software cages. Dryfeld would purchase an entire compartment, six broad seats, and progress in the dignity of a pasha; stabling his wheeled steed and book bags in unaccustomed splendour. I would travel with him, as confidant and betrayer.

I hadn't set eyes on the man for months, not since the advent of his overnight fame. Feeling, correctly, that the old sources, the clandestine bookshops, had been pillaged by book fairies and part-time dabblers, Dryfeld produced a vitriolic booklet listing them all in microscopic *samizdat* typeface: providing the only true and accurate portrait of their virtues (along with a wholly inaccurate stab at their phone numbers and opening hours). It read, to civilians, like some entrancing fiction: the *Pilgrim's Progress* of the Enterprise Culture. The *Guardian* picked up on it at once, rolling out Richard Boston to retrieve the mysterious author from among the stacks. A three-second TV flash of man and bicycle – and the image was buried in the brain-pans of even the most submerged members of the trade. Dryfeld was now so successful that it was a matter of weeks before he found himself in the bankruptcy courts, hammered by lawsuits, lovingly embraced by creditors who had fallen for the optimistic rumours of his death. His inviolate lack of social identity was detonated. He existed: as a National Resource, an eccentric who had gone public. It took an extreme effort of will – and a few hefty bribes – to duck under and out, to reprogramme his ice-worn routes.

Seeing me, he launched unprompted into the monologue he had broken off when I tipped him – chuckling over the strokes he had pulled in Mossy Noonmann's pit – on to Steynford Station one cold December afternoon. I heard his remorseless and inelegant dissertation on male nipple piercing, all the way to the A1's escape ramp, as I gunned the motor in celebration of my release from his overwhelming presence. The odour of electroconvulsed apricots followed me all the way to London.

'Begging!' he announced, spreading his newspapers across three seats, wedging the bicycle between us, and drawing down the tasselled blind to remove such feeble distractions as the external world. 'I've decided to give it a real go.'

The intended purpose of my trip on this (or any) railway was eliminated by Dryfeld's ill-considered action. Before the viaducts were built the middle classes had no opportunity of spying on the lives and habits of the underclass, no chance of peeping into tenement cliffs for jolts of righteous horror. Nor was there any excuse for the card-carrying voyeur to swallow *Rear Window* snatches of brutalist sex in sauce-bottle kitchens: the aphrodisiac scent of burnt onions and damp armpits. The elevated railway provided the first cinema of poverty – open-city realism – as the trains cut through the otherwise impenetrable warrens of metropolitan squalor.

'Begging has got to be the next great adventure for disaffiliated free-range capitalists like us,' Dryfeld continued. 'I had my virgin pop at it last week. Went to my favourite veggy restaurant with a woman I knew would give me trouble. I took no money, said I'd been mugged; didn't tell her it was by the Revenue. The stupid bitch had more sense than I gave her credit for: she walked out before I'd finished my second bowl of soup.' He smiled in remembrance of the incident.

'Never feed them first,' he advised. 'And never feed them after. They eat too much.' He stroked his hairy lapels – and sneaked a crafty glance at his reflection in the darkened window. He had the vanity of a craftsman among embalmers.

The voice roared on. It had outlived its host. Dryfeld was free to admire his tweeds to the point of cerebral orgasm. 'Found myself ejected into Greek Street,' he said, 'while the manager held on to the Katherine Mansfield I'd intended to flog to the lady. I quite fancied her, so I was only going to treble the price I first thought of. I soon discovered the first rule of scrumping for cash: don't mutter something about "20p for a cup of tea" – *demand* a fiver for a taxi. They'll think you're one of them. Money talks to money. These vagrants are all amateurs. They stop as soon as they've got enough for a wet. And – worse – they share it!' He shuddered at the notion. 'I cleared the price of the meal in ten minutes. Had to celebrate. Went back and ate it all again. Begging's a definite winner – as long as you're not a beggar.'

His alarmingly ruddy face glistened in beads of sweated blood; glowed like a respray. He scowled in complete self-absorption from beneath malignant caterpillar eyebrows. The bony ridges of his profile were shifting and sliding to reform, chameleon-like, in a simulacrum of the railway butcher, Franz Müller; whose sepia-tinted mugshot had been thoughtfully placed where the mirror should have been. I responded, tamely, by the defensive magic of fingering my imaginary watch chain, and accepting the damaged etheric identity of Thomas Briggs, the ill-fated Lombard Street clerk.

My bullish companion had once more recognized a shift in the market, in time to work his ticket and move on – before the forty-quid-a-week small-business mob snapped at his heels, blaming their empty begging bowls on a failure to secure the best underground tunnels. By the time they steeled themselves to fork out for his guidebook on 'How and Where to Make Your Poverty Pitch', Dryfeld would be ankle-deep in his latest survival hijack. Keep stomping, stay alive.

He even had word of the 'Outpatients'. First the good news: they stumbled on a Publisher going through a sticky patch who was prepared to unload a few sacks of high-culture rejects for the OPs to flog on the streets at one-third of cover price. Or, if that was too tough to calculate, for anything they could get. The OPs set themselves up with a stall on a windswept patch of river frontage alongside the National Theatre. The initial miscalculation came when they attempted to sell the same titles – wafer-thin playscripts – that the theatre bookstall was unsuccessfully promoting a few yards beyond them. The second mistake was fatal: they acted on the enterprising notion of carrying back all the valuable books to the Publisher's door, and claiming half the cover-price as 'returns'. For a few months all went well, the world they had ripped off was in chaos, shuddering from the threats of corporate raiders: they lived high on the hog, purchasing new saddles for their bicycles, no longer scuffling through the dawn markets; pigging out on a pharmaceutical cornucopia. They floated, glazed and benign, over Camden Town and environs: envied among their scriptless peers.

Then the roof fell in; they were rumbled by accountants, denied, cut off without even a fire-damaged copy of Kenneth Baker's *Little Britain* anthology. Their prelapsarian tip of a stall was glimpsed in the corner of the frame during one of Prince Charles's documentary attempts to

announce Himself as the latest Martian poet. He was drifting downstream, confidently stacking the similes, ready to dive out of the sun and
strafe this architectural abomination (carbuncle/ashtray/training centre
for thought-police), when the transfixed management noticed a troop
of scarf-dangling renegades touting for trade – like refugees from some
unsponsored touring version of the *Marat-Sade*. They screamed for
'Security', and bulldozed what was left into a skip. The contract for
'unofficial remainders' passed on to a discreet and respectable dealer –
Henry Milditch – who marketed his salvaged pulp with such skill that
he was soon able to retire, as something resembling a gentleman, to the
Suffolk littoral. And the Publishers were free to trawl once more for
designer casualties from the rock industry, Irish poets whose rhetorical
flourishes could be tamed to suit the requirements of English examination boards, and 'one-off' vagrants with a story to tell.

Crushed, spurned, spiritually overdrawn, the OPs didn't have the
bottle for another assault on the frontline jumbles; which were now, in
any case, the territory of much friskier locusts. They simply vanished,
gave up the ghost, blankly wandered the precincts, skate tracks, and
concrete walkways. Lepers, bell ringers: they hid themselves behind
sob-story placards. They were culled. One of them was fished from the
river, swollen and unidentified; the others were beyond tracing. Old
enemies might recognize them by an ineradicable vacancy, a born-again
naïveté that was almost criminal.

The train had, randomly, stopped and started a dozen times; obedient
to the stutter of the Docklands Lightrailway force-field. (Lightrailway
or Railway of Light? The only illuminated path over the Plains of
Outer Darkness.) While Dryfeld was preoccupied with the arrangement
of buttons on his waistcoat, I released the blind and leant from the
window to look at the lumpy and shimmering moonscape. We had
halted on an embankment that afforded an unrestricted vision of a
graveyard, or untended corner of parkland. The branches of deformed
trees brushed the damp ground, living ghosts ready to move in greeting
towards the stalled carriages of the dead. (I remembered Joblard's tales of
the white 'mourning' train shuttling the stiffs to Nunhead: white
curtains, white upholstery, white-suited conductors carrying white
toppers. The train must have slid silently through suburban halts, like an
avatar of death itself.)

The railway had casually amputated a dream site (caterpillar dreaming), encroached on gardens I now recognized as the burial place of the
Aboriginal cricketer, King Cole. The dream was maimed, but not
destroyed: disregarded. Inside our padded compartment the restored
gaslight hissed and spat: we were trapped in a blasphemous parody of

the confessional. Dryfeld was a mad, potato-picking axeman, ready to dribble out some tale of mutilation and necrophilia. The great wheels of his bicycle stood between us like a cage, webbing his raw-skinned face in faults and veins. I began to understand something of the terrible conspiracy between victim and murderer.

Through the square of open window, the night – salted with corruptions – pressed on our thoughts, dictating all the lies buried beneath us: forcing *us* to speak. I was overwhelmed by a sense of the Lombard Street clerk's hysterical conformity. His life was as bizarre and desperate as that of the unemployed German gunsmith. His fancy took him inwards, tighter and tighter, *soliciting* the blow that would set him free. The decoration of gold chains was an invitation: he wanted a postal suicide. But Müller's will was weaker: he was seduced by movement, America, diamond hills, rings, hats, walking sticks. He would be kneeling in scarlet restaurants before women, the wives of merchants – who would, without breaking off their brittle playhouse conversations, lift up their heavy skirts to allow him passage. The scent, the slithering silks, the tan of laced hides! They would roll, laughing, on to their strong bellies; while their complacent husbands, licking on sea-green Havanas, initiated him into the cabala of the stock market. Measure wealth in squares on a map of the city. Herds of red beef, defecating, slid towards the primed bolts; drift on an escalator of hooks, like levitating cardinals. Buy them! Buy them all!

The box shrank on us, sweating out the uncensored instincts. It was unreal: the train was somebody else's nightmare. The station announcer did not name the proposed destinations. It was necessary at peak hours to discourage passengers: villages went into limbo, were struck from the charts. But for Thomas Briggs the train is a clock. The structure of his life is regular. He has only his possessions to protect him. He demands, in his terror of loss, the death-blow that Müller is forced to deliver: an act so abrupt and unconsidered as to appear a preliminary to self-murder. The nerves of this mirror-divided couple could not survive the artificial confrontation.

Our train has been released, is moving; jerks, shudders. The rails glisten in the night, a frosty ladder. Dryfeld closes the window.

'An alky before I was sixteen, I was arrested twice on suspicion of being a child molester. Lies! But they believed them. Did time on the liquid cosh for GBH. "Yours or mine?" I shouted. They hacked out a piece of my brain without local anaesthetic. "Make your own, smart ass, out of fear-secretions." I use the truth as a last resort.'

Was that his voice – or something squeezed from the headrest? His lips were trapped in a sullen pout: photographed for the files of Special

Branch. I wanted to drive my face against his fist. To throw open the
door: snap it like the spine of a book. Plunge into the air. How could
Briggs have been discovered so carefully positioned *between the lines* –
like a bog sacrifice, cut from the peat, placed on a hurdle to be carried to
the village? Why didn't he bounce, skid, tear – a parcel of meat – tumble
down the embankment?

I could feel the blood running from my ear. Tongue thickening in my
mouth. Eyes milking to pebbles. Briggs's hand flinched from the first
rung on the ladder of steel. Cinders frayed the lacquer from his scrab-
bling boots. He climbed through the dirt, face down, towards Hackney
and the stars: this wild, inhuman persistence of the victim, the dead man.

No prisoner of the past, Dryfeld noticed nothing. His case-hardened
ego saved us. To him, this day was already scrubbed from the record. He
began to hum, tuning himself to ravish the most recent of Hackney's
'early-retirement-from-secondary-education' bookshops. It was cruel to
watch. They always opened in a frenzy of unjustified optimism: fresh
paint, cut flowers, and lovingly hung prints of 'Defoe's House', or 'The
Country Residence of the Prior St John of Jerusalem in Well-Street'.
Nothing could be less like the classroom: to be surrounded by books,
with no grubby kids allowed over the threshold. First-day visitations
from Dryfeld and Milditch, and a couple of tentative raids by the Stoke
Newington scufflers, stripped the few genuine assets. Then the interminable, dreary years of nerve-strung boredom – with nothing to look
forward to but another collection tin dangled by rampant gangs of
ethnic 'steamers': the revenge of the pupils.

Franz Müller was confessed, hooded, taken out to meet his public. He
had been seduced, as Mr Baron Martin remarked in passing sentence, 'by
the devil in the shape of Mr Briggs's watch and albert chain'. Like
Dryfeld he could not give himself over to 'railway time'. His madness
was firmly anchored in the realities of movement, dealing, seizing,
holding: intelligence without imagination. All transactions with fate
were politely declined.

III

Another victim had been found: in the scrub woods near the Springfield
Park Marina – by a party of nature ramblers. The trademark that
allowed the police to identify the killings as being 'the work of one man'
had not been made public (not yet invented?). The bodies had all been
discovered within half a mile of a railway station. Which didn't mean
much: after the 'privatization' that description covered most of London.

The same could be said of burger bars, mini-cab firms, video-rental libraries, and (at least three) estate agents. But the presumption remained: the killer used the railway as a means of prospecting for victims, then vanished down the line into some rival system. These tributaries were often absorbed, or adapted to another leisure pursuit, before they were even listed. The tabloids were on heat; dusting off the usual rumours of martial-arts loners, civil servants steeped in the black arts, 'butchers, Yids, and foreign skippers'. They purchased dubious polaroids that seemed – from the moral high ground – to rebuke the victims for levity in the face of death. They were unworthy of the circulation-boosting role for which they had been definitively nominated. The dead girls laughed over wine glasses, or wrinkled their noses on sun-blasted poolsides: PARTY GIRL SHOCK. THE PURSER'S STORY. EXCLUSIVE.

The phone rang. Davy Locke wanted to fix a meet in Well Street. He sounded flaky; speaking so slowly and deliberately that I was forced to imagine an attic of eavesdropping spooks: paranoid shadows straining, with uncertain shorthand, to transcribe every last word.

Davy was waiting outside the shell of a fire-gutted house. It was cold, a Siberian wind cutting across the marshes: he stamped, flicking away the liquid pearls that slid from his wide nostrils like lighter fuel. He wore a docker's jacket (the docker didn't need it), and groin-enhancing ballet tights. He had his arm around the inevitable racing cycle; the best tool for a fast getaway. His tight, knotted hair and formidable beak gave him the look of an exile, a Lithuanian, or a tranquillized Marx Brother. He had made the call from the kiosk on the corner. That had taken him most of the morning. (These new vandal-proof headsets have been commandeered throughout the East End by heroin dealers. They supply the perfect excuse for hanging around, doing nothing: and nobody can put his foot against the door to trap you.) The rat-scab character in possession had the phone off the hook, and was saying nothing. He was in no state to punch the buttons. The shivering lookouts were nodding off on their feet. The tom-tom (main man) was a twenty-stone black freezer, festooned in chains like a contraband Christmas tree (nothing works like role-dressing), who sat at the open window of a paint-trashed Cortina blowing empty pink speech bubbles. Nobody cared, or gave them a second glance. We were well off limits. Davy didn't want to talk about it; he wanted to let me see for myself.

The windows of this Grade 2 'listed' husk (illegal post-1709 sash boxes, flush with façade) were boarded over, the door was padlocked: Davy had the key. As we passed into the hallway, he began preparing me for the room we were to visit. The smell was appalling, it met us at the foot of the stairs (painted soft-wood banister, whose knotty and 'anaemic' surface was hidden beneath many layers of cheap gloss): burnt feathers in a flooded executioner's cellar. A friend of Davy's, from the obscure anarcho-libertarian group of which he was the active element, had asked him to open up this attic chamber and make a series of slides to record exactly what he found. He would learn no more of the events that created this abused environment, until the slides were safely handed over.

The room was low and dark, a loft for feral pigeons, high above the dim traces of a street market; odd shops doomed by the changing patterns of traffic. The sort of time-lagged patch in which to consummate minor drug deals or fence stolen radios. Orange peel stuck to the windows of defunct cobblers; magazine racks stank of libidinous tom cats. There was nothing to buy except cigarettes, condensed milk, and ostracized dog food.

Davy pulled the boards from the windows and revealed the paint-covered walls. I had never seen anything quite like it. Or, rather, I *had* seen pale versions, bowdlerized segments: ink-blot tests, Pompeian bath houses, subway graffiti, Mayan codices (treated by William Burroughs). It was startling that an uninhabited room could carry such a cacophany of voices – protests, denunciations – and still stand. Every inch of the surface had been painted over, sprayed, scribbled with messages, invocations, pyramids, ankhs, oozing lingams and lightning strokes of despair. We had forcibly entered a book that now surrounded us. It was diary, shopping list, calculus, and anthology of quotations. '*Love and man's unconquerable mind.*' '*Love is the law, love under will.*' '*The Familiar Spirits are very prompt – it is well to occupy them.*'

Water had been flung on the walls in a crude attempt to eradicate these terrifying assertions – but they had returned, time after time; smeared, but firm in their outlines. '*I ACCUSE ...*'.

There followed the names and telephone numbers (where applicable) of local informers, bent coppers, Fallen Angels, Vessels of Iniquity, Vessels of Wrath, Incubi and Succubi. Footpaths and broken vein-tracks jolted across the mural from childlike hospitals to sparrows crucified upon hills. There were sailing boats and steam trains. The world had been recast, populated with bears, talking fish, horned gods: a true *Mappa Mundi*. Pages from pornographic novels were collaged with the faces of musicians and terrorists. Orton and Halliwell's bedsitter in Noel Road was the *Habitat* version of this. The contents of a mind at the end of its tether had been spilled: a lurid spatter of brain grit.

The floor was clogged with mounds of damp sawdust – as if the furniture had been eaten and, conically, excreted. Bas-relief torcs of blood were splashed over the skirting boards. 'Dogfights,' Davy explained.

The house had been torched so many times that the landlord had given up and gone back to Ireland (where a grant had been found for him to make a start on his memoirs: fictions of the unlitigious dead, Flann O'Brien, Behan, Paddy Kavanagh, Julian Maclaren-Ross, the Two Roberts). Squatters moved in, and the girl followed them. Davy didn't know her name. But she was the tenant whose work he had catalogued. A weekend job for a friend that would last him a lifetime.

There were incidents with the local constabulary. The girl imagined she was being watched: bricks shifted in the wall. Pencil beams winked in the darkness. (Peepholes were cut between railway compartments in the wake of the Thomas Briggs murder. They were known as 'Müller's Lights'. But customers, valuing their privacy, complained loudly: the scheme was abandoned.) She would not remove her clothes. Astral messages were being transmitted into her head from Atlantis; which was, apparently, located beneath Horse Sands, off the Isle of Sheppey. She took down what she heard. Atlantis was a pirate radio station: an offshore fort where they babbled of sacrifices, dream lovers, and the coming birth of the light.

It had all been too much for her boyfriend, who had moved out: gone back north. Left alone, the girl fed the demons with smack. Paid her way with shaming services. She was visited by agents with skins made of glass. Her visionary exultation increased. Once she talked for seven hours at a stretch to a complete stranger, leaning against the exterior wall of the Hackney Hospital. He said nothing. She left him there. It was raining heavily: wet hair masked his face, he was splashed by the traffic. Deep stains blotted through his baggy poplin suit. He rocked his head, helplessly – a blinkered stallion.

She was listed as a suicide. Nobody took much interest. It didn't rate a mention in the *Hackney Gazette*. She had been cremated – bones spun and crushed, mixed with strangers – before her boyfriend heard a whisper. He would not accept the coroner's verdict: wanted images to project and study, commissioned Davy.

'I found out,' Davy said, 'the Hoxton Mob ran dogfights here. That's the blood. They had sacks of sawdust for the pit, boarded the windows; heavy metal on the turntable, and muscle on the door. Plenty of interested punters; both sides of the river, both sides of the law. Anyone with a wad. Bare-knuckle boys. Low boredom threshold. Had to start blinding the animals.'

His informant was a garrulous old lag who had leeched on to Davy's congenital innocence, eager to fill him in on the activities of an *agent provocateur*, operating out of Heroin House. This phthirus on the un-sullied *polis* of Hoxton was denounced, with all the pressurized moral fervour available to a man who had spent most of his adult life commuting, in high-security vans, between Wandsworth and Durham. Hoxton was dead ground: botched social experiments, beyond the wildest fantasies of developers. The perfect territory for breeding pit-bulls and grading hooky electrical goods for Club Row. The shelter of con-men, junkies, sneak thieves: every known degree of villain.

Davy learned they were going a bit green at the Eagle Road nick; recycling all the confiscated drug hauls. They also massaged the arrest statistics by pulling in a few of the slow payers, rapping the odd knuckle, and snipping the tendons of the lippy minority. They doubled the car pound as a freelance export warehouse: villains – who knew how to show their appreciation – picked the cream of the crop (the Mercs and the Jags) for Italy or Nigeria: the old Tilbury run.

Davy traced the curvature of the girl's river with his finger; dodging the demons, snakes, and voodoo masks. The paint was still wet enough to stick to him. He would never sell these walls at Sotheby Parke Benet.

It was probably time to disappear, I told him. The slides had been handed over and he had his money. None of this story, he could be certain, would ever see the light of day – even in the agit-prop columns of *City Limits*. Certain risks were naked masochism. On your bike, son. There is nothing left to exploit.

IV

'Blot out the landscape and destroy the train'

Mary Butts

There was once a woman whose job it was to entrain daily for Greenwich to capture and fetch back the 'right time', so that the watchmakers of Clerkenwell could make a show of precision, repair their damaged stock with transfusions of the real. I like to imagine her gold-cased instrument wrapped securely in folds of green felt (billiard cloth), carried, egglike, in a wicker basket: a Romantic icon. There is an almost disgracefully sexual charge in this solitary figure; long-skirted, widow-veiled, standing unhurried on the rural platform. Beyond her are the fields; woods, masts, the white tower of St Alfege. And the useless masculine impatience of the city; waiting, primed, for her return.

Late-travelling gentlemen, the loungers, obviously speculate upon her identity, and the purpose of her journey. Some of them doubtless involve her in their fantasy lives, make a mistress of her – savagely, or with self-hating tenderness. Poets nibble at her presence. None of them begins to approach the elegance of her secret. It is like an unconfessed pregnancy.

The railways pre-emptively 'privatized' time, put it to work on a grid system; an exploitable resource, they branded it with their own copyright: 'railway time'. Before passengers demanded the printing of timetables, time could be a local affair – whatever the village clock said that it should be. Time died at its own pace, suiting its transit to its location. But now, by decree, anywhere and everywhere had to come over, check in, attach themselves to the machine (heart) locked within the dome on Greenwich Hill. The telephone conspired against them. Each station down the line had to conform with Lewisham, 'clock in'; slaves to this unbending fiction. And, if time spent fishing is not deducted from the allotted span of your life, then time spent on the telephone counts double: beware!

A few remote and bloody-minded hamlets (disciples of Chesterton) refused to play the game and surrender their defective versions: take us as you find us, or leave us alone. They remained out of synch with the system; those five or seven minutes were their own – kidnapped, unaccounted for. Trains smoked out of the city, upholstered in comfortable certainties, removed from the rush of dirt and commerce. The passengers dined, took port, cut their cigars and consulted their pocket watches. But they would never arrive at a destination that was unable to accept their account of the journey. They disappeared into a void – dim light in a tunnel, a suspension, an entropy, where the lost minutes mounted into lost lives. The competing descriptions of time peeled away from each other, until a single carriage could contain travellers from many eras: not quite seeing each other, and always seven minutes away from the world.

The myriad routes and branches that followed on the unrestricted planning permission granted to the railway companies meant that time was also deregulated, released from its bureaucratic prison: now anybody with voting shares could call the shots. We were recklessly plunged into a lake of temporal Esperanto; and with no Stephen Hawking to guide us. We shook loose the spectres trapped in unopened Baedekers. We beat coprophagous adulteries from the smoking rails. Heavy secretions from elbow rests clouded the windows with crows' feet. I came to believe that the railways could be *operated mediumistically to unravel all their own mysteries*. The sightings of Spring-heeled Jack were no more than the first exhibitionist raid on the warp, a showy

example – a mild preview of the horrors to come, clubbed from the
trees by the sightless charge of capital.

It was for this reason I paced the platform at Homerton, ready to
attempt my experiment on the North Woolwich train. I walked along
until I found an empty compartment. There was no point in dragging
bemused civilians into a potentially morbid temporal anomaly. I sat
beside the window, with my back to our potential destination. I took
out my grandfather's presentation chronograph ('by his patients on his
leaving MAESTEG in appreciation of his services, Xmas 1898'), the
work of 'H. White of Manchester'; inserted my fingernail into the
necessary slit and began to wind the hands 'backwards'. But back to
where? *Back* only in the sense of defying the tidal advance of the clock's
crafted mechanism. The shuddering movement of the train on this lost
nocturnal route might be tuned by the *intention* I expressed in my
physical actions: the deed itself had no other meaning.

I heard her voice before I saw her face. '*Love and man's unconquerable
mind.*' The Voice was light, steady, uninflected, quoting more than
extemporizing: the voice of an actress at the final run-through.
Mocking? Ironic? The accent was one I couldn't pin down – either shore
of the Great Lakes. Detroit? Toronto? The train was moving now,
gaining speed, but we were 'going' nowhere. What I saw beyond the
window did not change. This is difficult to explain. It was much more
than basic back-projection, or travelling matte: when I forced the
window open – cold air rushed against my face. I could taste the usual
cinders. The perspective was quite normal; we were devouring a diminishing ladder of track. The escarpment leant away from us; stacked
with institutional blocks, whose outlines remained defensive and sharp.
The carriage shuddered over sleepers with a soothingly regular ration of
clicks and clacks. If you tried to lift a coffee cup to your lips, you would
deposit the contents in your lap: everything was normal. Yet the ground
beyond the tracks *remained fixed*. However fast the wheels churned, the
landscape was static. Lights shifted through the windows of the Hackney
Hospital – like a self-propelling lantern of mercy. Trees lost their leaves.
Black clouds revolved like a diorama, unwound to plunge headlong into
the silver smokestack. 'Here' could not shift: it was incorruptible. We
slid sideways, backwards, ahead – futile as wasps animated by the false
sun of autumn.

'What I did not reveal to you,' the woman's voice continued; floating
across the carriage, sometimes overhead, sometimes breathing on my
cheek, 'when you began to fictionalize my story – to follow up clues I
left, to quote my friends, and visit places where I had never been, forcing
me to give them mind – was something of great importance: a link

confirming the strength of my solitude. It happened when I was searching the glass-powdered decks of the hospital for a room to use for the children. I saw a light burning on the upper floor of a wing that I knew had been abandoned. They were closing down more and more of the outlying units, allowing them to fall into disrepair – so that the debts would be impossible and it would be easier to hand the site over to the developers. When there is nothing else to sell, you sell yourself.'

A band of cheesy, orange light excited the empty carriage, transforming the headrest into a face without features. The white cloth was printed with charcoal shadows that I could interpret or ignore.

'Later that evening, when I was travelling home, on this line, wearily drowning myself in a Virago reissue of Stella Bowen's *Drawn from Life* ...' The Voice, having engaged my full attention, dropped dramatically. It was becoming almost flirtatious. '... I recognized the very words that came into my head as I walked, exhausted, along the corridor to the room with the solitary light. Everything depends on these connections. Serendipity, don't you agree? What does Eliot say? "*We are born with the dead: / See, they return, and bring us with them. The moment of the rose and the moment of the yew tree / Are of equal duration.*" Everything we say parrots words that have already been spoken. We speak in quotations. And what we struggle to bring into focus has certainly inspired some other woman, years before we were born. We are at the mercy of our grandchildren. I wanted no more than to repeat the words I felt I had caused Stella Bowen to write.

'"*Homerton was a nightmare. I wish I could say that my social conscience was born from that moment, but it wasn't. I wanted to run away from it all ...*"

'I grew impatient with Stella. She was too reasonable, phlegmatic, too much of a colonial – putting her own abilities into storage, while she created unstressed domestic enclosures for her man, the artist, the talker. She fed on such modest resentments; indulging this walrus while he "agonized" over meaningless infidelities. He didn't have the courage of his own corruptions. Why didn't she poison him? But, despite my antipathy, our selfless careers moved in tandem. In this place, of all places – in Homerton – Stella met the person I myself discovered still trapped in a forgotten hospital wing. She felt the same dangerous, *involving* excitement, and the fear that I felt. She described that person in my words. "*A flaming object ... with her scarlet hair and white skin and sudden, deep-set eyes.*" The woman who had been called Mary Butts.'

Now it was my turn to vanish. The Voice required no supporting actor. Unheard, it existed. The story had outlived the storyteller.

'In Mary Butts,' the Voice said, 'I came into my own time. In her aggression, I let myself slip the leash. It was like one of those dreams in which we are able to interrogate the famous dead. We find the teachers we need. And they are so reasonable, so amused.

'From outside the hospital window I watched myself taking her hand. She smiled, but her eyes were always moving away, across the room, deeper into the darkness. She never spoke. But I understood, instinctively, what she was saying: the words never stopped. Sometimes I turned, as I was making my way back to the wards, looked at her. The small white face would be shining, her lips painted, a great gash of red – but the wide-brimmed hat was already eaten with shadows, it was fading: I was frightened that she would fade with it.

'Gradually, I came to piece together her story. I didn't need to read about her, the footnotes in Parisian memoirs, the sketches by Cocteau. She was a woman unable to contain the energy she generated. She made men uneasy, aggressive. Her social work meant nothing to her. She was stretching beyond it, sustaining herself with retrieved images of a sensual and eternal past: the house, the woods, the paintings, the sea. She was locked in a battle for survival with her mother: a single self-devouring organism. This conflict was more important than these broken-down urban wraiths in their desolation and anguish. She wanted to confront Whitechapel in quite another way – through John Rodker. She would challenge, possess and destroy it: the anarchy and the ugliness.

'She had such extraordinary style that she could stand up against all the demons she raised in confirmation of her own strength. The crisis, of course, came in a battle-to-the-death with that monumental slug, Aleister Crowley, the most authentic of fakes – and in the battle's more deadly analogue, her addiction. She saw – and this was unbelievable to me – in her prophetic sufferings, the visionary nature of this swampland hill, this bone-mound. She saw it *as it ought to be*: an unviolated site, *temenos*, ring of trees; antler-crowned about a river of trout and darting sunlight.'

The Voice was fulfilled. It yielded. In the artificially charged silence that followed, the seat across from me began to bleach and fade. Colour was sucked from the cloth: it crackled like water-resistant skin. It was brilliant and white; taking the form of a mourning cloth, or cloak. It was a coat, inhabited, shaped, lifting with the warmth of a human presence – but empty, self-supporting.

Earth ran on to the floor of the carriage, like a shower of sand. I saw the outline of a girl emerging from a fault in the upholstery. Head hung down, her long red hair covered her face. Her dancer's legs stretched out along the seat. She was startlingly pale, powdered in arsenic, white lead. Her lips were blue. Her skin had dried, and cracked like paint. Another Antigone, this girl had been buried alive: to honour her brother's death, and her father's crime. Therefore, she lived; trapped in the memory of life. Unlike David Rodinsky, who – building his own grave – walked free. Alive, he had been a dead man: clay in his mouth, 'hesitant in conversation'. Now the room absorbed his pain.

I knew that I was looking at Edith Cadiz, the invented (and self-inventing) victim. I had no idea how to release her, or how to procure my own escape.

'Corpse-maggot! Suckler of Semites!' A distant male growl – gravel and lethargy – forced the succubus to shift and falter, to adopt a more martial form. Under these accusations, Edith Cadiz became Mary Butts. '*Soror Rhodon*: the faithless, red-haired grub who rejected my cakes of light.' Aleister Crowley had been summoned, to complete a forgotten quarrel. There could be no advance without the intervention of this contrary.

Too ripe: the ribs of the carriage collapse. The succubus is provoked to reveal her other face. Melting wax flesh. Scarlet cap of hair. A viscid, pus-queen slithering, yellow, from the wounded steel. Breath of decay. A grey, mutton-ooze sweating from her hands. The compartment darkens and shrinks. Light is repulsed. The seats swell, crushing us together. I taste the mud and the poisoned spines. Her sharpened nails are dragging across the conjunctival membrane of my eye. I no longer have place in this, even as an unreliable witness. I do not possess the technical language to justify the completion of my account.

Now the male thing rolls and lisps; stuttering its obscenities over the insect-ka of the woman. It probes, blind, for a thoracic duct from which to drink. We are enclosed in a 'formless horror'; lost to the world. The window panels smoke to slate. The whole box is no bigger than a fist: or a camera with a capped lens. We stick to the coated film, like flies. Butts invokes her master, the Assyrian bull-demon.

The train shudders in fever, its woodwork creaking and splintering. The roof tears away like skin on a custard. The night rushes through us. The wheels glow to scarlet over the melting track. Uprooted trees hurtle against the side of the carriage. It cannot be sustained. The wind drops and, in the stillness and the painful silence, the landscape gets away. Buildings are sand-slides, scrub-woods replace them, flake and peel, are themselves replaced by fires, snowstorms, bears, wolves, shapeless predators.

Our eyes are covered by the leaking terracotta of our hands. Night and day are a single moment. Our throats obediently anticipate future terrors. The train is a projectile fired through damage and hurt. The unrecovered desolation of Stratford. The fire raids. Phantom bombers dropping below cloud cover to follow the quisling ribbon of mercury

that is the Thames: to target destruction on the wharfs and refineries of
Silvertown and Custom House. Gaunt churches stand in fields of ruin.
The dead chatter like starlings in the flight path of rockets. The purgatory of George Gissing smoulders around us: '*pest-stricken regions of East
London, sweltering in sunshine which served only to reveal the intimacies of
abomination; across miles of a city of the damned ... stopping at stations which it
crushes the heart to think should be the destination of any mortal; the train made
its way at length beyond the outmost limits of dread ...*'

   And if there is a destination, beyond the nightmare, it is North
Woolwich; graveyard of engines. I step out, tentatively, on to the
morning platform. The fresh chill of the river greets me. Cold, clear
sunlight outlining a reassuring solidity of objects: benches, barriers,
bricks in the wall. The Telecom 'saucers' lift like promiscuous mush-
rooms; rat-bitten on the stalk. Everything has been swept, scrubbed,
polished; made safe. The station is now a Museum of Steam, a tamed
mirror-version that would deny its own madness. We are soothed; we
enter a past that is narcotic, careful to avoid any engagement with
present furies. It removes itself, with condescension, from the debate of
opposites; remaining an attractive fossil. North Woolwich is nowhere,
sleep's terminal: I welcome it.

V

Too weak to resist, I made my way towards the Old Station Museum;
an obtusely grand sibling of Greenwich, boasting its nautical connections, eager to service the fashionable crowds destined for dances and
assignations in the Royal Victoria Gardens. The style is 'Italianate',
ennobled in its senility, because it has survived, because it can be
favourably compared with more utilitarian sheds and shelters. We are
invited to admire the four Doric pilasters, the acanthus-decorated brack-
ets, and the rusticated quoins – while dodging juggernauts and burger
vans as they hot-pedal to make the ferry.

   The welcome inside the Museum is unnerving, quite unlike the
assault course on offer in any functioning station. There are no mere
travellers to clog up the works, irritatingly wanting to go somewhere:
the immaculately presented staff can give their undivided attention to
the 'day-release' nondescripts who wander in to escape the weather. I
keep my head down, avoiding interrogation; passing, with significant
pauses, among the cases of old tickets, scale models, shovels, buckets,
overnight bedpans, heavyweight soup plates (porcelain disci) from the
days when soup was still on the menu. I veer gratefully into the

unattended Ladies' Waiting Room, where a section has been set aside to celebrate 'Notable Marine Disasters'.

And it was immediately borne in on me – by the chief exhibit – that I had grievously misdirected my original version of the tragedy of the *Princess Alice*: Gravesend Reach was Innocent, OK? I needed to relocate upsteam, call for a Second Unit, overtime; push against the tide from Northfleet Hope, Greenhithe, Erith Rands, Frog Island, through Barking Reach to Tripcock Ness, a mile below Woolwich.

The *Alice* left Sheerness at 7.40 P.M., put in at Gravesend without incident, passed the Powder Magazine and the Beckton Gas Works, holding to mid-stream; the sun ahead of her, leading her, dropping – like a fireball – on the city, breaking the stones into living clusters of light. To starboard: the jaunty boasts of a military march reverberate across the flinching water from the pleasure gardens; strolling couples linger by the river wall. A woman notices a three-masted collier, discharging black smoke, cutting inevitably towards the *Alice*, as she positions herself to come alongside the pier. Her gentleman friend, indulgent, squeezes her bare shoulder, explains the technicalities of the well-rehearsed manoeuvre that makes any collision impossible. The rules of the river.

'It was like a spasm, a whirlpool.' The head of the ship lifted out of the water like the jaws of a great shark, passengers slid helplessly down the black shaft: the Thames was 'like a sarcophagus'. A strong ebb tide ran some of the bodies back down to Rainham and the Ferry Boat Inn. The limbs of the dead ones moving in the wash of the sinking vessel. 'They appeared to be swimming.' Halfway Reach; they gave up the ghost to Dagenham and Hornchurch Marshes; were laid out on the tables of the pub: an indigestible feast.

I fled: escaping from the accumulated evidence to the scene of the crime. Away from the station, out along the riverside, towards Gallions Reach and the guilty Thames: an exquisite, still morning, sunlight disguising the squalor, varnishing the slogans on concrete, the upside-down motors sinking in mud, the corrugated fences, blinded buildings, drills and excavators. On the south shore the born-again hills shone with promises, releasing the names of power from grim chains of circumstance, *Lesnes Abbey Woods, Belvedere, Temple*. It was beyond me; I was drained of energy. I turned back.

In one of the cases in the Old Station Museum they keep the artefacts recovered from the river, small traces of the human snatched back from the swoops of fate. There is, for example, the corroded outline of a key, salvaged from the wreck of an East Indiaman, the *Albion*, put out from Gravesend, 16 January 1765, ran aground, gulled into following the

Horsedon, standing fast with 'no signal of distress'; waiting for the tide to carry her off the sandbanks. We don't have the key itself, only the chemical reaction that it caused. The ruin that surrounds it. The shape of its absence. The chest, to which it grants access, remains buried in the silt of the seafloor.

I did not yet feel ready to face the journey up the line to Hackney; I cheated by directing myself through the door that led to the fake station. The clerk in the ticket office was decently subservient: he was sculpted from wax – brushed, laundered, trimmed, his hair sleeked with axle grease. He was so obliging that our transaction did not require the usual lengthy consultation of the Book of Changes, or the ritual snarl of insults. Let us hope these men become part of the standard fixtures and fittings on the New Railways. Cancellations can be left on a pre-recorded loop.

I sauntered, unchallenged, on to the platform of this unreal terminus; denied myself the bench labelled 'Angel Road' (I leave *Hypothania*, the domain of angels, to Joblard), and sat instead in a restored Victorian carriage, to wait for a steam engine that would never arrive. I whiled away the time by studying the postcard I had purchased, Tenniel's prophetic illustration, 'Alice in the Train'. There was enough material here to last me a decade.

The details by which Tenniel's 'box set' diverge from Lewis Carroll's studiously surreal text indicate minor but significant shifts in interpretation. It is easy to believe that Tenniel's image *preceded the author's account of it*. The artist crops the compartment to eliminate the inessential players; he tightens the drama, sponsoring an almost lurid element of suspense. The Beetle, seated beyond the Goat, is replaced by the artist's monogram (a dead Beatle?). The Horse (hoarse), whose voice is a disturbing (if familiar) pun, is also dispensed with – but we can only enter the scene from his point of view. He is the unremarked double of the Guard who leans in at the window. Carroll lets it be known that the Horse is male. Of course.

The two travellers in whom Tenniel does feign an interest are 'the gentleman opposite' and the Goat. The gentleman (described in the text as being 'dressed in white paper') is depicted in a perfectly proper white suit, a Suez Canal speculator. He ghosts the popular Punch-icon of Disraeli; civilized, worldly, Semitic, with a wisp of beard – kissing cousin to the Goat. His hat is a folded triangle of paper; a pyramid, a toy imperial yacht. The words 'white paper' perhaps gave Tenniel the executive hint he elevated into a full-blown caricature. His oily nabob leers disagreeably over the top of his journal, which is innocent of print – an obvious voyeur's trick, these folded blank sheets disguise something peculiar and repellent, artichoke-leaved, that is emerging from the Gentleman's waistcoat pocket. His unequivocal designs on Alice will supply the missing headlines for the scandal sheet: in this case, certainly, no news is good news.

The Goat bides his time, masking his folklore attributes in a show of sleep. These dreams are better left unvisited. But the position of the Gentleman's crossed leg, with bulky folds of material at the knee, supplies the Goat with a mythically engorged member. He has been anthropomorphized in all surface details, but remains handless: a sinister deficiency, summoning intimations of future slaughter.

With the advent of the Guard at the window – asserting his status, inside and outside at the same time – the illustration lays claim to a moral complexity that is the cartoon surrogate for 'Las Meninas'. His dark figure is backlit, aping the pose of the courtier on the stairs. The panels of the train windows are echoed in the mirror and the portraits within Velázquez's studio. The focal point of both compositions is a long-haired unsmiling girl, attended by two acolytes – with the presence of an ambiguous witness to block our only means of escape, and to lead us back into the heat of the composition. The girls are sullenly incubating the poltergeists of puberty: curdled infantas, lethal as landmines.

Tenniel has proposed a toy theatre, in which his 'types' wait for the invention of cinema. Velázquez, the king's *apostentador*, is trapped – by his genius – at the easel: it is his shadow, the queen's *apostentador*, who pauses at the door. Tenniel too stands outside, beyond the compartment's absent wall. At his signal, the static train will be rocked on its cradle – and the journey will begin.

It's not hard to dislike the uniformed Guard, with his diamond-shaped belt buckle, his face hidden in his hands: a face which is suspiciously hirsute, and – not to put too fine a point on it – furry as a bear or lion. Neither am I comfortable with that leather tongue of a window strap that dangles so flaccidly in front of this man, ready to insinuate itself, as soon as the train jerks forward, in Alice's lap. The binoculars with which the Guard moons at his flaxen-haired temptress are an invention of the artist's. Carroll is quite specific concerning the categories of implement employed in the operation: 'first through a telescope, then a microscope, and then through an opera glass'. But Tenniel is not satisfied with those puny dimensions. He gifts his forked creature with a pair of vast, adjustable lager cans. The Guard is much too busy to speak, but we quake before the thunder of his voice. '*You're travelling the wrong way.*'

An area of furious cross-hatching spreads like a stain from the knees of the Gentleman in White to Alice's hooped stockings, tracing the undisguised coastline of Africa. The Guard, in his salvationist's peaked cap, is travestied as 'Dr Livingstone'. He sweeps the hot plains with his binoculars, eager to be confirmed in his latest identity by a wave from Henry Stanley. His concentration falters and the sharp lines begin to swim. The pale windows re-form as a lantern-skull, above the pithecanthropic jaw of Africa. It is the voodoo idol from *King Kong*: the binoculars are the eyes that pin Alice to her seat, where she calmly awaits her poisoned kiss of fate. In the tight square of sky behind the Guard, a black gull drifts, a swerving *V*, hinting that the river is close at hand, accomplice to the whole affair. Tenniel's carriage is located: I am sitting in it, holding it down. The moment of risk is eternally imminent.

But all of us, puppets and audience, are dominated – transfixed – by the mongoose-will of the blonde girl. Self-contained, she sits as if she were attending a lecture, with slides, on Faraday's electro-magnetic current, or the Discovery of the Source of the Nile. She has sunk into a cataleptic trance: the other figures are flattened projections, beings lifted from a magic lantern account of the 'news'. They are icons from an historico-mythical matrix: Disraeli, Livingstone – and the High Church Goat, an Oxford man, about to embark on some Anglo-Catholic schism. Alice can cancel them all, reassert the sanctity of the carriage, travel alone. They are shadows. She indulges their whim of travelling incognito, outside their public personae; swimming in the flow of time; gathering strength in some primitive, but decently padded, orgone accumulator.

Only the *anima* of this girl can lift the train from its rails. It is like the will of my daughter, of all daughters: mothers of daughters. The ghost-conductor inspects Alice three times: through the telescope of lust, the microscope of investigation, the opera glass of envy. She allies herself with the order of birds; a feather grows from her severe black torque. She is handless, like the Goat, hiding within a live muff, a hideous dog-thing. A handbag, that classic fetish, rests beside her. It is independent, surgically detached; no relation to Wilde's capacious theatrical prop. The effect is elegantly pornographic: furs, purses, unbound hair.

Carroll closes his account (which should be published in the *Notable British Trials* series) with a revealing fugue. Dr Freud revolves his cigar. '*In another moment she felt the carriage rise straight up into the air, and in her fright she caught at the thing nearest to her hand, which happened to be the Goat's beard.*' After this the exhausted author expires in a milky spurt of typographic stars. Fourteen of them, arranged in groups of five, Aleister Crowley's 'averse pentagram': numbered, perhaps, to indicate the desired age of the heroine. And, as with Hitchcock, only blondes need apply.

Beyond the author's phallocentric seizure is another interesting question: why does Tenniel make it perfectly clear in his version that the Goat's beard is far from 'the thing nearest to her hand'? Carroll's leap at priapic occultism is not tolerated by the illustrator — who is playing an entirely different game. He is playing detective. I believe that he codes his etching with the solution to the railway murders that had not, *as yet*, been committed; but which we can now unravel on his behalf.

The first suspect is traditionally the man in uniform, the Guard; a faceless voyeur, a wolf in wolf's clothing. He watches everything, has access everywhere; can pick his victims from deserted platforms, or use his pass key to enter locked compartments. But the evidence against him is all circumstantial. The stern *V* of his elbow signifies kinship with the flight of gulls: but that was another country and another crime. The four birds *are* implicated, but not in this affair. Tenniel keeps his establishment hitman (another Netley) outside the carriage; links him to the river.

Then what about the sinister 'gentleman dressed in white paper', who leans forward to whisper confidingly in Alice's ear, '*Take a return ticket every time the train stops*'? He is eager to prolong the encounter; 'busy' beneath the folds of his newspaper, but that is as far as it goes. He is, I'm afraid, out of stock, standard issue, the Levantine red herring. He will soon undergo a sex change and donate his albino wrappings to Wilkie Collins (inadvertently founding the English Murder Mystery). For the moment, he is no more than Peter Lorre lost inside Sidney Greenstreet's Hong Kong-stitched castoffs. We can dismiss him with a caution.

The Goat also plays with our prejudices. Tenniel, in giving him no hands, signals his innocence. He claims to have dozed through the whole thing. He is cancelled by rapid horizontal strokes of the pen; cast into the river with the other fall-guys. His name goes into the files of the Black Museum, along with his spectacles, his cufflinks, and his wing-collar. After a decent interval, he will be 'fingered' by Colin Wilson — as a blood-guzzling ritualist. His horns will be mounted on the wall of Donald Rubelow's office. His 'suicide' will close the case. The pebbles from his pocket will be returned to the proper authorities.

We are left, once again, with the classic Agatha Christie railway solution: *they orl dunit*. Railways beget conspiracies: Ethel Lina White's *The Wheel Spins* (filmed by Hitchcock as *The Lady Vanishes*), with nuns in high heels, injections, bandages; or Patricia Highsmith's smoking-car collaborators, exchanging crimes (also translated by Hitchcock, with the 'help' of Raymond Chandler); or so many more of the 'Master's' nightmares from the first *Thirty-nine Steps* to *North by Northwest*. This man, a true son of Wanstead, must be pulled in for questioning.

Tenniel's dark frame is a trailer for *Rear Window*. And we have established by now that being dead is no excuse at all.

In making his drawing look so much like a *film noir* production still is Tenniel telling us something? He makes us consider the role of Lewis Carroll as a compulsive photographer of nymphets. He reminds us that Carroll's text is an elaborate chess game: '*the final "checkmate" of the Red King will be found, by any one who will take the trouble to set the pieces and play the moves as directed, to be strictly in accordance with the laws of the game*'. There are no counterfeit tricks: follow Carroll's moves closely enough and he reveals his own guilt, as we all do. He plays the self-inquisitor, employs whimsy, teasing so savagely that he bruises his flesh. He has the arrogance to scatter incriminating messages he is sure we will be too stupid to interpret.

Have other 'psychic detectives' penetrated this mystery years before us? The only crimes worth solving are the ones that have not yet been committed: they are still formally immaculate. William Hope Hodgson narrates his 'Carnacki the Ghost-finder' tales through the medium of his own 'Late Watson'; a narrative 'I' who is unmasked as 'Dodgson' (Charles Lutwidge, perhaps? Author of *Phantasmagoria and Other Poems*: the 'real' Lewis Carroll) in *The Gateway of the Monster*. The supernumerary trio of disciples who attend Carnacki's 'evenings' are frequently named: Arkright, Jessop, Taylor (Science, Cricket, Neo-Platonism?) – but 'Dodgson' is, I believe, mentioned in only two tales; 'The Gateway of the Monster' and 'The Hog' (which did not feature as part of the original Carnacki canon, and was not included in the wrappered summary of 1910, nor the Eveleigh Nash collection of 1913). 'Dodgson' reports the adventures (fantastic-domestic survivals from the Looking-glass World), but – unlike Dr Watson – he is never a participant. Both these men are, of course, the true authors: they are able safely to share the terrors no outside agency has invoked. '*Some evening I want to tell you about the tremendous mystery of the Psychic Doorways. In the meantime, have I made things a bit clearer to you, Dodgson?*'

Tenniel, like Walter Sickert with the Ripper murders, mistook his own obsessions for guilt. He invented elaborate fables to account for his involvement *in the knowledge* of these terrible sacrifices. Sir John, it should be remembered, joined the staff of *Punch* in 1851, and produced, after the death of Leech, its principal weekly political cartoon. Now look again at the artist's heraldic sigil in the bottom left-hand corner of 'Alice in the Train'. It is exactly the same as the initials you will find imposed in the same position in that most famous of all 'Ripper' icons: 'The Nemesis of Neglect' (the hooded, knife-wielding spectre with CRIME printed on its forehead). Sir John Tenniel was responsible for both images. (A 'lost' word – part-rune, part-mirror script – is buried on the floor beneath Alice's feet: like the whispers on the dead track at the finish of the *Sergeant Pepper* LP.)

The collaboration with Carroll, and the production of this clairvoyant illustration gave Tenniel the chance to accuse the killer, whose identity he knew – because he had, *at some level*, shared in the crime. His capped (or crowned) Guard wears the Diamond and stares, eyeless, at the girl: because he is, or stands for, the *Red King*. He is checkmated. The Goat accuses him, a Tarot Devil, representing 'ravishment, force, fatality'. So Tenniel is able to put into his depiction of Alice the details of the murders that the police have never made public. The hands of the victims were always tied in front of them – as Alice's are, within her muff. They were all strangled with a knotted scarf, such as the one that Alice wears. *And a single feather was knotted into their hair.* I rest my case.

But wait a minute: didn't Joblard procure a quantity of these same gulls' feathers for his installation in the London Fields gallery? I must check the files. Yes, it's there in the *Flash Art* review: 'From the dereliction of the East End one passes into the labyrinthine interior and then via a metal staircase (under each step of which a feather has been placed – the Angel's wing of ascension) to the threshold ...' The feather or quill is an obvious invocation of the idea of 'inscription', with its darker twin – confession. Joblard is the guilty man: the Bird-Revenger.

No, no, no. It's worse than that: if the details of the murders have never been made public – *how do I know what they are?* I put up my hand, confess. The relief! In the end every writer confesses. It proves nothing; a kind of boast. I must draw on the anger of women to escape from this quilted cage, a strength we will never understand, and transcribe as 'will', 'stubbornness', or some other biological imperative.

I allow the conceit of my house to form around me: the armour plating of an insect-samurai. I can stick the Tenniel postcard, with a stub of sugar-free gum, on to the window of the phoney carriage – and walk out, be somewhere else. That is the power of the narrator. I need to consult *The Crystal Cabinet* of Mary Butts, and I climb the rackety ladder into the attic, to search for it. ('*The equivocal nature of the contact between visible and invisible, the natural order and the supernatural.*')

I sit in a hutch of darkness, holding a torch, illicitly leafing through John Symonds's account of Mary Butts visiting Crowley at Cêfalu, the Abbey of Thelema. The Great Beast offered Butts 'cakes of light' – the Host, in the form of 'a goat's turd on a plate'. Which she, unceremoniously, declined.

I am walled in by cases of books (unsold stock, forgotten purchases) that will only be read by torchlight. Extracts. Quotations. Specimen sentences questing for meaning. Any one of them could alter the balance of the tale, and postpone that hideous moment of silence – when your turn at the fireside is concluded; the audience demand that you sit down. (*Just a moment more.*)

This awkward space has none of the spontaneous chaos of Rodinsky's room. It contains all the material that no longer fits into our lives: clothes we do not wear, letters we shall never again read, cricket bats with lumps knocked out of them. I was finally able to suspend my unfocused quest when I came upon a drawing book in which my daughter, aged about three and a half, had executed a sequence of curious sketches, featuring bubble-headed, tendril-writhing figures. Her mother then took down the child's terse 'explanations' on the opposite leaf. The point was that the illustrations preceded the stories, and explained the unexplainable – only because her mother expected it. The child was perfectly capable of obliging some formal requirement, and 'doing her own thing' at the same time.

What interested me, in my present state of compulsive associationism, about these Rorschach doodles was that several of the 'stories' concerned railways. Two of these followed each other, but were not necessarily connected. '*The lady walked down the track. The train came and ran her over, but she got up. And she took the baby home.*' Then came a hot whirlwind, a vortex of crayoned blues and greens – on the perimeter of which was a pink blob; invertebrate, with dangling, threadlike legs. '*The water dripped on the lady's hand and made her die. The candle showed her the way in the dark.*'

I could let it go; leave it here with this marvellous soup of worms. By the restored power of the child's 'candle' I could pluck a book from the sack, some forgotten favourite, and carry it back down into the electric house. Kafka's *Trial*. The brutal termination of Joseph K. that I had chosen to suppress.

'But the hands of one of the partners were already at K.'s throat, while the other thrust the knife into his heart and turned it there twice. With failing eyes K. could still see the two of them, cheek leaning against cheek, immediately before his face, watching the final act. "*Like a dog!*" *he said*: it was as if he meant the shame of it to outlive him.'

7

Prima Donna
(*The Cleansing of Angels*)

Prima Donna (*The Cleansing of Angels*)

'A locomotive jumped its track and smashed Poe's tombstone'

Guy Davenport, *Olson (The Geography of the Imagination)*

Cec Whitenettle, a lifelong abstainer, poured out his second half of Bacardi, making it familiar by the addition of an orange cordial. He swallowed it grimly down; his scrawny neck convulsing, his thyroidal cartilage bobbling like a drowning chick. He drank where he stood, in the centre of the room, feet apart, awkwardly 'at ease'; taking care not to spill a single drop on to his uniform. His glass, as he returned it to the table – in a mindless hydrolic gesture – was coated in thick felt.

Water was steaming from the tap into a blue plastic basin. Cec watched the spiralling thread of its descent: from behind a plate-glass screen. He had no recollection of initiating this incident. He was utterly estranged from it; as from the rest of the objects that surrounded him. The cut-throat razor opened silently and smoothly. Foam curled in a lazy worm on Cec's open hand, and was mechanically smeared across his face. He slapped at his cheeks, feeling the reassuring rhythms of the contact, *feeling* the sound. Cec welcomed his 'auditory disability', his deafness, the only tangible souvenir of those best remembered years, in the battery: the earth-shuddering pounding of the 4.5s, pitted in the Isle of Dogs. That night, 4 September 1940, when the men realized they themselves had become the principal target. That was their only achievement.

And the bleak mornings: river mist; the desolate mud field, gun barrels tilted at the skies, looking from the road like so many collapsing chimneys. Nothing could compare with it. The solitude and the friendships.

As he shaved, Cec avoided the eyes of the man behind the mirror. He pinched his nostrils shut, lifted them to scrape at the ill-disciplined hairs, emerging to trespass on that narrow trench of puckered labial flesh, with its finicky, inaccessible ridges. The skin of the whole face was drawn back, stretched, inadequately attached to the bone armature beneath. Cec was terrified that the knots would give, the mask would slip, and collapse into folds – never to be ironed out. Already the pouch-cups under his eyes were bruised with anguish, scratched, wax-filled. His large asymmetrical ears stood, naked and proud, from a helmet of cropped and water-combed hair. Surface-nerves flinched as he paddled a cruel application of scented acid into the reluctant pores.

A flask of sugar-saturated tea, marmalade sandwiches, a copy of yesterday's evening paper, were waiting in the canvas satchel. Cec took his wristwatch from the drawer, advanced it by one and a half minutes, and slipped it over his wrist – with the solemnity of a marriage vow. Time to go: 2.55 A.M. Two-handed, Cec lifted his peaked cap from the chair. No trace of irony: from the instant it touched his head, he was on duty.

He hesitated; returned the cap to its resting place. One for the road: a final shot of Bacardi. Given time, he could develop a taste for the stuff. He licked the glass; refilled it, threw it back. It wouldn't matter now if his wife did notice. She only kept the bottle for her sister, New Year's Day. A quick one. She would be sleeping like a sow: tossing about, rolling herself in the sheets, snorting, fingers in her privates; *breathing*, saveloys and whisky. Shelley Winters's nightdress, up round her belly – at her age.

The cold air refreshed him. His ungloved hands felt no chill as they scraped the thin filter of frost from the car windows. The world was at its best: it was uninhabited, all its shocks and alarums were sheathed in a prophylactic darkness.

On Morning Lane he waited obediently for the lights; he would have waited for ever. There was not another car on the road; but without rules the universe falls into chaos. He drummed his fingers. The old childhood fancy came back over him: waking one morning to discover a deserted city, from which all the other inhabitants have flown, slipped away into another dimension. He would walk towards the centre, always through the same leafy squares, the memorials nobody else appreciated, touching them, fingering Coade-stone gods; nymphs, goats, griffins. He would tiptoe, unthreatened, on the crown of the road – until he arrived at one of the great department stores, blazing in a costume of coloured lights; where he would wander down avenues of ladies' things, dabbling perfumes, tasting cosmetics, running silks between his fingers, brushing against furs, curtains of animal pelts; testing himself against all their secrets. The mirrors would loose their magic. He would not disturb them. Unobserved, he would be naked as the day he was born.

Cec let the car steer itself down Homerton Road towards the marshes: he was enclosed against the night, the fingers of wind, the buildings of eyes. Tonight, nobody else was alive: a molten stream of fire-insects swarmed endlessly along Eastway, in a mad chase to escape from their own headlights. The marshes were nothing: grass over rubble; coarse turf, impacted by generations of footballing oaths, hid the cratered terraces of dockland. You could rebuild Silvertown from this midden. You could excavate the names of all the eradicated villages. The incendiary warriors were still waiting for the kettle to boil on the primus.

He crossed the imaginary (but irrefutable) border, cut down Temple Mills Lane, and was lost among the enormous shadows of the reclaimed mounds of Stratford. The hoists, the containers stacked into unoccupied babels: this was a transitional landscape that would never achieve resolution. Out of the fire-storms had come industry; out of ruin, imagination. We were promised a life of marvellous changes: no more poverty, no mean and pinched lives. So everything was cleared to make place for a dystopia of fenced-in goods yards, coldstores, bonded warehouses. Railways replaced rivers. Now 'docks' could be anywhere that capital chose to nominate. This demarcated zone was made ready to service the latest panacea, the concept of 'The Hole'; a tunnel that would connect these infertile swamps with the threat of Europe, and future prosperity. On this wild gamble, all regulations were suspended. Today was too late. Dig it first, discuss it later. Steel jaws ate the earth, with all the frenzy of orphans searching for their fathers.

Cec nodded to the security 'bull' on the gate, who hit the button and lifted the barrier, without bothering to look up from the climax of the snuff-video he was running under his counter. (Some footage had been 'sampled' from Sam Fuller's *White Dog*. Actuality – in the form of hand-held shots out of a car window, as the victim was run down – was planted alongside. The chase peaked. The white dog pounced. A thick smell of fear leaked from the machine, converting it into a defective microwave.)

The car shower needed no human agency: it was triggered by pressure points hidden in the road. The green light scanners cleared Cec, his uniform and his satchel. Even the technical equipment could find no interest in the man. His laser-coated pass carried him safely through the triple cage, and out on to the deserted platform. The nighttime 'special' sulked, steaming like a horse, under rows of overhead sodium-vapour lamps, that stretched a genetic chain of rusty haloes all the way between Hackney Wick and Canning Town. The train, a power-charged demon, had been disguised in panels of mud: its number-coding was standard, but it remained an officially sanctioned pirate. It was not here. It did not exist. The volatile silver canisters held their glowing million-year-old rods within laboratory-cushioned milk churns. Cec's engine was ready for its advance on Mile End (and its 'detour' through Stepney Green and Whitechapel to pick up the drums of reprocessed material from Barking, that did not show up on any manifest – but which were delivered, with the utmost precision, to the cosmetic shell of Liverpool Street). The rest was not Cec's business: the airstrips of Suffolk, or the lost estuaries of Essex. He knew no more than the comfortably receding lines of track.

Volunteer and they throw the works at you: lie detectors, hot wires, flash-frames, sensory deprivation, stress-curves, cranial measurement, pads on the tongue, anal dilation, scrapes of nail dirt, litmus nappies, ancestor research, criminal record, political affiliations and Tarot reading. Cec had been turned down for the buses on the grounds of 'poor road sense'; but the spooks found him perfectly suitable, a clean profile. He was deaf, impotent, suffering the onset of premature senility; a psychoneurotic depressive, prone to paranoid anxiety. He had a bad marriage, and no friends. His moral judgements were untrustworthy. He was just about capable of keeping his hand on the steering column. The ideal man: he fitted the job description to the letter.

The hermetic isolation of the cab was his prize: the line ahead was virgin, ready to be swallowed. The platform floated like a tropical island above this mud-churned dereliction. The red warning light flickered, then died: it was time to move out.

II

Anyone who has ever written anything about Whitechapel, or the Whitechapel Murders, will soon discover they have issued an open invitation to every conspiracy-freak who is not actually under lock and key (and who is able to raise the price of a phonecall). It starts even before your book is published, almost as soon as the typescript receives its ultimate correction: as you slide the drawer shut, the phone rings. It's always late at night; the caller has no name – his manner is circuitous, a shade abrupt. The voice is a vibrating needle of glass: you sense the veins knotting, the controlled resentment, the white hand clenching and unclenching. There is no time for, or interest in, your evasions: a message has to be delivered.

'Mr Sinclair? I am able to reveal to you that I am in possession of privileged information (hopefully, to be published before the year is out), *comprehensively* refuting all previous theories. All the books you have read, those manufactured bestsellers, have been nothing but a tissue of lies, illegitimate confessions sponsored by ... by ... The truth has nothing, absolutely *nothing*, to do with the Royal Family, the medical profession, or the Masons. I am the only one who has pieced together the entire story. It's all going to come out. But, as yet, I can tell you ... nothing.'

Significant silences, painfully indrawn breath: all the inevitable grey-room warnings, whispered so loudly that they wake the children in their cots. *Let it alone!*

Then, shortly after your book is launched (one copy on the reserved shelf in Camden Town, twelve ordered from Glasgow – author's name sounding vaguely Scottish – returned on receipt, with request for refund against postage), the postman is knocking with the first bulky envelope; taped and double-sealed, stuffed with obscurely menacing news cuttings. 'Has anybody official tried to dissuade you from publishing?' ('Only the publishers,' I mumble.)

Evidence accumulates in the form of photocopied accounts of spontaneous combustions: 'MAN BURSTS INTO FLAMES. *Paul Green, a 19-year-old computer operator, was walking along a quiet road in De Beauvoir Town, Hackney, around midnight when he suddenly burst into flames. He doesn't smoke. He thinks the blaze might have been set off by a passing car but he doesn't remember hearing any vehicle pass him. Police have spoken to Paul and examined the scene but are still puzzled by the fire. Paul is a holder of the Duke of Edinburgh's bronze medal, and has two O levels.'*

Or, some local-history buff will point out, rather crossly, that 'Nicholas Lane', the seemingly innocuous name of one of my fictional characters, is also a respectable channel, severing King William Street, where a Hawksmoor church is lurking – and where, apparently, T. S. Eliot spent his days as a banker, buried beneath the pavements, peering at typists' legs through squares of sea-green glass. More and more; madder and madder. '*Elderly man critical after two-ton concrete and steel block plunged on to his car killing his wife. The couple were driving in heavy traffic along King William Street.*'

I am deluged in accounts of corrupt surgeons, victims sprayed with kerosene, amnesiac detectives croaking out incriminating details in south-coast retirement homes, death-bed confessions occurring simultaneously (and word-for-word) in Adelaide, Buenos Aires and Copenhagen; clairvoyants, quacks, syphilitic poetasters; cocktails of feline blood (granting invisibility), showers of bread loaves, transported cathedrals; Russian-Jewish anarchists, Helena Blavatsky, M. P. Shiel, Sherlock Holmes, Queen Victoria. As one of these documents –

truthfully but inelegantly – concludes: 'The only exit therefore eventually left would be access to the zoo.'

To retain my sanity, it was necessary for me to cultivate the spittle-bibbed rudeness that is second nature to any antiquarian bookseller, to brush aside these twittering, but harmless obsessionists who cling to some personalized fragment of the past; determined, beyond reason, to wring every droplet of meaning from the soiled fabric. The events of nineteenth-century Whitechapel have been overtold to the point of erasure; confirming nothing beyond their eternal melancholy. The puffers, sniffers, scribblers and scratchers are determined to keep that small flame dancing in the circle of their sour breath.

John Millom was, I thought, different from the others only in degree: he was the most extreme example, the ultimate 'Ripper' nut. There was something so fixated, so dementedly popeyed, in the stuttering urgency of his phonecall that I found myself agreeing, reluctantly, to meet him, to examine his long-accumulated store of documents. It would, he assured me, change my life. There was a manuscript, I would know as soon as I looked at it, would *have* to be published. I had the ear of paperback editors, didn't I? I even had permission to call a few literary agents by their christian names.

Millom would be waiting on the platform at Leyton from eleven o'clock on the morning of 3 December. He would be wearing a dark 'business' suit and a tie with the insignia of the local Round Table. I, in my turn, would hold aloft a carrier bag issued by the Forbidden Planet bookshop, with their logo prominently displayed. I couldn't say what I would be wearing. I didn't know what I was wearing now.

My attitude was inexcusable: I needed Millom more than he needed me. I had no intention of doing anything with his offer, other than pressganging him (as a prime freak) into my book of tales – which was in a critical condition; and likely, without a speedy transfusion, to collapse under its own density, like a dead star. This compulsive scavenging took me to many places better left unvisited: Leyton was the worst of them.

III

Whitechapel Station comes more nearly to resemble a Berlin checkpoint every time I use it. There are barriers, scanners, plexiglass enclosures, money-eating slits. Remote-control uniforms (that may or may not be inhabited) demand tickets and passes. How would you recognize your own face as it flattened and bent across the visor of a helmet? Travellers are required to submit to a primitive body-search before passing into the tunnels. They are groped by buzzing hoops, pulled from the line, questioned against white tile walls.

'Fucking surfers, mate,' 'Tiresias' the newspaper seller (so named because he had 'foresuffered all', and never ceased to speak of it) told me, as he struggled, disapprovingly, to heft a copy of the *Guardian*, 'still shovellin' 'em orf of the track. Took 'em in buckets dahn the 'ors-pital, dint they?'

I nodded, meaningfully, as if I knew what he was talking about; he was spitting doom at the next customer, so I didn't hang about. I was already late: I'd planned to visit the Whitechapel Gallery on my way – to pick up a Yiddish phrasebook. I should have known better, the place doesn't open until eleven o'clock (culture breakfasts late in these islands): two or three mitching schoolkids and a solitary vagrant were mooning about outside, eager to get into the refurbished snack bar. I had to satisfy myself with sampling the blue Wedgwood plaque polyfilled to the Library wall in celebration of Isaac Rosenberg. Then a speedy browse through the repro maps and the tables of redundant stock, now offered for sale. (I selected a well-worn salmon cloth 2nd imp. of G. Scott-Moncrieff's *Café Bar*, July 1932: 'A Novel without Hero or Plot'. Joey the Jumper had once recommended it.) Soon there will be more texts outside in the 10p bins than on the library shelves.

Another odd thing about the station entrance is that any space not dominated by badge-flashing muscle has been colonized by an indiscreet hullabaloo of male whores, rent boys, and tasty runaways; most of them favouring the style known as 'Goth' (or 'Vandaloon') – sooty-black rags, white faces, chicken crowns. The undead in lethargic rehearsal. This seemed to confirm one of Millom's more off-the-wall pronouncements. He claimed the police were refusing to make public the fact that the victims of the most recent spate of railway murders were *all male*. (Some of his best chums, so he said, were on the force. And they were 'sickened' by what was going on. They feared a backlash. Lynch mobs. Homophobia. And feared it to the extent that they were busy formulating a policy of pre-emptive strikes. Hang a few 'cornholers' by the testicles. *Décourager les autres*.) The authorities were gravely concerned about a 'wave of panic' hitting the balance sheets of the New Companies; commuters shifting their always fickle allegiance to the collapsing road system. It was true: cars were, at this moment, honking swinishly in bumper-to-bumper jams that stretched all the way back to the Bow Flyover; tempers fraying into clinical psychopathy. There were 'incidents', fights, screaming women: panicking 'weekenders' trying to fight their way out of Timber Wharves Village in heavily provisioned Range Rovers were terrified by the very real threat from marauding Highway Gangs – who were ready to strip them to the springs, and add another bushel of hysteria to the telescoping zone of chaos.

Millom had ranted about plague, enforced sodomy, pyorrhoeal kisses, neck bites, genital stalks bitten off in Dionysiac ecstasy: the victims, in their turn, becoming predators – the entire railway network rife with plasma-drooling vampires. He warned of maniacs with endemic viral erections, flesh dripping from their bone faces like cooking fat, never stepping ashore, sleeping with their eyes open, ever vigilant in the quest for new victims. An eternity of travel, with no destination, no memory of life in the settlement: restlessness, hunger, hatred. The system was racing to a standstill; blocked by ghost trains, cruising for clean meat. Millom wouldn't step outside his door, he claimed, without his swordstick. He would make rashers out of the first gay who so much as asked him for a light for his cigarette.

The stamina, such as it is, of these weary Vandaloons is carelessly expended on subdued attempts at begging (that would have provoked Dryfeld's undying scorn). They risk no more than the exhibition of an unwashed hand: the full chart of their ferrous deficiencies. Many have sunk on to the ground, doing nothing and knowing nothing. Their interest in life is minimal, and does not stretch far beyond the recognition of this station as a worthy place to haunt.

And so it is: an off-balance, unplanned assembly of tunnels, spidery stairwells, bridges going nowhere. The station appeared to be linked, by undiscovered passages, to the London Hospital, and a gaunt warehouse on Durward Street (overlooking the Jewish Burial Ground and the cobblestones where the body of the Ripper's first victim was discovered). Dust-licked windows bell out over the track; swollen curves of Flemish bonded yellow marl bricks are shored up with proscribed medieval timber. There are watchers everywhere.

I descend, pass along deserted platforms, climb stairs that float in space, unattached and shifty. I glimpse apertures of remote light, occulted details of the hospital, slogan-plastered walls, a narrow footbridge surreptitiously edging over the track, from sealed attic to sealed attic. I am almost ready to abandon my rendezvous with Millom; to give my allegiance to the derelicts, go no further, find a hole, a forgotten office, and dig in.

The sun has exploited a fault in the leaden skies above this labyrinth of unfulfilled ambitions: the mist begins to shift, to infiltrate the smoke from a fire some workmen have lit beside the track. A man, a hunched solitary, is standing at the far end of the long platform, beneath a bank of television screens that play back an idealized version of this necropolis

junction: pearly, dim, soft. These pictures have the quality of trans-
missions from a diving bell in the deepest ocean trench. Eel-grass fronds
of morbid light flare from the black hole of the tunnel: an extinct
monster's last breath.

It is probably not worth the effort of asking this man if he knows the
place for the Mile End train – but something about the epidural rigidity
of his stance, the bulging pockets of his white coat, the incongruous pink
cap, makes me think he could justify a line or two in the notebook. He
has absorbed events, without participating in them. They have stuck to
him like a quilt of burs.

'Is this right for Mile End?' No response. It would be as useful to
question the angels on their green plinth at the station entrance. But the
television sets, in a reprise of some primitive short by Lumière, were
now featuring that twin-screen classic, *The Arrival of the Train*. I could
even make out the word – UPMINSTER – advancing like a special-effects
title. I was about to turn away when I noticed one mildly disconcerting
detail. I was quite alone on the slippery silver dish: my co-star had taken
personal modesty to the extreme degree of *remaining invisible*. His etheric
double was not there.

The train in dutiful longshot slid across the frame, hit its mark with
the precision of an old pro, and disgorged a few flower-bearing tourists,
determined visitors of the sick. I could still see, and admit to, an
ill-performed parody of my lean and noble figure, sullen cap pulled over
eyes, carrier bag in hand: but there was nobody beside me. I wheeled
towards the old man on the platform (that time-warped Gerontion): he
had not moved. He stared remorselessly at the screen; he must have
penetrated to a deeper channel. He gawped like an addict, untouched,
but unwilling to break free. I did not poke him, test his reality with my
fingers. The smell was overpoweringly authentic: it is only his ghost
that does not register. He slips, unharmed, through the electronic net;
ergo, he is not allowed to exist.

IV

'The wounded surgeon plies the steel
That questions the distempered part'

T. S. Eliot, *East Coker*

Nothing interrupted the complacent ruralist calm of Leyton. The
journey through the tunnel and out into the wide-sky spaces of Strat-

ford had been uneventful: no rapes, no violations, nothing to write home about at all. A warty red sun pitched over the rumpled post-bellum savannah, dissolving the blue-grey mist, and flashing across stagnant pools, car dumps, and portakabins.

The only action to be found on this platform was a low-intensity assault on a Reebok-sporting street-cred black by a mean cartel of uniforms. They were encrusted with enough badges to subdue a college of semiologists.

'Surfers,' Millom glossed, 'we're pretty hot on them in Leyton. These new trains can get up to fifty or sixty miles per on the clear stretch after Stratford: the drivers call it a "running road", gave it the bullet, then hit the brakes – late. Always shake a few woolly-heads out of the trees: we hand out a bit of a pasting, confiscate their footwear – they *hate* that – and turn 'em loose to limp back to their six-in-the-bed drug dens. They never learn, born ignorant, it's in the blood. Myself, I'd wire the train roof, turn up the juice, make 'em hop a bit. It's what they're good at. Am I wrong?'

The 'surfing' craze was a Brazilian import, that was taking a lot faster than Mirandinha in Newcastle. A real smack substitute: you mounted in Ongar or Woodford, caught the wave for the long skate to Snares-brook; felt the ripple in your spine, heard the wind talk – all the way to Leytonstone. You are *out there*, balancing on the lid of the snake, the power under your feet; swaying, jolting, snorting the colour, staying with it.

There were never more than three or four deaths a week: a few losers bottled out and grabbed for the overhead wires. They fried to a crisp; or suffered the harsher option – a disability ticket on the minibus.

It didn't take a detective to notice that Millom disapproved of most human activities, especially those involving more than one party, and the requirement of conversing in anything above a whisper. He had the soapy skin, the trembling handshake, and the averted eyes of an inveter-ate self-starting wrangler of picture books. Yet something told me that this was not the case. There was nothing wrong with Millom's sight; he examined me like a magistrate. No; he was way beyond the reach of *any* form of orgasm. His sex life, if we must consider it, resembled that of an unmutated cephalopod.

He scrutinized me, rapidly, missing no peculiarity of the scuffed boots, the rancid cords, the failed-its-first-autopsy jacket. He visibly flinched; decided he could expect nothing better from a writer; snorted, and limped off, flourishing what I took to be his swordstick.

The station stood on a mound that afforded a superb view of an enormous burial ground, a vision: thickets of white crosses, gardens of bone-trees, winged angels anchored to granite plinths. A mute army of the Catholic dead waited to be summoned; a snow harvest blazed to the borders of Wanstead.

'My digs,' Millom acknowledged, pointing to a window smothered in wedding-dress net, above an Indian pharmacy on the corner of Calderon Road. But that was not where we were going. I trailed in his wake, taking breath by admiring the clusters of lilac, lime, and virgin pink that riotously fruited around the doorways: the nuts, pines, and grapes. 'Personalized' flourishes burst from the closet in a scream of genetically-risky varnishes. The dim terrace sung out loud against the morbid oppressiveness of its fixed location.

'Ever read him yourself?' Millom's tight-lipped sneer came back at me, like smoke from a crematorium. 'Calderon? *The Surgeon of Honour*? Tell you why later, and you'll understand. Honour, my friend, is something I set my stall by. Am I wrong? It may have gone out of fashion, but this Calderon person knew all about it. When I saw his play – down Walthamstow, at the College – I got that very special feeling, you follow me? I knew what was coming: I could have written the thing myself, take away the language.'

I could not believe what I was hearing. It was like eavesdropping on Charles Manson, and catching a dissertation on the troubadour poets. (Indeed, it was even *more* spooky. Sooner or later someone in San Quentin is bound to turn Manson on to Ezra Pound. The rest follows.)

'A Spanish Duke of some kind, a nob, discovers that the King's brother has taken a shine to his wife, right?' Millom hadn't finished yet. His statements were cast as questions: the stunned silence of his audience was interpreted as a tacit collaboration. 'Honour must be preserved, right? Say what you like about the wops, they know about honour. There's your Mafia, your Falangists, your Inquisition: *omerta*, silence. Am I wrong?'

Millom pinned me against a privet hedge, pumping with his finger, as if he was chopping cabbages. I was forced to nod, disguising a yawn as a gasp of admiration.

'Anyway, see, this Duke, Don Gutierre, follow me? You're a writer, a literary man – what am I telling you? Falklands War? Yes? I don't have to spell it out. You're getting the picture. The Duke speaks to the woman, his wife – but in *the voice of the bloke who wants to give her one*, the King's own brother. He's got her. Am I wrong? Traps the cow. *Not* her fault? And some! If she's been had, *even in mind*, if an illegitimate party has *imagined* himself doing it – you with me? – she's soiled, damaged, ruined. She's no good to him any more. *His* honour is tainted. Right? Know what he does?'

Calderon Road had given way, with a good grace, to North Birbeck; from which source, doubtless, further anecdotes, allusions, and portents would flow. It looked like being a long hard afternoon. North Birbeck had its pretensions: it fronted the burial grounds. There were windows tricked out with bull's-eye glass: hideaways for the better class of vet, and a few under-qualified abortionists. We jumped from the safety of the pavement to dodge through a flotilla of black stretch limos, in which mourners struggled fitfully to freeze solemn expressions while enjoying their rare outing in fan-blown luxury. We shadowed them through the portentous gates of St Patrick's Roman Catholic Cemetery.

My path was blocked by Millom's upraised cane. 'He doesn't kill the King's brother, does he? No need for that. *He employs a blindfolded surgeon to bleed the woman to death.* Very astute. The King gives him a commendation and furnishes him with a bran'-new wife, a *virgin*.'

We plunged, unguided, into a spinney of plaster arms – raised in surrender like an abandoned winter army: bladed wings, crucified midgets. We were soon lost among negative forests of exiled Poles (*Bors, Tomczak, Balawender, Pitera, Pelc, Sieczko*); colonies of replanted Italians with sad sepia photographs, albums of grief; cellars of Irish, dismissed Republican taskforces.

'A blindfolded surgeon bleeds her to death, wonderful!' Millom was furiously revolving the tip of his swordstick among the crust of leaves. I expected a wisp of smoke to rise from the frozen ground. 'Drop by drop, razor cut by razor cut; he describes her – leeches her from life. Takes the heat out of her. Irritates her skin with expectations of pleasure. Am I wrong? An adultery of slow wounds, a salty painless sleep. Imagine the succeeding chain of ecstasies that rolled through her dreams. That's what the Whitechapel butcher was after. He wanted to bleed their fallen natures, let time drain the corruptions. But he was always interrupted; they harried him. He became frantic, botched the job. You understand? These things can only unfold in an ordered society. You can't force the pace of a culture. It took thousands of years for Rome to evolve. Yes?'

This narrative was, I felt, beginning to take a dangerous turn. Millom's agitation was increasingly seismic. He was being cannibalized by his own metaphors. His breath came in rasping seizures, gusts of recycled aniseed. His starched white cuffs were flashing mirror-gauntlets; as he jerked and jabbed and twisted. The rusting dog-fox hairpiece slithered on his moist scalp, ready to make a run for it. Suddenly, and without warning, he drew the blade from its narrow sheath and drove it into the earth, a couple of inches from my boot: an uneasy moment.

'You're standing on her,' Millom whispered, relishing the theatrical effect, 'the final victim! A girl of twenty-five, a beauty; *Prima Donna*, the whores called her. She was left without a cup of blood in her entire body. It has been revealed to me that the man who did this thing drank it, believing it would make him invisible. And *I know* who that man was. Or "is", because I'll tell you something else for nothing – *he's still alive*! He punished himself with immortality. You understand? The last ritual *was* successfully completed.'

By reflex, I looked straight down – ready to meet the dead girl's accusing stare. The grave was freshly dug, blanketed in red and white carnations, on which an inverted crucifix had been carelessly tossed. There was a splendid new headstone, listing badly to port – as if someone (in escaping from the earth?) had tried to pull it over: *The Prima Donna of Spitalfields. And Last Known Victim of Jack the Ripper. Do Not Stop to Stand and Stare Unless to Utter Fervent Prayer. (Mary Magdalene Intercede.) Dedicated by John Millom, 3 December 1988.*

'I had her moved. Dug out from a paupers' pit and placed here; beside the ground I have already reserved for my own interment – when the time comes. Am I wrong?'

The man was obviously moved by the enormity of the implications he had floated. Pulling a vast scarlet handkerchief from his breast pocket, he trumpeted ostentatiously. I averted my eyes in shame. Frosty silver trains were rattling and shuddering beyond the graves; defining the perimeters of the dead in a shower of sparks, hobbling the ghosts with thin fire.

John Millom was kneeling. Thinking himself unobserved, he dug his hands into the turned soil – and filled his pockets with damp clay.

V

The cheesy net curtains did nothing to filter out the inhuman entropy of High Road, Leyton; an embolic flutter of muddied Transits, partially resprayed Cortinas, and an angry boil of citizens scouting for the first rumours of the bus pack. The street had no evident purpose, beyond proving the Third Law of Thermodynamics ('Every substance has a limited availability of energy ...').

Millom's apartment smelt sour, unused: he had rented a ledger of unfranked slights, and half-digested resentments. The furniture was impregnated with ancestral flatulence (bad meat, verruca'd potatoes, cabbage boiled to a nappy-like consistency): it asserted a strident eagerness to be elsewhere. Grossly fragrant vapours, rising through the Axminster from the Pharmacy beneath, did nothing to sweeten the atmosphere. They suggested experiments with feline essences and mouth-violets intended to disguise the more active stinks of chicken vindaloo and illegal chemistry. Everything Millom owned was accounted for and in its place: unloved. A lighter touch was provided by the cloth-texture reproductions in their ornate frames (obviously ordered 'sight unseen', or left behind by some previous tenant).

The room described a reversed *L*, or mason's square (the Egyptian 'foot' hieroglyph); taking in views of Calderon Road to the north, and the High Road to the west. The proportions were unsettling, tending to slip and drift: a lozenge with a single shrine-invoking focus. I perched on the rim of a leatherette chair, struggling to repel its alarmingly adhesive embrace. At any moment the points of the golden compasses would close like chopsticks, and I would vanish into the only 'window' open to me: John Millom's emblematic map.

This scroll, or chart, dominated the east wall and had taken, so he said, three years to assemble. It was a socio-alchemical portrait of Whitechapel; featuring, of course, events from the autumn and early winter of 1888. They spiralled in ropes of demented imagery from a sulphurous heliocentric furnace: a Sun-Father. The words were engraved with marker pen on a marly field. Victim faces, hacked from magazines, were imposed on the courts and furtive alleys: heads bigger than houses, black eyes like dew-ponds. A rash of sticky heat raised these transfers of redundant obsession: names became stars, became pentacles; trees were swords. The circumference was cut by a scarlet thread drawn from the fixed point of the steeple of Christ Church, Spitalfields. The craftsman's own interpretations and comments were too intemperate to await some anecdotal occasion: they blazed free. '*I SAY TO SCOTLAND YARD: WHY PRETEND TO FORGET YOUR OWN LIES? Knight picked the WRONG GODFREY. WHO has the KEY???*'

'Like it?' Millom smiled, proudly. 'Now you can see I know what I'm talking about. It's all clear. Right? I learnt how to lay out information effectively when I ran a crack sales team. My time, your money. Am I wrong? We ate it up: Loughton, Chingford, Billericay, Stanford-le-Hope; west as far as Enfield, even Potters Bar. Heating equipment, bathroom suites, brassware, sanitary ware, boilers, tanks, polypipes, plastic plumbing systems: we handled the lot. Just get your basics right, I used to drive the message home. *GOTH*: Gather, Order, Transform,

Harmonize. Then, when they'd proved they could cope with responsibility, I'd slip them a big one – *JAH*: Jettison, Assert, Hazard. Take risks. No pain, no gain. Am I wrong?'

He stood back, mesmerized by the enormity of his achievement, ogling the chart with dubious paternal pride. It was, like all the other 'treated' rooms I had encountered, a map of nothing but its maker's brain. For these people, there was no 'outside'. Their rooms were works of fiction that fought to quell, through partial confession, the vessels of wrath. My very own job description.

'I always told them at group meetings,' Millom blathered on, 'remember *JAH*. Number One: Jettison. Cut out inessentials; fall-guys, stoolpigeons, false accusations. Number Two: Assert. Put down the *facts* in the clearest possible way. Dates, times, locations. Number Three: Hazard. Don't be timid, don't be bamboozled by so-called "experts", with their mouths full of language. The man we want couldn't have been more down-to-earth: he had a practical solution to a practical problem. Am I right? He was a pragmatist. I'm telling you. My solicitor is one hundred per cent behind me on this one. Won't stand still for any loose talk about "Royals" or "Secret Societies". All anarcho-socialist long-hair propaganda.' He tapped the side of his nose in a gesture that trembled with import.

'Reach under the red carpet and you'll soon get your fingers around our circumcised friend, the ringleted Israelite, unpicking the woof of an ordered society: exclude him at your peril. Marx, Trotsky, Rosa Luxemburg; Charlie Chaplin, he was half-Jewish, a Comintern agent. They kicked him out of America. Am I wrong? My solicitor doesn't think so. He holds duplicates, in his safe, of all the Protocols. Anything happens to me – he has his instructions.'

I wanted to pursue the matter of the key (???), for some reason it haunted me. (I suppose I was still thinking of Davy Locke's sunstreak epiphany.) But it was not easy to put Millom, in his cuff-twitching, finger-jabbing flow, on hold.

'Key? Key?' he pursed his lips in a vinegar pout of denial; trying to cover up the guilty words on his chart with a damp and boneless hand. 'The Jews didn't find out about that, did they? Your media czars – Bernstein, Weidenfeld, Lew Grade, Victor Gollancz – they're all in it. You won't see the key on the television with Michael Caine, will you? Am I wrong?' He slid open a drawer and took out a cigarette packet from which he extracted something wrapped in tissue paper.

'This was the pass key, made from a corset-spring, with which the man I am not yet at liberty to name picked the lock of the private madhouse and escaped into the streets. I acquired it, through mutual associates, from an official, no longer employed by the hospital: a favour for a favour, so to speak.'

I looked at the meagre object, which seemed hopelessly inadequate for the task of carrying its burden of iconic signification. It was more of a fish-hook than an implement of power. It lay, unactivated, on the occasional table: a symbol with nothing to symbolize. I tried to bury myself in the unyielding chair, to escape Millom's presence: the engorged veins, the carmine flush coursing through the unripe pallor like an over-administered hit of embalming fluid. He was holding his breath, sucking in the flaps of his cheeks, preparatory to some momentous announcement.

'You've shown you know when to keep silent,' said Millom, with a choreic twitch of approval (as if I'd had any choice in the matter!), 'now I will return the compliment and let you have first sight of the document you will publish on my behalf. But I must make one thing absolutely clear before you read it: though every word is transcribed in my holograph, *I did not write it.* It was dictated to me – by the one person who could have known, without dispute, the full secret of the Whitechapel Murders. I have used my own methods to "go over", cross the line, make contact. I have been granted access to the voice of that lovely young girl, the victim of the locked room, the madonna of that oven of meat. She will speak to you through my hand.'

The lights had come on in the High Road: Millom stood before me, continuing to demonstrate the progressive degeneration of his basal ganglia. He jerked like a pantomime demon: black-browed, corvine, streaked by the lurid beams of rush-hour traffic. The seediness of the situation was intolerable, but my criminal curiosity stifled all repulsion: I accepted his bundle of blue lined paper, unknotted the pink rose ribbon, and began to read.

VI

The Prima Donna's Tale
(As transcribed by John Millom, Calderon Road, 1/1/89)

I had not, I think, been dead beyond two or three months when I dreamed of the perfect murder. Perfect? No, hardly that – inevitable; pure in design and execution. My murder would be an exercise of memory: I would recover something that had, perhaps, never taken place, and I would *make* it happen. Now the past could be whatever I wanted it to be. I had surely earned that right. My power was absolute.

I saw the outline of a girl's body, frosted with unstable light. I saw my own double, kneeling sadly over that body, then moving into the shadows.

A cracked window pane. Muslin belling over a chair-back. The guttered stub of a candle in a broken wine glass. Something shapeless and made from felt smouldering in the open grate.

The room was an oven. But the smell was of incense, not of meat.

I couldn't hold any impression of the girl's face; dark hair was drawn across her throat like a wound. She would certainly have been called 'handsome', 'strong-bodied', 'gay'. But she had turned awkwardly, her legs raised as if for the stirrups. I do not know her, nor do I understand why she condones such abject and degrading poses.

An east wind blusters the powdered snow through a congregation of deformed angels: their names are gone, their faces are without features. They press heavily on the frozen cloth of earth, inhibiting the drowsing dead: those who lack the courage to dream.

A shower of sparks from an engineless train, breaking before the icy station: a platform of chilled and stamping travellers. They have forgotten us. Our desires cannot trouble the banality of their thoughts. Snow faintly falling, like the descent of their last end; unnoticed, unrecorded. Oak and elm, a chaplet of heartsease. Memory anticipates event. A clear, young voice, beyond the courtyard: 'Only a violet.' It is too late. There is nothing to revenge. A dream to be shaped. Dreamt again, perfected. I move in that dream, I float on its surface. Once more I am sitting at the window, awaiting his step on the cobblestones. I have no power to change the order of the ritual.

This was the best time, the preparation. Self-absorbed, my actions mirrored my intentions: an uninstructed immediacy. There was no anticipation of pleasure, nor dread of failing to provoke an interest. Brushing and rebrushing my hair, half-remembered words of some song. In the elbow-chair, a heavy rug over my knees. From the window, the world at an angle: across the court, a bare wall. Or running my cold fingers over the shape of my own face, making it into a mask of glass. Letting the act collapse into the memory of the act. Bare-legged. A green linsey wrap. Tapping my nail on the sill. Warmed, lit from behind by the glow of a coal fire.

The resonance of a church bell runs a prophetic tremor along the board floor; a warning step, uneven on the cobbles. A single knock.

The door is opened, I do not move; yellow suede gloves of his manservant. Hair oil and horse ordure. 'I shall return, sir, upon the hour.' High, mud-spattered boots.

His hand, then, lifted; out in front of him, grey cotton; stretching to touch me – so lightly – on the cheek. Paternal. To confirm my agreement, to implicate me. His leather travelling bag is abandoned on the floor; hideous, a mastiff with its limbs amputated. Or, a soft pouch for transporting bees. He turns, turns from me to bolt the door. The key to the room is his; the knock a sham: another of his subtle cruelties. He does not speak.

She stood in the centre of the room while he undressed her with his gloved hands. A foliage of flame, fern tongues, disturbed the grate: a demented tangle of blades. Crippled shadows, across the wall, uniting them in urgent and repeated acts.

She sat in the elbow-chair, waiting; he selected a pair of intricately laced boots from the cupboard. Nothing is said. Mumbled threats, instructions. The heavy cloth of his coat pressing on her, greasy with spilled food, old smoke.

Then he was at the window, worrying a corner of grey muslin between his finger and his thumb. She was on her knees, water steaming from the spout of an old black kettle: washing him. They were helpless, without breath, sunk in their poses – when the knock came. They were drowned.

An unyielding hand upon his elbow. The blind surgeon is led away. Out of the court, through the warren, and across the highway to the lit building, the source of his power. The opera house of all her dreams.

It could have continued indefinitely. I do not remember how it began or how long it endured, who had initiated the affair, or who had set its terms. Our meetings succeeded one another with the remorselessness of a black letter text. So long ago, so far back; voices beyond the court were calling to the shore. Sparks from the train, like fire-sprites released from a shattered stone; like sun-specks on water. Abandoned. Forgotten. My consciousness divided, bound, tied in brown paper parcels: jogging on a one-horse cart towards some mortuary shed.

There were times when it was *his* pleasure to sprawl in the elbow-chair, my linsey over his knees, my reflection beyond him in the grime of the window, my long hair a wig to his glistening white skull. He required me to brush him, powder him, to gently stroke the pulse in his temples. There were times when he fell to his knees – as in a seizure – clasping my foot to his lips, an alabaster gull chipped from a fallen monument; his dry mouth rubbing, a sand beetle in a nest of dead twigs.

It could have continued, it did, the years, ageing together, ghost-tryst, shadows miming desire in a house of the dead, a museum of trapped reflexes: masked, we enacted obscure rituals.

I understudied my own mythology; I was withdrawn, I surprised him, inspiring the grossest intimacies. My hands behind my head, beyond him, I lay on a bare mattress, plunged back into the current that ran through my bones, dragging him on to me, his beard-splintered skull down upon my belly. I learned to split the ceiling, to prise open the roof-tree, let the star threads cut my brain into Platonic segments. Babylonian histories swept over me: brass and thorn and crocodile. There was neither contentment, nor suffering. He moved only as I caused him to move. It could have continued, if I had not known from the beginning that he was my father. He had no choice. He did not want me to live. He *had* to follow me into his own extinction.

The frozen field is compressed. The knock of a spade. Ice creases me. I am drawn up through the earth. I rest my chin upon my knees. Without sight, I am pure. The scratching of voles. Oak and elm protect me. My chaplet of heartsease is gone. I float in the dust of my own skin. Who is that standing over my bed? The plan forms: over the bare trees, the dark buildings, a vein in the clouds. From the lattice of old pains I infect myself once more with venereal promptings. From beyond my death, I am guided.

The surgeon's hand is become his emblem.

He entered; I crossed the room, barefoot – I slipped the bolt. He paused, uncertain. Divinatory shapes in a garden of flame; the decision was forming. I had oiled the lock, tried it, but still he was startled. Directly, I initiated the new ritual: he was suppressed, stiff, anxious. He submitted. Rigid spine, fists clenched; the struggle etched stern lines around his empty sockets. A Mosaic will troubled his flesh: the skin of a glove left too long in water.

I would anticipate the motives of his actions, I would forestall him. If he lost his certainty he would no longer be my father. I would not have to kill him. The close walls rub my shoulders, powder me in fine bone dust. It is an obscene wedding, a blasphemy. The grey muslin bells around my nakedness. His black coat is grassed by firelight. The gold ring is my virtue.

Water has been boiled, it has cooled. I pour it carefully into a blue stone bowl, spilling no drop of it. The salt runs through my fingers in a vortex. I stir the surface of the water, setting the flow against the direction of the sun. Against nature.

I kept him standing where he was. Slowly I removed his coat, waistcoat, chains, cuffs, collar, the long cotton shirt. I laid out his things upon the table. An altar of offerings, touched by him, warmed with use. The turnip-watch had a seal and a red stone hanging from it. There was a key, a cigar cutter, some coins. I spotted his pale skin with water. I circled him, four times, dipping my fingers into the bowl. Four times I touched him.

He flinched, twisting, helpless, towards the direction from which he would be marked. Forehead, base of spine, liver, heart.

Behind him: I pressed myself against his back, my chemise between us, his as much as mine. My lips to his neck, whispering, whispering the names. I held him. My strength flowed out of me. Our veins were opened. My finger raced, rapidly, over his ribs. His nipples stiffened. I bound his wrists, lacing his thumbs together: a split sex.

He wanted, then, to turn. But I would not allow it. He was engorged; the thick vein pulsing in his neck. He was a painted statue. I saw the salt burn in him, his skin tightening to crystal scales. He was crowned with wild light. Priest, lion, sacrifice.

That autumn the skies over the city were scarlet, the market buildings and the tenements standing against them: plague islands. High windows were stained with this fire and the derelicts babbled millennial threats. It was the right time; I drained him, I milked his venom. The tower of the church, white ashlar blocks, was Egypt. His mouth was dry – he cried out – his tongue black: locusts. I fed him, dripping the salted water from the nipple of my finger. My tongue went into his mouth like a fish that becomes a knife. I wanted to slash his vocal cords, to make him speechless as well as blind. I wanted to give him rubies instead of eyes. To wrap him like a pharaoh.

Thunder shattered the mirror. A slate. Each segment, a forbidden syllable.

The hour had expired, his man was at the door. Yellow glove on the claw of the handle. A subtle pressure at his elbow. The surgeon hesitated, turning his great dim head towards me: a ceremonial ram caught in a thicket. My back was to him, I faced the fogged window. He was led away, slipping on the cobbles, unprotected, his face brushing through old sacks. This evening's victim was already naked on the cutting bench. Hiss of naphtha.

Sleeves rolled to the elbow, he washes; the audience is seated, expectant, the blade is placed in his hand. Twice as long as the neck is wide, without flaw. No break in its perfected edge.

Now he *cannot* leave my room. Stretched upon my bed, his hands behind his neck, his breath slow: out of his element. There is only light as we remember it. His man fidgets in the yard, muttering of appointments, digging at his groin.

Red incense in a brass mortar; smoke like the visible traces of an unheard sound. He loses all orientation. His man is dismissed, with no interval set for his return. Smoke scarfs the surgeon's face, eroding his individuality – unsexing him. It is warm, it insinuates; it whispers. He seems to be on fire. The smoke connects him to the brass mortar. It is without origin.

She is moving, barefoot, circling; white chemise. Man without eyes, her equal. A night when neither sun nor moon are to be found. She has painted a tree of bones over his spine. And he is made to lie upon her bed, his face to the open sky. The incense is pure. It takes his breath.

She is moving, all around him: the names. He is not aroused; stretched out, his length upon her bed. He rests on the painted tree, the tree of bones: it supports him.

One ceremony became another. The first ceremony – the stirring of salt, and of water – was repeated. His skin drying to leather. He sleeps. Oak and elm. Beyond the courtyard, a girl's voice, 'Only a violet I plucked for my Mother's Grave.' Each new beginning brought something fresh to the ritual; was, in its turn, absorbed and transformed. He is partly conscious, conscious for part of the time. The hospital was another life; a fiction, an excuse. Duties, rewards: a wife somehow implicated in his guilt, broken. Memories, pre-visions of a crime that has to be committed: a terrible act that remains *just* beyond the horizon; a service, an unavoidable savagery ...

His visits to her were restricted: thirty-seven visits, thirty-seven ceremonies. The incense of salt. The smoke. The smoke erasing detail from time, making the room a cell, drawing the walls in against his shoulders. Always circling. The same names, whispered. She unrolls a flint blade from a wrapping of felt. She marks him. The knife is his own. Now there are only eleven blades on the surgeon's desk.

She pressed him from behind. She held him until her life was his life. Her pulse in his wrist. Now her hands have acquired his skills. He is handless. They lie together in darkness. She is alone, dead leaves scratching on the lid of her coffin, flakes of disturbed alabaster: the heavy door to the mortuary shed is locked and chained. An east wind rushing among the chipped effigies. Snow falling. It lay thickly drifted on the crooked crosses and headstones. She sees with his skin.

Oak and elm. Dull wheels ringing through the packed black earth. Earth in her throat. The shiver of root hairs. Who are these men standing over my bed? Mud feet across the slope of the sky. Dreaming, open-eyed, of a murder that is not a crime. She is dreaming his dream. He has absorbed her anger, and her strength. He will act for her and *condemn himself beyond all hope of remission*.

Seasons, years, a century; bones into sand. He was young, he was moist. Weed-flowers breaking through the cobbles, splitting the black stone slabs. The church tower overbalances, topples towards him: a crisis, moral vertigo, a new fear. The tower is flint: *shechita* blade, white ashlar blocks. And now – as he rests in the elbow-chair, at the fogged window, worrying the grey muslin between his finger and his thumb – she covers his eyes with her hands. Trust. Warm, fresh bread. Clay. She draws them, suddenly, back. No warning. And he is pained. With light. The chamber streams with uncurtained brightness.

There was no hope for him this time. The serrated brilliance of snow. *The pain!* The white angels. The chipped and mutilated congregation of the dead, the witnesses. Casually severed fingers, fallen into the slush, are carried deeper into the undergrowth by disappointed scavengers. A thought fox, an outcast. Brambles bleed the plaster ankles.

Undefended outlines. Ghosts of objects that have disappeared from his memory. Unnamed shapes that he cannot use. He is driven back upon the bed, an ice hand cupping his heart – drawing it from him, a virgin's lantern. His breath screams. He is drowning in silt. Choking. Yellow blood. A snow of muslin.

She is forcing the slit of his bag. She has all the bright instruments; the secret tools, forbidden implements of power. The touching sticks. The bones of chrome. The perfected edges. *His* knowledge. She has leeched him of his will. But she cannot *see* these hieratic weapons. She can know them only by stitching her eyes, by moving in the thick certainty of darkness. This ceremony is the re-enchantment of life. The scalpel follows the heat-path of the scarlet tracings she has already inflicted upon his white skin.

The threads of his being are drawn out from his belly. He must reclaim the dream that was her existence. She is no longer trapped in his story, like a fly in amber. He is quite ignorant, he does not know her. He is effaced by a sudden scatter of snow. An unrecorded effigy on a dissenting tomb. His small heart. His heart-bird lifts. The threads are unpicked; he is scattered. The moisture of life. Her lips press against his wounds.

She looks from, and she rests in, the prescient socket of his eye.

She holds, in her hands, the womb – in which she should have been conceived: she is reborn. A dream of life. A key turning in a well-oiled lock.

In the elbow-chair, bare-legged. The glow of dissatisfied embers. Black kettle with a transmuted spout. Something shapeless and made from felt is smouldering in an open grate. The guttered stub of a candle in a broken wine glass. A cracked pane in the window, cold air belling the muslin. She wraps herself in darkness. The room closes on her; she has no further need of it. The intensity of that single moment scorches her lips. There is nothing more to say. The shadow of the church tower falls uselessly across an empty chair.

'Murder – Horrible Murder!' Shout at the dead. The door, bolted from the inside, is broken down: the servant (blood on his gloves), men in uniform, neighbours, barking dogs. A gay woman, an unfortunate – disembowelled. Throat cut to the spinal cord, kidney on thigh, flesh stripped from the ankles. *Horror!* Lock it, seal it, bury all trace.

Where is the surgeon? Gone, vacant: an empty house. Seizure? Madness. He is confined: there is no life in him. He stares into a frozen fishpond, his mouth agape. Toothless, spoiled. He is absorbed in a cup of cold water. He exists only in the vapour of the clouds racing through the high windows. Where? Anywhere, nowhere. Leytonstone. Whipps Cross.

Footsteps on the cobblestones, and a single knock at her door. The dream of a perfect murder fades.

VII

Beneath the odd, parchment-shaded lamp, a meniscus of pale light: the room quilted in bulky darkness. The bundle of blue papers has stuck to my hands in a single block, heavy as stained glass, interleaved with lead. Millom's face is bestial. He insinuates, whispers, rasps: fixes me with his sunken, chalk-rimed eyes. His fleshy lower lip shivers in a mime of humour. He is amused. He leans over; his buffed pike-teeth glinting voraciously. White hands break free of his cuffs, to flap around the lamp, as he signals his triumph. 'Gotcha!' He has implicated me in horror, infected me with a small corruption from which there is no immunity.

'You understand the nature of her triumph? Yes?' Millom preached, determined to poison the silence with a redundant afterword. 'It was *indifference*: "surviving death through death". The blind surgeon wanted something that excited him more than honour, more than sanity, more even than life. He wanted the one crystal absolute she denied him – yes, apathy; he wanted it so much he was prepared to pass over the borderline of identity, become her, and suffer her vengeance *within her flesh*.'

No. I didn't want to be drawn into giving mind to this fiction, but it seemed to me that Millom was wrong, completely wrong. As wrong as it is possible to be. I repudiated his terms: 'vengeance', 'apathy'. I could only read the crucial 'exchanges' between the woman and the surgeon in terms of the madness of love-death – the 'little deaths' of physical ecstasy. Within this tale, the woman exploits those out-of-the-body post-coital experiences, where both partners become the loved one and the lover: the metaphysical poets' mingling of souls. Through the focus of repeated ritual acts the woman infiltrates the surgeon/father's consciousness – so that, when the inevitable moment comes, she takes responsibility for her own death; leaving him with nothing, an achieved emptiness.

'The woman, the woman,' Millom twitched on. He was talking to himself. Without having 'written' anything, he found himself an author. His performance was magisterial in its self-deceit. 'The woman *allowed* the surgeon to enact the deed that was his inescapable destiny. She could not change the events of history, but only the meaning. In the freedom of death, she used her more potent memory, her older soul, to avenge herself by trapping the killer in the seductive mirror of her youthful skin. His sightless blunder damned him. His act of sacrificial slaughter, releasing her (as he thought) from an inherited taint, was, in fact, the very movement that brought him down, crushed his over-weening pride. You follow me now? He is the man, and he is still "alive". He has no need of a name; his identity is transferable, so he's immortal. He wanders the city, seeking out the fatal woman, like a benign host desperate for the only satisfying plague bacterium – the one that is fatal. Hopelessly, in drinking clubs and hotel bedrooms, he feels the contours with his trembling hands, face after face after face, search-ing for his own earlier self, his woman soul. He is prepared to commit any crime to avoid the dreadful ceremonies that have *already taken place*.'

Millom brought his jerky moth-catching hands together in a clap of self-satisfaction: he sealed the circle of morbid light. 'Am I wrong? Only the dead have the time adequately to revenge themselves. Their sense of honour is older than the sun; but the damage they inflict upon the dream of their lives is terrible. They die in obedience to some posthumous whim.'

It may have been the unconvinced nature of the light in this room, or some failure of nerve among my retinal fibres, but it now appeared that the manuscript sheets had lost their colour: the lines had faded and the blue escaped. Millom's double-spaced, tightly controlled Italic script had narrowed, spidered, speeded into an over-familiar black scrawl; a sequence of Bic-incisions intended for decoding by the author alone. *The manuscript was in my own hand.* The writing of this tale had nothing to do with Millom, nor with the 'Prima Donna of Spitalfields'. It is mine: lost or suppressed. But I have no memory of its composition. The risks were too great. I had sworn to finish with all this compulsive nightstuff. I locked the story away, and dropped the key into the canal. How then had it come into Millom's hands? If he was 'communicating' with anyone it was not the dead. I discounted the possibility that he (or his agents) had simply broken into my house and stolen these papers, from among all the stacks of ruin. Could John Millom have evolved some psychic 'fax' machine, the ability to invade my sleep? Was it possible that I functioned, in some ugly, involuntary way, as a scribe to the worst of the sites that I was foolish enough to visit?

I knew that, *whatever the price*, I would have to carry the bundle away from this place and destroy it. The thing was too volatile. It must never be published. The bargain it represented was no longer one I was prepared to honour. I clawed myself, frantically, out from the hissing leatherette chair.

Millom put his hand against my chest. I was relieved to find that it did not pass directly through the mantle of flesh. He signalled for me to follow him.

'I have a gift already prepared for you. Take it when you go, but be sure not to open it until you are safely back indoors.'

I agreed eagerly, intending to drop whatever it was, sight unseen, into the nearest bin. Millom blocked my path and – swivelling on his heels – opened a door which led into what might have been a bedroom. He scratched at the walls, looking for a light switch. Nothing had prepared me for this.

I would not cross the threshold. I remained outside, staring into a chamber of blasphemy, from which escaped bands of stifling air, the low smoke of wet leaves burning. Millom, in a palsied dance of celebration,

waved the corset-spring key in my face. This, I realized, was the heart of
the matter, the revelation he was desperate to share.

'Shaped,' he whispered, 'like the Egyptian character for *neter*, the one
supreme God; this insignificant metal tool activates the entire operation.
Its outline describes the passage through which we travel to communi-
cate with the world of spirits.'

The only spirits I was interested in, at that moment, were in a bottle. I
needed a stiff pull before I could take another step. But nothing of the
sort was on offer. The floor of the room was divided into lettered
squares; in its centre was a circular raised platform, a table masquerading
as a bed. Placed, obviously, at the four cardinal points were narrow-
lipped jars, filled with something dark, earth or ashes. Millom now
reached into his jacket pocket and – ceremoniously – added the latest
graveyard transfusion to the eastern jar. Silver wires ran from these
earth-batteries, across the canopy of the bed, to a gilded ring, a serpent
swallowing its own tail; on which Millom laid the key. The canopy
itself was a grey and lumpy conglomerate: rags of faded cloth, ribbons,
dried flowers, hair curls, maggoty earth-meat. *A body had been shaped*
from pillaged clay, dressed in wisps of net; wigged, laced, booted.
Sufficient space had been left on this necrophile altar for the unthinkable
implication that Millom himself would lie beside his mud-bride in a
form of vermicular marriage.

'With this key,' Millom said, 'the dead man, whose rituals ensured
both his invisibility, and his immortality, escaped from the asylum.
Without memory, or a past, he paddled over the marshes, to pass
unremarked among the houses and the traffic of East London. He left
behind his pentacle of victims – not as a barrier warding off future evils,
but as an achieved act of occult geometry, sealing the secrets of that
room for ever.'

The burial place had been physically shifted, cup by cup, from the
cemetery into Millom's chamber. He had dug his nails into corruption:
listening attentively while his mind split, and branched into previously
untested chapters of madness. This self-recording conjurer was trapped,
under a carapace of hysterical conformity, in degradation. He personi-
fied all the furtive impulses of his time and his city. Like a ruthless
bibliophile, he collected dead whispers. He walled himself in bad faith,
in fantasies of decay. He attempted to demonstrate with his septic wax
tableau, the ultimate extension of horror. He had earned the right of
becoming, in his own words, 'one of us'.

If the council had provided a litter bin anywhere between Calderon Road and the station I would certainly have dumped the whole loathsome parcel straight into it. It wasn't an item to chuck in the street, or to jettison on an innocent doorstep, along with the milk bottles. ('Must be the new telephone directory, dear.') And so, when the train halted in the tunnel, between Stepney Green and Whitechapel, and the lights began to flicker and dim, I make the excuse that I needed some intricate task to occupy my still trembling fingers.

I slashed the twine with my clasp knife (only slightly amputating my little finger), and unwound the stiff skirts of brown paper. I was left, after a short struggle, with nothing more alarming than a copy of my own novel, *White Chappell, Scarlet Tracings* (made 'safe' by the addition of a prophylactic glassine wrapper). By habit, I leafed through the opening salvo, taking a slightly guilty pleasure in the company of these refreshingly materialist monsters. The pages were virgin; mercifully untainted by Millom's attentions. The Bodonia paper was fresh as when it came from the hands of Sig. Mardersteig in Verona. But, with the introduction of William Withey Gull, a chronic dementia of red-ink annotations spattered the margins: '*NOT TRUE!!! Wordy evasions — grip the FACTS, boy. EVIDENCE? Stolen from other men's books.*' Revisions breed in the white spaces, feverishly overwriting the original version, to clarify some imagined authorial intention. Millom worked the pages like a speed-crazed collaborator. He was the uninvited Ford to my sullen Conrad.

The train labours, shivers, jerks; shudders a few yards forwards, stops. The lights go out. I am left in a comfortable darkness, polarized by those ever-active bulwarks of local history: the London Hospital and the Jewish Burial Ground. It is easy in this enforced silence to imagine the novel on my lap as a brick of impacted light: a freak reaction has converted the text into a pack of unrepressed images. They have a startling *bacterial* luminescence; giddy and dangerous. If I dared to turn the pages I know that I would reveal all the word-inhibited secrets: the steel engravings would begin to move, stone figures would shake off their shadows; white buildings would open their flaps to disperse the panicked basements. There would be a remission of violence.

When the lights came back on the book in my hand was a square of black cloth: the dustwrapper had slipped on its glassine hinge to reveal Millom's final critique; an effort coming as close, as his nature would allow, to a jest. He had pasted a reduced photocopy over the snapshot portrait my wife had taken for the rear flap: Tenniel's illustration of

Alice in the Train. The windows have been Tipp-Exed; Africa reduced
to a phantom. The linear whirlwind of the railway carriage is now a
radiant plaster skull – with Alice and the 'gentleman in white' clinging,
pathetically, to the zygomatic arches. They are the handles of a drinking
vessel, balanced in the symmetry of perpetual confrontation.

Millom knew from the start that I would open his parcel as soon as I
got on to the train. He had probably succeeded in 'withdrawing' enough
electricity to hold us in the tunnel. That was his message, or his warning.
But there is something else: bookworms, I can accept, but Millom's pun
is grossly literalist. A slithering sightless string-inch breasts the fore-edge
of the novel, like a Polish cartoon; wriggles free, drops on to the
tartan-covered seat. The heart of the book has been hollowed out, cut
away; scooped like melon-flesh. Millom has filled the wounded cavity
with contraband earth. Moist pink and grey things are knotting on the
carriage floor, covering my boots; multiplying. The shape of a key has
been pressed into the miniature grave.

IX

The spiteful pulsing of the rods in their frozen canisters became the
pulsing of Cec Whitenettle's heart. His hand squeezed gently on the
geared control. The power of the track travelled through him, so that
his hair turned to fire. He was the messenger of the immortal ones. His
softly lit cab did not move: it was the tunnel that rushed past him, a
hood of black velvet. He was restored, revived; he outpaced the darkness. Rodents scuttled to escape his bladed monster. The slanting walls
of the embankment washed over him in green waves. The train was a
water snake; it twisted and burrowed beneath the sleeping streets. It
absorbed the dream-jungles of all the sleepers. The streamlined observation window became the visor of a winged and wired helmet. Cec
listened to a scatter-speak of voices, living and dead: the controllers. It
had happened; he was himself the core of the fusion, the germinator of
the force he was riding.

It was only with the switch to the branch line, the plunge into the
Whitechapel burrow, that the old fears returned. Every night, without
fail, a red beast, a kind of deer, stood waiting for him on the curve. He
did not touch the brake, but always drove straight on – at it and through
it. He would not allow the creature's presence (or its meaning) to
trouble him. His cab was monitored: if the central computer showed
him slowing, anywhere, he would be surrounded in seconds by bala-
clava'd security-men, armed snatch-squads eager to redefine the 'rules of

engagement'. He would be rapidly converted to an unemployment statistic – waiting for his number to be called in some linoleum-carpeted retirement home; doped to the eyeballs, nodding through a remorseless procession of soap operas and advertisements; wetting himself.

Cec *knew* there was no living deer: no animal had been reported going over the fence from Victoria Park. The animal was a two-dimensional cartoon; lurid, sticky with varnish. It was the Roebuck of Brady Street, moonlighting from its pub-sign pasture. Now, apparently, even this mild territorial guardian was infected with panic, and obliged to understudy its own apocalypse. One of these days, Cec decided, he would confront his fear – go down the Roebuck, order a drink, sit with the Irish and the Maltese, talk about car auctions.

What did the quacks know anyway? Giving him placebos, coloured smarties, like some kid – pretending that would cure him. 'See how you go. Come back in a month, Mr Whitenettle. We can adjust the prescription.' Was it *reasonable*? Who would want to achieve marital intimacy when the whole world was dying? Do apes hump in their cages? Not bleeding likely: they wank themselves stupid. Cec had read all the relevant stuff himself, down the library. *Transient Global Amnesia*, *Automatism*, *Psycho-motor Epilepsy*: your hands can never break free from the controls because they are part of a circuit. A single fracture will destroy it all, lay waste the landscape. The power is in the machine. We have only to hang on, put all our trust in its deeper wisdom.

The roebuck is waiting for him. 'Hold up, you fucking Bambi. I'll have you.' The creature, for the first time, faces the train – head on: gone rogue, its eyes full of blood. Cec cannot break his grip. The harder he strains, the more power he releases. The engine bucks, leaps, rears. The track hisses like a punctured hose, heats to orange-white: the rails open like the ribs of a clattered Buddha. They are liquid spears of rage. Cec starts to laugh. It hurts his stiffened face. He is a jockey, a monkey mounted on a mad dog. It is no longer his affair. *Let* the train jump its brook; let it tumble down the perilous chasm between the banked windows of the hospital, with all its revenging monsters, and the eternally poisoned site of the first sacrificial murder.

Rattles the crossing: nothing now will halt the fire lizard. It will bury itself, beyond sight, on the far side of the buffers, the sand traps, in a dead-end tunnel: a drain for anguish. Excused by the formal density of madness, Cec lies on his back, smiling: the stones of London are his heaven, and they move. They slide. He will excavate remote sources of darkness. He is redundant, the train needs him no further: it will travel on, through yellow clay and blue rock, ferrying the solemn dead in search of incorruptible rivers.

X

Tattered and exhausted, Arthur Singleton, haunter of stations, prisoner of White Chappell, planned his escape from the treadmill of time. The field of his 'life force' was too weak to interest the cameras: undetected, he hooked his rope over the crossbar of the gantry that supported this spy system. Like a first-plunge swimmer, he lay groaning; then edged forward, ready to lower himself into the shallow abyss. One foot clung to the platform, the other searched for the neck of the roebuck. It was foretold: only the Triple Death of Llew Law Gyffes could release him.

From the deep pocket of his moss-stained overall Arthur drew out Count Jerzy's massive service revolver, stolen this night from behind the bar of The Spear of Destiny. Its cold barrel, greased and foreign, was inserted in a toothless mouth. He would pull the trigger at the moment of impact. As the train tossed him into the air, so would the rope from the gantry snap his neck; flying, he would squeeze his finger, in a come-hither reflex, spilling his brains into the night – like stars. The unwitnessed silence of his act would stand in place of Llew Law's 'terrible scream'. The falling gunge and the smoking pink cap would be one; an eagle in the dark. Arthur would, at last, get out from under the responsibility of myth. He would be nothing, nameless; *unrequired*.

The eye of the rapidly approaching monster filled the tunnel: it was scarlet, a steppewolf dribbling fire. It pawed the ground. Arthur knew that the engine was no machine, but a living thing. It was cloaked in vegetation, it was alive; rich with green leaves and secret veins. It was fruiting, streams of clear water ran from its side. The engine had transcended speed, arriving before it was understood: a torrent of fruitfulness, challenging wrath, carrying life and birth, deserts, storms; the jaguar and the stone. The ancient rubbled fields were scorched by a path of new light.

Arthur, in that instant, glimpsed his vanished river: it was unchanged. He did what never can be done, he stepped into it for the second time.

8

Art of the State
(*The Silvertown Memorial*)

Art of the State (*The Silvertown Memorial*)

'A lustreless protrusive eye
  Stares from the protozoic slime
At a perspective of Canaletto.
  The smoky candle end of time'

T. S. Eliot,
Burbank with a Baedeker: Bleistein with a Cigar

One morning ... the newspapers loud with her praise, the *Sun* in its heaven, banked television monitors floating a cerulean image-wash, soothing and silent, streamlets of broken Wedgwood crockery, satellite bin lids flinging back some small reflection of the blue virtue she had copyrighted, filmy underwear of sky goddesses, clouds of unknowing ... the Widow rose from her stiff pillows – bald as Mussolini – and felt the twitch start in her left eyelid. She ordained the *immediate* extermination of this muscular anarchy, this palace revolt: but without success. She buzzed for the valet of the bedchamber, a smiler in hornrims. He entered the presence with a deferential smirk, hands behind back (like a defeated Argie conscript), bowing from the hip: he was half a stone overweight, creaking with starch, and greedy for preferment. He disconnected the 'sleep-learning' gizmo, the tapes that fed the Widow her Japanese humour, taught the finer points of cheating at stud poker, and provided an adequate form forecast to the current camel-racing season. She was a brand leader, she did not sleep. 'A' brand leader? *The* leader, the longest serving politico-spiritual Papa Boss not yet given the wax treatment, and planted in a glass box to receive the mercifully filtered kisses of a grateful populace.

The golden curls were sprung and twisted, lacquered into their proper place. The valet held up the wig for her approval. She made her choice from a cabinet of warriors' teeth, toying between the chew-'em-up-and-spit-out-the-pips version and the infinitely more alarming smile-them-to-death set that the boffins never quite managed to synchronize with her eye-language. The Widow was a praise-fed avatar of the robot-Maria from *Metropolis*; she looked like herself, but too much so. The 'blend of Wagner and Krupp' (in Siegfried Kracauer's memorable phrase) had suffered a meltdown: it was gonzo, dangerous to its living soul and the souls of all other life-forms. She was a prisoner of the rituals she alone had initiated. If she ever appeared in her original skin the underclass would riot and tear her to pieces. And so she suffered the stinking baths of electrified Ganges mud (bubbling like Malcolm Lowry's breakfast), the horse-sized 'hormone replacement' shots. Even now the lab boys were grinding a fresh consignment of monkey testicles in the mixer. The eyedrops, the powder, the paint: she censored the morning radio bulletins. Not a breath of criticism, nor a whisper of forbidden names: all was analgesic 'balance', the cancellation of energy. Muzak for the hospitalized, garden notes for the dying. Jollity was unconfined; house-broken 'rogues with a brogue' winked and blarneyed, and sold. But *something* was not right.

She was a couple of years into her fifth term in what was now effectively a one-party state and a one-woman party – what *could* be wrong? True, there hadn't been a photogenic disaster for several weeks, a crash, a bombing, some dark débris-scattered location she could avoid – only to appear, phosphorescent with concern, a Marian blue manifestation, primed, lit from her good side, serene and comforting among the bedpans, eager to press the wound with a white-gloved hand: or again, severe with grief in tailored black, stilting on four-inch heels, at some well-guarded memorial service. Never, *never* (she had been advised), at the graveside: there must be no subliminal associations with mere mortality. 'Rejoice then!' she quoted the Bhagwan Shree Rajneesh with unironic relish. Ambulance chasing was a thing of the past. (There were no ambulancemen left to drive them.)

The Widow scuttled, lurched, towards the full-length mirror; a mother hen who has recognized a significant lump of her first born in the feeding tray – an eye perhaps, or a tine of red comb. She lifted her plump arms in a vague, archetypal gesture; flashing hazardous sharply jewelled knuckles, while the valet swooped with the Ladyshave and the environment-friendly roll-on. Her survivalist instincts, which some commentators felt were preternaturally acute, nagged: a nerve surfacing in a diseased molar. A fresh initiative was called for, a grander set of photo opportunities, a rallying cry: a lift from lethargy.

Perhaps she should summon a team of 'our' boys from Hereford to take out a few Paddys or stungun a Bedouin tent-show? But who was left with the clout to carry the front pages? It was counter-productive to sanction too many 'natural' disasters, to whistle up winds she could not bring to heel. The relatives tended to behave so badly, wailing and protesting, asking nanny for 'compensation': let them buy a share in the sewage racket. Palliative tele-prompts only muted the whingeing proles until the next share issue. There had even been whispers, brave and foolish (from the submerged wine bars of Stoke Newington), that she was not altogether innocent – how *dare* they think it – of her beloved Consort's death. He 'passed over', it is true, at a particularly flaky moment: the Widow's stock had dropped a couple of points in the wake of a Sophoclean chain of takeover scandals, buggers bursting from the closet, call girls with carrier bags of banknotes at railway terminals, episcopal suicides and low-level resignations – Defence Secretaries and the like. But *that* was a trick that couldn't be repeated. She was married to the nation now, divorce was out of the question.

Another impassioned bull on matters ecological? She'd already worked her way yards deep into the lectures of Gregory Bateson (as delivered to the Fellows of Lindisfarne). Time has, she discovered, this marvellous facility for civilizing the most recalcitrant material. Stuff that would have put you at the head of the Prevention of Terrorism Index in the 1960s, when it was still prophetic and active, could now be broadcast from St Anne's Cathedral, Limehouse, in a safely retrospective form. Let us keep a tidy house and sing loud – with William Blake – for vanished green glories. Let the Prince have his Palladian toy town around St Paul's. Let him bleat about planning, proportion, rustification, the *piano nobile*. It was a sideshow, a box for chocolate soldiers – popular as Bourton-on-the-Water (and with about as much clout); serviceable for Royal Weddings, which could be timed to coincide with unconvinced by-elections. She'd outmanoeuvred him, shifted the axis downstream: stuffing Wren's overloaded Roman bauble by rededicating Nicholas Hawksmoor's unfrocked riverside monster, that 'masterpiece of the baroque', as her personal shrine. She could float by barge, in viceregal splendour, turn with the tide, disembark at dawn, or make a progress, a torchlit procession, with heraldic beasts, courtiers, cameramen, brownsnouts, to be greeted on the steps with a lick of the hand from her faithful *gauleiter*, the mad-eyed Doctor. (Another refugee from *Metropolis*, visionary social architect, crazed as Mabuse himself, planning a world-assault in Baum's asylum.) The whole gaudy epic (a pastiched version of Rubens's 'Arrival of the Queen at Marseilles', made suitable for family viewing) would be slapped down on previously primed canvas, by an official War Artist, and hung in the National Gallery before she had swallowed her second gin and french. Get your heritage in first. Build your museum while you still have the muscle to control it.

There were still a few dodges she was not too proud to steal from Ambassador at Large, Richard Milhous Nixon.

Acknowledging the crowds she saw as a featureless throb of pre-coital discomfort with a limply dropped wrist, she remained tormented by unease: there was an unidentified splinter lurking beneath her perfectly manicured fingernails. 'You'd have to be a stiff to get better coverage,' she muttered. She was 'prime time' with all the majors and most of the disk cowboys who cared about their franchises. *That was it!* Why hadn't she thought of it before? What were her so-called 'advisers' playing at? Those brilliantined lounge lizards, those neutered toms who fed at her table. What on earth was going on at the Agency, for goodness' sake? Off with the velvet glove (and the velvet hand inside it!). Were there any lard-haunched half-Brits left to bounce? That was always so popular with the back-bench lynch mobs.

Dead, extinguished, excused parade. The Judas kiss of cold marble. The ultimate camera call. Victoria R came up with the same solution when she was beginning to slide back in the ratings: a Memorial to her dear departed husband, her companion, her inspiration. Dead meat, a Consort could still be pressed into service. *What are you waiting for?* Put a call through on the blue line to the Sh'aaki Twins. A State Commission must be set up immediately. Yes, NOW! Of course, this morning. No planning permission is required. Flatten Greenwich if you have to. Next time they'll think before they vote.

II

The Steering Committee convened at the London City Brasserie (Silvertown) had been democratically nominated. Eleven places were laid at a shimmering linen table, that was crowded with surgeries of Georgian silver, light-manipulating facets of crystal. It was possible, by peeping through a captive tobacco plantation, to cop a vision of the grey and choppy waters of the King George V Dock: a subdued and unmeditated *absence*. The Brasserie exploited one end of the upper deck of the City Airport; the other was reserved for perpetual trade exhibitions, maquettes of riverside apartments. A weekly flight hammered its way, too low to be tracked by radar, to the Channel Islands, weighed down by the lumpy packages of money-laundering service industries. Otherwise this was a showcase with nothing to show.

Brendan (Clancy) Mahoun, a former dock labourer, perhaps 'lifted' by the booze (on the strength of his redundancy money), claimed to have seen Our Lady walk upon these waters. Otherwise cold-blooded and calculating investors are always eager to leap on any sign or portent; they grovel for the soothsayer's blessing. They decided that pilgrims would very soon be rushing the turnstiles from every farflung corner of the Catholic empire. An airport must be constructed. The theory paid off (eventually) at Knock. The sheds were booming: not with alms-jangling shrine hoppers, but with country boys frantic to emigrate. And that was the only way this place was ever going to work.

Ten of these *complaisant* diners had been nominated directly by the Widow herself, and the eleventh by a conga of 'practising' artists (sculptors, window dressers, creative book keepers and the like). The conga had been brought under starter's orders, a month in advance, by the Widow's Press Secretary, wearing his other hat as (the entire) 'Council for Arts and Recreation'. It had been a tricky one, at first blush, finding the names to cloak the event in bogus respectability. In the end, the task devolved, quite satisfactorily, on those heavyweight players, the Sh'aaki Twins, who picked a few hungry faces from among their own holdings. A good lunch was better than the promise of a postal order.

'I think it behoves us to tie this one up fast,' announced the Chair, a banker, and director of thirty-two City companies; who was not keen to expend one second more than he was being paid for at table with the great unwashed. His own scowling portrait had been perpetrated by the late Oskar Kokoschka (one of his flashier efforts): to a background of bridges bursting from his waistcoat like exploding ribs. This shameful object was soon relegated to the boardroom, which the Chair never found the time to visit. 'All agreed? A show of hands; no dissenters, no conchy abstainers – then we can address ourselves to the more complex and rewarding decisions demanded by an eight-course luncheon.'

Professor Catling, the distinguished sculptor, had jumped the gun, and was washing down an indigestible knuckle of knobbly, over-boiled octopus with a thimble of salt-rimmed *mezcal*. His fingers dipped expertly into a side salad; stiff fronds of arctic lettuce, endive crinkly as well-oiled pubic hair. Catling had once been the leader of the 'Walthamstow School', now he was merely its last survivor. English Cinema, which Truffaut claims (with some justification) does not exist, is stuck with two festival-hogging tendencies – both are derived from Walthamstow, the legendary SW Essex Technical College and School of Art; training ground of Ken Russell and Peter Greenaway. For 'Art Cinema' we should read 'Art School Cinema'. And remember Walthamstow.

Catling's work (when he practised it) was of the Third Kind: uncomfortably direct. (A man treated to a full spaghetti dinner is then given two or three pints of salted water to drink. The camera, unblinking, records the result.) No, Catling had been elevated to this company for three quite distinct reasons. He possessed a very presentable chalk-stripe suit, in something close to his own size. (It wouldn't frighten the ladies.) His work was so obscure and recondite that it could not remotely come under consideration for the project-in-hand: it was years since anybody had set eyes on it. (No whispers of a fix.) But, most importantly, he had a pan-European reputation as a trencherman. He'd keep his snout in the trough with the best of them, and sing for his supper with gems from his repertoire of superbly timed and delivered smoking-room anecdotes. He'd be far too busy licking the grease from his fingers to question any *realpolitik* decisions with nitpicking aesthetic quibbles.

The Chair resumed, while his fellow freeloaders wet their lips in iced Perrier: he rapidly and succinctly outlined their brief, informing them of the conclusions they would reach in time for the circulation of the port. The Widow wanted a fitting memorial to her Consort. It would have to achieve an epic scale (Valhalla), soar above the docks – signifying her courage in the face of adversity, and also the courage of the nation, the 'little people', Britain-can-take-it, 'Gor blimey, Guv', it's only *one* leg, ain't it?' A memorial to the spirit of the Blitz and a torch to Enterprise. It should make Prince Albert's cheesy stack look like the heap of bat guano it would, in truth, soon become. No rivals were tolerated: Gilbert Scott's 'memorial of our Blameless Prince' had already been condemned as a dangerous structure and would be demolished within the week; the Ross of Mull granite, the marble, the bronze figures, the Salviati mosaics redistributed to rusticate wine bars and industry parks in South Shields or Humberside, or wherever some discreet patronage was required. For too long there had been an elitist *focal* around the 'Royal' Colleges, the Museums, the Albert Hall, the under-exploited parklands, the subsidy-swallowing Palace. Our memorial rising above Silvertown would shift the whole axis downriver: not Canaletto, nor Turner – but William Blake! The horses of instruction feed in silver pastures. ('Can Wisdom be put in a silver rod?')

The Architectural Adviser (who was able to speak only while pressing his tongue with the ear-grip of his tortoiseshell spectacles) had visited his latest Rotherhithe development, and was 'absolutely appalled' to discover that so mean a site had claimed one of the city's grandest viewing platforms. He was selling customized bijou residences in Cherry Gardens to half-solvent media lefties, who had to cash in their life-insurance policies to raise three hundred and fifty k! (It was a real drag dealing with social-climbing paupers.) We're not having interviews with Shadow Cabinet ministers conducted *directly* opposite George-in-the-East, with the whole curved bosom of the river spread to the eye from St Paul's to St Anne's, Limehouse; insinuating undeserved notions of imperial grandeur. History doesn't come cheap. The word, therefore, is *move out* — lay down some action in swamplands. Bus the punters by water, or by chopper. Start the turnstiles clicking. Without a major feature, 'focused on cultural excellence', and spread through the supplements — OK? — you might as well shut up shop. It's been costed, won't top fifty million.

'But, surely, Mr Chairman,' piped the Laureate's Wife, smiling a swift incision, appealing to Daddy, 'we should, at least, be allowed to *advise* on the choice of artists to be involved in such a morally significant venture?'

The Chairman, covert stag, flared his spidery nostrils in acknowledgement of that lady's mythical fragrance and — with effortless condescension — soothed her ruffled sensibilities.

'Plenty of time for the small print, my dear. You chaps can argue up and down the cheeseboard about the drapes and the colour co-ordinates. I'm booked on the three o'clock flight for Zurich.' (Handled that rather well, he thought. They only want to be noticed. He debated a compliment. Would her *earrings* be too personal?)

The Architectural Adviser, bronzed, beaked like a peregrine falcon, grinning the full zip, leant confidentially forward, gesturing expensively manicured hands in a spray of transatlantic eloquence.

'My initial brief was to locate an adequately site-specific piece. It was felt that we must insist on a "language of symbols" and so, as a consequence, we took steps to eliminate from our discussions all the currently notorious practitioners of *bricolage* ...'

He leered significantly at the Twins, who had amassed uncatalogued tons of the stuff in their North London bunker.

'What in God's name is the man talking about?' demanded the Chair, winking boyishly at the Laureate's Wife, and sneaking a glance at his timepiece.

'The scavengers, sir,' returned the Architect, bravely, 'the beachcombers. Cragg, Woodrow; those people. We *could* turn them loose down the defunct rail lines, or let them abseil among the cooling towers — but, we tended towards the notion that they might not be altogether ... reliable. They have this bias towards unstable metaphors: "singularities" straining beyond their rational event-horizons.' (He had been reading extracts of Stephen Hawking and was looking for the opportunity to unburden himself of some of this language, before he lost it.)

'What about David Mach?' said the Last British Film Producer, brightly: he had been watching too many late-night arts programmes, and it was beginning to show. He clawed at his pepper-and-salt beard, grooming compulsively, as he had done while playing for time in so many interviews. He had been persuaded, against all his baser instincts (the ones that bought the place), to instal a Mach folly at the Mill House: a tumbling waterfall of never-distributed histories of the National Trust, in which a wild hunt of pink jackets, pikes, cuirasses, and drumsticks were drowning, soundlessly.

The Architect sucked the wax sheen on the arm of his spectacles. He was enjoying this. The illusion of authority. Not a critic in sight. 'Too visible, too impermanent. The Widow, it has to be admitted, does not enjoy humour. Doesn't understand it – or approve of those who do.'

The Producer, a dues-paying conservationist, paled, cruelly reminded of the 'biographical details' he had skittishly allowed his secretary to forward for inclusion in the project's Official Brochure: 'Tottenham Hotspur Supporter, bicyclist, knitter of Shetland sweaters, patron of David Mach, and occasional film-maker'. The Widow was probably looking at the thing at this very moment, asking somebody to explain what it meant. He could forget the peerage. A crippling spasm of yellow pain shook him: he clutched his gut and made a rush for the Gents, where he pounded the digits of his cellphone, trying to reach his Artbroker before the close of trade for the Holy Hour.

'Sell Mach! Take a loss, anything – get shot. I need *weight*, formalism. Get me into marble, or forget your percentage, baby. I want work that takes a crane to lift it.'

'I must admit,' the Laureate's Wife elevated her bone-handled fork in the direction of the Chair, 'to rather a soft spot for Gormley's "*Brick Man*".'

'Over my dead body!' screamed the Architect, who was involved in a running battle with an unpronounceable critic who had written of the figure with trenchant enthusiasm. The Architect wouldn't lift a finger to support anything his Hackney-based rival *might* (for want of a better idea) editorially endorse.

'Put up a thing like that,' said the extrovert Twin, 'and you'll frighten the aeroplanes.'

'*What* aeroplanes?' retorted the Chair, waving an empty glass towards the deserted runway: a gesture the hovering Cypriot waiter read, correctly, as a request for a 'top up'. More sycophantic laughter. 'You don't seriously imagine anyone in their right minds would risk flying out of this cut-price lagoon – a hundred yards of couch grass in the middle of nowhere? The original notion, fatuous as it now appears, was that the terminal itself would be the big attraction – pulling in charabancs of manipulated imbeciles eager to gape at their own reflection, then stagger home with a trolleyful of gimcrack souvenirs. Now the taxi drivers won't touch the place. They tell their fares it's been closed down, run them to Stanstead.'

The Architect, fearing the conversation was drifting away from those areas in which he could decisively demonstrate his erudition and understated humanity, slid a sketch of Anthony Gormley's brick giant across the table. It was instantly skewered by a flash of the Chairman's steak knife.

'Damned thing's got no willy.' His euphemism was tactfully pitched at a level suited to mixed company. 'The creature's a eunuch, sexless as a gilded Oscar. Dickie Attenborough'll blub if he comes within a mile of it. Ugh! An impractical dildo: won't be up a week before the Paddys have the bricks away to front some King's Cross sauna. Jumping Jesus, can you imagine what the Widow would do if her husband's sacred memorial was shanghaied into the retaining wall of a wankers' bath house?'

'Couldn't we talk about Barry Flanagan?' The Laureate's Wife ached to shift into a more life-affirming territory. 'His dancing hares have got such *animal* spirit, such dawn-fresh vitality. He's a true shaman; his drawings come alive before your eyes.'

'Flanagan?' snorted the Chair, 'feller in a trilby? Looks like a bookie's runner? He's a potato basher. Quite out of the question.' (The Producer was relieved. He had shifted swiftly out of Flanagan when the soft furnishings started to cost more than a year's subscription to *Country Life* or a modest assignation at the White Tower.)

'Just so. The *gestalt* is now most definitely "on the floor". We have to prepare ourselves for an assault on new forms of reality.' The Architect clawed back; causing Professor Catling to raise the tablecloth, fearful he had missed out on some notable side dish. 'Flanagan's latest proposal excitingly combines a performance element with his always scrupulous truth to materials. He wants us to validate – bear witness to – the construction of a *hole in the water*. This would have such a miraculously transitional quality, a metamorphosis of liquid into air ... an anomaly, I believe, of enormous resonance.'

'If you think the Widow wants her saintly husband remembered by a hole in the water, you must have a hole in the head,' snapped the Chair, muttering something further to an attentive aide, who instantly passed the message on to a pocket tape-recorder. (The Architect was on his way back to the Masonic one-night stands.) 'Look here, haven't we got a couple of these johnnies on the payroll? They should do something to earn their gravy. The Civil List's not a gentleman's club for bloody civilians.'

'Sir Eduardo,' said the Architect, eager to stay on the ball, 'is occupied in laying out an Aztec mosaic somewhere beneath the Elephant and Castle. Sir Anthony, it was felt, had done such sterling service at Millbank that he should be considered for compassionate leave – before he suffered the debilitating effects of front-line trauma. He's an artist, first and last; not an administrator.'

'I think,' said the irrepressible fenland châtelaine, 'we are all in danger of forgetting the true purpose of this gathering.' Her remarks were floated in such soft but narcoleptic tones that the disadvantaged drinkers (male) froze in mid-hoist. An unconvinced frog's leg jerked spastically from the Architect's open mouth, as if deciding to make one last pathetic leap for freedom. 'Our brief is to commemorate the aviators who died protecting these factories, deepwater docks, and mean streets.' She dangled a bloodless hand (so white it seemed to have been kept in a bath of milk) in vague benediction towards the shapeless mounds of masonry that hid the river from their privileged viewing station.

'We are required,' she continued, with all the confidence of one who has received absolution from the highest court in the land, 'to offer our suggestions for the erection of a National Shrine; a place of quiet and meditation, a place fondly to recall those who have gone before, an inspiration to those who will follow.'

'What *did* the old boy do in the last show?' enquired the Chair, 'apart from blasting out a few craters on the golf courses of the Cinque ports?'

'Not known,' the Architect, subdued, whispered into his hand, 'stricken from the record. "Mentioned in despatches", certainly. Something biological. And intelligent. Very hush-hush.'

Flash frames of shredded files. Laser-enhanced index cards. Chemically-inspired memory transfusions. They swept over the gob-struck assembly like a hazchem plague. Take your pick: droplets of blood beading the windows, dead fish pelting from the clouds, black and gungy smoke belching in spasms from the fluted stacks of the Silvertown Sugar Mills. And now, operatically, as if orchestrated by Leni Riefenstahl, at this moment when all the secret nightfears of the heart lay exposed on the linen table, a silver chopper skimmed in over the dock, ruffling the hide-thick surface, to land within sight of the petrified diners, on the uncropped grass of the man-made isthmus. Goons, too highly strung to wait for ladders, leapt to the deck, wheeling as they fell, scanning dim horizons, shrugging and twitching inside their Burberrys; patting themselves for the reassurance that they weren't toting an empty holster. A child, scrubbed and pink, backlit, emerged from the open door of the Sikorski, as if for his first day at prep school, clutching an executive-size briefcase (from which the price ticket was clearly visible) to his bosom. He was dressed in unbruised cricket flannels. A wet bob faking it for the parents' match.

'The Minister,' announced the Chair, 'early as usual. Come to take our soundings back upstairs.' Surreptitiously, he slid a magnum Havana back into its pigskin case.

Before the guilty reflex was complete, the praetorian guard were hustling their juvenile lead into the open-plan dining area, were taking up crouched positions among the rubber plants, and gibbering killspeak into faulty handsets.

The Chair was not alone in his guilt. The Lady from the Fens had a distinct 'thing' about men in cricket gear. It began when she'd been dragged along to Lord's, because her husband, after some characteristic reverse, needed to maintain a high profile, show himself, rub shoulders with the nabobs, share the banter and the chocolate cake of the radio box. She had been bored out of her skull, until she had taken up the fieldglasses to watch this beautiful black fellow (Michael Holding?) walk back to bowl, rubbing the ball in the most intimate way on the side of his thigh. There was an awful, addictive languor about the whole performance. The slow build-up. The springy stride into the wicket. The ball fired like a bullet. The cringing batsman. Ahh!

This sense of innocent eroticism was not shared with her husband (nor indeed with the Minister – who had not enjoyed his compulsory charity match: either under siege, and in danger of voiding his bowels, or banished to the mindboggling inertia of the outfield). Did nobody share her dream? A wide bed, her lover helping her to change the sheets. Christopher Martin-Jenkins on the radio. Describing, let us say, Imran Khan's flight to the wicket. The leap. The delivery. Her lover in white. She is in lacy black underwear. Neither one touching the other, separated by the bed. And he is dressing to leave. As she undresses, a warm afternoon, to lie back, listening to the cricket. The curtains flap. He hesitates. He cannot bear to turn away. Apple blossom in the orchard.

'Did you score, Minister?' She blushed, as the Chair put his toadying question. 'Pick up any wickets?'

The flustered youth ignored him. (He hadn't; but that was nobody's business.) 'Your deliberations are complete, Mr Chair.' It was not a question. The youth lisped in a still small voice; implying that if he did not get his way he was quite capable of 'screaming and screaming and screaming until he was thick'. He was under visible pressure. One of those who feel they should be somewhere much more important; and who keep glancing down to check the zip of their flies. He squeaked, like a cheeky cartoon mouse being dubbed by a seventy-year-old actor who has not yet been told that the polyps in his sinuses are malignant.

Closer inspection, in the hush that followed this incursion, revealed no youth, but a shrink-wrapped young man – who had forgotten to climb out of his lightweight suit before sending it to the cleaners. Or some kind of quantum leap in the field of headshrinking. The Minister looked like a ventriloquist's dummy – which, in a sense, he was: the latex exception that proves the rule. The rest of the Widow's gang split neatly into the Uglies (shifty, weasel-twitching Goebbels clones who breakfasted on razor blades and seven-week embryos) and the Bunters: smooth, fleshy, near-identical, bum-faced nonentities in Savile Row suits and bulletproof spectacles. Apocalypse-resistant unflappables. The Uglies had lost ground recently, the time for cracking skulls was past. They were ennobled, sent to the city like feral cats. No longer the nights of broken glass, lycanthropes and zoo-rejects with burning brands: it was the mid-term era of soft sell, Brylcreem condomed, safe-handed boys, and public men of conscience (and private fortune). We gloried in the exploits of the agitated one (nicknamed 'The Albatross'), the Sumerian fish-totem, whose role it was to be seen wandering, gape-mouthed in pin-stripes and hard hat, from one disaster to the next, blinking like a nocturnal animal caught in the harsh lights of the rescue services; lips trembling, ready to blub out his patent sincerity. A scapegoat begging for slaughter.

This boy, the Minister, had been picked because he smelt like a political virgin: he was fresh, oven-ready, blatant with coal tar and Old Spice; bubbling, enthusiastic, popping up everywhere with endorsements that kept him spinning dizzily around the outer circle; never quite 'one of us', but very useful as a fag and disposable messenger. He had been rewarded, as Minister of Sport and Recreation, by being given in addition the very minor Arts portfolio. (In his spare moments he was supposed to sort out the weather.) But he remained, basically, a whipping boy: buoyant enough, and stupid enough, to deflect heat-seeking missiles from such entrenched citadels of the left as the Church of England, the Royal Opera House, and the *Sunday Telegraph*.

'Your decision, gentlemen – and, excuse me, Madame,' (he smacked his lips in a dinghy-inflating pout) '*if you please*,' the Minister trilled, grinning bravely about the placard-sized identity card pinned to his lapel, as if he was still an evacuee. (Without it, civil servants kept 'losing' him. And he wasn't allowed in to the premières of grown-up films.) 'I'm obliged to show my face at the First Round Losers' Cup Second Replay at Plough Lane. Now we've got rid of those beastly beer-swilling spectators they expect a few celebs to make the broadcast a bit sexier.'

A show of hands was called for: all reached dutifully in high salute –

except Professor Catling who was fully occupied with the cheese cutter and a brace of ripe walnuts.

'Of course, Minister, we give our unqualified support to the scheme as outlined.' The Chair ritualized the verdict.

'But no scheme has, actually, ever been outlined, has it?' said the Laureate's Wife, to subdued titters.

The Minister, superbly, without a trace of self-consciousness, performed his smiling-at-the-ladies smile. He snapped open the steel skin of his attaché case and produced packs of hi-tech brochures. They had the heavy paper and the gloss finish of the best international art magazines. There were photographs, half-tones, tints, bleeds, elevations, concertinaed maps, detachable numbered etchings: all the tricks that disguise the thinnest dribble of text. The margins were so generous that modernists might have imagined themselves holding a set of one-word columns from Tom Raworth.

'We're going to take off from the defunct Crosby/Sandle "Battle of Britain Monument" projection. That's been our inspiration. It's a definite mover. It's got all the elements – in fossil form, naturally. But the bottom line is that we, as a Government, have the guts to sink our dosh in an uninhabited swamp. We must summon up the courage of the Dutch, when they built their polders against chaos, or helped us design the great fortress at Tilbury, repulsing the Spaniards and extinguishing for ever the fires of the Inquisition.'

He bowed, held his breath for the statutory forty seconds, waiting for applause – while the committee members scrambled frantically through the brochures, attempting to convey, by coughs and significant nods, the impression that they had heard of (and wholeheartedly approved) this cracker-barrel pitch.

'Crosby has grasped the salient point: the first duty of any decent monument is to pay its own way, and not to simply stand around for a few hundred years waiting for history to kiss its ass.' He had the grace to blush, most becomingly. 'You art wallahs can sort out all the retrospective justifications. I can promise you prime-time television and the best crews available (none of that hand-held stuff, straight from the ad agencies). Make this clear: Crosby's underlying theme is absolutely spot on – *celebration*! It can't be shameful to rejoice in our God-given victories; and our joy will take the specific form of a stepped pyramid, bathed in banks of coloured light. The very beams that once swept our London skies, seeking out pirates and invaders, will now illuminate a transfixed block of time; in which a Heinkel bomber plunges to its doom beneath a brave little Spitfire. Gentlemen, we're going to top the Eiffel Tower, the Statue of Liberty, the Colossus of Rhodes in one hit.'

'And where would this monument be sited, sir – exactly?' enquired the Architect, with lapping khaki tongue.

'Here! Where else?' The Minister allowed his impatience to show by tapping his black brochure on the tabletop. Someone had not done his homework.

'I'm sure,' he continued, uncreasing a disfiguring scowl, 'our friend from the cinematograph can help us to stress the value of a professional presentation. Wall-to-wall sound systems, the right choice of themes … *Chariots of Fire*, *Dam Busters*, *Kwai*, Elgar, Paul McCartney. Nothing too sophisticated, nothing rabble-rousing. No German melancholy.'

The Producer nervously groomed his beard, searching for his mouth, which had dried and contracted to a useless ring of gristle. 'Yankee names above the titles, home-grown technical facilities, plus Jap finance (with maybe a Colombian top-up). Am I close? Logos from brand-leaders tactfully showcased in positions of maximum visibility – right?'

'*Right*? You're in Disneyland, baby. We're not pitching for a Cola franchise, or a sweetener from Virgin Atlantic. Think Armada, Festival of Britain, Churchill's funeral. We're talking heavy ritual here. Leo Von Klenze, the Egyptians, the Mayans. What does Crosby call it? "A place of pilgrimage … a viable commercial investment … with side-effects which are unpredictable."' He rapped imperiously at the window, causing three of his goons to flash for their shoulder holsters. 'The monument will be sunk in that dock. Work to commence immediately, contracts tendered and awarded.'

A modest smile crossed the Chairman's face: as a director of both the firms involved he could not lose. He had ruthlessly undercut himself, juggling the tax concessions and the Enterprise Zone allowances.

The Minister was inspired: a vision appeared to him on the face of the waters. He saw things as they ought to be, he *believed*. 'Visitors will enter through a maze of submarine pens, based on Sandle's preliminary drawings. They will be "mood-graded" by a discreet soundtrack, quoting from those wonderful films of our boyhood, *Above Us the Waves*, *Sink the Bismarck* … Johnny Mills, Jack Hawkins, John Gregson, Ordinary Seaman Bryan Forbes … all that bleep-bleep, glug-glug, Up Periscope stuff. On through glass-walled tunnels, from which the humbled punters glimpse phantom U-boats, white sharks, limpet mines – maybe a hologram *Belgrano*. *Gotcha!*'

He whacked his hands together. The lady screamed. And the chief goon shot himself in the foot. And was carried, bleeding, to the chopper.

'Then it's into the pyramid itself, a Cave of Remembrance. Sober. Solemn music. On the walls could be carved elevating sentiments from the great philosophers and leaders. We considered using that Scotsman who is, apparently, something of a whiz with a chisel (to show we don't harbour grudges and also to do our bit for unemployment north of the border). But now we're informed the chappy is an over-sensitive, litigious blighter. The frogs are quite convinced he's a card-carrying Nazi.'

'That's a cross we all have to bear,' murmured the Chairman.

The Minister was not to be diverted. 'A continuous frieze of speeches by Winston and Margaret will remind us of our duties as citizens, prepare us for the tapes of ack-ack guns over Dagenham, cones of concentrated fire, tracer shells. White parachute discs over the Isle of Grain. A distant thunder from the Thames Estuary. Stamping jackboots. Criss-crossing searchlights windmilling above the dome of St Paul's. Vast processions. Boy scouts, landgirls, aviators. Cheering. Travelling camera. Flashing bulbs. Cheering and clapping to the rhythm of a beating heart; clapping and stamping; cheering building to a soul-purging climax. *Yes!* All the razzamatazz of Nuremberg, without any of the chthonic excesses. The showbiz side, if you like. They certainly knew how to throw a party!'

'Right!' enthused the Producer, his eyes moist with the possibilities. 'Those production values! Technically speaking, *Triumph of the Will* stands up; it's a hell of a movie. Give me extras from the old school who'll really go for it, give me a monster-monster budget – and anything is possible.'

'We ascend,' the Minister dropped his voice to a cathedral whisper, 'in an open-fronted elevator ("a vertical ghost-train", it has been called); climbing silently through all the strata of wartime desolation: fire-raids, rubble, water jets, Mass Observers, nigger bands in smoky cellars. We re-experience the primal energies of conflict – so cruelly denied to many of us in this comfortable world, where all our enemies have been defeated. Then, at the summit, in the hush of the final chamber, we come upon a still-life tableau of striking simplicity. A sunken pit ringed with plain wooden stools, and a table on which the waxen corpse of the Consort has been laid out, among all his ribbons and honours; his favourite golf clubs bound like a bundle of rods (*fasces*): the symbol of a lictor's authority. We back away in awe. From the portholes, we kneel to look down over the battleground of the city, the sun-capturing towers of Canary Wharf, the silver helmets of the crusaders of the Thames Barrier.'

'I see it, I see it!' the Architect cried out, with all the agony of a convert. 'You're reviving Speer. I've thought for some time – though one has been reluctant to admit it – he's quite a respectable figure, once you remove him from the sleazy *milieu* in which he operated. In fact, he seems to have more genuine "bottom" than many of his fellow Neo-Classicists working not a mile from here in the deregulated sector. Acting as muse to a carpet-chewing dictator may, in the long view, prove a worthier calling than fudging some pastiched Byzantine cladding for a cartel of grinning orientals. Isn't Speer's the very stuff that HRH has been advocating all along? (More havoc from the socialist planners than the Luftwaffe?) Speer had that unifying vision, the epic sense of scale, without which there is no *polis*. In time he may very well be recognized as a minor master, and given a retrospective at the Hayward.'

'The overriding object,' the Minister had clamped his case, and was preparing to depart, 'is to shift the river axis. The City of the Future must be a phoenix rising out of the ruin of docklands. Abort the flattering urbanities of Canaletto, the pastoral fancies of Turner: we must assert the primacy of William Blake and his "Hiding of Moses" (page twenty-four in the brochure). Twin pyramids honouring the swamp, a curve of water guarded by a lioness; the precise hieratic steps of material progress. I leave it with you.'

And he bounced from his perch. His perfectly pink head, level with the tabletop, passed among the peaches and pineapples like a runaway sweetmeat, an exotic blancmange. Professor Catling, spoon in hand, stared longingly after his rapidly diminishing form; a trickle of drool starting from the corner of his mouth.

III

The move into the Bow Quarter hit Sonny Jaques like a jolt of mainline adrenaline. Here he was – in the heartland – aligned with the feral energies of the heroic and legendary East End. Scrap the ear-stud (lose that Kit Marlowe boy-prince image), shave the skull, climb into Chagall's bleached blue jacket, and an aircrew cap. Look at me, Ma: worker/artist, Constructivist poet articulating the inchoate scream of the masses.

The Quarter also promised a kidney-shaped pool, an indoor jogging facility, and a panelled library, stacked to its girder-enforced fake ceiling with all the latest blood 'n' boobs videos. Sonny pumped iron. It kept Kathy Acker looking good – and he was ten years younger! There she was in *Time Out*. But he was going to make the cover. (He hadn't decided yet if a tattoo would be construed as bourgeois narcissism, proletarian solidarity, or a brand of brotherhood with the primitives of the Third World. Would it help to pull the chicks?)

The buzzword was *realpolitik*; clear-eyed, stand-up-and-be-counted, a streetgang of warriors. For less than £150,000 you could purchase a few cubic feet of the old Bryant & May match factory, a kiosk tricked out in the style of a blue-ribbon transatlantic liner (tourist class, natch). Or, more accurately, as if the set for such a vessel had been tastefully vamped in plasterboard, chrome, and plastic mouldings for a Noël Coward revival (*Sail Away*?) This former cathedral of industry was now partitioned into a series of mock-deco hutches: waiting rooms for some futurist dentist. And everywhere the gaunt spectres of the sulphur-jawed skivvies were invoked in sepia-tinted prints. The Bow Quarter was a shrine to the authentic. Volunteer inmates were barricaded against the outside world, eager to turn a blind eye to the railway, and the ramps of petrol-burning lemmings who dirt-tracked within yards of the perimeter fence. (If this is the Bow Quarter, who needs the other three-quarters?)

Sonny paced between fridge and window; where he gazed, olive carton in hand, ruminating, upon the squadron of builders' skips that packed the inner courtyard. It was time to put a flame under a few dozing projects. Obviously, Spitalfields was burnt out (caned by the supplements) – but Bow was effervescently marginal, a desert crying aloud for re-enchantment.

'I think we've got a genuine lever here,' Sonny lectured. I had agreed to meet him, not because I had any expectation that our film project could be resurrected, but because I felt that the Bow Quarter itself would stand a little research. It was a fortress for New Money, not for the seriously wealthy river-spivs. These proper people, the traditionally liquid, had staked out Wapping, years ago, while the here-today-gone-tomorrow boys ravished the Isle of Dogs, laundering their blagswag: leaving such previously despised outposts as Bow to small-change tobacconists, hairdressers, media hustlers, and oral-hygiene mechanics.

'Francis Smart has flitted – the producer who once met your mate, Eric Whatsisname – so Hanbury's script is on the spike. It's in limbo. It won't be cancelled, but it won't be cleared either. Forget the kill fee. There's no fizz left. They're putting Hanbury out to grass in Dorset, Open University rap, the Valium beat. Smart has cashed in his credits. Now – this is strictly off the record – I don't want to read it in *Private Eye*, you must promise ...'

'Oh, naturally,' I replied, smirking with insincerity, 'I know the rules.'

'Well, what happened was – the old fart let some Oxford chum run a graveyard series on "The Chivalry of War"; twenty episodes, bottle-necking Sunday nights. Hours of dreadful stock footage, voice over, rostrum trawls across *The Rout of Ran Romano*; flutes and drums, talking heads; purple, cabbage-skinned passed-over brigadiers thumping maps – and young Lochinvar poncing about in tailored sour-cream fatigues around every battlefield he could think of from Carthage to Marathon, Bull Run to Saigon. The expense sheet's been framed: it's a legend. And in exchange, *quid pro quo*, Smart gets a sabbatical year, recharging the batteries among the dreaming spires. He'll shuffle back at the end of the cricket season to see if there's anything on the boil at the Palace: tread water until the knighthood comes through. Might put in for Controller of Channel 4, or cop the Arts Council as a consolation prize. Then there's always *The Times*. And the antiquarian bookshop.'

He yawned, bored with the inevitability of it all. 'The fat cats,' he continued, 'the boys in the red braces have packed away their cellular phones and departed. You can't make a deal anywhere in the Corporation. It's all accountable. I'm trying to get a hook on "The Last Show", our latest attempt to put insomniacs on a culture drip. The rolling credits look hugely impressive – until you read the christian names. Strictly, "son of". Kindergarten Athenaeum. But they do need plenty of fillers (they don't use anything else). We can change the title of your treatment and resubmit. Take a few more snapshots, find some new faces. Pop in the odd cutting from the glossies. You'll be on for a research fee. Your agent cops his percentage. Everybody's happy.'

Without further debate we plunged recklessly into the streets, the broad channel of Bow Road. 'I'm getting the twitch,' screamed Sonny, above the traffic. 'We're on to an activated possibility.'

I agreed: it was my policy at that time to agree with everything, to play Russian roulette with whatever fate threw at me, to break – by paths I could not anticipate – into the madness of the city. I would lead Sonny to the redoubt of Imar O'Hagan, the secret Bracken Bunker. Sonny was beginning to see the shape I had already prepared for him.

'I like it!' he shouted, as he bounced a pensioner into the path of an oncoming 35cwt van. 'It's got *realpolitik* and balance. This solitary anchorite, O'Hagan, labouring in his cave. Modest, employing horizontal forms, working only with what is available to him – free of sponsorship. A re-enchantment of that which was never previously enchanted. Yes! And we set that against the state art of the Silvertown Memorial, those bragging *vertical* energies, laying claim to emotions they have not earned. The public river and the unregarded wasteland. God, it's almost a title! We've got it. We've got our pitch.'

Sonny beat his hand against his side (altogether missing the historic tablet that stood with its Noah's Ark, named Courage, to honour the memory of the match-girls). He was awkwardly squaring his fingers to screentest the statue of Mr Gladstone that rose out of the curve of the

Gents on an island in the middle of the road, around which swept an enraged scum of drivers, catapulting from the flyover.

'Who *is* that? What's the church? Bow? The bells? You mean, this is *it*? The epicentre? We're there, in there, *there* there, at it – we've arrived.'

He advanced at a run towards Gladstone, emitting idiocies like a froth of ectoplasm. The Grand Old Man's right hand gestured prophetic scorn back towards the Bow Quarter, in bird-limed resignation.

'Brilliant! This anonymous vision of the great liberal patriarch. It's biblical. Decency. Authority – by respect. An earned authority. Feel the humanity burning in those eyes. My God, he's actually supported by a cairn of books. What's that? Dante? Of course, *Juventus Mundi*. And a third volume whose title is turned away from the spectator; thus preserving the essential mystery of personality. That's us. The third force, the mediators between spiritual heaven and material hell. We must shoot our film with the same sense of unegoic communality espoused by the modest craftsman who created this statue. Come on, yes – do you see it? – let's go.'

He vaulted the protective fence, to hurl himself among the hog-run of cars. I could not bring myself to point out the sculptor's name, larger than life, cut into the side of the pedestal: Albert Bruce Joy. Sonny spun past corrugated fences that surrounded soon-to-be-demolished municipal mausoleums: the fences were plastered with fly-pitched posters for rock groups whose names had all been lifted from the canon of modernist literature. A hyperactive collage of quotations; many from William Burroughs, some from Joyce, some even from Jean Rhys. Authors whose works would finally exist only as names on hoardings: *memento mori* to bands who went out of business before the paste was dry. The hallucinatory wave patterns of the fence metamorphosed a leering Derek Jameson into an avatar of the Elephant Man.

Devons Road opens to the north from a submerged precinct, half-developed, half-boarded for the bulldozers: nothing happens until you duck under the railway bridge. Sonny was rambling euphorically, pirouetting in tight circles: panoramas of blight – 'yes, yes' – grass humps, horizons of aborted social experiments. These were the final killing fields of the welfare state: bleak towers, mud gash, red cliffs of hospital charity. 'Yes, yes, yes!' Sonny's camera/eye swept from the dead nettles of the embankment to the spark-grid of the south-flowing railway cutting, from the marshes to the distant docks. This island earth: a dab of infected lint helplessly staunching a terminal haemorrhage.

He chanted an ecstatic litany of road signs: Fern Street, Violet Road, Blackthorn Street, Whitethorn Street. 'I can see for ever,' he said, 'an open vein, the lifeblood of London, a trail of light. Devons Road converting to St Paul's Way, filtering and fading, dying as Ben Jonson Road. Do you realize that Ben Jonson's first known work, *The Isle of Dogs* (1597), was suppressed by the Privy Council as "lewd, seditious and slanderous"? It earned him ten weeks in the Marshalsea, where he was plagued by two narks, government agents; one of whom, Robert Poley, was present at the death of Christopher Marlowe in Deptford. Now the play's lost, only the record of the punishment remains.'

'There's something unlucky about the mere mention of the place,' I replied. 'It probably vanished with Jonson. There's no other reason to go there; you can leave the known world behind. Let it be struck from the maps.'

'Poets knew how to live in those days,' Sonny accused. 'Jonson was branded, rope-scorched; an angry, sweating, pock-marked, ungodly man. He killed the actor Gabriel Spenser on Hoxton Fields with a sword. This empty arena lets all those things flood back. Do you feel it? It's a flattened book, ready to snap shut, and kill us like flies. We're there, and here. On it, in it. Found. A slice through the wedding cake of culture, a geological section: a *self-preserved* dereliction.'

It was true. We had stumbled into the Borderland, the space between the fortress developments of New Money to the north and the *De Stijl* colour-charts and pineapple-dressings of the riverside oases to the south: between the poisoned swamp of the Lea and the Limehouse Cut was one last slab of unclaimed territory.

Beneath the railway embankment was a wide allotment band, neatly tended, five-year-planned, baled with straw; a medieval strip system, generously sooted by the constant fret of passing trains. Commuters could glimpse this rustic scene and imagine a greening of the inner cities. The hospital barracks conveniently blocked out the uncontained acres of industrial graveyards. It was marvellous: we were floating between Empson Street and Purdy Street – the austerities of the Cambridge School and the fine baroque flourishes of homophile decadence.

Kids used the mud slopes to road-test their liberated BMX bikes, while barefoot freaks spun and stabbed in exotic Tai Chi ballets, like white-faced 'Nam vets exorcizing their trauma in some crummy Holly-wood guilt trip: Nick Nolte, or the cheapest available beefcake. One solitary end-of-terrace pub, the Old Duke of Cambridge, stood in the middle of the wasteland. It was somewhere for the demolition men to drink, while waiting for the loot to come through, so that they could step back on to the street as fully-fledged brickies for yet another motte and bailey canalside folly.

.A pirate cable had been run over the wall from the Docklands railway to a fugitive scrapyard, where blue flashes from welding guns lit the gloom with nerve-destroying bursts, as they cosmetically sculpted new wrecks from a mound of old ones: spare-parts surgery.

Sonny did not know how to handle this. He kept twisting, grand-mother's footsteps, muttering: an *aide-mémoire* for his 'Last Show' synopsis. 'Gladstone ... City of Towers ... the sump ... anarchist aubergines ... Colin Ward.' He did not recognize what stood directly before him, what I myself had only vaguely sensed, until Imar O'Hagan, the anchorite, the snail painter, had pointed it out to me. This dim field had been, very slowly, and very precisely, rendered as a scale model, smoothed and graded, of the Silbury Hill-Avebury-Windmill Hill complex. Imar, alone, had worked for years, digging and measuring, planting out. So that now Sonny stood, arms raised, on the East London Silbury, the burial place of kings: he trumpeted aloud his brazen affirmations of everything that was not here.

IV

Bracken House was the kind of set you encounter only in radical documentaries about 'Chasing the Dragon', or in reruns of 'The Sweeney'. These places had no official existence; they had been wiped from the books, transferred from the housing list to some directory of naff locations. Unpeopled balconies, madly angled, relished their independence – beyond the reach of stairs that went nowhere, connec-ting only with other stair systems. Numerology had run riot: doors and walls were defaced with columns of figures (like equations that would never come out, predicting a sun-swallowing black hole). Every dustbin was numbered, many of them several times over. After slashing your way through a yard of booby-trapped motors you can enter the labyrinth, and never be seen again. Your finger bones discovered in the foil of a Chinese takeaway. Rabid infants snapped the wipers from the vans of social prowlers, or set fire to the rags that fluttered on the wire washing lines, from which some trainee psycho suspended the occasional cat.

Imar O'Hagan had converted his flat into a stunning workshop/cave, a vibrant green cell, the walls electric with a Baconian brew of fish oil and reconstituted snot. It was heaped with piers of axed firewood, gathered from the wilderness of Tower Hamlets Cemetery. An aban-doned mangle had been transformed into an etching press. One glimpse of Imar's wild-eyed charms and Sonny was filling in the application for his Equity card.

Trays of lascivious snails betrayed one of Imar's current obsessions. A visit to the fridge revealed the other: blocks of frozen vampire bats, shipped in from the German labs (like an airline breakfast of compressed leather gloves), fought for space among the melting sparrow hawks and other assorted dead things that friends charity-faxed from the Dorset backwoods.

Sonny timidly refused the offer of a carton of blue-green yogurt, uncapped among this ice-furred carnage. We voted instead to broach an interesting bottle that contained either Monte Alban worm-water, or turpentine.

A postcard self-portrait of Chaim Soutine honoured Imar's master. The Bracken hermit had successfully brought Minsk to Bow. Notebook flashing, Sonny gazed longingly at the dark curls, the high cheekbones, the profile chiselled and chipped by adversity. Fired by our interest, Imar's predatory smile broadened: he shone in an aureole of red-gold light, as he piloted us through his portfolio of deformity: the darkly etched abortions, the pathology crayons, the *quattrocento* dementia of snails and hands.

Finger-drumming, Sonny stared – with a costive pout – into the courtyard. He had almost completed the draft treatment he would offer, as soon as he could reach a telephone, to the top corridor of teenage producers. 'The FRIDGE as Storehouse of Magical Possibilities (cf. Joseph CORNELL). Any chance of working in Eli LOTAR's slaughterhouse photos for Bataille's *Abattoirs*? (Check with Sofya.) Outsider Art. MUD location (Voice over: Eliot reading from *Wasteland*). Studio; Talking Heads – Januszczak? Ignatieff? Some woman??'

(The prime advantage of these jokers with the outlandish monikers is that your godfearing Englishman will only accept that something is 'cultural' if it comes with a music-hall accent. Foreigners may be an inferior product, lacking true *spunk*, but they do know about art and cooking.)

Sonny would not sit: a mistake. He refused the luxury of another era, a row of salvaged tip-up cinema seats. He could not let the moment breathe; he was impatient to drive on, impale all the facts, achieve some grand conclusion. He began to read aloud from his preparatory notes. 'The bunker?' he blurted. 'I thought there was a bunker. I need a definite bunker for our title: "The Bunker and the Monument". That essential contrast of vertical and horizontal energies, the secret and the showy: the glitz of Silvertown and the modesty of Bow. All those nightland images. I want some of the great Henry Moore drawings on our rostrum. *Tilbury Shelter Scene!* The sleepers and the dead. What a metaphor for the condition of English *kultur*. Epstein's pietà attached to the Headquarters of the London Underground. Thick-lipped mothers of gloom!'

'It's bad karma to watch people sleeping,' Imar frowned. 'Better to put your eye to the keyhole and watch them fuck. It's *especially* bad to watch a pregnant woman sleep. That's taboo. The whole quality of the experience is so intense.'

'No, no, no,' Sonny yelped, 'I want the *heroic* side. People taking action for themselves, capturing their own space; taking their destiny, *forcibly*, into their own hands. That blitzed community of sleepers, dreaming their archetypal dreams, recapturing previously excommunicated territory – railway tunnels, sewers, bridges. Photographs by Bill Brandt evoking communal memories: lovers nestling against each other ... the face of an old hag in the crypt of Christ Church, Spitalfields ... timeless! ... she could have known the Ripper. Or those orthodox Jewish fathers in the Brick Lane shelter. The dignity! Undisturbed, carrying on their work, Books of the Law. What Brandt does ... here, look.'

He shoved a photograph towards Imar.

'What? A shed of gassed chickens?' Imar responded. 'Mouths agape, toothless, arms flung out – they are nothing but victims.'

'I see the shelters,' Sonny persisted, 'as a "concrete armada". This is one of the highs of our history, a time for the people, and we've got to link it with what you're doing now – not with the madness of Crosby's Tower of Babel.'

If the Silbury Mound field was a strong, though imperceptible, public statement, then the Bracken House bunker was one of the most notable single-handed achievements I have ever encountered. Imar, in the guise of a remedial gardener, had been granted access to a stark exercise yard, imprisoned on three sides by tall blocks of windows. Every move he made was viewed by the other tenants; and yet his master plan went unremarked, if not exactly a state secret.

Beneath the grass-flecked clay of this sombre garden was the formal geometry of a wartime bunker, harmoniously divided into four self-contained chambers. Platonic truths had been reasserted in these *gnomon*-activating depths: invisible passages between the world of elements and the race of life. Imar had excavated the entrances, one by one; had listened carefully to the oracle of falling water. He waited for clusters of eolithic light to break from the tainted darkness.

We sat on a log at the bunker's edge and let the night swallow us: solitary windows flared, glimpses of movement, opera snatches muffled in rapidly drawn curtains. This welfare rookery had fallen into the hands of the only people prepared to relish a Soviet-style glamour: students, archivists, state-sponsored artists. A gibbous moon slid from its cloud cover, offering – in the unwalled southern sector – a carnival vision of the most outflung of the Docklands studio-bivouacs; a pointless flurry of trapped waves, portholes and marine quotations. A pleasure boat grounded one nautical mile from the river.

It was time to go under. We slid our spades beneath the squares of turf that Imar designated, and dug – until we heard the clink of metal upon metal. A trapdoor was located, prised open, lifted. We lowered ourselves, feet scrambling for the rungs of a ladder, into the clammy darkness. We advanced, hesitantly, inch by inch, through unconvinced puddles of light afforded by my pocket torch. We found ourselves, at last, inspecting an icehouse, in which time itself had been chilled, slowed, handicapped. Even in the breath of our heightened expectations, the bunker remained obstinately less than it was.

The antechamber was steepled so high with industrial fallout that the only entry to the inner sanctum (the heart shrine) was by way of an obstacle course, perilous enough to deter any respectably mercenary tomb robbers. 'I let an old rag and bone man stash his stuff,' said Imar. 'He asked if he could leave a couple of things here – just for a few days: then came back with a pantechnicon.' What was on offer? Washing machines so ancient they must have been pedal-driven; useless slices of bicycle; sodden briquettes of paperbacks, congealed into twelve-deckers; enough folding chairs to sit out a square dance; Marcos-rivalling collections of single shoes; artificial limbs for dogs; gas stoves; lavatory bowls; columns of rusting paint tins: a fully-stocked museum of folk memories. We picked our way, admiringly, among the exhibits. And, as we stumbled blindly forward, we snapped off the spears of occasional stalactites; limey droplets plicked irregularly on to the flooded tile floor. In the torchlight the low ceiling shone like a dome of radium-licking insects (about to become stars). An eidetic cinema.

The secret inner chamber had been successfully dammed, mopped, dried, polished. The walls had been scoured of bureaucratic symbols and the blood oaths of cadet gangsters. The chimney pipe had been cleared of dirt, dead birds, rags: it was possible, once more, to light a fire. 'You should see them heave shut their curtains, when they see smoke rising, without apparent cause, from the old grass hump,' said Imar. 'Legends are spreading. Civilians keep well clear. They think some berserker mob are incinerating inconvenient human evidence.'

Oozing goodwill, and cackling with pleasure at his own strategies. Imar was no 'divine light' zombie: his vision could have been realized only through an immensely powerful self-belief (and many man-hours of vein-popping muscular effort).

'I determined, when I first heard rumours of this heretical Silvertown monument,' he announced, 'to counter it with one of my own. To work faster than they could work. To start digging while they were still farting around with brochures and flogging the circuit of merchant banks. Look at the blasphemy of it.' He jabbed fiercely against a projection of Crosby's river, pinning it to the wall; then swept an avenger's hand over this plucky attempt to align such reservoirs of the eternal spirit as the Museum of Design, Tower Bridge, and HMS *Belfast*.

'Can you believe it?' he stormed on. 'These people want to erect their obscene stack, a heap of inert and spiteful weaponry, upon the most potent site on the aetheric highway between Greenwich Hospital and St Paul's Cathedral. They actually intend to deflect the path of light, opened and acknowledged by Nicholas Hawksmoor; the ley that runs down from Blackheath – without drama or fuss – *exactly* through the gap between the twin domes, across the river, over the malign Isle of Dogs, to circle and recharge at the Tower of St Anne, Limehouse. As the light travels, it fades from our sight, but its influence does not pale: the Jews' Burial ground, Whitechapel ... King Cole's eucalyptus, the cater-pillar dreaming tree, Meath Gardens ... Victoria Park fountain ... Well Street. It blesses and touches all those unacknowledged and marvel-provoking enclosures; a spine of hope. How *dare* Crosby misread Turner's "View of St Paul's from Greenwich" (the Maze Hill eidolon)? Turner is careful to place an antlered deer in the foreground, and also a buck – so insubstantial that you can see the canvas beneath. These are the animal familiars, the spirit guides. Turner must never be dragooned into the enemy's camp.'

Sonny's frustration at not being able to take notes in the dark, and not knowing *what the hell* Imar was talking about, made him pathetically eager to escape our confinement. A smothering, claustrophobic sense of being 'out of it', beyond telephones – perhaps for ever – contributed to his unease. He was now quite certain that if we ever should re-emerge into the real world, *there would be nothing left*. The flats would be a cliff of termites, and the wasteland a robot-controlled industrial estate. Even his beloved Bow Quarter would have regressed to supplying matches to a phantom army of beggar girls. Surely, that was impossible. The Bow Quarter would never fail. But Imar's voice had that quality: an under-tow of mad humour that threatened to freeze into uncensored prophecy. He laughed aloud as he savaged Crosby's demonology of bad faith.

'How did you develop this concept of ... lines of force?' Sonny demanded, revealing, all too candidly, that his *realpolitik* was in tatters.

'By watching randy molluscs. I was sitting on the wall in Island Gardens, sketching a snail (*Helix aspersa*), as it inched towards its mate:

they can orgasm, you understand, for days at a time. It's been suggested that the more advanced mesogastropods returned to the sea. I wondered if this couple – in their slow-motion ecstasy – were going to make a dash for the river.' Imar smiled at the recollection. 'I happened to notice, to my amazement, that the dome of the Royal Observatory, with its turreted brick body, suggested a perfect snail silhouette (*Pomatias elegans?*); and I had an immediate vision of these irradiating hoops surging across the entire country, knotting the globe in right-hand spirals. I saw a translucent shell of unexploited energies. The "lines of force", as you call them, were created by the measured burn of mating snails, tracking each other down lucid paths of sticky seminal joy: a silver glide visible only to hermaphroditic life-forms. A condition to which I have always, subsequently, aspired.'

Sonny snapped – sure now that Imar was taking the piss – and bolted for the escape hatch. Our submarine was sinking straight to the bottom. We followed. Sonny cursed as he splashed, ankle-deep, through the flooded outer chamber. Paint tins clattered in his wake. We let the trapdoor fall into place behind us, and covered it once more with earth.

'I've been given permission to take casts of angelic forms in the Fitzwilliam; so I shall surround this square with twenty-four winged beings, their fingers reaching to make a connection,' Imar said. 'I don't want frozen salutes, baptized warriors holding their sword-arms out of the river. I'd rather amputate every limb. I want polysexual transcendent bliss – like snails, male and female together, mutually fucking and being fucked. I'll be *ready* if they ever try to build that monument, that Beelzebub nob. My work of defence has already begun in the bunker's unopened fourth chamber. When the time comes, I'll turn it loose.'

I slurped through the mud on Sonny's trail. The boundaries of his concept had burst, and the only solution was to wipe the slate, cut out, pick it up again in Silvertown. Another day, another notebook.

V

There comes a time in every successful meeting when the warring egos tire, and blanch towards the compromised satisfaction of having survived, intact, a potential trauma. The gathering at the London City Brasserie had mellowed through all the layers of port, stilton, champagne, strawberries, boredom, claret, gin and terror. Convulsing throats thirsted for silence. Inane fragments of conversation lay heaped on the floor like shattered saucers. The interminable afternoon had stretched into a star-bright evening. The Chairman, to general yawns of relief, had been stretchered out, choppered away to his next free meal. The atmosphere lightened up — to the extent that the Last British Film Producer tried to interest the fastidious Sh'aaki Twins in 'doing a line' of something. Professor Catling was stuffing his pockets with bottles of Armagnac and sniffing at bundles of cigars. Previously unstressed, but potently real ambitions were beginning to surface. Aware of his chamber reputation, as a ram among rose-spectacled bleaters, the Architect was pitching it strong at the Laureate's Wife. He was quite indecently horny, his cream slacks bulging with overstated pistols. A gamy reek of hormonal secretions blended with the madeleine of meat-steam on the airport window: horse-radish, pestled garlic, basil, Gauloises Caporal.

The building had now — officially — closed down and sad clusters of under-employed aliens were dumped, long coats covering their uniforms, at the riverside; to wait on a gale-tossed pier for the shuttle to Wapping, Cherry Gardens, London Bridge, and Chelsea Harbour. The cartel of pigged-out gourmets were the only humans still conscious between the sugar factory and Barking Road. A royal box of candlelight flickering over the angry black waters.

'And why not?' She shrugged. 'What the hell.' This sort of boardroom grapple happened all the time (usually at the end of chapters) in her husband's sweaty, screen-tested fiction. (If not in his private life; which she thought, on reflection, was not very probable.) She could never bring herself to try his stuff. She granted it all the credibility of a government-approved white paper, without any of the literary flair of the Wykehamist mandarins. His books, she assumed, were only purchased by smart young women on the promotional side of publishing, who wanted to create a sensation at dinner parties by boasting, to howls of derision, that they had actually *bought* one at Kennedy — and read it!

Unashamed, she met his arrogant gaze. She stared back — her firm breasts rising and falling under the simple Ralph Lauren sweater — into those smoky, steel-blue orbs. The darkened picture window over the King George V dock was the screen of a word processor. Green sentences stuttered and rushed at her, syllable by syllable, line by line; bringing the hot blood to her cheeks. *She must not give herself away. But she could hardly contain the mounting excitement she felt as she admired that sharp profile, the Roman brow, the consular authority. This was a man to command crucifixions. Those slender, cruel lips could compose passionate speeches, or soothe a high-blooded stallion. Cacharel, Eau de Toilette? She knew instinctively that his fierce mask hid a gentler and more sensitive aspect. The Katharine Hamnett storm-trooper jacket hung easily from his powerful shoulders. He was coolly, openly undress-*

ing her with his eyes. How lucky then that she had slipped into her sheer black Dior stockings and her peach-coloured Janet Reger underthings. She was unafraid. She wanted his hot maleness. She could wait no longer. Her fingers tore at the buttons of his collarless Calvin Klein shirt. How sweet and traditional he was! How unaffected by the dictates of quotidian (Cancel. Illegitimate. Type again. Substitute: 'everyday') *fashion. 'Take me, take me,' she sobbed, as she fumbled to unbuckle his sadistic* (Cancel. Illegitimate. Substitute: 'snakeskin') *Benetton belt. 'Take me here, now – make me yours.'*

The romantically enhanced appeal of this sensual and yielding creature was, for the moment, wasted upon the Architect. In his first, bug-eyed, response to her grab at his pleasure principle, he had inadvertently dropped one of his contact lenses into the sorbet – and was now impotent with fear, trying to convince himself that the crunching sensation in his mouth was caused by nothing more alarming than a shard of lemon-flavoured ice. Tiny slivers of deadly plastic were – he could *feel* them – targeting his intestine, eager to slash their way to freedom. And bugger the consequences. Was it not a fact that the post-mortem lens would carry the imprint of the unconscious assassin? Some swampland pathologist would tweezer up this curved miracle of micro-technology, and have a better idea of the woman's looks than the disadvantaged Architect would ever enjoy. He didn't want to check out while humping some blue-stocking turkey. But there was no time to validate her status (in the centrefold department): his trousers were around his ankles, and the life force was returning, in spasms, to his battle-scarred member.

Dear God, had she noticed that his eyes were, quite suddenly, different colours? Maybe she was turned on by freaks. He breathed heavily on the back of a silver spoon, and polished it on the cloth to reassure himself, in this distorted mirror, that she had not spotted the tiny distinguishing mark – do not call it a wart – in the cleft of his chin. Ladies of a certain age apparently considered this trivial flaw leant a saturnine quality to his otherwise classical (Stewart Granger?) good looks. They also went for men who limped. But there was no opportunity to try that one. She was astride him and ripping the shirt from his back.

A curious sensation rippled upwards from the soles of his feet, to break – in hair-raising confrontation – on the waves of involuntary surrender, spiralling blindly down the freeway of his spine. All six chakras were in critical overdrive. He licked his lips like a man drowning in sand. Was that a bowl of yogurt? What *was* she up to? 'Eh? Eeee. I–I. Ohh, you-uuuuu!' he vowelled his distress, rupturing in a single convulsion the elocutionary pretensions of a lifetime. She was, very slowly, devouring him. He couldn't stand it. He was lifting from the

runway, surging through railway tunnels, breaking over rocks, pounding the white buildings, waterfalling; with a singular greed to rewrite all
previous definitions of ecstasy.

At this hour only the Sh'aaki Twins were not pissed out of their
skulls: they were getting rather silly on lime-flavour carbonated water.
They were playing the game of spinning an empty claret bottle:
whoever it pointed at could choose an item from his brother's
collection of contemporary lithographs. Nobody was keeping score, but
it appeared that the one remaining wine waiter (who slept on the
premises) was now the proud possessor of forty-eight prime examples of
Kitaj, Schnabel, Kieffer, Koberling, Penck, Bellany, Baselitz, Polke,
Johns and Warhol. Indeed, the man was able, in a modest way, to set
himself up as a respected dealer, and adviser to new investors in this
notoriously high-risk field.

The Film Producer, who had snuffed his way through his own
supplies, was starting to 'freebase' the sugar basin. It was, as Professor
Catling judged, the optimum moment to make his outrageous pitch.
'We've dutifully rubber-stamped the shitty Bayreuth we were convened to bless, OK, fine; but now we have a chance to make our mark
and – within the same budget – initiate another project, an *original*
proposal that can slip through on the back of what the grey men require.
We can recover our reputation for probity, hold our heads high among
the community of artists. Let us act with stealth and in a way they will
never suspect – until it is far too late.' He let his balled fist drop on to the
table, startling the recumbent Producer, and throwing the Sh'aaki
Twins into a fit of the giggles. His rhetoric expired over a palpitating
dunescape of naked buttocks that strained, diligently, to make the earth
move. 'We don't want our names in lights,' Catling said, 'but neither
will we allow them to be scribbled on the water.'

He flicked open a scuffed sketchbook and gave his own interpretation
of the defiant dogma of that utterly obscure sculptor, S. L. Joblard. He
translated, with impressive fluency, these pages of frantic thaumaturgic
doodling: the mineral metaphors, the pencilled ghosts, the chalky erasures, the leagues of angels.

Professor Catling, prepared to travel in the quest of visionary stimulation, had 'discovered' Joblard's work in a remote gallery on the edge
of London Fields, Hackney. An old drovers' patch of no consequence
whatsoever that was notable only for lending its name to a spirited work
of lowlife fiction by John Milne. Joblard, it seemed, had conceived the
idiot-simple notion of borrowing the ice-making machine from the Lea
Valley Skating Rink to freeze the western dock, the second eye of the
Silvertown skull, to create a polar ocean. In the ice would be embedded

the salvaged wrecks of several whaling vessels. *Fram, Terra Nova,* and *Discovery* would be represented, however dubiously, within sight of the North Woolwich railway. The rubble of demolished riverside terraces would be dumped, then layered in foam or polystyrene chippings, to suggest Mt Erebus. Tattered canvas tents, war surplus (Brick Lane), would be despatched to the most far-flung regions, to double for Scott's camp sites. A dart-nibbled builders' shed would stand in for the shore base. Expenses would be minimal. There might even be a small profit to be earned in clearing such unexploitable relics. Outdated tins of bully beef, prairie beans, dog food, and pemmican could be buried in flag-marked cairns. Wind machines could guarantee a force-ten blizzard. Brave spirits, at the flash of a Euro credit card, could relive the noblest failure of them all – the dash to the Pole. Junior executives, under compulsion, would build their characters, hone their cutting edges, in a race against a team of Russian sailors from Tilbury (prepared, for the price of a night among the Soho slot machines, to fake it as Amundsen's hardy Norwegians).

Joblard of course had other – darker – notions he would tack on behind this preposterous smokescreen: shamanistic ceremonies concerned with lunar eclipses, molten lead, horse skulls, brick ovens, ice spears, the invocation of animal ancestors. These, Professor Catling had the tact not to mention.

The thing was put to the vote. The Sh'aaki twins sniggered, took out an option, and accepted. The Film Producer was already on his way home, via the Limehouse nick, in a canvas sack marked 'DOA'. The couple under the table, locked into writhing (and interchangeable) combinations of hunger and tumescence, continued to heave like huskies: they rose to the occasion, offering up tacit moans of approval. And so, to the sounds of feeding time in the wolf pen, a ribbon of pure madness was innocuously inserted among the footnotes. Professor Catling signalled for the waiter to summon a taxi.

VI

In that refurbished cattle truck, shuddering on some embankment ledge, above fenced mud fields, over paludal wastes into which sacks of paper credit had been tipped as ballast; in that rattling, enclosed space, pressed hard against the smeared, cold window – I began to understand the concept of breakdown. Complete, absolute despair. The ego extinguished. The power of the centre, the unviolated heart of my being, was tattered and frayed. I tasted vomit on my lips. And felt my angel shiver to be free. Sonny spoke aloud, but his voice was untrustworthy. It was my mother's voice, calling out in the darkest hour of the night, addressing me with my dead father's name.

The quality of the desolation outside the carriage's window-screen altered; it shifted and shook, as I drove my knuckle against the ball of my eye, feebly opposing this accumulation of evidence with mere pain. I pulled my cheek from the dirty glass, leaving behind a negative frame: the portrait of a ghost, a man without moral substance. I had never confessed to being anything but a jaunty witness, a paddler in the narrative shallows. Now there was nothing else to look at. There was no 'story'. The landscape had withdrawn its labour: an unsettled greyness. This heat-printed trace, this copied man, stared back into the train with an unfocused, autistic gaze; and saw Sonny sitting with some straw-stuffed bundle of laundry. Borrowed clothes, borrowed skin; the inevitable carrier bag of other men's books.

The catastrophic rump of Stratford and Plaistow, Canning Town and Custom House became, as the train moved, the blast furnaces of Margam, the rolling mills, the fire-tongued stacks belching their gritty deposits on to the salt breeze; creeping over low hills, to strip ancient damp oaks, or gift the valley folk with lush cancers and squamous growths; dying among the inhuman lightless depths of conifer plantations, in which foxes hid from squadrons of shotgun-toting foresters. I was back in Wales, being driven down the coast road, west, following the coffin. Pieces of that journey lodge, and overwhelm my lack of interest in yet another East London railway adventure. Salient flashes of the Thames, between wrecking yards and stiff-necked cranes, burn into the persistence of the broad flat Severn. I saw the shell of Margam Abbey, and the roofless chapel on the hill above the maze; while, all the time, we continued to jolt towards the business of Silvertown.

Sonny still danced to a self-inflicted cattle-prod tango. 'If we can borrow a standby crew from "Local News" or "Blue Peter",' he said, 'we'll simply compose with their tired utilitarian footage. Exploit banal images that have no resonance, no sense of being inhibited by meaning. The method has distinct possibilities. Found art, construction by selection: editing is the really constructive stage anyway. Give us your raw material – formulaic establishing shots, over-emphatic close-ups – and we'll electrify the air waves.' He broke off to hammer at the walls of our designer-vandalized compartment. 'An Art Train! Dziga Vertov! *Kino-Eye!* Montage is the true engine of the lyric. We'll plunder those reservoirs of unconscious aspiration. Take whatever we are given, and *cut/cut/cut* to the heartbeat, to the rhythms of the breath: engines, wheels, statues falling, racing clouds, the quaking towers of the city. Futurists of a New Reality!'

Sonny's lips were moving but the sound, mercifully, escaped from me; ran out into the overhead wires, leapt towards Canvey Island and Shoebury Ness, bearing false messages of revolution and hope. His gestures were wilder and faster. His teeth dazzled like Mexican bone dice. It was like watching a madhouse charade in which some flesh-scorched depressive mimes his remembered account of the Book of Deuteronomy. Without warning, I experienced an excruciating pain in my ear (how crude are the body's metaphors!); as if Sonny's irrepressible torrent of enthusiasm was splitting the incus, the anvil, with a tiny (and blunt) cold-chisel. Each blow projected a scarlet flash on to the ceiling of the carriage: cooling towers, the moulded angel on the side of the Custom House, the black and silted canal. I tipped forward to rest my head in my hands. Sonny was pouring the landscape, in the form of an ointment of honey and melted film stock, into my external auditory meatus. It was slipping, sticking, soothing; inwardly sealing my father's voice, which prompted me towards actions I could not begin to understand.

Absolute madness! Sonny had no mandate from the Corporation. We were without cameras, crew, or recording equipment. We had no budget. We couldn't raise a production number between us. Our epic looked certain to qualify as one of those masterpieces that exist only in the conversations of film buffs. The fewer people to see them, the fewer to contradict the legend. Eventually you have world rights on a cockney cut of Orson Welles' *It's All True* – and without exposing a single foot of film.

I was drowning in the psychopathology of obsession: the harder I drove myself in composing this account, taking down the voices (the intrusions from 'elsewhere'), the more exposed those around me became to repeated and meaningless mischiefs. My lacerated ego puffed and swelled to a critical state: I began to believe that, by some magical trope, unwittingly enacted, *I had moved ahead of the events I was describing*. Or even, and this is hardest to swallow, by committing these fictions to paper, I had ensured they would occur. I found myself, a sandpaper-pored Richard Burton, opening my newspaper with palsied hand to have the latest atrocity confirmed. *Vessels of Wrath*: 'angels that failed', revengers, river-inhabiting, tied to the earth (but not part of it), deluding with false divinations, whispering into the wires, toying with stop lights. Light bulbs exploded as I touched the switch. The typewriter cut out as I pressed the first key (I considered shunning the letters 'j' and 'k', but that was insufficient penance). I fell prey to the temptation to destroy everything I had done – as if that would revoke it; to pitch the whole mess into the fire. As soon as I completed my narrative of the Whitechapel train-fury, typed the final paragraph, I slumped in front of the television set to receive equally distant, but more compelling, versions: blood, carnage, suffering. I began to wrestle with the present tale of widowhood, memorials, monuments, and I was telephoned with the news of my father's death. If I moved on, as I proposed, to crucifixions, cursed motor launches, Islands of the Dead – what could I look forward to?

Walking away from it all – escaping – the house, the desk; a Saturday morning, down the Waste, for old time's sake. And I found in a box on the floor a curious, awkward, Germanic engraving: 'Descent from the Cross' by A. H. Winter. It was very cheap. I bought it to resell, as I hoped, at the next Book Fair. But succumbed to temptation and held on to it, hung it on the wall. A slumped Christ; maimed, extinguished beyond all hope of resurrection. The peasant disciple, mongoloid with shock, fingers hooked beneath the lifeless shoulders, struggles with a dead beast-weight. The twisted neck, the veins of the kneeling woman. It was unutterably bleak.

I recognized the cross, a monstrous concrete tree, as we turned off the motorway and down the private slip-road to the crematorium. Red furnaces against an overcast sky. Perimeter fences of the steelworks. Out of the window of the Silvertown train the whole reel was available, now, today, at this moment, the film of life: event by event, second by second, a procession of single frames. It is all there, all within reach; birth to grave – and beyond: it requires only the courage to *stop everything* and to look.

I pushed the heel of my hand against my ear and succeeded in muffling the pulse of pain. Held firm by the gravity of sick pride, I remained exactly where I was – and nowhere else. There was no further expenditure of stolen time. The trauma was safely frozen.

Sonny is nudging me, opening the door: Silvertown platform. It is as mauve, silky, stocking-filtered, fey, day-for-night as Delvaux's 'Night-watchman'; used on the dustjacket of the American edition of Julio Cortázar's *Around the Day in Eighty Worlds*. Obscure, semi-official buildings. A snake's nest of rail tracks. Hills in the distance – across the river? And the river itself, that self-renewing avenue of escape? Denied to us. I grant no credence to this preposterous set. If this is reality – pass me a paintbrush.

We have to arrange, somehow, to re-enter our narrative, to advance; or stand for all eternity, shivering in this dogmatically transitional limbo. (I flashed to John Clute's warning of my 'not remarkably powerful grasp of narrative syntax'. But I am powerless to act. It is like being handed a plague card.) I allow myself to be dragged, club-footed, a storm anchor behind Sonny's still bustling pilot boat.

Silvertown, sadly, makes little attempt to live up to the glory of its name. It would have to be acknowledged even in the most optimistic auctioneer's catalogue as 'distressed'. Subdued by the deconsecrated ziggurat of the Sugar Factory, the thin main street – once active in the field of nautical exploitation – now reluctantly let chaos greet chaos; it tumbled into more and more boisterous characterizations of squalor and decay. The once fire-stormed hamlet was now a glittering beach of sugar. The air was thick with a viscid sweetness; inspissated droplets fell, without fear or favour, like a sleet of poisoned nostalgia. As you smiled, charmed by this version of the picturesque, the enamel of your teeth was stripped to the nerve roots; the periodontal membrane dissolving into black lace.

We crossed and recrossed deleted railway bridges, trying to find our way to the City Airport, the Royal Docks, the site of the almost completed memorial to the Widow's Consort (known locally as 'Dirty Den's Knob'). The tracks always petered out among the same tangles of wire, giant wheels of extinct machines, columns of treadless tyres.

A mustard-plaster Victorian Gothic church, St Mark's, primed with a terrifying bestiary of gargoyles, oversaw and dominated this principality of unemployed apparitions. S. S. Teulon's masterpiece, with its hollow ceramic blocks, was caged in wire and no longer approachable. Soon it would be returned to the populace, the eager communicants, with a new identity – as a storage shed for the local history collection of the Passmore Edwards Museum. An unnecessary conceit: the entire canton should have been under a bell jar, with a neatly engraved *sans-serif* label. Even the inevitable First War cross was beyond our reach. I pressed against the fence, striping my cheek: a refugee from the razor gangs. The words (*Courage, Remembrance, Honour*) exulted the dead 'whose names shall live for ever'; but not here, where the sugar-smog has already eaten the gilt from the sandstone, and erased the lost squadron of claimants on our sympathy.

It was long past the time to look for a drink.

VII

The kids leant in wonder on the antlers of their BMX bicycles, as Imar O'Hagan walked inside the wicker head across the Bow wastes. He disappeared into a shallow pit and – for a few minutes – they saw nothing but the crown of the great head itself, the shell-crusted eyes, floating towards them. They mounted up, cowboy fashion, standing on the pedals to race back to a safe distance. The Wicker Man and his double were within a breath of life.

Lacking honest, friable Dorset chalk, Imar had whitewashed the x-ray of the Cerne giant on to one of his lesser mounds. The creature's arm was stretched out in a gesture of reconciliation; not grasping a warrior's club, but a shamanistic twig that resembled nothing so much as a favourite niblick. The face was decorated with a pair of Rotarian-approved spectacles. His vertical manhood fell short (by several yards) of the generative potency of his two-thousand-year-old rival.

When the wicker head was lifted into place, the revenging Twin, the basket case, stood ready on his scaled-down Silbury. He stared fiercely across an empire of compressed slurry towards the southern horizon and the coronation of his Silvertown rival: this false sibling with its feet set in concrete.

With a hoe Imar raked up the living grass, the mud and the worms; he stuffed his creation (his Adam, his angel) as he would a cushion. Balls of old newspaper (carolling wars, disasters, corporate raids, rape, surveillance, child abuse) were fed through the cage of his curved white ribs. He kissed the head full upon its lips. He aimed a sharp blow at its paper heart. The physical work was done.

Sitting at the foot of the mound – with slowed breath – Imar opened his sandwich box and gently lifted the twelve snails from their leaf. He was prepared to follow their instruction. Their silver threads would set the destiny of the monster.

VIII

Our search finally yielded, among wine bars fretful to parasite upon the flanks of the City Airport, an old dockers' pub, an unrestored end-of-terrace barrack. The ham rolls were reassuringly authentic: crusted in oven-tanned plaster of Paris, concealing a pink slick of reconstituted animal fat. The Guinness was warm and slightly soapy. The wallpaper had not been pasted to the wall: it had grown like a fungus. And was growing still.

The only other customer, sitting under a photograph of the wreck of the *Albion*, was Henry Milditch. They fitted so well together, these blatant props, that they might have been artfully posed by the management in a patriotic tableau; an advertisement for extra-strong cough drops. Milditch was dressed like a seafaring man. He was bearded, grizzled, red. I could have sworn he was suffering from frostbite. He blew on clenched hands: his eyes narrowed to menacing slits against the glare of sunlight on pack-ice.

'What'll you have, boys?' Milditch offered, with unprecedented generosity. 'I've landed a beauty here. Polar trek across the Royal Victoria: two hours a day, three days a week. Five hundred notes in the hand. Can't be bad. And a possible "voice over" if the "South Bank Show" bites on Joblard. Catling's been dropped, or there'd be a clash of chalk-stripes with Melvyn that would devastate the horizontal hold. It was no contest, I walked the audition. I still had the costume I'd liberated from the tele in Greenland; I thought it would come in handy for winter mornings down the Lane. It's promotion for Milditch, boys. I've made it from base-camp gopher to Captain Oates. I was the only applicant with his own gear. So it's hard tack and horsemeat all the way to Christmas.'

It made me shiver talking to him. We dosed the shakes with remedial tots of rum. Milditch had even taken to a pipe. He poked and scraped, puffed out contemplative streams of blue smoke; hummed the odd Music Hall chorus. He offered to take us with him on to the Great Ice Barrier. We could participate in the ultimate bulldog fantasy.

The broken-backed *Albion* hung above us, trapped and framed (a crocodile trophy), as we killed another bottle – holding our wake while we were still around to enjoy it. Royalty fanciers on overcrowded and inadequate piers had been swept away in the tidal wash of the *Albion*'s launch. Respectfully dressed to the nines, they drowned where they waved. Their sacrifice authenticating the loss of the vessel. They were 'justified' when their small tragedy afforded the opportunity for some strikingly purple cadenzas in the national press.

Arm in arm, wrapped in a shaggy cloak of spirits, we staggered up the slope towards the City Airport; battling through a whiteout of sugar-fires, the darkness at noon, the huskies howling in their quarantine cages.

IX

The naked hubris of the Consort's Monument was startling: a scaffolded Colossus, an Ozymandias touting for copy from a gossip-column Shelley. The stack, knitted in coloured searchlight beams, could achieve its apotheosis only as a ruin, a *Planet of the Apes* arm, lofted from future sands for the gimcrack inspiration of stoned romantic poets.

Chained barges were linked across the King George V dock. Choppers worried and swooped. Marksmen crouched on roof tops. Dogs sniffed for plastic explosives and cannabis. (That Janus-headed horror of drug-crazed bombers!) A babble-speak of spooks licking their own gloves. Then the Widow herself clattered on sawn-off stilts into a hail of exploding flashbulbs. She was padded like a Dallas Cowboy; smoke-blue, she chicken-danced towards a nest of microphones. Her head was unnaturally tilted (as if it had been wrongly assembled after a motorway pile-up), but her hair was obedient. A swift, over-rehearsed smile preceded the ankle-stamping homily. 'And you know ... you know you know you know.' The blade-shredded acoustics fed her catchphrases back into the prompt machines, to blare in frantic reverb from speakers which had been hung (like so many skulls) around the perimeter fence for the benefit of the uninvited masses.

'I can only echo the words ... the words the words the words,' she uncurled a fleshy white arm, like Gypsy Rose Lee about to peel a long black evening glove, 'of Captain Robert ... Robert ... Falcon Scott. "For God's sake look after ... after after ... our people ... people people." That has always been ... been ... and remains remains ... our first principle. Looking after our own people.'

Over at the Victoria Dock they were testing the strength of the ice by airlifting the Royal Vegan. The Widow had timed her oration to the second, the recorded applause would steal his thunder, and neutralize any potential whingeing about 'traditional values' and amateur heroics, the boy-scout stuff. Anyway, why dig up that Polar fiasco? Didn't the bloody man *fail*, beaten by a gang of Viking lager louts? And what had we salvaged of the fabulous mineral wealth of the continent, to say nothing of the buried occult deposits, the blue hollows guarding the Spear of Destiny? Sod all, that's what. Enough ground for a five-a-side football pitch.

A sad knot of anorak-draped proles had been bussed in from outlying geriatric hospitals and day centres to stand at the dockside, waving-by-numbers at the overalled maintenance workers; while being deafened by the thud of ice-making machinery, the sinister hum of Joblard's privately generated magnetic field, and the low-level raids of helicopter gunships. A day to remember. Or so they were told.

Milditch ushered us towards the Customs Sheds where my old friend the sculptor, S. L. Joblard, was mumbling his final instructions to his regular wild bunch of razor-cropped assassins. These were revealed, on closer acquaintance, as a trio of mild-mannered, obediently impoverished art students, who happened to look like warders from a Hogarthian asylum. Joblard would lead us in our push on the Pole. There was no difficulty about our joining the team. We were winched into sets of bloodstained and stinking parkas, balaclavas, vast gloves on which the fur was still growing. Then we were given a swift onceover by Make-up.

'We'll have to do something about the suntan, lovey,' Make-up trilled, patting Sonny down with arsenic powder and a copydex laminate. 'Very persistent, isn't it?' Stone-faced, we received our quota of lip sores, blains, blisters, tissue trauma, and rime-spiked dogfur fringes. We staggered out on to the rink like tipsy rejects from a VD clinic. Milditch, the old pro, leant contentedly on a stick; puffing at his pipe, absorbed in a suitably jaunty *leitmotif* from his headset: *Blood on the Tracks*. The familiar sage-spiced odour of the herb calmed us.

Joblard had retreated into himself: his social persona had shifted to something unformed and private. It was like watching a detailed reflection drain from a mirror. Joblard no longer reacted to external stimuli. He was quite alone. The polar pantomime meant nothing to him: a convenient method of funding some arcane and potentially unstable ritual. His motives were also opaque. They were not satiric, nor political. He flattered nobody and wanted nothing in return for his efforts. He made no boasts. He listened intently for the return of some sound he had initiated in a previous existence.

It struck me that Joblard had reversed Stevenson's polarity: Hyde had succeeded in manufacturing his own doctor, in the form of Professor Catling. This mask of respectability granted him leave to slip the bear from its chain.

We were undistinguished extras. Joblard would soon break away from our plodding troop of bogus adventurers and strike into the solitary distance, bent against the storm of shredded asbestos that his assistants tipped over the propellers of the wind machine. He would 'tap' the ice floor, searching for a spirit hidden within a secret hermetic chamber, a presence of 'concerned agile violence'. He would cast the moon in lead; deliberately inverting the process and meaning of alchemy. He would make a necessary sacrifice. I only hoped that we were not a part of it.

We followed Milditch out; and were ourselves followed by a pre-recorded cacophony of sledge dogs. It felt as if we were about to be hunted to the death. Awkward as underwater divers in our stiff and cumbersome gear, we slid and shambled down a short ramp and on to the ice. Drooling exemplars of Hurler's syndrome gaped at us from the windows of a rank of lime-green minibuses: so many selenotropic vacancies. Helpers jollied them into twitching their miniature union jacks. An orange flare curved against the darkening sky; the wind machines began to clatter and grind. It was impossible to stand upright: we tumbled, a heap of rags, against the dockwall.

Crouching, with gritted teeth, cursing; we were strapped to our sledges. Roped together, unable to speak, or hear the word of command, locked in our individual hells, we manhauled our ballast (of undistributed Crosby/Sandle brochures) over the thunder of a ground sea – somewhere in the general direction of Southend.

The Customs Sheds and the Airport buildings vanished in a total wipe of stinging plastic pellets. The creaking icebound vessel, the *Terra Nova*, fell behind us: our last icon of escape. A lingering look at its frost-webbed rigging and we were alone in a wilderness of negatives: all the dark shades whose power we had invoked (and insulted) were out there, and they were waiting for us.

'Stone-crazed lunacy!' Sonny screamed. 'I only hope someone somewhere is shooting this. We might be doing the stuff for no reason at all. What if we get back to the cutting room without an inch of film?' he gibbered. 'Maybe, yes, wait. What if, ah, yes yes. We'll scratch the film like those Brakhage freaks, like Norman McClaren, Len Lye. We'll scrape storms out from the emulsion. Cave-painters. Get at the elemental force. Flood it with raw sound. Uncover the primal images. Yes, great. What a breakthrough!'

Henry Milditch remained at ease, comfortable, ganja-loose, marching with steady rhythmic strides; not exerting himself, modest in courage. Oates had joined him, or so it appeared; giving us all the strength to follow. He was, as he told me later, quietly running over the list of junk shops he hadn't checked out in the last month, between Billericay and Westcliff-on-Sea. He was rehearsing the mantra of phone numbers he would need on his return to the terminal.

I cannot guess how many hours passed: we twisted and writhed in our harnesses, our savaged faces always into the wind. We could see no more than ten or twelve yards in any direction. There were no longer any buildings, no walls, no bridges, trees, birds, vehicles – no other people. We were microbes twitching pathetically on a lens of ice: we obeyed the laws of physics, responded blindly to forces we could not understand. A circle of visibility followed us, as if we were held, wherever we moved, within the spotlight beam of some perverse and experimental theatre.

Now I began to sense the presence of other creatures on the ice, strange familiars whose articulate breath surrounded us: melted by human heat, the speech-mist released whispers of false doctrine, fatal advice. ('*But when I look ahead up the white road / There is always another one walking beside you.*') They guided us between blue crevasses and snow-powdered obstacles: dumped motors, or inconvenient canisters that hissed when you brushed against them. Dog forms pressed on our legs, leaving them chilled and trembling. Snarls of meat savagery forbade us to turn our heads and look back.

Suddenly the load increased; Milditch, leading us, held up an arm – Sonny had fallen on to his knees. We were dragging his dead weight. He was weeping, the hot tears cracking channels in his grotesque white mask. 'Nobody can shoot in these conditions: we've got to negotiate for time and a half. Or I'm pulling out.' Negotiate with whom? Out where? The dock, by my calculation, was not quite a mile long – maybe a little over two miles, if we had strayed through on to the Albert or the George. *But they were not frozen!* I suppose the machines could have gone ape, mindlessly responding to this atmosphere of trumpeting euphoria. Perhaps the sledges were slowing us to such an extent that we were hardly advancing at all. We had been marching for at least three hours by any real estimate; therefore, we should be out on the Thames itself, and heading for the North Sea, Spitsbergen, and the Arctic Ocean. I believe the Thames itself had magnified our mood by freezing up like some Baltic port: it had plunged into its own past, sealing plagues under a coarse skin of jollity, ox roasts, fire. A green-white membrane was creeping from Woolwich to Bermondsey. The tower of St Alfege would lift from some glacial tongue like the tusks of a trapped mastodon.

Milditch snapped the spell. He had spotted a dark shape that he took to be an emergency cairn, hopefully containing food, medical supplies, and rum. Supporting Sonny between us, we stumbled towards it. There *was* something, a shape in the snow, a mound. We scraped with our gloved hands, scratching and tearing at the unpleasantly glutinous solution. It peeled back in strips, an obscene fruit; or an egg laid by something half-human. We were looking into the face of a woman drowned in air; flattened against the glass, puff-cheeked, rigid – her eyes open. We had unwrapped some casual crime of passion. Another victim entombed in a car. The kind of journey, begun in fever, which frequently ends in the River Lea: hauled out, dripping, white legs in a police net. The blue shirts smoking and sharing a thermos: 'pacing' the paperwork to enjoy a fine spring morning. But this woman was behind the wheel, clothed, undisturbed: she must have taken a seriously wrong turning and been swallowed alive in a web of soft white rubber; denied breath.

Whatever it was that she saw, before she gave up the ghost, was still out there. She was still seeing it; it was in front of us. And as I became aware of this, *at that very moment*, a narrow crack, or passage, opened in the mantle of mist. We could see for miles – but only through a mean slit, a keyhole. Everything was sharp, brilliant. There were precise, elegant shadows. A radiant landscape; too clear to be true. There was grass again, all green things; and a firm cloud on the crest of a hill, getting slowly bigger, coming towards us. We did not dare to breathe: our fernlike exhalations turned to glass, chimed and shattered. The cloud grew into a forked human figure, or something more than that, an unfleshed diagram of veins, sinews, scarlet pulses: a walking tree, a giant.

There was the ugly interference of a monogrammed helicopter overhead, a cone of lights to confuse us; the snow powder swirled and stung, the figure was lost. The Royal Personage was evidently making his appearance. Around us the ice began to creak and strain, to protest: our boots were surrounded by pools of water. It looked as if, very soon, we would have to start swimming; still chained to the weight of our sledges.

We began to slide, to skid, to scramble for the dockwall. But which direction should we take? Away to our left we caught the orange glow of a fire and, irrationally, pulled towards it; towards a primitive source of comfort. We advanced on the patch of ice that would be first to give. Joblard's cauldron of lead was about to be tipped, his liquid silver spilled. I feared for him. It was always the big men, the bulls, who went fastest: Petty Officer Evans, a legend, a tower of strength, 'so confused as a result of a fall that he could not even do up his boots'. The culling had to start somewhere: we were too many in too small a place.

The lead hissed at our feet, a scimitar; a moon was cast, a delicate, rough-edged meniscus. *THE MOON IS THE NUMBER 18*, I flashed; how I'd puzzled over that title of Charles Olson's, intrigued but uneasy, until I discovered the tarot, and its interpretation. 'Hidden enemies, danger, calumny, darkness, terror, deception, occult forces, error.' Is that all? It felt much worse; those were pinpricks available anywhere. A few pages deeper into Olson another title lurked: *AS THE DEAD PREY UPON US*. The purity of Joblard's act under these extraordinary circumstances was post-human. What drove him to it? The preparations and the difficulties were everything. He worked best under pressure. He searched for someone to hold a harpoon to his throat. The object itself was redundant, self-erasing, an embarrassment. Joblard hunted the irritation of motive through blocks of inert fat. I can accept anything from these artists – except their justifications: the laboured, stuttering language-seizures forced upon them in their attempts to procure some pitiful dole of credit. 'Take a bath, man. Don't explain.'

The smoke from the cauldron thickened, and resolved itself: a giant figure had entered our circle. It had shaken free from an antiquarian's gazette, a *Gentleman's Almanac*: a Wicker Man, tongued with fire, his lineaments blazing, a mane of crackling whips. We could see through him, and see ourselves; mesmerized, inadequate. Sonny had wet himself like a frightened child. The Wicker Man was helmeted like a *poilu* in a spiral of shell. His frame was warted with snails; they popped, and spat hot oil as he burnt. A Job, he was magnificent in a cloak of boils. His wooden ribs breathed fire, but were not themselves destroyed. Gladstone's effigy had marched from Bow in stern rebuke: his arm stretched out, pointing beyond us. Frankenstein's Adam come to his end, prophetic, goaded further than his capacity for forgiveness could bear: he was cast in pride. '*I shall die, and what I now feel be no longer felt. I shall ascend my funeral pile triumphantly and exult in the agony of the torturing flames.*'

The ice, with cracks like fired timber, was breaking up all around us; we were afloat. Clumsily, we twisted free of the sledge harnesses, and searched for something with which to paddle our floe for the shore. All of Joblard's machines were sparking, smoking, failing. The wind dropped and the fog lifted. A sour lemon sun revealed the Boschian scope of all these Earthly Delights.

The Consort's Folly, the stepped pyramid (its lions, and friezes, and elevators) was a black torch. Flames tore at the sky. Sirens screamed. Masonry crumbled. The concealed steel joists, supporting the Heinkel, buckled; then gave way. The bomber nosedived into the dock, wrecking a rescue launch that was attempting to take the panicked official party to safety. The sound system pounded out anthems of rage. Crimson fire engines ineffectually jetted high streams from both banks: they crossed, married, fell short. Glistening liquid arches converted the dock into a cathedral, and the memorial stack into an altarpiece.

The Wicker Man was stepping, with single strides, from barge to barge. The embalmed corpse of the Consort hung from his arms; leathery and fire-blackened, wood in its veins – a bog sacrifice, or Grünewald's Isenheim Christ. The pair were expelled from the world of men, exiled in a collaboration at the heart of the flames: the sudden chill of the furnace's fiercest cell.

We had passed unconsciously through some warp, crossed the border, and were viewing gospels of the future; but we were frozen, trapped, floating helplessly – unvoiced witnesses. Like Mallory and Irvine ('still climbing when last seen') we had reached our summit, our Everest; but we could neither return, nor report. We were no longer required. We had all travelled far beyond the possibility of any useful participation in the resolution of these events. The fire erased us. Let somebody else interpret the preserved shadows, the thin prints of lead, the irradiated wafers of light.

9

The Isle of Doges
(*Vat City plc*)

The Isle of Doges
(*Vat City plc*)

'I am not sure the bubble has burst, I would
prefer to say there has been a realignment'

Alan Selby (Estate Agent),
Débâcle in Docklands

'Hath a dog money?'

Shylock, *The Merchant of Venice* (Act 1, Scene 3)

Yes, we have no bananas. A nightmare then? How does one run a credible
banana republic without them? Child's play. The ingenuity of our fiscal
cardinals, our thinktank of snapping turtles, is needlessly invoked. Sell
what has already been stolen and let the victims of this sleight of hand
believe that, in some miraculous fashion, their long sequestered property
is being returned to them. The zebra-suited pirates, puffy pink faces
innocent of all corruption, are rewarded in votes and adulation, in *yen*,
Deutschmark, *krugerrands*, *dollars* – credit! 'Interest' is a distorting mirror,
its own contrary. Let the plant wither on the vine, but the deal must go
down.

It all began when South Wales, from Caerleon to the cathedral
city-hamlet of St David's (the grail dreams of Arthur Machen to the
seven cantrefi of Dyfed), was 'leased' to Onokora-Mishima Investments
(Occidental); and a Shinto shrine was erected at the epicentre of the
Bridgend Enterprise Park. A gold-crusted phallus was set in a rectangle
of raked white sand (gathered from the radiated ruins), to frustrate the
ambitions of corporate raiders and to abort the flight plans of locusts.
Half-naked, male worker/slaves built up the ridges of their upper
bodies, glistened and chanted: admired, from afar, by fluttering painted
bird-boys in travesty. *The Sun Dragon!* The ancestor-worshipping
rituals of rugby football were honoured by the people of both cultures –
living on a pauper's diet of bitter memories, and conquests celebrated

only in song. The aboriginal *Cymry*, natural quislings, greased back their hair, shifting allegiance from Gene Vincent to Toshiru Mifune: finding solace in Germanic oratorios, and the seasonal slaughter by fire of innocent estate agents. Their racial pride, a sour thing, was made tame by a cargo cult of hi-tech toys, filling the cupboards of their immaculate hutches. They lived, gratefully, by a creed of strong bellies and limpid poetry.

Norfolk, from Lakenheath to Sculthorpe, went to the Dallas Cowboys. The decision was close, requiring a plebiscite by male suffrage. The benefit-drawing underclass and the mentally disadvantaged (Liberals, Gays, Book Collectors) were rigorously excluded; which resulted, inevitably, in a low turnout of weekenders, east enders, and media gypsies. Who voted, after searching the darkest recesses of their psyches, over many a dinner party, to exclude the Washington Redskins. The pinks and the greens could not live with the word 'Washington', and the right-thinkers (*sic*) were not about to invite some ragtag of landless Blackfeet to camp in their lush back yard (despoiling the habitat of so many recently discovered toads, coypus and birds of passage). Lock up your daughters. The Dallas Cowboys it was: by a neck (size eighteen, ruffed in fat like prime beef in the stockyard).

But all this was no more than making legitimate a contract which had been, *de facto*, in place for generations. The whole inheritance of abandoned tactical airstrike bases was up for grabs: a dying tundra of miniature golf courses, conifer screens, radiation-free bunkers (conversion-friendly as DIY hyperhyper-markets), baseball diamonds, and American Rules football pitches, complete with electronic scoring facilities (with Early Warning playback and 2,000 provocative sponsor's messages from the Big Book). '*The Lord shall smite thee in the knees, and in the legs, with a sore botch that cannot be healed.*' (Deuteronomy, 28.35).

The local dealers, car-boot traders and pensioned 'wreckers', swooped early to carry off the stacks of Gold Medal paperbacks, the snuff videos, porn aids, uppers, downers, heroin, crack, speed, Southern Comfort, deep-frozen grits, fetishist flying suits and helmets (beloved of skateboarders). It was Saigon revisited. The whole strip, from Grimes Graves to the Wash, was cropdusted with defoliants, bulldozed, burnt, cleared as a pre-season training camp for those genetic braggarts from Texas (bulls, bears, guards, fridges, fleetfoot blacks): the infertile steroid-pumping popeyed gladiators. Museum fodder! These games were a logistic embarrassment run for the benefit of the root-beer and popcorn franchises. Teams would soon confront each other – separated by thousands of miles of water – by shovelling strategies, game plans, meat statistics, favoured plays and form guides into the computer, and taking bets on the outcome. A potentially rich territory was opening up for baby-faced console jocks and goat-slaughtering snake-brained fixers. They were bending the future under the shame of bad money.

The ice floe was breaking. Mother London herself was splitting into segments, the overlicked shell of a chocolate tortoise. Piggy hands grabbed the numbered counters from the table. The occult logic of 'market forces' dictated a new geography. Banglatown, as it was vulgarly known, replaced the perished dream of Spitalfields. The 'born-again' Huguenots dumped their Adam fireplaces, and ran. The stern fathers of the One True Faith sent columns of black smoke twisting skywards as they redressed the violations of the culture of drunkards and apostates that surrounded them. Vulture priests, percolating hatred beneath their turbans, bearded in a nest of absolutes, spittled their chanting congregation with infallible accusations. *It is spoken.* Fundamentalist guards patrolled the border tracks (Cable Street to Cannon Street Road, to Bethnal Green, to Commercial Street); white-eyed, reciting the scriptures, AK-47s dangling from their shoulders. Children stoned adulterers, unbelievers, and White Hart Lane heretics. A time of angels and visitations: angels of revelation, angels of death, trumpeters of the resurrection. Now the censors alone have the melancholy duty of reading books. And condemning them to the flames. The marketplace blazes to a life unequalled since the Marian barbecues. The Brewery, indecently eager to confess its blasphemy, sold its holdings; and was smoothly translated into a prison for theological dissidents, common criminals, and journalists.

We had lost the capacity for experiencing surprise. We were immodest. Nothing Davy Locke told us could bring the blood to our cheeks. The *Book of Revelation* was as familiar as the *Hackney Gazette*, but tamer. We knew that the Isle of Dogs had been sold to the Vatican State, and we did not care. It was a natural consequence of Runcie's merger. One of the shakier assets that had to be stripped. The peg of uncircumcised land was known to the outlying squatters of Blackwall and Silvertown as 'The Isle of Doges', and to the cynics of Riverside as 'Vat City'. This deregulated isthmus of Enterprise was a new Venice, slimy with canals, barnacled *palazzi*, pillaged art, lagoons, leper hulks: a Venice overwhelmed by Gotham City, a raked grid of canyons and stuttering aerial railways. A Venice run by secret tribunals of bagmen, too slippery for Vegas; by relic-worshipping hoodlums, the gold-mouthed heads of Colombian cocaine dynasties.

A temporary alliance of Milanese industrialists and pro-Albanian social purists had made things too hot for the established Papal Mafia; a move from the homeland to some more relaxed set of mercantile codes was advisable: and soon! A few hours ahead of the sequestrator's pantechnicon. Nowhere, no rum-crazy atoll, was looser than Docklands. They've torn up the rulebook. Open City, Scum Town. If you can imagine it, then it's been done.

The Princes of the Church threw a few Raphaels into an overnight bag, crated a nightclub of tight-buttocked boy gods, a spare set of silks — and did a runner.

The Isle had passed from the hands of the simple bullion thieves who first correctly identified its present malaise, its untapped potential, bought the wharves cheap, and laundered their grubby millions (to make a far greater fortune than their under-exercised imaginations could encompass). The indisposed loot became rapidly critical. It reproduced itself in an orgy of self-love. It went off the scale of human greed, and into some borderland of wallowing swine demons. The cartel of Deptford clubowners (company directors and bloody-knuckled bouncers) took the advice of their bent brief and evaporated.

Now serious predators with multinational connections moved in, grabbed their percentage, and let the place collapse: skins tore from the buildings, radiation-sick lizard flesh. Many were never completed. Only a much-photographed frontage existed: colonies of rats multiplied behind exhibitionist façades. The cosmetic dentistry of the project was revealed. Sour smells crept west from the unrepentant swamps. Nervous settlers formed themselves into wagon trains, hired native guides, and galloped for the causeway. Tinkers crept out from under railway bridges, out from inoperative building sites, out from holes in the ground. They stripped the portable fittings, the scrap, the engines and tyres: they trashed the software, left cold turds floating in disconnected bidets. They cruised in unlicensed vans, with hooks and chains. Speed-freaks incubating sawn-off shotguns sprawled in pickup trucks, blasting the heads from inquisitive rodents, setting them free to find a higher plane of existence. Even the lowlife, blood descendants of river vampires and cannibal buccaneers, were uneasy. There were no cargoes left to pilfer, no household goods unofficially to pawn. It was a time to let it all go.

Armed guards, in a rehearsed manoeuvre, synchronize their multi-functional watches, and pull out from the fortresses. Pearl of the East, Dogtown. Screams. Sirens. Panic in the unpaved streets. Gold-card boatpeople stammer aphasically as they trundle their suddenly ridiculous rowing machines, their Pierre Cardin business suits in zipped bags, down to the water's edge. The bleeping of half a hundred hyperventilating paging devices: cicadas in a fire-storm. Khaki-complexioned tremblers in designer jogging suits are waving frantically on rotten jetties for river taxis to carry them back to civilization. They see it now. It was all the most ghastly mistake.

And, as they made good their escape, a fleet of labouring transport planes, freshly painted with the Papal Tiara and the Triple Cross, spilled their grim cruciform shadows across the hop fields of Kent; a circuit of Sheppey, and they followed the renegade river to belly into Gatwick. The chopper shuttle to Mudchute hill began under the flag of diplomatic immunity: locked files, treaties with dictators (living and dead); shop-soiled shrouds, bleeding plaster virgins, crates of sanctified bones (barking and bleating), pre-stamped pardons, thongs, nails, hair-shirted statues, masonic hit lists, the phone numbers of reliable accountants and vestal hostesses with medical clearance, and enough fragments of the True Cross to build a Bailey bridge to Greenwich.

We were hiding out in Imar O'Hagan's Bow bunker: the three of us, twitchy, defensive, booze-brave – conspirators looking for a conspiracy. The world beyond these concrete walls had lost all credibility. Bad dreams were the accepted currency. Strangeness was palpable. It was hard to draw breath. I felt the mould creep from the earth floor on to the membrane of my lungs. Our hands shook, and were cold: held rigid in trays of iced water. Imar had a wild, blood-rimmed grin: something cornered and eager to bite back.

'I'm convinced,' said Davy, 'we are confronted by a demonic entity, a blue-rinse succubus draining the good will of the people. That woman can't be stopped without a stake through the heart, burial where four roads meet, a fist of garlic up the rectum. She's a force of nature. But she's not self-created. As Jane Harrison says, "the gods are our needs made manifest". They describe the thing we most desire. The Widow is the focus of our own lack of imagination; the robot of our greed and ignorance. Therefore, she is indestructible.'

'Right!' I chipped in, 'the culture that ignores Doug Oliver's *The Infant and the Pearl*, and compels him to live in exile, gets what it deserves – nothing. We have earned the freedom to live by a more popular text, *A Dominatrix's Log*. The mindless worship of our silver-skinned abbess of pain.'

Davy was lucky to be alive. (If that was still the preferred state.) He had the hunch something *big* – millennial palpitation, Zoa shifting – was going down in Vat City. He was set on penetrating the outer defences of the Isle of Doges, to find out what that monster was; to witness the shape of the thing, and if necessary – if that is what it cost – to celebrate his martyrdom at a time of his own choosing. He decided to go in as a civilian, a tourist. He bought his rail ticket with the regular flock of bead-worrying, St Vincent de Paul-shepherded, halt and lame at Bow Church.

The unpiloted observation truck floated down its fairground track, guided by the hand of the saints, who offered a fine scenic view of Imar O'Hagan's Ridgeway terminal, his earth mounds and hill systems, and beyond that – the deleted catalogue of housing 'solutions': vertical graveyards, glass jars stacked with dishonoured ancestors. Potential pilgrims (at Devons Road, All Saints, and Poplar) were scanned by spies in bullet-proof booths, who rang their suspicions down the line to the border post, which utilized the bankrupt Billingsgate Market. These chilled fish-packing sheds were conveniently, and economically, lit by the vaporous glow of radon daughters, fluorescent waste products with a half-life of a thousand years.

Davy's train halted under the Vat City symbol: an Atlantean cross within the wobbling tonsil of the Island. The pilgrims were on their knees, muttering about sins of omission and emission, guilty desires, furtive and transitory pleasures: they were ready to wipe the slate clean and to dive, with renewed vigour, into the same old quagmire. The crippled outbid each other in deformity. The amputee *demanded* precedence over the slightly rickety. A torso on wheels was bathed in an aggressive nimbus of sanctity that followed him like the beam of a searchlight. The shadowy minders kept their heads down, sighing with all the concentrated apathy of bingo players. No time was wasted. A pre-recorded absolution, triggered by an electronic eye, was broadcast as the truck moved over the final bridge. But, if the others were soon cleansed of their sins, Davy was the goat among sheep: the necessary sacrifice by which the faithful obtained grace.

Swiss Guards, holding back snarling Rottweiler dogs, frisked Davy for membership cards from masonic lodges, the Diners Club, Opus Dei. They found nothing but a lapsed ICA season ticket. They dragged him from the train to the fence, and swung him out by the wrists and the ankles. He was flying: a skeleton forest of scarlet and nightblue cranes, sunlight strafing the buildings, a skullcap of unblemished sky. Then, pedalling furiously, he fell ninety feet into the dock below. Bruised, choked, spluttering; he paddled to shore, and crawled back to the bunker. A failed suicide. We would have to plan our next assault with much greater care.

'They're incubating the Antichrist!' Imar burbled. 'Everything you report proves it. This is an age of fraudulent dystopias. Some bleak *Nova Atlantis* replaces the possibility of a *City of the Sun*. They've turned from the rule of a Philosopher King to the power plays of a mad voodoo priest.'

'True,' Davy nodded, spinning on his heel, excited by these images of cosmic alienation. 'They've laid down an apparently impenetrable mental grid. They've protected themselves with an *actively* malign geometry of earth and water: formal canals, fire-towers, black glass temples. The street itself has become an outmoded concept. "Street Cred" is something to be sucked up by a vacuum cleaner. You can see it all from the first bridge. I glimpsed it as I fell – vast avenues, empty, unpeopled. All movement is mechanical, zombie-urgent, other-directed.'

'And you *still* want to find a way into this madness? And, worse, to drag us along for the ride?' I said. I had the obstinate conviction this was not one of Davy's better ideas.

'Of course!' he howled, 'don't you want to be there when it happens? Don't you want to be the first outsider into Pivot City? The business of the Island is hidden from sight. The action is all under the ground. It just needs a firm hand to spin the buildings and bring these blood-matted cellars up into the light.'

Reluctantly, I agreed. I looked on swift annihilation as the simplest solution. I slumped on my chair in an abject spirit of self-accusation, convinced that everything that had happened was a consequence of my casual invocation of the Vessels of Wrath. I knew what the Isle of Dogs meant. An unlucky place, anathematized by Pepys; and identified by William Blake with the Dogs of Leutha, whose only purpose was to destroy their masters. Even the nineteenth-century maps register a desert occupied by three houses: *Folly, Chapel, Ferry* (Insanity, Prayer, Escape). The island has always been shunned or exploited for its dark potential. ('*Till he came to old Stratford, & thence to Stepney & the Isle / Of Leutha's Dogs, thence thro' the narrows of the River's side, / And saw every minute particular: the jewels of Albion running down / The kennels of the streets & lanes as if they were abhorr'd ...*')

Imar laughed aloud, intoxicated with glory, a *kamikaze* pilot, clapping his hands at the prospect of the biggest buzz of them all: straight into the dock at a million miles an hour.

We each in our own way submitted as Davy outlined his brain-fried plans on a squeaky blackboard. Vat City, it appeared, was protected by a chain of deepwater docks. They looked in Davy's diagram, set down within the lingam of the Island, like the symbol of a new religion, a triple-barred cross metamorphosing into a football rattle, in honour of the rabid ghosts of Millwall. The West India Docks had been rebaptized.

The blunt tip of Davy's chalk scratched in the new names: *Maggiore, Lugano, Como.*

Water, according to Davy, would be our only way in. The major custom barriers at West Ferry and Prestons Road effectively sealed the Island. This was too narrow a track to breach. Tight valves controlled the passage of blood to the heart. Justice was summary for detected aliens – with the bridge jump as the softest option. And the railhead was even more fiercely scrutinized. Journalists and freelance couriers of *samizdat* literature found themselves doing a twelve stretch in one of the Island's custodial monasteries. Bread, rainwater, and prayer: endless repetitions of the Holy Names. They became generators of a spiritual force to be tapped by the Council of Elders. An unnatural resource, a privatized power station.

No, we would have to slide in covertly, by night in a primitive craft of Imar's construction: cockleshell heroes. We had struck our individual contracts with the dark gods, sanity staked on a single throw. We sucked on jam jars of Imar's poteen, letting the enamel peel from our teeth; turning them, before battle, into black razors.

With the ugly leer of a serial killer unveiling his latest atrocity, Imar pulled back the rug which covered his vessel. Vessel? The thing was a mess of warped ribs: the carcase of a sheep, picked dry by crows. It would never circumnavigate Victoria Park paddling pool, let alone conquer the tidal reaches of the Thames. But the design, Imar insisted, was an ancient one. He had researched the Voyages of Brendan the Navigator, and of Maeldune. They had survived Isles of Ants, Birds, Whirling Beasts, Fiery Pigs, Peltings with Nuts, Laughing People – what did we have to fear?

What did we have to fear? An encyclopaedia of potential monsters flooded, engraving by engraving, through our minds, inspired by Imar's modest listing. We stared at the 'boat' in utter disbelief, as Imar gloatingly pitched us a few of its more spectacular characteristics. The urine-cured skins we were able fully to appreciate, without prompting from the donor. They were overpoweringly authentic in the close confines of the dripping stalactite bunker, our cave of nightmares. The craft was more of a coracle than a canoe, more of a coffin than either. There would be no opportunity for test or rehearsal. We would set sail (figuratively speaking) that very evening – before the fumes of fire alcohol lost their efficacy, and reality returned to jeer at us.

Silently, putting aside all thoughts of our loved ones, we prayed that we had achieved the correct bardic numerology for our hero voyage: the archetypal mix of Maker, Warrior, and Holy Fool. The exact division of these roles was still open to debate. But Imar swore, by the white cow of St Malachy of Armagh, that he could paddle us, noiselessly, wherever Davy required the craft to go.

What Davy required was simple to tell and almost impossible to execute. And what charm lay in that 'almost', what spine-chilling speculation. Our bowels fluttered to water at the mere recitation of the plan. After dark we would hoist the coracle onto the chassis of an old perambulator, and pack it with rubbish – as if we were, according to local custom, about to dump the thing in the canal. Down Bow Common Lane to the Limehouse Cut, through a gap in the fence, and on to the water. East to join the River Lea; then south, meandering between gasworks, to Bow Creek; into the Thames itself. We hoped, before first light, to come up with the tide to Coldharbour inlet; then slip through to Como deepwater dock with its prophetic vision of all that Docklands attempted: '*barren mountains of Moral Virtue*', dreams, flights; an eagle sun lifting, behind us, out from the night river, firing the stepped Mayan folly of *Cascades*. We would be *in*. Or so Davy, modestly economical with the truth, assured us. Reality slept somewhere ahead in an unopened ledger: sculpted in steel, with pages of human skin.

II

The currach is a blunt egg, turning on itself, reluctant to face the responsibility of nominating a direction of travel, eager to drift. Our slightest movement, adjusting a buttock, or twisting to view the pale spectral draw of the houses, threatens catastrophe. The poisoned canal is the thickness of a snake's skin beneath us; slippery with promises of Weil's disease (leptospirosis). My liver, unprompted, goes into a detoxification mode: sobering me in seconds. *Can this be happening?* Davy's single paddle swoops at the scum. His silhouette is confident, precise in its necessary movements: shaman of the backwater ways. I will relieve him on the Lea, and Imar will tackle the Thames. No return ticket is available: the only direction is onward.

We are spinning, dizzy but not yet sick, down a sewer with its lid lifted away. Starless: low night. I sink into a condition that is neither sleep nor wakefulness. I allow the spent dreams of these terraces to invade me. I see shapes struggle in the water, escaping from our insanity: dog pieces, things in nets, sphincteral mouths adorned with silver hooks. I am shocked to find myself erotically aroused.

Imar is soundlessly fingering a penny whistle, calling to his snails; seeking a justification for the route we have chosen. And, in all probability, the snails answer. It is their territory. Nobody else would want it.

Light thins. We have mastered the Cut, navigated the river, the broad creek; been drawn up on the tide towards the Island. Our coracle bumps against the high wall of the Coldharbour Lock.

Now Davy's truth assails us. If this is a Lock and we have the key, we must be afloat on Alice's Pool of Tears. I remembered the trap that she was in: 'either the locks were too large, or the key was too small'. These closed water gates have been stolen from some medieval fortress city. They repel invaders by their scale: the very *idea* of them is enough to make any thinking mortal call up a previous engagement. The gates are massive, studded in iron, nailed forests, crusted in slime: fearsome. What do they hold back? Tons of water, the weight of small countries. Our spirits are crushed by the immensity of natural forces heaped against us. This is why a single guardhouse suffices. There is no way into Como without passing through a double lock. What did Alice blurt out, as her nerve broke, and 'language' rushed, uninvited, into her mouth? '*Are you – are you fond – of – of dogs?*'

Our walnut shell debates the tide: soon we will be swept away, ignominiously, visible to the shore guns, a prime target – as the light finds us somewhere between Gandolfo Gardens and Greenwich. It is over.

The beam of a torch flashes through our self-generated gloom. This clamour of despair (thunder of heartbeats) has doubtless alerted one of the guards. There is nothing to wait for – except the bullets. Is there a *quality* of sound to appreciate before your brain-pan shatters? Is there a microsecond in which to prepare yourself, to let the old Adam go?

Davy is nudging Imar towards a ladder set into the dock wall. A metal-runged, slithering scramble into ungodly darkness. To reach for the first rung, as we pitch on the tide, is to experience a delicious surge of vertigo. More of this would be excessive. I'm no glutton. I revert to some mud-guzzling Devonian coral form, an *ichthyostega*, or a jawless fish. I have no desire to 'better' myself, to drum in the air, turning my skull to the stars for inspiration. I'll sink where I stand. Imar, above me, has already 'evolved', disappearing into the limitless night.

'Climb!' Davy prods, reinforcing that suggestion by slitting the belly of the coracle with his clasp knife. Water laps playfully around our ankles. I climb. Davy is behind me: our only means of escape is now a fond memory. (You can recall the leg-irons with affection when they move on to the thumbscrew and the rack.)

The grasp weakens; the climb is eternal, equal in horror to the final ascent of the Tower of St Anne at Limehouse, when the wind revenges itself on your presumption, cutting through the sharpened angles of hieratic masonry. Is it possible to advance, to command the muscles, in such a state of terror? Imperceptibly, the awfulness of the situation evens out, smooths; the horror becomes another norm. It is almost comfortable. It is what we are used to. We climb through the night and out into a new world.

The torch again. The briefest of winks. A monk, a Dominican. We have been nabbed, netted. It is jump or burn. The black friar holds the torch beneath his chin, offering us a portrait in the Spanish style of his own decapitation. He is the ultimate fanatic: bald, thorn bearded, thin-lipped, skin picked raw by spiritual devotions. Undoubtedly a flagellant, an ecclesiastical storm trooper. His burning fire-coal eyes skewer deep in quest of confession. I am ready. My guilt spills gratefully from paper-dry lips.

'This is Tommy Clayden,' said Davy, making the introductions. 'He's the guv'nor at the *Gun*. The last publican on the Island. And the first sinner. He'll show us the way in.'

Tommy grasped our hands in his misshapen mitts, as if it was the most natural thing in the world; as if we had met on the terraces at Upton Park, or down the Lane on a Sunday morning. Another one who could have been a contender, if he hadn't developed a taste for his own stock. He *liked* getting hit. And he liked drinking. He'd be boasting about how he could 'take it' when they shut the fridge door on him for the last time.

'Right, lads.' Tommy cut it short, and produced a bottle from beneath his robes. 'Have a pull. Then fuck off. These cunts'll be shouting for their double egg and bacon as soon as they unstick their eyelids. That's what I'm doing here.'

We drank, sucking like lambs at the teat, burning the lining of our throats to sandpaper.

'It ain't much fun, mate, but there's only one way you're going to make it.' Tommy threw his arm around Davy's shoulder. His foot tapped against something metallic. 'The pipes, my son. The workmen stop off down the boozer for a bit of something, but they have to be on site by half seven – or they're banged up with two hundred years in purgatory. No panic, but the sooner you get stuck in, the more chance you've got. It ain't no harder than wriggling back into your mother's belly. If you haven't made it by the time work starts, relax: you're in there for good.'

The beam of Tommy's torch obligingly lit up the open mouths of two red pipes that ran along the side of the dock, one above the other, passing within a few yards of the guards' black glass observation kiosk.

They continued, so Tommy promised, beneath the perimeter road, and the fortified bridge, to the lock, and finally to the edge of Como itself. A distance of no more than one hundred and fifty yards: as the worm slides.

Already the sun was crawling treacherously out of Blackwall Reach; intimations of a fine spring morning darted along the furrows of the dock, spun against the mirrored temples. It was spellbinding. A remission from the wheels of time.

'You've got three minutes to get yourself into the pipes. Then I take a pot of coffee to the guards and wake 'em up,' Tommy said. Davy was enjoying this: heaving and shoving, he inserted Imar into the upper bore. A headless torso, Imar thrashed his legs to propel himself from our sight.

Ladders, if they are firmly attached to a wall, I can manage; but crawling *blind* into the unyielding intestines of some obscure (and probably boobytrapped) system, becoming a parasite – a tapeworm – with only the faintest hope of ever reaching daylight – that is something else.

Davy, foaming at the mouth, frenzied as a Khan to the slaughter, followed Imar. I withdrew my last lingering breath from the sour dock (how sweet it tasted!), and plunged into the lower pipe. Anything was better than having Davy's boots kicking in my face. It was hard for those first few yards, the light lost behind you; churned and squeezed in this unforgiving alimentary canal. After that, of course, you settle down. And it is all quite impossible.

III

'How bright the sunlight was, on the warm grey stones, on the ripe Roman skins, on vermilion and lavender and blue and ermine and green and gold, on the indecent grotesque blackness of two blotches, on apostolic whiteness and the rose of blood'

Fr Rolfe (Baron Corvo), *Hadrian the Seventh*

Rolling our shoulders, snaking forward, driven by intestinal spasms: we progress in a bloodless sexual dance. Creep through circles of pain from our elbows and knees, where sharp bones lack that necessary cushion of flesh. Often we collapse. I hear heels drumming above my head. And I am convinced the pipe is filling with water. I hear it. Distorted whispers, voices. Pursuit. I suffer instants of deep sleep, microdreams. I lie with my cheek against the cold metal, until the metal chills to ice and threatens, if I move, to peel away my face. I can't turn back. There is nothing behind me. This journey has no past. We have been here for ever. Only the pipes themselves can eject us; contract, expand, tip us into a bowl of raw light – like some waste product dredged of its virtue. Our vitality has been absorbed by the machine. Motionless, huddled into a defensive ball, we slide towards whatever strange birth awaits us.

The traitor sun has outpaced our lizard shuffle. The waters of the dock scintillate, braided in threads of light, gilt and silver; clusters in which sparks have been struck, colour separations in slicks of oil. But this vision is alienated, trapped in the black iris of the tunnel. It is the lie of a telescope that cannot be brought into focus.

Davy's curly head swings, upside-down, into my pipe, blocking the radiance of light, which streams behind him. 'We can't move,' he whispers, 'until the bells ring for Mass. Then we can slip out and join the procession. I don't know exactly what's going on – some kind of festival. Holy images carried aloft, mutilated martyrs, drums, pipes, hooded penitents, incense: all that stuff.'

Imar is already on the dock. He has spotted a mound of packing cases and pallet boards. Davy signals. We are free. We can squat: peep out from between the slats, and wait for it to happen. Our heads sink on to our knees; we doze.

Plop. Ploppp. Plip. The sounds move gently away from us. Mild rings of disturbance chase each other across the dock. It's like listening to a procession of frogs leaping into a pool, while trying to provoke a *haiku* from some monumentally dim Zen monk. The world is rotating so slowly. The objects (whatever they are) are being thrown further and further out into the water. I have no interest in this – a marginal annoyance – but, after watching indifferently for ten minutes or so, the duty of keeping a true record compels me to stick out my head to search for a rational explanation.

From the top deck of one of the black glass *palazzi* (anchored around the dock like a phantom fleet), a burly man in full cardinal's drag was hammering golf balls out in a loop over Como. They fought bravely for life, reaching into the empyrean; then they failed, lost faith in their own abilities, dropped with a satisfying sound into the unforgiving water. The cardinal snarled, spat red, sickened by their weakness. He took a replacement from a golden bucket, judged its courage between wrestler's fingers; squeezed until the veins popped. He set the fresh white communicant on to a tiny purple stalk – a doll's house champagne glass – and thrashed it into the sky. He was now concerned only with distance, with metaphors of his own power, not with style. He expelled the balls, he cursed their lack of faith: he excommunicated them to the limits of his considerable strength. They were ex-balls. They should no longer enjoy his indulgent patronage. Let them sink or swim.

Lathered in flecks of creamy sweat, the cardinal rested his cattle-felling forearms on the rail, and puffed for a moment in meditation on a green cigar, rolling it between curiously prim, feminine lips: wetting it, tasting it, sucking and chewing. 'Goddamn their greaser eyes,' he snarled. 'Never was a wop who knew fuck about offing a stooly. Always got to make a production out of it – ropes, stones, hocus coonshit pocus. Dago assholes, turn a hit into a fucking Verdi opera.'

He resumed his exorcism, his ballet of lift/pause/swoop/strike. *Thwack. Thwack. Thwackkk.* Black, petro-chemical grease trailed down his bony scalp, wounding it: the heat dissolved the hair dye into a velvet skullcap. He was hooded, pouch-eyed, circled with lack of sleep: a dead tree. Fat knuckles flashed with scarab rings; as if he had been grabbing locusts to gobble in his open hands. One of God's uglier minders.

The bells! The bells! A recorded tintinnabulation doubles these canals and fetid lagoons – another Venice – summons albino crocodiles from under the rotting piles. Slithering from their bolt holes, the sick legions of the invertebrate faithful creep into the morning light, protecting their eyes behind dark glasses, huddling under umbrellas: fire-damaged turtles. They tremble towards some unknown cathedral. It is time for us to join with them: to walk upright into the Holy City.

IV

Shuffling along, eyes on the floor, we are disposable extras in some monochrome spectacle: the megalomaniac nightmare of a one-eyed Austrian dictator, whose celluloid epic will be acclaimed for exposing the myth of totalitarianism. (How many times have we heard Lang's account of his interview in Dr Goebbels's office? The hands of the clock. Money in the bank. The Paris train. Polite expressions of the Führer's admiration for *Metropolis* and *Die Nibelungen*.) A premature anti-Fascist, prophetically announcing the coming of the long knives, *Kristallnacht*; wolves from the iron forest skulking into the suburbs. But prophets are redundant on the Island. The worst has already happened.

The avenues! Treeless, broad, focusing on nothing. Dramatic perspectives leading to no revelation: no statues of public men, no fountains, no slogans. Nothing. No beggars, no children, no queues for buses. This city of the future, this swampland Manhattan, this crystal synthesis of capital, is already posthumous: a memorial to its own lack of nerve. It shudders and lets slip its ghosts. It swallows the world's dross. Isle of

Dogs, receiving station of everything that is lost and without value. A library of unregarded texts. Escaped pets. Abortions. Amputated limbs. Hiding place of Idi Amin, Baby Doc Duvalier, Martin Bormann. There must be a showcase tower that contains nothing but the collected shoes of Imelda Marcos. There must be a pyramid filled with the severed heads of torturers, waiting for the quacks to steam them to reincarnation. Their red-veined eyes move, like the eyes in portraits: they watch us. There must be a gambling hell for all those who blaspheme against fate by calling themselves 'Lucky': a sullen moustached Lord Lucan 'greets' a toothpick-chewing Luciano, who slips him a counterfeit nickel. There must even be a shrine where collectors of military fetishes can worship the single testicle of Adolf Hitler.

We tramp through award-winning piazzas where all the monuments fake at collapse: heaps of loose honey-coloured bricks have been cunningly arranged to suggest the frisson of real disaster, metal fatigue, earthquake: jagged fragments of Rivera and Orozco murals have been imported from Mexico City. But there are also once-active dockworkers entombed beneath wrecked apartments that were pushed too high in worthless materials, held together with bandaids and unbonded cement. Pastiched catastrophes overwhelm the dusty traces of true archival pain.

We find ourselves sniffling into our sleeves, exposed to all this emptiness, to nothing beyond the *dementia praecox* of the buildings themselves. They confess, they boast, they lie; they make us ashamed of the tired remnant of our humanity.

How much further? The procession of charcoaled communicants winds among tombs of vanished dish-hogs, the heavy players who put their trust in sky-sucking satellites. They slink down sirocco-buffeted canyons of damaged glitz that swiftly repudiate any notion of pedestrianism. The desire to lift our heads to the stars, to admire the pulsing lights on the summit of these alcazars, is immediately blocked by a jungle ceiling of tracks from the elevated railway, as it shuttles in another cargo of relic buyers, grit-tongued penitents, architecturalists with cameras, endlessly repeating the same reflected images, flattening the city, carrying it back out into the world; lecturing, proselytizing, extending the screwball aesthetics of collaboration and surrender.

There were no streets in this paradigmatic city, only public boulevards, and tributaries linking the basins of dark water, the unmeditated pools. But even in their obscurity these tributaries had to be named, and the names set in alabaster to mock them: *Ambrosiano, Gelli, Sindona, Ortolani, Marcinkus. Marcinkus?* Why not? It might have been the Bishop from Cicero, Illinois (home of Alphonso Capone, Jake 'Greasy

Thumb' Guzik, Frank 'the Enforcer' Nitti), we saw on the rooftop, wasting the golf balls. The Bishop was no longer a name; neither living nor dead, he remained perpetually incommunicado, an exile in his Tower of the Winds. There was still too much he could tell. Let him spit in the water.

We were evidently closing on the heart of the place. The grand boulevard was zonally marked; so that we passed through colours, states of consciousness – perhaps of grace – through Platonic harmonies towards the cathedral of all the mysteries. Blinking, we emerged from darkness (base lead) to approach the painted spokes of the sun, an hallucinatory scintillae of Byzantine gold. The formal stages of our initiation were designated by Neo–Classical letters tooled in silver upon the scarlet brick road. *P V, P IV, P III, P II* ...

The light blinded us, bent wantonly back from the pyramid at the peak of the Magnum Tower, eight hundred feet above the scutal bowlers of the pilgrims. It remained London's tallest man-made structure: a fortified nest, an angled chamber, the nearest point to the hand of God. He had only to uncurl His finger to touch it.

William Blake's interlocking columns of words were the armature around which the monster's panels had been bolted. The Magnum Tower

> ... *frown'd dreadful over Jerusalem,*
> *A building of Luvah, builded in Jerusalem's eastern gate, to be*
> *His secluded Court* ...
> *Dens of despair in the house of bread, enquiring in vain*
> *Of stones and rocks, he took his way, for human form was none;*
> *And thus he spoke, looking on Albion's City with many tears:*
> *'What shall I do? What could I do if I could find these Criminals?'*

By indulging in these ethical speculations we have fallen far behind the other communicants. They look at nothing, advance with regular, zombie-piston tread on the portico of the Anubic Temple. I am willing to pause in admiration of the twin deities, the basalt throned jackal-headed guardians on their granite plinths, who oversee this pilgrimage of dead souls; but Davy is tugging at my coat-tails, pulling me away from a fatally seductive vision of Cynopolis, City of Dogs. We escape from the central boulevard, dodge down one of the tributaries, a blind alley that leads inevitably to another fenced building site, a ziggurat shrouded in flapping black nylon.

Alien footsteps, creaking spars, subdued voices: we press ourselves back into the shadows, lurk behind the hollow pillars of a false atrium, watching. We expect, at least, a Conradian bark or Twelfth Dynasty funerary barge, sliding down the herring-bone road to disappear among the floating draperies of the wrapped mound. But there is only the noise: a dragging, bumping grind of some recalcitrant cargo over the uneven mosaic of bricks. The performance is not far behind. Two priests, a fat one and a thin one, tethered like oxen to a grand piano, shudder and shake; their faces pasty and flushed above soiled white bibs. They struggle past us without lifting their heads, mopping themselves with rags of altar cloth. This listless Laurel and Hardy couple have been sentenced to perform this bizarre penance, as I imagine it, for crimes against children. Roped together in a sterile hermaphroditic marriage, they debate the Pelagian Heresy while orchestrating, with every step forward, a hideous discordant jangling. We have penetrated some latter day version of *Pilgrim's Progress*: moral lessons are being made *visible*. We have only to interpret them.

The surreal audition fades and we run for the fence. It has been disguised, in playful *trompe l'oeil*, with a painted forest. Uccello's 'Hunt by Night' surrounds us: crimson tunics, spears, straining hounds pursue the unseen prey into the deepest realms of darkness.

The secret of the mural's perspective reveals a loose board. On the far side of the painted forest are living horses, chained to a stake, quizzical, coquettishly tossing their axe-shaped heads. A yellow Hazchem container has been converted into a dormitory for tinkers. A few men sit around a bucket of fire, cleaning their shotguns and drinking from unlabelled bottles.

'Massive!' said Davy. 'Canary Wharf to Cannery Row in the blink of an eye.' Curs were foaming on short ropes. None of the men looked at us, no movement was apparent anywhere; but, walking slowly towards the fire, we *knew* that we were covered from all sides. Shotguns nestled comfortably in laps, impatient fingers stroked trigger guards.

'Where are the women?' Imar blurted. 'Did you ever see a tinker site in daylight with men still on it? And where are the kids?'

'That's right,' Davy mused. 'Not a female to admire since we got on the Island. Even in the crocodile plodding to Mass. No tribal mothers, vinegar spinsters, no repentant harlots. Not a single one.'

'They're death in this place.' One of the tinkers spoke, without looking up from the fire. A long lank, shivering, red-haired dodgem-car jockey. He picked a crust of scab from his nose, wiping the silvery snot on to his sleeve. He hunched his coat-hanger shoulders, quivering in seizures of uncontrolled and unmotivated laughter. 'Any bitch found here is taken. The black skirts can't stand the heat of 'em, the smell. Raw fish eggs.' He spat into the fire bucket and watched the spittle cook.

'They bring in a few whores in an ambulance for the Bishop: the rest of 'em make do with *castrati* and the odd bout of solitary snake-strangling.'

He mimed an obscene and frenetic form of boxing-glove onanism. He giggled. 'Keep women out of it and the black skirts'll leave you alone. Fuck your own fists, boys.' He nodded; his head loose as a dummy. He laughed until bubbles of lager ran out from his nose, to be lapped up on a pustule-decorated tongue. He gobbled a heap of downers from his open palm. His dog-yellow eyes were already mad as one of the coal-dancing damned.

'They've got the enforcers,' Davy told us, 'to make it stick. "Swiss Guards", they call them, so they can pay them in cheese: lovely bricks of soft yellow gold. Far worse than the Tonton Macoute, these beauties. More dangerous. Psycho-police eavesdropping on your nightmares. They "anticipate" every outbreak of heresy. Dawn raids. The generators and the water baths are running before you hear the tap at the door. Torture as a fine art. They have no other interests.'

'You've never been here before,' I mumbled, 'how do you know the moves to make?'

'Well Street,' Davy replied. 'I discovered, by accident, the means of interrogating an empty room, holding an oracular séance with the voices trapped in its walls. I was drawn back, when it was all over and the photographs were taken, to the place where the girl-junkie died. I slept there two or three times a week. It became obsessive. But it was never the same as dreaming. You can take any room where there has been some form of interrogation – torture cell, psychiatrist's study, confessional, lovers' afternoon hotel – and the activity does not cease simply because the participants withdraw. The true monologue (these exchanges are inevitably one-sided) soaks into the plaster. The interlocutor is unnecessary, gets in the way, clouds the issue with his feeble attempts at "drawing out" and giving unacceptable visions a rational form.'

Davy creased his knuckles, trying to depress his eyes into their sockets; forcing back the things he had seen. He only succeeded in bringing them into a sharper focus. He drew breath. He was shaking. But he went on.

'I opened my hands. I ran my palms over the walls. I made them bleed. I circled, I squeezed. The voices were there. They came back to me. I asked nothing; I lay on the floor. The heart of her fear was opened to me. But it was held within another thing I could never understand, a hoop of sticky light: wasps, wax, corn-dust. I tried to touch it. It was playful, sliding across the walls. And then all her prints, maps, words came rushing out from the distemper. I had whitewashed over the crazed and panicking graffiti. But it *insisted*. It was immortal. And the horror was that … *it started to make sense*. You know the symbol they use? The jackal-headed guardians of the Island lingam? Dog Island, Isle of…'

'Cunt!' The red-haired tinker was at Davy's throat, blade open: its tip pressing against the jugular vein. 'Shut it. Can't be said. Nobody speaks it, the old name. Your tongue'll be ripped out like the page of a book. They'll do you up.'

Worse than the superstitions of theatricals, with their 'Scottish Play', their 'break a leg!': the same curse. The same treaty with the dark side. The same abdication of courage. 'Don't say it!' To name is to cause, to set in motion. Once spoken, never recalled. The name lives: is independent of its begetter. A power these people clearly understood. Titles out of the past were forbidden; bringing to mind, as they did, more honourable times. This was the treaty under which the tinkers made their camp. We were forced to comb our thesaurus of euphemisms and allude to the 'Heresy-free Zone', 'Capital-friendly Isthmus', 'Islet of Saints and Savers'.

Imar turned his back on us and took out his penny whistle. And as he played, something crawled out from under the container; something white and snail-slow, a Permian reject, a dead man returning.

'Him's better than any of your women.' The tinker grinned. 'Got a bung'ole like a glove filled with garlicky butter.' He licked his broken teeth, and prodded the creature with a surgically-abbreviated shotgun.

The gelded monster crawled agonizingly towards the fire, and Davy recognized, with dread, the former Well Street landlord, Elgin Mac-Diarmuid. His condition, once boastfully reprehensible, was now terminally forlorn: broken, trembling, unshelled. Two damp peaks of sweat-soaked hair suggested the horns of a snail. He was naked under a grease-stiff gaberdine. His feet useless in layers of flapping bandage. They pulled him into the light on the end of a sharp pin. He had the fatal softness of a grub and the self-justifying mean spirits of the reformed drunk. He had swallowed his heart.

'Blessed Mother of God, help me. Jesus, Holy Lamb, help me. Sweet Babe of Heaven, bless my suffering. I'm not ready.' Elgin supplicated, in tears; arms flailing like the flippers of a seal, sweeping sawdust in some ring of shame. 'I *beg* you. Don't let them crucify me. I ran away once before. You remember? I was younger, I had my strength then. I could tear in half the telephone directory for the city of Cork. I went back, oh mothering bitch. *The nails!* Do you understand? They drive them through the wrists, not the soft palms. Hang me bleeding like Medhbh's pig? And for what? I was "pricked" once for the priesthood. Talk to the

Christian Brothers. I could have been a Jesuit. Why do they allow this thing? I was at home, holding on; gathering my thoughts, getting ready to write – until they put the accursed television into every bar from Stillorgan to Finglas. Couldn't get a drink for it. McDaid's, Toner's, the Pearl Lounge. "No no," I screamed at them. The curate winked. "Right, sir, sure enough." He switched the channel, thought I wanted the racing from Punchestown. I knew they were watching me out of that little spot that never goes away even when you switch it off. I needed a ticket out. Not too far gone to recognize the arch-blasphemer, Shamus Joys himself, sneaking in by the back door. On the steps of an aeroplane, with the pilgrims at Knock, sniffing good Irish air. The blackguard! Didn't he try it before? With his cinematograph? His Galway whore? Brandishing the blackthorn like the devil's own pizzle. Did he ape the Pole and put his lips to the sod? He did not. Come back, Elgin. They'll have you. They want to nail me to a Jew's tree.'

Elgin tried to rise from his knees, but he couldn't make it. Thick salt tears slid slowly down his gelid cheeks. Nothing could halt the flow of his keening lament. 'One of us had to go. The country couldn't hold the both of us. I bummed the boat fare from the uncle. They were glad to see the back of me. Mother weeping. "All for the best." Plenty of honest work on the other side. Kilburn? Did they think I was a common labourer, a paddy from the bogs? I had a year's heavy engineering behind me. UCD. Wasn't it founded by Cardinal Manning himself? I had commendations, letters from Tony Cronin. Don't lift me on to the golden throne. I don't want the Pontiff's crown. Can't eat, not here. Intestinal problems. Negroes masturbate in kitchens. They make the soup from it. Put drugs in your coffee. You wake in the Papal apartments, breakfast tray served by the nuns of the Congregation of Maria Bambina. Orgies. Filth. And they're measuring you for your shroud. They say it's a portrait in oils. That's a lie. The man's the official mortician. Look, listen to me. I didn't ask for any of it. All I wanted was an introduction to an intelligent middle-class woman. His wife, your wife. A graduate with a taste for theatre, a bit of spending money and a double bed. Was it too much to ask? The time to finish my monograph on Douglas Sirk?'

The redhead jerked on the chain and Elgin fell into the mud; lay where he fell. We could not insult our hosts by asking for his release. He was almost as valuable as a crippled horse. They would rather kill us all; 'found floating'.

'There *is* a way.' The tinker's conspiratorial grin reminded me of someone, years before, a book thief on the markets, who had vanished overnight into rumour, or Amsterdam, run off with a nympho speed-freak. 'For a price, I could get you in. For a reasonable consideration. Right to the top, the Holy of Holies: the Magnum Tower. I deliver you to the building – the rest is your own business. But don't try and stop them, whatever you see. They'll shred you and feed you to the crows. The equinox is closing on 'em, they won't wait.'

Davy listened with intent, while compulsively squeezing the bulb of his nose. The redhead fumbled through cavernous pockets, pulling out lengths of string, apple cores, biscuits, coins – before he located the three badges. They were stamped with the inevitable symbol (the lingam and the water crosses), and they bore the legend, in 'Perpetua Italic', *NIHIL OBSTAT*.

'Of course,' yelled Davy, 'the conference! The Jesuits cobbled it together, to prove to the world how open-minded they've become. All the cameras will be there. The international correspondents. It will go out, via satellite, at the very moment the secret ceremony is enacted in the pyramid of glass: the one that is intended to halt time, wound its membrane, and give them access to unimagined powers. This is good, very good. The long lenses will be tight as warts, in a phallic cluster, on the face of Stephen Hawking, as he lectures the princes of the church on cosmology. A classic example of the "divine illumination of intellect". What paternalism, what benevolence! A new era of enlightenment is upon us. Dogma challenged by revelations from the furthest stars.'

'Hawking *here*?' I gasped.

'It's not so shocking,' Davy said. 'They've already wheeled him in for an audience with the *Capo di Capo*; laid down the guidelines. "Anything you want, Professor – we're men of the world – up to, but *not* including, the Big Bang. That alone is God's affair. The instant of creation." What do they think God is? A cosmic wind?'

I wondered if Sonny Jaques was on the bus. He would have loved this. What a scene was in prospect! The TV boys, the *hungans* in red braces, wetting themselves in anticipation. Hatchet-faced video directors (with millennial razor-trim hairstyles) leased from the ad agencies. The Professor, the brain of the universe, wired to his special-effects voice-box, as he faces the tiers of expectant ascetic faces; skull caps, crimson robes. *El Greco!* Ten full days to work on the lighting. Simultaneous translation into every known language. The lecture already previewed in the *Listener*, so that the media vermin can get their pieces written before the programme goes out. 'Space-time is finite,' Hawking states, 'but has no boundaries.' Wow! Beautiful! When that little bombshell hits the fan the pyramid alchemy will be activated: we'll all be halfway to heaven.

'No panic,' said Davy. 'Hawking knows where it's coming from. He's sharper than any of them. It's not for nothing he was born exactly three hundred years after Galileo Galilei. He knows the risks he's running. He's well aware that they'll spray him in images of reincarnation, heresy, old mistakes made good. He can carry it. And we'll be right there with him. Three hard-boiled prime-time news hounds: collar and tie strictly optional. Let's do it, let's join the professionals!'

V

A bruised wind, frustrated, bounced the tall buildings, sibilating like a host of linkpersons struggling with the revised pronunciation of 'Rushdie'. It chopped the slate waters of the dock into small waves, broken anvils. The light dropped to pewter, with glints of sick plum; martyr stains spreading an irrevocable wound. The evil silver-green hulks of decommissioned Polaris submarines rode the swell, converted to wine bars, the private dining facilities of Vat City news-laundering executives.

With his lupine features set into what he proposed as a clerical sneer, the drooling redhead waved us on. His rickety legs were trapped in tourniquet trousers that finished six or seven inches shy of his sockless ankles. He stabbled at the dirt with blade-sharp shoes. *Mycosis fungoides* erupted from the grassy duffle coat that enveloped him; conferring, he imagined, a miraculous respectability. We stalked his heels, indian file, cockily flashing our *Nihil Obstat* badges at the shuttered glasshouses.

Sticking to the dockside, lashed by icy droplets flicked into our faces by an increasingly sullen wind, we crept beneath towering tributes to the service industries: excess information, sky-trawling disks (humming with morbid radiation), self-cancelling messages from the stars. Anything could happen, as long as it happened *fast*. Nothing was made – except the deal. Immaculate telephone consummations. Fax machines mindlessly reproducing themselves in pin-sharp detail. High-profile offices, lit to be photographed, were unsullied by human occupation.

Replacing the Flour Mills (the Rope Works, Chandlers, Ship Repairers) were faceless dung-beetle enterprises, with designer stationery, offering fast food / muscle tone / wet bikes / hire car / personalized chemicals / *Galleria* / wine vaults / lingerie / roses / blowjobs at your console. 'Selling' was too important, too rarefied a skill, to be tied any longer to mere products. It was an autonomous artform, practised for its own sake, creating insatiable hungers even among the most resistant of all targets, the other salesmen.

A narrow alley between boarded-up lots returns us to the central boulevard. The path towards the Palace is before us, lined with hierarchies of guards. First, the *gendarmeria pontifica* in dark glasses, leather corsets, belts, holsters, jaundice cigarettes, sub-machine pistols; then the *guardia palatina*, leaning on ceremonial halberds. We fall silent and bunch together, close in on other groups of media wannabetheres, as they scramble unenthusiastically from the car-park crypt with their video cameras, furry soundsticks, cellular telephones; their unshakable cynicism. But something in nature has been affronted: the wind tears at them, flicking back the tails of their trenchcoats, unshuffling the sculpted layers of their hair. Revenge is imminent. Tangled balls of razor-wire roll down the avenue like tumbleweed. The glamorous cladding on the architectural anthology of the towers starts to unpeel, to flap and clatter: an unserviced facelift. A dustbowl of semaphoring scarecrows, we are tossed against the plinths of the Anubic guardians; offered as unworthy sacrifices to the jackal-headed gods. We abase ourselves, scrape our foreheads in the dirt. And crawl up the slippery marble steps into the Temple.

We were swiftly assigned to the care of a certain Father Healy, an insignificant other, a vertical worm. Contempt poured from him. He sweated his distaste: a heady mixture of onion soup, eau de Cologne, and Sweet Afton cigarettes. (Could this be one of the Galway Healys? The traditional collectors of customs? A relative of Nora Barnacle?) He slid us from trophy to trophy, in the company of a gang of handrubbing *frotteurs*; spoiled priests, rotten with sanctity. Healy gestured, with supreme arrogance, at the dazzling concourse of Popes hanging on the walls: 'Innocent X' by Velázquez, 'Julius II' by Raphael: even Francis Bacon, it appeared, was now an acceptable investment. All fakes, of course, more lustrous than the originals.

The shrine at the heart of the Papal Palace was kosher. The great black ecclesiastical fortress had been constructed around the ruins of the medieval hermitage and chapel of St Mary, lost for so many years to the citizens of the Island. It was shrouded in a climbing frame of girders; wafers of cladding that suggested Nicholas Hawksmoor's white fossil-filled blocks of Portland stone. The simplicity of the shrine was overlaid by mandalic diagrams, defended against all known heresies. The vaulted ceiling came alive (at a signal from Healy) in a stunning fresco of light, a laser-constructed version of Michelangelo's Sistine masterpiece. Only the 'Creation of Woman' was missing, expurgated and cast into outer darkness on the advice of a committee of responsible aesthetes, recently 'let go' by our Museums of State. Even the spoiled priests hushed their chattering, the programmed responses, as Father Healy – with a tremendous salute – flung his arm aloft, to release, in an ascending cloud, the soapy odours of excessive self-mortification. The Sistine vision bent around the available wall space in convincing deceit: all the iron-pumped carnival of gesture and counter-gesture; expulsion, ecstasy, pride. A Cinecittà pleasure-beach supervised by Vittorio Cottafavi; complete with time-cracked varnish, correctly insinuating the final vulnerability of flesh.

'Gentlemen, Brothers in Christ,' intoned Fr Healy in a lucid gargle, 'you have before you the cinema of the gods, *ab ovo usque ad mala.* Its upkeep is no trivial matter. Your cheques will therefore be gratefully received; earning you respect among your peers, and probable remission in Purgatory.'

The lard-faced penitents scrummaged forward to drop their folded promises, their plastic tickets, into Fr Healy's open briefcase. They froze momentarily in the act, like politicians casting a public vote for the benefit of the newsreel cameras. The Celtic Father blessed them with a limp wave. They filed out, heads down, ignoring the triumphant murals (for which there might well have been an additional cover charge). It was left to the three pagans, the fifth columnists from the Bow Bunker, to acknowledge the magnificent walls of this chamber. We made our private choices between 'The Miraculous Expulsion of Heliodorus from the Temple', 'Attila Repulsed from Rome by Leo I', and 'The Symbolic Marriage of John Paul II with the Church of Poland', consummated before a backdrop of the Gdansk shipyards.

We stood silent, hands knotted together over the organs of generation, while Fr Healy gloatingly evaluated the pillaged treasures. He clucked. His Clara Bow lips pouted, as if closing around the nipple of a peculiarly sharp lemon. They were discreetly glossed. His malachite-green cheeks had received the faintest blush of powder.

It was time for us to enter the *Sala Rotonda* for the conference on Cosmology. We assimilated our final instructions with impatience. We were asked to maintain a dignified and responsible silence, and to remember, always, where we were.

'Our mode of discipline anticipates the performance of the crime, and requires no vulgar enforcement. *Suaviter in modo, fortiter in re,*' Fr Healy warned with a smirk. 'Do not forget for one moment this is not only a place of worship but also the home of the Holy Father, the lineal descendent of St Peter. He, in his infinite wisdom, has invited you here for a purpose; a purpose not to be revealed to his handservant. He has pronounced, *ex cathedra*: it is so. *His* will be done. Execution is tautologous.'

Allergic to cant, Davy sneezed. A tiny goaf of sputum elapsed down the halva-textured marble: a sea-green snail. Suspending all disbelief, it crawled – under Imar's benevolent patronage – towards the exit. The portent was not difficult to interpret.

VI

Professor Hawking leant forward in his customized wheelchair, tieless, large-eared, a fruit bat quivering with intelligence, smiling the huge smile of the enthusiast, absolutely at one with his discourse. He was flanked by MIT-certified gophers, Mormon types, corn-fed hulks in sleeveless shirts who operated the Japanese speak-your-weight voicebox: an unborn mid-Atlantic bass interpreting some dim shade of the great man's argument, dipping the diamond clarity of his equations in bursts of silicon language. The machine spat Hawking's wild truths into the lap of the hogs. The physicist's speculative leaps were calmed by the necessary hesitation between authorial grunts and filtered translation. It all sounded so perfectly reasonable. 'Space-time has no beginning, no end. There was no moment of Creation. The boundary condition of the universe is that it has no boundary.' The Jesuit fathers, wordly and toxic, nodded in unison: dangerous, inherited smiles. They were already rehearsing the destructive brilliance of their inquisition. Their scalps shone, shelfed pebbles of bone. They were eager to audition before this captive audience of television producers. Always room for another housebroken 'talking head' from across the Irish Sea.

From our insignificant position in a cage at the rear of the hall (with representatives of technical journals and footnote puffers from giveaway property sheets), we edged towards the door. We had done our homework and clocked the glass-fronted elevators, with their ornate jackal-embellished thrones (presumably designed to facilitate a quickfire Papal Audience, in transit to the skies). The elevator was our only route to the secret seminar in the heavenly pyramid. The wide Carrara staircase was nothing but decoration, an inflated metaphor for 'time made subservient to form'. It was guarded by a regiment of Palatines, who increased in stature at each turn, thereby fostering an illusory and disturbing perspective. Each step was as sterile and polished as a cutting bench. The supreme tribunal, the *segnatura*, was elsewhere.

We were unchallenged. The long corridors were deserted. The guards were statues. Distortions of Hawking's speech blared from disguised speakers. 'Imag mag mag inary time is sss real ti ti time.' We watched our own ghosts hesitantly approaching the doors of the lift.

Our shallow breath left no trace on the glass. Imar pressed the button. Nothing happened. We waited anxiously: Davy fingering the embossed symbol of Vat City, the silver and gold crossed keys.

As he touched the key, the heavy doors slid open with a surprised hiss. 'Everything in this building is contrary,' he muttered. 'The key should always be the symbol of a closed system. That's what I discovered about Princelet Street. The synagogue was open to all. Every man who used the place had his own key. And so the ancient rusted thing in Rodinsky's drawer was not the clue to some hermetic secret, but a badge of conformity. His membership of the *shul*. He belonged. The key hung on a string around his neck. The string rotted away, its flax devoured by rodents; the key survives within its oxidized shadow. Its continued presence in the drawer grants Rodinsky a family and a living place.'

The ascent began as soon as Davy spoke the word 'key': our stomachs turned, and we shot irreversibly up towards the *sanctum sanctorum*. We drifted past open-plan terraces on which scarlet cardinals sat at their consoles, revising history, tapping Index-approved lies into the ever-lasting files, wiping all unauthorized versions. They translated agency reports into dog latin, sensually airbrushing the rogue images.

We were invisible. The clerks looked through us: an unoccupied throne in an empty elevator. We were unremarked even in the halls of the torturers. Heretics dancing in electrified baths did not turn to us for recompense. We could not smell the crackling pork flesh of the scorched sinners.

Wind demons surrounded the Magnum Tower, frantically wavering between a celebration of this latest blasphemy and the desire to tear the whole stack out of the ground. Turbulence surged and spat. A night-crow's head on the body of a feathered snake. It shuddered the windows, uttering threats; so soon to be performed. It butted and stamped. Something had been released that could not be earthed. The Cardinals had let a virus escape from their chained units: an unripe grub was eating the Books of the Law, reproducing itself, feeding on fear, marrying the operatives to their terminal screens. Whatever they imagined was made instantly visible. The wind rippled in a wave of pandemic chlorophyll from screen to screen, floor to floor, face to face, absorbing all their attention. It gave form to their worst nightmares. Cinema-generated plagues shattered the curved glass. New rat species were conceived from forgotten bacterial formulae. *Pasturella pestis*: deadly creatures evolved to justify the *sound* of those words. And they bit like corrupted saws. White growths manacled the wrists of the Cardinals as they struggled, screaming, to drag themselves from their keyboards. Orange bile seeped from the wires: they slashed them, like so many living vines, in a fever to break free. A low apple-green radiation licked at their wrinkled eyelids: their genitals withered to worms of ash. Dead statistics and natural disasters poured, unchecked, over their masks of terror.

We were nothing. Unseen, we rose through the vertebrae of the Tower like the three Jews in Nebuchadnezzar's fiery furnace. And the fire did not know us. If we had come so far it was because our report had no external significance. We were summoned as witnesses to confirm the validity of the event that was about to be consummated. We were here because the powers wanted us to be here.

A fourth man was with us. A disembodied voice. The euphuistic rhetoric of Fr Healy intoning his prophecies of doom. Sheep's wool saturated in lanolin. The sky-pilot's warning: *Fasten your seatbelts, extinguish your cigarettes.*

'Brothers,' said the voice of Fr Healy, 'the time has come for you to leave the mundane world behind. You have been elected — for your singular qualities of imagination, courage and copper-bottomed stupidity — to be flies on the wall: the expendable, disinterested third eye at our glorious ceremony. And it will cost you nothing more than your preposterously unconvincing lives.'

The lift had come to rest. We were within the Magnum pyramid. But only as far as the line of our chests. We were stuck into the chamber like men buried in sand. No more of the lift emerged than was needed to form the surface of an altar or shrine. We could see everything, but we were powerless; we could not intercede. Neither was there any possibility of escape.

'We have stood St Peter's Holy City on its head and pitched our tent among the stars. The business of the world is now far beneath us. We are purified, and ready to bring forth a New Order.' Fr Healy's words no longer required any physical voice. We salivated obediently, like dogs wired to a bell.

VII

La-place, the master of ceremonies, stepped towards us, machete upraised, tongue like a dagger, leading a procession of white-hooded *hunsi*, penitents and magicians. Objects, which we could not clearly identify, were passed to him. He arranged them on the roof of the elevator: bowls, pitchers, candles, photographs tied with ribbons, live things that scratched.

Directly in front of us was a throne, the *sedes stercorata*, the pierced chair. It rested on a circular carpet of human skulls. The penitents, attached to leather hoops, hung from the slopes of the pyramid like hypnotized studies for Dali's Glasgow 'Crucifixion'. Lanterns were suspended from their necks: an inconstant light making the skulls glitter and grin. A muffled drumming as the exterior panels bucked and flinched from a shower of bizarre terrestrial objects hurled against them by the furious wind. We were under siege. *Agau vâté vâté. Li vâté, li grôdé*.

The voice of Fr Healy reverberating in our heads let us know that the sound system would amplify every breath from the chamber. We would not miss a whisper, a cockcrow. But we must not ourselves, on pain of death, utter a sound. The first ceremony, the sexing of the Pope, was about to begin.

A huge man was lying face down among the skulls, an oil slick on a beach of limestone pebbles. We had taken him for a ritual carpet. He moved. He was draped in ostrich feathers, monkey fur, patches of yellow silk: prayer satchels were strapped to his massive, leopard-clubbing arms. He rose up and strode towards the throne: turned to face us. A grin like an elephant's graveyard. We were confronted by Iddo, the Hausa bookman, bathed in magnificence; his skin gleaming red in the light of lanterns. He called aloud. He bellowed the name of Agassu. He invited possession. Then he lowered himself on to the chair, let his robes cover it, offered his splendid nakedness to the crouching sexers, the dwarf twins hidden beneath the throne. Their conclusion was never in doubt. Iddo Okoli would be crowned with the triple tiara. He would be the Anti-Pope to carve an incision in time's living mantle, to glorify in all the coming madness.

The dwarf twins, the sexers, crawled out from beneath Iddo's skirts. Split kneecaps granted independent articulation. Sacred monsters; they were petted, indulged. Tortoise abortions. Honoured in their deformity. Chosen ones. Two of the white robed figures advanced on them. A challenge. Spears at the throat. As one, stitched into a single skin, they raised their free arms to parade the egg of silver and the egg of gold. All the members of the *segnatura* beat their staffs upon the ground, rattling the skulls like so many melon seeds. The masculinity of the Pontiff was proved.

A soft pattering; nails scratch on hide. It begins. Automatic writing. Forbidden transcriptions in the air. Drums. *Pititt, manman*. The paired, married drums of *petro* ritual. Struck with the flat of the hand. A regular insistent rhythm, broken by wilder surges, trance-inducing seizures. We are locked to this nerve-pulse. It unpicks our conditioned consciousness. It speeds. Voices of rain and rushing water. The anger of prophets. The sweating drummers hammer at their maps of skin.

Now a dark figure steps out from the unknown, from behind the elevator: flapping tails of greenblack cloth. A shirtless *maître d'hôtel*, top-hatted: tramp, clown, medicine-show huckster. He limps, dragging a dead leg. He leans on a cutlass. The dwarf twins kneel before him, lick the rust from his blade.

The blade has a life of its own. It is magnetized. It boxes the compass. It hums, moving between them: an undecided pendulum. It whistles. Strikes.

The dwarf who committed the blasphemy, who dared to handle the stones of potency, was butchered. The blade drawn across his throat. Severance of larynx, trachea, gullet, carotid arteries, jugular veins, vertebrae. Abrupt, indecent termination of all signals. Darkness. The Baron holding him by the hair. An icon, a gorgon head. Life-blood bubbled, drained into an earthen cup; a *zin*. It was offered to Iddo, who drank, dipping his fingers to bless the lucky brother, the ex-twin, the survivor. Iddo kissed him on the mouth, his sanctified fool.

Baron-Samedi passes the cutlass to his master. Iddo receives temporal power, the power of forged steel, of life and death. The initiated blade sweeps over the heads of the assorted penitents, the shuffling dancers; spotting their laundered robes with visceral chutney. It red-strokes the Baron's whitewashed face. Baron-Samedi is the returned avatar of Todd Sileen. His dark side, his double. The black will made albino in its magic. The dead man.

The witnesses drew thongs from around the waists of their costumes. Each man stroked the shoulder of his neighbour with a knotted cord, caressingly, in time to the muted rhythms of the drums. Then more sharply. The tempo quickened. They scourged, they flailed. They groaned in ecstasy of pain. Soon the thin white robes were criss-crossed with dark, wire-grid patterns: relics to be cased for future interpretation, premature miracles. They howled and chanted. They writhed. They twitched like monkeys. Baron-Samedi stood silent, his arms folded across his naked chest.

Iddo led them. He was their voice. They were his echo. This was his place. This was where he surfaced. As Amin hid among the Arabs, the hereditary slavers, and Hercules among the women, so Iddo faded from sight among these colonists of Christ, the huntsmen of aboriginals. He was the only diamond of life in the swamp island, the last redoubt of a dying faith. The white eyes of the dancers revealed his glory. He roared his latinate responses. He was on fire. The lanterns polished his flesh to leather. He was varnished in man-sweat. He was worshipped.

But the red wind was angry. An irreversible prediction. The deck of limey birdsnot screens warned of falling markets, collapse, disaster; and the markets obeyed this failsafe logic. Sell, sell, sell! The wind screamed out of a tumbling fiscal vortex. Unload wheat. Get out of coffee. Dump rubber. Shaft property. Hailstorms of alphabet glitch. The spook tornado swept up everything in the world that was not chained to the ground. Bread loaves, umbrellas, grandfathers. Wounded branches bleeding resin, gale-torn limbs, whole forests thrashed against the arm-oured walls: in opposition to this trashy exploitation of a primal power. (Slash and squirm novels, gut-bursting orgies of special effects!) In the black dome the stars threatened to shake free from their fixed positions. The wires were snipped on the abacus of time. Professor Hawking, directly beneath us, was building his argument to its climax. And when those radiant connections fused ... light would become truth, truth light: it would stretch, bend, *warp*. We would be damp spaghetti-vests hanging from a tree.

The surviving dwarf crawled down a sandy avenue that penetrated the carpet of skulls. He held out twin bowls for Iddo's inspection: a bowl of salt and a bowl of sugar. All feeding is a search for essence. Food is never more than a disguise. Exercise for unhealthy bowels. Iddo re-volved a thumb in the sugar, withdrew it without tasting. He drove his tongue – to the root – deep into the crystals of salt: a fluorescent fish, a crusted poignard. He bared his teeth. The choice was made. The sugar bowl was smashed with a single blow. Sticky grains scattering on to the skulls; sharp-edged slivers of porcelain falling without divination.

Bearers advanced on the throne. Iddo settled himself; accepted, from Baron-Samedi, the Papal crown. Placed it upon his own head. Three times the throne was raised. Three times the trumpet sounded. Ancestors acknowledged him. His title was made known. The Pope whispered his new name to the dwarf. And the dwarf announced it. *Cephas Agassu Ogu*. The penitents kneeled to receive their communion.

I was beginning to have some slight misgivings about my oft-stated policy of witnessing anything and everything, taking whatever was put in front of me. Those excuses would stand no longer. They were a cop-out, the hyena journalist's justification for paddling in horror. We have to take full responsibility for what we choose to see. My choice of action, on the other hand, was strictly limited. I could observe or I could shut my eyes, block my ears; refuse all belief. Claim the privileges of the condemned cell. We were very close to the edge. It might be prudent to accept zombie status, give up our souls – before we slid helplessly across the border and became participants, or even sacrifices, in the abomi-nation that was about to occur.

The light shared my doubts. It drained from the sky in cracks of rust, rivulets of morbid purple. No longer the irradiating waves of our familiar sun but a sulphurous heart-scum, the memory of an exiled planet: sullen heat from a core of apostate metal. The pyramid chamber had loosed itself from its host, the Magnum Tower. *We were floating free.* The glass shields started to sweat, to melt, turn back to water. We were at the mercy of pre-human transactions between excommunicated elements. Wind had captured the Island. The Wild Hunt ravaged the sky fields, romped unchallenged; the red-grey Dogs of Annwfn, *Cwn Wybr*, howled to the dead in us, bringing the ghosts out of our skin: a procession of lost fathers. The flooded river covered all trace of the drowned lands. The Isle of Doges had nothing more to say. It had served its purpose. It was deleted.

Davy kicked at the door of the elevator, aiming his blows at the crossed keys. He pedalled in air, lashed out. There was not the faintest rattle of submission.

Imar had never feigned an interest in the climax of this video nasty. He rejected it. It was not happening; fast-forwarded to oblivion. He hunched his shoulders against the whole performance. He squatted in a corner, plaintively calling with his penny whistle on the wisdom of snails. Tracks of luminescent gum oozed from his jacket and across the glass, a filigree of unresolved impulses; but the beasts themselves, the guides, would not appear. Neither martial arts, nor the quaint visions of primitive molluscs, could aid us. Some action, too fictional to command belief, nagged at the extreme limits of my consciousness. It refused to come any closer. *Trust me*, it said. Only the imagination itself can rescue you from this labyrinth of mirrors. You have willed it, *you* must break it.

I turned to the chamber, hoping that my heretical qualms would have tempered the action. Shut your eyes and it'll go away? Bishop Berkeley was comprehensively refuted: the unthinkable was the only channel still in play. The dwarf was riding towards the Papal throne on the neck of a goat. He was supported by two penitents. He bowed to his kneeling followers. He gestured, and blessed them. He flicked droplets of water into their faces from a large leaf. Baron-Samedi halted his progress, grasping the goat by the horns. He spoke to the animal. It reared up, as if struck with a crop. It stood on its hind legs, a man in furry jodhpurs; it boxed the air – tipping the dwarf down among the appreciative skulls.

Rumpelstiltskin, the bruised pet, grew whimsical; cavorting among the penitents, lifting the skirts of their robes, pinching them, or darting his tongue at their buttocks. The drummers allowed their rhythms to ape him in his eccentric flight: their fingers creeping across the hide, then rushing in a crescendo of excitement as the sanctified fool ... reamed hairy vertical smiles.

The dwarf sprang to loosen a belt, rip open a habit that revealed the body and sex of a woman. *Vodû-si*, a consort of the gods. No stalk-legged hireling, painted, and shaved to the taste of fashion; she stood firm — strong bellied, scarred by life, shockingly real: her blue vein clusters, her creases, her thick black thatch of curls. Her breasts were full and heavy, not exercised into some pneumatic mode. She *was*. Neither virgin, nor victim. She participated here as an equal partner. There were demands she wanted to articulate. She stood naked before them, as they were naked before her. The only indignity was that her face, her identity, remained hidden within a conical hood.

La-place lifted his snake staff and crashed it against the ground. The whole congregation followed his beat. And they chanted. *Cephas, Agassu, Ogu. Cephas, Agassu, Ogu. Cephas Agassu Ogu. Cephas Agassu Ogu. CephasAgassuOgu. CephasAgassuOguCephasAgassuOguCephas* ... Faster, faster. *Faster*. It became a single sound. A manifestation of the wind. In that long rush of breath the wind gained access to the chamber. Curled itself familiarly around the upraised staff.

Cephas rose from his throne, lion king, priest-emperor, flung out his arm. He opened wide his mouth and roared with mad laughter. Roared and shook. Roared until the congregation grew silent and trembled in fear.

Baron-Samedi, saluting in turn the woman and the goat, threw back his tailcoat and drew out, with a showman's flourish, the severed head of the dwarf, the arbitrarily remaindered sexer. He held it over the prostrated white-robed figures, like an owl lantern. They twisted their faces deeper into the sand.

The skull had a tongue in it, and spoke. A liquorice teapot: its jaws clattered. Baron-Samedi played ventriloquist to the mesmerized flock. The skull jabbered: the morse of castanets. 'Beware, Cephas — bathed in glory. King and martyr. Arch-impostor. Beware, Agassu. Blood god, patron of waters. Beware, Ogu — of the Beast who is coming. The *dajjal* killed by Jesus at Lud. Mahdi, false redeemer, speared on the twelfth step of the staircase. Believe in nothing, deny nothing. Neither omens, nor portents. I am a prophet foretelling a prophet.'

This mock-Cawdor millennial rap was terminated when the dwarf-fool snatched his brother's head and carried it away upon his shoulder, setting his own face into a mask of alabaster, letting the skull speak for him. Or yelping with the bloody egg in chorus, duetting, chanting; reverberating like an oracular cave. He wore a strange apron sown with a sporran of lead, the kind of self-constructed garment that early x-ray technicians adopted to protect their gonads. He bowed before Cephas, and placed the head — as a trophy — in his emperor's capacious hands.

But, as soon as the great man was occupied with silencing the loquacious caput, the dwarf opened the jewel-crusted Papal robe and tied it behind Cephas's back with a silver tassel.

The goat is sprinkled with water. The woman feeds him with palm leaves. Baron-Samedi conducts the wedding. Now the extent of Cephas's urgency is evident to his shocked subjects. Time is repulsed, withdraws. Faces appear on the surface of the woman's crisply ironed hood. Dreams that the dead dream. Snatched moments. Suspended memories. Illusory frames promising more than they can deliver. 'This is me. Now and for ever. This is the truth.' All the ages of the woman in a flicked concertina of static images. Mary Butts in London. A party face, flashing with laughter. Red-gold hair. Illusion of movement. Cocteau's Paris: surrounded by gulls, the ghosts of her young men. They perch on her lap. The Abbey. Heat. Scorn. Solitude. The light drowned in a western ocean. Sennen. Ignoring the camera's tired inquisition. Lifeless, without interest. Edith Cadiz. The face in performance. Face of terror. Well Street. Fire-window. The park. Face of death. White linen. Earth crumbling into her open mouth. Alice.

Leading the goat, her bachelor, the woman walked towards Cephas. The drumming stopped. There was no wind. There was silence to the end of the world. The cutting edge of the pyramid.

Strengthen my disbelief. I took Davy by the wrist and reached for the wrist of Imar. We formed a triangle within the square of the box, within the triangle of the pyramid, within the square of the detached tower, within the revolving lingam of the Island. We had to believe more strongly in some other reality, a place beyond this place. To feel the curvature of time, which is love: to resolve the bondage of gravity. To move out along that curve, to have the courage to make that jump. I willed a mental picture of the only other site on the gulag for which I felt any affection (muted, ambivalent): the slight elevation of Mudchute, a remembered field. Afternoons of children and animals. And, at its perimeter, the original windmills of Millwall. An engraving in the Nautical Museum. *See it.* The view towards Greenwich, the classical vision of form: hospitals, avenues, churches, order. I willed the others to see what I saw, and to hold to it. *Now.* As time was made to hesitate, stutter. The will towards madness; using our terror to escape from terror.

The walls of the lift shook and shuddered: snail-cracks ran through the glass, a system of veins, a fern garden. The crossed keys became the map of another place; a river defence, lines of fire. Earth jars crashed from the roof, and shattered. Rum and salt. Essences of the unborn. Dead sugars. Our nanosecond of resistance to the spin of time was aborted. The goat was dead; the knitted entrails steaming in the hands of Baron-Samedi. The grinning waiter in a cannibal restaurant. Cephas was crushing the shoulders of the only woman on the Island. His breath drawn so deep as to steal all the oxygen from the chamber. We were choking, cobalt-blue: our brains dying on the stem. She was webbed within a curtain of eyes. The *hunsi* were queueing inside Cephas's hunger for a share of the sweetmeats: a singular gangbang.

The woman pulled off her conical hood, shook out her hair. Cephas hesitated. He was looking at death. He was looking at a face without features, an empty mirror. The flesh was as blank, as uncontoured, as linen. Wild light from the south streamed through the pyramid, down the reopened ley, from Blackheath and Greenwich Hill, over the dark waters, cutting through the blasphemy of the architects. It rushed to meet itself. Imar's heated snail-path silvered the coupled contraries in gummy radiance.

We closed our eyes, gripping each other's wrists, gasping for breath. We felt what we saw: grass. Moved our hands, brushed the steel floor. The springy, sharp resilience of grass breaking through the walls of the elevator. Tickling our shocked skins, dewy blades. A green cell, a wind from the river.

We lifted our heads. We did not need to open our eyes, we *saw*. The pyramid was pulsing — a drop of sweated blood — far in the distance; reaffirmed at the summit of the black tower. Far, far away, above the terracotta roofs of this morning-fresh medieval city, this transported Siena. Beneath us, along the riverside, a parade of windmills: decent samurai. The first, the true, the unexploited Island. Marsh grass rustled by breezes from the Reach. The outline in the earth, the foundations of the Chapel House. Coarse fields split by a single urethra track.

And we began to roll, to tumble, laughing, cheeks pressed in the cool damp grass, down the gentle slopes of Mudchute hill.

VIII

We had come through; but at what cost, we preferred not to consider. We touched our arms, patted ourselves, tenderly feeling for bruises and broken bones. We stood up. It was morning. Ridiculous. Soft white sheep bleating on toy hillocks. The stacked, angled roofs of some Italian city-state; some hill town celebrated in guidebooks. Bells. Church bells across the deepwater docks. There were even piglets with corkscrew tails churning up the mud. All the excavated silt from Millwall had created a token farm for the brochures of developers: a grass enclosure around which to heap their defiant fortresses. The edge too had been worked, planted with market gardens. Even the windmills had been restored. Only the uprooted trees, with their huge earth-bowl bases, witnessed the night of storms.

'There's something very strange about those windmills,' Imar remarked, 'even with a fresh river breeze, the sails are not turning.'

'Obviously heritage fakes,' said Davy, 'carefully sited along the riverfront to hide whatever is going on behind them.'

'Which, I suppose, we have to investigate,' I groaned wearily, 'before we consider some way of getting out of here.'

'Unless,' Davy persisted, with relish, 'unless the freezing of time has had some darker consequence. You realize we may actually have been flung back into an ahistorical anomaly: a confirmation of Hawking's absence of boundaries, a liquid matrix, a schizophrenic actuality that contains the fascinating possibility of finding ourselves placed in post-modern docklands and *quattrocento* Florence, *at the same time*. So that all those greedy pastiches have become the only available reality, "real fakes", if you like. We arrived here by an act of will: *was it our own?* What if the inevitable return of our natural cynicism and disbelief has let slip Conrad's *Heart of Darkness*, renegades from Dickens's prison hulks, or any other composite monsters – including those from this fiction you are supposed to be writing? If the imagination is primary, then anything we can imagine must lie in wait to ambush us.'

We strolled carelessly down through ancient overgrown apple orchards towards the windmills; passing among unconcerned sheep, ruminant philosophers, skull-faced Augustans, and their loose-bowelled lambs – urgently worrying at their mothers' dugs. Our speculations were comfortable: the chalky prattle of tutors perambulating an enclosed quadrangle. We knew that the savage world was safely distanced on the other side of a high wall.

We didn't need to come any closer to the windmills to see that Elgin MacDiarmuid's living nightmare and his dying ambition had both been fulfilled. He had been crucified, in the Roman fashion, between a pair of tinkers. The windmills were all crucified men, staked, to face the river: a warning, or a boast.

Our contemplation of this latest atrocity could not be prolonged. No aesthetic reveries; no measured comparisons with Mantegna or Grüne-wald. Late Gothic or early Expressionist? The unacceptable sound of skulls falling into a petrol drum. The wind returned: from the crown of the hill, in the shape of thundering hoofs that churned the soft brown earth. First, the scarlet pillbox hats, the buttoned tunics; then the rearing, foam-flecked horses, monsters of stone; the stretched hounds, the spears,

running men, shouts of triumph. Uccello's 'Hunt by Night' had come
loose from its hoarding. We knew now what they were hunting.

'Split up,' screamed Davy, 'run!'

'The tunnel!' Imar shouted, already ahead of us; tearing, with wild
erratic strides, for his talismanic vision of Greenwich and the snail-
domed observatory.

'That's no good, man,' warned Davy. 'They've flooded it. The
foot-tunnel's drowned.'

Too late. Imar had vaulted into the goats' pen, sprinted, stumbled,
checked, fallen, lost a boot, gashed a leg, slithered through a yard of
dozing sows, and out again, shit-plastered, on to the perimeter road.

Davy yelled that he would double back towards Glass City, link up
with the surviving tinkers; or, failing that, dive into the water: swim for
it.

I decided in an instant – what other choice was there? – the last human
street on the Island, Coldharbour, was the place for which to aim. The
ground beyond the Gun, a derelict terrace, was my target. Already
future fictions were accumulating around those images of honest decay.
We were divided, the power of the triad was broken; we lost sight of
each other. We fled from our separate mounted demons; the sharp spears
ripping our clothes, the teeth of the dogs tearing at our sinews. It is my
fear alone that gives life to these chimeras of pursuit.

At last, after so many words, the metaphor is workable: escape.
Flight. Careering across an alien landscape, the unknowable vacancy of
another man's dream. Running, and putting the world behind you.
Escaping from it, or letting it swallow you whole? Nothing remains.
No trace of being. No history. No tools of language. *Don't look now*.
Try to confirm the reality of the final set. The dark barrel of the Gun.
Then hide, vanish, become zero, a ripple on the tide: the crazed
anchorite I am already supposed to be. Enjoy the luxury of silence, exile,
cunning? Forget it. Posthumous sediment at the bottom of a bottle of
yellow wine.

The perspective of Uccello's time-hurdling Hunt ordains a single,
distant figure of prey. One victim only, but which of us should be the
lucky man? It might prove interesting to find out.

10

The Guilty River

The Guilty River

(In Homage to Nicholas Moore, poet, who died
in Orpington Hospital, 26 January 1986)
'*... Pocahontas histories
Left trailing in the wind. O visionary ...*

Nicholas Moore, 'Yesterday's Sailors'

Weak: weak rather than sick, I followed my sickness to the river, willingly anticipating its arrival – the tickle in the throat, the raw and bloody eyes. (Are we not all, more or less now, sick? Who cling so stubbornly to the cities? Sicker on some days than others. *Noticeably* sick. Unable to stand up, retching. Sick in the head. Wanting to inflict damage, editing those encounters – or walking, head bowed, into the path of a car. The viruses, the newcomers, spread in a blush of shame, disguise themselves, return home; kissing the damp chicken-flesh. I remember in 1967 talking with R. D. Laing in a waste garden alongside the Roundhouse. A garden? The Roundhouse? R. D. Laing? He had this messianic intensity – which is relish, celebration – going on about an artist who *chose* to live in Manhattan, because he liked feeling his lungs grind to tissue, black lips, fevers; he took it on, the early version. How remote it sounded, how intriguing. In the sunlight, which was Belsize Park to Primrose Hill; the trees. The bloodymindedness of hanging on, *knowing*: watching the tremble, the crazy runners racing after themselves, clutching at their hearts; the filth – the fatalism of an apocalypse clique. End of sermon.)

I wanted the smoothed tapeworm of the North Woolwich shuttle: the unlisted halts, the elevated views over frenzied sections of motorway, sun scars flashing on curved windshields. Only in the train could I step out of time and hear its brazen doors bang behind me. All notebook-twitching novelty had long been drained from this journey. I could use it like a contemplative retreat. A weekend visit to the Trappists – with the bonus of moving *scenery*.

What is it with trains? The line of doors slam shut like a collapsing house of cards, or – seen from above – oars on a prison galley. Nailed into our juddering coffins, we slide down the rails towards the furnace: in fits and starts. That might be it. The train generates metaphors, similes. (And without much self-criticism: no revision capacity.) It's ready (indecently eager) to be everything except itself. If I could hold my mind still, hold the compartment in one place. The only movement is in time; *sideways*. Parallel loops of film. The wheels of the train running backwards. Which train escapes the station? Jumps the line; an oblique reality, an unexpected angle. (Not angles, but angels.)

I can't forget that story Bruce Chatwin tells in *The Songlines* (one of the italicized fillers: captured 'On the train, Frankfurt–Vienna'). It's a clever piece of writing, its moral judgements slanted into this dark fairy story with no visible strain. A 'pallid', fleshy, airless youth is travelling to Vienna to meet his father. Chatwin opens the carriage window to breathe in 'the smell of pines'. The inevitable fabulation awaits his return.

The father, a rabbi, survives – but his story is a terrible one. In 1942 the Nazis painted a star upon the door of his house in Romania. He 'shaved his beard and cut his ringlets. His Gentile servant fetched him a peasant costume … He took his first-born son in his arms' and fled into the forest. Worse than Grimm. He left behind, with a final embrace, his wife, two daughters, and infant son. All died in Birkenau.

The rabbi was sheltered by shepherds, fed on slaughtered sheep 'that did not offend his principles'. The Turkish frontier. America. Time. Despair. Europe again. Vienna. And, late at night, the doorbell. An old woman with 'bluish lips', carrying a basket. His Gentile servant.

'I have found you,' she said. *'Your house is safe. Your books are safe, your clothes even. For years I pretended it was now a Gentile house. I am dying. Here is the key.'*

The key returns, fate: a wrist tattoo. *I am dying. Here is the key.* Trains promote confessions, as cruising yawls promote the leisurely spinning of tales. I was wrong about Rodinsky. Now I can open the letter I received this morning from Mr Shames. I had written asking for his permission to quote from his original letter to Michael Jimack in my Spitalfields story.

Stoke Newington

Dear Mr Sinclair,
    Please forgive delay in reply to your letter for which I thank you.
    I herewith have your article dated Aug 1988 which was most

interesting, but I must correct your assumption about David Rodinsky. Firstly, I knew him when young, a pasty-faced chappie who always looked under-nourished. He was not Polish, but born in London, he was a tenant together with his mother in two rooms let to them above the Princelet Synagogue, not a scholar, his sustenance was given to him and his mother from Jewish charities.

Neither was he invisible. My daughter Lorna spoke to him many a time, & she remembers him well, it was I that named (pardon me) his mother 'Ghandi' & is mentioned by my sisters-in-law to this day.

The Synagogue was cared for very well by Bella, even after her late father died, until she decided to move away & it was closed. All prayer books & Torah scrolls were returned to the Federation of Synagogues, together with their silver appurtenances, & thereby closed an era of East End Jewish history. As a member of the synagogue, I was Mr Reback's son-in-law, having married in those premises. I can assure you that some of my contemporary members included Dr M. L. Barst, a most likeable practitioner, also some wealthy merchants, like the merchants who dealt with government clothing contracts, three brothers who were master bakers, the Rinkoffs, the Olives, wholesale & retail umbrella merchants, cloth merchants etc, their names have been forgotten in my memory.

It was in 1948 I last saw & spoke to David, it was at a bar-mitzvah of my nephew, the son of Monty Fresco, the press photographer, & author of *50 years in Fleet St*. It was then I related to him about my experiences in the Middle East, Egypt, India & Burma.

At that occasion he told me he had learned, while resident in a home, Arabic. I spoke to him in Arabic, & his reply was understood by me, & I guessed his Arabic teacher was an Egyptian Jew. He was taught Arabic, like myself using English vowels & consonants; I too was taught Arabic & Urdu during my service in the canal zone.

To conclude, I had pity on David, he kept himself interesting during his short life, but unfortunately attained nothing, this was due to his low IQ. With people like him, they know not of having an ambition nor the initiative to get somewhere in life. David invisible? Definitely NO! My daughter Lorna, also the Reback family living at the Synagogue always treated him well. He had a sister Bessie, she paid occasional visits to Princelet St, but she too had a mental illness & was a patient in Clayberry mental home, from my deduction she may be there still.

A word about myself. In my travels I returned with many 'objet d'art', I possess a collection of gold sovereigns from George III to the present day, as well as a fine collection of Israeli proof coins.

Today, in my garden I have two vines, black grapes growing on one wall, white grapes growing on the opposite wall – this year's crop is a record due to the long summer. From the grapes I make a black portlike wine, the white grapes make a fine dessert wine. So at the age of seventy-six, I'm still pretty active.

To close, I sincerely hope this finds you well, if you have an hour to spare you are always welcome to see some of my collections.

Best wishes,
I. Shames

The speeding train leaves no visible wash. The uncertain past is erased by its passage. My early tales vanish behind me; they are not to be trusted. But each new version of the Rodinsky legend only increases its interest for me. Was his life so 'short', if Mr Shames met him, capable of conversing in Arabic, in 1948? Were his attainments so negligible? How could a man scratching by on doles of chicken-broth charity have left fifty-three cases of books worth removing to the Museum of London?

I was standing once more on the banks of the river. Deleting the dead versions only cleared the track ahead – on! Throw off the rattling tin cans, the barnacled anchors. The river *is* time: breathless, cyclic, unstoppable. It offers immersion, blindness: a poultice of dark clay to seal our eyes for ever from the fear and agony of life. Events, and the voices of events, slurp and slap, whisper their liquid lies: false histories in mud and sediment; passions reduced to silt.

I let my sickness lead me where it would, to discover its specific 'spot' on this dull ribbon of shore. The Telecom saucers were lanced skywards: the harm was there to be imagined. No immediate lacerations were available, no blistering, hair loss, no cankers or amputations. Future damage would be required, at the insistence of the courts, to invent a more distinguished parentage. The silver funnels of the Sugar Factory gleamed in the Reach: a death-kit, a plug on its back, blunt prongs wounding the sluggish puffball clouds.

Yard after yard, step by step, I dragged myself past the Royal Pavilion (its red, river-facing sign: COURAGE); and on into the pleasure gardens. Downstream once more to bear witness to the sinking of the *Alice* in Gallions Reach. As if, by staring into the leaden waters, I could clear the shame of my obsession, could see the jaws of the paddle steamer rise from the depths – healed – band playing, smoothing its circuit of water, reversing on to the pier; its white-faced voyagers stepping ashore to join the perambulation of other ghosts on these geometric paths. A whelk-stall Marienbad!

The gardens were an extension of my pre-emptive convalescence. I would get that out of the way before the blow actually fell and fever boiled my blood to water. Shrubs remained unshakeably calm in their pools of shadow. Willowy transplants (willows?) from more exotic regions drew me in among their yellow-gold skirts of sunlight. The bark tasted of freedom. Even the tennis courts were painted amulets, untroubled by the dance of ball-punishing fanatics.

But there is always a territory beyond the gardens (there *has* to be), a wilderness that makes the tentative notion of a garden possible. Beyond music (gossip, ease, assignations, French kisses, sticky fingers, cigar smoke, sweet Muscat) is a concrete balcony, a fierce ramp aimed at the suck of the river: an unshaven wall of threat, sprayed with curses, among which I notice the delicate invocation, 'Acker'. The tide is teasing the rug away from under the usual catalogue of broken bottles, pieces of chain, grievous bodily weapons that failed their audition, lukewarm motors escaping the net of insurance investigators. Yellow river-sick plasters the hubcaps. This is where you will find (should you so desire) whatever is spat out when all the meat has been picked from the bone. A last run of wild ground which heavy plant instruments are obscurely, but inevitably, eliminating. A brief no man's land. An Edenic flash in an atrocity album. A truce between the mental gardens and the Creek-mouth Sewage Works. I can go no further.

I sit on a stone block in a sheltered hollow, and look from my map (Landranger 177) to the river, and back again: the sun dance, the golden float of midge-bright particles. The love soup. Teasingly, the light reveals itself. The tainted water is marked on the pale blue that represents the Thames with a heavy cross of ink. (There could be no mistake.) The death place, between Gallions Reach and Barking Reach, is named: Tripcock Ness, or Margaret. The chill of that baptism inflicts, as if by ordinance, its own shock waves of ruin. Margaret mines the channel, exacts her toll, visits the drowned; a succubus, she drinks their terror, licks the weed from their mouths, irradiates them with her glory. Punitive strokes of benevolence flay them to the last wafer of skin. A curtain of nuclear winter hangs across the river – a second barrier – a thin line of artificial snow, a mantle of ash through which all traffic must pass.

I let my anger die in the distance. And, as so often before (when i walked beyond Woolwich), I found myself meditating on the poet, Nicholas Moore, somewhere on the other bank, in a white hospital ward, dying in exile. After long years of neglect, blind struggle, the satisfaction of pitching it all into the flow of the river; that molten crucible of light – splitting desire into a chimeric insect pattern. *Maya.* Illusion. Nothingness. Without ego; freed at last from the persistence of your ghosts. (How we load our own burdens on to the defenceless dead!)

The south shore then became a place of interest. (Literary associations stick like dogdirt to the turbulent mouldings of our boots, as we plod through 'Eliot's' East Coker, 'J. C. Powys's' Montacute.) Some life, in the form of new hope in the sky, *had* escaped down these unconsidered tributaries of Thames. And I wanted very much to learn about the accidents that brought Nicholas Moore to this dim sprawl, where he lived for so many years, sustained, energized, possessed by the poems he wrote. Until the day came when words could no longer offer any protection. There was nothing left to articulate in that form. ('Reconciliation and relief after immense suffering'?) Impertinent to speculate. We need to know more than there is to tell.

> 'Night. Night thoughts. *Nacht und Traume.* Dreams
> Of the old. *Greisengesange.* Turtle dreams.'

I decided to visit Peter Riley, the poet and bookdealer, in Cambridge; to tape an interview about his pilgrimages to St Mary Cray (to talk with, and assist, Nicholas Moore). I would transcribe some sort of record and include it, as a testament, among my twelve fate tales. There should be a bridge of light, however hallucinatory (and self-willed), to span the guilty river.

My state of mind was strange enough (put it down to the fever) to risk this evil town, to which every excursion was another failed attempt on the record for being buried alive in peat slurry. Fen consciousness has never really recovered from the retreat of the North Sea: the life-forms are Jurassic. Already, the cold chalk of Templar enclaves has worked its way under my fingernails, as I bite them in frustration, trying to find a way into the deconstructed shell of Liverpool Street Station.

I stepped on to the train, with an air of assumed bravado, carrying a tape-recorder, and two or three of Nicholas Moore's books for the journey. We jolted pleasantly above all the familiar East End secrets. Soundless, they were no more troubling than an in-flight movie.

I followed Peter's directions out of Cambridge Station, across the car park – soft drizzle – into a web of narrow streets that clung for support to the railway. I bought some cheap cigars from the Bengali corner shop, as a gift. Nothing better was on offer. We could have been in ... Crouch End?

The house was easy to locate, an unfraudulent artisan's terrace, now shifted in use and status (down?) And, after the usual preliminary courtesies (the peek at the poetry shelves, the soup, the coffee), we settled to make our tape.

II

A Conversation with Peter Riley, at Sturton Street, Cambridge, 1 March (St David's Day) 1989

IS: How did you come to visit Nicholas Moore in the first place? And why did you decide to go and see him?

PR: I simply wondered what had become of him. I made a few enquiries around and nobody knew where he was, or thought he was still alive. Eventually, I found an address which I wrote to – and it worked.

Nobody published him: but, although he wasn't publishing, Nicholas Moore never gave up hope of publishing. He was constantly producing 'Selected Poems', constantly sending things to periodicals like the *Spectator* and *TLS*, who did not publish any of it.

He must have produced a dozen different typescripts of 'Selected Poems', which went to every possible publisher in the country. He was writing a lot of deliberate doggerel – he called it 'satire' – with serious poems, now and then. He'd write all day long, he did nothing else. In the morning he'd hammer away at his typewriter – most of it was rambling, rhapsodic – but, generally, towards the end of the day, he might get around to a serious poem.

He sent people bundles of this stuff, which just gave them terrible headaches: then it all came back.

IS: You got an address for him, dropped him a line?

PR: Ummm, yes. I wanted work like that to do. I said I was interested in collecting his work together – little realizing that I was talking about something like three thousand poems.

I got an address. He responded. And I called in.

IS: What did you discover?

PR: He lived in St Mary Cray. It's near Orpington. Estate houses, of about the 1930s, '40s, '50s, covering several hillsides; mostly semi-detached houses, let off into maisonettes. He was in a downstairs maisonette, on his own. His second wife had died two or three years earlier.

I turned up and found this little man, with one leg, in a wheelchair, in absolute total squalor. Through the front door, then along a corridor. Several rooms open off: a bedroom, and the room he lived in, a back study which was now disused, a totally squalid kitchen, and a bath which was full of lumber and detritus. There was coal everywhere. It was absolutely filthy. He was perfectly happy in there and very organized.

The place he lived in, the room itself, was incredible. You couldn't see the furniture, except for the table and the chair he sat in. It was piled up with food and rubbish and biscuits and bits of paper: old newspapers, magazines, books, and records.

It's strange that this should have happened to him. Nicholas Moore was a very successful young poet – as early as 1939, and on through the war. It was the war that made this possible. A reaction to the left-wing liberalism of the 1930s, Auden and that generation. During the war things got published that would never otherwise have got into print.

IS: Nicholas Moore had been part of a Cambridge group?

PR: He was the son of the philosopher, G. E. Moore, and was a student at Cambridge. As such, he was interested in joining all the forms of modernism together in one movement: taking whatever he wanted from America, from Wallace Stevens, and from Surrealism, jazz, Picasso, Henry Miller and Durrell.

His friend, George Scurfield, said to me once, 'We thought in those early days we could stop the war.' He was referring to the polemic activities of that student group in Cambridge. They were fellow-travellers. They thought they could forge a link between Britain and Russia. But how they were going to do this with student magazines is not clear.

People's university careers ended and they disappeared; but Moore carried it on. He took it to London and collaborated with Tambimuttu.

IS: Why wasn't he actively engaged in the war?

PR: He was a conscientious objector.

IS: Did that mean he went to prison?

PR: No, he had to go and work on farms in East Anglia, digging potatoes. That didn't seem to last long; for the last years of the war he was commuting between Cambridge and London.

IS: He thought of poetry as being his career? And then the war ended and it was all over?

PR: Not very suddenly; it was a process which took the rest of the 1940s to work itself out. As the poetry-reading public increased, and became something more like Auden's public, so Nicholas Moore's personal readership diminished and diminished. A completely new set of poets had taken the situation over.

IS: During the war, he lived in London?

PR: No, he lived in Cambridge, and commuted to his work in Tambi's office. He took no part in that Soho scene. He carefully steered clear of it. When he finished work, he went back home – and left the others to drink themselves insensible.

IS: When did he move to Orpington?

PR: That's part of the great crisis which occurred to him around 1948. Unfortunately, this worsening literary situation happened to coincide with three or four other crises, which amounted to a total reversal of fortune.

IS: Presumably, he wasn't making any money from the poetry? Even when he was successful?

PR: No, I shouldn't think so: not much. Tambi was paying him, he'd got work. But very little specific payment for writing. But in 1948 everything, which had been going so rosily for him, collapsed in a short period. Only the poetry was not sudden. That was a slow haemorrhage of readership.

IS: Wasn't that, then as now, a general condition?

PR: It affected a lot of people: Wrey Gardiner, David Gascoyne, and W. S. Graham (who ended up living in Cornwall, in penury). Perhaps George Barker too. Many of them left the country.

IS: Was this normal, everyday indifference? Or did society need to revenge itself on them? Was there no longer the imagination to tolerate their very existence?

PR: It's difficult to know the basic reasons for this. But it's to do with what the readership of poetry is, and their expectations.

IS: The readership of poetry seems to consist only of other poets, the peer group, and those looking for a way into the racket. Was there ever a readership of people not involved in the practice of writing the stuff?

PR: There was for Nicholas Moore and his associates during that one brief period. There was an intellectual following that was a continuation of the following the modernists had during the First World War, Pound's and Eliot's public. Their books were professionally produced by Poetry London and the Grey Walls Press.

The reason these poets weren't at Faber is that they thought they had their own publishers. Then, of course, those publishers collapsed; and Moore and his colleagues were left without a publisher at all.

There were also financial disasters. The supportive money from Moore's family was no longer there. His wife, Priscilla, left him. Half his early poems are dedicated to her.

That was the big disaster for Moore; he was left with no wife – which devastated him. She went off with somebody else. No wife, no money, nowhere to live, no publisher. He was helpless: so he went down to London and found himself a job.

He'd always been interested in gardening, had become expert at cultivating new species of flowers. He got himself a job in a horticultural shop, a seed merchant's. He was wandering around the West End and saw an advertisement in a tobacconist's window for this flat in St Mary Cray, near Orpington. He took it, and lived there for the rest of his life.

He continued to work in this flower shop, commuting to St Mary Cray. He married a second wife, a very different sort of person. She was more of a local product, a daughter of the bourgeoisie of those suburbs.

The 1950s, as a period, is dark and obscure. He wrote less and less. He was on the train every day, into Victoria. Then there was a child. He was in a very difficult situation by the middle or late 1950s. His wife began to get mentally ill and couldn't cope with looking after the children. He had to do all the work in the house himself, while struggling with other things, and doing some writing. He began to get very ill himself. The child, his son, was put out to a foster home. He found he'd got diabetes – which he had for the rest of his days.

IS: When did he have his leg amputated?

PR: That was much later on. He continued with the diabetes for quite a while, under treatment. But it gets worse, whatever happens. So that brought him, more or less, into the situation in which I found him.

He started writing again, in earnest, around 1965. It had become a totally private activity, although he always had hopes of making a 'comeback'. He never gave up. He remained in touch with Tambi – who likewise had schemes, was going to make it back into the limelight. But never quite did, not properly.

IS: He was more prolific than W. S. Graham, for example?

PR: Oh yes, his method was to write: he didn't think. His poetry wasn't concentrated in the way that Graham's was. But the poetry kept him alive, I believe.

IS: Did he hope that at some point circumstances would turn around again? Did he feel it was an accident that nobody read him any more?

PR: He might have thought that at first, but after thirty years ... If he hadn't kept going there would have been nothing at all.

IS: Did he greet you warmly when you arrived?

PR: Oh yes, various people had taken an interest in him before that. There was Barry MacSweeney. And, around the time he published *Spleen*, there was some short correspondence with Andrew Crozier and Jeremy Prynne. The thing was that Moore kept up to date with poetry. He was a subscriber to *Grosseteste*, and he bought Ferry Press books.

     He was stuck out there in a wilderness, in outer suburbia, in the most dismal place you could possibly think of living in.

IS: It wasn't anywhere near a river? His writing is filled with images of water.

PR: I think that started in Cambridge. The dream images are of the Cam. His father's house was a few yards from it.

IS: I wondered what his sense of that location, the place he lived in, was?

PR: He thought it was an accident. A fairly pleasant place, when he first moved. His house was on the edge of the development, next to fields. But within a few years, of course, the whole area had been covered in suburbia. Nothing in sight except identical houses. He had really established a personal island, or islet, in the middle of a huge mud estuary.

     There is no sense of movement. In *Lacrimae Rerum* there's a dream sequence about wandering endlessly through anonymous streets: pavements the same, trees the same, round corners and up hills. That's suburbia. It doesn't crop up much in his poems, only at the end. He had an island, this dingy room in which he lived. He maintained all the things which had been part of that student enclave in Cambridge: jazz, cricket, gardening, modern art – also pots, especially Lucie Rie pots. He actually ate his dinner off Lucie Rie pots, which were worth thousands of pounds. And, occasionally, he broke one.

IS: When you turned up ... did Nicholas Moore see you as a messenger from the same tradition, a couple of generations on? An initiate?

PR: He didn't know I came from that background. I suggested it to him later on. But he had begun to feel pretty bitter about the whole poetry world. He didn't sit there like a church father and calmly accept what had happened to him – as if he was a hermit in the desert.

There was a large sense that poetry is very important and was everywhere abused. He felt that what he was writing was important, and that the world was losing it. There was no access to the world. All he could do was keep on producing. In phases. Faster and faster. Until, as his illness got worse, it tailed off. He was in and out of hospital. There'd be two or three years with an upsurge of poetry. He always went to the same hospital, Orpington Hospital.

Writing was now physically very difficult. Diabetes affects your eyesight, you go nearly blind. He didn't wear glasses. His vision was very blurred and minimal. It was a 1940s island, without television. Hospital meant the radio. You're stuck in a bed for weeks and weeks. There's nothing to do except put on your earphones. There's only one station: Radio One. So he was caught listening to John Peel. It's extraordinary. He sent poems to the BBC and John Peel. Peel had slight intellectual pretensions.

Nicholas Moore had built up a world which was not just poetically self-sufficient, it had to be culturally self-sufficient as well.

Of course, his wife was with him – but that was more of a problem than a help.

IS: Did you visit him in hospital?
PR: Only latterly, yes.
IS: Did he know he was dying?
PR: No, he'd been in so often. He didn't look after himself. His cultural thing included good eating and good drinking. He wasn't going to give these up just because he'd got diabetes. He was certainly not going to stop drinking wine. He was something of a connoisseur of wine. He ate himself through diabetes with French chocolate biscuits. He lived ten years longer than anyone in his condition would be expected to live; perhaps because of the drive that kept him writing poetry.

The diabetes got worse. He developed gangrene somewhere, along an extremity. In his remaining foot. There was talk of that having to come off. He was imprisoned in a wheelchair. But he still gardened. I've had terrifying descriptions of Nicholas Moore and his wheelchair, gardening with one hand, the chair tilting over at forty-five degrees, while he dug holes in the ground. He'd recently given it up when I first met him. The garden then became totally overgrown, grass sprouted up.

There was a move by the family to get him to Cambridge – which Moore strongly resisted. The reason he gave was that he couldn't abandon his garden. The garden looked like a wilderness, but the pattern was still there, underneath. All it needed was weeding. This was a great creative work of his. He cultivated his own hybrids of irises and Michaelmas daisies and *sempervivums*. He had pieces of rock – limestone – which he said could not be moved to Cambridge. He'd have to stay there with his rocks, whatever happened. And yet, of course, a few weeks after he died the house was sold and the whole thing was razed, beyond trace.

He had a beautiful flowering cherry in his front garden, a rare Japanese cherry. I have never seen one before. It grew up beyond his floor and emerged in front of the window of the tenants upstairs – and had to be trimmed, because they said it impeded their view of the council houses. When the house was sold, the tree was uprooted.

IS: He was living in a condition of sentimental exile, like Guy Burgess in Moscow?

PR: Yes, an exile in which the postal services had stopped taking messages back to his native country.

IS: What was his state of mind, in hospital, when you visited him for the last time?

PR: He was under painkilling drugs, so he was speaking very slowly. He was most concerned that nothing should be lost. He didn't think in terms of archives; when he'd written poems, he threw them on the floor. When we were clearing up the place, afterwards, there were poems everywhere: under the kitchen sink, stuffed into flower pots. He didn't want any of them to leave the flat, even if they got screwed up and dirty.

IS: The 'Last Poem', or *(THE LAST POEM)* as you have it, published at the end of *Lacrimae Rerum* ... was that written at home, before he went to hospital?

PR: It was written in his head. He wrote everything in his head, before he started to type it. He wrote very little in longhand, because nobody could read his longhand – not even himself.

He said the 'Last Poem' was in three parts. He told me what it was about. But it wasn't very clear whether he was reciting or summarizing. He typed the first part, neatly. The second part he typed, roughly. The third part was still in his head. He was going to do that when he got home. He was concerned that it shouldn't be lost. He mentioned this very particularly. But the third part is lost, yes. And will never be recovered.

In spite of the neatness of Moore's cultural isolation, the work was a sprawl, a mess. He was producing these typescripts, all day long, which were utter doggerel; and casting them around the room, spilling things on them, and eating off them.

Writing was so difficult for him. He had to put his nose against the keyboard and type one letter at a time. It's difficult to think of a poem when you're doing that.

The last year, he almost stopped. There were too many problems. If I hadn't come, and taken an interest, *Lacrimae Rerum* wouldn't have existed at all, hardly any of it.

It's interesting – you have to be metaphysical – but he makes continual reference to 'islets' in his work. Which is a metaphor to him. He was living on an islet, a rock in the sea. Also, the seat of diabetes involves things called the *Islets of Langerhans*.

When I first saw this term I thought it was some place he had visited during a holiday in Austria when he was young. But Langerhans was a German pathologist who described the islets, small groups of cells scattered through the pancreas.

Those translations he did from Baudelaire, *Spleen*, are all to do with diabetes: the sluggish slowing down of the bloodstream, turning green, thickening to bile.

IS: You seem to have a taste for searching out these old men, the survivors? When you went to see Nicholas Moore were you, in any sense, nominating a father?

PR: I hope not. There *is* a feeling that you like to relate to father generations; but you don't know what you want, or expect, from them. If you've got parents like mine, who are non-intellectual, perhaps there's a tendency to hunt around. On a personal level, I like helping old people. I enjoyed going to Nicholas Moore and picking up the things he dropped, reaching for things he couldn't reach, trying to make some order out of the appalling chaos he'd got his manuscripts into.

We'd be talking about poems and he – suddenly – would think of one which he considered was very important, and we *had to find it*. So we'd start, turning things upside-down, moving piles of records and books, moving furniture, looking for one little thin piece of paper. Which nine times out of ten we didn't find. Then it was time for me to go. He knew what colour the paper would be.

If anyone ever published a 'Collected Works of Nicholas

Moore', a three-volume job, a thousand-odd pages, his real achievement would be lost in it. Nobody would be able to find it.

As, finally, nobody could find him. He didn't relate to this locality in any sense. When he wrote about it, it was a dream image. It was an unreal world outside.

IS: The reason he was there was the simple fact of the railway, conveniently connecting him to his city seed shop?

PR: Yes, that's why he was there. But it wasn't a pleasant place. He had to put up with neighbours chucking stones through his window. The local kids looked on him as some kind of witch, because he was going round in a wheelchair, with his one leg. The house was obviously derelict, the windows coated in dust.

IS: He never attempted to sell off his books? The obvious reflex for most writers?

PR: No. Nobody wanted to read them, so why should anyone want to buy them? He'd got three or four copies of that very rare book of his, *Recollections of the Gala*, mint copies in a drawer; which he could have sold, even in those days, for £30 or £40 each. That's not to mention all the signed presentation copies from Wallace Stevens.

He lost his correspondence with Stevens. That was one of the things he did realize was of some value. He was still hale and hearty, he'd just arrived in St Mary Cray. So, instead of letting them fall among the detritus, he carried the letters from Stevens around in his wallet. Unfortunately, his pocket was picked while he was browsing in a street market in London; and they were lost, never to surface again.

III

'When your ghost comes to me, I will tell you
What it is that I now pursue ...'

Nicholas Moore, 'The Last Poem'

I had my testament, the evidence of the tape. But was it admissible? It could be replayed. (It *had* to be, endlessly, inch by inch; a finger-blistering chore.) It could be verified. (Always the same sounds, until the tape pulls loose on the cassette, called upon to perform once too often, this brown slick of dental floss. The miracle of the machine is finite. In my case, *very*.) And, yes, the version offered in this book has been abridged, with minor details corrected; obviously, I tried to focus on the elements useful to my theme. (I left out the side of near silence, when I pressed the buttons in the wrong order.) I was trying to discover how much the contemporary Cambridge poet felt that he was ready to accept the role of scapegoat, the condition of exile. If the culture at large refuses to imagine your existence, how strong is the impulse to spit in its eye? Or: do you stick modestly to your last and wait (to the death) for a tap at the window?

I always leave these meetings burdened with an obscure sense of guilt. Something to do with the ambivalence of dealing in books and failing to write them (and: writing them and failing to 'deal' in them). Cambridge itself is the corporate manifestation of guilt, the brand leader, the architecture of guilt – corridors of the stuff; moulded, sprayed and cast. A memorial park themed in stalled art: morality tribunals programmed for one verdict. *Guilty!* Paragraphs by Henry James that can be un-wrapped only in spasms of blushing shame.

The meeting happened, devoured its time, as I planned that it should. There is a colour photograph of Peter Riley, at the end of the table, side-on, half-turned to look down on the microphone, the silver weapon. The casual details accumulate: the wine bottle (drunk to an inch below the label), the bowl of oranges, low-fat spread, carton of fruit juice. Then; the pale-yellow door (its paintwork bubbling under the abrupt severity of the flash), the garden beyond, the slate-blue bookshed. It is possible, with care, to make out the titles of a few oversize volumes in the corner cabinet: *A Pictorial History of Jazz, Antisuyo, Paris Imprévue*. The focus is very slightly soft, but the occasion is there to be remembered. Parts of it are fixed.

Yet I was not quite satisfied. I had got no more than I set out to get. The taped interview, like its flashier television counterpart, necessarily gives you no more than you ask for. The answers are all implied in the questions. If the 'subject' dares to break into some thicket of improvisatory parentheses, he has to be dragged back – kicking and screaming. Truth never did climb off the cutting-room floor.

My thesis had to take a more extreme form. Pain, madness, mutilation: all the showbiz shamanist tokens that would authenticate my quest. I put a photocopy of Nicholas Moore's 'Last Poem' in my pocket and set out to follow the River Darent, from the Thames at Crayford Ness through Dartford Marshes, until it divided, to be rechristened as the Cray. I hoped to track the stream as it meandered south, between tumps of undifferentiated settlement and the open-field illusion of golf courses, hospital woods, cemeteries, and humiliated farms. At St Mary

Cray I would identify Nicholas Moore's house, and take the snapshot Peter Riley requested, as we stood talking on his doorstep.

I clung to the irrational belief that the third sequence of Moore's final poem, the 'lost' coda, would deliver itself up to me in the course of my pilgrimage: and not, as Riley claimed, stay 'stored as electrical connections' in the dead poet's brain. Irretrievable; 'out with him'. Holding page sixty-one, the blank (expectant space) finish of *Lacrimae Rerum*, Moore's posthumous selection, to the light reveals a reversed text; the editor's 'note' coming through like a spirit message from the far side of the paper. It cannot be interpreted, but it offers a ruled garden on which the number (*III*) signifies the gap in which the poem could still resolve itself. A sinistral, mirror world in which the italicized word ꙅonꙅꞁƆ stands out.

In the second section of the 'Last Poem' (though addressed to the loved one, or Muse) there is a deliberate Hamlet-echo of pursuit, inheritance, chill: the elongated boredom of unfulfilled death. And the cold. The words evaporate in the tall corridors of a skull-castle. A son's father returns with questions, dripping earth: ventriloquist of self-inflicted guilt.

This paper voice tracked me, folded and refolded into a zipped pocket, as the train jolted once more towards North Woolwich, and the ferry crossing. Despite official radio warnings — I *couldn't* wait in the house long enough to drag a coat from the cupboard — it was a fine, bright, high-cloud morning. The 'free' ferry celebrated its role in the narrative by carrying no other passengers. *Do they know something?* They have all shuffled down the foot tunnel. The green river shines like crocodile mud. The south shore is more of a promise than a threat. The rail connection to Erith offers intriguing glimpses, scrub-covered slopes on which to imagine the *Abbey (rems of)* Lesnes. And the more recently imposed fantasy of Thamesmead.

Detrained at Erith, it is a considerable effort to shake free from the town. The river is guarded by a succession of scrapyards, metal fanciers, suppliants for brazery, machine cannibals: only the most dog-footed plodder, sampling each fresh lane, will eventually clear the buildings; and then the fields open gloriously to the waterline. The Thames is almost domesticated, frisky, Edwardian, a tributary of itself; pleasure boats ride at anchor. I walk, among tethered horses, on an elevated pathway: distant flashes of Dartford. The revolving shadow of the radar scanner on the Crayford Ness beacon plays on a low wall. A peaked sun projects this illusion: the silhouette of an amputee wrestler, frenetically warming up. The creek mouth has a scimitar tide of driftwood, cans, plastics – an over-eager Richard Long installation, an unscavenged beach.

There is a formal, twin-towered rivergate where the rib of the Darent splits from the Thames and begins its own journey. Lost land. Game birds thrash from cover at my approach, shoot out over the water, decoying attention: rubbish fires drift gritty blue smoke from fenced yards. Dumper trucks, far away, grind and drone, tipping out the endless intestinal waste of the towns. The young river wanders, is alive; its surface shimmering, burning with gold scraped from the rims of heavy coins. I cling to the bank until the Darent parts from the Cray, and the view to the south-west is of mean over-settled hills.

The Cray, according to Barry MacSweeney who walked part of it as 'a hack on the *Kentish Times*', was once a 'first-class trout stream, used by Henry VIII'. At its mouth it is still unspoilt, a surprising thatch of river wheat, tawny with feather-headed rushes. A small Egypt, Mosaic in implication: a removed place.

But here a path cuts between hedges, back towards Slade Green: a solitary track across Crayford Marshes. An old man, black-jacketed, plods down this narrowing tunnel of perspective; limping, leaning on a stick. I stop to watch, and (of course!) to project on him the spectral avatar of Nicholas Moore. Let him go. I force myself to heed Douglas Oliver's warning about believing 'every lame man was a messianic sign'. The figure recedes very slowly, weak-footed, lurching inexplicably from verge to verge, avoiding the gravelled camber at the centre of the lane, tapping for grassy softness.

He was hooked, for a long time, on a stile. I was hooked also, watching him; thinking of nothing else. The ground between us. He became part of the stile, inhuman, a sack balancing on the rim of disaster. He was forced to look back the way he had come, and to face me: while he lowered himself, tragically slow, legs stiff as planks, towards the expectation of solid earth. I must have appeared to him, at that distance, if he noticed me at all, as a stump or post. And even though I now withdraw all the meaning I can discover in this occluded incident, it will not suffice. I am listening for something else, a voice, a sound: something Peter Riley cites as Moore's dominant mode, 'the speech of a variety of statues'.

If the walk so far has been coated in sensual pleasures, the riposte is swift; the path runs into a storm-fence and further access to the river bank is denied. I am expelled, forcibly parted from the Cray, deposited on a mudslide slope, where lorries (Hell Drivers), cursing from a weighbridge, gun the short track that separates them from the A 206. On either side of this slithering hazard are pens of chemical threat, sacks marked HOPE, inadequately sealed skull-drums, hissing valves: behind which rises a tower, proclaiming itself the ultra-Mosque of Vitbe Bread. Its business is to convert the river wheat to uniform envelopes of white shame.

The pub is worse. Any traveller is a leper; a dusty, sweating renegade. A carpet fouler. Born-again barpersons target the Industrial Estate with reflex smiles: Canada Dry, Booker, Chef's Larder ('Caring About Catering'). The empty, vaselined suits of salesmen are serviced by over-obliging waitresses in cruelly laundered jeans. The soup of the day is pink, slightly saline, with a limp leaf floating on its custard-like surface. Something lumpy and white has struggled for life in it. And has lost.

Now the problems really begin. I am disoriented by a fury of traffic, screaming to get away, or cutting – with no signals – into one of many identical service roads. Unknowingly (fume-crazy), I drift north-east, losing all the river's wisdom: go back on myself towards Erith and the Thames. The first roundabout is a vortex of unconvincing promises: no offered destination holds the slightest attraction for me. Feebly, I aim for the highest ground and shuffle into one of Nicholas Moore's night-mares: unlittered streets, clean cars, safe margins of grass, lace curtains that twitch faintly as I pass, like the last flicker of breath in an oxygen tent. I shadow the railway embankment, hug to it, a lifeline, a false river that peevishly deposits me at Barnehurst. A nameplate attached to nothing: a subliminal cancellation, an early-morning travel flash. Bad news.

Hours have been lost (to say nothing of the river). The ticket collector, consulting his wall charts, denies any possibility of a link to St Mary Cray. The only hope lies back towards the city. In savage despair, I hop a suburban cattle car to Lewisham: flicker of white graveyards, roof estates, slate churches. A twenty-minute wait on a wind-exposed platform. Then the slanting run south to Petts Wood, in the company of independent, well-tailored ladies gazing sternly out of the windows. Peripatetic anthologists? Raiding the margins of our journey for a South London literary pot-pourri: Conrad's Greenwich, Paul Theroux's *Family Arsenal* at Deptford, Muriel Spark's Peckham Rye, Pinter's Sidcup.

I have only to walk away from the station (Petts Wood), pick my track through a set of mental-health charities, estate agents, windows of cream cakes and wedding dresses; march east, slogging to the crest of a slow hill. 'St Mary Cray?' 'Right direction, dear, but it's quite a step.' The distance melts. I am in cruise gear at last: drawn on by a destination that is 'getting warmer' with every stride.

An avenue of ancient, thick-girthed oaks leads away from the main road and down towards the poet's secret grove. The estate developer, with fond memories, more probably of Richard Todd or the English TV series (written by a blacklisted Hollywood leftie) than of the Errol Flynn/Basil Rathbone extravaganza, and with a dozen sturdy trees *in situ*, went for the obvious theme, Merrie England and the liberties of the Green Wood: Lockesley Drive, Friar Road, Lincoln Green Road, Archer Road, Robin Hood Green.

But the oaks *are* a truth, unembarrassed repositories, bare of leaves, black against the setting sun: dark magistrates. In their presence the temperature drops, my pace slackens. This zone is … just as I imagined it. I have often shared this pituitary nightmare, floated along these unpeopled cul-de-sacs. The houses can be seen only through diabetic lenses: they are constructed from slabs of coarse sugar, liquorice timbers, bull's-eye windows. My crazed persistence is rewarded, and I enter the vision that was present all along, that buddied my quest: the beached vessel (Islet of *Longueurs*?) in which a poet was free to live undisturbed, except by the voices to which he was constantly forced to attend. The voices of fabulous statues. Cold sublunary passions. Metopal logic, the wit of chalk. But this 'harsh holocaustic unlife' was not without its rewards. To be left alone: who has the courage to ask for that?

Oakdene Road is an afterthought, an apologetic addition, succumbing – with little protest – to a plague of pavement-hogging tricycles, motor scooters with L plates, open-jawed Cortinas: a blue-collar compromise between ambition and expediency. The twitchy pretensions of the high-contour semis have wilted within a hundred yards to a boisterous meanness. I don't want to linger. The pain is palpable. A grey-blue migraine helmet.

Moore's left-hand maisonette is a pebbledash and red-brick affair, oddly angled. I had visited it often in dreams – of which this was only the most recent version. But 'my' house was a mirror image. I pictured it on the other side of the street: where my childhood home would once have been situated, on its steeper hill.

But what made me particularly uneasy was the absence of a door. A flushed and ugly block faced the world with muslin-carpeted windows; offering no entrance, no exchange. The door was a social gaff, shunted to one side, where necessary commercial transactions could be rapidly despatched – away from prying eyes.

I scarcely broke my stride. I snatched a full-frontal snapshot, featuring the stump of Japanese cherry tree (which had not been uprooted, as Peter Riley believed, but hacked off, mindlessly amputated). Yolky flower heads were nudging through the untended grass.

I jogged on down the hill, towards the *idea* of the river, hoping to reconnect with that possibility. Then pulled up. Turned on my heel, aware that nothing had been resolved (or made clear) by my visit. The roof bristled with aerials. They were equipped to monitor the galaxies. Nicholas Moore's house was number eighty-nine. Its immediate neighbour was eighty-five. Idly, I wondered what had happened to eighty-seven. (Had it been sucked into the skies? Or offered a more select location?) My oblique (low-angle) view framed an awkward Kurt Schwitters (use what you find) arrangement of doors, window slits, coal-bunker lids. An 'extension' that provided an external stairway, while effectively blocking my prospect of the famous garden. Unmoved, an elderly cat stared me out; yawning, breaking wind, and attempting halfhearted press-ups in an upstairs window.

Safely lodged on the train, and returning to the welcoming soot of the city, I took out the folded sheet of paper with Nicholas Moore's 'Last Poem', to examine once more the irritating blank of the final section. I had, of course, now scribbled my own shorthand notes on the verso; possible clues when I came to write about the incident. *MILLENNIUM MILLS (train window, Custom House). Royal Pavilion (COURAGE). Darent miander, sun on water (pieces of clock?). Old man bad leg black jacket stick. River wheat. Chemical wilderness, sacks HOPE. Vitbe Bread. Oak Avenue. House, mirror image of dream. Cat.*

The page remained frustratingly bare, beyond certain mantic creases, like the footprints of … statues? And from the margin the green waves of Juliet Moore's dustwrapper illustration were encroaching; cardiac tracings – converted in reproduction to healthy strokes of black. The tide was turning from a knitted electrical stream to a fevered voice-print, soliciting computer analysis. It was all there, but would we find the time to hear it? The instruments to interpret the steps of the dance?

Crossing the fold of the wrapper's edge were two leaf fingers: the tall bearded iris. The poet's flower. Recurring through time: Bellini, Dürer, Leonardo's 'Madonna of the Rocks', the Ghent Altarpiece of the brothers Van Eyck. 'Band of iris-flowers / about the waves' (H.D.) Iris, personification of the Rainbow. Black iris: *Verité, Starless Night.*

The word I wanted was the one my transcription of Peter Riley's tape sent me to the dictionary to check: *Sempervivum*!

II

The Case of the
Premature Mourners

SPRING-HEELED JACK,
THE TERROR OF LONDON.

"SIR ROLAND," SAID SPRING-HEELED JACK, "THIS IS A MERRY NIGHT FOR US TO MEET."

The Case of the Premature Mourners

'Civilization ends at the waterline'

Hunter S. Thompson,
The Gonzo Salvage Co

There had been no point in sleeping. The dreams were too bad; they coloured the days that followed them. They previewed the agonies ahead of us. And anyway, after the first three months, you lose the habit. Then it does get interesting: guessing which strip of water you can safely walk across. I sat with my back, resolutely, to the river, and waited for Joblard to surface. The sculptor was grinning as he snored; an empty bottle nestled in the crook of his arm. It rested content: a sated babe. Primly, Joblard clucked his lips. He patted the bottle; and, waking to the light, smiled. He had forgotten what faced us.

It was no more than a stroll from the wasteground behind the Gun to Folly Wall: time enough to sober us for the task ahead. I had pestered Joblard to use his network of contacts to procure some craft, anything that stayed afloat, to carry us downriver: beyond the known station of Tilbury towards the potential mysteries of Sheerness. From the Isle of Dogs to the Isle of Sheep: a pilgrimage towards hope, and for Joblard a quest for his origins. But his motivations were hedged in ambiguities. The orphan, who had for so many years – and wisely – left his parentage as an uninvestigated secret, was now prepared to risk a chance encounter with his closest blood relative. (The pouch of sea, the memory bed.) His mother might serve us our first pint. Ghosts lurked among the marine pleasure shacks, waiting to claim him. The man that he was, the identity he had chosen, could be lost for ever. He might be forced to abdicate the rare privilege of inventing himself. This journey by water also celebrated the news of his lover's pregnancy, his fatherhood. He was going joyfully backwards to greet the unborn child, returning.

Our pauper's budget (we were so poor – winos kept waving their bottles at us in greeting) did not run to either a reliable craft or a reliable pilot. (*Judea of Shadwell*, Do or Die.) We took what we could get. A friend of a friend of a friend. A name with an answering machine that spat 'one liners' like a borscht-belt comic on speed, and a flat on the nineteenth floor of the only surviving council-owned towerblock on the Island: the last refuge of society's lepers. 'There is no such thing as society,' stated the Widow. And, observing this rat pack, it was difficult not to agree with her. Ordinary families had long since decamped to become housing statistics in some less 'progressive' borough. What was left couldn't be cleared with a blowtorch: post-mortem optimists, chemically castrated 'outpatients', spittle-flecked psychos too temperamental to be approached without a high-voltage cattle prod ... Latter Day Outpouring Revivalists eager to greet the Final Trump (where better?), stamping and chanting and calling down the black, wrath-primed stormclouds.

The agreed meeting place, on the Amsterdam Avenue slipway, was deserted. So far, so good. We had been warned not to leave a car in the neighbourhood. The tinkers would have carved it into saleable segments before we cleared Blackwall. (No problem: the car had long gone, to pay for the railway tickets.) This neat estate (a tribute to the glaziers) was too new to appear on any maps. But it already featured a wine bar and two shops. The first sold property and the other displayed naughty knickers. A pair of open sewers had been cleverly adapted, by the ruse of mustard-yellow bricks and dinky wooden bridges, into Dutch canals. Any disorientated (schnapps-crazy) burgher might reasonably have mistaken the quadrangle for one of those West Polder communities that cluster around Monnickendam. Sharp-pointed red-tile roofs (and anorexic balconies, for pot plants only) looked out on the scrapyards across the river; the crushers, the lifting plates, the foothills of rusting motors.

An ugly tide licked at the slipway, leaving gifts: pressed cans, detergent bottles, ends of rope. It was hungry to run us down to Tilbury, and whatever lay in wait. I no longer wanted to burden it. I was happy to sit on the wall, watching these reflex spasms – the cough of mud – as I brooded on other rivers, better days.

A few harsh bars of 'Dixie' on the klaxon of his horn announced the arrival of our captain. 'No,' I said, 'absolutely not. Let me out of here.'

In that moment – as I turned from the simple savagery of the river to stare in disbelief at the two customized Cadillacs (welded together, as if they had met in some monster smash and never been separated) – I knew we were in *serious* trouble. Then there was the scarlet boast emblazoned down one flank: GOPHER IT! And worse: HEAPUM GOOD JOB, NO

COWBOYS. Six-wheel independent drive. A black tank bouncing on white-rimmed balding tyres. Our pilot, mercifully hidden behind his tinted windshield, was a card-carrying soldier in the New Confederate Army. The war had been lost. But they fought on: as electrical contractors, respray jockeys, pine strippers. The surviving remnant of Robert E. Lee's greybelly cavalry is hiding out in the swamps of East London. They had the flags, the stetsons, the sideburns. Did we dare to climb into anything driven by a dude who looked like Richard Harris after two or three decades riding across New Mexico, tracking renegade redskins, under the command of mad General Sam Peckinpah? I waited for Warren Oates, Slim Pickens, L. Q. Jones and the rest of the good ol' boys to roll, hawking and chawing, out of the pickup.

This creature, our self-inflicted Ahab, hitched his pants and lurched, bow-legged, towards us. He couldn't make up his mind whether he wanted to be a cowboy or an Indian. He had the bronze skin of a reservation Apache, and the last non-institutionalized Frank Zappa moustache on the planet. A shockwave of snakecurl hair had been tipped over him: like well-mashed seaweed.

He wore a checked shirt, jungle-green combat vest, baggy cords, scummy loafers. He looked dangerous: focused on a badge of light that was rapidly arrowing into the past – straining to reconnect those ECT-toasted synapses. It was too late to escape. Our fear had heated our interest. Could we resist it? This was time travel without the hardware. Straight back into whatever had come through, in critically mutilated form, that sad decade, the 1960s. A paradigm of the Weird was whinnying to break free from the Sanctuary.

Introductions were made. The Confederate promptly forgot our names; they were of no importance. He had enough trouble hanging on to his own: remembering which alias was current, and in which country. His ego had been broken into powder and snorted. The snuff-stains on the drooping ends of his moustache had more grip on reality. His mind had lost all adhesion. It was a grey tongue of outdated flypaper. We slid down it without leaving a smear.

'Jon Kay,' he admitted, sounding surprised. He punched a fist into his open palm, to reinforce the fleeting inspiration. 'Right,' he nodded, noticing the boat for the first time, 'let's do it. Let's hit the water.'

Immediately, one of my more reasonable prejudices came into play: avoid at all costs that fateful combination of letters, J/K. And certainly never trust yourself in an open boat with anyone bragging of them. Was the man Victim or Assassin? The evidence of his face suggested an evil compromise. He had taken a few good hits, but he was still smiling. (My God, was nothing sacred? It flashed into my head – the Confederate had that effect on people – that Conrad was christened *Josef Konrad Korzeniowski. J/KK*. We were betrayed even by our mentors.)

The slogan-sprayed tank was backed up to the slipway, and the craft, on its trailer, was winched towards the slurping water. Joblard had his boots off, ready to wade aboard. He was soaked to the waist, and grinning like a bear.

Kay emerged from his catatonic lethargy to bawl a few nautical quotations he had overheard in riverside dives. When his repertoire was exhausted, he slipped back to the glitzed hearse, fumbled in the glove compartment, swallowed something – and returned, bouncing, to the action. He was sharp enough now to register my examination of the boat's licence; which, reassuringly, was only illegal by a matter of four years.

'It's yours,' he said, 'three hundred notes in the hand. Two-fifty – no, two hundred – if you pay me *now*. And you'd better have it away, sharpish. They're going to repossess tomorrow. The car, the flat, everything that isn't nailed down.'

The face of the dog, with its liquid accusing eyes, watched us from the rear window of the jumbo Cadillac. A deserted mistress. A golden sunbeast, long-nosed: some random collision of labrador and collie. Lassie meets White Fang. The creature knew all too well what lay ahead. And celebrated the prophetic nature of its blood with prolonged and marrow-chilling howls. Seeing what it saw, the dog's small-brained courage was such that – weighing the odds – it begged to accompany us. (A pathos that would have sent tears coursing down the sandblasted cheeks of crusty protection racketeers competitively hurling back fire-water in the Grave Maurice, Whitechapel Road.)

Drawn by the noise, from their innocent game of hurling milk crates from a third-floor balcony, a gaggle of urchins gathered on the river wall. Silent harbingers of doom. Further back, in the shadow of the flats, tinkers in breakdown vans watched us, pricing the craft with greedy eyes, counting the salvage: unhurried bounty hunters. They could well afford to wait. They gunned their motors, prepared to track us all the way to the finish.

Kay hauled the trailer out of the water; climbed into the car; set the wheels spinning and smoking on the slimy ramp. He was allowed, *this time*, to escape the river. He parked. Leaving the dog behind, as guardian; locking its painted cage with an enormous bunch of keys. (The antelope curry smell of improperly slaughtered leather.) Kay rattled back to us. A ghost pirate: his bones were riveted brass.

We waited on the water. But before Kay had rolled aboard, the urchins were all over the Cadillac: chiselling at the hubcaps, bending back the wipers. The dog was snarling and foaming, hysterical with impotent rage. They would get to him later.

None of this mattered. We were afloat. Kay wrestled with the whipcord. The stubby craft swung its nose towards the money-magnet of the city. It was no more than a tub of baby-blue fibreglass, a tray with a cabin, an unplanted goldfish pond driven by an elderly forty-h.p. Evinrude outboard motor. The name on its rump was *Reunion*. With what, or whom, or where … we were not deranged enough to imagine.

Under instruction, I punted us out with a boat hook; churning up swirls of dark quag. Joblard ripped open the first can of lager. The engine fired. Kay took the wheel.

'Which way, boys?' he howled, above the rage of the spluttering outboard. 'Just point me in the right direction.'

'Don't you have any charts?' I asked, innocently.

'Charts are for wimps,' he sneered.

'Haven't you ever been to Tilbury before?' demanded Joblard, increasingly convinced he was booked on an inspirational outing.

'Tilbury? Tilbury? Where's that? I go zubbing under Tower Bridge, skate up the Prospect, sink a dozen frosties, and float home on the tide.'

'Stick her nose downstream and burn it until you smell the sea. You can't miss it. A big green thing,' Joblard instructed. It was almost as if he was going to be the one underwriting this excursion.

The motor coughed, died, spat out a rinse of hot oil; fought for life. Jon Kay cursed. He flogged it like a mule. He kicked. He wanted to see our nose riding out of the water: lacy white furrows ploughing behind us. A steepling kerb of wash to drown the engrammic tracery of these mean bayous.

The teeth of the Thames Barrier were approaching: helmeted Templars, flashing with signals, arrows, red crosses – warnings. As soon as we negotiated this psychic curtain, we would quit the protection of the city. Kay tried to fire the motor, shame it into a more manly performance. He entrusted the wheel to Joblard. That decision alone convinced me: we were dealing with a man whose judgement made Humphrey Bogart, rattling his ball bearings and grinding his molars as Captain Queeg, look the very model of sound sense and marine probity. I hoped I would live long enough to stand witness at the Court of Enquiry; to pick up some punitive damages.

Joblard was hunched in concentration, peering dimly through thick, spray-smeared spectacles. His pathetic orange lifejacket was strapped across the bulk of his shoulders like a dowager's paisley. It wouldn't keep him afloat for a second. He'd wallow face-down on the tide, a cetacean Quasimodo, vividly targeted for the harpoons of Japanese whalers.

There's something hideously familiar about Jon Kay's face. You want to sneak away and check the illustrations in the latest Charles Manson biog. His whole persona is one that any sane civilian would take considerable trouble to avoid. The scab of some ancestral, suppressed trauma is waiting to be picked from his skin. He is a karmic experience of horror, buried alive in the psyche: a dodgy deal in the silver market, a newspaper-wrapped parcel oozing blood fat in the stall of a condemned urinal.

Then he half-turns, he asks for the time – he's fiddling with a toy TV set, a flat miniature offering random interference, mantic sunstorms – and I remember. Remember it all; the whole squalid story.

Joblard and I, fifteen or so years before, were cutting the grass on the south side of St Anne, Limehouse, when we discovered the wreck of a boat (an Ark?) rising out of the jungle of a neighbouring yard. We sat on the wall. Took a blow. The thing was as unlikely as an helicopter gunship excavated from a Carthaginian amphitheatre. Joblard rolled a cigarette, while I fell to musing on images of flood, inundation, fire and lightning. I glanced up at the tower of the church. A man was swinging out of the octagonal lantern, attempting to lever the clock-face from its fixed position. He was loosely attached to the crumbling masonry by an umbilical length of rope. Old rope, frayed rope. Hangman's twine. He was swaying nicely in the breeze: enjoying, simultaneously, nose-scraped close-ups of the fossils in the stone and wide-angle longshots of the river and the dying hamlets. His legs thrashed against the clock, predicting the hour of his self-destruction. We judged the distance to the ground, and we waited. 'The things you see,' commented Joblard, 'when you haven't got a camera.'

It's a pleasing thing to sit on an old brick wall in the early-spring sunshine – the grass cut, the sepulchres cleared of weeds – and watch a lunatic wrestle with a clock. His heels kicked among the Roman numerals, causing them to crash like shrapnel on to the path below. The man persisted, against all nature. What was left was now worthless. But that did not quell him. He was in a man-to-man, eyeball-to-eyeball duel with time. And he was losing every round. He aged with every swoop of the rope pendulum. The creature they would siphon from the shrubbery would be less than the dust in a beaker of impacted cockle-shells. No joy here for the resurrectionists.

Finally, the man snapped; put all his weight on to the minute-arm of the clock, and succeeded in forcing it out, horizontally – so that it pointed in accusation at the watchers on the wall. Time, which had been costive in Limehouse since the First War, now leapt into another dimension. It attacked. Smoking lines of longitude surged back towards the Greenwich meridian. The rulebook was shredded. The arm broke away. It plunged; embedding itself in the soft earth, like the lost Spear of Destiny. (Joblard had it wrapped in billiard-felt, and tied to his bicycle, before it stopped quivering.) But the defenestrated villain was left helpless, suspended by his ankles – an impatient suicide, a bungler – tangled in a web of sisal. He substituted for the missing clock-arm. He marked the scarcely perceptible passage of time for the citizens of the borough, the immortal community of vagrants. They studied him, furtively, through the dark glass of their liquid telescopes: brown apertures of serially emptied cider bottles.

These were still the good old days when the vicar chose to spend his afternoons hearing confession in the Five Bells and Bladebone. We had, wisely, taken the precaution of getting the church keys copied. We had access. We were the unofficial sextons and celebrants. Unhurried, we climbed the tower and hauled our man in. Jon Kay (*aka*, Paul Pill; *aka*, Harry Whizz) was not especially grateful. He did not allude to the affair or to his failure in it. He had moved on. The clock was history. And not, therefore, to be trusted. Winners wrote the story. Losers lived on lies. He thought we might be interested in humping the great church bell into his van. He'd worked out a way to shift it, with fresh ropes and a beam: swing it at the tall west window – right? – shatter the opaque glass, the pigeon shelves, the whole bloody crust of feathers. The bell was strong enough to survive the fall. It would float through any holocaust, like an acorn cup. We had only to lift it and loop the rope around its skirts. He'd see us right. There was definitely a drink in it. No danger.

Somehow we hustled the maniac down the narrow bore of the tower, skating in linseed curls of pigeon dirt as he went. He couldn't be hushed. I dragged him from in front, Joblard kicked him from behind. He yelled as he trotted. 'A few organ pipes, boys. I've got a blowtorch in the van. One angel then. Let's do a couple of sodding stained-glass windows. I'll shift them down the Passage first thing Wednesday. Be *realistic*. A bible! Who'd miss it? I'll tear the plates out without moving it from the lectern. Gimme a break, fellers.'

As the most recent incumbent, the Rev. Christopher Idle, remarked to the *Observer* newspaper (5 June 1988): 'Over the past twelve years we have suffered most when the church has been locked.' Sneak thieves are the least of his problems. The Parish Magazine shudders with pulpit-thumping bulls denouncing pyramid-worshipping satanists, mendacious television producers (*all* television producers), occult tourists brandishing yellow-back Gothic Romances (in impenetrable verse), oil painters who think the church a fit place to exhibit twenty-foot snail portraits (waggling their horns like the legions of hell). All the dispossessed phantoms of lunacy are screaming at the windows. 'Let us in. Give us a break, fellers. One angel. A piece of the action.'

Jon Kay. How had this prohibited life-form survived? What miracle had preserved him to rebuke these dark days? Some deathbat brushed its wing against his face. He was too far gone to be affected by mere memory. Electrical connections twitched and sparked. Red cells perished as a septic tide rushed into his cheek. Memory, for him, was a form of sympathetic jaundice. Veins collapsed (like landslides) in his mollusc eyes. He poured with sweat and clawed at his palpitating belly. There *was* a cure. He scanned the horizon (to check that he was unobserved) and announced: 'I'm just popping below to write up the ship's log.' He bolted the cabin door, and left it to Joblard to bounce us over the boiled milk skin of the sun-polished waters, exuberantly to search out the wash from larger and more powerful vessels.

It's curious how different people notice different things. 'What a freak,' Joblard said, as soon as Kay was out of sight. 'Did you clock his arms?' I hadn't dared go that far. I was still in shock after dealing with his face. We couldn't, either of us, dodge that: the missing eyelid, the permanent wink. (The story came later, but I might as well throw it in. How Kay had sat on his dark glasses while watching a live sex show in Barcelona. How he'd superglued them together again, along with his eyelid. How his mate had hacked him free with a stanley knife. He never felt a thing.)

The narrow band of visible flesh above Kay's wrist had, inevitably, been disfigured by the usual blue cartoons of flying fish and grinning skulls: epidermic graffiti too commonplace to merit Joblard's attention. 'The skin, eeeugh! Hanging in a nicotine flap. A wilted support-stocking. Bubbled up, percolated. He's had it *cooked*. And the graft hasn't taken.' 'Who could blame it?' I thought; not caring to picture the events that lay behind this trivial deformity.

Joblard, in his turn, paid no attention to the detail I'd picked up on: the overpowering blast of the weed seeping through the deck-boards like compulsory nostalgia. Our captain was a dope fiend, and he was making an ominously early start. He stayed below for about thirty minutes and emerged, red-eyed and tooting, to search for a pair of wraparound shades. (O Save us from that Lidless Stare!) He wanted another shot at raising the ghosts from the aether of his pocket TV, the faulty snuff set. He was hooked on some fantasy of pre-pubertal jailbait, squealing Saturday-morning t-shirts: a mail-order catalogue for the Bill Wyman tendency.

We were drawn together now in what Conrad's Marlow refers to, ambiguously, as 'the fellowship of the craft'. The worst was surely over. We were *Three Men in a Boat*. 'Three, I have always found, makes good company,' remarked the jaunty Mr Jerome. But he was another*J*/*K* (JKJ), and not to be trusted. It struck me that we had embarked on a contrary statement of Jerome's Thames journey. Our motives were not dissimilar. The trip was a rehearsal for the book that would follow. It was flawed therefore. Impure. Vulnerable. Upstream for Comedy, Downstream for ... whatever it was we were involved with. We had wantonly chosen the wrong direction. We would never pull gently, at our own pace, back towards the river's source; the spurting puddle in a Cotswold field. We sought dispersal, loss of identity: *'moremens more ... Lps. The keys to.'* We were fleeing in desperation, in pieces, letting the water devils out of their sack. We could never implode through comic exaggeration into the mildest and most human of excursions. We would never be reprinted. Never repeated and abused on video. We had forgotten our striped blazers and our cricket caps. We were verminous, hounded from the society of men: a bottle of plagues, expelled like Lenin in his cattle car. We were escaping into an uncertain future.

But Jerome did not set out to provide raw material for institutional whimsy: books at bedtime, television pastiche, fat cats in Portobello blazers too boyishly enjoying themselves. He meditated a grander concept, *The Story of the Thames* (no less): a journey, limited in duration, which would cunningly open itself to episodic seizures by the *son et lumière* of history. He would be possessed by guidebooks, architectural jottings, myths gathered from waterside inns. But, as always, the fiction achieved an independent existence that overwhelmed him, tearing the publisher's advance treatment to shreds. The feeble (premature heritagist) pageant collapsed. The vigour of the past ambushed him at every turn in the river. It was alive, unexorcized. And not hiring out for exploitation.

The Victorian boatmen were 'real' characters: George Wingrave (a bank manager), Carl Hentschel (who worked in his father's photography business), and Jerome K. Jerome (an author?). It was once possible to visit them, to interrogate them on the degree of accuracy in the report of their adventures. Only the dog was a lie. He was the conscience of the quest. Without him, it was all meaningless. Our beast was alive – but we had betrayed him, left him imprisoned within the black Cadillac. Even now he was measuring its air, panting against the sealed windows. He *had* to survive. This was his story. The rest of us were wraiths, unsound fictions, diseased figments of the dog's (oxygen-rationed) imagination. If the tale belonged anywhere ... it was in his mouth.

Jon Kay felt our panic: my terror that our fate remained a prisoner on the Isle of Dogs. 'That fucking animal!' he roared. 'He'll tear the seats to ribbons. He'll throw up on the fur rug. He'll piss into my restored leather upholstery.' And he made this the excuse for another heavy session below decks, chainsawing the ship's log into kindling. Now you could hear him draw the smoke to his lungs with hungry bronchial gasps. He was drowning in his own breath – mimicking the dog's plight. Even Joblard, gripping the wheel like a length of chicken-neck, careering wildly over the river, realized something inadmissible was going on. Six inches beyond the reach of his sea boots.

The cabin door burst from its hinges. Kay was too far 'out of it' to work the bolt. He reeled towards us, holding the door in front of him like a barman's tray. He was in the wrong script. He was looking for the head of John the Baptist. He pitched the door over the side and collapsed in a boneless heap; sprawled, face-down, in a puddle of what might once – at the kindest estimate – have been water from the bilges. We watched him closely, ready for anything.

He was silent for a few moments (the mercury tension leaping at the thermometer): he stared morosely into the ever-shifting depths. The surface was perilously smooth. The glass was beginning to melt away, just like a bright silvery mist.

Clinically, Jon Kay could be diagnosed as suffering, in one hit, all the symptoms of cannabis misuse/overdose/withdrawal. He was euphoric, relaxed, talkative, disorientated/fatigued, paranoid, irrational/hyper-active and crazy as a tick. A loose-tongued compulsion took him – a returning fever – and he began to rap.

'We were bringing a couple of keys across the desert. No, Turkey. Was it? Istanbul. Early evening. I had the wheel. Really loose. Handle it with my eyes shut. Sheeew! Don't ever go off the road there, man! Stay in town. Two wrong turnings and they've got you penned in a concrete pit, a ramp. Streets with no names. Dead ends. No way out. And hundreds, hundreds of these little kids … wow … out from the ground … skulls with rats' teeth … climbing on the Land Rover. No, man! Smashing the lamps. Bending the mirrors. Slicing the canvas. I tell you, we were beating them off with tent poles. *Give us cigarette. Ficky-fucky. Suck your dick?* I'm trying to reverse. Can't see. Faces. Windscreen covered like a blanket. Termites. And then, then … the worst thing … the very worst …'

It was all too much, too far away. He aborted it. What did it matter? He ducked under; rattled around, searching helplessly for his misplaced stash. 'Got to get some speed on, man,' he burbled, on his return, 'or we'll never make Tilbury. I've handled real boats, boats with balls, boats that *jumped* from wave to wave. They had to, man. Give the horse his head, or get blasted out of the water.' He swivelled, arms outstretched, demonstrating the Wall of Death aerodynamics he demanded. 'Skidded, planed. Right? Sharp curve down the moving wall of noise? Dropping a cargo for the Aldeburgh fishermen. Then – whoooooosh! – away ... before we're even registered on the radar. *Yeah!*'

He barged Joblard from his perch and guided the *Reunion*, with unexpected delicacy, in alongside a rotting red hulk. The old 'Powder Magazine', he called her. And he made us fast to her chains, while he tinkered once more with the *Evinrude*.

Joblard pierced another can; and shut his eyes, wedging the glossy green-and-red spout between nose and lower lip – while he glugged in naked satisfaction. We relaxed and enjoyed the morning. It had been, so far, one of the best. Suspended time. The hours on the river are never held against you. We drifted back and forth, cradled between memory and forgetfulness. Superb clouds, menacing and charged with iron, squadroned in from the sea: continents of cloud, shaping and parting, overlaying the last brave peepholes of blue. The scene was pure narrative, a conversation piece: horizon to horizon, unchecked, a revelation of 'England's End'.

We had not yet escaped Woolwich Reach. We pitched and bumped against the Powder Magazine which might, for all we knew, be still active. Nobody had anything to say. We were submerged in the sounds of the tide rushing past our captive craft, and the steady trickle of beer, flushed in choking gulps, down Joblard's capacious throat. But it was coming back on me. After-images of unredeemed pain. The fixed present was slipping, getting away: under siege from the combined forces of the poisoned light, the solidity of the water, and the low-lying, feverish marshground. We were ephemeral to the singular quality of this scene.

I saw a tier of chained hulks, as they had once been – or perhaps as they were about to become. I saw them as prisons. (*'What's Hulks?'* said I. *'Answer him one question, and he'll ask you a dozen directly. Hulks are prison-ships, right cross th'meshes.'*). The prison service was collapsing, overwhelmed with technical offenders, swollen with the evicted mad, the helpless, the demented. Market forces suggested privatization on the American model. But we had our own well-tried methods. We had thousands of years of dark history to draw on. The hulks had been pressed back into service. I could not believe what I told myself I was seeing.

Men-of-war, old Indiamen, burnt-out relics of the Falklands campaign were chained together, another Thames barrier, a malign thunderhead. We lay among them. They were low in the water, patched with canvas, rotten, decayed. The pollution of the river met all the diseases of timber in an illicit and riotous embrace. No name but 'hulks' would satisfy this graveyard fleet. The deck planks were cemented by grey-green mosses: spores migrated on to the raw skins of the sleeping bilboe-shod convicts. They scratched, they tore at themselves – sunk too deep in exhaustion to wake for such minor annoyances. Blackened fingernails opened wounds in which bred a pomp of maggots. Woolwich was swiftly returning to its former glory. (A red-white-and-blue illustration on the lid of a matchbox.)

Dissenters and criminals (marginal to the needs and legitimate desires of the state) were once spilled into the wilderness of an unmapped world; where they fought for breath with savage aboriginals. The hulks provided a neutral zone, removed from the land's heat. To live here was to lose your memory. You could not vote or speak. But the outbreak of the American War of Independence made it impractical to transport these brutalized slaves. They were held in perpetual transit: a floating Gatwick, without the duty-frees. The only destination was death. Which was also the only product of their labours. Dame Cholera. Work was the only freedom. '*Punished by being kept on Board Ships or Vessels properly accommodated for the Security, Employment, and Health of the Persons to be confined therein, and by being employed in Hard Labour in the raising of Sand, Soil, and Gravel from, and cleansing, the River Thames …*'

Now the hulks were occupied once more, under the co-sponsorship of English Heritage, who had lovingly restored them to the last detail of authenticated squalor. This daringly simple solution had been unveiled by the Widow in her keynote Marshalsea Speech (subsequently recognized by commentators as the moment when the perceived identity of Britain changed from Orwell's colonial airstrip on the fringes of the civilized world to a land which had, successfully, made a reservation of its own history).

'From this day forward,' the Widow began, with a defiant twist of the head, a lift of the nut-crusher chin, 'let it be known that We are no longer to be considered the prisoners of history. We have forced open the great iron doors of mystification, self-doubt, self-critical inertia. We have walked, unafraid, into the sunlight. History has been conquered. *Rejoice!* We have summoned up the courage to recognize – after decades of misrule, lip-service to alien gods – that *anything* is possible. If We will it. If it is the mandate of the people. The future is whatever We believe it to be!'

Hysterical (orchestrated) cheering continued until the Widow lifted her hand: to preserve the health of several of her key ministers who were empurpled with enthusiasm, to the point of spontaneous combustion. The fanatical ranks of the faithful (*flog, maim, crush*), gathered for the ceremony of throwing wide the Marshalsea gates (reconstructed for the purpose by Stanley Kubrick's design ace) to welcome the first beneficiaries, fell silent.

'After We have finished speaking to you today, there will never again in this noble land of ours be such a thing as a prison,' she continued, unblushing. 'A prison is a state of mind. And, unlike our opponents – who are fettered in ritual dogmas – *We* sincerely believe that We can *all* be released from outmoded concepts of state care. And, in good faith, We make you *this* offer: let every man become his own warder, protecting the things he loves best: his *family*, his *home*, his *country*. Then, and only then, will We discover what *true* freedom means.'

Sir Alec Guinness shuffled forward, doing some marvellously observed business with a red-spotted handkerchief, touching the side of his nose, dissociating himself from his actions. He smirked, cancelled a cough, and cut the ribbon. The Marshalsea was reopened as a Dossers' Dormitory. Vagrants were driven in (by the container load) from their cardboard camps. They should no longer give the lie to the Widow's rhetoric of achievement. Corporate Japanese in white raincoats (like gulls, they tracked the action) fussed at the lowlife with their cameras, giggling over the quaint ritual of 'slopping out'. From the viewing gallery above, they composed eloquent longshots as these tattered vacancies perambulated their circuit of the yard, under ferociously pointed walls. The 'guests' of the hospice paid their way by posing for polaroid versions of Doré's anguished etchings: which, incidentally, were on sale, mounted and framed, at the gatehouse. All credit cards accepted.

The hulks were the flagships of a new social order. The shirts of the prisoners hung over the side, as if in surrender: 'so black with vermin that the linen positively appeared to have been sprinkled over with pepper'. Benevolent plagues carried off the inadequates. The succubus kiss of Dame Cholera made room among the hammocks for an ever-increasing army of offenders, fit-ups, unbelievers, and political heretics. The parson, a white-livered clown, planted himself on the poop deck of the vessel; claret bottle in one hand, a bible in the other. He was afraid to accompany the corpses, as they were stretchered in their dozens, by mask-wearing trustees, to the burying grounds, away among the marshes. Alone, he read the burial service, at a rattling trot, dabbing his carbuncular nose with a silk handkerchief soaked in eau-de-cologne. When he arrived at 'ashes to ashes, and dust to dust', he let the handkerchief drop: a strangled dove, fluttering, stalled, caught in a contagious thermal. And the bodies, at this signal (captured by the sergeant's telescope), were lowered into their lime pit.

I had moved apart from the others. There was a hatch in the cabin roof through which I squeezed my head and shoulders. I could not move my arms, but I could see everything ahead of us. Kay fired the engine. And we roared back out on to the river. The noise dispersed the ghosts. I could hear nothing my companions said. I was driven over the marbled waters like a wooden figurehead; mute, powerless – but inconveniently sensitized to every whim of the light, every *memento mori* in the running tide. The river outpaced my fear of it: a tightening roll of mad calligraphy, scribbled wavelets, erasures, periods of gold. I was buffeted through a book that had turned to water.

We left Woolwich behind us; its barracks, Arsenal, Museum of Artillery: we dodged the trundling ferry, and scorned the gaunt mushroom field of Telecom discs on the north shore. We relished the clear water of Gallions Reach. There were no other craft. A torn-paper outline of advancing headland. A carpet of clouds.

It could not last. Even Jerome, safely upstream, had his unexpected encounters: he found 'something black floating on the water'. A suicided woman, around whom he spun a sentimental fable. But I was staring into the dark spaces between the wave crests, letting the ink run, *willing* some apparition to justify our voyage, as we retraced the fatal track of the *Bywell Castle*, midstream, closing on the beacon at Tripcock Ness. Navigation lights. The *Princess Alice*, visible over the murky ground – a land vessel caught among the dead branches, the hooks of thorn! Her red light and her masthead light. '*Stop the engine! Reverse full speed!*' The thing was inevitable. We passed through the wings of tragedy. I could not turn away. It was too easy to enter the consciousness of Captain Harrison, who also travelled here from the domestic safety of his Hackney villa. I was repeating his account of the journey. And I was aware of it.

Harrison of the *Bywell*, I learnt, resided in Cawley Road, Victoria Park. One of those strong, ugly, family houses taken on in later years by exiled Poles. The hobbled green of Well Street Common lay to stern; the ocean of the Park broke, tamely, over the bows. The house, a brick-built collier, rode at anchor, between voyages. But it could catch the tide at an hour's notice from the owners.

Cawley Road survived into the 50p edition of the *London A–Z*, but it has subsequently been purged – leaving Henry Milditch, the thespian bookdealer, who lived directly behind Harrison, and who stalked his destiny like a herring gull, with an unimpeded view of the Park.

Milditch, red-bearded (as of this A.M.) – worried, wrinkled like a preserved fruit – stared over Captain Harrison's shoulder at the familiar prairie. He was sunk into the immortal melancholy (stateless, land-locked) of a man who knows that, however well his affairs prosper, it is only a matter of time before the Cossack hordes thunder out from the Lido. Grass liquefied before his tired eyes. The Burdett-Coutts Folly was an island – on which the child, Jerome K. Jerome, claimed to have met and held a prophetic conversation with Charles Dickens. Authors of Destiny!

Milditch saw none of this. In his hand was a telephone. He smiled as he lied. In an empty room he made appointments. He withdrew books he had already sold. He smoked a cheap cigar. Captain Harrison, the dead man, was cleared to sail to his fate.

The sense of wellbeing, the anticipated pleasure of a short voyage, was such that Harrison carried his wife with him in a growler to Millwall on the Isle of Dogs. An unlucky thing, a taboo broken: a woman brought on board. A rival to the jealous spirit of the river. (As they clipped through the south side of the Park, the Captain noticed a gang of workmen repointing the stone alcoves, the London Bridge trophies.)

The Captain asked Christopher Dix, a pilot of thirty-four years' experience, to scour the riverside drinking dens for 'runners': family men, far gone in drink, who would sail to Newcastle, but no further. Purcell, the stoker, was – even by the long standards of his craft – outrageously drunk. Skewed, damaged, blotto. He stank of doom. Wharf rats backed away from his reeling shadow. He rambled incontinently. Two strong-stomached runners supported him up the plank to the *Bywell Castle*. (Do or Die? *Pass the bottle.*)

The first collision came when the *Bywell Castle*'s propeller inflicted a cut on the port chine of a barge that drifted across her path as she ran on the ebb tide from the outer Millwall Dock. This was a sober rehearsal. Grander sacrifices were required. The collier dutifully aligned herself with the High Victorian demand for drama (and with our desire to write about it). Panther-feasting poetasters, trained for years on stock drownings and suicide sonnets, let rip in a flood of privately printed chapbooks. The gross weight of public sympathy was forcing the boats together (like the mating of pandas) before they so much as let their hawsers drop on the quayside. All that good will could not go unre-warded: 640 deaths was the most reliable estimate. Rescue services can justify themselves only among the dying. The health and security of any society is measured in regular cathartic doses of mayhem. The *Alice* was split and its human cargo spilled into the water.

The account of what happened after the sinking belongs to Purcell.

The strange incident in the cutter. Purcell and Mullins (a Somerset
runner) pulled downstream for Erith. They trawled for corpses –
finding four, including a young woman, '*warm and supple as though she
was still alive*'. They were in awe of a tall stranger, handsome, flame-
bearded, who sat with them, though they did not know him, nor where
he came from. The men spoke later of his enveloping 'boat cloak' and
the stovepipe hat that he clutched to his head. His hair was unusually
long. Certainly, his manner was that of 'a gentleman'. He spoke only
once – sharply – in warning to Purcell: 'Hold your row.' The keel
scraped on the slipway. The boatswain crossed himself. Moonlight.
Two gas lamps illuminated the landing place. The stranger had vanished. And was never seen again. Neither among the crowd giving
statements, nor in the Yacht Tavern, nor even at the Inquest.

Purcell. The bodies taken from the cutter and placed in a handcart. A
constable painstakingly entering the particulars into his notebook. Age,
height, weight, clothing. Mullins carried an old man, more dead than
alive, on his back to the tavern. 'Better to have let him ride in the cart,'
said Purcell. 'They'll measure his length before the night's out.' They
took brandy and later beer. Purcell seemed strangely elated. Said he had
spilled some silver in the bottom of the cutter. Returned to the river;
alternately lifting a pint pot and a lantern. He found a halfpenny down
among the scuppers. Was visibly shaken. His dampened moleskin
trousers bulging comically over his engorged member.

Before dawn he had accused the Captain and the pilot of being drunk.
These were serious charges. 'Take care what you say, man.' 'Boozed, sir?
Every blood bung. Soaked – all of us.' Purcell: shivering in shirt,
moleskins, calico cap. Borrowed a jacket off Harris the confectioner, got
some warmth from the fishtail burners: 'a pleasant yeasty smell'.
Accepted cake and ginger beer. Returned. This time he was not followed. The body of the young woman on the landing stage, under a
policeman's cape. Her feet and her ankles uncovered. 'Warm and
supple.' Hot brandy to her lips. 'Boozing all the afternoon long,
guv'nor. As I'd report before my Maker.' He had the skirts up, bruised
her white thighs with his thumbs. Sniffing at her – a dog – for warmth,
for the smell of life. He would not look in her face. Rolled her. They
thought he was after jewellery, hidden coins. It was worse. Or: it was
the only human reaction. He let down his trousers. 'A call of nature,' he
claimed. To piss back into the river. Turn spirit to water. He climbed on
her. Mounted. Entered. Spent. They drew a bucket to pitch over him.
Mullins put a fist in his mouth. The cur! He spat blood. Tobacco juice.
Called out, justified. *Daughter!* He believed there was life in her still.

Harrison recalled the navigation lights crossing over the headland. 'Like lamps on a hansom.' Margaret, or Tripcock Ness. 'There was singing from a multitude of voices.' The ship's orchestra. The dancers inherit the party. A bass viol floated away on the tide: an inflatable curate. A varnished torso. The bow fetched up in Gravesend. Bodies drifted ashore between Frog Island and Greenhithe. The victims chose an unlucky hour to enter the water. They were discharging the sewage from both the north and the south banks into Barking Creek. Outflow. Mouths open, screaming. Locked in a rictus. Rage of the reading classes. Public demand for the immediate provision of swimming pools for the worthy poor. Let them learn breast-stroke. Letters to *The Times*. Eels suture the ragged wounds. Good, traditional fare, served in public houses: The Angel, the Mayflower, Town of Ramsgate, White Swan, Blacksmith's Arms. Begetting potency. Lead in the pencil. Oil on troubled water. Tanned, condom-skinned sliders. Toyed with (forked aside) by fastidious matrons. Ripe green: catarrh. 'Two continuous columns of decomposed fermenting sewage, hissing like soda water with baneful gasses, so black that the water is stained for miles and discharging a corrupt charnel-house odour.'

Later. The city vermin, pouring out of excursion trains ('Derby Day', hampers, buttonholes), tramped the marshes, grinding down the tussocks. Pickpockets, inebriates, ladies' men, gay girls. Sensation seekers rowing in pleasure boats to the beached wreck, the afterpart of the *Alice*; breaking off pieces of wood, relics to carry home. Watermen fought each other with oars and boat hooks: five shillings for each body recovered. Eyes lost. Traumatic injuries. Ruffians, far gone in drink, drew their shivs on the constable guarding the site; swore to slit any bluebottle who got in their way.

Lines of sleepers. False claimants (legions of Tichbornes) searched the corpses in the dockyard. Crocodile tears, intimacies. They felt for earrings. They assessed the silk of undergarments. They moved among the dead, weeping and stuffing their carpetbags. By night, inconvenient stiffs from other locations were added to the platform of the unburied. Numbers rose, confusing the statisticians. Foul murders were 'inspired' by this golden opportunity. It was as if the graves opened in sympathy. The dead multiplied as they lay in state. They coupled in fertile embraces.

Madness on madness. Dig them under. Hide them. War rockets fired over Plumstead Marshes: the feeble and transient shock of magnesium flares. Spirit photographs. The darkness floods back, covering the ground in decent obscurity. After-images. The sad legend: little pale-blue flowers with purple leaves, *Rubrum lamium*, grew only over the graves of criminals. Tender, unobtrusive. A starry carpet, visible (*there*) for a single instant of trust.

Wilder and wilder stratagems. The idea of the cannons. The heavy artillery of the river defences put, at last, to use: sixty-eight-pounders with a range of 3,000 yards; muzzle-loaders, firing 250-lb shot, to rock the casemates. It had been suggested by W. Aldridge (plumber, house decorator, wholesale oilman) that gunfire would bring some of the bodies swimming to the surface. '*I have seen it tried and have seen a body rise almost perpendicular. The cannon are there as the internal part decomposes gas is formed which renders the body lighter and then the concussion makes it rise all my household with my self, have wept over this sad affair.*'

An irregular bombardment shook the skin of the river, pitching the *Reunion* like a runaway rocking horse: lifting crows from their cover. But none of the anchored dead march of their own volition on to the beaches. We are the only craft to suffer this repeated concussion.

Something happens with the draw of time. With names. The *Alice*. Fleeing from the extreme interest of Lewis Carroll (weaving a labyrinth of mirrors for his English nymphet) into the tideflow of Thames. '*Can you row?*' the sheep asked, handing her a pair of knitting needles. Dodgson. Dodge-Son. Out on the river with another man's daughters: Lorina, Alice, Edith. 'Edith' rediscovered as the Tilbury–Gravesend ferryboat. Edith Cadiz.

I was returning from the Children's Hospital in Hackney Road, looking at the waxy yellow (Wasp Factory) light of the windows reflected in a newly dug ditch of water (a future wild-life habitat). I was brooding on the character of a fictional nurse: caring, competent, driven by her obsessions. Another (dream) life as a Whitechapel prostitute. Neither role cancelling the other. And, as I ran home along the southern boundary of old Haggerston Park, I noticed the name plaque of a street that no longer existed, weathered to the high brick wall. *Edith Street, E2*. Only the names survive; riding the tide of history like indestructible plastic. Without meaning or memory. Alice, Edith: the unplaced daughters.

If you need to understand nineteenth-century Southwark, you must float downstream to Deptford. The old qualities migrate, drift like continental plates, move out from the centre: rings on a pond. The faces Dickens saw in Clerkenwell are lurking in Tilbury junkshops. De Quincey's Greek Street chemist is a Travel Agent in Petts Wood. Everything escapes from its original heat. That is why, in error, I located the fatal encounter of the *Princess Alice* and the *Bywell Castle*, midstream, off Gravesend; which was, by historical record, merely the point of embarkation. Rosherville Gardens. No trace remains. The passengers, waiting to go aboard, were already dead. A few songs, a fine sunset. It was over. But nothing is lost for ever. It slips further out, abdicates the strident exhibitionism of the present tense: lurks like a stray dog, somewhere beyond the circle of firelight.

Subdued, the *Reunion* came into Erith Reach, like Purcell's cutter: heavy with corpses. I relieved Joblard at the wheel. The sky was a darker ocean, livid with portents. Our faces were stinging and raw. Red-cheeked as schoolboys. As brides on the staircase. There was an immediate surge of bliss. A connection with other voyages. Our small craft bucked over gentle waves, a sheep in open pasture: we had escaped. We had left behind the dense pull of the city, the bad will (hating, fearing) of a huddled and grasping populace. Channels of beaded sunlight opened their doors to us. We had only to follow.

Erith Rands. To starboard: the cluster of an old sea town, its slipways, gardens, taverns. A municipal facelift that had fallen behind on its payments. Then marshlands, horses; the revolving radar beacon at the mouth of the Cray. Crossing my own path. An unlucky thing? An accident? I saw myself plodding along, buoyant, grim-faced, quest-hungry – carrier bag in hand, map and camera. 'It's too late,' I wanted to shout. 'That story never worked out.'

I saw the hieratic river gate, like the entrance to a flooded temple. The local storm gods crowded above, perched like calligraphic crows. They assaulted the entablature, but were unable (as yet) to break through. The framed window of light shone with columns of grey and silver. It wouldn't last. It was a flaw, a fault, a forbidden glimpse. This presentation of emptiness was the (lost) third section of Nicholas Moore's 'Last Poem'. Words. They were not his words, but they came into my mouth. Uninvited. I spoke them aloud, startling Jon Kay, who tongued his spliff, swallowing the hot worm of ash in a small crisis of heartfelt loss. 'Remember me.' *Remember me*. The only goal worth striving for, William Burroughs has always stated, is immortality. *Remember*. The museum of memory. No more than that. Gardens of river wheat. Feathers of golden truth. Another path opening; a meandering tributary to the ocean of the world's business. A possibility. I remember. Charles Stuart, on the scaffold – to Bishop Juxon. 'Remember.'

But Jon Kay was growing increasingly agitated: his stash was gone, his thirst raged. 'Remember me.' His life was dedicated to forgetting. He wanted out. He snatched the wheel and drove us, head on, towards the industrial jetties at Purfleet. We skimmed the shallows, churning mud. I fought to regain control, while Joblard screamed in his ear – the sculptor's long-suppressed stutter erupting into a paroxysm of sneezes –

that Tilbury was around the next bend. We'd all take a break: a long and liquid breakfast.

II

Tilbury Riverside and the Custom House had vanished. They were hidden, we assumed, behind two white cruise liners, basking, back to back, like sharks (with Red Stars rouged on to their slumbering snouts). The skies above were monumental, a union of warring republics. They were heroic, drawn up in lines of battle. Tanks buried in snowdrifts. Ruined cities. The river was brown with the sweat of the fields. With the blood of military martyrs. A montage of symbols assaulted us: flags, waving sailors (in flat, bobbed caps), anchor chains, rushing agitated clouds.

Kay needed a drink. He had fulfilled his side of the contract and brought us down to Tilbury. It had been ominously easy. He believed (as these freaks always do, against all evidence to the contrary) that he had, somewhere, just enough smoke to get him home – if he could still remember what 'home' was. Now he *demanded* a couple of big stiff ones. He ran the *Reunion* in between the Russian liners, and he tied up.

We stepped ashore in a foreign land (*more* foreign than the rest of it, than Rotherhithe or Silvertown). No word of English fell on our ears. The seamen shouted at Jon Kay. And laughed. They mimed the universal hand pump of derision. Kay had to be dragged from the security fence that blocked our access to the Gravesend Ferry and the path to the World's End, which lay beyond it, in the shadow of the Fort. We were waved, by uniformed officials, towards a covered walkway: a crazily angled gangplank that disappeared into the citadel of the Custom House. Even the signs were in ... Polish? PASAZEROWIE POZOSTAJACY W LONDYNIE PROSZWE SKRECIC W LEWO. Sunlight laid a ladder of immigrant abstractions along the tilted boards of this glasshouse tunnel. A cleaner stood, motionless (like an onlooker at some spectacularly messy accident, who thinks he might be in the frame of the newsreel cameras), staring at us; two brooms and a shovel rested in his hands. The atmosphere was one of unrelieved Baltic gloom.

A hunched figure trudged ahead of us, plodding on sea legs, hands sunk in sullen pockets: his red, fungic chin slid chestwards in defiance of the inevitable bureaucracy on the far side of the frosted glass. He had learnt how to wait, and how to express his unbending disdain – by the slightest movement of his upper lip. A movement that offered the controlled exposure of a powerful dentato-laciniate bite. He came ominously close to actually relishing the challenge of hours of form-filling tedium: the repetitive cycle of questions in the snuff-coloured room. The boredom of ashtrays and official calendars. He was a stocky, balding man; collared and hatched in a dark blue donkey jacket. An Estonian stoker soliciting political asylum? Or a Basque pornographer caught with a suitcase of bestial snapshots?

We trailed behind him, accomplices, vacuumed into an eddying zephyr of guilt. But the benefits of quitting the river grew more doubtful with each step. Amphibian reptiles, we knew we had been tricked: there was no way back. The cleaner, self-consciously, threw open the Custom House door and gestured with his broom. Dutifully, we turned left: towards the winking red eye of the camera.

'Mmmm, all right. OK. I s'pose that'll do,' commented the director – with a notable absence of vitality – in a toast-dry Birmingham Ring Road accent, that was still quite fashionable at the cutting edge of the visual arts. He was a tall man and a tired one. He didn't believe in anything he could see in front of him. Why bother? A certified deconstructionist. Who had lost his faith in the validity of performance. Actors, hot for motivation, could hope – at best – to witness his struggle to pretend that they had already gone home. They were obstacles blocking his heartfelt longshots. And the state of their hair ... Those *sweaters* ... He shook his head. Satisfaction, we discovered, was expressed as: 'I don't want to sound over-enthusiastic, but ...'

The methodical Pole (a sewer-rat Cybulski), who had led us into this trap, stalked over to the window; distancing himself, as far as the limits of the hall would allow, from the film crew, whose antics were no more than a source of potential embarrassment to a man of his achievements. It was Milditch, of course: earning a crust.

The Corporation has its own mausoleum for spiked scripts. Files of unachieved treatments that have not yet been infected with the black spot. A sperm bank to counter some future threat of a strike by the Writers' Union. A prophylaxis on ideas. A drought of projects: empty restaurants. There has to be the occasional reprieve for the corridor of suggestions unblessed by accountants. 'Yentob thinks it's mega-interesting, baby, but too many calories. Try Channel 4.' There have to be sleepers to foist on 'difficult' directors coming to the end of short-term contracts on 'The Last Show'. That nervy collage of brilliantly achieved trailers. That culture-clash headache.

Which explained this Custom House invasion. I had abandoned my three-month 'rewrite' somewhere back among all those lunches and phonecalls, the motorcycle messengers waiting on the doorstep for urgent revisions – which only elicited further phonecalls. Which elicited further lunches. Which elicited ...

My Tilbury story (erased history) was finally being shot under the impossible title of 'Somdomites Posing': which, apparently, made reference to Queensberry's illiterate and insulting card (the fate card), left for Oscar Wilde at the Albemarle Club: 'To Oscar Wilde posing Somdomite'.

A new director (on his way to the knacker's yard of pop promos), Saul Nickoll, replaced the emotionally bankrupt Sonny Jaques. He determined to blow what remained of the year's budget on a single grand gesture: the least likely script he could find. Mine was the worst by a comfortable margin. It was so far off the wall that nothing could save it. 'Don't worry,' said Nickoll, 'if things start to make any kind of sense ... we'll throw in a few clips from your home movies. Keep 'em guessing. Red frames. Bogus surgical procedures. Fountains of blood.'

And Milditch, being both actor and bookdealer, was type-casting as the paranoid, doom-laden author/narrator. I was being impersonated by a melancholy and balding market trader of doubtful reputation. Why didn't they go the whole hog? Cable for Charlie Manson?

'Milditch looked *terrible* in *Spotlight*,' said Nickoll, gleefully. 'And the portrait was seven years old. He's perfect to play you.'

Milditch knew now he had made one of those mistakes that destroy a career. Like Dickie Attenborough doing John Reginald Halliday Christie. There's nowhere left to go – except the colonies. Or the other side of the camera. He'd finish his days in blackface, a loincloth and a turban. This part would have been well within the compass of a 'walker'. Even so, Milditch was ready to do the business, give it the cold-eye stare. But Nickoll wouldn't talk to him. Nickoll wouldn't, if he could avoid it, talk to anyone. I was beginning to appreciate the man.

Nickoll had the slight, forward-leaning stoop of a man used to looking down on people: on actors, who tended to be dwarfish, with neatly husbanded imperfections the camera was ready to forgive. Nickoll forgave nothing. He *understood* it; but he did not forgive it. He suffered, and he dubbed a world-weary smile. A Spanish saint on his way to the gridiron. He was darkly clad, of course; in the usual gulag chic. And he favoured a quotably minimalist haircut, close razored and modestly abrasive. His appearance was a statement. 'No comment.' But he *was* something of a connoisseur of haircuts. He collected them, pigeonholing the entire newsreel of human history by its length and style. His method was universally acknowledged as more accurate than carbon-dating. 'Mmmm, all right,' he'd drone, 'late 1950s ... '58? No,

'59. Joe Brown at the Two Is.' And he'd stroke his notionally shaved chin.

He modelled blue crombie overcoats, left behind, in something of a hurry, at the Old Horns (Bethnal Green), and white mufflers. He disliked conversation. He had a wonderfully practised way of turning his back on anything that offended his haircut religion. Milditch's functional crop, which looked as if it had been performed inside a coal bucket by a gang of blind chickens, gave him palpitations. He had the trick, under these distressing circumstances, of switching his attention to shoes, one of his lesser interests: until he felt able to cope with the shock to his nervous system. The aesthetic damage.

There were two ways that he signalled his emotions. When things were going badly, and it was all getting away from him, he chewed his hangnails. He gnawed voraciously at the celluloid meniscus, spitting out grey chippings like mangled grape seeds. When it was not *quite* so bad, and he was able to watch a scene without putting his head in a black rubbish sack, he put on his serious spectacles and gazed into the distance: to avoid the possibility of an involuntary smile.

I had every confidence in Nickoll. If anybody could turn my humble disaster into a millennial catastrophe, he was that man. He gave the impression – even now – that if only he could heave Milditch into the dock, with concrete flippers on his feet, get him out of the way, he might be able to deliver some definitively controversial footage. Meanwhile, he chewed his fingers down to the knuckles, and gummed unhygienically on soft cartilaginous tissue. He was picking out lumps of white skin from between his excellent teeth.

The teeth of the little Scottish script girl, on the other hand, were chattering like the typing pool of a fictional tabloid. The sound man (her lover) glared at her in a proprietary rebuke. She tried to invent some way to describe, for editing purposes, the fantastical lack of event unfolding in this refrigerated hall. The sound man, buried in quilts of arctic down, was in despair. There was *nothing* to record. Not even the lugubrious hoot of tug boats or the wind whistling through miles of corridor. He had only to keep sound *out*: neutralize the turbo-props battling to reach the City Airport, or the getaway drivers rehearsing a screech of three-point turns along the quays of the empty dock behind the Custom House.

Nickoll, irritated by his moping underlings, now revealed himself as a closet humanitarian. He noted the script girl's lead-blue lips and frostbitten nose and felt obliged to pass some comment. 'I'd rather be skinned alive with a blunt razor blade than wear a jersey like that. It puts pounds on you, girl.'

He twitched in agony: the awful embarrassment of being confronted, *in flagrante delicto*, by the author of the very farrago he was trying to animate. He wished he could simply hurl back in my face the pages of high-flown nonsense I had so wantonly cobbled together in some warm study, far from the front line. Authors were sick men: punishing themselves, and wallowing in the pain. And worse, much worse, expecting to implicate innocent readers by conning them into turning the first few (inevitably comic) pages.

I shared the director's repulsion. But I had written none of this. This chamber had no place in my text. It was worse than even my damaged mind could imagine. I wanted Tilbury Fort, Highlanders in tunnels, catacombs, waxworks, cricketers, the Mahdi. I wanted the World's End populated with post-orgy catamites and Ripper-yarning clubmen. I wanted corpses to rise out of the river, shrieking in accusation. I wanted the past to resolve itself, and the present to become habitable. I wanted fire angels, warrior/priests, horses that spoke in Latin couplets. I wanted an absence of dogs. And, most of all, I wanted this shifty troop of inadequates to have to drag all their cumbersome equipment into the deepest, darkest, dampest of the subterranean passages: the pools of stagnant air, the trapped voices of prisoners. They should confront everything that cannot be transferred on to videotape. There was no hell hot enough for the man responsible for converting *Vessels of Wrath* to bland stutters of electrical impulse. (Was *I* that man?)

The Beta-Cam, so they said, cost £50,000. It was a nasty, flat case on a thin tripod: an executive ghetto-blaster, a mail-order toy, with a trumpet of lenses protruding from its side. And it was useless ten feet from daylight. 'Sunguns' had been vetoed by the electrician. His word was law. The catacombs were therefore expendable. The script girl, under instruction, deleted them with a stroke of her felt-tip. British Rail (most of whose income came from facility fees from advertising agencies) wanted £200 an hour to let this mob loose in the derelict Tilbury Riverside station. They sent along a female trouble-shooter to tot up the score, minute by minute, on her pocket calculator. 'We had Kenneth Baker yesterday,' she said, looking me in the eye. 'Beautiful manners, a *real* gentleman.'

Nickoll now proved he had the essential quality of a great film-maker: the ability to burn money. He was well on the way to landing the Corporation with a seven-minute version of *Heaven's Gate*. Questions in the House would certainly follow. Resignations were in order. Heads would roll. The Widow was, at this moment, being fitted into her largest set of tombstone gnashers.

Jon Kay shuffled around the crew trying to bum a cigarette. They looked at him with open contempt. Send for wardrobe. That hair! They were green and clean, and pink of tongue: apple-cheeked, scrubbed, concerned. In perfect dental health. Snugly confident in the overweening freshness of their underpants. Milditch simply turned his back on the nodding time-warp spectre, and lit a cheap cheroot. To blow away the bad memory.

If we hang about, thought Joblard, we might score a free lunch. 'Don't forget to keep your bar bills,' he warned. 'And any others you can pick out of ashtrays or spittoons.' Get your invoices in *fast*: that's the first rule. And that was all we'd ever be likely to take out of this fiasco. A couple of corn-crusty cheese rolls and a bottle of gassy Guinness.

We retreated. Left them to it. Watching Nickoll work was like watching hairs grow from a wart. We staggered into the Passengers' Lounge, and sat, spark out, under a mural of palm trees, coral islands, straw huts. It had been executed in a tequila sunburst of radioactive colour: Bikini Atoll, in the shimmering realization of the impact of fifteen million tons of TNT, courtesy of a bomb named *Bravo*. This Robert Louis Stevenson espresso bar was clearly intended to jolly the cruise victims into the mood for the high jinks ahead of them. Its effect on less well-prepared browsers was instantaneous. We slumped, heads in hands, mute, cattle-felled: contemplating a snap preview of all our best-kept fears. Fallout, mouth cancer, plague, famine, bereavement, premature burial: these were the lighter passages.

Sofya Court, the researcher, sat with us. A human presence, she subtly distanced herself from the rude mechanicals of the film crew. She was a modest exile; but with the will and persistence to have twitched this lifeless project into an active mode. She doubled, androgynously, for the authority of the director. There are, after all, many more subjects to be researched than directed. A chequered Hibernian overcoat, studious spectacles, trousers, black shoes. Neat badge-sized earrings to emphasize the delicacy of her ears. Fine hands. The dial of her watch on the inside of her wrist. Time hidden.

'What happened to Sonny?' I asked. I was mildly curious, but the effort of putting the question was enough. My interest in him had, I found, faded before she could reply. Sonny was out of it. Out of the screenplay.

'Ah, yes,' she smiled; so transiently it was possible to miss it, 'Sonny.' He evaporated as she mentioned his name. A shadow slithering across a tile floor. Moisture at the pool's edge. 'I do see him sometimes in the corridor. But what's left to say? We can never decide who'll nod first.' Freelance producers, it seems, come and go with the seasons: the *realpolitik* marches on. Only researchers are immortal. 'I believe they're

sending him to ... Paraguay.' She made it sound like a one-way ticket.
They don't want him back. *Ever*.

This whole episode was cranking into back-lot Dostoevsky. The
unshaven beer-breathed trio, in from the river; rancid with boredom.
Swamp scum. Drooling, mumbling glossoplegics awaiting their next
appointment with the Grotesque. Outpatients sharing a squeaky ban-
quette with their fantasy salvation, a golden-haired Slav. A soft-spoken
waif who *chose* to live and work in Whitechapel; to involve herself with
demonstrably unhealthy material, morbid life-forms. And all to the
despair of her family who suffered so much, and worked so long, to
escape the place and all its memories. Our children, in one afternoon,
unpick the ambitions of a generation. How innocently they enact our
unspoken nightmares!

Jon Kay, ever the literalist, tried to lay his head on Sofya's lap. He
leered up at her. A lost soul crying for a mate to share his purgatory. She
made a tiny adjustment to the line of her coat. Kay's pipe-dream died.
He slid floorward, and began to snore.

Sofya probed me, discreetly, about the fate of my tale, *He Walked
Amongst the Trial Men*, which had initiated all this termite activity:
brought us out on to the rivers and railways. (That stuff had been
recycled more times than a Brick Lane pint.) It was her business to
gather information, to interrogate, to forget nothing. The story, which
she invoked, had originally been commissioned by the magazine, *Butts
Green*, a defunct student publication from Cambridge, kibitzed into
multinational stardom by the hard-nosed marketing strategies of Bull
Bagman, its American proprietor. The magazine, which had previously
limped along on a diet of unpaid effusions from E. M. Forster (Ted
Hughes, Sylvia Plath, Thom Gunn – and anybody else who wanted to
audition for Faber), now showcased the hottest properties in World Lit.
If you were a near 'name' or a future 'maybe', one issue would confirm
your bankable status.

But Bull and I shared a trivial secret. I knew all about Bull's previous
identity. He was once a terminally distressed fenland bookdealer, going
under the stagename of 'Mossy Noonmann'. Fame, in the form of a
libellous caricature in a forgotten novel, did him in. Put paid to the old
lifestyle (if that is what you could call it). Tourists clogged up his cellar,
staring at him in disbelief, as at a chained lunatic. And worse: the
landlord noticed the long months of rent arrears. The commercial
advantages of an instant eviction. Mossy was defenestrated, unhoused,
cut loose. Most of his 'stock' gave itself up voluntarily to the exter-
minator. The rest made a dash for the drains.

Two months later, and forty miles south, Mossy was riding into

Silicon City. A change of name, a change of pitch: he was a power in the land once more. And this time – it was for real! The wilder his schemes, the more the bankers loved it. He couldn't ask for enough money. But he could try. He'd been trained in the right school. All the 1960s scoundrels were getting out of books and into publishing. Much more scope on a sinking ship. Room to manoeuvre. And, anyway, the Americans had stopped buying antiquarian literature and started collecting imprints, conglomerates, prestige Georgian properties.

'Bull loved bits of *White Chappell*,' said the worthy young man, deputed to make the offer. 'He never finishes anything. He skim-reads. But he has the hunch you could work up something lowlife, London, topographical – basically, *downriver*.' I didn't answer. I was lost in admiration for the style of my potential patron, who was occupied with a courageous, single-handed revival of the Colin Wilson look. Drab: with balls.

We were sipping our tepid half-pints in an unlikely hostelry, off Trafalgar Square, crammed to the doors with paroled business folk. I hadn't partied in this zone since my eldest daughter was born in the (transferred) cockroach hospital around the corner. The ambulance, on that occasion, had broken down a mile shy of its destination. We walked the streets, carrying our suitcases (how much stuff do you *need* for an unborn child?); into the building, stepping over the sprawled ranks of junkies puking on the floor of Casualty.

'I hope you don't object to line-editing,' warned the bespectacled go-between. 'Bull likes to keep a tight grip on the text. That's the house style. Delusions of empire building. He thinks he's putting out the *New Yorker*. He chops everybody. Except Jeanette Winterson. And Martin Amis, of course.'

I was caught off-balance: being *asked* for a 'piece of writing', and promised real money, the front window, display space alongside the cash register. I went along with it. I should have known better. But now, a year and a half later, I was living (*living?*) on kill fees; and feeling like a resurrectionist when the graveyard has just been covered in concrete.

I showed Sofya the great man's final letter of rejection. '*I'm confused by it, confused about what is being depicted ... I remain at a loss.*' We were, up to that point, and despite our cultural differences, in complete agreement. The man had sweated as he wrestled with this thing. The typescript was devastated by saline smears, honey blobs, burns, wine-spits. Holmes could have gathered up enough ash for a library of monographs. Bagman truly wanted it, wanted to hack and slash, transplant, transpose, transform: until *his* 'piece' came into a focus that would hold. He wanted to achieve a finished object that could be honourably exploited.

I dragged the spurned and tattered rewrite from my pocket and shoved it across the table. Pencilled comments speared the margins: a messianic tutorial. '*Who is "I"?*' was the first controversy. An existential dilemma that stopped the present writer dead in his tracks. On that single incisive challenge the whole schmear hangs. '*Who is "I"?*' Answer that riddle, or get out of the maze. The slippery self-confessor, the closet De Quincey (I, Me, You, He), speaks of 'the Narrator', or 'Sinclair': deflects the thrust of the accusation. The narrator exists only in his narration: outside this tale he is nothing. But 'Sinclair' is a tribe. There are dozens of them: Scots, Jews, Scribblers, Masons, Cathars (even Supernaturals, such as Glooscap, the mangod of the Micmacs). It's an epistemophiliac disguise. A small admission to win favour: a plea bargain. And what gives this self-designated 'I' the right to report these events? How deeply he is implicated? Is he (I) a liar? Can we (you) trust him?

This was beginning to pinch. I ('I') let my gaze drift down the lovingly assembled beds of words until I ('we') arrived at the sentence reading: 'The man who had shot, and lost, the definitive Minton.' '*WHAT IS THIS?*' screamed Bagman's reasonable pencil. *What* is this? As if he suspected it (Minton) of being some species of effete English porcelàin. Should I have provided a footnote on the Soho Scene in the 1940s and 1950s, on John Deakin the photographer, on John Minton? Should I have credited Daniel Farson? Was Minton now forgotten? Even among all the kiss-of-life attempts to revive the flaccid corpse of British Romanticism? Did it matter if these strange names remained unidentified, mysterious? Which names, if any, *would* have been acceptable? Mervyn Peake? The wrong sexual persuasion. The Roberts? Colquhoun and MacBryde? Worse. They only exist as fictions in the untrustworthy memoirs of Julian Maclaren-Ross. Francis Bacon, perhaps? Too many of them. And they're all too famous. (But you will notice if you check back to the first tale that I have, in fact, acted on Bagman's excellent advice, and rejigged the sentence.)

Now the editor was warming to his task. He made short work of the knockabout book-dealing picaresque featuring the Nigerian, Iddo Okoli. (Racist? Afro-American sales?) A firm grey line removed it entirely. We (Bull and I) limped along in a nervous truce for several more pages. 'Destot's gap' was the next provocation, eliciting an agonized '*HUH???*' The medico-theological debate over the point of passage of the nails, hammering Jesus the Nazarene to the cross (palms of the hand or gap in the wrist?), had gone unremarked in Cambridge. And why not? There were sexier topics out there in the slums and shanties of magical realism. Travel was sexy. Poverty was sexy. The New Physics was sexy. Sex was *not* sexy. (Except for Martin Amis.)

The jig was up. All patience expended, Bagman bombarded the innocent pretensions of the flinching text. 'Bishopsgate Institute?' he snarled, '*what* Institute?' The *Princess Alice* went down for the third time, cleaved by the editor's anguish. 'Too compressed. *What* slaughter? *What* psychopath? *What* nickname?' Guilty. Guilty on all counts. Tumbled. I (I,I,I,I,I,I,I,I,I,I) have been found out. Deconstructed. *Spike it.* 'Let's do lunch sometime and talk about happier things.' Bull remains 'a big fan' and begs to be the first to refuse further 'sketches', 'evocations of the city not dissimilar from Tilbury'. So there might still be an outside chance of getting my spoon in the gravy.

'That's *Butts Green* for you,' said Sofya, 'those dinky sentence rhythms, straight out of Enid Blyton. I love Bull. He'll change tack when he stops having to read bedtime stories.'

The trouble with *Butts Green*, I believe, is not Bull – but his readers. The magazine is a huge market-forces success. A jewel in the Widow's crown. It's a way of participating in literature without getting your hands dirty. It synthesizes and it addicts: culture crack for provincials. Mail-order sampling. 'The Last Show' in your pocket.

I was rapidly being written out of my own story. 'Saul didn't think you'd be up to doing yourself,' Sofya said. 'He thought you were too shifty and, basically, too bald. He's changed his mind after two days of Milditch. But he's absolutely ecstatic about Dryfeld. He told me to thank you. It's really the haircut he's fallen in love with. We're calling Dryfeld's agent as soon as we get back to the office. Saul wants him under personal contract.'

Dryfeld? It was getting worse. If we had to have Dryfeld in the film – couldn't we afford an impersonator? I knew that Raymond Carver was dead, but I'd settle for Alexei Sayle. We'd have to act fast. The medics kept telling Dryfeld if he didn't stop drinking, he'd be dead in six months. The man was a teetotaller.

I'd only ventured to Tilbury in the first place because Milditch put me on to a junkshop that turned out to be a howling dog. I asset-stripped a few of the more blatantly fictional elements – and ran for my life. I was then bullied by *Butts Green* into cutting and cutting again; line-editing, clarifying, glossing, paraphrasing and – finally – casting to the winds. Only to discover, as I lurched from the river's grasp, that my fragmented nightmare was being captured on videotape. The film existed before the book could be completed. The book had therefore been declared redundant by all interested parties. And they wanted the advance returned by the first post. If I could find an even hungrier hack to 'novelize' the mini-saga then I wouldn't have to pursue this madness to its inevitable climax. I could sit back and read the pulp version in the comfort of my own room. Later, after relishing the exhibitionist wrapper, I could sell it.

Sofya told Nickoll we'd walk on, ahead of the crew, to the Fort. They had only to can a selection of failsafe cutaways and it was a wrap. They could break for lunch. The technicians wouldn't, at any price, eat a second time in the World's End. They were going to shoot off with their Egon Ronays to road-test a place near Stanford-le-Hope.

Joseph Conrad lived there once, I thought. But the only scholar I knew (an ex-postman) who had tried to search out the house, achieved nothing more remarkable than an old man, spitting in a hedge, claiming descent from Tunstall, who – he said – either shot, or was shot by, Billy the Kid. He couldn't be sure. But it was definitely in the film. One of the family came over once from New Mexico, wearing a white stetson and a string of liquorice around his neck: took photographs. 'We're searching out all the living Tunstalls in Essex, England. And then in Ireland.' The old man didn't say whether he qualified. He'd never heard of Conrad anybody, not in Stanford-le-Hope. No Poles of any description.

The road between Tilbury Riverside and the World's End is the strangest in Europe. A bank of earth (mercifully) hides the river. Unwary tourists usually opt for the elevated route, enjoying an uninterrupted vista of mud and tide: the timeless roof-stacks (in slate, mustard, replacement vein tissue) of Gravesend. Distance lends a false appeal. Imagined pleasures will never be sweeter. And yet some lingering masochistic fret sends us trundling down the low road: at the mercy of white-knuckle winos in clapped-out Cortinas, convinced that last orders have already been called. The marshes, to the north, are the training ground for a pack of the rat-hunting undead; who are armed with nothing worse than lead-tipped clubs and blood-rusty forks.

Sofya pauses to take a snapshot. It is certainly a spectacle: this foolishly reclaimed swampland. Let them have it, I say. Give it all back to the waters. Erase these sunken levels, these broken industrial toys. Sheds. Straw bales. Pylons. Ditches. Undeclared violations. I'm beginning to love it. That's how far I have degenerated.

Jon Kay can't cope with the size of the sky. He's snorting like a horse, an asthmatic Welsh cob. Joblard and Sofya are relishing the discovery of a scatter of teenage female runaways, lying in (rag) heaps beside the road, legs spread, auditioning for *La Strada*; smoking with little dry-lipped sucks, not inhaling – blowing out a suggestive rinse of bad air, picking brown tobacco shreds, with chipped and scarlet nails, from between their tiny teeth. Self-packaged White Trash hopeful of Russian sailors. Ready to lean over backwards for international relations. By the state of their dress, they have been waiting for months in the couch grass.

The set was far too theatrical for us to consider: a promo-nostalgic 1950s blackout. Jon Kay felt comfortable for the first time since we stepped ashore. He even scored an American cigarette.

Manhandling a multicolour bicycle towards the World's End was a glamorous dyke: a stone-freezing scowl and bellow of greeting revealed the exotic creature as the lowlifer's lowlifer, Dryfeld. The perceived universe of logical linear progressions was coming apart in front of our combat-weary eyes.

'Great ass – for a bull,' Kay acknowledged with a low whistle. 'Must be the cycling. I bet she really stomps those pedals.' He leant forward to test with a shaky paw the tightly-corseted pudding, the muscular cleavage of his fantasy. He was lucky to miss. The rest of us were too far gone in civilization to allude to Dryfeld's startling change of image. He must have grown tired of beggars and golfing tweed. He was getting too well known. Women rushed up to touch the hem of his skirts. Children threw stones.

He had cracked Milditch's legendary junkshop, while waiting for his turn to face the cameras. There was nothing else to do. He'd eaten two breakfasts. And the nearest *serious* bookshop was sixteen miles down the track. So he put the frighteners on the junkman and came away with a satchel of trade catalogues. The film business excited him. He was crazy with energy. He out-wolfed Wolfit. He laughed so loud and so long that falcons lifted from the grain silos, to hover like heraldic totems gone, badly, to seed. They'd been brought in, so Joblard informed us, to finish off the pigeons. It didn't work. Now the silos themselves were awaiting demolition.

We cowered, and pretended that we did not know this all-too-public aberration. Dryfeld was putting the wind up even the hardened drinkers, lying under the warped pear trees in the pub garden; their faces buried in grey alopecic scuff. Tottering on six-inch heels, he gave the best imitation I have ever seen of the Widow's television walk: the way she reels at the camera, hurdling across hot coals, and expecting some able-bodied male, some promotion seeker on the far side, to hold out his arms and catch her.

The pub was of no interest to the fruit-sucking Dryfeld. He stormed on towards the Fort. And – as he swayed and pitched – he roared out the story of his transformation: to our shame and to the undisguised delight of a party of smutty schoolboys with loosened ties and substance-abused blazers.

It appeared he had developed a fancy for the company of children. Young children. He liked to spend money on them. And hear what they had to say. He could freely indulge in childhood pleasures denied at the first attempt: helicopter flights, picnics, museums, opera – the spread of the city. He developed a decided craving for the position of Nanny. (Eat your heart out, Bette Davis.) Also: he wanted to model the uniform. He knew he had the legs for it. Sadly, he met with a series of unreasonable and unnecessarily abrupt rejections. Most wounding. He was discriminated against. The job specification required the applicant to be experienced. And female.

No problem. Surgery was on the cards, but King's Cross was nearer. (He was buggered if he'd live with all the other stitched changelings in Hay-on-Wye.) He'd read in the *Guardian* about a place where you could get yourself done over in an afternoon. 'It was amazing,' he repeated, entranced, reliving the experience. 'Quite amazing! It lasted three hours. Assisted shower, powder, underclothes, razor, seminar in make-up. They wanted to shave off my eyebrows. I wasn't having that . "Tuck 'em under a Veronica Lake wig," I said. I drew the line at forking out extra for a studio portrait, "built in from the shadows – in the style of Edward Steichen". They couldn't guarantee I'd look like Marion Morehouse, so I told them to stuff it. Marched across the road to the station, and queued, with all the other claimants, for the photobooth. The transvestites seemed to be army officers. It was like a regimental reunion in there. They collected their snapshots in plain manilla envelopes; tore them in half, unopened, dropped them in the bin on the way out – and were home in time for dinner. Sheer waste! I'm auctioning mine to the highest bidder from a rival magazine.'

There was an armed guard on the Watergate of the Fort. We were scanned and registered by the red eye of a swivelling, vulture-necked camera. Another heritage prison. Alcatraz among the marshes. Visit the felons in complete safety, and rattle their cages. A day out for all the family. Test the electric chair at a carefully monitored voltage: snug in a pair of authenticated rubber bloomers. Amuse the kiddies.

They'd sold more tickets in the first two weeks than in ten years of boring Armada tableaux, restaged battles, cases of waxworks. The dummies had been melted down and replaced with genuine recidivists. Even as we stood waiting for the machine to process Sofya's pass, another black-window van pulled up and shook out a stock of assorted Scotsmen: poll-tax refusniks, street-fighting parliamentarians, ginger-haired nationalists. The underground catacombs of the Highlanders were waiting. They had been whitewashed and fitted with pallets. Credit-worthy villains were given the opportunity to buy their own cells.

My outlandish improvisation, in advance of the truth, was made actual. But Sofya, a professional researcher, could not escape from the woeful inadequacy of mere facts. An unpleasant inclination towards verifiable evidence. She cruelly pointed out that the prisoners taken by Butcher Cumberland after Culloden had not, according to historical records, been held underground – but were housed in the now demolished barrack block. The passages of the powder magazine were an addition from the last war. Therefore my story was pure fiction. And my fiction was corrupted by its desire to tell a story. Lies, all lies. The text was untrustworthy; especially when it lectured its audience like a logorrhoeic tour-guide.

But still I shouted: BELIEVE ME! I developed, on the instant, a theory of the shunting of place by time. (In itself, a slippery performance.) The validity of received emotion migrates through all civil and temporal boundaries. It is a wild thing, to be seized without reference to the proper authorities. To have any real understanding of the spiritual plight of the Highlanders, it was clearly necessary to shock our complacency, our endemic cynicism. To activate the image of the tunnels.

Wind-scored men held fast in dripping darkness. The list of dead names *is* 'true'. The clansmen and brothers were buried here: or thrown overboard in passage to Van Diemen's Land. I would not libel their suffering. You can purchase that list for £1 a sheet at the Gatehouse. The cells which were illegitimately populated by real ghosts are occupied once more. Manacled men shuffle through the cobbled parade ground. Kilts are issued to every prisoner. It is impossible to outrage the baroque realism of the dying century. Imagine the worse, and then double it.

The chief electrician of our skeleton film crew was cursing at the wheel of the silver Mercedes he'd spent the morning turtle-waxing, on time and a half. His Rolex said one o'clock. And that was it. 'Sorry, love. No can do. Dodgy ticker. I was up Harley Street, wasn't I? See the quack, Saturday? No heavy lifting whatsoever. He placed a definite embargo on it. And no tunnels. That's gospel. My life.'

He wedged a cellphone against the side of his head, like a malfunctioning electric razor. 'Market's jumpy, darling. Bit of a panic on. Shittin' theirselves in the City. Don't like the vibes I'm getting off of Tokyo. Resignations, sex scandals. Respectable blokes topping theirselves. They're wading through blood out there. It's the old knock-on effect, know what I mean? The Mexican Wave, that's what you've got to look out for. I'm thinking of taking a bit of a poke at property. What d'you think? An option on a slaughterhouse in Poplar? Fancy a spin down there before it gets dark?'

Saul Nickoll could forget the Fort. As of now, the script was Fort-less. 'Nahh, take hours, *hours*, to light it. You're looking at two days, darling, to nick your first shot. Always the same, innit? These poxy location jobs are a real fucker.' Advised the electrician, the last mastodon of the studio system. He screwed in the bulbs, pulled the switch, and waited for his redundancy cheque. Meanwhile: there were free lunches, petrol, and telephone bills. Can't be bad? The entire shoot revolved around the mood swings of this crusty mercenary.

As we backed off, Sofya touched my arm. She had an apology to make. 'Graphics', it seemed, had lost the only illustration of the *Vessels of Wrath*. I had lent them the photocopy that Joblard made for me from a book of cabalistic ceremonies. They wanted to use these demonic forms to pep up the credits. Now the sheets had vanished into the corridors of the Corporation. And Joblard couldn't remember the book's full title. Was it published by Lackington & Allen? Was the author Francis Barrett? The London Library had no record of its existence. *Mammon, Astaroth, Apaddon* were cast upon the air. *Magot, Katolin, Dulid* and *Kiligil* skimmed over the surface of the waters. The princes, sub-princes, servitors and spirits were loose in the cutting rooms. *Anything* could happen.

We heard the crackle, and felt the heat, of a great bonfire in the centre of the parade ground of the Fort. Through the slit of the open Water-gate we saw the orange flames leap. The archives were being cleared. Barrows of paper, bundles roped like sacrificial sheep, were wheeled out from the chapel. Old uniforms, furniture, ledgers. Ancient corners of paper floated over our heads like scorched moths. Teasing fragments, inconclusive extracts. Climbing and twisting, as they drifted above the wall and across the landscape: a nuclear snow falling in yellow mud, riding on the river.

Joblard stuck out his hand and caught a few of them: pressing them, without stopping to read or decipher, into the uncharted depths of his wallet.

III

> 'Were there two sides to Pocahontas?
> Did she have a fourth dimension?'
>
> Ernest Hemingway

On the slipway beneath the gardens. We had crossed over. The fort slides from our sight behind its fortified wall. It might never have been built. A column of black smoke hangs in the still air like an Indian massacre. The comfortable Monopoly tokens of the Power Station, the

Pub, and the Custom House dominate the riverline. But we are safely out of it. Put ashore. Gravesend. I've humped a couple of cans of petrol a mile back to the boat. Joblard has emptied the shelves of the off licence and the pie shop. And Jon Kay has secured two tiny plastic tubes from a car-accessory store to replace the broken oil pipes in the engine. Will he agree to push on around the bend – through the Lower Hope into the Sea Reach?

Water slaps invitingly against the boardwalk. The *Reunion* rides the swell, almost as if she meant it. She was ready to sail on without us.

Eight hundred yards is the distance at which Tilbury becomes an acceptable reality. The gaunt figure of Saul Nickoll strides along the battlements, arms swinging stiffly at his sides. Sofya follows, hands in coat pockets, blinking behind silted spectacles: a refugee. She is fleeing from the culture of talk into the terrors of night and storm. And then Nickoll actually performs that terrible director's thing. A lenshead! I would never have believed it of him. He makes a frame of his fingers, glares at the gun emplacements, the sky, reads the light, blows on his fingers: soberly, shakes the brain oil, and waves the crew back to the cars.

The Whitbread Best Bitter trickles down Joblard's throat as he flogs the green cylinder to ease out the last brown droplets. He turns his attention to Jon Kay. 'Where did you pick up the retread?' he asks, direct as always; pinching a fold of the junkie's loose skin between his finger and thumb. Joblard never meets a medical man without demanding a full and detailed account of his *very* worst experience: arms sucked into slow mincers, tongues amputated from freezer units, meat gangrene, internal organs cooked by microwave leaks.

Kay is lying at the water's edge: a missing engraving from the *Princess Alice* portfolio. His cheeks have hollowed, decompressed around an ice-lolly stick which has to double for the unlocated roach. All mortal expression has drained from him. The life-force has collapsed. His face is an old man's sarcoidal nates, penetrated by a rectal thermometer. He gawps in disbelief at the lead-curtained sky: the brown wash of body liquors. A marbled bar slab wiped of its stout puddles. Light is being slowly crushed towards the waterline.

'We were crossing the desert. No, wait. Hold up. It was Turkey, was it?' All Kay's yarns opened to the same formula. It steadied him. 'Italy. Italy, man! We almost made it.' He smiled at his own presumption. 'We pulled into an olive grove to check out the grass. Got to know just what you're selling, right? Before you monkey around with it. My mate's a bit road-crazy. Off-beam. Heat shivers. Those mirror things? Mirages, right! Been at the vino all morning. He sits down on the reserve petrol can.'

Kay laughs. An ugly sound. And we laugh with him. His foot, with a misplaced twitch of morphic resonance, drums against *our* red can: the one I lugged through all the recobbled walkways of Gravesend. The twin pictures begin to fit rather too neatly together. Gravesend, having no viable present, needs somewhere else to go. 'The can's like a primus, right? My mate's wearing cutoff jeans. He's scalded. Jumps in the air. The cap blows. The can hits the ground. Wow! I'm drenched. And he's pissing himself, my mate. Drops his spliff. Ball of flame? Fried like a chicken, man. And I'm screaming; calling him every name in the book. Five months in some shitty clapshop in Naples. They peel my ass. The arms never took, did they? Stayed wet. But the tattoos came through. It wasn't a total disaster.'

After that, we drank in silence. A rusting container hulk, the *Paul Kelver*, Liberian-registered, ghosted like a phantom down the deepwater channel. Horses were penned in a makeshift corral on the deck: nervously, they sniffed the salt air. Dog food on the hoof. Gamey steaks for Belgian tables. Spavined *ragoût*, retired from the shafts of brewers' floats.

Pocahontas didn't want to go 'home'. This was where they carried her ashore. She knew there was no passage back down the river. No way to re-enter the womb, without dying. The first seal had been broken. The waters had burst. She could never be readmitted to the society of the forest. She was crossed, baptized in holy water. She was another. She was Rebecka, 'daughter to the mighty Prince Powhatan, Emperor of Attanoughkomouck'. It was her husband, John Rolfe, the established man, who was forcing her. She had become the prestige symbol of the Virginia Company: the silver band on a cigar, a cigar-store Indian. She was more potent as a symbol than as a living woman. Her husband was willing her death. He was colluding with darkness.

Coming into a strange land, she was installed at the Belle Sauvage, Ludgate; where William Prynne the pamphleteer denounced the performance of the *Tragical History of Dr Faustus*, with its 'visible apparition of the devil on the stage'. A time of freaks and harbingers. The Scottish showman, Banks, exhibited his silver-shod horse at the same inn: walked it up the short hill to old St Paul's, where it succeeded in climbing to the top of the tower. (A horse with the eye of a crow? The river, once only, a horse map?)

London was posthumous. She had dreamed it. A child in the forest. Trees became the pillars of a great court. Gods appeared, painted in gold-and-white lead; shining, buried in layers of stiff cloth until they could scarcely move. The sun, the moon, and the stars were trapped upon a ceiling of overhanging branches: dark, feathered arms.

Twelfth Night, 1617. Pocahontas attended the court masque. Ben

Jonson. She was accompanied by her stone-faced warriors, the Chicka-hominies: scornful, proud, holding to the costume of their tribe. The Indian Princess was modest; correct in manner and dress. She maintained an unsurprised dignity before these spectacles of savage transformation: she-monsters delivered of dancing puppets, clouds that spoke in rhyme. She was initiated into the mysteries of new and dangerous gods. It was the price of the bargain she made so many years before: when she reached out her hand to touch the apparition of a stranger.

John Smith was the first. But not her husband. She had been eleven years old when she saw him. He would not live by what he was. He would not live by what she knew him to be. The memory of the forest is not a recent memory. Memory is recognition. The people know this. Fate is memory, memory fate.

Returned to his own country, Smith delayed his visit. There was an awkward interview at Brentwood. 'You did promise Powhatan what was yours should be his, and he the like to you; you called him father, being in his land a stranger. And by the same reason, so must I do you. Were you not afraid to come into my father's Country? Did you not cause fear in him, and all his people? And fear you here I should call you father? I tell you then, I will, and you shall call me child, and so I will be for ever and ever your countryman. They did tell us always you were dead, and I knew no other.'

Betrayal. What is spoken cannot be unsaid. 'Your countrymen will lie much.' But when their word is given in the way of business, they believe, it can be taken back. It will not stand. They look for interest, returns. Circumstances alter cases, they say. Each day is new. We wake to a different sun.

For Pocahontas, all this is heresy. A promise is a contract honoured to the final breath. Her beauty was in strength. The firm set of her mouth. The broad nose. Her features held no appeal for the courtiers, the men of affairs. Rebecka. Eleven years old, looking on John Smith (nameless name): divorced at once from her father's gods. Smith was her father. 'Okeus, who appeareth to them out of the air. Thence coming into the house, and walking up and down with his strange words and gestures.' His presence revealed by freak winds, or 'other awful tokens'. Her desire for him gave him a human shape, an outline she could bear. He came to the forest. He sat at the strings of the death-cutter with Purcell and Mullins. He spoke whatever it was they feared most to hear.

John Rolfe carried her aboard the *George*, in enforcement of duty. Along with their young son, Thomas. She was his to command. She knew she would die of it. Rolfe brought a dead woman on to the vessel. The houses of the city were grey, limed, huddled: a graveyard. Downriver: the fortified places, the church at Erith. The bleak marshlands, treeless, offered no cover for the spirits.

She was sinking. Lifted ashore in great pain at this hithe. We step aside, make room; we watch. She passes us: carried to the Inn on a seaplank, by four sturdy sailors. Another corpse, beached and scrubbed. Another narrative claimant.

The shadow of the statue in St George's church fell across her window. A replica of William Ordway Partridge's Jamestown monument. More Hiawatha than daughter of Powhatan. Single feather, arms open, palms spread: making entrance in some lumberjack operetta. She was divorced from herself. There were two of her.

She opened her hand on the flowered bedspread. Stone entered her heart. What she was offering could not be accepted. The city was half-born, unmade. A plague dish. Let her become a charm against fever. Let her preach a quiet ruin upon the dockyards, the timbers. Soon the forest will march back to claim her. The sap to varnish her cheek. Her breath is wood smoke.

Our fuel tanks were topped and ready. We were invaded by waves of shame and courage, fear and anger: an inhuman desperation. (Like reading a letter from one of those unloved poets who turn rejection into full-blown martyrdom by way of the correspondence columns of the *TLS*.) 'Let's do it,' said Joblard. 'Let's try for Sheerness.'

Together we dragged Jon Kay aboard. If necessary, we would lash him to his own wheel: like Dracula's helmsman. We no longer needed a pilot. We were hot to quit this final landfall. The taint was choking us. There was no more protection in wood and plaster. No tax shelter in memory, in other men's tales. Out then, out on a running tide. Eastwards.

The engine fired at the first touch of the rope. The *Reunion*, with previously suppressed reserves of omphh, surged gratefully off the chart. There were no maps for where we were going.

IV

The ductile spread of the waters cooled, in a moment's narrowing of the diaphragm, into a blanket of unrelieved latex. The pluck and suck that gives fair warning, but does not slow our progress.

Now there were only container ships, hugging the Essex shore, blocking out the oil refineries: Mucking Flats, Lower Horse, Deadman's Point, Canvey. 'Cowards!' howled the resurrected Kay. The tide was with us. The wind. The light. We were expelled, cut loose. Good riddance, said the stones. There was nothing to go back for: the world disappeared in our wash. We skated on the edge of an abyss. Jon Kay had his hands on the wheel. He spat in the face of the Furies. He'd already taken off his dark glasses and flung them over the side. With his winking lidless eye, he looked a thousand years old. His flapping tent-show skin. He was something carried in a cardboard box from the crypt of Christ Church, Spitalfields. He grinned like a mummy. His teeth were black wood. He haemorrhaged sawdust from every seam. He had locked himself totally into some older journey. Outfoxing the coastguard: Harry Morgan off the Florida Keys. *GOPHER IT!* We had run beyond our permissions. We were bouncing towards the mystery of Sheerness. It was written. Fate.

The light was infected, a bead curtain of airborne droplets. It was bad light. Bugs burning up. You could smell it. The peculiar intensity of a sunstream revealing a circle of jungle floor better left in dampened shadow. Things crawled. White eyes flashed beneath the wavelets. The clouds were at war, split by the beams of heavy searchlights. Smoke solid skies, bone smoke. Foreclosing this petty adventure. The river became all rivers. The James, the Congo, the Amazon. Eliot's Mississippi. Let the green vegetation creep down the banks. Let it smother the storage tanks. It will not yield. The river is the agent of transformation.

'Is that the Isle of Grain?' I pointed to a headland that shone on the distant Kent shore. Nobody knew. It was unreal, a promise. It could be the beacon at Egypt Bay. It could be Allhallows. The light played with our expectations; offering a *visible* destination at which to aim our craft. It was all too easy.

Against all mythic prohibitions, I looked back. Black gouts of engine oil were gushing from the outboard into the water. A torn shark. Surely, I thought, this is not right. This shouldn't be happening. I nudged Joblard. We were bumping against something. Jon Kay had fulfilled his potential. He had run us aground.

'But this is *impossible*,' he bleated. 'I don't believe it. The river is three miles wide.' He gunned the motor to a scream: churning us deeper and deeper into the quaggy filth. With a groan of hurt, and a radical crunch, the propeller-shaft parted from its blades. Kay had done it. Give him his due. He had put us on to the notorious Blythe Sands.

We were not the first. We fought for space in these temperamental paddies, these bury-yourself swamps, with the wrecks of East Indiamen: colonists, convicts, merchants, brides, and rum-soaked soldiery. We hardly merited an entry in the log of nautical disasters. We had nothing to leave in the sands except our bones. Many vessels waited for months at Gravesend: commissioned, provisioned, crewed –

needing clearance, a letter from the owners. They came so soon to grief.

, An old acquaintance, the *Paul Kelver*, had anchored on the borders of the sandbank, to wait her turn for the pilot boat. We could see the condemned horses, as they fretted and stamped. Joblard rubbed his hands. Nothing made him happier than the arrival of a long-anticipated trauma. Now it could only get worse. He unzipped a Jacobean gash of teeth.

The fates were in the mood to indulge him. The skies darkened, lost all muscle tone, and fell. They pressed on the horizon, leaving us with nothing to admire but a thin mercury column. We were imprisoned in a radiation helmet, a black chimney of soot. We were blinking at what was left of the world through the slit of a visor. A wind of hate rushed past us, spitting and gobbing, kicking green water over our bows. A sheet of rain (a rain hoarding), solid as steel, swept towards us from the open sea.

'Can't we pull ourselves out of here?' I asked, bright-eyed as a Rover Scout. 'Isn't there a rope?' Kay cackled until he shook. His eyes were rolling like lubricated bearings. His single lid shorted and twitched. He drooled. He knew it was all over. This was the image he had spent his life searching for; driving through deserts, begging for mayhem. This was IT! To run aground with two blustering inadequates in the middle of the widest stretch of the Thames, the tide on the turn, head-on to a gathering storm. *A* storm? A storm among storms. *The* storm.

The winds were the Vessels of Wrath, named vortices of bad will – self-inflicted, and gaining in strength. Rushing (fleeing) into the vacuum of our fear. They did not hesitate to expose all our defects: greed, violence, jealousy, hatred. We had left behind the safe harbour of boredom and complacency, we were defenceless. We saw, in this personalized weather, all the things we had never quite dared to imagine.

Rain stripped us in a hail of blades. Our shirts were rags. Joblard's orange (distress flare) jacket stuck to him like an acid-attack skin. We were drowning where we stood. But I didn't want Jon Kay for company on that journey. I decided to go over the side. I pulled off my sodden corduroys, and jumped.

The water came halfway up my thighs, and the sand was firm. Joblard, lurching like King Kong with a migraine, followed me. He had lost his spectacles and was blind to the horrors that surrounded him. He could have gone under and never noticed it. He grabbed a boat hook, wrapped the tow rope around his shoulder and took off in the general direction of Norway: a deleted icon of St Christopher as a sumo wrestler. I shoved at the stern. The boat had taken plenty of water: rain was filling it like a moulded birdbath. But it moved. It shifted.

Jon Kay sat on the cabin roof, tailor-fashion, and watched us. The calm epicentre, the target. He was crossing the desert again. (Sand to water. Water to sand.) The rope stretched out. Joblard vanished, deep among canyons of rearing swell. Waves broke over his head. He roared. He shouted something we could not hear. For a moment, we glimpsed him again, clinging crazily to his staff: blowing and swallowing and gasping for breath. Broken spears of lightning pitched from the black skies. Antlers of white fire. Cracks in the glass. Sounds of rending and tearing; ripples of thunder. The night guns were all blazing, booming and echoing. Stereophonic shock waves tagged the mucoid dome: bringing to life the theoretical fire pattern of the shore defences. They fizzed and short-circuited in sprays of pinball madness.

One of the horses, driven to risk everything, smashed free of its pen and plunged from the side of the pitching container ship. It was immediately lost in deep water: swimming or drowning. The elements were all assembled for a minor apocalypse. They posed, daring some fool to try and describe them.

I left the *Reunion* and fought my way towards Joblard. The sea was now the darkness of ignorance. I saw Jon Kay in a sequence of flash frames, lit by strokes of lightning. Electrical anomalies played tricks with my vision. I saw *two* men in the boat. Kay was crouched in the stern, trying to coax the outboard into life, frantic to escape from the thing confronting him on the cabin roof: a second, and more convincing, portrayal of himself. This minatory being was cross-legged, webbed in a graft of inky shadows. His wet hair rose into stiffened peaks, horns. His finger pointed in accusation at the heavens. Kay saw himself as the Beast, the Other: the Stranger in the cutter, Okeus, John Smith, Spring-heeled Jack. The names meant nothing. He had run out of aliases.

The stranger's long arm hung over the side, obliterating the 'E' in the boat's title. Jon Kay had undisputed command of the motorized ashtray, *Runion*. He cowered like the sailor's wife with chestnuts in her lap. From the Scottish play. He waited on the coming of the witches, the bearded women.

Then the lightning found its target. The irritation of the matchbox television, still flickering its feeble interference, guided the jagged discharge towards Jon Kay's trouser pocket. The *Runion* was a fireball. Cheap plastic wrinkled, and contracted like an anteater's mouth. Kay was on his feet, naked, winged with flame. Wrestling his double. He was magnificent. He soliloquized defiance. Holding and damning. The scorched skin justified, at last, its pensioned deformity.

'So there you have it,' as Fredrik Hanbury would say on 'The Last

Show', wrapping up some number on how water resists all attempts at privatization. Is provoked. To answer back. With an anti-commercial, in which we have a featured role. Bottomless budget. The camera becomes an industrial vacuum cleaner, sucking down the skies, draining the sea – and all its flotsam.

I was holding a limp rope. I was attached to nothing. I called out for Joblard. I listened. I was standing in the middle of the estuary, neither in sea, nor on the river: somewhere uncharted between Canvey Island and St Mary's Marshes. It was too far to walk, and too shallow to swim. The direction to follow was the erased track of a panicked horse. The guide whose whims no pilgrim could anticipate.

12

The Sexing of Stones

The Sexing of Stones

'I see them rising! Save me from those therrble prongs!'

James Joyce, *Finnegans Wake*

It's so hot the Indians have dragged their mattresses on to the flat roof. Lloyd warned us never to set foot on it. 'That roof's as strong as a fistful of wet twin-ply toilet paper,' he said. 'Stroll out with your post-prandial cigar – and you'll drop straight through into the supermarket.'

This was probably no exaggeration. I'd witnessed one of them, in his best suit, during the last of the spring storms, pouring *wet* concrete feebly into a crack the size of the Californian fault. His best boy respectfully held a ladies' plastic umbrella over his head. When torrents of rainwater (sky scum, washed dirt) gushed through the ceiling, fusing the strip-lights, the cashier had broken open a special offer of candles: then, when the shop was quiet, climbed to the roof and stuffed the holes (mine-shafts, UFO craters) with Pampers and sanitary pads.

The Bengalis know I'm watching them (some of the time), but they don't care. They noticed me at once. There are no curtains over our window. It means nothing to them. They are wholly absorbed in their own affairs. *Video, jacket, cassette. Cassette, jacket, money.* The shifts change, but the lights never dim. The noise of sewing machines, an infernal river, never falters. Day and night. Winter and summer. I think we'd miss it. This avian tide of chattering, *fulfilled* voices. Money, money, money, money.

Some of them, young boys, male with male – even solemn married couples – are spirited enough. If the roof can stand their devotional humping, it can stand anything. Straight off shift and on to a very recently occupied, still steaming mattress: hot for it. Uncovered acts of love, without emotion. Graciously conducted. Few words, fewer blows. Other men – solitaries – lie there among the chaos (the heaving, the groaning), staring up at a narrow rectangle of sky. An older man, a grandfather, drops at once into bottomless slumber. His territory will be claimed soon enough. He does not enjoy the luxury of dreaming his own dreams. He shares whatever is left in the horsehair: laughter, delight, the music of the gods. Inky leather jackets (welded and creaking), polished skirts (in scarlet nail varnish), cattle coats: they pour from the building in a perpetual haemorrhage. A blood circuit, a wound path. Down the twist of stairs, into the open-mouthed vans: away. Up West. Gone.

I always knew I'd come in the end to this place. I've no more connection with it than any other. I passed the house so many times in the course of my ramblings, looked up at the windows, making statements I trusted would never have to be justified. But the change in my life has been a magical one. I *have* to believe that. I do believe it. I have never been so vulnerable, so content. It's risky: I am finally getting the things I said I wanted.

There's not much furniture: a settee under a dust sheet (better left that way), a draughtsman's desk that runs the length of the room. A desk for a team of draughtsmen. Lloyd left this behind, but will almost certainly get around to claiming it back for one of his other properties. You might even recognize the thing. Lloyd featured it in several of his staged photographs. (What do *they* go for now? What's the swap? A car? A year's water rates? Another house?) What else? The usual cardboard boxes and black polythene rubbish sacks. Odd glasses, half-empty bottles, a pram. Bits and pieces scavenged from old performances and reinvented for domestic purposes: an illuminated globe, an oil lamp from the operating theatre in Southwark. And *projects*. On the desk, pillows of white paper. Sketches, notes, clean thefts. The time to work it all out. That's what I'll never have.

The proportions of our room are peculiar, but satisfying. I relish the knowledge that this was once the living quarters of a Rabbi and his family. I welcome the tradition, without the obligations. The synagogue beneath our feet has been converted into a storeroom for sides of salted fish, brightly labelled tins, hot spices. The Ladies' balcony is heaped with sacks of Patna rice. The last recorded sighting of David Rodinsky, so Sinclair tells me, was in this room: a party of some kind, a ceremony, bar-mitzvah, Kiddush. 'It was as if he had become another man,' Sinclair wrote. He found some letters about it in Princelet Street. 'The familiar self-consciousness left him. He was fluent in Middle Eastern tongues. What had once appeared a caul of sullen idiocy, stood proud: a performance of wisdom that touched on arrogance. He shone. He seemed to know his own fate.'

I'm convinced: the agent of transformation is still active within these walls. I recognized, but did not fear it. I avoided mirrors. I breathed slowly, with comical deliberation. I knew I would have to come back, sooner or later, to this trap. All those years picking at the scabs of Whitechapel, fondling safe (confessed) images, visiting the butchered sites as if they were shrines: paddling in mysteries. I held off the frenzy, stayed out of it, within rigidly defined margins of safety: a well-informed tourist. I faked it, molten orgasms of righteous indignation. There was always another house to return to, a home, locked within never-revealed systems of protection. It's terrifying how quickly all that can change. A few abrupt twists of fate. A phonecall extended beyond the demands of courtesy. A third drink. I've paid my dues to the furies. And here we are, on set, in the long room, looking affectionately down on the business of the streets; or back, the hidden courtyards, the sleepers on the roof. Shameless. I live here. I belong.

I tasted my coffee. The jiffy bag lay unopened on the desk. I had no desire to break this moment and unstaple the honey-crusted package. Sinclair's runic scribble: it gets smaller all the time. He has to write now. The phone's been cut off, and he daren't set foot in Whitechapel. With his bald dome and spectacles, his notebook, he might be mistaken for Salman Rushdie. They'd hack him to pieces on the cobbles of the brewery. The atmosphere has been fouled up for ever. Gang fights. Banners. Burnings. Aggravation. We all feel guilty, guilt as a constant, a hangover of guilt: even if we haven't read a word of it. There are no sides to take.

The padded envelope, with its franked red exhortation, is obviously a communication from Sinclair's publishers, used for the second time. KEEP COLLINS INDEPENDENT. 'Colin's what?' I ad-libbed compulsively. Sinclair thinks I can't punctuate or spell, that my lips move when I read. I don't disillusion him. That's one of the least offensive of his fictions. This portrait of me as a genial drunkard (lowlifer, mutant, dabbler in the black arts) is all nonsense: a shorthand convenience. I'm no Jonsonian 'Humour', ready for my knockabout interlude when the narrative drive is flagging. But I go along with it. It leaves me free to pursue my own much fiercer self-interrogation. It's too comfortable to present ourselves through our flaws, to play them up, become clown, dupe, holy fool. Like a type in a medieval passion play, you finish by impersonating a single quality. 'The Man Who Stutters' or 'The Man with One Leg'. You are gulled into wearing a mask that somebody else has selected for you from the literary prop basket. You are the failure of another man's inspiration. I want to fail in a grander cause.

It amuses Sinclair, after three or four Russian stouts, to pretend to believe my name is really *Jobard*, the French for 'ninny', 'simpleton'. *Joblard (sic)* is how he has addressed the jiffy bag.

It might be a book. I'll have to open it. I'll risk a squeeze. At least, it won't be a bill. The electricity can't be cut off. We haven't got any. We live by the natural rhythms of the day. Even among all this chaos – *especially* among this chaos – everything is slow and calm. Dust motes spiralling in trumpets of sunlight. The persistent drip of water wearing away the basin. We are waiting on the unhurried dictation of an unborn child.

The large jiffy bag contains a smaller one, too small to hold a book. It is addressed to Sinclair in a hand I do not know. What could this second bag have contained? Sinclair has nothing but books. He eats books. He pays with books. He sleeps on them. He'd probably sleep *with* them if he could. He begets books. There's also a letter. I'll save the letter. One thing at a time. Heat more water in the pan. We still have gas – until the end of the month. Another filter paper, another mug of coffee. Getting weaker with each infusion: no more than an *aide-mémoire*, recalling the sensation of previous cups; and – by way of that sensation – the cluster of thoughts and images, the day dreams, floating to the surface as I sipped before, and as I sip now; my eyes firmly closed in creative indolence. Somewhere, there is half a Gozitan cigar to be found: marking my place in a notebook, shredded by the opening and closing of the hinges, perfuming the creamy paper with dark and oily resins.

I dig out the staples from the fat lip of the envelope – one by one, with a fork; lay them around the circumference of my plate. The hooped silver bones of a centipede. I study the arrangement. Pick up one of the staples and lick it. Uninteresting, flavourless. I shake the packet. Something wriggles out, falls reluctantly on to the table. This is much better, the colour is superb. A bruised purple, infected with carmine: that must have been the original state. Soutine's impasto. Colour that's hung on a hook until it's ready to declare itself. It shifts. It prevaricates. It broadcasts its history. Dies, regresses into a morbid, flagellant blue. A slate licker's punishment. I lift it on my fork, bring it close to my lips – as a rasher of dead veal. A grey corpse cut. Waggling. Six inches of meat fallen from a hanged man's mouth.

What am I dealing with, *exactly*? The pith of a skinned lizard? Too dark; too much blood in it. The tannin-dyed cock of a Tibetan priest, beaten out flat on a stone? I don't want to think of this sample as what it actually is, or was. Or what it is now intended to be. What does it want – *of me*? It's altogether less painful to stall, to speculate, construct post-Martian similes. The thing has been savagely divorced from its natural setting, the purse of wet meat, the talk box. A human tongue is, at the best of times, an obscenity. A naked muscle, slithering with bacteria-marinated mucus, food memories; its papillae travestying lime-white kettle fur. And this tongue has not been decently amputated; it has been torn, uprooted, ripped from the throat. It lies on the desk like a silent scream. As I poke it reflectively with the tines of my fork, it twitches. It persists: it has something to say. It is still eager to rap, to taste, to forewarn of pleasures as yet unrisked. Scorpic to the end, it arches to the touch. It spits defiance.

I swear this is not my affair. I don't know the tongue. The tongue does not know me. The smaller jiffy bag is clearly addressed to Sinclair (or 'St Clair', as they have it). It's his business, his mess. Now I will have to read his bloody letter. The usual see-through copier paper, crammed to the margins; but – this *is* rather remarkable – it's written in his own hand, his holograph. No typewriter. He must be serious. Desperate. He's cracking up. I'll throw the thing away. I'll try another coffee transfusion. Kill the taste of the water. The taste in my mouth.

II

Haggerston, 198–

Joblard:

a favour. You will by now have opened the mysterious package and performed your own autopsy on the small gift that arrived for me this morning, innocently lurking among the usual clutch of threats, begging letters, final demands – and poems written in red Biro on lined paper, postmarked HALIFAX, and emanating, without a doubt, from Hebden Bridge.

That's the time of day to live through. From then on it's a quiet slog to survival. I squeeze my heart back into my chest. I start to shake as I listen for the postman's footsteps. I'm crouched behind the door, sweating. I've been there for hours. All night? Possibly. I've forgotten what it was like to sleep in a bed. The rattle of the brass flap, the aggressive slither of envelopes cascading on to the mat, has become – for months now – something of an ordeal. My hands tremble. I can't decide whether to smash what's left of the furniture, or to break into tears. Often, I'm done in for the day. Another one gone, shot. Dealers are ruthless in setting up meetings, for which they never show. Poets? Poets are the worst. Don't *ever* get involved with poets. Stick with the pulp boys, the rippers and gougers. They're pussy cats. Edit the belly-bursters, the revolving head merchants. All delightful conversationalists. Poets? The sound of the word and my knuckles are turning white. They are rabid correspondents, openly psychotic, proud of it, proud of their galloping paranoia. They issue threats by the hour, polemics, circulars of hate. You take your life in your hands if you reply to one of their mad spiels. Carry heavy life insurance before you offer veiled criticism of a stanza. Reject one? You're dead. Accept one? Worse, they want to sit on your shoulder and watch you love every last syllable.

It's cruel. My creditors are pressing cheques on me, but they return like homing pigeons. Tax assessments, all different, all massive, double by the week; invoking punitive penalties. Publishers sue me for work I have no recollection of taking on. I've promised 'afterwords' for books that have not yet been written. I won't bore you with the domestic traumas: death, disease, cash-pleas. The usual lightweight stuff. I can *taste* madness, see it from the window. It would be a relief to let go, to gibber like all the other blanked cancellations; wander off down the middle of the road, looking for the right bone-crusher. So what's new? Nothing. There's just more of it. And my ability to climb out, to watch it happening, is going, going, gone. How long can I stave off the onset of stone craziness by the trick of writing about it?

By now you will certainly have smoked the second half of your mandrake root cigar, and you will have succumbed to another cup of coffee before turning, reluctantly, to my note. That's good. (Do you feel that you're playing a part in a spiked fiction? I used to. It was OK. When it's scriptless, that's much tougher.) The slippery hint you are poking around on your plate is not a subtle one; though, you might consider, not without its own bleak humour. Don't worry: I can identify the source of the tongue (ugh!) The pathology, with which we have been confronted, has been squeezed like tomato paste in a Mafia video. But I'm afraid it's more serious than that. The thinking behind this gesture is coolly pragmatic. In other words, they know exactly what they're doing.

'They?' you ask. *They.* Here we go. The old conspiracy circuit. Bear with me. Please. The object itself, the glossa, was stapled to a portion of card torn from a bookdealer's catalogue. There's a man I know in Upper Tooting who trades under the flag of convenience of 'Ferret Fantasy', and who habitually fills in any space left at the end of his price list with a few lines of domestic intelligence or biblio-banter; before, cordially, signing off. His name is Locke. The torn corner of lemon-coloured catalogue which formed the base for the uninviting open sandwich I received in the post had the single word, *Locke*, ringed in felt-tipped pen.

The dealer, of course, has nothing to do with this. A jest on their part. A warning against fantasy, tale-telling. The gathering of arcane information. Imaginative speculations of no concern to civilians.

I know now that my friend, the over-inquisitive anarchist, Davy Locke, was the one who did not make it off the Island. He fell among Doges. He was worried by dogs. You are looking at what is left of him. I wish (with my life) that he could be reconstructed from that blood porridge exclamation. I know also that from here on in, I'm mute: a stone. A pebble on the beach.

I spent a long week combing the bunkers and the waste-lot gardens before I found Imar O'Hagan, who accompanied us to the Island on that phantasmagoric adventure. He'd lost everything, except his enthusiasm. His hole in the ground had been mysteriously flooded and his flat burned out. He was fanning the ashes with court orders. The trays of frozen bats and snakes, the birds of prey were melting on the floor under a black and twisted fridge. Total extraction. Oral catastrophe. Pathetic lumps of flesh coal, feathers of tar. A death stink rising through the forensic acids. Imar's still crazy, still grinning. He's taking to the road. And he isn't coming back. He swears he's on the trail of an industrial tunnelling gimmick, pipes that eat their own way into the earth.

When he dropped in at the pub, the Old Duke of Cambridge, for a farewell drink, the night before I found him, the landlord had a package waiting under the bar – delivered by hand. Nothing for the studio. A pair of ears and a key, rusted with blood. The full matador's tribute! Imar was being offered some friendly advice concerning 'activities incompatible with his status' as marginal artist, and supplicant on the tolerance of society at large. Our delight in exploring and exploiting the anomalies and perversions of the secret culture (islands, docks, stations, airports, churches) had waned: it was, frankly, detumescent, limp as lettuce. Which brings me to the favour I want to ask.

My project, the grimoire of rivers and railways, is almost complete: its spiritual wellbeing is critical. I've gone over the top, invested too much. I'm sure it's very close to the end, but it lacks a final *tableau vivant*, a magical getout. The one that lets the narrator melt from the narration. Can we make our escape while the witnesses (the readers) weigh the plausibility of some tricksy conclusion? I can't carry on; or, rather, I can participate, provoke the action, but I cannot report it. For a whole dreary catalogue of reasons, this has become impossible. Anything I touch transforms itself into a fresh metaphor for pain and anguish, burns those around me, leaves me unharmed. I want to offer you the protection of the narrator's role: I want *you* to keep the record of our trip to Sheppey.

You know what this year has been like: a motor-neurone shuffle between surgical wards and crematoria, with the occasional day trip to the Magistrate's Court or a bookfair thrown in for good behaviour. Now the ultimate blow has fallen and my typewriter, a senile heavyweight I have nursed for months, indulging all its petty-minded eccentricities, has decided to go ape. It's had enough. It's sick of the depressive muck and filth it's been forced to process. I didn't get my story done in time. My rental with fate was revoked.

Apparently, nobody will touch a Silver-Reed. 'Pity it's not an IBM, John,' they mutter, backing off. 'Can't get the parts. Not worth bothering, mate. Only go wrong again in three months, then where are you? Know what I mean?'

Grimly, I started up Holloway Road (forty minutes at the wheel and five years beaten out of your ticker): to the place where I bought the thing. At least, they couldn't deny that *somebody* used them. They didn't have to. They had the perfect answer. The shop was gone. Decamped in the night, with all its booty of iffy keyboards and illicit phials of Tipp-Ex for primary-school sniffers. The site had been grabbed by yet another estate agent. They were staggering in with the palm trees, as I went for a death-or-glory U-turn.

Next, on a tar-bubbling, three-shirt day, to Roman Road. The good old Roman. You can trust the Roman. 'Bring 'er in,' they said on the phone, 'we'll take a look.' A blink was enough. I was bounced out of a side-door, a blanket over my head, like some terminal junkie, so far gone he hits the same chemist four times in a week with his pitifully forged paregoric script.

Finally, in raging despair, I tracked down a mechanic, hiding out in an attic off the Bethnal Green Road, who said he'd try *anything* for cash in hand. I'd have to schlep the monster up three flights of stairs. He couldn't collect it. His motor was temporarily 'off the road'. I explained (personally taking on all the guilt, as for a defective child) that every *W*, every *H* repeated incontinently, turning my camera-ready sheet into a duff concrete poem.

A fortnight later the repaired machine was back on my desk. Feverishly, I whacked out the first sentences of the twelfth (now never to be written) tale. And was returned a few random lines of gibberish. The keys I hammered bore no resemblance to the symbols that defaced my page. For example: my attempt at 'From this point, I'll write by hand' emerged as '*Fff- thjy jfjttf Jjuu yfjtt hy hftu.*' 'I'm going crazy' was spat back as '*Jf- -fjt uffty.*'

'That's it,' I said, and dropped the sick beast out of the window, narrowly missing next door's neutered and basking tom cat. The ex-machine, a set of fat steel dentures, grinned back at me as it fell: hit the stones, and exploded, sending a long repressed spiral of mania sawing through the overgrown weeds, the lovingly transplanted hart's-tongue ferns, the metal-green dust on unpicked raspberry warts.

But my conscience – stabbed by the loss of a companion who had, whatever her faults, carried me so far – left me twitching and sleepless. I crawled out of bed, crept into the garden, and humped the disembowelled veteran on to my shoulder: to jog through the streets to London Bridge Station.

'What crackpot therapy is this?' you ask. 'What primal agony fad?' (I know you lay the letter aside and walk across to the window to see if the pub has opened. It hasn't. Carry on.)

At five A.M. the early-morning punters were a heavy presence in the town. If they are not actually allowed to sleep at their consoles, they're panicky to get back to them before the sun rises – like vampires to their coffins. There might be a flicker in the overnight price of peanut butter. These mercury-complexioned sleepwalkers ignored me. Anyone demented enough to hoist a wrecked Silver-Reed must be coming from the dark ages. A head case. A money hater. Unlucky to see, dangerous to approach. I loped in a lather of self-celebrating masochism along Bishopsgate, past Leadenhall Market. I was in pursuit of a fugitive image from a television documentary about South American Indians, road runners, who chew coca leaves and race (God knows why) in dusty, marathon relays, trundling monster tree stumps.

The journey took two hours and involved three changes of train. (I had, by the way, chickened out of the notion of manhandling my burden *all* the way on foot. Life's too short for absolutes. This was an instant penance.) My first taste of Sheppey. We were halted for twenty minutes on the bridge over the Swale, no man's land, a limbo between the living and the living dead. Too much sky. Wide flat fields; maggoty sheep cropping the flame tongues of

blast furnaces. Something evil and mean had insinuated its way
into a minor Plantaganet tapestry: had poisoned the natural infu-
sions of time.

Later, in Sheerness, on the streets, I saw the inhabitants as
wraiths, doubles, fetches, tricksters. They were bloodless, secret-
ive. They were the humble dead going about their business. A
colony of the dead (like the end of Jim Thompson's novel, *The
Getaway*). They could not touch me. I wasn't there. My typewriter floated among them, a levitating soup tureen.

I buried it at low tide, with a vision of Southend (that fault-
cloned Miami) away across the water, rising from its archipelago
of untreated sewage. A bone-white jewel in a bisto sea. I ate a
lively breakfast (still squirming on the fork), and returned by the
first available train – taking care to work my way through a pack
of zany local history pamphlets. 'The Legend of the Grey Dolphin
Becomes Fact'. 'The Minster Miracles'. 'The Gatehouse Gallows'.
'Minster's Stonehenge'. 'Pagan Gods in Minster Abbey'.

I have to get out from under the burden of a narrative which
includes my request to be released from the burden of a narrative.
Which includes ... Even this letter is part of it; the mess, the
horror. The swamp that follows me around. And *your* response to
my letter, the way you are rubbing your chin with your thumb;
or the way – now – you are cleaning your spectacles with your
shirt-tails. You *will* do it. I know you will. A few pages, that's all.
It's a lot to ask, right? The barest report in any style you favour: a
pastiche of what has gone before, some off-the-wall neologisms to
catch the eye of Anthony Burgess. There is, I assure you, a measure
of safety in being the one who holds the pen. 'I' is the man in
possession, but *he* is also possessed, untouchable. 'I' is immortal.
The title of the survivor. There has always to be *one* witness to
legitimize a massacre. Aneirin at Catraeth. My best hope is to offer
you that role.

Don't you find the world is an increasingly mirthless hallucination? Fredrik Hanbury was waiting on the doorstep when I
arrived back from Sheerness. The *Guardian* had been on to him,
could he deliver a message? Did I dream about the Widow?
Would I care to describe those dreams in no more than two
hundred words? This whole book is a sleep of revenge. But the
logic is hers: the dreamlife of a woman who never sleeps. Isn't it
bad enough to be forced to share (to co-author) her bleak fantasies,
without having to talk about them to the *Guardian*? So this is their
latest shot: boredom. This is what they have come up with. To

hobble her. A perpetual-motion machine, a non-sleeper: a mantis that does not stop to pray.

But possibly, just possibly, at long last, the omens offer a favourable reading: the rats are gnawing through the skirting board. Can you hear it? A noise like a bonfire of banknotes, like newspaper being trampled underfoot, like the biting of lightbulbs. They've caught the first (unidentified) whiff of fear: salty, sweating, chill. The electroplated daemon of the air waves is beginning to tremble. The colour control is bending blue into scarlet: watch those pupils flare to bubbles of blood! It's putting a blush of shame among the radiant silver scales. Why do they talk about 'the Widow's Britain'? It should be 'Britain's Widow'. We made her in our own image. She is the worst of us. But once the masses (we, you, all) sense they've been conned into worshipping nothing better than the synthesis (stolen hate sleep, stains, tabloid news smear) of their defects, it's over. They'll tear her to pieces like a rag doll.

The trouble is I will have to go down with this particular ship. I've hooked my credibility on to a pantomime of horror. I've exploited the darkest of times for comic routines that only flatter and fatten the monster: give it a tongue job. All any self-respecting demonic entity needs is attention: criticism, vilification, and ridicule are its life-blood.

I feel utterly submerged and powerless. There is no interest anywhere in texts written under my own name, but I've had an offer I can't refuse to knock out a sequel to William Hope Hodgson's *The House on the Borderland*. The fact that the book winds up with the end of the Universe (Multiverse!) – time, life, hope (all those fat magazines) – is a mere detail. I can grasp it. I see a small career opportunity in necrovestism: impersonating the dead, spook-speaking. There's a definite gap in the market. All I have to do is forget who I am. To snip the memory connections. Is *that* a problem?

The TV film at Tilbury was, so I hear, something of a disaster. That's what Dryfeld tells me. And he didn't even watch it. That's what the boys on the street tell him. Yentob rang from his limo on the way home to congratulate the producer, dynastic son of some cardinal of comedy, for sponsoring such a sharp spoof on the *avant-garde*. He's convinced, despite rumours to the contrary, that I'm a figment of Patrick Wright's imagination. Some arcane, *London Review of Books*-type joke. He doesn't see the point, but he'll back his minions all the way. I return the compliment.

Yentob? You can't be serious. The name has to be some sort of anagram gimmick. Zen Yob, Yob Tab. Whatever.

So that's about the size of it. Either *you* (S. L. Joblard) become 'I', or the story ends here. In petulant recrimination. I & I can only wish you luck.

Sincerely, *S*

III

Is Sinclair completely gonzo? Has he screwed himself so deeply into his paranoid fantasies that he's imploded in a shatter of mutating icons. Does he *mean* it?

I don't, of course, have to accept his spiked commission. Why should I strap myself to this improbable fictional double? Sinclair has exploited – exclusively – the burlesque aspects of the role I have performed to gain acceptance in the world; and now he wants me to collude in this cheap trickery (this dreary post-modernist fraud) by writing as if I truly were that person he has chosen to exploit. My first difficulty. Which I intend sharply to counter by writing my account of the Sheppey journey as if he were imagining me writing it. In other words, I will write *my version* of him writing as me.

That's fine as far as it goes. But there is also a much richer deposit, a territory I can reach by using this 'fixed' expedition as a cover. I have been dogged for years, from as far back as I care to remember, by the impulse to return to a place where I have never been: to Sheppey, an imaginary and an actual island. Sometimes the shore shines, and is bright with miraculous potentialities. Sometimes it is the manifestation of all my most secret fears.

It has been comfortable, and it still seems true, to remember my childhood as a series of rooms, buildings that no longer exist, streets that have been erased. I have not made any of this up. But these places, worn grooves, are no more real than what remains. They cannot be verified. They've gone. They breathed – as in a page of prose by Arthur Morrison. I 'narrate' my childhood by the simple act of thinking about it. The tones become warmer, more conversational; golden-brown at the edges. I walk to school. Wood shavings and strong glue. The furniture factory. Juvenile gangs roaming the baked mud banks of the Surrey canal with slingshots and air pistols.

Myself in photographs: a serious stranger, awkward in shorts and National Health spectacles. The expression the child has is the terror of what he will become. This solid ghost in the grey garden, caught among relatives, is older than I am. The boy stares back at his future self, a pretender, fondling the bent photograph in his huge, acid-scorched hands.

I am walking alongside my dad to East Street Market. Tired fruit. Linoleum. Sunday roast. The war? India. Visits to museums, as to cathedrals of a disestablished religion. We are the last of our kind. Nose pressed against the cold window of the bus. Smooth chin rubbing the greasy silver rail.

There was nothing missing in this sketch. I felt no absence, no shortfall. I did not need to know who – or what – my blood parents were. If the woman who gave birth to me came, once upon a time, from Sheerness ... let that remain a curious, but unurgent fact. Relegate it to the margin. My mother might have been a day-tripper. She might, just as well, have stepped ashore from Whitby or Aberdeen, Hamburg or Tromso. I did not need to act on the little I knew. To plunge into some corny *Citizen Kane* quest. I'm not propositioning a mini-saga.

I have never felt half-born, unfinished – though I suppose, considering it, that is precisely my state. Incomplete. An old soul, unconnected to the embarrassing accident of parentage: the spasm in the car park, the shudder on the shingle. There is an exhilarating sense of freedom (of risk) in the absence of this banal information: my father's father's father, rising and falling fortunes, a sentimental procession. I hate those novels that begin with grandfather catching a glimpse of grandmother at some bucolic hop. Who cares? They are imposters. Why are they dressed like children? They have nothing to do with the case. They insist on telling us things we do not need to know. The orphan is special; touched, chosen. He can be useful. He completes, for some otherwise unsatisfied couple, the illusion of a family. He gives form to something that is missing. He is desired, but without obligation. He can become whatever he wants to become: warrior, coward, poisoner, priest. He is without guilt. He can even refuse to join the game at all. He can lock himself away; troubled, shivering, never quite in focus.

The chance has come to return to this shunned island, and I will take it, only because ... *it is no longer my story.* But this time you *have* to accept my version: I am the sole recorder. Sinclair is pursuing the trail I have laid for him. His brute persistence is extraordinary – but predictable. He simply cannot resist my casually deployed hints. He has no independent imagination. No capacity for invention. He recognizes. He begs me to do the thing which can only be attempted in this very peculiar context. It's a one-off. It is written. It *must* be. I am writing it. I am scratching away at a tablet of slimy slate to recover what I always knew was there: the text I have yet to formulate.

My life had entered a new seven-year cycle. A lot of clutter, human and otherwise, had been left behind. I was beginning to realize it was not quite as simple as that: I would soon have to accumulate some more. We are defined by our possessions – even when they are invisible. But I felt confident the years of physical lumber (things, memory-hooks) were done with for ever.

I could risk suspending my absolute faith in my own instincts, my treaty with the irrational. Let the past, if it would, do its worst. Let it bury its claws in my heart. If we will not listen to the babble of the dead, how can we defend ourselves against the tragic inquisitions of our children?

I was quite ready to cut loose from my oldest fears, the ones I had fondled so affectionately that they became a kind of masturbatory totem: vagrancy, Whitechapel, alcoholic despair. He has gone, he's faded, split: the projected figure in the solitary dosser's room, clutching a tattered photograph of the son from whom he is helplessly parted. Tears running down his grizzled cheeks into a salty beard. *Bollocks!* I wasn't going to play the Blind Beggar of Bethnal Green to satisfy anybody's mythology.

My early separation, from the couple whose far-reaching instant of pleasure *got* me, was neither an accident, nor an act of deliberate carelessness. Why make more of it? It had no deeper significance than my childhood in an unspecified district of South London, my temporary tenancy of an unfrocked synagogue. The only necessity is to stay sharp, stay open, refuse nothing. I was determined neither to remain a prisoner of some fantastical version of my past, nor to dodge the suspect, stomach-churning advances of my future.

Interrupted by some marginal irritation, I broke from my meditation. I *wanted* a way out. It was boring; it was boring me, I almost understood what I was trying to say. This other voice was in the room: one of those snatches of TV dialogue from the supermarket below that come – with selective hindsight – to take on a prophetic *gestalt*. In truth, they are meaningless: sound pebbles. Monkeys hammering out, if not the plays of Shakespeare, the plays of Joe Orton. Eavesdropping on the eavesdropper. TV is an endless loop of self-cannibalizing drivel into which we can dive to discover anything we want, any soundbite applicable to our purposes. I'd seen the film before, a deathwatch special: Frank Capra's *The Bitter Tea of General Yen*.

'*Orphans! What are they anyway? People without ancestors, nobodies!*'

I dug out my heaviest boots from a rubbish sack. I filled my tobacco pouch. I found the milk money. I put on my smoked glasses and folded half a dozen clean white handkerchiefs into my breast pocket. I was ready for the assaults of pollen. I was ready for Sinclair. I was ready for anything.

IV

'Much that lies dead in us is alive on an island of voices'

Douglas Oliver, *An Island that is All the World*

The first time on the island was a mistake. It came back to me as I plodded through the tunnel between the ticket barrier and the platform at London Bridge, I *had* been here, once before. In the train, years ago, basted in some unclarified domestic estrangement, I never noticed the crossing of the Swale. It was one of those spur-of-the-moment trips that attempt in their mimed spontaneity to lift a chronic depression, but which succeed only in confirming it, focusing it on an innocent location that is, for all time, cursed and banished from the memory.

We jumped out at the first halt, Queensborough. Anything was better than the train; trapped in each other's company, with nothing left to confess. The shadow of blast furnaces, smoking stacks, migraine hammers: black air. I choked for breath. The sea was hidden. We skulked around a few mean streets, not knowing what we were looking for, nor why we had bothered. I glanced, with dread, at derelicts, dribblers, dwarfish vacancies – there were plenty to choose from (the authorities culled anyone over five feet) – as if any of these gimps should touch me, my father. A man ruined by a single heated spasm, an alien penetration: one bliss shot. The jest soured. My wife flogged it, relentlessly. I felt no fellowship with these stunted, lightless zombies. These grey-necked turkey peckers. Who refused to cross the water.

We took the first train back; I buried the horrors of that afternoon beyond harm's reach – where they stayed, sleepers, until this moment.

Now on a damp fresh, late June morning, there was a much more seductive (washed-over) edge to the town. Sheerness, a mile or so down the tracks from Queensborough, is another world. I sat in the grease caff and waited for Sinclair. I had armed myself with a notebook and the full breakfast. Which was superb: a karmic trembler swimming in bacon juices, pig sweat, pressed tomatoes, root gristle, salt-caked pressings of blood, essences of panic. I savoured, at my leisure, a heady blend of greed and guilt. I suicided, slowly. I licked the platter with bestial relish. (Is *that* close to the way he would see it?) Then I unfolded and reread Sinclair's latest note, while I punished myself with a second cup of sweet-sick coffee. He was precise: *Rendezvous, 7 A.M.* He would be here. For a man who never seemed to know what century he was living in, he was a disciplined fetishist when it came to the niceties of time. He could never bear to be late for an appointment of his own making.

I looked up at the brass ship's clock, bolted to the wall above the proprietor's smirking portrait: a sad self, twenty years younger, with the same criminal bow tie. Bottom-of-the-bill ventriloquist, professional child molester. The hands jerked obstinately towards the fatal hour. Sinclair sat down opposite me. He toted the inevitable camera.

There has been a distinct, a difficult to describe sea-change in these last months. I'd be guessing, but I believe that after his father's death he absorbed, or took on board, a share of the old man's qualities. An immediate laying on of hands. They want you to look hard into the open coffin. It's part of the ceremony. Something comes across that was not around before: a sense of calm, of slowing down? Ironic observation? But this is coupled with an acceleration in the fever of his old obsessions: desperate not to let time go, sand running helplessly through his fingers. He knows he's the next man on the springboard.

Physically, he's not much changed. A flannelled Lord Longford: on sulphate. His scalp gleams, wrinkles in a secondary grin above a crown of shocked wool. Tipp-Exed couch grass tufts out of every available fissure: he looks like a fire-bombed sofa. His deep-set eyes, bloody with concentration, roll alarmingly, in contrary directions, as he tries to relate anything to everything. And back again. His abrupt movements threaten the crockery. The other gourmets rush to the bar, fling down their coins, and escape. Blunt (socially inept) colours come and go, using his cheeks as a transit lounge. His temples are bruised, hollowed, marked by the forceps that dragged him into the world. He twitches, undergoing – at irregular intervals – pulses of electroconvulsive therapy. His skull's too heavy, surfacing slowly from the dredge of sympathetic autism. He's moody, submerged; longing to spittle his victims with the dubious wisdom of an idiot. Self-condemned. Speechless.

Has he walked here? Or have they fished him out of the river? He's mute. Stone dumb. He explained in the letter. It's not a zen challenge, a spiritual discipline, nor even a protest against the moral turpitude of the nation. (He did float some bravado subtext about considering his book a failure if the Widow clung on to power one year after its publication; but this was, I assume, a joke of sorts.) No: he is simply, at this time, unable to speak. He can't do it. A condition of benevolent trauma, post-operative shock. It doesn't matter. It might make things easier. He knows where to go, and what he is after. He's searching for those curious, unique details that confirm his hunch, and lend a superficial credibility to our version of the Quest. The details that boast: we were there, we did it.

I'm not sure why I'm here. (If I was, I wouldn't be.) I feared the worst: that the whole island was a taint, just another riverside wilderness, and that the 'mysteries' (such as they are) of my birth would be an arbitrarily imposed fiction. But already we have gone too far for that. This time it's real. Fiction would have copped out with Sinclair's letter. Fiction would have said, 'Pull the other one. Send on the heavies. Where's the flesh interest? The suspense? What's the hook?' Sinclair has brought me to a place from which we cannot both return. And I have the whiphand, I'm the narrator. I think he wants me to kill him.

He rises without warning, and I follow him out. We strike towards the shore, passing through the skeleton traces of a Jurassic pleasure park, an insurance write-off. We fall rapidly into our invariable order of battle. We have tramped the chalk from Winchester to Salisbury, and on – via the UFO-haunted declivities of Warminster – to the serpentine water levels of Glastonbury. We have bumbled over the Black Mountains in wet mist, seeking out bogus abbeys or remote pulpits where Giraldus Cambrensis preached the Third Crusade. We have cruised the South Downs on Blakean awaydays, and crawled on our hands and knees over the sharpened limestone combs of Gower. The routine never changes. He strides ahead: I plod, drawn into the vortex, stumbling, blistered, taking the time to observe the land across which we scorch our skid-tracks. I poke among pebbles, gather the bones of sheep.

He told me once that his solitary walks were a rehearsal for eternity. He's practising, getting warmed up, finding his rhythm. He's certain he'll be walking for ever through a blasted landscape, a smoking lava desert. Humping a knapsack, the weight of a four-year-old child. I think he's looking forward to it.

The Sheppey sky is low, moulting, shifty. Container ships wait on the tide, hobbled and without enthusiasm. The water is glass-green, unusually clear. Sheerness responds to my mood. Its rain-washed roofs glisten and gleam. Despite myself, I am drawn to the place: solid marine architecture, gracefully proportioned Victorian pubs on the corners of terraced streets. The best day of the summer. The first pint you drank. The dizzy search for a wall to piss against. Tame fields are floating behind the houses. I hang out my tongue to taste the clean bright air. Movement is luxury. The town streams back in a sequence of painted, emblematic banners. Red walls. Salt-dulled brass. Bow windows, weather-smudged, opaque. The angular frame of a missing child's black swing, with chains and seat never replaced. And as a constant, keeping company with us, the short steep beach. Its shells and stones have been scrubbed by a fierce tide, polished, individually nominated. The beach is numbered like a geological chart. An illustration. The dominant colour is a fugitive pink: pubic coral. Fragments, sea-brick, corners of Dutch tile – sharp enough to perform a mastectomy. I imagine a table laid with these strange, tide-scoured china rejects: half a cup, the open mouth of a blue saucer, the handle from a soup tureen (like a porcelain moustache). A dozen separate shards go into the construction of a meat dish. I picture the compressed cubist family who might have partaken of this fractured feast. The single yellow (dog) eye of the father. Grandma's chocolate-crusted teeth. Mother's smoothly pumiced shoulder. The two fat white hands of the alabaster child, gripping the unsupported bar of a lipstick chair.

Sinclair has, I suspect, already identified this stone slide as the section of beach where Robert de Shurland's mythic horse, Grey Dolphin, swam ashore after they had both battled more than a mile out to sea, to reach the king's ship. Seeing the rogue knight as the survivor of a trial by ordeal, Edward II offered him a pardon for his capital crimes of treason and heresy. Robert stood accused of killing a priest, by burying him alive in the open grave of an unknown sailor recovered from the channel. Dragging himself ashore in triumph, Shurland met a demented woman, weird or devil-possessed, who warned that the horse would be the death of him. Robert slaughtered the beast, and covered him with shingle. Years later the knight, walking in penance along the circuit of the island, pierced his foot on a needle of bone from Grey Dolphin's skull, and – dying – fulfilled the prophecy. That's the gimmick, that's how it works. Death is like stabbing your finger at random into an open book. It's an anthology of doom quotes, waiting to be justified.

My pockets are bulging with pebbles. I feel like Monty Druitt; an over-obliging Masonic sacrifice, a voluntary redundancy from a Suicide Partnership. I can't resist the unique quality of these stones: the colours they have drained from sky and sea. Alchemical essences. I fondle them. I weigh them in my hand: eggs. I sniff. I lick. I listen for the pulse of life. I have also to carry away a lump of rusted iron in the shape of a pike's head: a flaking battle helmet, a shamanistic blood-tool out of John Bellany. I arm myself against ease. The weighted awkwardness rubs against my thigh, chaffs at every step; satisfying my demand for discomfort. The hair shirt that wards off annihilation.

We leave the shore and Sinclair begins to open out his stride pattern. I thought at first that he was limping. No such luck. There is some peculiar hereditary disease lurking among the males of his family, some cold-water Jacobite slash of guilt, some inbred sinew-eating fetish, cargo-culted from the tropics: a sex wound. He is waiting impatiently for it to announce itself. While he can walk on his heels, he is safe. He does not fear the arrival of this flaw. He has convinced himself it is an honourable one. But now, as we climb through all the seafront development scams that died in the mixer, he decides to put his weakness to the test. He increases his pace to a steeplechaser's lope. He seems to feel personally responsible for all this speculative dross.

The exotic bungalows are obviously staging posts en route to the Costa del Crime. Somewhere to wait for that dream plot you have reserved within barking distance of Ronnie Knight and the Hoxton Mob. Florid inventions: customized with picture windows, Moorish arches, car ports, security cameras, fretwork signatures. Salvador Dali retirement homes for poodles. They boast a cabin cruiser on every lawn; hooded in tarpaulin, like a bullion stash. Rest and recreation for bent security guards, long firm operatives, video pirates. The only visible occupants are hungover designer dogs, tanned and lacquered like cocktail sausages.

As we suffer the steady pull of the gradient between Scrapsgate and the Minster, it is clear that the flog-a-gaff clusters have been confined to the lowlying swamplands: a ghetto of carrier-bag cash, the actual stuff, the grubby fifties. Now, uphill, the stained-glass arcady of sunrise suburbia mixes unself-consciously with captured farmhouses. We are cutting through social and temporal distinctions as precise as geological strata. My blisters are the size of spring onions. The worse my surroundings, the more I suffer. Perhaps Sinclair senses this; he pauses. There is a heart-stopping vision, back down a tributary street, to the sea. One of the container ships is floating into the liquefied sky, a signature, an ephemeral plague transport. Cloud under it, and cloud above. Masts have grown from the telegraph poles. A portent, a death ship; a black galleon moving, with the inevitability of a Jamesian paragraph, into a darkened stadium of rainclouds.

One curious thing: the condition of my feet deteriorates catastrophically but my spirits, perversely, rise. I am sufficiently uncomfortable to encroach upon the borders of ecstasy. Move over St John of the Cross, I'm levitating. This is a homecoming. I cannot walk, I can hardly crawl; I slide, weightlessly, over hedges and neat envelopes of lawn. The long bend at the crest of the hill — before we turn to the business of the Minster and the Abbey — shelters a cottage hospital. We have to investigate. My mother was a nurse. This is (what's left of it) the only hospital on the island. So much I know. I have never before wanted to push matters any further. To any revelation.

Dead on cue, Special Effects sends a raft of rain in from the sea to blind us. Soft, persistent; streaming. We were soon drenched to the bone: a slow soak, layer by layer, through jackets, undershirts, trousers, pants, socks. Garments, dulled by familiarity, clung in a promiscuous embrace; a new skin, a hybrid of cold rubber and wet fleece. We steamed where we stood: a pair of drunks, not sure whose leg it was we had just pissed down. But the discovery (the hillcamp) was worth it.

From the street the hospital was unexceptional, a white-flag victim of the cuts in the health service. Empty offices flickered with faulty, epilepsy-inducing light tubes. Everything portable had been wheeled away to the nearest junk dealer. We were not discouraged. We penetrated the standard semiotic confusion of contradictory notices, warning the radically infirm, the malingerers, to seek help elsewhere. Treatment was off. Wounds would have to be self-stapled, while traumatized casualties swam to the mainland. Impressive boards listed all the services that the hospital did *not* operate. Temporary wartime huts offered the reward of physiotherapy to anyone fit enough to reach them: without the effete assistance of a discontinued bus service.

Beyond all these mist-shrouded props, we found it: the site we did not know, until now, that we were searching for. The enclosed garden. It was overlooked by an ivy-contaminated tower that rose from the main barrack block of the hospital. But it remained hidden in an overgrown hedge of thorns. Its shape was a bruised oval; a drained swimming pool, innocent of flowering plants and frivolous decoration. I was gripped by an excitement that scarcely related to the modest attributes of this exhausted patch. I led the way down a dim tunnel of arched and dripping greenery, and in through the concealed gateway.

I don't know what I expected to find. This was a place defined largely by what it lacked: twisted stirrups of iron suggested that something had recently been torn from the ground, which was gouged and ripped in the struggle. The purpose of the garden was to provoke images of absence, elimination. The people, the plants, the objects that had gone. How should we read the scars? Orthopaedic benches? Meditation platforms for the terminally ill? Floats for the performance of death chants? Classical statuary? Hothouses? Furnaces? The primitive chapel of a fever sect?

Then I noticed the gravestones, and my madness had a focus. This was so much the scene I should have expected that I was shocked; shamed, gobstruck. It was quite unreal. In the fictional twin of this event, which was playing simultaneously in my mind (as Sinclair intended it should), I would now uncover a startling and significant secret. My mother's name, or some other scrap of family history, would be chiselled on to one of these fire-blackened, moulting placards.

I leant forward to examine the weathered markings on the ring of a recumbent stone figure. The hand moved. It clawed at my throat. 'I knew that one day you would come. Now I can die in peace. Kiss me, son.' The old gardener sat up, reaching out his arms. The disgraced surgeon who had stayed on, anonymously, to tend this bleak sanctuary.

That would be the conventional ending. The curtain call. The bullshit. I laughed aloud at the inadequacy of my invention. I'm no Edgar Poe. I can't stack the adjectives like H. P. Lovecraft. There was nothing, nobody. No message. A graveyard had been cleared, tidied away, to create this lachrymose and unvisited park. The bones of the dead must have gone into some communal pit. The larger memorial slabs rested – a convocation of umbrellas – against the thorn hedge. Lichen invaded the powdery whiteness, the death cosmetic. I stared hopelessly at forgotten names. Nothing. Let them go. I smiled at the discovery of a 'Julius Caesar', whose pretensions ended here, smothered in poison ivy.

I moved from stone to stone, running my fingers into the trenches of meaningless letters, tracing the words, mouthing them like a convict with reading difficulties. The quest could have ended on the instant. I had no urge to continue. I was ready to join the stones. The trenchcoat I had bought in Holland, a respectable field-green, was transformed by the remorseless panels of soft, seafret rain. It petrified. It was spotted, blotched, soaked with grey earth: flecked like an apple leprosy. I was drip-fed on stone. Meltwater ran down the channels of my spine.

Why didn't the bodies float out from their pit, logs of leather? The rain was here to stay. It was apocalyptic rain. Washing the gravestones clean. They were propped open, a Book of the Dead. Stone pages. The language was impenetrable; it meant nothing.

Lights burnt in the hospital tower. Birth. The knife. I forced myself back into the pain of my raw heels. I rubbed them, with steely purpose, against my stiff new boots. I provoked the pain to answer me: my only oracle. I was insanely determined to find endorsement in this drowned field. Or to die in the attempt. I had no idea how much further we had to walk. This was one of the great moments of my life. A true epiphany, without hope of reward.

Sinclair (of course) has his camera out. Poking it in my face. Hoping that some meaning he can subvert will be returned to him in a flat packet from the chemist's shop. He knows there are spots of rain on the lens, which he hopes – by an act of faith – to add to the truth of what he has captured. He shadows my movements, watching and frowning as I open myself to the experience: he exploits, annotates, measures, anticipates the final stages of the journey. There is never anything he needs to find: another one, one more, a new sentence.

I had been wrong for so many years, living under an inhibiting illusion. *I* was not the orphan. My father might be anywhere. Here. From this damp hilltop, I felt his breath of freedom: the space, the scraggy fields running down to an ordinary sea. I felt his life: voyager at Sheerness, surgeon, mechanic, porter, imbecile – it didn't matter. I was charged with a liberating rush of irresponsibility and courage. I could not be condemned to repeat a life that had never happened. What I had of my mother was her youth. And that lives on, that is what I retain. A girl of twenty-two walking towards the Court, arm in arm with her own mother, both dressed for a day in town. Now I was able to accept the image related to me as a family fable. I remembered (without seeing) the movement of it; lurching and knowing and wanting. An infant on my adopted mother's shoulder, carried to the chamber where our relationship would be formalized. I was looking back, grinning – as in recognition. The involuntary exercise of my lips later interpreted as a smile. 'He saw his real mother and he blessed her.' In her youth. Then. She is fixed. I will leave her, leaving nothing; losing nothing, holding on to that strength. The blessing of a *double* parentage, of blood and of habit. The habit of love. Years of trust bringing me back, returning me to a new beginning.

But my loss has to be exchanged: the wet green stones become mirrors of transformation. Sinclair (the watcher) is the true orphan. His father dead – and his mother, apparently, detached into a mental realm to which he is denied all access. A dream country where the landscape of childhood is trespassed by a son who is older than her father; a place where unavoidable damage occurs, heals, readies itself to strike once more. Familiar gardens are made awkward by the presence of a one-legged dog. There are afternoon encounters with condescending royalty. 'I'm so glad to hear that your son is having some success at last, Mrs Sinclair,' said the Queen Mother. 'We all follow his career with the greatest interest.'

It is clear. *He* is the solitary. A deep black pool has spread out between himself and his ancestors. They are benevolent, remote; but they no longer see him. He does not interest them. He is alone. And yet – at the same time – because he led me here, my own sense of family and belonging is so intense that I can turn on my heel, walk away, and never again need to look back.

V

The vicar who had posted in the porch his 'Seven Reasons Why Women Should Not be Ordained as Priests' simply did not notice us.

He cannoned into me, and recoiled with a leap of undisguised horror. The notion of anyone wanting to poke about in the building before banking hours was abhorrent to him. As always, the Church Commissioners had appointed a Harvard Business School jock to neutralize a site that could, however remotely, be connected to folk memories of ritual and mystery. Medieval shrines are invariably guarded by an unenthusiastic dogma; a plodding sense of responsibility towards the world at large, and nowhere in particular. The further Synod can remove their prayer-negotiable problem from any sanctified enclosure, the deeper their concern. Ethiopia, Mexico City? Always worth a poster. The church is a multinational octopus in the process of rationalizing UK branches that refuse to pay their own way. Our hypermetropic iconoclast obviously loathed every last legend-infested stone of his inefficiently designed and expensively lit workspace.

I sat on a chair near the De Shurland tomb to excavate my feet, plaster over the showier blisters. It was difficult to adjust to this concentrated atmosphere. The light was dust. The church itself an ivory sepulchre. I steamed like a gun-dog brought in from the marshes. Shurland ignored me. He had worse problems to consider. He lay on his side, back to the world; his legs twisted in the rigours of an attack of acute appendicitis. He offered his cheesy skirts to the penknives of amateur calligraphers. At his feet, well within kicking distance, was the mantic skull of Grey Dolphin: his death, his familiar.

This was certainly a curious object, uncontoured by generations of hot hands – like the buttocks of a much-loved public lady. The relic had been fondled into a high-definition sheen: irradiated. It could have served as a lantern for primitive amputations. It gave off a talkative, smoky-grey light which had the capability of penetrating flesh and all of its shadows. But it was mutilated. The spiked ears were gone: enforcing silence, releasing other attributes. The long skull was a bandaged hammer. It reminded me of something I once made, based on a study of Siberian horse sacrifices: but which had subsequently disappeared. And was therefore a special favourite. The Minster carving looked more like a sick crocodile than a horse. A crocodile imagined by someone who had only read of such creatures. A blind craftsman working from distantly relayed messages must have made it. A mail-order croc. The rictus of its fat-lipped mouth had been most unnaturally extended by the Swiss Army knives of boy scouts, frustrated by an annoying scarcity of stones in the hoof. This was a talking horse; a wiseacre, bridled into silence. If I gazed long enough at the skull I would find myself stuck with transcribing and interpreting its miserable monologue. (I knew it would sound like a choric wail of poets, blathering about the Arts Council, the metropolitan critical nexus, the iniquity of publishers' readers.) I avoided the dead eyes; pebbles hammered into sockets too tight to hold them. The head was spooked, triggered. It was open for consultation.

Worse was to follow. I glanced from my exposed and swollen foot to the leering equine skull: the connection was unavoidable. There was a close family resemblance. My foot, neatly severed and dipped in plaster of Paris, could stand in – sorry! – for Grey Dolphin, when he takes a sabbatical to roam the shingle. And there is something else: the wretched *caput* is a three-dimensional map of the Isle of Sheppey. The split of the mouth is the Long Reach of the Swale. The right eye is the hill of Minster. The left eye, distorted by the angle from which I view it, marks the still sacred church of St Thomas the Apostle at Harty; once a separate island. And now the last refuge of the light. A blinding flash from Sinclair's camera scorches the dim recess. The skull winks.

I'm catching his madness. I'm starting to believe what I see; or – more accurately – I'm starting to see what I believe. The three-dimensional map is a conceit. The head is no more than a topographical model of what the island *should* be. A model to which every pilgrim has contributed by scratching his rune into the chill flesh, or cutting his initials into a ploughed field. Mutilate the horse's stone skull and you mutilate the living earth. The land is forbidden to respond.

Sinclair is lurking behind me, somewhere in the shadows. I am articulating *his* vision: that is the effect of his silence. I am *forced* to remember another map, so detailed we could have dug it out of the ground and used it for navigation.

It was the first anniversary of the planting of the eucalyptus tree in memory of the Aboriginal cricketer, King Cole. Sinclair insisted on dragging me all the way along the line of the railway track from Shoreditch to Meath Gardens, dodging among industrial properties, schoolyards, gaunt estates: we held firm to our elevated ladder of sparks, as to a great tribal river, an uncompleted folk song. I told him it was pointless. We were wasting time better spent in the Roebuck. The tree would be uprooted, torn to ribbons, scattered to the winds. This did not matter to him. Once he had adopted ('written in') a site, he was bound, in honour, to revisit it: that site had become a repository of meaning, a place of consultation. A blood relative.

A soft rain was falling as we passed under the arch and into the old burial ground. Strange atmosphere. The earth furrowed, twisted, shaken; lashed by some trapped dream-demon. (A caterpillar released from physical laws? A lizard quicker than light?) This slowing of time gave a momentary illusion of calm, soon replaced by a genuine fear of vast serpentine energies held in reserve.

Sinclair felt that we had been readmitted to the day of the original ceremony. Which itself rehearsed earlier ceremonies. Respected future acknowledgements. The trees were a dominant gathering, a parliament of presences: shaped, trained, set free to find their own forms. They ventriloquized the wind. Malign cartoon spirits shuddered among the agitated leaf scales. A priapic mouse-head was grafted on to the torso of a bear.

And I was, as usual, quite wrong. The eucalyptus survived. But the plaque, which Sinclair told me had been screwed into a wooden block beneath the tree, had vanished. He showed me the photograph when we went back to his house: 'In memory of King Cole, Aboriginal cricketer, who died on the 24th June 1868.' This might be the only surviving record; slightly out of focus, the pious blessing lost in dreamtime. No casual stroller will know the origin or meaning of this alien tree. The park itself is remote, shunned, hidden behind the mean energies of Roman Road.

The theft of the plaque had caused a dark stain to form in the varnished pine; the now untitled volume. A distinct shape was caught within a rectangle of screw-holes: the outline of the Isle of Sheppey, every creek and headland. (Sinclair had photographed this too. And set the Ordnance Survey 178 version, successfully, inside it.) King Cole, whose fate was obscure, whose legend was nailed to this place, was free once more. His dream had published a tobacco-spit path, and our walk would attempt to complete (retrace) its circuit.

I had to break out of this trap. Turn away from the sick magnetism of the De Shurland tomb and the knight's spear, which ran along the edge of it: an object I coveted above all others. This was the weapon I had never yet forged to my own satisfaction. Its soiled, putty-coloured mantle had been rubbed away, enamel from a dead molar, revealing a stick of black tar: iron within stone, a liquid vein. With the wounded lance, Robert had worried the margins of the sea, asserting his rights of salvage; stamping (on Grey Dolphin) through all the treacherous shallows. I saw the heated metal hissing in cold winter tides, turning the feudal ocean to a lake of fire. The sleeping knight had turned away from this ritual implement, which was also his spine, his staff of memory: he twisted in agonized slumber. But the challenge was explicit: to drag the spear from the lid of the tomb and bring down the shamed building. Reduce it to rubble. I was not ready. Not this time. I censored the impulse, and moved across the body of the church to admire its lesser curiosities.

The parson trusted us with the key to the side-door, while he stepped through the garden to the vicarage for a late breakfast. This was a symbol of power, too large for any pocket. Sinclair held it in his hand like a policeman's torch. The parson had pointedly switched off all the church lights, except the one above the table of souvenir mugs and dishcloths, the postcards and collecting boxes. We drifted without shadows, ghosts among the sepulchres. Craftsmen had laboured long to hold the Minster notables within their deep plaster trunks, confounding them in an excess of heraldic detail. We became the nightmare inflicted on the noble dead. We were the future horror tormenting their slumber. The revenging peasants, the pilgrimage of lunatics.

The effigy of the supposed Duke of Clarence has been devoured beyond recognition by the spirochaetes of time. He is chiselled out of rancid wax. He exploited the privilege of blood to nominate his method of execution. And was drowned in a butt of Malmsey wine. 'So far so good,' he thought, sampling the first sweet quarts. But 126 gallons is a long pull for the thirstiest toper. He surely came to regret the sugar-retching sickliness of his chosen vintage, and longed for the dry bite of a Canary sack.

Now Clarence floats over a stone tank that contains all his brown body liquor: a subtle blend of blood and wine in constant and heretical transubstantiation. High-collared, sour in breath, he waits to be released by some brave spirit who summons up the courage to tap the flood, and drink.

Hidden in an eclipsed alcove, beyond Clarence, is another knight; excommunicated among the reserve collection of loose and nameless rubble: broken stone tusks, tiles, calcified toads. This sleeper frames, between praying hands, a carved scarab, a stone mirror, on which it is just possible to identify a shrunken version of himself: a miniature (*shabti*) to share his experience of decay. I lean over, letting my breath moisten the cold skin. I strain to interpret the blunted detail. I notice that the homuncular double is also holding, between *his* praying hands, a scarab; on which − I have to accept − there is another knight. And another knight. And another. And another.

The trap has been baited, and sprung. The watcher is telescoped backwards through an infinite progression of fears. Oval cards click in a reductive tarot. My features lose all their hard-earned flaws, their history. I vanish into the thing I am seeing. This is one of those places where it would be all too easy to lose your balance, to topple, to give entry to the cold damp air: to halt and never move again, while exhausted flesh finds repose in a condition of alabaster. To cease.

Sinclair has the key in the door. We have indulged our tame speculations. We are rested and dried. We are almost comfortable. It's time to

step back out into the storm. To find out which one of us is not coming
back.

VI

Devouring a set of cold-meat pasties (folded marble, stuffed with
varicose bandages), we process down the spine of the island towards
Eastchurch. A plague penance. Cars lurch out of blind bends to scrape
our knees, or drown us in their wash. I have to make a loud noise to
avoid being flung into the crunching mechanism of a refuse truck by a
gang of white-eyed zombies: a dismissed mercenary troop roaming the
highways in flapping layers of rope-tied fertilizer sacks. The road is a
slick river for panic-crazy millennialists, racing to escape from whatever
lay ahead of us. Only the black siren-vans move in our direction;
hooting from behind, as they hurtle towards a secret prison complex,
dug out of a distant hill. Domes and bunkers. Cruel shapes suggesting
freelance experiments in social and chemical control. (In happier days,
Joe Orton holidayed here. Took a six-month body-building course at
our expense. For collaging library books.)

My Achilles tendons have gone (both of them) and my knees are
beinning to lock. I'm walking like a bad (taste) Douglas Bader impression. Sinclair, a man possessed, is flinging himself into the eye of the
hurricane. I know the bastard is enjoying this. Pellets of hail are soloing
like Max Roach on his bald crown, a rattle of drumsticks. The landscape, within this storm bell, is transformed by the strangest underwater
light. I have to hang on to Sinclair's faint blue-grey outline, as he hauls
me, yard by painful yard, into the parasitical prison-hamlet of Eastchurch.

Only one window, down the dreary length of the village street, is lit:
a wacky lesbian mini-cab outfit, obviously targeted at carrying wives
and girl friends out to the prison. An uneasy ride made tolerable by
freedom from (male) sexual harassment. The office is dominated by an
alsatian-draped sofa and a cage of parrots, most of whom are wearing
lipstick. I press my face longingly against the glass; but nothing halts the
solitary stalker, the headcase. If anything, he speeds up. He wants to
shake free from the taint of this nest of collaborators, to get back to the
shoreline, the fretting sea. He barely pauses to register the shrine (school
of Michael Sandle) to the pioneer aviators. Dynastic porcine heads
strapped into fetishist flying helmets. Old war is new porn. Cloudy
white stone. Primitive Magdalenian aeroplanes rising in relief from the

columns of dead names. Aeroplanes as imagined by wrecked, rape-surfeited Danish raiders. Zero visibility over the marshlands. Threat vapours. Fear-induced thunder. I know Sinclair can't resist sampling the monument; but rapidly in a portfolio of off-beat snapshots. He logs the anomalies, to work (somewhere) into the final mosaic. The spiralling connections. *Not now.* His head jerks, a clockwork owl. *Yes yes yes. Got it. Let's go.*

We double through a predatory scatter of breakfast bars, clocked by the android eyes of warders, gobstruck with their dripping meat forks halfway towards their faces. They can't believe we've avoided captivity. Any society that allows the likes of us to roam unmolested down the public highway is sick. Terminal. Finished. Order another breakfast. Nobody on the island eats any other meal. A twenty-four-hour morning. A perpetual hangman's dawn.

Sinclair's map is useless. It has regressed to pulp in his sodden pockets. Damp blots have rearranged all the salient features. He abandons its untrustworthy guidance and leads us, by will alone, to Shurland Manor. Or what remains of it.

This is another of those moments I enter reluctantly, only to find myself overcome: breathless in dumb recognition. We slither down a private road, made anxious with warnings, and are greeted – across an authentic duck pond – by the sight of a red-brick manor house: lifting the unprepared onlooker straight back into … *what?* A time that never existed, but which instantly activates all the simpering ducts of senti-ment. I find myself transfixed: staring through the rain-curtain, over luxuriant chlorophyll meadows, at the preserved façade; the ancient blackwood door, the asymmetrical arrangement of windows. It works superbly as a backdrop, but it has no substance. The stone-dressed hide is stretched on a framework of scaffolding: a nomad's tent. The body of the house has gone. We are left with an exploitable exterior for costume drama: a photogenic sweep of wall to disguise the empty gardens. I have no business with this place. Yet I am both grinning and weeping. My response to the dangerous combination of colours in this wind-thrashed circuit of trees is as unexpected as it is absolute.

Sinclair is standing beside me, nodding his agreement. His gouty white fingers too numb to slide open the lens cap of his camera. Our walk has degenerated into a series of poses in the teeth of the English scenery (the weather!): on to which we are determined to project some meaning, some significance we can achieve in no other way. The history of our day is expressed in a morbid checklist of roadside halts. And this is, Sinclair would blasphemously assert, also the history of England.

VII

The long march to the sea ends at Leysdown; or, as I keep calling it, Leytonstone. There is nothing more. The Leytonstone Keys: a scrofulous gathering of subhuman shacks, huddled together in order to limit the damage to a single location. We are entertained by the freakishness of Venice (California), without the carcinoma additives, and without the boringly self-justifying eccentricity of its inhabitants. Would it be ethical to make our discovery public? To endanger this time-warped reservation? Leysdown on Sea is the ancestral dreamsite of a Lost Tribe: all the aboriginal cockney characteristics, celebrated in fiction and in song, have migrated here – and have been buried alive in pitches of caravans, mobile homes, wooden sentry boxes (inner-city privies), and upturned tin boats, veterans of Dunkirk. The displaced dwarfs of Camberwell, the ex-stevedores of Millwall, the draymen of Whitechapel have drifted in on a mindless tide. This is the Last Redoubt, the final stand. Beyond the groined and squelching shore is the German Ocean: a cocktail of mud and filth and regurgitated burger-gristle too rich even for the grey-complexioned molluscs. The now almost extinct qualities plagiarized in hop-picking documentaries struggle for breath on this remote gulag. *Walthamstow. Leyton High Road. Kingsland Waste.* The dead villages gasp for air.

A cloud of murderous buoyancy assaults us. Nuts us, head-butts our melancholy. We can smell the noise: winkles, whelks, chip fat, the onion sizzle of crematorium takeaways. We are storm-shaken ghost prospectors struggling into town, empty-handed, with no energy to look for the action. Everything is on a funfair scale. As 'clock' is to 'golf', so Leysdown is to Leytonstone. We should have ingested shovel-loads of criminal substances to suffer this. Morally shriven, we can only gape at pubs the length of Brabazon hangers. You'd have to be a shrunken head to relish the atmosphere. Every discount warehouse on the North Circular would have to empty itself into these saloons to make them appear less deserted and terminally sad. Slot-machine brothels pull back from the main drag like professionally vandalized cathedrals: drills of sick light (redgreens), crippled bandits, junk symbols, wobbly fruit, shake-til-u-retch bikes, revolving drums of strawberry-blonde snot-corn.

And what if all this is my true inheritance? Sinclair can enjoy it. It's so vile he can hardly believe his luck. For him, Leysdown is just another 'routine', another paragraph. Break out the showboating similes, the patronizing travel rap. I have to accept the contagious hamlet as part of my story, give it equal weight to the graveyards of Minster. I have the shaming and inexplicable urge to search the local phonebook for traces of my mother's family. I drag Sinclair, smirking complacently, into a waterfront dive.

It's a hundred yards long and hires out, in off-peak months (September to June), as a bowling alley. We're the only *bona fide* customers. One old man in the corner has died. But nobody's noticed. We share the space with a coy Rottweiler, who has an uninhibited pork-scratching and fag-packet habit. We stand in dripping puddles, pretending not to be Travellers, while we order our Pils beers with Irish whiskey chasers. The barmaid yawns. She couldn't care less if we piss on the floor. No Irish. No call for it. Settle for Teacher's. Our sheltered window on the ocean. Red-felt banquettes. Low, kneecapping tables. Women in dresses too small for their daughters, drenched to the skin, writhe and hobble across the wharf to the bingo hall. Formal hairstyles collapsing into turbans of boiled string. If any of my family *are* still living here … I'll walk straight into the sea and finish it.

Sinclair puffs on a cheap cigar and swabs his spectacles on the flowered curtains, while I circle all the possibilities in the phonebook, scratching the numbers into a wet Carlsberg beermat. Too stupid to escape, my abdicated name lives on in columns of strong black type. I'll carry the beermat away, hidden in my wallet. And one starless night, when the world is on its edge, I'll use it. The phone in one trembling hand, a loaded pistol in the other.

This is the end of the claims of civilization. The feeble encroachments of humanoid life-forms. From this point on, we are free. We have expunged all our tribal responsibilities. We have marched through the terrors of the morning. The rain relents. I begin to imagine a new light in the sky. And to consider the nature of the final act that Sinclair has prepared for us.

He leans forward in his chair, innocently rubbing his eyelids. What does he want of me? A vitality lacking in his portrait of the island? An *engagement* he can never share? I am critically exposed. We are the only sentient beings left in the land. There is no protection in the slumbering benevolence of my nature against the warped and ruthless instincts of this man. I believe he would kill us both, without a qualm, if that was the most satisfying way to escape from the burden of the story. But he doesn't know. Not yet. He doesn't know how it ends.

VIII

'Is it still us that all this is about?'

Gert Hofman,
The Parable of the Blind

The rain has indeed slackened to a light and refreshing drizzle. The horizon retreats, and is defined. The stalk towers of an offshore fort appear from the mist as an uncharted hazard. The beach is our private territory. None of the caravan people ventures beyond Leysdown. They are happy to curse the weather, and abuse the pinballs; to drink, smoke, gob, gab, break wind, snore, scratch, and – very occasionally – dangle a fishing line into the water. But the spatter of sewage pipes and the slobbering black-green gunge that rots the old wood pilings has no real appeal for them. Nothing can compare with the gloriously toxic rancour of the Limehouse Cut or the Hertford Union Canal. They have no enthusiasm for a space they cannot dominate. They are comfortable only when the path is sealed by hampers, umbrellas, transistors, dogs, and sandwich boxes bursting with maggot life. Our way is clear. No condoms squelch underfoot. The whole strand could be mined from Warden to Shell Ness. Amorous entanglements are consummated in bucking Cortinas, parked outside neon and roughcast concrete bar rooms.

An heroically direct track leads to the island's south-east tip. A puddled red dirt road, out of some grander tale, is caught between retreating telegraph poles and the deserted beach. We can share the fantastic Icarus flights of the pioneer aviators, high above luminous green fields and out over a blanket of grey sea. Smoke columns. Fires among the cabbages.

Our two-man procession slowly absorbs, and celebrates, the energy of the curve: a wild sweep into open marshland. (The liberating spin, the tilted world!) We can follow the whims of a modest dyke path to the drowned fiefdom of Harty. Totemic birds shelter at a distance, nicely calculated, from the parking place of sharpshooters, the bicycles of fish-hook-casting juveniles. Crested, nodding lapwings hop over the quaggy ground, cackling at their own abundance. Let them remain what they are. Make no demand on them as symbols. The White Goddess is dead, and all of her triads.

This is not what I expected. This is not the barnstorm finish. I *can't* come back. I was prepared to confront another self, a double, a fetch. To be carried away, sucked like a prophet into the clouds. It's all too easy.

Saltmarshes, tidal flats, water meadows: a remote agitation of fat white sheep. A new vocabulary is required, creating a new mind. I am transformed by the previously unknown beings I am required to name. I whisper the terms like an invocation: 'sward', 'fleet', 'sluice', 'raptor', 'passerine'. I begin to let go, to fade from the path; to lose my always fierce sense of individual identity.

Small craft buck over the Swale in unaccustomed sunlight, dipping and chopping against a running tide. And yet the older boats at anchor barely stir. All movement seems unreal, made in defiance of this pastoral landscape, this panorama of recall.

The long grass wraps my feet in a sodden poultice, giving them a fresh strength. I am renewed by an expectancy of healing. The path (a green serpent) doubles back on itself, hesitates between the slate modesty of the river and the promise of small fenced hills. Teal, shoveler, wigeon, pintail. We can expect them all. They are listed on a notice board. A short-eared owl breaks from cover and glides, wings spread, in confirmation of our track.

Sinclair waits for me. I feel the accusation. He is pushing so hard. He wants more than there is. His imposed silence is developing into a threat. I am no longer able to follow in his footsteps. His challenge is a shadow I must step across. He wants me to share his madness, to refuse my comfortable graph of success: to fail. Or am I taking my duties as storyteller too seriously? Am I reading motives into the silence of contentment? I'm probably being as literal-minded as the students of those early Russian montage experiments that cut a neutral close-up against images with different emotional values. He wants none of these things. A blow, a rest from words. He turns back to the path ahead. He is only pausing while I draw breath. He doesn't want to lose me. Not now.

I am the sole prosecutor. Should I have made myself a *Kultur* shaman of fire and ice, a lead-scratcher, another Anselm Kiefer? Should I bring all that Nordic apparatus, that clutter, into galleries? Lock myself in cages with wild beasts? Produce myself as the wooden tongue of wisdom, the articulate mask? The choice is mine alone. This has nothing to do with him. What happens, happens. The third man, the unacknowledged one, is joining us. The other: feeding on his grim and remorseless belief in the quest. I abdicate my reserved status, and enter the narrative. He conned me. That was his trap. Fictional puppets have all the freedom of action. They can deny their creator. They can refuse his manipulations. They can abandon him.

Our own messenger floats down towards the rush-fringed fleet, disappears. This is an island that is *not* the world. It is removed, discrete;

one of those transitory border zones, caught in uncertain weather, nudged, dislocated by a lurch in the intensity of the light. A special place where, I'd like to believe, 'good persists in time'.

These are not my thoughts. This is not what I want to say. 'Good', if it still survives, is sustained by its concubine, 'evil'; its sullen dependant. There is only the *will towards good* asserted by these unnoticed landscapes. And the quality we discover in ourselves as we are drawn towards them. 'Good' is a retrospective title. To be used when it is all over.

As I stare in mongoloid fascination at Sinclair's heels, I realize I have accepted a new doctrine: there *is* no third person. There never was. The watcher and the watched are one. And that is just the first stage. My analeptic concentration on the rhythms of the walk drowns all lesser motives, restores me to myself, reinforces the visionary dynamic of the route we have chosen.

Now anything is possible. I can see the ash-shaded body of the church of St Thomas the Apostle at Harty: pebbled walls sinking into the soft ground. A low sun picking out the pinkness in the stones. Turf is rising to cover it entirely. I see the dark oak of the muniment chest with its jousting knights, as it was salvaged from the Swale. The building has no further use for its priest and congregation, no concern with pilgrims and baptism in black tidal waters. But a procession of penitents and plague-fearing believers resist this apathy. They rush, slithering and stumbling, on to the mud flats; edging narrowly ahead of the darkness. They renege on wicker fire-gods, pitch themselves into the cold white hands of the saint; bleating with terror, they beg for immersion.

And I see the other side also. The architecture of repression: bunkers buried under protected lands, unlisted blockhouses sheltering beneath a promise of sanctuary. The preservation of wild life is seen as nothing more than a charter for the destruction of all other kinds. The long-range binoculars that log the coupling seabirds also warn of the approach of unauthorized witnesses. Bird wardens double as security guards. Under the boastful photographs of rural England are cells of elimination, torture, death. Romantic watercolours pipe and wash over broken bones. Modesty is an avatar of ignorance. Curiosity does well to hesitate at the perimeter of any open space. When there is nothing to offend the eye, beware. The green hill above Windmill Creek is the dome of a prison.

I see into subterranean honeycomb laboratories where monkeys in suits are testing blasts of radiation. Their thin bones print the grey cloth like stripes of chalk. They look comic, but there is no relief from this joke. It goes on for ever. Fur falls out in scalded patches. They suffer shock and chemical assaults. They have the skinned foetal cast of veteran rock stars at society weddings. They are dressed up, traumatized, trembling. They are deaf. They lipread the lab assistants' obscene banter.

Addict monkeys. Researchers on their backs. '*The sustained administration of maximum doses of morphine, heroin, and codeine on healthy monkeys (MACACUS RHESUS) in conditions more extreme than those to which humans could be safely exposed. These pictures were taken after the animal had been on morphine for seven and a half months.*'

A pregnancy of pain; conditioned nightmares. I see the blueprinted textbooks emerge from shelves of morbid dust. Sheets of heavy gloss paper (bedsheets) fall open, part, with a noise that is almost sexual. Cool analytic prose undermines the hideous static poses. We finger the fore-edge, flicking the illustrations into a parody of life. Monkeys gibber and shriek on stoneblock altars: damaged, senile children.

Hastily convened families of the unclaimed dead 'volunteer' to sample the force of controlled detonations. They are arranged, by the Widow's sponsorship of Mrs Beeton's domestic virtues, around tables spread with contaminated food. Wooden cutlery is wrapped in silver foil. They consume. They are glutted with possessions. The unmortgaged dead. They can boast of fridges made from paper and cardboard televisions. Flesh linen dissolves into gangrene and mutton, soot, carbon, corpse-cheese. They are photographed, described, measured, recorded; buried in earth. How deep can we go? How much clay does it take to smother these sights?

Enough. I don't have to write about this. I see Sinclair forging ahead once more. I don't know how long we have been walking or what distance we have covered. He has seen the things I have described. I have accepted the things he has seen. Our track is undisturbed. We turn from the Swale, uphill. Climb a stile, and are welcomed by a tumble of abandoned tractors, broken pallet boards, rotting turnip heaps. The safety of unfarmed farmland.

A red car was parked on the road alongside a tyre cemetery. The kind of chaotic, labyrinthine (high-risk) dump kids are instantly attracted by. I needed a rest. Badly. I searched out a dry tyre on which to collapse.

'Wouldn't sit there, boy,' said a conversational mangel-wurzel, 'not if you'm courting. Some nice ol' rats live in them tyres. Biggest fucking beasts I ever seen.'

A character in a greasy cowboy hat stuck his head from the car window, and followed it with some kind of high-velocity combat rifle. 'Farmer don' mind,' he said. He was waiting for twilight. 'Best sport to be 'ad on the island. Blow them fuckers' heads off, watch 'em run for it. Twenty, thirty yards down the road.' He drooled, and spat. A copycat redneck with a six-pack and a box of cartridges.

What does this oaf *think* about as he sits fondling the safety catch and keying himself up for the moment when the mutant rats make their suicide dash from Tyre City to the pyramids of mouldering potatoes? He seemed calm enough, and well-adjusted – by Sheppey standards. He may just have been drunk, or waiting for the pills to wear off. He didn't even take a friendly potshot at us. The man probably voted Green, and worked as an accountant. He was certainly the tallest male we'd encountered. He must have been almost five foot two, without the hump. A potential relative, a kissing cousin.

I led Sinclair up the yellow road by a dozen paces. I didn't break my stride until I could see the bell tower of St Thomas the Apostle. And so we came at last to an enclosure on which I had absolutely no claim. A building I could respond to openly, without hope of reward – or fear of punishment. A circuit of grass that shone in the afternoon sun, that existed without my description of it; that was suspended from the narrative.

Pale, uncontaminated land. Fields of peas were pressing on the path; dripping from the recent showers, brushing against our coats. I picked a pod and split it with my fingernail. The peas were blunted, squarish and very sweet upon the tongue. The density of 'green' that now surrounded us was almost unbearable. Light recovered from the storm, charged light. It called for blood; axe splashes, unmotivated crimes. This was the perfect frame, the correct exposure: the meadow of death. But not for me; it was not my story. Sinclair did not turn in at the church gate. He wanted to see what was on the other side.

IX

'I used to watch the line where earth and sky met, and long to go and seek there for the key of all mysteries...'

(Prince Muishkin) Fedor Dostoevsky, *The Idiot*

The landlord of the Ferry House Inn was waiting for us. 'You'll have to get a move on, lads. Or you'll miss it.' The track swerved away from the flagged terrace of the pub, and down to the old river crossing; where a fancy-dress group stood stubbornly around, as if they expected – against all the odds – that the discontinued ferry service would operate one last time. Perhaps, lacking the imagination for any other occupation, they had simply refused to budge when the ancient boatman retired. They looked ridiculous: sub-actors, professional extras forgotten by the crew – somewhere out of reach of the railways.

I was beyond shock, but the landlord registered my self-doubt. The lack of trust in my eyes. 'The day of the match,' he said, 'isn't it? The cricket on Horse Sands. Been happening this day since time immoral.'

Sinclair came back to life. He rubbed his hands. And worse: he took from his coat pocket a varnished, red leather ball and began to pick at the seam. I bet he knew all about this, the evil sod. I *hate* cricket. I despise the hours of contentless boredom, punctuated by threats of occult violence (too far away to be interesting). And I abhor the nagging danger of sudden grievous harm, perpetrated against even the entirely innocent spectator, who is trying to sip a glass of cold Rhinish wine, and dip into a novel of urban mayhem, until it all goes away. 'The classic art of hurling hard balls at soft ones' is his friend Dryfeld's terse but accurate definition. I'll have nothing whatever to do with this. It will certainly end in tears.

Horse Sands was a shark-shaped islet of river mud that emerged at low tide from the Swale. Apparently, once a year (on the anniversary of some repulsed Viking raid), an eccentric cricket match took place on the sandbar; lasting just long enough for the already inebriated participants to get their feet wet, lose a few balls in the river, and work up a raging thirst. Nobody kept the score. They made up the rules as they went along. They turned out in absurd and unsuitable costumes. And took it all, in the English fashion, with the utmost seriousness.

The walk out to the wicket could be the trickiest part of the game. But the batsman waiting to receive his first delivery in the middle of all that water – wondering if the ball will be flung at his head, or drop at his feet in the mud – has nothing of topographical interest to contemplate beyond a botched prospect of Faversham. The cultivated cricketer (the Fry, the Brearley, the Raffles, the Roebuck) will think of murder. *Black Will* and *Shakebog* hired by *Mistress Arden* to assassinate her husband. Apocryphal ghosts in an unperformable drama. He will also recall, with guilty affection, all those tearjerking John Ford set pieces. Monument Valley. Huddles of wind-whipped repertory faces gathered, yet again, at the river: to praise some arrow-punctured corpse. *John Wayne, Ward Bond*, the other *Ben Johnson*.

I don't want it. I'm not going down there. Enough is enough. I'll nurse my Guinness on the terrace, and watch. I'm not falling for that wide-angle sentimentality. The rhetorical assumption of a man (shot low from behind) striding out from a square of darkness into an over-exposed furnace of action. This time I'll wet my lips, keep my notebook open on my lap, and make the report. The narrator cuts the cord.

The boat arrives to carry them over. A low flat-bottomed skiff, paddled from the stern. The cricketers wait at the slipway in an awkward huddle: they nudge and josh, or fiddle obsessively with their laces. A choir of rejected Spy cartoons. There is a bull-necked, waistcoat-bursting man, who has not quite decided whether he will impersonate Dr Grace or Sir William Withey Gull. His chin juts aggressively, but his beard is patently false. A Herculean bat swings from his hand. There is a woman dressed like a Red Indian. Or a Red Indian dressed like a woman. A dead one. Her clothes and skin are the colour of oxidized copper: a drowned and ugly green. She moves towards the water, her arms stiff, raised: as if to encourage the other fielders to close in for the final over before the tea interval. A circus dwarf in a light-brown derby is flicking and catching a boomerang. His face shines with white lead, his huge eyes are outlined in black. He is pushed aside by a limping, cursing man – who struggles to unravel himself from an umpire's floor-length dust coat. A fantasy nurse, in breathless costume-hire uniform, pushes a heavy bicycle. Sinclair helps to manoeuvre the vulgarly exaggerated telescope of a Pacific islander with a bone through his nose. All we need – and I think we are about to get it – is the arrival of the *Reunion*, with her griddled pilot still chained to the wheel.

Something *very* strange is happening. I grip the arms of my chair, tighten my fingers around the slats of the table. I want no part of this. There is a remission in the gravity of time, a period of involuntary 'feedback'. Our script is in turnaround. If I do not resist – I will be written out. It'll take over, write itself. Uncensored. On this day the river disgorges its dead. I swear that one man, his pockets bulging, crawled from the water on the far side of the sands. He pulled himself upright, feeling his way like a blind man, tapping, and resting on an antique bat. A faded pink cap, tipped forward over his eyes, made him look both clownish and bald.

The stumps are unevenly set. They sink at different levels into the mud, so that the bails will not sit across them. Neither will the ball bounce. They've been playing for hours, and nothing has reached the batsman. He is patient, lifting his weapon, and then lowering it again, as each attempted delivery falls far short of the crease. The dead balls are left, buried in the sand like infertile eggs. The players are all so solemn. There is no sense of competition, only of collaboration in an eternally recurring ceremony.

I look down at my glass. I've been pulling steadily, all this time, at the gravy-coloured froth; but to no effect. The level of liquid is unchanged. My Leysdown cigar remains half-smoked. The blue ring I puffed into the still air hangs exactly where I launched it years before.

Before *what*? How long have I been here? How long has *here* been here? Long enough to unspool twelve parallel wheels of fate, twelve concurrent dreams? The remote white figures are unburdened. I cannot dismiss them, call them in. A crackle of wraparound noise: wind mischief, a territoriality of birds, unsounded bells; silent bell towers directing the circuit of cooling air. Spasms of gunfire from across the darkened fields. My cousin, the humpbacked ratter, has lived to see the twilight. The tide insinuates itself over the tongue of sand. The outfield has already been squatted by an extended family of diving ducks. An oil-feathered pun, an English score card floating from sight.

I'm weary, burnt-out, blown. I'm sick, I'm tired of sweeping up the parrot droppings from the floor of his mind, but there's time for one more. One final crackpot theory. I'll fake the soliloquy, talk for the ghost. Sinclair proposes that a cricket match is essentially a trial of psychic health. He finds he performs most effectively when he is run-down, exhausted, or injured in some way. It is only then that the conditioned reflexes relent; they are inhibited, and his modest *will towards failure* grows weak. The act of bowling, or striking the ball, fulfils itself without his egoic interference. Writing this book has been a Wagnerian rollercoaster: tree-felling drives, followed by legless first-ball gropes. I don't know if this proves his thesis or destroys it. But the conclusion must be: the sickest team wins. Wait until this gets out! They'll be pressganging the terminal wards, digging up plague pits, injecting our South African mercenaries with wet beriberi, malaria, trypanosomiasis. We'll be a power again. We'll be contenders.

The Grace/Gull impersonator throws Sinclair the ball. 'Get rid of it, chuck it in the river,' I want to scream. It's his turn to inflict some damage. He counts out his twelve paces and scratches a mark with his (sick) heel in the sand. He checks his grip, shuffles, jogs on the spot, runs in close to the stumps, and lets it go.

For a moment I think nothing has happened. The batsman plays no shot. The fielders are lifeless. A freelance wound, a lengthening suture of red advances from the West, from Fowley Island. The ball – if it was ever delivered – passed through, and on, without harming man or wicket. It connects with, and disappears into, the long rays of the setting sun.

Now there is a quality of yolky golden light revolving in a benign cartwheel along the course that the ball should have taken. Something calm and bright and inexhaustible. A spinning nimbus of maize and bees and song. A bowling hoop of sticky radiance: wasps, wax, feathers, corndust. An Egypt, a linen sail. A spiral of white sand. A waterfall turning back on itself. A rush, a dart, a hymn. And as this pulsing yellow trawl, this phenomenon, bounced across the estuary towards the cancelled land, an umprompted description came into my head. A set of alien words. '*The opposite of a dog.*' I have not the slightest idea what that means.

I am without desire, and outside time. I hold my drink in my hand, but there is no longer a glass to contain it. The tide has caught them. I think the sandbar has vanished. It's too dark to see. The fields close around me. I hear the snorting and stamping of horses. I want to come back to this place, to bring my family, my children; but I don't want to be here now. I must ring the ladies of Eastchurch for a cab to ferry me out. Until that arrives I'll just sit here, and keep my eyes firmly closed.

X

The oppressive closeness clears. A sudden violent storm had left the streets of Whitechapel fresh and wet. Sofya Court walked home. She had given the swollen jiffy bag into the hands of the cashier at the Indian supermarket in Heneage Street. To be delivered to Joblard on his return. Her duty was discharged.

'*HERE AT LAST IS THE GRIMOIRE,*' she had written, '*WHICH WE SO CARELESSLY MISLAID. I HOPE IT'S NOT TOO LATE TO CONSTITUTE A HAPPY ENDING?*'

November 1989, London

Acknowledgements and Confessions

My thanks to Mr Shames (of Stoke Newington) for granting me permission to quote from his letters. And also to Peter Riley (of Cambridge) for time and hospitality; as he recounted his memories of the poet, Nicholas Moore.

The rest of the book is not so reliable. Much, I'm afraid, is mere fiction (i.e. it hasn't happened yet). My journalistic accounts of verifiable newspaper incidents, such as the planting of the eucalyptus in honour of King Cole, live down to the ethical standards of that trade. (You can't believe a word of them. *I* was there; but Meic Triscombe, Edith Cadiz and the rest were floating in the aether.)

Professor Stephen Hawking, as far as I am aware, has never set foot in the Isle of Dogs; nor yet the Isle of Doges. The words I have entrusted to him are derived from his published works. (The interested reader will know that Professor Hawking did 'attend a conference on cosmology organized by the Jesuits in the Vatican'.) His appearance in my narrative is a (desperate?) quotation of virtue.

I can't go so far as to claim that 'this version of history is my own invention'. It would be more truthful to suggest that these inventions are versions of my own history.

Finally, I would like to express my gratitude to those twelve (unknowing) souls who accompanied me through my grimoire of rivers and railways. They deserve to remain anonymous.